# Requiem

CLARE FRANCIS is the author of seven international bestselling thrillers, *Night Sky*, *Red Crystal*, *Wolf Winter*, *Requiem*, *Deceit*, *Betrayal*, and, most recently, *A Dark Devotion*. She has also written three non-fiction books about her voyages across the oceans of the world.

# CLARE FRANCIS

# Requiem

PAN BOOKS
*in association with*
*William Heinemann*

First published 1991 by William Heinemann Limited

First published by Pan Books 1992

This revised edition published 1994 by Pan Books
an imprint of Macmillan Publishers Ltd
25 Eccleston Place, London SW1W 9NF
and Basingstoke

Associated companies throughout the world

In association with William Heinemann Ltd

ISBN 0 330 33962 1

10 12 14 13 11

A CIP catalogue record for this book is available from
the British Library.

Typeset by SetSystems Ltd, Saffron Walden, Essex
Printed and bound in Great Britain by
Mackays of Chatham plc, Chatham, Kent

For those patient and loving friends who have sustained me through the struggles of the last five years; and for all my fellow sufferers who are still fighting their way up the long path to recovery.

# Chapter 1

IT WAS JUST after midnight when Nick slipped away from the house. The moon cast shards of pale light across the wide parkland and illuminated the beeches like giant white-sailed ships. The shadows were very deep, and he wondered if he would be able to find his way up through the glen. He'd never walked the glen in darkness before; usually he drove, and then in daylight with Alusha or Duncan, the estate manager, at his side. He could have done with Duncan's special knowledge to guide him now, but Duncan had been told nothing of this little expedition: he wouldn't approve.

From the post-and-wire fence marking the end of the park, rough pasture rose gently towards the dense woodland which covered the lower slopes of the hills. The direct route to the glen led diagonally across the pasture, but anxious to avoid the obvious paths, Nick struck off at a tangent, making for a dark mass of oak trees on the fringe of the woodland.

He paced himself for the long climb ahead. The shotgun in his hand felt awkward, absurd and rather obscene. He wasn't sure why he'd brought it. Maybe because here, in what was possibly the safest place in the world, he still felt unsafe. Time had done nothing to alleviate the unease; if anything, it had increased it, and he needed the reassurance of the weight in his hand, even if the idea of ever firing the thing frightened him to death. He had no skill with the weapon. Duncan had given him some rudimentary tuition

on pointing it in the right direction and not accidentally
shooting friends in the backside, but even Duncan, with his
boundless optimism, had given up hope of making a good
shot of him. Alusha hated him even to pick up a gun. She
would be far from happy if she knew he was carrying one
now – and far from happy if she knew he was out here,
playing cops and robbers in the middle of the night.

But he couldn't have stayed away, the chances were too
good. For a week the weather had been foul even by West
Highland standards, with blustery westerlies, lowering
clouds and almost continuous rain. Then early that evening
the sky had cleared, the wind had died, and a brittle blue-
washed moon had risen over the hills of Cowal. It was then
that Duncan's prediction had flashed into his mind, the
prophecy that they would come after the rain, as soon as
there was a touch of moon to light their way up the glen.

Almost as he thought it, the outline of the approaching
woods became less distinct, blurring into the sky, and he
saw that fingers of cloud were creeping across the moon
from the west. Would the cloud be enough to put them off?
The thought brought him a mixture of disappointment and
relief. But it didn't make him turn back; it was too late for
that now.

On reaching the woods, he had intended to follow a
small footpath that wound between a succession of overgrown dells and hazel thickets, but the darkness was so
great that he lost the path almost as soon as he found it
and was forced back to the pasture, to skirt the edge of the
wood.

At first he had been conscious of few sounds except his
own breathing and the soft squelch of his feet on the
sodden ground, but now, close under the trees, the night
came alive with faint rustlings and scratchings and suggestions of movement. He felt an absurd pride, as if the
untouched forest, complete with its small unseen residents,
was his very own creation. And in a sense it was. Duncan

was forbidden to touch this part of the estate, apart from cutting the worst of the bracken and erecting protective fences around rare plants. Fallen trees rotted where they lay, saplings were left to compete for light in tangled thickets. In the early days this non-interference policy had driven Duncan mad but, despite dark mutterings, he had never actually quit. Nick liked to think that, after eight years, Duncan was beginning to see the point of it all.

The clouds slid past the moon and the trees sprang into relief again. Coming to the corner of the pasture, he re-entered the woods, taking the path that would lead him west towards the deep cut of the glen. Now the forest was mainly oak and sycamore with the occasional Scots pine, the trees high and well-spaced, so that the moon filtered down onto the ground in delicate droppings of light.

As he hurried on, the distant whisper of the river grew steadily until the rush of fast-falling water drowned all but the most distinct sounds.

A pale ribbon appeared through the trees: the track that ran up the glen in a long lazy loop from the house. Stopping just short of it, he crouched in the shadows and, glancing up and down the empty road, strained to hear over the gush and rumble of the water. He became aware of how ludicrous he must look, hiding there like an overgrown boy scout, and, whether from nerves or amusement, he chuckled aloud. The chuckle died in his throat as the shadows at the bend in the track shifted and sent his heart thudding against his ribs. The shadows quickly settled into the benign shapes of trees and shrubs, but after that nothing seemed remotely funny.

Once his heart was back under some sort of control, he tried to plan his next move. How would the men come? By car? If so, there was only one way they could get onto the track without driving past the house itself – something even they, brass-nerved as they were, wouldn't dare. Some quarter of a mile down the glen a narrow overgrown track, hardly more than a wide path, ran off the main track towards the lochside road. Entry to this path was barred by a gate which Duncan had reinforced and locked with a massive padlock and chain. This hadn't stopped their visitors from entering in the past of course; they'd merely used larger bolt cutters. Nor had a three-night stakeout by Duncan and the local constabulary – all two of them. The enemy had merely bypassed the gate and trailed up the glen on foot.

So what would they do tonight? Would they break the padlock and drive up? Or come on foot?

Whichever way they chose, they were bound to use the track, which followed the glen and the racing river for miles, up through the forest to the high moorlands. It wouldn't be a good idea for him to be spotted dawdling along the middle of the road. On the other hand, he wasn't too sure he could manage the full commando approach, crawling through the undergrowth with a mud-daubed face.

Taking a final look both ways, he crossed the stony surface of the track and entered the woods on the far side. Here the ground fell steeply away to the river. Clambering down through the undergrowth, he made for the narrow path that ran close beside the rushing water, and began to follow it up the glen. Now and again, when the moon slipped behind the clouds, he had to reach a hand out in front of him to feel his way forward. Once he stumbled, jarring his shoulder against a rock and the shotgun barrel struck the surface with a loud crack. The sound was quickly swallowed up by the thundering water, but he paused, sweating coldly, before pressing on. Finally Macinley's Rock came into view, a massive outcrop that obtruded into the river, deflecting the flow against the far bank and squeezing the water into a thundering cataract. Above the rock was the Great Pool. According to Duncan, this was where the vermin, as he called them, were to be found.

Twice since April Duncan had found evidence of their visits in the form of trampled ground, cigarette butts and peg holes.

It took some time for Nick to find a suitable spot for his watch. Finally he picked a rocky ledge a few yards up the sloping bank, opposite the widest section of the pool. It was rather open, but if he'd gone higher the trees would have obscured his view of the approaches.

He lay on his stomach on the damp grassy earth, and peered over the edge. The Ashard was by no means a broad river – for much of its ten-mile length it was only a few yards wide – but after heavy rain the Great Pool flooded into a wide basin some fifteen yards across. After the commotion of the lower reaches, the pool was quiet, its surface satin-smooth in the moonlight, only the occasional ripple hinting at movement and eddies beneath.

A mournful bird-cry made him start slightly. It sounded again, a cross between a moan and a hoot. A tawny owl – well, an owl anyway. He wasn't quite up to positive identifications; *The Oxford Book of Birds* wasn't something one got to grips with overnight.

He rolled onto his side and felt something sharp dig into his hip: the shotgun cartridges in his jacket pocket. He pulled one out and fingered it. An unpleasant thought came to him. Might they be carrying a shotgun too? As he understood it, there was a sort of unwritten code in these parts, the sporting men's version of the Queensberry Rules, which said that gamekeepers waved shotguns and sometimes even fired them in anger, but that poachers remained unarmed and bolted when caught. He hoped the rules would be in full operation tonight.

If they weren't carrying anything, would they turn and fight? He nursed the idea with a mixture of fear and unexpected excitement. He'd been no hero in the early days. Once, years and years ago, after a gig in Sunderland, a group of the local lads had decided to exhibit their

particular brand of machismo by lying in wait for him at
the stage door and beating him up. He'd put up the best
fight he could muster, which wasn't saying a great deal, but
all that his meagre bravery had got him was a broken jaw
and the lost earnings from five cancelled gigs. Not long
after, he'd sworn a personal non-aggression pact with the
world. It had lasted a long time – something like fifteen
years – until six years ago and the incident in the Fifth
Avenue apartment.

After that, all sorts of things had developed the power
to make him angry. Most of all anybody or anything that
threatened Alusha. Then, as a close second, anything that
threatened this fabulous patch of earth that had somehow
become his own. Yet it wasn't because Glen Ashard
belonged to him that he was up here playing games in the
middle of the night – though that would have been enough
for most landowners hereabouts – it wasn't even the idea
of all his and Duncan's painstaking work being ruined; it
was the thought of having his space and peace invaded by
money-grubbing oiks that he really couldn't stomach.

He never admitted as much of course; he talked about
responsibility, a word he used to avoid like the plague but
which he now said quite often, along with other words like
obligation and conservation, which in these feudal parts
were usually bandied about by tweedy aristos and retired
army officers. According to Alusha, it was all to do with
middle age. She said he was finally growing up.

He put the cartridges back in his pocket. There didn't
seem much point in keeping them out, when he had no
intention of loading them.

It was well after one when the moon dimmed for the
last time, lost behind the rim of the hills. The darkness
wouldn't last – the midsummer night up here was barely
three hours long – but would they have the gall to come in
the light? He resigned himself to the possibility that, if they
were coming at all, they'd have shown by now. Yet he

wouldn't leave, not while there was still the slightest chance. He rested his head on the crook of his arm, pulled his jacket higher round his neck and, ignoring the damp chill of the earth, tried to doze.

He woke after what seemed a very short time. Shifting his body a little, he tried to settle again but was seized by a tickle in the back of his nose. He drew breath, waiting for the itch to trigger the satisfaction of a good sneeze, and it was then that he heard it. A sharp sound. His mouth still poised for the sneeze, his lungs full, he jerked his head up. The sneeze hovered, refusing to die. He clamped his fingers over his nose and squeezed viciously until his eyes watered. Finally, reluctantly, the sneeze faded and died.

Another sound. A scrape, like metal against stone. Then the murmur of a human voice some way off. A second later, a second voice, much closer. Slowly Nick rolled onto his stomach and peered over the edge. At first he could see nothing. Then he spotted a movement – a black shadow against the gleaming surface – and heard the sloshing sound of someone wading into the water.

For a while he was frozen by indecision. He hadn't thought this bit through. Should he stand up and yell? Should he creep up on them and give them a fright? Though it was questionable as to who would be getting the bigger fright. He decided it was worth the risk of heart failure for the satisfaction of seeing them jump.

Taking the shotgun, he rose into a crouch and began to creep slowly down the bank, testing each footstep for loose ground, reaching a steadying hand out to the slope above him, all the time keeping his eye on the man in the water. It wasn't hard to follow him: he was splashing a good deal and leaving a long trail of ripples. There was one nasty moment when a voice called out, but it was only to say: 'Loose off.' A moment later a reply came floating on the air, but the words were muffled by the water.

A filigree of shimmering light rose above the pool as a

thin line broke the surface: that would be the net. The excitement rose in Nick as he realized he was going to catch them right in the act.

They appeared to be dragging the deepest part of the pool immediately behind Macinley's Rock. But where would they pull in the catch?

Nick decided on the likeliest spot and, keeping in a deep crouch, worked his way round to a point nearby and waited.

But they weren't bringing in the net, not yet. There was a tapping, like a mallet on wood, and he realized they were pegging the net to the ground, leaving the current to do some of their work for them. If he stayed where he was, it was likely to be a long wait.

He crept closer. He saw the shape of a man's head against the night sky. A moment later he heard a sloshing sound as a second man emerged from the water. Were there more than two? He couldn't be sure.

There was the flicker of a match and the glow of a cigarette, and the low murmur of voices.

It was now or never. Gripping the shotgun, aware of a quite ridiculous fear which had somehow turned to elation, with his heart exploding against his ribs, Nick stood upright and walked steadily towards them. He felt amazingly conspicuous: they must see him, must hear him at any moment, but by some miracle no shout came, no challenge; there was only the glowing cigarette end and the suggestion of two shadows in the darkness. With only a few steps left, he was overcome by a bizarre sense of unreality – was he really going through with this?

Suddenly they saw him. There was a sharp exclamation, a loud oath, and the two men jumped apart. One of them dropped into a crouch, as if to make a run for it.

'Stop or I shoot!' Nick heard his voice come out of the distance, as if it belonged to someone else. Had he really said that? It sounded like something out of a B-Western.

They made no move. Then the one who'd been crouching straightened up slowly. There was a long electric pause. Nick tried to make out their faces, but it was too dark. What did one say next?

He began: 'What the hell do you think you're doing?'

One of them, the much taller of the two, relaxed his stance. There was something insolent in the gesture, as if he no longer considered himself at risk. That was it, of course: the fellow had realized that, far from facing the dreaded Duncan, who never had any compunction about peppering poachers' backsides with shot, he was dealing with an altogether softer opponent.

Nick held the gun higher to be sure the tall man could see it. 'Who are you?'

The man gave a grunt which was almost a laugh. 'I'd say that's for me to know an' you to find out.'

Nick's anger rose over him like a hot sea. 'I wouldn't take that attitude, if I were you.'

'No?' The man sounded unconvinced. 'What attitude should I take with a weapon pointin' at me? Intendin' murder, are you?'

'Why not – you're murdering the river!'

'I've never heard of a river bein' murdered. It doesna' look dead to me.' He was sounding very sure of himself now.

'But it soon bloody well will be. Then you'll have a chance to see what it looks like – when it's too bloody late!'

'Och well. Somethin' to see then.'

'You don't give a shit, do you?'

'I wouldna' say that,' came the cool reply. 'But then, why should I? An' then again, why should *you*? They say you're rich enough, eh?'

'What the hell's that got to do with it?' Nick's wrath wasn't helped by the realization that the tall man knew exactly who he was.

The man pushed his head forward and spoke in fierce virtuous tones. 'You come in here, you buy up the place an' you think you own the entire country. You've no knowledge of our ways, no notion of our customs – '

'Your customs! You call years of wholesale poaching a custom! Christ – '

'No notion – '

'It's you who's got no notion, chum. The world won't put up with your sort any longer. Perhaps you haven't heard of conservation up here, but believe me the rest of the world has.' Nick waved the gun in a vaguely southerly direction.

'The rest of the world? Och, I beg your pardon.' The voice was heavy with sarcasm. 'It's in the name of conservation, is it, that your friends come up from London in their grand cars an' lord it over the place an' boast how they caught a salmon all by theirselves, eh? It's in the name of con-ser-vation' – he drew out the syllables scornfully – 'that we have to put up with your kind tellin' *us* what to do, is it?'

'There's been no fishing on this river for three years,' Nick cried in exasperation. 'And there'll be no fishing for years to come either – not while you go on draining the bloody river dry.'

'No fishin', eh? Is that a fact?' The voice was both mocking and uncompromising. 'The folks round here will believe that when they see it. Let me tell you' – he raised a hand and Nick took a step backwards, momentarily misreading the gesture in the darkness – 'we've been comin' to this river for longer than any of us can remember. It's our right. We're not about to stop, not for the wild ideas of some loony pop star.'

Trembling with rage, Nick heard himself snap hotly: 'Songwriter.' No sooner said than regretted: what a time for accuracy.

A bow. 'Och, I beg your pardon.'

Nick flushed in the darkness, and let his anger carry him forward again. 'As for wild ideas, Christ, you can talk. You can't see any farther than the next easy buck. You don't give a damn about what happens to the river – '

'That we do!' the rough voice interjected, sounding injured. 'We want the fish back. It's not been good for us – '

'But they're not your fish!' Nick cried.

'An' what makes you think they're yours?'

'Damn it, they *are* mine!'

The other man didn't reply and Nick had the impression he was pulling a contemptuous face, even a laughing one.

Nick rushed on: 'Not good for you – God, you've a bloody nerve. If we're going to talk money, how much do you make a night, eh? Three hundred, five hundred? Who's the rich guy, then, eh?'

The comparison was a mistake, Nick knew it as soon as he said it. But the tall man wasn't about to bother with words, not when action would do, not when Nick had forgotten all about the gun and let the barrel drop. He came for the gun with a speed and confidence that caught Nick totally offguard. Grabbing the barrel, he drove his body against Nick's and carried him backwards until Nick staggered, fighting for balance.

Finding his feet again, Nick held grimly on to the gun. But the tall man had the better grip and the better leverage, and as they grappled Nick could feel the weapon being slowly wrenched from his grasp. In his blind determination to hold on to the weapon, it was a moment before the vital realization seeped dimly into his brain. The gun wasn't loaded, so why the hell was he battling for it? Even then it took a conscious effort to overcome the instinctive urge to clutch on to it at all costs, and let go.

He was an instant too late. Just as he released his fingers, a powerful blow hit the back of his knees, knocking his legs from under him. He had the sensation of falling, then a jarring explosion came up and hit the side of his head and his brain was filled with flashes of brilliant light.

He had no sense of time when he woke. It took him a long while to remember where he was and why he was there. His head hurt with the sort of intense dagger-like pain that he remembered from spectacular bicycle crashes in his youth.

By screwing open one eye he registered the fact that the surface of the pool was reflecting the grey light of dawn. By swivelling the eye very carefully – he wasn't about to move his head, not yet anyway – he saw that the pool was deserted. The men had gone, and the net, and with them what would inevitably be a ruinous number of salmon.

His pride hurt almost as much as his skull. As a victim, he had been a gift. The tall man was probably laughing at this very moment.

The daggers began stabbing at his skull in earnest. He concentrated on feeling sorry for himself, an emotion he felt he richly deserved. He pulled his jacket closer round his neck and dimly registered the fact that something else had been placed over him, a coat of some sort. The coverings didn't prevent the cold from seeping up through the ground into his body, nor the sharp lump of rock from digging into the small of his back. But despite these aggravations, he no sooner closed his eyes than he fell into a heavy drug-like sleep.


Duggan was not at his best in the mornings, and certainly not when forced to get up at such an ungodly hour. It was four thirty when the alarm went off, and it was only the recollection of his precarious financial position that per-suaded him to sit up and face the ugly little room with its single overhead light. He felt rotten. Having heard the favourable weather forecast the previous evening he'd been careful to keep off the booze – even in his most despondent moments, and there were all too many of those, he wasn't so stupid as to risk his licence – but he'd been hitting it hard earlier in the week, and for some obscure reason the hangover seemed to have caught up with him a few days late.

It took him ten minutes to dress, run an electric razor over his face and get downstairs. The landlady had said she would leave some food out for him and he peered expectantly into the darkened dining room, hoping for a pile of bacon sandwiches and a flask of coffee, but the shaft of light from the hall revealed a loaf of Mother's Pride, a pot of garish yellow margarine and a jar of runny marmalade. With weary resignation he slapped a sandwich together and went out to the car.

It was a ten-minute drive to the airfield. Automatically Duggan cast an eye at the dawn sky. No cloud, very little wind. He breathed a prayer of thanks. It was high time the weather went his way. He was paid piece rate – no flying, no money – although Acorn Flying Services Ltd did provide what was laughingly called a bad-weather retainer, a derisory sum that barely covered the cost of beer.

As he drove alongside the field he saw that the mechanic had got the generator and the two floodlights going, and was already poking around inside the Porter's engine. Outside the Portakabin which served as the local office of Acorn Flying Services (AFS) Ltd, Duggan was surprised to see a smart BMW, very shiny and very black. He could think of only one person who might have such a flash wagon, and when he had parked and stomped into the cabin his suspicions were confirmed.

Keen was at the table, poring over some papers. He was the executive director of AFS Ltd. According to the company's letterhead there were two other directors, who were so non-executive as to be invisible. At least Duggan had never met them, and he'd been here about three times as long as was good for him. But then Keen wasn't exactly a familiar face either; Duggan had seen him only once before when Keen had interviewed him at what was glowingly referred to as company head office – a couple of rooms in the converted stables of a country house north of Glasgow. During the interview Keen had spent all his time rattling orders down the phone to what appeared to be a host of operational offices at airfields all over Scotland. It was only later that Duggan had heard the rumours, which like all worrying gossip had proved to be absolutely true, that AFS was down to two aircraft, both of which were leased on short-term contracts, and, until the recent upsurge in business, had had severe financial problems. The mention of financial difficulties had made Duggan nervous – he had quite enough of his own, thank you very much – but as long as the pay cheques kept coming through on time, then it was no concern of his.

Keen acknowledged him with a brusque nod and a frown at his gold Rolex. 'About time. Here – ' He tapped the chart spread out on the table. 'We've got a lot to cover today. Got to make up for all the bloody weather. Take-off at six, preferably sooner. First job is the Drunour Estate. Three hundred acres of pine.' His finger stabbed a red-ringed area on the chart.

'What about the schedule? I thought – '

'No, Drunour first,' Keen interrupted testily and without explanation. 'Then we'll go back to the schedule.' He flicked through the typed sheets. 'Yes – job number 563 next. Then 568 if there's time.'

Duggan glanced over the job sheets and knew without making calculations that the three jobs would take him well over his official flying time, but made no comment. He needed the money too badly.

'No,' came Keen's voice. 'Forget that last one. We'll wind up with a little job by Loch Fyne.'

Duggan liked the way Keen talked about 'we', as if he himself was going to be up there all day, sweating it out in the poky cockpit of the Porter. Keen was red-pencilling a block of forest on the north side of Loch Fyne. Duggan cast an eye over it. A little job it was not. A hundred and fifty acres at least, and bloody hilly. Could be tricky. And tricky or not, he'd be lucky to get it finished that night. He glanced at the schedule: the job wasn't even typed up.

'It's not typed up,' he said.

'I'll write a job card now,' Keen said heavily.

'I won't have time to recce the site. And what about placing the Hi-Fix?' The electronic spray guidance system required two black box transmitters to be placed on high ground so as to give cross-bearings over the target area and thence, by means of a decoder in the cockpit, to guide the plane along corridors of precisely the right angle and width. Normally the black boxes were put in position by the second member of the ground crew, a singularly brainless oaf named Reggie.

Keen said with elaborate forbearance: 'You can do it on reciprocals, can't you?'

It wasn't worth arguing. Things had been hectic for weeks, ever since the panic about this new bug or moth or whatever it was that was gobbling up all the local forests. Duggan said: 'Allow me an extra fifteen minutes' flying time then.'

'Fifteen minutes?' Keen threw him a pitying glance. 'I thought you ex-fighter boys could do it backwards with your mind in neutral.' Duggan ignored this; he was used to facetious remarks from small-time flyers like Keen.

'What about the notifications?' he asked.

'I had assumed that Jeannie could just about manage that,' Keen said with heavy sarcasm.

Jeannie, who would drift in later, constituted the complete staff of the Portakabin office. Normally she sent the prior notifications to the local police, the local Health and Safety Executive and the properties adjacent to the spraying area by post a good couple of weeks before the expected spraying date, although in all the recent rush Duggan knew she had got behind. How she would cope with the need to leap into sudden and urgent action remained to be seen; even by local standards she wasn't exactly dynamite on the telephone.

Keen scribbled on the job card then, muttering something about going to see Davie the mechanic, hurried out of the Portakabin, leaving Duggan to ponder on the reason for his master's unexpected visit. Money troubles, probably: he had the look about him. Duggan should know; he saw a man with money troubles in the mirror every morning. He made a mental note to ask for his next week's money in cash.

Lighting another cigarette, Duggan settled down to look through the job descriptions and match them against the Ordnance Survey maps. The idea of double checking was to try to get the details right, details like spraying the correct forest, which was always a good start. Only a month before, he'd drenched a large corner of Forestry Commission land by mistake. Then, just last week, he'd showered a flock of sheep in a field that shouldn't have been there.

The sheep episode had refused to leave his mind, not because it was the first time such a thing had happened – it wasn't: cattle, sheep, horses, he'd given them all a dusting in his time – but because of the small dot of colour that had imprinted itself on the periphery of his memory – a dot glimpsed before it vanished under the wing, a dot that wasn't in the slightest sheep-like, a dot that should not under any reasonable circumstances have been there.

He got up to make a coffee and drank it with his fourth cigarette of the morning.

He reckoned up the flying time for the day. Even if he cut short his lunch break to the bare minimum, he'd be hard-pressed to finish all the jobs before nine that evening, uncomfortably close to twilight, and so far over his permitted flying time that it wasn't worth calculating.

As he glanced through the job card Keen had just scribbled, something caught his eye. It was the specification for the Loch Fyne job, a new chemical Keen had sent them out of the blue the week before, something which Jeannie had been writing up as ZXP, but which Duggan, congenitally allergic to technicalia, referred to as the new gunk. Duggan saw that Keen had used what must be the full name: Silveron ZXP.

The question was, would it be compatible with the old gunk they were using during the first half of the day? If not, they'd have to flush out the tanks, which would waste valuable time. He supposed he should ask Keen, since he seemed to be the only one who knew anything about the Loch Fyne job, but when Keen reappeared he was in a flap to get the show on the road and Duggan, not taking kindly to being goaded along, wasn't in the mood to ask.

In fact, what with having to fold an unusual number of charts and failing to find an aspirin for his growing headache and having to put up with Keen breathing down his neck and, most irritating of all, discovering that there was only one Mars Bar left in the box under Jeannie's desk, Duggan's temper was at rock bottom. And the day had only just begun.


At the edge of the forest Nick leaned against a tree and recovered his breath. Gingerly, he fingered the lump on his head and hoped it wasn't going to show. It would be better not to get embroiled in explanations. Alusha wouldn't understand. She'd give him that sideways look of hers, the one that asked him how he could have been such a fool, and he wouldn't be able to give her much of an answer.

It'd been hopelessly naive of him to think he could have

a discussion, even an angry one, with a man in the act of breaking the law. And quoting conservation at him, that had been pie in the sky. The tall man was as likely to think green as to donate salmon to the poor and needy. As for the idea that everyone was going to stick to the quaint rules of conduct which required villains to turn and bolt – well, that cosy little myth looked pretty stupid now.

It wasn't the only myth looking shaky in the first light of day. He'd harboured this ridiculous idea that nothing unpleasant would ever happen at Ashard, that by settling his mind to it, by putting all his energies and emotions into the place, Ashard could become exactly what he wanted it to be – beautiful, flawless, safe. Now, with the night still fresh in his mind, nothing felt too safe any more, and some of the old bitterness and guilt come sourly into his mouth, and he remembered the suppressed rage that had haunted him when he and Alusha first left New York.

Yet, even as he looked out over the enormous panorama before him, he felt the place begin to work its old magic again. Light was expanding over the eastern hills in a brilliant show of gold and yellow that radiated into the tall blue dome of sky above the loch. The water itself was hidden under a thin grey mist, its surface dusted with gold as it caught the early light. There was a wonderful stillness to the air, broken only by birdsong and a sort of vibrant whisper, like the sound of the earth coming awake.

As the familiar delight began to creep through him, he folded the poacher's jacket into a cushion and settled down at the base of the tree. It was five thirty; until the rest of the world awoke this all belonged to him alone. Beneath him, the ground sloped gently away in a long sweep of rough pasture to the richer green of the wide park, with its tall beeches, oaks and cedars, standing like scattered sentries. Then, where the land flattened out slightly before continuing its onward fall to the loch, the house itself stood in its circle of gardens and lawns. There was a faint mist around the house, giving it an even more unreal and extravagant air than usual, like a castle created for a film set. A product of the nineteenth-century baronial building boom, Ashard came complete with mock keep, flagstaff and crenellations. It was not a beautiful house – the stonework was heavy, with reddish tone, the effect dark and sombre – but it had a solidity to it, a dependability that gave it the air of a large and ancient family pet. It was what Alusha called a house of character.

Despite encouragement from his friends, Nick had refrained from flying anything from the flagstaff. A local heraldry expert had assured him that with a good Scots name like Mackenzie there'd be no trouble in finding a coat of arms, but having been born and raised in Chertsey, the depths of green-belt London suburbia, having come nowhere near Scotland for the first thirty-five years of his life, he felt that stuff like flags and coats of arms was not only inappropriate but ludicrously sentimental. Also, flags and pageantry might make Ashard look something of a joke, which it most certainly wasn't, a point on which he was particularly sensitive. Ashard was a working estate, the house his home, and he liked people to know it.

He'd never really wanted to live anywhere else, not since first seeing the place. Certainly not in the house in Provence that he'd owned briefly and visited three or four times, nor the place in the Bahamas he'd kept until last year and secretly hated, and certainly not the apartment in New York. Getting rid of them was the best thing he'd ever done. The only place he'd kept, apart from Ashard, was Caycoo, a small island in the Seychelles, where he and Alusha went every winter. Much as he loved Ashard, winter was not its best season.

He got up and stretched. He decided to walk the long way home, mainly to kill time. If he was going to pretend he'd gone for an early walk, he could hardly return yet.

He picked up the poacher's jacket and, taking the gun in

his other hand, set off along the edge of the trees, heading east across the top of the pasture. His head ached at each step and he winced as his feet jarred over rough ground.

At the eastern corner of the pasture he came to the small dark round hill known as Meall Dhu – which meant, in the way of Gaelic names, dark round hill – and climbed it. It wasn't very high, but from its summit he could look out over the whole of this side of the estate and see high above him, rising over the tree line, the moorlands, daubed gold by the first splashes of sun; and beneath them, reaching as if to his feet, the wide band of mixed deciduous forest that was so much a feature of the Ashard Estate.

To the east the woodland curved round in a narrower band from one to three hundred yards wide, marking the estate boundary on that side. Beyond was the next-door Fincharn Estate. Owned by a London-based insurance company and run solely for profit, it had been turned over to plantations of fast-growing Sitka spruce. Rising over a prominent hill, the dense regimented rows dominated and overshadowed the soft woodland and, to Nick's mind at least, spoilt the view.

He made his way slowly down the hill towards the railed paddock and Alusha's pony Rona. Rona, normally sedate and unexcitable, tossed her head at the sight of him. 'No treats,' he called out to her. 'Sorry.' Coming to the rail, she inspected his empty hands before turning her substantial buttocks on him and trotting off towards her stable.

He continued down, heading directly for the house. The mist was rising from the loch revealing waters the colour of gun-metal, very still and very dark. The loch was long, some forty miles from its head just beyond Inverary to the Firth of Clyde. Though Ashard was a long way from the open sea, he could often smell the salt in the air and sometimes, when up on the moors, he liked to imagine he could glimpse the open ocean beyond the distant Kintyre Peninsula, although he'd been told it was impossible.

He strolled down the steep slope that led from the paddock towards the walled garden, and stopped abruptly. A figure had appeared at the back of the house. It was Alusha, walking in that slow purposeful way of hers, her head high, her hair loose, a basket in one hand, like something out of a pre-Raphaelite painting.

Nick hesitated. He'd been intending to slip the shotgun unobtrusively into the house. Now, he realized, he'd have to think again.

Breaking the gun open, he hung it high over the branch of a rowan tree where it would be hidden behind a screen of foliage, then, after a moment's thought, hung the poacher's jacket alongside it.

Alusha had gone into the walled garden below him. He could see the top of her head as she bent to pick some vegetables. After a moment, she straightened up and stood very still, her face upturned. He knew exactly what she was doing: looking at the light spreading across the sky. The scene was so perfect, she looked so lovely, that his despondency lifted.

He touched the side of his head, checking the lump. It hadn't got any smaller. To cover it he agitated his hair into some sort of uniform confusion, then, brushing down his clothes, entered the walled garden by the nearest gate. Alusha was picking spinach.

'Well!' she exclaimed with a laugh. 'There you are! Where were you when I needed you?'

He gave her a brief kiss. 'Oh? What happened?'

She gave an expressive little shrug. 'Too late now.'

She had a way of being both suggestive and innocent all at the same time. A tantalizing smile hovered on her mouth, and he kissed it again. What he really wanted to do was hug her very hard, not only because he loved her, and today more than ever, but because just looking at her was enough to make him feel the night had been nothing but a bad dream.

He settled on a small squeeze. Normally he wasn't at his most demonstrative before noon and anything more would have made her suspicious.

'What do you think our guests would like for breakfast?' she asked.

Nick had forgotten about them. 'Mel's never been a great one for breakfast,' he said. 'As for David – coffee I should think.'

'And you?' She looked up at him and her smile turned into a small frown. 'What have you been up to? Digging with the rabbits? You're covered in dirt.'

Nick ran a hand over his cheek. 'Don't laugh,' he said. 'I fell over.'

She laughed. 'What were you doing?'

'Tripped over a bramble,' he said, avoiding the question.

'Next you'll tell me you grazed your knee and need a sticky bandage.'

'A sticky plaster,' he automatically corrected her. It was a habit from the days when Alusha's English was fragmentary.

'Poor love,' she murmured with a soft laugh, and reached up as if to stroke his head.

He ducked quickly away. 'Must go and shower.' He blew her a kiss to stifle the faint surprise in her face. She watched him for a moment, narrowing her eyes in a sidelong glance that was both affectionate and suspicious at the same time, then gave a small wave, a slow fluttering of the fingers, before turning back to her vegetables.

It took him a while to find something for his headache. Pills and potions, though not exactly banned at Ashard House, weren't encouraged either.

As Nick crossed the hall, the phone rang.

'Mr Mackenzie, if you please.' It was a male voice with a local accent.

'Yes.'

There was a pause. 'Is that you yourself, Mr Mackenzie?'

'It is.'

'You're back then,' the voice said.

Nick stiffened, then, as realization came, he almost laughed with incredulity. 'You've got a bloody nerve!'

'An unfortunate mishap, Mr Mackenzie. Ma friend, he didna' mean for you to fall on the rock. He wasna' thinkin'.'

'Wasn't thinking! He almost killed me.'

'It was the gun,' the voice chided. 'If it hadna' been for the gun nothin' would have occurred, I think you'll agree.'

'Agree! My mistake was not using the bloody thing. Next time I won't make the same mistake.'

A short pause. 'In that case, Mr Mackenzie, it might be wise to try loadin' it.'

Nick gripped the side of the table. 'I'll remember that. Thank you for mentioning it.'

'Not at all. I trust your head mends good an' quick. An' if you'd leave ma coat by the back there, I'd be obliged. You've a wood store, have you not. If you would leave it there, just inside the door.' There was a soft click as he rang off.

Nick wrenched the receiver from his ear and, holding it inches from his face, stared at it, unable to speak.

Then he gave a short exasperated cry. He was still muttering when he stepped under the shower.

# Chapter 2

SATURDAY, SATURDAY. DAISY awoke feeling guilty, and it was a moment before she remembered that there was no need. She felt a wash of relief. No need to jump out of bed to push oranges through the expensive Californian juicer, which took hours to clean, no need to pound down the street to fetch newly baked croissants, nor feed freshly roasted coffee into the grinder whose screech carved right into her brain.

But then Richard would have put up with anything to get these things right. She knew the end had come when he decided it was time to get into heavy opera, and, not being one to do things by halves, had made her sit through over five hours of *Götterdämmerung*. She wouldn't have minded if opera had been a genuine passion, but like most things with Richard, it was a matter of social éclat. Something that had to be endured to get his lifestyle into shape.

At the opera, during one of the all-too-short intervals, Daisy had failed to live up to cultural expectations in front of Richard's friends by allowing her south London accent out of its cage – as often happened in times of exasperation or stress – and asking who this Wagner geezer thought he was anyway, rambling on for longer than *Ben Hur*, giving people stiff bums and tired brains?

She was so used to waking to the sound of Richard showering – a signal that the rush to create the perfect breakfast must begin – that it was a moment before she identified what had woken her. It was, she realized, the ring, click and buzz of the answering machine. A little early for a social call, which was the only sort she was interested in, but she got out of bed and checked the machine anyway.

'Daisy, something's come up – '

'Oh no, it hasn't,' she said switching the machine firmly off. She didn't need Alan's voice first thing on a Saturday morning, not when she'd heard it all week in the office. What she needed was some calls from her friends, an invitation to a party or two, and while she was waiting for that, a bit of self-indulgence. Now that it was no longer an offence to be a slob, she wanted to go the whole hog – milky Nescafé, the *Sun* and the blare of Capital Radio while reclining on her uncoordinated sheets. And for afters – yes, a bowl of Coco Pops with full-cream milk – none of your skimmed stuff – and a heavy lacing of white sugar, followed by toast made from steam-baked sliced muck from Gateways.

She pottered off to the rabbit-hutch of a kitchen and five minutes later was back in bed with a steaming mug of coffee which, coming straight from the jar, tasted like nectar. The newspapers, despite being yesterday's, weren't bad either, mainly because for the first time in months she passed straight over the *Guardian* and the *Independent* in favour of the tabloids and read all the silly bits.

Skimming through the papers was a regular item in her life, and when pushed she could get through all eight of the main rags in twenty minutes without missing anything very important. She took cuttings on most environmental articles, whether or not they related directly to Catch. Three years ago, when she'd started with Catch, she'd been lucky to find as many as three Green articles in a week of tabloid-reading. Now the office files fairly bulged with Green news, views and opinions.

Anything on chemicals or toxicity was of special interest, of course, but then she usually knew when something like that was coming up. The press, being short on time and information, and lazy to boot, often contacted her for their facts. After she'd done all their work for them she'd give them an earful on the government's environment policy – not a subject she ever felt reticent about – before spelling out Catch's name in full – the Campaign Against Toxic Chemicals – and telling them to put it in big letters near the top of the article, preferably with an appeal for funds. They never did, of course, but she lived in hope. If she hadn't been a dedicated career optimist she wouldn't have been in this job in the first place.

At eleven, when she'd exhausted the last gossip column, she finally got up and, pulling on some jeans and a sweater, went down the hill to Mr Patel's to fetch the Saturday papers.

She still wasn't quite sure why she'd chosen to live here on the borders of Tufnell Park and Upper Holloway. To the east was a ragbag of two-roomed flats and bedsits and crumbling terraces that housed every nationality, and a few more besides. To the west, ranks of grey-brick villas undulated over the switchback of hills that led up to Highgate. Inhabited by writers and academics, classless *Guardian*-readers and women who did pottery – professionally, mind you – and precocious chess-playing kids, it was another continent after the conspicuous consumption of SW3.

And Richard's consumption had been particularly conspicuous – designer haircuts, hand-made shirts, car phones, restaurants six nights a week – though, pig that she was, she'd miss the food all right – and a BMW convertible, for God's sake, which had taken a bit of explaining away at Catch, where the employees – a grand total of three including Daisy herself – were on wages that would have caused the tightest employer to blush.

Daisy hadn't always been poor. In fact until she gave up her job as a solicitor specializing in family law her salary, being firmly tied to the divorce rate, had been buoyant and rising fast. But three years ago, taken by the thought that there had to be more to life than the breakdown of the family unit she'd decided to go for broke, quite literally, by joining the anti-chemical group. She hadn't regretted it. Well, only when she was stupid enough to worry about money.

The newspapers didn't get any lighter, not even when Mr Patel handed them over with an apologetic smile. By the time she had bought Coco Pops, milk, jam, butter (a cholesterol no-no in SW3), a tin of mackerel, fruit, and a sticky cream cake (roughage-free), the walk back up the hill to number 50C Augustus Road became something of a trek.

Climbing, she planned her day. Coco Pops, papers, then work on the flat. The word flat was estate agent's hyperbole really: it was more of a one-roomed space with cubbyholes daringly described as bathroom and kitchen. The place was a new conversion of a Victorian house in a shabby terrace, and it was only after she'd moved in that she began to understand why the rent was affordable. The ceiling was so thin you could hear the two Greek waiters in the flat above arguing, which, being lovers, they did frequently; the fittings were so flimsy that the lever-type plastic door handles had assumed permanent downward curves, there was a chronic shortage of hanging space, and there wasn't a single door that wasn't slightly warped. That said, it was on the first floor with a large bay window which faced south, and the girl she shared it with, a social worker called Anthea, spent four days out of every seven at her boyfriend's.

She struggled in through the flat door just as the phone rang. A social call. One lived in hope anyway.

It was Alan again.

'Don't want to hear from you.'

'Didn't you get my message?' he asked. 'Listen – your Mrs Knowles. Something's come up.'

'Oh?'

'She's planning a one-woman demo at some agricultural show in Berkshire.'

Daisy groaned softly and said, more to herself than to Alan: 'What does she want to go and do that for?'

'Don't know, but it could spoil your coverage.'

Daisy didn't need reminding. She'd been working on the Knowles story for two months and now it was within a week of being ready to tout round the quality press as a subject for a serious investigative piece. The last thing it needed was Mrs Knowles making scenes at some agricultural show, and having the tabloids make her look like some kind of agitator.

'How did you hear?' she asked.

'Local pressman. Left a message on the office machine. Wanted some background. Apparently Mrs Knowles has talked to him and promised him the whole story. He says he's going to try to string it to a national.'

Daisy sat down heavily on the bed. 'Why, for God's sake?'

She could almost see Alan shrugging at the other end of the line. 'Finally got to her?' he suggested. 'Flipped her lid?'

'Don't even mention it.' But the thought had already occurred to her. Alice Knowles was under intolerable pressure; many lesser people would have cracked before now. 'When's this meant to be happening?' she asked.

'At three this afternoon.'

End of quiet Saturday.

Daisy tried calling Alice Knowles, but there was no reply. Already left for the show, perhaps. Or lying low, avoiding the phone.

There was nothing for it then, not if all the work wasn't going to go up the spout. Quite apart from anything else, she rather liked Mrs Knowles; it would be dreadful to see her disappointed, maybe even humiliated.

The case was typical of many that came Catch's way.

The Knowleses were a farming family with seven hundred acres of good arable land not far from Newbury. Nice hard-working people, reasonably prosperous, distinctly law-abiding. Like most farmers, they worked with large quantities of chemicals. But unlike most other families they had been unlucky or not careful enough, or both, and now things had gone wrong.

But was a demonstration going to help? Daisy tried to imagine what sort of protest Alice Knowles might be planning. Handing out leaflets, setting up a stall? Not so bad. Banner waving, shouting, speech making? Not so good. In the minds of much of the press any sort of jumping up and down was still firmly associated with weirdos and political agitators, and while they might print a two-line protest story, they were unlikely to give the item the space it deserved. Alice would be written off as an isolated old woman with a grievance, and Daisy's chances of getting a serious investigative piece would be that much reduced.

But there might still be time to pre-empt things. Leafing through her address book, she found the number of Simon Calthrop, a *Sunday Times* journalist she'd just met. Simon was a committed environmental reporter, just as he'd been a committed consumer affairs correspondent two years before, and a dedicated investigative reporter the year before that.

He sounded grumpy when he answered the phone. 'Can't do anything this week,' he began unpromisingly.

'As a human interest story then,' Daisy suggested. 'You know, how ordinary people are driven to desperate acts. It could make a good photo feature.'

'Mmm.' He sounded unconvinced. 'So tell me about it.'

Daisy told him about the family and how the medical tests had shown them to have high levels of pesticide residues in their bodies – the residue of several pesticides unfortunately, and not just one or two, so that it was impossible to know which particular chemical or cocktail of chemicals might have caused their troubles. But Daisy had her suspicions. For years the Knowleses had been using the pesticide Aldeb on their potato crop. She reminded Simon that Aldeb was under notice of withdrawal in the US because of fears that it was carcinogenic.

'And in Britain?' he asked.

'Here?' Daisy gave a derisive laugh. 'You know how it is – everything takes a little longer. The ministry did their usual trick and rejected the US research on the grounds that it was inconclusive. Aldeb's still heading the bestsellers' list.'

'Mmm.' He wasn't sounding enthralled by the story so far. 'Aldeb's who, remind me?'

'Morton-Kreiger. They've just announced their results. Worldwide profits of three hundred million, give or take the odd million. Pounds, that is.'

'And what's their response been? You've contacted them, presumably.'

Daisy was beginning to realize that, for all his erudite environmental articles, Simon still didn't know everything about the workings of agrochemical companies. 'What response?' she replied caustically. 'You must be joking. I'm always referred to their legal department.'

He took the point, though she could sense that he didn't appreciate it being made so forcefully. Tactlessness – and instant regret – were such a regular feature of her life that she automatically backtracked, adding quickly: 'What I mean is, they've been less helpful than they could have been.'

'Listen, this isn't exactly straightforward,' Simon said. 'If there's a story, it could take weeks to dig out. I really don't think there'd be much point in covering this woman and her demonstration this afternoon, not at this stage – '

'Maybe not, but let me come over with the file,' Daisy urged. 'It's impressive, I promise you. The story could be an important one. At least we think so. And if we're right, then a lot of farmers could be at risk.' He was silent, but Daisy could sense a flicker of interest. 'Needless to say,' she added, 'you'd have full access to all our material.'

Another pause. She'd almost got him.

'Where do you live?' she asked.

He lived in Islington. After a detour to the office at King's Cross to pick up the Knowles file and the draft press releases, she made it in forty minutes. His flat was on the third floor of a tall house in a rubbish-strewn street off the Pentonville Road. The main room was basic but comfortable, with a couple of deep sofas, a Habitat dining-table and an expensive-looking Scandinavian hi-fi system. There were a few good etchings on the walls, a dying fig tree in the window and on the floor several piles of magazines and newspapers. A functional if untidy kitchen was visible through a half-open door.

A typical bachelor flat – or was it? She found herself casting around for signs of female occupation, and was surprised at herself. Was she making room for a new man in her life? More to the point, was she considering the rather dry, unemotional Simon?

He emerged from the kitchen with two mugs of coffee. He was wearing the rumpled but carefully assembled uniform of the north London intellectual: well-worn jeans, open-necked safari-style shirt which, if it had encountered an iron at all, had met it only briefly, and old tennis shoes. He had a pale face, glasses with minimal gold frames, dark eyebrows that feathered over the bridge of his nose and heavy black hair which kept falling over his eyes.

She took him through the file, item by item. Eventually he said wearily: 'It could make a small item, I suppose . . . Or a major investigative piece. But I can't see anything in between.'

'Okay then,' Daisy said immediately. 'Make it a major investigative piece.'

He gave a weighty sigh. 'I've got two big features on the

go at the moment . . . I couldn't possibly start on anything yet. Not for some time, in fact.'

'But soonish?' She was pressing him, she knew it, but it was vital to screw some sort of commitment out of him, however tenuous. 'We could get more data, I'm sure of it,' she said more out of hope than certainty. 'Other victims and that sort of thing.'

'Oh? Where from?'

She had to think quickly. 'Umm, the unions. The NFU, the Transport and General Workers.' She had in fact already spent long hours with the health-and-safety officers of the two unions, combing their files. The National Farmers' Union had produced a number of cases which might be traceable to Aldeb, but the evidence had been sketchy even by Daisy's undemanding standards. There were hundreds of cases out there, Daisy was sure of it; the victims just didn't know what had hit them.

'Okay.' Simon gave another, sharper sigh. 'Find what you can and when I've got the time I'll have a look at it.'

She had to settle for that. She took another coffee off him all the same, partly to satisfy her curiosity about him, partly to argue her case again should the chance arise, which it soon did. If she was being dogged, it was because in this line of work opportunites had to be grabbed as they arose and then shaken into life. It wasn't enough to have right on your side; that never got anyone anywhere.

'Of course it *has* been known for the Americans to get it wrong,' Simon said. 'They can over-react.'

'What, on Aldeb?' Daisy exclaimed. 'Have you seen the evidence?'

He shrugged, as if nobody of any sense could seriously believe that anything, even scientific evidence, could be taken at face value. 'To provide balance I'd have to interview Morton-Kreiger. Get their side of things.'

'I wish you luck,' she said drily. 'I'd be interested to know what they have to say.'

Simon, making an obvious effort to be sociable, asked about her background. She told him about being brought up in Catford, famous for the greyhound stadium, how her father had encouraged her to get some A-levels and try for a law scholarship to Birmingham, which she didn't get. Her parents had sent her all the same, though it was a strain financially. 'They thought education set you apart. It did, in Catford at least. None of my school friends ever spoke to me again. I had a best friend called Samantha who thought I'd got totally above myself. The last I heard, she was earning a thousand quid a week as a nude model. My only consolation is that my assets are likely to hold up longer than hers.'

Simon's forehead creased. 'Assets?'

Daisy studied him carefully but he wasn't having her on.

Comprehension finally slid over his face and his mouth cracked into a nominal grin. 'I'm a bit slow this morning. Late night,' he said with a hint of pride, and she wondered what – or who – had been keeping him up so late.

Letting it pass, she went on with the story, about her years at Birmingham and coming back to London and all the divorces she'd processed and how she'd despaired at married people's general desire to tear each other apart, and how she'd wanted to bash their heads together when they fought over the children. 'The only thing that kept me going was the light relief. After five years, what I didn't know about sexual proclivities wasn't worth stamping on a pinhead.'

Her life story had never been particularly exciting, even when she spiced it up a bit, but it was still disconcerting to find Simon staring past her towards the window, looking preoccupied. If there was potential in a relationship with Simon, then it was failing to reveal itself.

'Well,' she said, 'a pity to cut this short, but I must be going.'

He looked mildly sorry, which was a surprise. 'Ah.'

'I've got to go and see Alice Knowles.'

'I'll give you a ring next week then, shall I?' He shot her a quick glance. 'There's a good film on at the Screen.'

So it was to be social? Was he keen after all? If so, he'd done a brilliant job of concealing it. More to the point, how keen was she?

Perhaps he caught the doubt in her eyes, because he blinked at her through his spectacles and said: 'Sorry if I've been less than ... er ... *compos*, you know. But I was up till four. Working.'

'Till four? God, they push you hard.'

'No, no. I was working on ... well, my novel.' He looked defensive, as if he'd just let her into a devastating secret and wasn't sure how she'd take it.

'Your novel?'

'Yes. Nights are the only chance I get.'

This explained the preoccupied look, and in her mind his image underwent an instantaneous metamorphosis from harassed journalist to tortured novelist. She agreed to go the cinema with him later in the week.


Daisy's W-registration Metro was perfectly adequate for London, but in recent months it had started to balk at motorways, and, reaching the M4, it began to grumble. A mechanic had told her the suspension was on its way out, a problem which hadn't sounded too serious in Chelsea, but which here on the open road was definitely ominous. She stuck to the slow lane, ambling along with the family traffic and swaying caravans, and hoped there wouldn't be too many jams getting into the show.

A few miles short of Newbury it began to rain, solid permeable stuff that seeped in through the bodywork, but it eased off a little as she took the slip-road and followed the signs towards the showground at Newbury racecourse.

The traffic, though heavy, was still moving and she made it into the field-cum-car park by a few minutes before three. The rain, choosing its moment, fell heavily again. She did not have an umbrella. Getting out, her feet sank ominously into the sodden grass. She pulled her jacket over her head, mainly to protect the sheaf of press releases that she had under her arm.

Green wellies, dun-coloured waxed jackets, headscarves with chains and anchors; horsy women who talked in loud authoritative voices, farming types with jutting chins and grouchy expressions who looked as if they shot everything that moved, and probably did; also people, like Daisy, in unsuitable shoes, men in thin shirts and women in summer dresses sheltering from the rain. It was a big show and she had to ask the way to the agrochemical merchants' stand a couple of times before finally locating it half-way down an aisle of large marquees, lodged between a bank and a brewery.

Nothing. No Mrs Knowles chained to the railings. No Mrs Knowles brandishing a large placard. But there was a young man dripping quietly under the porch, sheltering a camera under his jacket, wearing the watchful lugubrious expression of a pro.

Daisy retreated to the bank next door and waited beneath their tented porch on a boardwalk. Three fifteen. Still no sign of Mrs Knowles. Then Daisy spotted the small purposeful figure in brogues and a long raincoat marching up the avenue of stands with a flat parcel under one arm. She was flanked by four men, and Daisy recognised the long waterproof jackets and energetic strides of provincial pressmen.

Alice was travelling fast. Daisy hurried to intercept her before she reached the agrochemical stand.

She didn't seem surprised at the sight of her. She even managed a faint smile. 'Oh, hullo, Daisy,' she said, stepping neatly past her and continuing her onward progress.

'Mrs Knowles – Alice – look, are you sure this is a good idea?' Daisy said, hurrying to keep up.

She didn't slow down. 'Well, something's got to be done, hasn't it?'

'Yes, but ...' Eyeing the reporters, Daisy dropped her voice. 'What about our press release? What about the evidence and the meeting with the man from the ministry? I thought we were going to wait, like we agreed.'

Alice narrowed her lips and said firmly: 'Can't wait any longer.'

'But why now, Alice? Why so suddenly?'

She snorted and shook her head. 'Got a letter from the government safety people. Told me I was talking rubbish.'

'But, Alice – one letter.'

'Four years' hell and the blighters aren't even listening,' Alice retorted. 'Can't wait any longer.'

Daisy took her arm and whispered: 'I know how you feel, Alice, but listen – people aren't going to understand something like this ... It might actually put them off, you know. They're going to think – well, that you're overdoing it a bit.'

'Oh?' Alice Knowles stuck her chin out. 'Well, we'll see, won't we?' Her hair, normally grey and bouncy, was plastered darkly over her forehead. Rivulets of water ran down her cheeks and hung from her nose in droplets. With her square face and jutting jaw, she looked like a bull terrier, small and very determined.

'Alice – I really don't think this is the best way.'

'If Jane Fonda can protest and get her picture in the paper, why can't I?'

Oh my Lord, Daisy thought, there's no answer to that. About the only thing Alice Knowles and Jane Fonda had in common was their age.

'Alice – '

But Alice wasn't listening any more. Having given her face an abrupt wipe on her sleeve, she was tackling the wrapping on her parcel, which looked uncomfortably like a placard.

'What's the story?' a reporter murmured in Daisy's ear.

Where did one start? Tragedy sounded trite when reduced to a few sentences. Instead, Daisy fumbled under her jacket and pulled out one of her press releases.

'Thanks.' The reporter skimmed through it. 'Can this be proved? I mean is it certain that this stuff killed her husband?'

'Depends what you mean by proof,' Daisy said. 'We've got two doctors' opinions. Aldeb was found in his blood and body tissue – '

'But is that proof? You know . . .'

She knew all right. He meant, was it signed and sealed and agreed upon by the entire scientific community, the whole medical profession and all the various government departments. The answer was, of course, no. In fact: no, no and no. Not one body or group agreed on anything. Quite the opposite in fact: many so-called experts would rather die than admit to the possibility of agreeing with other experts in their own field.

'As much proof as one can ever get,' she said truthfully.

'Oh.' By the sound of his voice, he had lost interest and would probably have slipped away if the action, such as it was, hadn't been about to start.

The wrapping was off what was indeed a placard. Alice Knowles turned to face her audience, which consisted of the small knot of reporters and photographers, and a group of unsuspecting show-goers sheltering from the rain. She clasped the placard against her body, message inwards, so that no one could read it until she was ready.

She cleared her throat and began in a fierce emotional voice: 'I've come here today out of desperation. I've come to make myself heard because no one'll listen . . .' The show-goers began to shuffle imperceptibly backwards, as if this sudden burst of sincerity and passion might be dangerous. '... I couldn't let this thing go unchallenged any more. I have already lost my husband. Now I'm in danger of losing my son ...' The crowd had stopped shuffling and was now rigid with amazement. '... They were both perfectly healthy men, nothing wrong with them, never been to a doctor in their lives. Not until they made the mistake of believing wholesale lies. Not until they made the mistake of believing the totally meaningless assurances they were given by the manufacturers of Aldeb and the Ministry of Agriculture ...' The listeners weren't sure about that; nor, for that matter, was Daisy. *Too much, Alice; too strong, too moralistic.* The onlookers began to exchange glances and dive off into the rain in search of fresh shelter.

Sensing the crowd's restlessness, Alice faltered and seemed to lose her thread but then, fixing the reporters with her intense stare, she got a second wind and launched forth again. 'I want to prevent this happening to other families. I want to make sure no one has to suffer as we have suffered. I want these dangerous untested chemicals banned, and not just to protect people like us, farmers who have to work with these poisons, but to save every man, woman and child in this country. To save everyone who's eating and drinking these dreadful things and doesn't realize it.'

She went on for a bit, talking about the unrealized menace of pesticides, their role in disease – she quoted almost every incurable disease in the book, though where she'd got those ideas from, Daisy couldn't imagine – then, having repeated herself a few times, tailed off.

Daisy thought: Oh, *Alice.* It was a gallant little speech, bravely delivered but seriously misjudged. Daisy gave her a little cheer all the same. The pressmen looked less than bowled over.

Suddenly remembering the placard, Alice Knowles turned it round and held it up. It read: BAN DEADLY

CHEMICALS – BAN ALDEB – BAN POISONS THAT KILL INNOCENT FARMERS.

A photographer dutifully took a picture or two. A local radio reporter advanced on Alice and pointed a microphone at her. Daisy handed out press releases. But it was no good, she knew it was no good. The popular press didn't like one-woman demos any more than they liked stories about obscure chemicals, shadowy unseen things neither they nor their readers knew or cared to know about, not when there were good old bogey men like nuclear power to pick on, not when they had tear-jerking pictures of children with leukaemia, not when they had villainous substances that were certified guaranteed all-bad, things like PCPs, CFCs and leaded petrol.

Poor Alice. Husband dead of cancer. Only son fighting the disease. She'd believed that her evidence, with the opinion of two doctors, would be enough to get her some sort of justice; she'd imagined that the world would listen. Well, she'd learnt differently, and now she was going to be disappointed all over again.

Not that the event was over. The agrochemical merchants had finally woken up to the fact that someone was saying nasty things about one of the products on their stand. A small bullish man had shoved his way through the onlookers and pushed his face close to Alice's. Daisy couldn't hear what was said, but Alice drew back, looking at once nervous and defiant, then, rallying, pulled herself up to her full height, which wasn't very much, and stood her ground.

Daisy stepped forward. 'Can I help?'

The bullish man spun round. 'She's got to go, or I'll have to call the police.'

Daisy was soothing. 'She's finished now, I think. Just making a point. Quite peaceably.'

But he wasn't having any of that. 'Off – *now*. This minute.'

'Well, of course, if that's – '

Alice cut in: 'I refuse to leave, I'm afraid.'

'Right,' said the bullish man, vibrating with sudden rage. 'If that's the way you want it, no problem. I'll get the police to remove you forcibly.' And elbowing his way past Daisy, he swept off into the rain.

Not surprisingly, the pressmen had changed their minds about going and were now waiting patiently for their police-remove-lady pictures. They weren't disappointed. It was an ugly little scene, and Daisy felt a lurch of humiliation for Alice Knowles. Once the two policemen had established that she wasn't going to go willingly, they took an elbow each and marched her towards the showground entrance. As Daisy set off after them, she looked back and saw the bullish man pick up the placard and break it across his knee.

It took quite a while to get Alice Knowles back into some sort of shape. Despite her brave front, she was badly shaken. She'd never experienced the police in anger before. Daisy drove her to a motorway café and fed her tea and biscuits for over an hour before deciding it was safe to take her back to the ground to collect her car.

They sat in the Metro for a while, watching the rain course down the windscreen.

Alice gave a deep sigh. 'I suppose I've been a bit of an ass,' she said.

'I wouldn't say that!' Daisy said quickly. 'A bit of an optimist maybe.'

'I had to do something.'

'I know.'

'What next then?'

'Well, I'll have another go at the live wires in the ministry,' said Daisy. 'Beat them over the head, you know. Interrupt their tea break, remind them we're not going to go away and give up.'

'Do you really think they'll listen?'

It was hard to explain to people like Alice just how obtuse and convoluted were the workings of the Ministry of Agriculture, Fisheries and Food. MAFF had until a few years ago worked entirely on the principle that pesticide manufacturers were all frightfully good honest chaps, and should be allowed to run their own chemical safety scheme on a voluntary basis, administered by the ministry's Advisory Committee on Pesticides. The safety scheme was now legally enforced, which was a step in the right direction, but that didn't prevent the activities of the ACP from being secretive, and their findings unchallengeable. Worse, there was no proper watchdog in the UK, nothing like the USA's Environmental Protection Agency, no one to re-examine the manufacturer's safety tests to make sure they had been sufficiently thorough, no one to challenge the widespread official view that chemicals were all right until they turned round and bit you. Ludicrously, the Ministry of Agriculture, Fisheries and Food was meant to represent not only the farmer and the agrochemical industry – groups whose interests were often diametrically opposed – but also the consumer. And though consumers might have a number of vague worries about the amount of chemicals in their food, it was the farming and agrochemical lobbies that had all the clout. Outsiders, people like the Knowleses, found it hard to understand just how low consumer interests came in the pecking order. Getting information out of the ACP or MAFF was like extracting a tasty bone from the teeth of a fierce dog: almost impossible without a large stick and a lot of muscle. Catch had neither.

'We'll get to them in the end,' Daisy said with a conviction she didn't entirely feel. 'There's our tame MP, Jimmy. He's had four shots at getting a question at prime minister's question time. Might be fifth time lucky.'

'But it's no good, is it? Any of it.'

Daisy laughed. 'Blimey, Alice, if I thought that, I might as well tie my ankles together and jump in the river.

Honestly, I'd give up tomorrow if I thought I was getting nowhere. It's just *slow* that's all. Like swimming through wet concrete. But we'll get there in the end. I do believe that, Alice, I do, really, otherwise I wouldn't be bothering.'

Alice was slumped in the seat. Her hair had dried into a grey frizz. She looked exhausted. 'But they won't even speak to us, will they? Won't tell us anything. That's not going to change, is it?'

'Well – no, not for the moment,' Daisy admitted. Incredibly, information on certain types of pesticides came under the Official Secrets Act because the chemicals had been developed from nerve gases. No good pointing out that almost every belligerent country in the world – and there were enough of them, God only knew – was well aware of how to produce nerve gases. No good arguing that information on this type of pesticide was freely available in the US. The British loved secrets. Correction: the British *Establishment* loved secrets – a different thing. The information that wasn't protected by the Official Secrets Act was covered by that old stalwart of profit-making prevaricators – commercial confidentiality. MAFF and the pesticide manufacturers looked after each other very nicely, thank you. From the rosy picture the two of them painted, you'd never have thought there'd ever been a mishap, far less a disaster. No DDT, no 2,4,5-T, no dioxins. Very cosy, very frustrating, and very difficult to comprehend when all you wanted was the answer to a few simple questions like why and how, and can't this be prevented from happening again.

Alice blew into a handkerchief with a blast like a ship's siren, and shook her head. 'Just what will it take?'

Daisy knew the answer to that. Cast-iron scientific proof in triplicate. A silenced agrochemical lobby (that would be the day). Further disaster.

'They're banning it in the States,' Daisy reminded her. 'It'll get banned here in the end too.'

'But when?'

Daisy sighed. 'Good question.'

'What will it take?' Alice repeated, almost to herself.

'Money, I'm afraid, Alice. Pots of dough. On a scale I don't even dare think about.'

Alice nodded with weary resignation. She began to get out of the car. 'I'll send you a cheque when I can.'

Daisy's throat tightened. 'Oh, Alice, don't. Keep your money. You'll be needing it.'

Alice didn't reply but climbed out and slammed the door.

Daisy wound the window down and called after her: 'Sure you'll be all right?'

Alice gave a small wave and got into her car. Daisy watched to make sure she got away all right, thinking that if only worthiness and dedication were enough, then the Alices of this world would keep Catch going for ever. But Catch ran on hard cash, and it took a shocking number of small cheques from the likes of Alice to keep it afloat. And that was without any wild notions about an independent research programme.

Put off by the rain, people were going home early and there were long queues of cars leaving the ground.

A research programme or two ... And a proper press office, professional parliamentary lobbyists, a national membership organization, a glossy newsletter ... Well, the list was endless. All it needed was what Catch's accountant liked to call a healthy injection of cash. But then what campaigning organization didn't need that? The few outfits that had managed to trap a tame environmentally minded millionaire kept good and quiet about it – and who could blame them – and those that hadn't, which was an awful lot, sat like alley cats, waiting to pounce on a passing moneypots, fully prepared to scratch each other's eyes out in the process. Green campaigning wasn't quite the benevolent business people imagined it to be.

Finally getting away from the showground, Daisy

pointed the Metro in the direction of London, thinking about money, wondering what she could salvage from her press campaign on the Knowles story, and doing her best to ignore the grinding noises coming from the suspension.

# Chapter 3

—————

DAVID WEINBERG AWOKE with a sense of alarm. It was a moment before he was able to identify the reason. It was the quiet; a pervasive and sinister sort of hush. For David, a Londoner born and bred, silence was unsettling: it was the world standing still, someone else getting a deal, and being dead and knowing all about it, all rolled into one.

The sound of a car in the drive reassured him sufficiently to get up. His instinct was to reach for the phone and start worrying his way through the day, but he remembered this was Saturday, he was in the middle of Scotland and this was supposed to be a break, something people like him were meant to need, though he could never understand why, since leisure had never done anything for him except upset his stomach.

Once dressed, he wandered downstairs in search of Nick. The house was quiet, the doors around the large flag-stoned hall open, no sounds issuing from the sunlit rooms. Only in the kitchen were there signs of life: coffee on a hot stand, croissants in a warming dish, butter and marmalade on the table. He helped himself to coffee, added forbidden sugar, and looked for the newspapers. Then he remembered: Nick had told him they didn't arrive before late morning.

Without the *Financial Times* the croissant tasted bland, the coffee flat. The kitchen was pleasant enough – Nick had always spent a lot of money on his homes – but if David couldn't look at the share index then he would like some company. Shoving the last of the croissant into his mouth, picking up his coffee cup, he went in search of the household. The formal living room was, as expected, empty. The room was high and vaulted, with polished wood floors, Persian rugs, Victorian-style high-backed chairs, long damask-covered settees and a vast baronial fireplace crying out for stags' heads which, this being Nick's and Alusha's house, it would never get.

Nick called this the drawing room – a bit grand, David thought, even for such a grand room. There was something delightfully incongruous about Nick, whose family had never inhabited anything more impressive than a small lounge, talking about a drawing room as if he'd lived in one all his life. But then the Nick of Ashard House wasn't the same boy that David had first met in the poky Chertsey semi all those years ago – and that was just as it should be. Of all his people, David had been – perhaps still was – proudest of Nick. Nick had made the most of himself; Nick, as David's mother used to say, had made good. He'd never allowed himself to be taken in by the lunacy of fame and the endless flow of cash. Nick had gone his own way, in his own way.

Standing behind one of the long settees was a large drinks trolley, thickly forested with bottles. At one time Nick's way had included the drink, of course; but even then he had drunk with style, unobtrusively, almost secretively. Unlike Mel and Joe, there'd been no benders, no downhill races towards self-destruction, no stoking up on chemical cocktails. Not to say the drinking hadn't been a big problem: it had. Nick had drunk steadily and with single-minded concentration, as if mastering a new skill, and it was only after two unproductive years that he'd frightened himself into doing something about it. But once he'd made up his mind to stop, that was it. As David knew to his cost, Nick could be determined when he chose to be.

It was typical of Nick both to have such a lavishly

stocked bar, and to have it in full view, where it would provide a constant reminder and maximum temptation.

On the other side of the hall was the library, now a television and video room, which looked altogether more lived in than the drawing room. This too was empty. Back in the hall, David paused to glance at the visitors' book, a thick leather-bound volume, already more than half full of signatures and comments from what seemed to be a fairly constant stream of guests. There were a few big names – actors, writers, new rich – but in the main it was Nick's carefully chosen inner circle, none of whom, as David well knew, came from the music world. The dining room he didn't bother to check, but went straight along the adjoining passage to the studio. The padded door was open, a sure sign that Nick was not at work, but David looked in all the same, just in case. He was curious to see if the setup had changed and, though he hardly admitted it even to himself, to see if there were signs of work in progress. In the twenty-eight years he'd handled Nick, David had never once asked when the next song was coming. He liked to think that that was one of the reasons he was still around.

The studio was a fairly recent addition to the house, built when Nick had decided to move in permanently six years before. Like everything else Nick had a hand in, it was beautifully designed, though, unusually for him, the room was untidy. In the old days Nick had always been neat to the point of obsession, especially when it came to his work places, yet there were books scattered over almost every working surface, even the piano and synthesizer.

David peered at the titles. There were books on organic farming, broadleaf forestry and environmental protection. Nick had been interested in things Green for a long time. As far back as the early seventies he'd marched in protest against whaling – or was it sealing?

On another surface were two large expensive-looking books on, of all things, birds. The books were lying open

to show large colour illustrations of such feathered friends
as – David had to peer at the unfamiliar names – kites,
buzzards and ospreys. Beside them was a loose-leaf student's pad covered in Nick's spidery scrawl. David couldn't
help glancing at it. Under the heading 'Habitat' were
various notes on, as far as David could make out, the
nesting habits of ospreys.

He scanned the rest of the room. There was no sign of
anything like work, no scattering of sheet manuscript.
Sipping the last of his coffee, he returned to the open pad
and stared thoughtfully at the bird notes. When Nick had
first thought of burying himself up here David had been as
keen as anyone for him and Alusha to find a place where
they could get over the unpleasantness of the New York
incident, and had gone out on a limb to encourage him,
something he would normally have avoided. It was one
thing to be responsible for people's working lives – money
and deals had neat conclusions – and quite another to
interfere in their private affairs, which were always, but
always, minefields of the most lethal kind. The mildest
suggestion, the slightest offer of help, earned you nothing
but resentment, hostility and a lifetime's blame.

Having broken his own rule and encouraged Nick, he
had long since regretted it. He'd hoped this Scottish jaunt
would mark the beginning of a new era of productivity, but
far from stimulating Nick the place seemed gradually to
have stultified him. The first three years had been all right
– there'd been enough material for two albums – but more
recently the flow had dropped to a trickle. Three songs in
two years, not enough for an album, and worst of all,
unrecorded because, try as David might, he couldn't get
Nick near a recording studio.

Nick had hinted that he was working on some experimental material – there was a chilling rumour that it was a
modern opera-type piece using a choir, or something else

equally uncommercial. Whatever, it was a project rarely
mentioned and never seen, and consequently written off by
David. Yet Nick seemed perfectly happy. To David, this
was totally mystifying. How could Nick be happy if he
wasn't producing albums, wasn't using his gift? How could
he live without work?

There was a sound from the passage, the door swung
wide, and Nick strode in. He gave a start like a nervous
animal, then a characteristically quiet smile spread across
his face. 'David! Looking for the action, were you?' He
gave a wry laugh. 'Well, you won't find it here, I'm afraid.'
This admission didn't seem to upset him.

David gave a slow shrug. 'Just wondering where everyone was.'

'We were down in the new garden, looking at the roses.'
Nick shot him an oblique glance. 'You found some breakfast all right?'

David raised his coffee cup in reply.

'Sleep well?'

David made a so-so gesture. 'I was a bit worried when I
woke up. It was so quiet I thought I might have bought it
in my sleep.'

Nick laughed at that. 'No chance. You'll die at ninety.
Doing a deal with the undertaker.'

'Don't *you* find it quiet?'

Nick perched himself on the edge of a table. 'Too much
to do. The estate, the gardens – you know. And people to
stay. Alusha loves that. And so do I, of course,' he added
quickly in case David should think otherwise.

Nick glanced towards the door and whispered in a
theatrical voice: 'Got a smoke?'

'I gave up. Five years ago.'

'Of course. So you did. I gave up – when was it?'

'Four years ago. The year after me.'

Nick shook his head, surprised that David should

remember such details of his life. 'I wouldn't mind a smoke now. I didn't sleep much last night.' He patted the side of his head and screwed up his face, as if in pain.

'That's not like you.'

'It's your visit, David, it makes me nervous.'

He didn't look in the slightest bit nervous. David made a mild gesture of astonishment. 'Me? Why?

'Because you never say anything.'

'What about, Nick?'

'You know. About the next album. You should be beating me over the head and giving me a hard time. And you don't. It makes me feel guilty as hell.'

David didn't take this accusation too seriously. 'Nick – when did I ever beat you over the head?'

'I've just been too busy, David. There's been all the forestry work. That took an age. Then there was the farm to get off the ground.'

'Nick, you don't have to apologize to me, you know.'

He conceded this with a small laugh. 'I know, but . . . I feel everyone's hovering quietly on the sidelines, waiting for me to produce the goods.'

'I don't think anyone's complaining.'

'Not complaining. But *expecting*, which is worse.' He paused apologetically. 'They might have a long wait, David. I'm not sure when there'll be another album. Or even *if* there'll be another album.'

'Well, if that's the way it is, then that's fine with me,' David lied, hiding a sudden swoop of disappointment. He could understand Nick's reluctance to get together with Amazon again – it was thirteen years since the band was at its peak and ten since it was more or less disbanded – but to give up his solo career? After the last two albums had gone platinum? It tortured David even to think about it.

'But it's not so fine with Mel and Joe, I take it?' Nick asked, sounding beleaguered.

'Joe, he's got his Medea tour. I don't think he minds one way or the other. Mel, well . . .'

'What is it he wants? To get back together again?'

'I think so.'

This evasion earned David a mildly reproving look. 'The two of you coming up here. Looks like a deputation to me.'

'It was Mel's idea.'

Nick gave a slow nod as if he'd suspected this from the beginning. He went across to the window and stood staring out at the garden. 'I can't do the old stuff any more, David. I've moved on. I'm just not interested. I couldn't . . .' He lost momentum and trailed off. 'What does Mel want – an album?'

David moved across to a deep leather chair and sat down. 'I think so.'

'What – Amazon Ten Years On?'

'An album was one idea.'

Nick threw him a sharp glance. 'What was the other?'

David looked pained that he should even have to speak the word. 'A tour.'

'You're kidding? You are, aren't you?' Reading David's expression, he gasped: 'You're not. God. I never thought I'd hear that coming from Mel. Of all people.' He gave an incredulous laugh. 'I thought that was the one thing we were all agreed on. No more tours. What's made him change his mind, for heaven's sake?'

'I honestly don't know. You'll have to ask him yourself.'

Nick frowned for a moment then left the window and flopped into the chair opposite, stretching his long legs across the carpet.

'Kids don't want to see middle-aged trendies,' he argued. 'What's Mel – forty-eight? I'm almost forty-seven. That's as good as a hundred to them. They don't want to watch wrinkles and bulging tums and grey hairs peeking through gold medallions. Hell, they've got fathers of our age on their second coronary bypass.'

David knew the argument wasn't really about age or restarting Amazon or a shortage of the right material. It was all about touring being agony for Nick, who was too private a person to find the hysteria and clamour of the circuit anything but ridiculous.

'The Stones' US tour was a sell-out,' David ventured.

'They're different.'

'The Who, the – '

'Okay, okay. But turning back the clock? Trying to act twenty. Worse – trying to *look* it. They'd have a hell of a job tarting up my mug anyway.' Laughing, he rubbed a hand mercilessly over his face.

'You look fine,' David said, and meant it. Nick had never been good-looking – that accolade, such as it was, had always gone to Mel – but he was a striking man, with his broad strong features, sandy hair and pale eyes, made remarkable by having one of the most lived-in faces David had ever seen.

'It makes my blood run cold,' Nick added reflectively, 'to think of being sprayed into leather jeans and having my hair tangled each morning . . .'

David said: 'That's the biz though, isn't it?'

'I suppose so,' he agreed heavily.

'You'll have to talk to Mel.'

Nick gave a sigh of resignation or perhaps weariness. David didn't envy him the chat with Mel. Although Amazon had disbanded amicably, both Mel and Joe had regretted opting out. While Nick's solo career had rocketed, their attempts to go it alone had been less than successful. Which didn't come as any surprise to David, who'd never had any doubts as to who was the lynchpin of the group. Without Amazon, Mel and Joe were nothing, because they were nothing without Nick. Everyone knew it. 'It's not as if we needed the money,' Nick said almost to himself. He turned suddenly. 'We don't, do we?'

David shrugged. In his book one always needed more

money because money was the only reliable measure of success. 'No one *needs* the bread,' he conceded. 'Except perhaps Joe, but then I warned him about getting married in California.'

'Is it the live gigs then? I mean, is that what Mel's hankering after?'

David was careful to make a non-committal face, but Nick wasn't fooled.

'You know, don't you?' he accused gently. Suspicion darted into his face. 'What is it — a woman?'

David went through a last gesture of reticence, then gave a slow nod. 'She's eighteen.'

Nick rolled his eyes. 'Dear Lord. What *is* he thinking of? No' – he held up a hand – 'don't answer that!' He pushed his head hard against the back of the chair, his eyes screwed up against some non-existent glare. 'It's no good.'

'But with new material, new ideas?'

'What new material? There is no new material. I've been writing solo stuff, David. Or stuff Mel or Joe wouldn't want to use.'

David was curious to know more about this experimental material and what made it so unperformable – was it lyrical, like most of Nick's solo material, or was the horrid rumour correct and it was opera stuff? And, just as relevant, did it exist on paper or was it still an unrealized idea in Nick's head?

Before he could think of a way of framing an appropriate question, Nick stood up abruptly and smiled his gentle sidelong smile. 'Come on, David, I'll show you round the estate.' He said it with such anticipation that David got to his feet and, looking suitably enthusiastic, asked him to lead on.

It was one by the time they had inspected the forest, the new broadleaf plantation and the farm which Nick had added to the estate three years before. As Nick liked to recount it, he'd had to buy the farm to obtain manure for the vegetable garden. Being a purist, only chemical-free manure would do, so the farm was slowly being turned into an all-organic showpiece.

It was costing, of course. Though the estate was a limited company which Nick ran more or less independently, David had a pretty good idea of what was being put into it in the way of hard cash. Nick didn't stint when it came to staff: there was a workforce of three on the farm; four estate workers including the manager; two gardeners, and a couple for the house. But then apart from Caycoo Nick had no other drain on his income. There was no reason why he shouldn't amuse himself in this or any other way he chose.

Hopefully the fascination with this place wouldn't last for ever. Nick might never return to touring – that would be too much to hope for – but the regular albums, recording studios, London, must lure him back eventually. Even as David tried to convince himself of this, he looked across at Nick in the driving seat, his face a picture of contentment, and wasn't so sure.

When they returned to the house, a large cold lunch had been laid out in the dining room. David had forgotten what a wonderful housekeeper Alusha was. The food was a mixture of Scottish feudal – cold wild salmon with mayonnaise, tender cold beef with horseradish sauce – and Seychellian exotica – spiced fish, devilled chicken with a variety of sweet spicy sauces. David's diet suffered another postponement.

After helping himself from the sideboard he made for the nearest place at the table but Alusha, sweeping up behind him, waved him to the far end, near the window. 'The sun, we must sit in the sun,' she exclaimed. 'It's too good to waste.' She sat next to him and, though the others had not yet appeared, urged him to start. As they ate, she chattered brightly, breathlessly, charmingly. She was one of those people who had the rare gift of intimacy, the ability to make you feel you were the most important friend in the world. David was flattered to remember that she bestowed this gift with considerable discretion.

Her looks, both exotic and unusual, had seemed entirely appropriate for Nick when he was at the height of his touring career but here, in the richly panelled dining room, amid the tartans, watercolours and heavy oak furniture, against the soft northern background of trees, mountains and water, she could not have looked more incongruous. David had never enquired about her parentage, but it was said her father was French, her mother Chinese or Indian or, much more likely, a mixture of both. The result was arresting rather than beautiful, but that, to David, was a recommendation rather than a fault.

'Can't you stay another day, David?' she asked, widening her eyes at him. 'It's Sunday tomorrow.'

'I've got a meeting.'

'And if you didn't have one, you would make one up.' The reprimand was delivered with such a beautiful smile that it was impossible to take offence.

'You know how it is.'

'Nick would have loved you to stay. So would I. Can't you really?' Alusha, for all her gentleness, had a streak of tenacity. But it was just this mixture of charm and quiet determination that seemed to make her relationship with Nick such a success. Not many women would have made the move from New York to the back-of-beyond; fewer still would have stuck a life of organic farming and long country walks.

It was another ten minutes before Nick and Mel joined them. Mel looked stormy, Nick quietly pained: they had obviously had their discussion, complete with predictably unsatisfactory outcome.

Mel's mood didn't bother David; he'd been desensitized by eighteen years of Mel-instigated dramas. Alusha was not so hardhearted. She directed all her attention towards Mel, trying to soothe his ruffled feathers. Typically Mel was not to be placated so easily, and after a time even Alusha had to admit temporary defeat.

Nick, a peacemaker by nature, did his best to make conversation. Then, without warning, he said: 'What about that charity concert Amazon were offered some time ago, David? The one in aid of the rain forests. Are we still considering that?'

David could hardly believe his ears. The concert invitation had actually been for Nick, but that wasn't the point. Nick was talking about 'we', he was talking about Amazon. 'Well – no. You said . . . You . . . I turned it down. They've advertised it now.'

'Is there something else we could do? A one-off charity thing.' Nick shot a guileless look in Mel's direction. 'If it's all right with everyone else, of course. And if it could be fitted in on our way to Caycoo in the autumn.'

David recovered himself. 'It could be fixed, sure,' he said swiftly.

'Something worthwhile,' Nick continued. 'You know, something we all feel strongly about.' This wasn't just a small conciliatory gesture on Nick's part, it was a massive act of generosity, and David was relieved to see from Mel's expression that he had the grace to realize it.

'You name the charity, they've been asking for you,' David said. 'You only have to choose.' He immediately flicked his memory through the large quantity of requests that regularly flowed into the office and, inventing what he couldn't remember, listed a few ideas. The discussion roamed from whales to the ozone layer and back again, without decision.

'What about the clean water campaign?' Nick suggested. 'I don't imagine it gets much attention. Not glamorous enough.'

Mel dug himself out of his mood sufficiently to make a

typically unhelpful comment. 'Clean water – isn't that the government's bag? I mean, where would our money be going?'

Not surprisingly, Nick knew something about the subject and patiently took Mel through it. Not for the first time David was struck by the contrast between the two: Nick, articulate, rational, restrained; Mel, thorny, mercurial, forever a victim of his own instincts and therefore life. Nick had had some education – grammar school and a year at Newcastle University – while Mel, like Joe, had left school at fifteen. But the contrast went far beyond that. Sometimes David wondered how Amazon had held together for as long as it did.

Mel announced himself unconvinced on the clean water campaign and, it seemed, on most other ideas as well. 'Everyone's on that bandwagon,' he kept saying. 'It'd look like we were desperate to cash in or something.'

There was an inconclusive pause. Determined not to let the idea wither, David dredged his memory further. 'There's always famine. That's got a good image. Even better, famine and children. The Save the Children Fund are having a famine-relief drive for the Sudan, I think it is. You can't go wrong with Save the Children. Worthy. Caring image. One of their fund raisers has been after you for months.' The fund raiser had actually been after Nick solo, but he didn't mention that.

No one expressed wild enthusiasm, but then no one looked unhappy about it either. In an effort to leave no stone unturned, David said to Nick: 'She says she's an old friend of yours. The fund-raising lady, that is. Wife of an MP. Driscoll, is it?'

Nick gave a shrug. 'Could be.' Like everyone in his position, he'd met thousnds of people for a few minutes each. It was impossible to remember them by name.

'Perhaps you *do* know her,' teased Alusha, narrowing

her eyes. 'Perhaps she's an old flame.' She rolled her tongue round the idiom with obvious pleasure, as if she'd just learnt it.

Nick gave her a broad smile. 'Before you, my love, it's all a great big blank.'

Alusha laughed with great delight, as if hearing the remark for the first time, although to David's certain knowledge Nick had used the same phrase several times before. Perhaps this was the secret of a happy marriage: repetition, ritual and feigned delight at each other's jokes. He wondered how they were getting on with their attempts to have babies. He would be careful not to ask. The last he'd heard Alusha was about to try yet another fertility treatment.

'Is it agreed then?' David pressed. 'Shall I pursue the Save-the-Children idea?'

Nick gave him an imperceptible wink of encouragement. Mel shrugged in what was not, apparently, disagreement. David breathed a sigh of pleasure and profound relief; against all expectations it seemed that Amazon was back on the road again. And from one charity concert, who knew what might grow?


Duggan felt the sweat dripping down the side of his face. His eyes flicked over the instrument panel: engine temperature normal, no malfunctions. Cockpit heating off; vents discharging cool air. What the hell, he was just hot. Hot and tired. The headache had settled into a sharp stabbing pain behind the eyes. He put the Porter into a steep turn and lined up for the next run. Only three more runs before the end of this job, thank the Lord, then back for a feet-up. He pulled the throttle back, dropping the machine quickly towards spraying height. This was a little game of his, to see how quickly and proficiently he could level out at the magic spraying height after a rapid drop. On a good day he could hit it in one, on a bad day – and there were plenty of those – he levelled out too high and had to ease her down. Now and again he gave himself a fright and dipped a bit too low. One way or the other, it relieved the boredom.

As usual, the job was forest. The terrain was almost flat and the trees of fairly uniform height, a doddle compared to ground crops, which were apt to be surrounded by tall trees, roads, telephone wires and houses with irate people.

He found his height at about fifteen feet over the treetops, throttled down to a steady ninety-five knots, located a visual marker at the far end of the run, and, fifty yards from the edge of the plantation, engaged the atomizers. He glanced briefly back through the scratched Perspex, saw the answering cloud of vapour, and looked ahead to the marker. The marker was less than adequate, but since dear gormless Reggie had somehow managed to cock up the placing of the black boxes and the Hi-Fix wasn't working, he had no choice but to rely on eyeball fixes, reciprocal bearings and old-fashioned seat-of-the-pants stuff. He had to estimate the spray widths, calculate what he'd already covered and find some landmark to keep him straight on the next run. Inevitably the spraying would overlap a bit. Just as inevitably there would be the occasional gaps. But he'd only get to hear about them when the angry proprietor complained about swathes of rampant bugs.

He completed the run, and the next. He noticed that the wind had got up. That was all he needed. Not only did it make flying more difficult but it caused excessive drift, blowing the spray off-target. His theoretical wind limit was eight knots. It might be close to that now, but since he had almost finished he wasn't going to let that get in his way. One more run, then it was back to the Portakabin for a couple of well-earned cigarettes, a large cup of coffee and one of Jeannie's lead-lined ham sandwiches.

He turned and came in for the last time. He switched on

the atomizers, automatically glancing at the flow meter
as he did so. He did a double-take. No spray. Red
light. Cursing, he disengaged and re-engaged the atomizers
several times. Still a red. He fiddled the control valve.
Nothing. He spun it again, then punched at it viciously.
Finally he was rewarded with a feeble green light and the
sight of vapour when he glanced back. Too late for most of
the run: the end of the plantation was approaching fast.
The question now was, would the blasted spray turn off?

Only with great difficulty, he discovered. It took several
flicks of the switch and a fast turn of the control valve
before the spray trail finally thinned and vanished. Looking
down, he saw he was overflying a clearing with a fleeing
deer.

'Sorry about that, old girl.'

Gaining height, he turned sharply and headed back to
the air strip. Hot and weary, he half hoped the mechanic
would be unable to fix the trouble so that, though it would
mean the loss of much-needed loot, he could take the rest
of the day off.

# Chapter 4

As soon as lunch was over, Nick slipped away and strode briskly up through the park to the rowan tree. Wrapping the shotgun in the poacher's jacket, he made his way back to the house, feeling conspicuous as he walked stiffly and unnaturally with the gun clamped firmly against his thigh. But there was no Alusha to see him this time, nor anyone else, and he managed to return the gun to the secure cupboard in the corner of the boot room unobserved.

As for the jacket, he couldn't make up his mind about that. To leave it in the wood store would be to suggest that last night was forgiven and forgotten, which it most certainly was not. To keep the damn thing would be equally unsatisfactory. Putting the decision off, he finally hung it on a peg behind the door.

On his way out he met Alusha in the hall and almost gave himself away with a guilty laugh. Duplicity had never been his strong point. But if Alusha noticed, she chose not to mention it. Instead she invited him to walk with her to the paddock while Mel was watching the American football on TV and David was, inevitably, phoning London.

They stepped into air that was unexpectedly fresh. He stood looking around him, as he always did when leaving the house. The sky was clear, the hills were bathed in a light which seemed to have burnt the high moors an unaccustomed shade of ochre. The trees sparkled and shimmered, their leaves tinkling and rustling in the breeze.

They walked past the walled garden, through the

rhododendron grove and began the climb towards the paddock. Nick looped his arm firmly in Alusha's. Already the events of the previous night seemed a long way off and, if he tried really hard, he could persuade himself that none of it had happened.

Clear of the gardens the breeze was stronger and cooler, and he realized that, unusually for the time of year, it was coming from the north, maybe even a little east of north.

From the house came the distant sound of a car crunching across the gravel and a moment later Nick glanced back to see the unmistakable figure of Duncan coming round the side of the house. Nick whistled to him and Duncan, waving a brief acknowledgement, started after them. Even at that distance Nick could see that Duncan was using his angry walk: stride rapid, head down, arms pumping. By the time he caught up with them at the paddock rail, his complexion was a deep and dangerous shade of red.

'They've been at it again!' Duncan panted through clenched teeth. 'They've been at it again!'

Nick caught Alusha stifling a slight smile and frowned at her. 'Who has?' he asked.

'Those damned poachers! Up at Macinley's Pool, curse their eyes! Just when I was away for the evening.' Duncan had been in the business of outmanoeuvring poachers for thirty years, but it never seemed to occur to him that the opposition's intelligence-gathering system might be better than his own.

'We'll get them next time,' Nick said soothingly.

'Of that you may be sure! If it's the very last thing I do. Oh yes!' Duncan was momentarily silenced by his own indignation.

Alusha had entered the paddock and was calling Rona, who was going through an elegant charade of evading capture. 'I could get some of those image-intensifying things,' Nick suggested. 'You know, sort of night binoculars. Would that help?' This offering was made to mollify

Duncan, but also to assuage his own guilt at having cocked up a perfectly good opportunity for capture.

Duncan's eyes sparkled. 'Those things they use in the SAS?'

Nick hadn't thought of Duncan as a military enthusiast. He couldn't resist teasing him. 'I've only ever seen them in nature films,' he said innocently. 'But what do you think?'

Duncan chortled with unconcealed glee. 'Now that would do the trick very nicely! Oh yes. I could set myself up on the hill-side, with a two-mile stretch of river in my sights. Oh yes!'

The pony, after a last coquettish dance, had allowed herself to be captured and was following Alusha meekly to the rail. Duncan, his optimism restored, said brightly: 'Not riding today, Mrs Mackenzie?'

Alusha stroked Rona's neck rhythmically. 'No, not today.' She looked away slyly, secretively. This small evasion was so uncharacteristic of her that Nick allowed himself to read an unmistakable message into her decision, and felt his stomach tighten.

Turning quickly to Duncan he said: 'Anyway, I thought you were taking the evening off. Going to Oban.'

Duncan admitted to the possibility with a dismissive grunt. 'But I'll be back later,' he said significantly. 'And every night, by God. Until the river falls.'

Nick heard this with some alarm. A stakeout wasn't likely to be too productive; the tall poacher, for all his artfulness, surely wouldn't come back so soon, not after a fracas like that. Hastily, he invented a job which would require Duncan to be in Oban early the next morning, so that it wouldn't be worth his while to come back from the evening with his sister. They argued gently for a while. Duncan vacillated, looked unhappy, but finally agreed.

'It's that Alistair Campbell from Inveraray, you know,' Duncan said over his shoulder as he started back down the hill.

'Who is?'

'The damned poacher.'

Alistair Campbell. Nick didn't know the name, but he turned it carefully over in his mind, fitting it to the voice and the dark faceless figure by the pool. 'You're sure?' he called after Duncan.

'Och, I'm sure,' Duncan said heavily, and, giving a rueful wave of farewell, plodded back towards the house.

Alusha said: 'The police, can't they arrest this Campbell?'

'They'd need proof.'

'What about the salmon? His house, it must be full of them.' Nick regarded her fondly. 'Sold on by now.'

She gave him a narrow cat-like stare. 'And after you so nearly caught him.'

He was completly taken aback. 'I . . . caught him?'

Alusha unclipped Rona's halter and the pony shimmied away, picking up her feet and showing the whites of her eyes like some affronted spinster. Alusha ducked under the rail. 'You were out all night, weren't you? And there's that bump in your head.'

'On. *On* my head,' he corrected her. 'Does it show?' He put a hand to the lump.

'You've been touching it all day. And blood – I can see blood. Not much, but enough.' She gave him a triumphant grin. 'See? Easy.'

Alusha, as always, had an unfailing talent for rooting out the truth. Far from minding about this, Nick was rather proud of her for it.

Putting on a suitably sheepish expression, he said: 'It seemed a good idea at the time.'

'If you like to go falling over in the dark or whatever you did, well' – she gave a small shrug – 'what can I say? Playing cowboys and Indians. It's *almost* funny.' She raised her eyebrows to show how unfunny she thought it was.

A Wild West comparison wasn't the first Nick would

have made, but considering the gun and the ridiculous tussle by the pool she wasn't so far wrong.

Alusha prodded his shoulder. 'So long as no one gets silly, Nick. As long as no one gets hurt. That's all I ask.'

He thought for an appalling moment that she knew about the gun. But reading her expression, he saw that there was nothing deeper in her remark and pulled her into his arms so that she wouldn't see the guilt and relief in his face.

Breathing the musky scent of her hair, feeling the familiar shape of her body against his, he wondered not for the first time how it was possible to foul up so much of one's life and still end up with the first prize.

Then her last words drifted back into his mind, and he complained mildly: 'But I *am* hurt.'

'No sympathy,' she said firmly, pulling away from him. 'Serves you right.' But she couldn't have been too cross with him because she put her hand into his as they walked down the hill.

Nearing the house, Nick could make out David's figure in the rose garden, wandering between the beds, examining the flowers, but stiffly as if he wasn't quite sure what to make of it all.

From long habit, Nick and Alusha made a detour through the walled kitchen garden. But unusually, they walked in silence as they made their inspection of the vegetables, the burgeoning raspberry canes and the vine in its long glasshouse.

Nick gathered his courage. This was the obvious moment to ask the question that had been hovering between them for days, since the time Alusha had stopped riding Rona.

He got to the point of opening his mouth then, hesitating disastrously, turned away to examine the grapes. His courage ebbed away. It was superstition, it was nameless fear, but he felt that asking the question would only invite disappointment, and he wasn't sure he was quite ready to face that yet. Postponement offered a sort of promise that seemed to go hand in hand with the perfection of the day. Anything, perhaps, was better than the blunt certainty of failure, although in some curious way the hope of children had been with them so long that it was almost enough in itself.

The sun was warmer here, the breeze soft, the day perfect. Later, when everyone had gone, the moment would come.

Squeezing her hand, he talked instead about the visit to Perthshire they were planning for the coming week.


David was first into the car, getting into the back with his briefcase at his side, doing his best to look sorry the visit was over.

Mel came next, sauntering jauntily out of the house, chattering with Alusha, kissing her warmly, as if the weekend had been an unqualified success. An afternoon in front of the television seemed to have restored his humour. As he climbed in, Nick started up the Mercedes. Alusha put her head to the open window. 'You'll come back soon, both of you – promise?'

She had pulled back her hair into a long plait and donned her workman's kit, a pair of baggy overalls. Nick tried to remember what she was planning to do for the remainder of the afternoon. Painting perhaps – she'd taken a watercolour course – or renovating an old lamp she'd bought in London.

As the car rattled over the cattle grid Nick glanced in the mirror and saw that Alusha was still there, waving slowly. Something about the sight of her small figure standing in the wide expanse of the front sweep bothered him, but he couldn't pin it down. He slowed the car to give himself time to think, but Mel shot him a questioning glance and, remembering that they had a plane to catch, he pressed on.

'I can see the attraction of this place, you know,' Mel said as he surveyed the spectacular beauty of the loch. 'Unadulterated escapism.'

'Escapism? I wouldn't have called it that,' Nick replied amiably. Purposely choosing to misunderstand, he added: 'There's no need to escape from anything here.'

'No, I mean it's places like this you escape *to*,' Mel explained, impatiently. Then, catching Nick's expression, he closed his mouth abruptly before commenting: 'I wouldn't mind a place like this myself, mind. No aggravation. No pollution. No stress. And all that organic food – I tell you, you'll live for ever if you're not careful.'

Nick smiled. Sometimes, when he thought back to the early days, he could persuade himself that he missed the companionship, the running gags, the buzz one got after a good show. On the other hand, he only had to remember the horrors of the attendant nonsense, the tensions and disagreements and crises that used to spring up with unbelievable regularity to miss nothing at all. 'Is this for ever?' Mel asked suddenly.

'What?'

'This stopping the world and getting off.'

'I haven't got off. Not the world, not anything. You make me sound like a recluse or something.'

'I'm only asking if it's for ever.'

Nick was aware of David in the back making a poor job of pretending not to listen. 'I don't know, Mel,' he replied honestly. 'I really don't know.'

He knew what they were thinking. That the New York incident was years ago now, that he should have put that behind him, that he should be back where he belonged, producing an album a year and, while he was about it, throwing in a few gigs and an album or two to get Amazon off the ground again and put Mel and Joe back in the way of money and success.

One charity show wouldn't be enough to satisfy them. He should have realized that. They didn't understand, either of them, that he was quite happy alone at Ashard with Alusha and his work.

They came into Inveraray, with its main street of neat white-painted shops and hotels. A string of tourists dawdled along, staring into windows packed with tartan dolls, plastic bagpipes and miniature haggises.

A car drew out from in front of the Spa grocery shop on the other side of the street and came towards them. He recognized the car, and saw one of the occupants wave. It was his housekeeper, Mrs Alton, and her husband. He waved back. The vague concern about Alusha clarified. He realized that, with Mrs Alton here in town, all the staff were either off-duty or away. Even Duncan, who lived barely half a mile from the house, would be on his way to Oban by now. Alusha was on her own at Glen Ashard.

He calmed himself. He hadn't chosen a house in a remote corner of Scotland with automatic gates and high fences for nothing. Nevertheless, he felt guilt. Years ago, he'd made himself a promise never to leave her alone again. Now after all this time, he'd broken it and he couldn't for the life of him think why.

He pushed his foot down and the Mercedes leapt forward, accelerating out of Inveraray and along the winding lochside road. Another fifty minutes to the airport if he stepped on it and went in for some adventurous overtaking. He could be back at Glen Ashard by eight.

The afternoon sunlight was spreading a golden glow over the hills, like molten honey. Away to the right, above the ruffled waters of the loch, a small black dot appeared, moving smoothly across the absolute clarity of the sky. For a moment Nick thought that Helen in the estate office might have got it wrong and ordered a helicopter to take his visitors to the airport, but then he saw that it was not a helicopter but a light plane, and turned his attention back to the road.

The plane carried straight on, heading south-west, down the loch towards Glen Ashard.

Duggan wrestled with the Ordnance Survey map. The damned thing was not designed for small cockpits, nor for much else as far as he could tell. The multitudinous folds did not lend themselves to being pulled open and refolded. Though he'd prepared the blasted thing back in the Porta-kabin, he now needed to take a closer look at the terrain around the target area, specifically the area to the north-west, a patch he'd not planned on overflying, and would, under normal circumstances, have avoided.

But since his backup was as usual nil, and the weather information he'd been given by Jeannie as good as useless, he was having to think again. The north-westerly he'd been promised on take-off had developed a distinct north-easterly slant, and increased from a light wind to a firm breeze. The easterly twist might possibly result from the funnelling effect of the hills, but more likely the weather information was simply hours out of date. Whatever, he would have to look carefully at the approach angle. As far as he could estimate, the wind strength was ten knots or so. Well, maybe it was a touch more, but as long as he could fly crosswind on an east–west slant without hitting a hill on the way out, then it shouldn't be too much of a bother. Inveraray was down to starboard. The target area would be coming up shortly. With a last angry punch at an obdurate crease he finally got the map into some sort of order and started comparing the symbols with the land-

marks below. The target area was immediately obvious, a
large block of high-standing conifers, planted in serried
ranks with occasional fire breaks.

The northern and eastern perimeters were clear-cut –
the forest ended in rising moorland – but to the west and the
south the conifers blended into broadleaf forest with no
obvious boundary, excepting the contrast in colour. There
was some broadleaf forest in the south-west corner too, but
it soon gave way to pasture, paddocks and, beyond, a large
castle-type house belonging to the neighbouring estate.

Duggan made a couple of passes over the timber,
assessing the local wind conditions, gauging the lie of the
land, checking for livestock. The obvious run was parallel
to the high land, on a line south-west to north-east. The
approach was long and reasonably level, and the exit even
kinder, the land dropping gently away to the open pasture.
Plenty of turning room. A doddle in a northwesterly.

The only problem was he didn't bloody well have a north-
westerly. And, trying a dummy run, he soon discovered
that the northeasterly that he did have was powering over
a wide cleft in the hills in nasty gusts, causing the Porter to
crab sideways.

He considered the possibility of flying on a south-to-
north line. But while it might be easier to control the
aircraft that way, it would also in all probability kill him.
Quite apart from an approach over sharply rising ground,
which was bound to be prone to down draughts, the way
out was steep and craggy.

This was not the sort of job Duggan needed at the end
of a long day. Not after an inadequate recce, not with
the corking headache that refused to go away, not with the
dodgy spray mechanism that might or might not have been
fixed. Davie had sworn it would be okay, but then he
would. Mechanics always said they'd fixed things even
when they'd patched them up with sticky tape.

For the umpteenth time he cursed Keen who, after

creating the maximum disruption and aggravation, had pissed off back to Glasgow in his vulgar little motor, throwing a last Hitlerite command over his shoulder to the effect that everyone had better pull harder or else they'd all be in trouble.

If anything, the wind seemed to be freshening. No point in hanging about then.

He took a swig of lemonade, pushed a toffee into his mouth and banked steeply to port to line up for a dummy run.

Rona snorted in sudden agitation. Alusha paused in her work to shush her. 'What's the matter with you? Go away.'

The mare stamped her feet, her shoes ringing on the hard standing in front of the stable.

'Away,' Alusha Mackenzie repeated. 'You're being a nuisance.' She waved her paintbrush at Rona and shooed her into the paddock. 'Off with you.'

The pony trotted off and stopped a short distance away, tossing her head. Turning back to the stable door, Alusha dipped her brush in the preservative and slapped some more onto the bare wooden door. The thin green mixture had an evil smell and instinctively she pulled back to avoid inhaling it.

Somewhere an engine buzzed lazily in the sky, like an insect in the sun. Rona snorted again.

Alusha laughed at her. 'What do you want this time, eh?' She finished the door and, fetching a large metal bucket, upended it and positioned it in the doorway. Balancing on it, she could just reach the lintel.

When it came to it, there was no decision really. It had to be the south-west–north-east line; Duggan wasn't about to kill himself to earn a mention in anyone's rule book.

Besides, he should be able to adjust his course to allow for drift. It couldn't be that difficult.

He found his height, lined up on an imaginary line a width inside the southern perimeter of the plantation, and, holding a steady course, hovered his thumb over the spray switch.

The conifers sped towards and under him. He switched on. There was an answering billow of vapour from under the wings. That was something anyway; he supposed he should be grateful. Eyes front again, he was surprised to see broadleaf trees moving in under his port wing. The gust must be stronger than he'd thought. He compensated, touching the rudder once and again, only to find that either he'd overdone it or else the crosswind had dropped suddenly, because he was too far into the conifers now. Cursing, he eased the Porter back on line, only for the same thing to happen again. He was weaving about like a bloody amateur.

Not a moment too soon, the end of the plantation loomed up and vanished beneath. He switched off the spray and swivelled his head back.

No change: the spray continued to course lavishly from the atomizers. He felt a vicious choking anger. Swearing loud and long, he flicked the switch rapidly back and forth, kicking the heel of his hand against it, then leant down and rapidly rotated the control valve beside his feet until, quite suddenly, the indicator light went off and, an instant later, the trail of vapour finally thinned and died.

He looked up. *Christ!* He was almost over the parkland; the big house was not far ahead to port. Instinctively he took the Porter into a tight turn to starboard, rapidly gaining height to clear the rising ground beneath.

He twisted in his seat to press his face against the Perspex and look back towards the park. Nothing. Thank God. No sheep. No small figure, face upturned, like that child the other week.

The relief left him exhausted. He knew exactly what he was going to do now: give up and return to base. And he knew precisely what he was going to do once he got there: telephone Keen. Rehearsing the exact combination of expletives kept him occupied all the way home.


The buzzing hung languorously in the air, faded, then got louder again. Rona, unseen by her mistress, sidled silently back towards the stable and, blowing loudly in Alusha's ear, gave her a terrible fright.

'That's it!' Alusha exclaimed, stepping off the bucket. She made a grab for Rona's bridle, but the mare was too quick for her and danced away.

Alusha held out some sugar. 'Come on, you greedy pig.'

The pony, despite her uncharacteristic nervousness, couldn't resist the sugar and within a minute Alusha had caught her and hitched her to the ring on the stable wall. 'And here you stay until I've finished.'

The soft drone grew louder again. Alusha shaded her eyes and looked up but, seeing nothing, returned to her brush and her pot and dabbed some more green fluid on the door frame.

For some reason the smell of the stuff suddenly clutched at her throat. It was incredibly strong, like ammonia or worse. She clamped a hand over her mouth and nose and tried not to breathe, but the stuff seeped into her nose and throat. She staggered off the bucket and retreated onto the apron. She coughed, and the act of coughing made her pull a deep draught of air into her lungs. Air that wasn't air; air that was sharp and burning. Inexplicably, the fumes seemed to have followed her across the apron. By the time she had raised her collar over her mouth, it was too late. The acrid vapour was eating at her lungs, her eyes were streaming, her head was weaving violently.

She tried to find her way back to the stable. She was

dimly aware of noise, of a clattering of hooves and sounds of alarm from Rona. But the collision, when it came, caught her by surprise. One moment she was groping her way back towards the stable, the next moment the bulk of Rona's hindquarters was barrelling into her, a solid weight that cannoned into her shoulder and toppled her over.

Her head didn't hit the concrete terribly hard – in fact, the impact was more like a hard knock than a solid thud – but it was enough to send her sliding into a grey land somewhere between panic and nightmare, a land in which her eyes saw nothing, in which every breath drew her deeper into some terrible darkness.

# Chapter 5

———————

FIFTEEN COLUMN-INCHES. Daisy pasted up the fourth and final cutting, already worn and ageing from the cutting agency's tardy service, and held the finished montage at arm's length. Not bad if one overlooked the origin of the stories – the *Newbury Chronicle*, the *Reading News* and such like – and imagined that the items had appeared in the national dailies. Alice Knowles' demonstration hadn't merited the attention of the nation, not in print, not on radio or TV. Nor had it, apparently, justified the undivided concentration of the journalists who'd covered it. One described Aldeb as a fumigant instead of a fungicide, while another talked vaguely about the dangers of processing potatoes as if the Knowleses ran a chip factory instead of a farm. All in all, the coverage was no better or worse than she'd expected.

The street door banged as someone arrived and Daisy heard the unmistakable sound of Alan clearing his throat, something he did so regularly first thing in the morning that she suspected him of being a secret smoker. Not that she dared say so; Alan wasn't too good with jokes.

She heard him enter the cubicle next door and shuffle around, the rubber soles of his shoes squelching softly on the lino-tiled floor. Catch didn't run to carpets or other such luxuries. Under normal circumstances it wouldn't have run to an office near King's Cross either, but the place had been let to them by a sympathetic developer at a peppercorn rent. Situated in the rambling basement of an

Edwardian house due for demolition in a couple of years'
time, with high barred windows and woefully little daylight, it was not the ideal workplace, and certainly not in
winter when, for lack of central heating, they had to suffer
the fumes of mobile gas heaters, an expedient which did
little for their corporate image let alone their lungs.

Alan appeared round the door and, sorting through the
mail, dropped a batch onto Daisy's desk. 'Can we have a
talk some time?' he said.

'Now, if you like.'

He hesitated as if he'd rather have put the moment off,
then sank into the chair beside her desk. Alan, dark and
slightly built with the stoic tenacity of the seasoned campaigner, had come to Catch by way of Greenpeace, the
anti-fur campaign Lynx and, for a brief time ten years
before, his own environmentally friendly cleaning products
company which had folded after six months, a victim of
being ahead of its time.

Picking up a bulldog grip, he started operating the jaws.
'The Knowles case. What exactly *are* we recommending to
the Committee?'

Daisy was on her guard. The two of them had discussed
this only the previous afternoon. Alan was well aware of
her views on the subject, so this could only be the opening
gambit in an attempt to shift her.

'We're going to recommend full backing for the
Knowleses, in their legal action and whatever else is
needed,' she reminded him.

Alan closed the bulldog grip on his finger, screwed up
his mouth in mild pain. Withdrawing the finger, he examined it carefully. 'I think it would be a mistake.'

'What – to help them?' Daisy tried to smooth any
exasperation out of her voice. 'But why, for God's sake?
We agreed – we should do everything we could – '

'Their case won't succeed.'

This needed to be taken gently, not an approach that

came naturally to Daisy. 'How can you say it's doomed? We don't know till we try, do we?'

'A case like that – it'll take years and God only knows how many thousands of pounds.'

'I know, but we're not promising the family a lot of cash, are we? Just a token offering to get them going.'

'*And* back-up – data, information, research, liaison . . .'

'Well, of course . . .'

'Which means a helluva lot of time and money.' Alan agitated the jaws of the grip so rapidly that they made a loud clacking noise, like the teeth of a mad animal. He looked up, wearing his most resolute expression. 'We decided right at the beginning, when Catch was first set up, that it would be absolutely futile to take on the agrochemical industry direct while we had such limited funds, that confrontation would be a sure way of defeating *ourselves*. Nothing's changed since then, Daisy. In fact, if anything there's even *more* reason to avoid getting bogged down in something like this. We're just as stretched as before, if not more so. Committed on too many fronts – the new newsletter, setting up all the regional groups . . . well – you *know* how it is. But a legal fight . . . it'd be a minefield, Daisy. We can't afford to go pioneering, not over totally untested ground. We just don't have the resources. The media – *that*'s our battlefield, *that*'s what we understand, it's the only place where we know how to win.'

Daisy let this flow over her; it was familiar, not to say well-trodden, ground. 'But it's not us who're taking on the case,' she pointed out. 'It's the Knowles family.'

'Quite.' He waved the bulldog grip in the air, as if he had just succeeded in explaining everything. 'The Knowleses should never have been encouraged to take legal action in the first place. The scientists are still totally divided, the evidence is too weak for any British court of law. You know that, I know that, but it seems the Knowleses of all people don't know it.'

'You're making it sound as if I pushed them into it,' she said defensively. 'You're making it sound as if I encouraged them. Which isn't true, and you know it.'

Alan shot her a stern look. 'Put it this way, perhaps you could have done a better job of discouraging them.'

'Thanks,' Daisy said sharply. 'And how exactly do you tell people that the law is a total waste of time? How do you tell them that their whole experience has been for nothing?'

'You tell them, that's what you do. You tell them because it's true.'

Daisy was losing ground but couldn't see how to fight her way out of it.

'Oh, the case'd get some publicity all right,' Alan went on remorselessly. 'On the last day of the case, that is. And maybe the first. But in the middle, all through the weeks and weeks of expert evidence and the months waiting for the second appeal, there'd be zilch. The only sure thing would be the catastophic expense and almost certain bankruptcy for the family.' He finished with a flourish: 'It seems rather a high price to pay for a little publicity.'

Daisy leant back in her chair and folded her arms tightly across her chest. 'So what on earth are we doing here then?' she said, unable to suppress the frustration in her voice. 'I mean, if we can't help people like the Knowleses?'

Alan stood up. 'You know the answer to that – to campaign. It's the only game we can play. More to the point, it's the only game we can – '

'Yes, yes,' she said wearily, 'I know, I *know* – it's the only game we can afford.'

A phone began to ring. Neither of them was in a hurry to answer it and it continued to sound eerily through the dingy rooms. Suddenly the street door banged and they heard the rapid tap of Jenny's metal-heeled boots as she ran into the general office to snatch up the phone.

In the silence, Daisy picked up her argument again. 'We

should be doing both. Campaigning *and* offering support. Honestly, Alan, what's the point otherwise?'

He gave an exasperated laugh. 'But, Daisy . . . It's always a mistake to get too . . .' He hesitated. She had the feeling he had been about to say emotional, not a word she would have appreciated. Instead he murmured: '. . . *involved* in these things.'

Jenny's voice called from the outer office, summoning Alan to the phone. Before disappearing he gave a gesture of regret, an affirmation that, according to his reckoning, he had won his point.

Daisy stood up and took a couple of turns round the filing cabinets, trying to make sense of her anger. It wasn't just the lack of money, though that was a continual problem, it wasn't even Alan's habit of putting a dampener on her most precious ideas, though he did that often enough to make her suspect that he got a perverse satisfaction from it. No, the worst part was the knowledge that he had a point, that much as she longed to see a case brought against the agrochemical camp it would be wrong to let it go ahead at the Knowleses' expense. However determined Alice Knowles was, however keen her son to find a purpose in his illness, it was doubtful that a case fought with such meagre resources would be worth the emotional and financial strain. Reluctant though she was to admit it, Alan could have been right, and she should have done a better job of talking the Knowleses out of it.

Dropping dejectedly back into her chair, she leafed through her diary, looking for a date when she could go and see Alice again. The weekend, as usual, was the only time she had free.

She started on the mail, automatically flipping the discarded envelopes into the box earmarked for recycling. Magazines, journals, reports, scientific papers, members' letters, non-members' letters: too much of it, always too much of it.

Opening a large envelope, she pulled out three smaller ones, each addressed to a box number at *Farmers Weekly*. In a guilty reflex, Daisy glanced over her shoulder. This was a little idea she'd forgotten to mention to Alan, but now was not, she felt, the moment to come clean. The ad had been simple enough: ALDEB. *Anyone experiencing health problems from exposure to this fungicide, please write Box No.* . . . Normally Catch accumulated their case histories through people like the Farmers' Union Health Executive, through newspaper articles or contacts made on Catch's behalf by friendly toxicologists. To Daisy these haphazard methods had always seemed inadequate, and she'd long been haunted by the almost certain knowledge that there were dozens of other cases out there, just waiting to be uncovered.

The first letter was not promising. It was from a lady in Wiltshire who'd worked on a chicken farm and wanted to know if Aldeb was the medicine they were always feeding the chickens, because if so, she thought it was responsible for her 'hormones'. She'd been under the doctor for months, had had several operations, but was still suffering all her old troubles.

Daisy put the letter to one side. Investigating chickenfeed wasn't within Catch's present brief, though if anyone bothered to analyse a modern broiler hen's intestines, it probably would be.

The next letter was from a Lincolnshire farmer whose wife had developed cancer. Their main crop was potatoes and, until they'd been alerted to the dangers of Aldeb the previous year, they'd been using the chemical continuously. The wife had been in charge of warehousing and storage, which involved regular applications of fungicide in enclosed conditions. Daisy felt a small spark of optimism: this was more like it.

The third letter was from a man with a Hertfordshire address. Daisy wasn't quite sure what to make of it. He said he'd come across Aldeb and would like to tell her about it. He was in London for a few days, staying at a friend's in Battersea, and suggested they meet for tea. No details, no suggestion of how he'd come into contact with Aldeb; it was all rather vague and unsatisfactory.

She went back to the farmer's letter and read it again. Definitely worth following up. She started to dial the number then, remembering that farmers were rarely home at nine in the morning, called Simon instead. He was generally in the flat at this time of day, bashing out his articles before going in to the *Sunday Times* at about eleven to do his telephone research at the newspaper's expense. The later part of the day was for interviews and meetings, the evenings for the novel. Between all this came Daisy, at least she thought she fitted into the picture somewhere, though it was difficult to be sure.

'Is there any medical evidence of a link?' he asked as soon as Daisy told him about the letter. 'She might have got ill anyway.'

'Not yet,' Daisy conceded. 'But if we run some tests on her and the results tally with the Knowles family – well, we might have something.'

'Even then . . .'

'Well, what?'

'Not enough, is it?'

'It's a start.'

'You could do with some more cases.'

Daisy thought of the Hertfordshire man who wanted to meet her for tea. 'I'm working on it,' she said. She almost asked Simon if he was working on the story too, but she didn't like to press him, not when she'd given him a second hard sell only the previous week. She didn't want him to think she was obsessive, not when she'd hardly got into her stride.

'How about that Truffaut film?' she asked lightly, putting a low inviting note into her voice. But if there were ways to entice Simon into sudden acts of recklessness this, apparently, was not one of them.

'I'm working tonight and through the weekend,' he said. There was a pause. 'Umm – Tuesday?'

Tuesday was four days away. 'No chance of a quick meal in between? Like Monday?'

'Can't. I'm going to the Ritz.'

'The life you lead,' she said. 'What is it – a discussion on North Sea pollution washed down with a dozen oysters?'

'Not quite,' he said disapprovingly. 'Morton-Kreiger are unveiling some plans. For an environmentally friendly chemical plant, something like that.'

'Not so far wrong. Champagne and canapés in the lion's den.'

'Well, they're trying at least.'

'You could put it that way.'

'They try harder than most.'

'That's because they've got more to hide.'

Simon put on his authoritative voice, the one he used to counter emotional and ill-argued opinions. 'You can't look at everything in black and white, Daisy.'

'Maybe not, but even in colour Morton-Kreiger looks pretty murky.'

'I'll see you on Tuesday, Daisy.'

'Don't forget to ask them about Aldeb,' she called, but he'd already rung off. Unfinished conversations seemed to be a feature of whatever relationship she was establishing with Simon. She had the feeling that, when it came to discussions, she failed to come up to his rigorous intellectual standards of debate. Well, she'd never pretended to be Oxford Union material. Jenny poked her head through the door, a fax dangling from her fingers. Jenny was a punkette, complete with gold nose-ring, leather miniskirt, black tights and hair the colour of an iridescent tropical bird. She had a degree in sociology and laughed a lot, which was just as

REQUIEM 83

well considering her working conditions. 'It's your Washington friend Paul Erlinger,' she said.

'Why do you say *friend* like that?'

'I think he fancies you.'

'I've never met him.'

'Well, I wouldn't let a small thing like that get in the way,' Jenny said archly, closing the door.

The fax read: *Dear Daisy, The good news – the EPA won the Aldeb appeal. The bad news – by only two-one, and Morton-Kreiger International have been quick to file for a rehearing in the Federal Court of Appeal, and a stay of order. At the appeal hearing MKI pleaded bias in the testing procedures at the research company they used for the retesting demanded by the EPA. Rich, huh? The mind boggles at what comes next. More bad news – they've got a hold on the publication of the complete retest data, so I've nothing more to send you.* Daisy muttered to herself, a quiet heartfelt oath. She had been banking on that data. She had been hoping to be the first to send it to the Advisory Committee on Pesticides, prior to pressing for an urgent UK ban. *At this rate the whole thing will get to the Supreme Court some time next century. I dreamed about you the other night – crazy, huh? Something to do with having your picture (courtesy the Catch newsletter) pinned over my desk. Will you ever make it over this side? Love, Paul.*

Morton-Kreiger would fight the Aldeb ban to the bitter end – she wouldn't have expected them to do otherwise – but what surprised her was how successful their tactics were proving, and in the States of all places, where the balance was more heavily weighted in favour of consumer safety than anywhere else. Delays, appeals, hearings; Morton-Kreiger didn't seem to run short of ideas.

She swore again, though it was more of a sigh this time, and felt her disappointment drift into something approaching acceptance. She began to draft a reply to Paul Erlinger, asking when he guessed the data might finally be released, and if there might be a dirty-tricks story in there somewhere, a few unsavoury facts about Morton-Kreiger's tactics which might be suitable for leaking to the investigative press. She also asked for details of EarthForce's most recent case histories, in case there was an obvious overlap with the Knowles case. His reply would make for a lengthy fax, but EarthForce could afford it. Their supporters numbered a healthy two-point-five million, rising fast.

She read the last part of Paul's message again. It was hard to know how to respond. She'd seen a picture of Paul Erlinger in the EarthForce newsletter, and she didn't have it pinned over her desk.

After some thought, she scribbled: *I'll meet anyman anytime anywhere who gets me that Aldeb report.*

She took the letter out to Jenny for typing and faxing, and, after sifting the papers for cuttings, spent the next few hours working on a report on the aerial application of pesticides, breaking off only to take a couple of calls, and, at eleven, to phone the Hertfordshire man who'd sent the odd reply to her ad in the farming magazine. In his letter he said he was staying in Battersea for a few days, at a friend's flat, and he had given times when he could be contacted there. Eleven to eleven-thirty was the first slot.

It was answered immediately, almost as if he'd been waiting by the phone.

'Is this Colin Maynard?'

'It is.'

'About your letter. From the ad in *Farmers Weekly*.'

'Ah.' There was a pause and a rustling, and she imagined him sitting down and getting himself comfortable. 'Yes . . .' He sounded distant, as if he was holding the instrument away from his mouth. 'Your advertisement was most interesting.' The voice drew close again.

'You've had personal contact with Aldeb, have you?' asked Daisy.

'Forgive me,' he slid in, 'but before answering that question I hope you don't mind my asking who's asking.' He gave a nervous little chuckle like a bank clerk smoothing away any awkwardness.

'Of course not,' Daisy said hurriedly. 'My name is Daisy Field and – ' She wasn't sure why, but she was reluctant to mention Catch. 'I'm gathering information for a research project,' she said, which wasn't too far from the truth.

'Really? A research project? That sounds most interesting. May I ask, is this something you're doing as a – Oh, you know, what is it? – for one of those things, those – what *do* they call them?' The nervous little chuckle again, a click of the tongue. 'A thesis – that's it, a *thesis*.' He said the word with satisfaction as if he'd just answered a question on *Mastermind*.

'No, it's an independent project funded by a charitable trust.' This, too, had a grain of truth, since a large charitable trust had once funded one of Catch's few research projects.

'How interesting,' he repeated, his voice dipping obsequiously. 'I hope you don't mind my asking but it's as well to know who you're dealing with, don't you think?'

'Of course.' Daisy tried to guess what Colin Maynard might look like, how old he might be, but his voice gave nothing away. 'And what would the name of the trust be exactly?' he asked in a tone that was at once insistent and ingratiating.

Daisy hesitated. Even allowing for normal curiosity, the conversation was disconcertingly one-sided. 'You suggested meeting for tea,' she said. 'How about this afternoon?'

'Oh.' A show of surprise, as if he hadn't expected to be so honoured. 'If you like. Why not. Yes – how about the Waldorf? I'm rather fond of the Waldorf. The foxtrot, all those *wonderful* Thirties tunes. Four o'clock all right for you? The Palm Court. I'll book. It's always best to book.'

Daisy rang off, wondering how a man so familiar with the Waldorf and things cosmopolitan matched up with Aldeb. He might not be anything to do with farming, of course; he might be on the marketing and distribution side of Aldeb, or even – the very thought – a renegade ministry man, complete with unpublished evidence of Aldeb's carcinogenic properties and cast-iron proof of the attendant cover-up. Well, one could always hope.

After lunch Jenny, who'd been out of the office on an errand for Alan, dropped in brandishing a magazine. 'Something for you,' she announced.

The magazine, a glossy gossip magazine with luscious 'pix' of stars reclining in their Hollywood homes, was not something Daisy normally got around to reading. Jenny had opened it at a page of news snippets and was pointing towards the lead story. It was about the singer-songwriter Nick Mackenzie and his wife Alusha. According to the report there'd been an accident on their Argyll estate. His wife – they referred to her as an exotic Seychellian – had been admitted to hospital after inhaling dangerous fumes.

Daisy murmured: 'Plenty of people inhale fumes.'

'But not many rock stars' wives,' declared Jenny.

'She's probably better by now.'

'They wouldn't have mentioned it if she was.'

Daisy was unconvinced. 'Most likely it was gas fumes or petrol or something like that.'

Jenny gave an expressive shrug. 'No harm in finding out though, is there?'

There would be no harm in finding out, but these things weren't that easy. By some peculiarity of human nature, people often preferred to remain in ignorance of the true nature of the risks they'd been exposed to, as if by ignoring them the dangers would in some magical way disappear.

It might be a waste of time, but she reached for the phone anyway. She had quite a few Nick Mackenzie albums back in the flat. In fact she was rather a fan of his. There was something about his songs, an intriguing quality. Also, he wrote songs about the environment and, as far as she could remember, had done so for many years.

A contact on the staff of a rock magazine gave her the name of Nick Mackenzie's management company, which was listed at an address in Covent Garden. Getting this far had taken five minutes, the next part took a lot longer. David Weinberg Management was not the most friendly of organizations, nor the most forthcoming, and it took Daisy ten minutes to get through the first line of defence which came in the form of a girl with all the impenetrable indifference of a minor official unleashed on a position of unlimited power. But Daisy was used to wearing people down – it was part of her job: nonetheless it took a determined this-is-really-rather-important approach and a firm assurance that she wasn't trying to sell anything before she finally got through to the next bastion. This was some sort of personal assistant and, Daisy realized, as far as she was ever likely to get. Keeping the conversation short, Daisy introduced herself and asked what the chances might be of getting a letter through to Nick Mackenzie.

'We can't make any promises,' said the clipped female voice.

'If he doesn't read it himself, will he be told about it?'

'I really couldn't say.'

'Suppose I asked you to forward it to him wherever he was, would you? I wouldn't ask except it really is important and I've got to find someone I can trust to pass it on.' Daisy heard the sycophantic tone in her voice. 'I'll be sending information – nothing more – but it's information he might be very pleased to have.'

There was a pause. 'I'll do what I can,' the assistant

finally conceded with great reluctance. Then, just in case
Daisy should feel too confident, she added: 'Though I really
can't promise.'

When Daisy came to write the letter there wasn't a great
deal to say. She pointed out that Catch had access to most
of the available information on common chemicals and
their effects on health, and could, if necessary, recommend
some good toxicologists. She also said she was sorry.

She sent two copies, one care of the assistant at David
Weinberg Management and the second to Nick Mackenzie,
Argyll, Scotland. Correctly addressed mail was sometimes
mislaid by the Post Office for no apparent reason at all but,
incited by the flagrant challenge of a two-word address, the
service could produce miracles.

Daisy wasn't sure what you wore to a tea dance at the
Waldorf but she was fairly certain it wasn't tight jeans,
patterned leather boots and a sweater of idiosyncratic
design and clashing colours. Her jacket, short and soberly
black, toned things down a bit, and she made a special
attempt to brush her hair into some sort of order, not a
simple matter when it was naturally curly and sprang out
from her head.

The Waldorf was a massive grey elephant of a building,
a Palladian–French-château hybrid in the Edwardian style.
It seemed to sit on the curve of the Aldwych with reluctance, as if it had realized its mistake in being built bang on
a noisy unattractive street.

A short flight of stairs with solid brass rails led to the
foyer and the entrance to the Palm Court. A queue of
people snaked out from the doorway, waiting to be seated.
The tinny strains of 'There's A Small Hotel' floated out
over their heads, and Daisy glimpsed a lone couple shuffling
gently across a sunken dance floor.

As the queue inched forward she saw a room decorated
in flat Wedgwood colours, dusty pinks and greyish greens,
with marble floors and pilasters and a raised terrace around

three sides of the room. There were a few palms all right, but they were small and emaciated.

The head waiter had been well primed: Maynard's name produced immediate recognition and a small bow. A young waiter led her round the terrace between tables of elderly ladies whispering across their teacups, giggly young people in Thirties-style hats, and terminally jetlagged tourists staring dully about them. Rounding a corner, the waiter stopped at a small table tucked in beside the balustrade and indicated a small grey-suited figure rising from the shadows of his chair.

He was young, in his twenties, and Daisy realized that she had pictured him as much older.

'What a pleasure.' He bowed obsequiously before straightening up to a height that was a good half inch shorter than Daisy's, and she wasn't that tall. She caught a strong whiff of the sort of heavy musk-like scent that Italians and Arabs splash on with impunity, but which Englishmen wear only at the risk of comments on their masculinity.

He hovered attentively while the waiter pushed in her chair. 'Now, first things first,' he began, settling back in his seat. 'The full tea or the not-so-full tea? I can't recommend the full tea highly enough. Sandwiches – very delicate, very dainty – scones, muffins. Nothing like it.' He gave a short laugh. 'A real touch of the good old days, I tell you. Then there are the teas to choose from – Earl Grey, Darjeeling, Lapsang Souchong.'

He couldn't have been more than twenty-eight or -nine, she decided, though he might have been even younger. He had a round fleshy face with a broad nose, pasty cheeks, a red full-lipped mouth and thick gingery hair that had been slicked back from his face with a lavish coating of wet-look gel. He was leaning forward in his seat, his pale indistinct eyes staring keenly across the table at her as if he were anxious not to miss her slightest movement or gesture.

Daisy chose the full tea although, at seventeen pounds, she rather hoped she wasn't going to be picking up the bill.

'I've been so looking forward to meeting you, Miss Field. I've never met a scientist before.' He spoke in the same mixture of servility and enquiry that had marked their telephone conversation.

'I'm not a scientist, I'm a researcher.'

He screwed his face up in an expression of apology. 'Oh, I do beg your pardon. Very remiss of me. One shouldn't make wild guesses, should one?'

'And you, Mr Maynard? What do you do?'

He blinked modestly, though it seemed to Daisy that he was overdoing it a bit. 'Ah. Now that's another story. Not a lot to tell, I'm afraid. How I wish there were. A modest accountant, that's all. With an insurance firm.'

Very Heep-like in his humility. Daisy tried to imagine Maynard bent over a ledger, working on columns of figures. The nondescript grey suit fitted the picture, as did the abject manner, but the plastering of hair gel and the heavy gold signet ring that adorned a thick finger appeared rather too flashy.

'And what's your interest exactly?' Daisy asked.

'Oh, I have many interests – golf, that sort of thing. Yes, golf mainly.'

'I meant in relation to Aldeb.'

He pressed a hand to his chest. 'Oh. *Oh.* Forgive me. How silly.' He screwed his face up and smiled at himself. 'Aldeb. Yes, of course, of course.' But he didn't answer her question. Instead he leant on the brass-capped balustrade and smiled indulgently towards the dance floor. 'Isn't this wonderful? All these old tunes.'

The band, who looked about the same vintage as the songs they were playing, had swung into a stately interpretation of 'The Blue Danube', a number whose higher notes were providing a considerable challenge to the trombone player.

The sandwiches and tea arrived. When she turned back it was to find Maynard staring at her. 'You were telling me about Aldeb,' she prompted.

'Of course. Well, it's like this, Miss Field. I've a sister, name of Jancis. Unusual name, isn't it? Most people call her Jan of course. Except me. I like to call her Jancis – such a pretty name, pity not to use it, don't you think?' He glanced at her constantly, watching her face, gauging her reaction. 'Quite a bit older than me,' he continued through the abject smile which seemed to be an almost permanent feature of his face. 'In fact, my half-sister, though you'd never know it. I mean, we're very close.' He creased up his ginger-lashed eyes to emphasize how close they were. 'She married a farmer, went to live in Northumberland. Then – oh, four years ago, she got sick. Her old man couldn't deal with it, couldn't cope at all. Went off with the neighbour's wife.'

He paused and, wrapping his lips delicately around a sandwich, chewed it rapidly.

'When you say sick, what exactly was the problem?'

He swallowed. His expression was unchanging, the eyes constantly searching her face, the smile expanding the corners of the heavy overblown mouth. For a moment Daisy thought he hadn't heard her question. 'They were never sure,' he said eventually. 'But she'd been working with Aldeb all right. Oh yes, she never had any doubt that it was Aldeb that had been the problem.'

Daisy caught the faintest hint of an accent. It wasn't one she knew, certainly nothing that came from anywhere near South London. The only feature she could pin down was a guttural twang to his c's and k's. 'You say they weren't sure what was wrong,' she said, 'but she must have had some symptoms, surely?'

He started on a muffin, eating with the rapidity and determination of a compulsive eater. Below the fleshy cheeks, a heavy neck strained at its collar and the loose shirt could not hide the swell of a well-padded belly. 'Oh, plenty of symptoms. Aches, pains, that sort of thing. Bad aches and pains, mind. Very bad. Had to take pills and potions all the time. An absolute slave to them.'

'I see,' said Daisy, trying to sort her way through this morass of vague information. 'Would she be willing to come and see us, do you think? To undergo some tests? They're quite painless. Just blood, that sort of thing.'

'She would have, I'm sure. In fact she'd have been only too pleased. Sadly, though . . .' He paused, frowning deeply, and continued in an unsteady voice: '. . . it won't be possible.'

'Oh. Why not? Is she too ill?'

'Not exactly,' he said with evident difficulty. 'No, you see she died last year.'

It was Daisy's turn to stare. Until just a moment ago he had been using the present tense. 'How awful,' she murmured.

Momentarily overcome, Maynard looked down at his hands. The fingers were blunt, she noticed, and there were gingery hairs growing thickly along the backs.

Breaking free of his grief, he picked up the teapot. 'More tea, Miss Field?' he asked solicitously.

'It must have been awful, Mr Maynard. I'm so sorry.'

'Colin. Please call me Colin.' He did the trick with his eyes again, crinkling them at the edges to demonstrate his sincerity, before topping up her cup and offering her a muffin. 'Yes, it was sad, very sad indeed.'

'But surely the matter was investigated. Did they establish the cause of death?'

'Ah. There's no doubt about how she died, I'm afraid.' Adopting a reverential tone he confided: 'Her car went into a tree.'

Daisy took a moment to absorb this. 'I see.' She didn't like to ask if this mishap was likely to have been a complete accident or not. 'How awful,' she said. 'I'm sorry.'

He accepted her sympathy with a small bow of the head. 'One has to bear these things, doesn't one? One has to be brave. No choice really.' Almost immediately the ingratiating smile was back.

Daisy made an effort to like him and failed. His desire to please was so palpable, so overdone that her instinctive reaction was to pull up her drawbridge.

'Tell me,' she said, 'what exactly did you want from me, Mr Maynard?'

'From you?' He gave a humble little shrug. 'I thought maybe you could make something of what happened. You know, do something useful with the information. So her death won't have been in vain.'

The orchestra sprang into a noisy Charleston. Some of the younger dancers hurled themselves into a frenzy of leg kicking and arm waving. Every table in the room was taken, Daisy noticed, and people were being turned away at the door. Maynard had been lucky to get a booking.

Daisy raised her voice over the blare of the music. 'Quite honestly, I'm not sure we can do very much with what you've given me. There's so little to go on, you see.'

'Little to go on? Oh, I see. I hadn't realized.' He chewed thoughtfully on a pastry. 'But now you come to mention it, I suppose there isn't.' A regretful chuckle. 'Oh dear, oh dear. I'm disappointed of course. I mean, I had hoped ... She was my sister, after all.' He popped the last of the pastry into his mouth. 'Well, well. There we are. There we are. One has to accept these things.' The smile slid back into place, and Daisy suppressed a sudden urge to wipe it off his face. 'So tell me, Miss Field, normally – when the person's available, so to speak – you can do these blood tests, can you? And what do they show exactly?'

'If we're lucky, if we catch the person soon enough, high levels of pesticide.'

'Just floating around in the blood, are they?'

'More or less.'

'And you've come across a lot of cases, have you?'

'Not as many as I'd like.' His accent: she had it at last. Unless she was mistaken it was South African or something very similar, an accent that time or determination had all but eradicated.

'Forgive me, but would that be tens of cases? Or hundreds?'

'We're not sure.' She explained how some people had been exposed to several pesticides and it was hard to know which individual agent or combination of agents had caused their illness.

'But Aldeb's the number-one suspect, eh?' It seemed to Daisy that there was a hint of slyness in his eyes.

'Not necessarily.'

If he was disappointed in her answers he didn't show it. He offered her the last pastry. When she refused it he slid it onto his plate and raised his pale eyebrows in disapproval at his own self-indulgence. 'And the organization you work for, Miss Field. I don't believe you mentioned it.'

'Didn't I?'

'You said you worked for a charitable organization.'

'Yes, so I did.' She was tempted to skirt the truth again. There was something about Maynard that did not invite trust, and his questioning, for all its caution, had an edge of relentlessness to it. At the same time she had nothing to apologize for, and certainly nothing to hide.

'I work for Catch,' she told him. 'The Campaign Against Toxic Chemicals. We monitor all sorts of chemicals and their impact on health.'

A look of wonderment came over his face. 'Really?'

'Some of our work is funded by charitable trusts, as I told you, but mostly we rely on subscriptions.'

'You have a membership, do you?'

'Certainly. Would you like to join? It's twelve pounds fifty.'

He gave the briefest hesitation and, though it might have

been Daisy's imagination, she thought she saw a flicker of calculation pass over his face. He beamed: 'Why, I'd be delighted.'

He insisted on paying in cash and drew fifteen pounds in notes from his wallet. She couldn't help noticing that the wallet was well stocked. He wouldn't accept any change. 'Let it be an extra little donation,' he said proudly. 'You will keep me in touch?'

She explained about the quarterly newsletters.

'And might I phone you just occasionally?' he asked. 'To see how things are going on the Aldeb front. If it wouldn't be too much trouble? It would mean so much.' He inclined his head timidly, though Daisy had got the feeling that timidity didn't come easily to Colin Maynard.

'There won't be much to report, not for some months anyway.'

He said hastily: 'In due course then. In due course.' He summoned the waiter and paid the thirty-five-pound bill without a murmur. Daisy couldn't help noticing that his lips moved as he calculated the tip.

# Chapter 6

—◦—

SUSAN DRISCOLL WAITED for the driver to hurry round the back of the car and open the door for her. She was perfectly capable of opening it herself, of course, but such perks were still novel enough to gratify and entertain her. Having stepped out, she walked slowly into the house, leaving the driver to unload the baggage and carry it into the hall after her.

Once inside, any fleeting illusion of high living came to an abrupt end, and her mood darkened. She looked irritatedly for something on which to focus her dissatisfaction, but the hall and the drawing room, glimpsed through the open door beyond, were just as she had left them, the scatter of cushions unruffled, the carefully arranged bric-à-brac unmolested, the picture frames straight. Even the dried flower-burst on the Queen Anne occasional table by the door, which the cleaner usually managed to displace, was for once undisturbed. The place, her painstaking and loving creation of five years, was perfect, and she felt an angry unreasoned resentment against it. However much guests admired it – and they did, lavishly – there was never any escaping the fact that she had exerted all her creativity on a house that was small, hemmed in by ugliness of immense proportion, and wildly inconvenient, being deep in an area which, up-and-coming in the great property boom of five years before, had failed to arrive. This street and two of its neighbours formed an island of yuppification in a sea of depressing council estates, run-down Victorian terraces and menacing inhabitants, most of whom were coloured, a fact which Susan wasn't allowed to mention now that Tony was a junior minister. Over the years guests had become infrequent – it was easier and, though Tony wouldn't admit it, safer to meet them in town – and now the house seemed a laughable, lamentable waste of effort.

The driver asked if there was anything else she wanted, but she knew better than to take him up on the offer. A shopping trip to Knightsbridge would have been nice – her wardrobe had failed to stand up to the test of two days in Paris – but Tony would need to make cabinet rank before she could get away with anything as frivolous as that. As the other wives had allowed her to discover the hard way, the lines of privilege were not to be overstepped.

With the driver gone, she flicked through the bills and wandered into the kitchen. Even a cursory glance revealed the reason the dried flowers had been undisturbed: the cleaner, due yesterday morning, had failed to show up. Susan felt a deeper depression: it was really impossible to get things done around here.

A pan lay in the sink, clumps of congealed spaghetti floating in its oily waters. This meant that Camilla, her student daughter, must be in residence, an unexpected but largely pleasant surprise confirmed by the fact that the answering machine had been turned off and replaced by a stack of pencilled messages.

Susan brightened up a little and, going into the hall, called up the stairwell to the top floor. It was ten, still a little early for Camilla, and Susan was preparing to call again when her daughter's head suddenly appeared over the banister rail.

'Mummy! Who's a clever girl then?' Camilla shrieked.

'Oh? Am I? That makes a change.'

'And I thought you were kidding.'

'What are you talking about?' Susan said, slightly irritated.

'I'm talking about Nick Mackenzie!'

It took a moment for Susan to absorb the implications of this statement. Incredulous, she said: 'You mean – he's called?'

'His agent. Phoned yesterday.'

Susan hurried back to the kitchen and shuffled through the messages. There it was: David Weinberg Management had called. They wanted to discuss a date for a concert. Would she please call back.

She stared at the message, read it again, then sat down on the nearest stool.

Nick hadn't forgotten her then. He had realized that the unfamiliar-sounding Mrs Susan Driscoll was really her and had said yes; agreed to the impossible, to the one thing they'd said he'd never do.

The thought filled Susan with vivid exhilaration and a sort of bitter-sweet triumph. It had been a long time since she had seen Nick – incredibly, almost twenty years – but despite everything, despite the number of women who must have been through his life in all that time, despite his marriage to the woman with the strange name, he'd remembered.

And remembered her kindly, it seemed, despite – no, why did she say that? – *because* of what had happened so long ago. Yes, and why not? They had been very young. That said it all, really: very young, very selfish. Looking back now, he must feel guilty – *yes*, and rightly so. He had been awful, *awful* at the end. Yet she was happy to forgive and forget – it was such a long time ago, after all.

Even as she convinced herself of this she felt an echo of pain and anxiety, like an old wound. Would he really remember her kindly? Would he?

Camilla breezed in and enveloped her mother in an embrace that was mostly long hair and floppy T-shirt. Susan kissed her absentmindedly and disentangled herself.

Camilla gazed admiringly through oversize spectacles.

'Mummy, you *are* a dark horse. I'm afraid I didn't really believe you. I mean, it sounded so unlikely.'

Susan smoothed out the message and tucked it into her bag. 'What do you mean – unlikely?'

'Well, you knowing Nick Mackenzie.'

'But I told you. I knew him well.'

Camilla giggled delightedly. 'Mummy!'

Susan gave her a long cool look. 'We were very close for a time.'

The laughter fell away from Camilla's face. She looked respectful. 'Mummy, I had no idea.'

Susan gave a small secretive smile. 'Why should you?'

'Was it . . . Were you . . .?'

'We were lovers, if that's what you're getting at.' Susan looked away, out to the small enclosed patio with its scattering of geraniums. She noticed that the white walls, painted only a few months before, were already streaked with grime. 'We met at a party in Chelsea. It was one of those instant things, across a crowded room. The sort of thing you don't believe in until it happens to you. Within a week we were living together. It was – well, special. For both of us. We were very much in love.' She was aware of Camilla's incredulous stare. Children, selfish creatures that they were, always chose the images of their parents which suited them, and youth and desirability they found very uncomfortable indeed.

'What happened?' Camilla asked in a hushed voice.

Susan half turned so her face was in profile. 'I ended it. I didn't want that sort of life. It may sound glamorous, a non-stop succession of concerts and parties and travel but, believe me, it was soul-destroying. The band was always touring. The pace was mad, the pressure awful. No one could survive that. It started to destroy me and it certainly started to destroy Nick. He hit the drink, you know. I couldn't bear to watch it. I wanted it to end while we still had something going for us.'

'Mummy, I can't bear it. It's so sad.'

'Oh, not sad really.' Susan gave a brave little smile. 'These things happen all the time. Right person, wrong timing. And vice versa. It's the story of most people's lives.'

Camilla gave an agonized groan. 'But, Mummy, if he'd been anyone else, I mean if he'd been *ordinary*, would you – well, still be together?'

Only an eighteen-year-old could ask a question like that. 'Darling, who knows?' she answered enigmatically. 'One can never tell about these things.'

'Of course, I should be glad – that you married Daddy, I mean. Otherwise I wouldn't be here.'

Susan's mind was back on Nick Mackenzie. What memories came into his mind when he thought about her? Good ones hopefully. The others – well, they faded with time, didn't they? She gave a small shiver.

'Not that Daddy's ordinary, of course,' Camilla rattled on.

'No, darling,' Susan murmured vaguely. 'Of course not.'

'And he *is* a minister. Which isn't at all ordinary, is it?'

'A *government* minister, Camilla,' she said briskly. 'If you say minister people will think he's a parson.'

Camilla burst out laughing. 'Daddy a parson! What a thought!'

Susan didn't reply. She was thinking ahead to the night of the concert and the moment when she would face Nick again. She would dress very carefully. None of the staid government wife look, yet nothing too glitzy either. A designer dress, very simple, very dramatic. Very expensive. She would buy it first and argue with Tony later.

'Will you have lots of meetings beforehand?' Camilla asked. 'If so, can I be your assistant? Notebook in hand.'

Susan hadn't thought of meetings, but of course there would have to be several, maybe as many as three or four. Perhaps one with Nick himself. In which case she might well take Camilla along. But not the entire committee; they

didn't deserve it. Though they were far, far too well bred
to say so, they hadn't really believed she could pull this
thing off. She would enjoy announcing her coup at the next
meeting.

Pointing Camilla in the direction of the sink and the
unwashed spaghetti pan, Susan hurried upstairs to unpack.
Only a few hours before, everything about her clothes had
disheartened her: frumpy, frowsy, second-rate. Now she
sang as she hung them up. Pausing in front of a mirror,
she cast a critical eye at her reflection, pushing her chin
forward, turning to half profile to find her best angle. Not
bad, really. She had good bones, and bones always stood
the test of time. She didn't look forty-something, more like
thirty-five. There were laugh-lines around her eyes, of
course, and the eyelids were going a bit crêpy, but what
could you expect. The hair needed attention though. The
style, layered but long, like a shaggy lion, really didn't suit
her. Too middle-class. Too middle-aged. She would go for
something sleeker, simpler, more classical.

Normally she made it a rule never to unpack for Tony,
just as she made it a rule never to wash and iron his shirts
– laundries were the best people to field complaints about
creases and late deliveries – but after this news she was
feeling light-hearted and decidedly generous. Tony had to
work hard in this new job of his; the three-day conference
in Paris had been preceded by two days in Strasbourg and,
before that, a hectic week in Parliament dispelling fears
about contaminated water in Lancashire.

His case contained a pile of dirty shirts, socks and
underclothes. There were an enormous number of them; he
must have changed shirts at least twice a day. She bundled
them into the laundry basket, hung his spare suit in the
wardrobe and placed his unused clean shirts neatly on a
shelf. In the bottom of the case were a few loose papers –
brochures and circulars – and these she placed on his
bedside table.

His sponge bag she put beside the basin in the bathroom, then, feeling really noble, opened it and hung out his flannel. She noticed his toothpaste was nearly finished and made a mental note to buy him some more.

She glanced at the brochure on top of the pile. A five-star converted château somewhere in France, complete with moat and drawbridge. Tony must have stayed there on his way from Strasbourg to Paris, before she flew out to join him. It looked gorgeous. How strange that he had said nothing about it. She opened the brochure out. Lying inside it was a slip, the sort they hand you with your key, confirming the room rate. At the top in French script was written: *Mme. Smith*, and a room number.

Susan sat down on the bed. It was several minutes before she moved. Then she got up and, going to the wardrobe, systematically went through the pockets of Tony's suits. Running quickly downstairs, she searched his overcoats hanging in the hall. Returning to the bedroom, she sat on the bed again for quite a time before going into the bathroom and staring at herself in the mirror.

This would take some thinking about.

As she turned to leave, something made her pause and look at the sponge bag again. At first she wasn't sure what it was that had caught her eye. Then she identified it. Just beyond the toothpaste, peeping out from a side pocket, was the corner of a small carton. Even as she stared at it, even as she reached to draw it slowly out, she knew exactly what it was, although that did nothing to prevent the rush of shock and anger.

The brand name was from the let's-make-condoms-jolly school. The packaging was bright and simple, as brash and innocent as a packet of sweets, designed to go with the bright young things' Porsches and post-modernist life-plans. Wishful thinking on Tony's part, perhaps. A middle-aged man's lustful little daydreams. Slowly she opened the packet. Her hand was shaking slightly. Out of a packet of three, there was only one left. No daydream, then. *Christ*.

Was she a bright young thing, this woman Tony was screwing? Had she been in Strasbourg with him as well as the château? Or even Paris? If Paris, she'd have had to be quick; Tony had been there barely twenty-four hours before Susan herself arrived.

Was it a long-standing affair? Did they meet regularly? Was she young and pretty?

God – was it a friend of hers? Worst of all, was it someone Tony actually cared for?

Mrs Smith. She might have been more original. Such a shabby little name.

As far as Susan knew none of her female friends or acquaintances had been at either the Strasbourg or Paris conferences, nor had any of the female research assistants or secretaries from Tony's office. Unlikely, then, to be anyone she knew. In which case Tony couldn't possibly see the woman with any regularity. He was too busy, his movements too well accounted for.

But someone he cared about all the same? Surely not. There would have been signs: he would have been tense, or particularly attentive or unaccountably excited. She cast her mind back, but for as long as she could remember Tony had been nothing but his normal plodding reasonably affectionate self.

She relaxed a little. This couldn't be anything too serious. In which case, did she really need or even want to know more? She was surprised to find that, mixed with her shock and anger, was genuine amazement that bordered on admiration. The cunning devil. Who would have believed it? For years their love-life had been so-so, very so-so in fact. She had put this down to the channelling of Tony's energies into politics and his impossibly long working hours. But now she realized that she had been rather naive to think this state of affairs could continue unnoticed and unheeded, at least on his part. In the final analysis, no man could resist all the little extras that power brought with it. Weren't people always saying – and with monotonous regularity – that power was the greatest aphrodisiac of all?

She replaced the carton carefully in the side pocket, along with the damp flannel she had recently hung out, and carefully zipped the bag up again.

'Mummy, I quite forgot – '

Susan gave a great start and clamped a hand to her chest. Camilla was peering in from the bedroom. Susan shook with rage. 'Never do that again! Never!'

Camilla put on her sulkiest expression, the sort children keep exclusively for their parents. 'Sorry. I only wanted to show you the paper. There's something about Daddy in it.' She gave a resentful shrug and tossed the newspaper onto the floor. 'Excuse me for trying to help,' she added with unnecessary sarcasm, and flounced out.

Angry with Camilla, angry with herself for having reacted so sharply, still catching her breath from the surprise, Susan reached for the paper. It was *The Times*. It took her a moment to find the item, tucked away in a political diary column.

One dark horse is the fast-rising junior minister, Tony Driscoll. Dubbed grey and undistinguished in his first post in Transport, he quickly bloomed at the Environment office, and has been credited with singlehandedly getting the government out of the Lancashire water pollution fiasco almost unscathed. Until recently considered a rank outsider in the Cabinet stakes, Driscoll's unsuspected talent with the media, his readiness to take on thankless tasks, and his quick wit on the floor of the Commons have the pundits tipping him for a more senior post after the next election.

Were they serious? Quick wit. Talent with the media. Susan reread it with bemusement. It was hard to believe they were talking about Tony. His jokes were museum-pieces, his wit schoolboyish. As for the media, she had to brace herself to watch him on television. His desire to impress was so transparent, his concern so palpably laid on, that she felt sure everyone must see through him at any moment.

'Unbelievable,' she said aloud.

She was still murmuring her disbelief when she dressed for dinner that evening. She wore her favourite black suit with a tailored jacket and a skirt of decorous length that came to just above the knee: shorter skirts, though fashionable, had been forbidden. Tony said they looked tarty. He was a fine one to talk, Susan decided, when he had a tart of his own tucked away somewhere.

She'd a good mind to embarrass him in the restaurant, to drop a hint over the soup. That would serve him damn well right. At the same time, now that she had got over her shock and was feeling an almost perverse satisfaction in having caught the silly fool out, her more cautious instincts told her to do nothing of the sort. Like something let loose from its bottle, a revelation, once made, might expand and take on all sorts of ugly shapes. Besides, they were going to the Caprice, and she didn't want to spoil her meal.

The doorbell rang just before seven thirty. She opened the door to a uniformed chauffeur who tipped his hat to her. Behind him was a Rolls, the large-bodied type of thirty years ago that sat high above the road and was usually packed with Arabs on their way to Harrods. She sank into the dark recesses of the interior, feeling suitably indulged, and thought: Bully for Mr What's-his-name. Directed to the reading light by the chauffeur she checked her pocket diary for the name of their host for the evening. R.B. Schenker, chief executive, Morton-Kreiger International, Agrochemical Division. Morton-Kreiger was one of those

vast corporations that made chemicals and pharmaceuticals, that she knew, but Mr Schenker she had never met,
not so far as she could remember anyway.

Tony had told her the man's first name on the way back
from Paris but she couldn't remember that either. R.B. –
Robert? Richard? But certainly not Bob or Dick. These
corporate men didn't like abbreviations: it invited people to
take them less than seriously. Robert or Bob or whatever it
was would be a bore, there was no getting away from that,
and she would have to survive the evening as best she might.

His name, as it turned out, was Ronald. He was a slight
man in his early forties, with dark hair which he brushed
over to one side to cover his sharply receding hairline. He
had a narrow high-boned face, a pointed chin and very
white skin. His eyes, which were quick and dark, were set
close together and stared at you with great intensity, as if
he was watching for your every move. He was attentive
and courteous, but without charm, as if he had taken a
half-day course in etiquette and had forgotten the lesson
about looking as though you were enjoying it. His manner
first embarrassed then irritated Susan. Mr Schenker had
obviously read in some how-to-succeed book that, on the
path to influence, no stone was to be left unturned.

Most of the time Tony and he talked politics, or rather,
Tony talked and Ronald Schenker listened. Mr Schenker, it
appeared, was not married – at least he hadn't brought a
wife with him – so that Susan often found herself left out
of the conversation. She used the time to think about Nick
Mackenzie and her husband, though not simultaneously.
Her mind flittered schizophrenically between euphoria,
biting uncertainties over the concert and wonder at the
sight of her cheating husband, butter incapable of melting
in any part of his anatomy.

As usual in company, Tony was animated, very – what
was that awful word? – forceful. It was all laid on, of
course, all part of his political persona. Away from the

limelight he was quite a subdued person. At least, with her he was.

Susan had always regarded him as safe and sturdy, the sort of quietly successful, middle-of-the-road Englishman who never let you down — but didn't give you too many surprises either. The success of his political career had been a little unexpected, to put it mildly, but then the most unlikely people often make it in politics. She was constantly struck by the number of dull, narrow-minded bores she met in the Commons.

Until today she'd always believed that Tony's staunch Thatcherite qualities extended to their relationship. Never, during the nineteen years they had been together, had it ever occurred to her that Tony would rock the boat. Even after what she'd discovered today, she couldn't imagine that anything would ever seriously undermine their marriage.

But that, of course, was precisely what all unsuspecting wives thought, right until the moment their husbands walked out of the door. She would have to watch her step.

Tony caught her stare, and gave her a perfunctory grin. She tried to decide whether he could possibly appear good-looking to other women. He was very ordinary, so very ordinary that she sometimes wondered if he hadn't come out of a mould marked standard middle-aged mark-one Englishman. He had always had a tendency to put on weight, a battle that had ebbed and flowed through their marriage, but which, with the frequent lunches and dinners, was finally being lost. He had thinning hair of a nondescript colour, large rimless glasses, rather pudgy cheeks and a neck that was beginning to squeeze out over the edge of his collar.

Yet he must have something special, something that gave him the edge on the political platform and, so it would appear, with this woman in France.

Perhaps Susan was missing something, perhaps she had

missed it right from the beginning. Perhaps Tony had charisma, that much overused word which always sounded to Susan like an unpleasant socially transmitted disease. But it was a hard idea to swallow. Charisma depended on sex appeal and Tony lacked the edge of danger that is the essential ingredient of sex appeal. Tony had always been unutterably safe.

She hadn't married him for sexual chemistry – she'd had quite enough of that and its attendant disasters in her early twenties – no, she'd married Tony for his dependability, his merchant banker's income, and because she was tired of having to look after herself. The merchant banker's income had disappeared soon after they married, when Tony had decided to earn his Brownie points by going to work for a big charity, but by then Camilla was on the way and she was rather taken by the idea of motherhood.

'Do you like opera, Mrs Driscoll?' Schenker asked with his rather stiff smile. 'We'd be delighted if you'd come to Glyndebourne with us next month.'

Susan glanced at Tony for affirmation and smiled graciously. 'That would be lovely,' she said. She didn't like opera, but she knew Tony would be keen to go, and everyone said the gardens were lovely.

'Good. I'll send you a programme then. There are four operas to choose from – Donizetti, Mozart, Tchaikovsky and Strauss.' There was a hint of hesitation and rehearsal in this speech, and Susan guessed Schenker had memorized the list especially for her benefit.

'We also take seats at Covent Garden. I don't know if you'd like that?' He watched her face carefully. 'Or the theatre?'

He spotted her flicker of interest and quietly seized on it. 'The theatre then? Just let me know what you'd like to see.' He waited, and Susan realized he was expecting her to name a play there and then. Mr Schenker was obviously someone who liked to nail things down.

'I'm not sure,' Susan replied. 'Any ideas, Tony?'

'Oh, you decide, my dear. You're more up to date with these things than I am. Besides, I always like the things that you like.' He raised his eyebrows at Schenker in a quick conspiratorial smile, as if they, as men, had conceived this ploy to keep the little woman happy.

Susan managed a thin smile, and named a popular musical you had to kill to get tickets for.

'Good. That'll be arranged then,' said Schenker, and Susan had no doubt that it would. 'The minister's kindly agreed to visit our new plant in Newcastle in September,' he continued, and for an instant Susan had to remind herself that this grand personage he was referring to was Tony. 'We would be delighted if you would come too. But of course, we'd quite understand if you'd prefer not to . . .' Schenker trailed off politely, awaiting his next cue.

Susan tried to think of something she'd hate more than a visit to a factory in Newcastle and failed. She put on an interested expression. 'A new plant?'

'Fertilizers. It's the largest and most modern fertilizer plant in Europe. We're very proud of it.'

'Really? How wonderful.' For a moment she was lost for anything else to say. 'But fertilizers aren't exactly environmentally friendly, are they?' She rolled her eyes in mock disapproval. 'I'm surprised at Tony having anything to do with it.'

It was not much of a joke, but she expected a favourable response. Tony did chuckle slightly, but Schenker was silent, the tight-lipped smile fastened to his face with difficulty, his small eyes unamused. Susan realized she had made the classic error of imagining that such a grey little man would have a sense of humour.

'Fertilizers have had a bad name in the past, of course,' Schenker said in a voice that was at once earnest and slightly reproachful. 'But as I'm sure you're aware, the agricultural industry in this country couldn't function without them. In fact food would cost four times as much, maybe more, if farmers were forced to do without them. But that isn't to say we don't take our environmental responsibilities very seriously. We do. Very seriously indeed.' The unblinking eyes stared into hers, as if he could convince her by willpower alone. 'In the last ten years Morton-Kreiger have spent millions and millions on developing fertilizers which are less likely to leach away through the soil and find their way into water sources – fertilizers which are kinder to the environment. Millions and millions. No one else has done as much as we have. No one.'

Susan said hastily: 'I'm sure that's true – '

'And it's the same story with pesticides. We lead the world in pesticide safety. Morton-Kreiger undertake more research than any other major company into producing safer products. Not only in terms of pounds and dollars, but in terms of the quality and thoroughness of the tests we run – '

This was getting tiresome. Susan said firmly: 'Mr Schenker, it was a joke. Really. Just a joke.'

The idea seemed to take him by surprise. He hesitated, absorbing the information, then nodded slowly. 'I see.'

'I think Susan was just echoing most people's misconceptions about my job,' Tony stepped in smoothly. 'They seem to think that an environment minister should go around banning everything in sight, rather than persuading manufacturers to adapt and modify existing products. If we banned everything the Greens wanted us to ban, then we'd be back in the Dark Ages, living in hovels and eating porridge three times a day.'

Schenker swivelled his eyes back to Susan.

'I'm not much of a one for porridge,' she said.

Schenker seemed to take her remark as a sign of approval, not only for what Tony had just said, but for himself and all his chemicals.

'Porridge.' He nodded and smiled, and Susan realized

this was probably the closest he ever came to laughing. 'And what sort of cuisine do you like, Mrs Driscoll?'

Susan suspected she was meant to say: do call me Susan, but she resisted. 'Well, I'm not complaining at this,' she said, indicating the newly arrived dessert, an artistic array of sorbet, fruit, raspberry *coulis* and sugar wafers.

'I see,' said Mr Schenker, filing the information away. 'Then we'll come here again, shall we? After the theatre.'

Irritated at being parcelled up so tidily, Susan had the sudden urge to disturb Mr Schenker's meticulous little world. 'What about you?' she enquired politely. 'Do you like French food?'

'Yes, indeed.' Anticipating the drift her questions might take, he pulled back a little. 'But nothing too rich.'

'What sort of things exactly?'

His courteous expression slipped into something altogether more guarded, as if he was beginning to realize he was on thin ice. 'Oh . . . their soups.'

'Vichyssoise?'

He gave the faintest of nods, and looked away, trying to close the subject. It was just as she had suspected: he knew nothing about food.

'And what else?' Susan persisted.

He did not like being pressed, not when he was being shown up. Moreover, he was beginning to suspect her motives. With good reason, of course. She was rather enjoying herself.

'The fish soups. They're very good too,' he said eventually.

'Bouillabaisse?'

This time he made no attempt to reply, but stared at her, the little eyes gleaming darkly. Mr Schenker did not enjoy being disconcerted.

'But you're not so good with the shellfish, eh?' Tony said. 'Made you sick as a dog, didn't they, Ronald?'

'Oh dear. What happened?' Susan asked pleasantly.

'Oysters,' Tony said. 'That's what happened. And it was me who persuaded him to try them. Not my finest recommendation. But you should have told me they were no good, Ronald. I would have called the hotel doctor. It could have been serious. Salmonella or something.'

'Where was this?' Susan asked.

There was a small pause. Susan looked up from her plate to see a shimmer of realization slide over Tony's eyes, a flicker of caution as if he were thinking his way rapidly out of something. But the shift, which was so small that no one else would have noticed it, was gone as quickly as it had come and he said with his usual ease: 'At this hotel in France.'

For once Ronald Schenker was not staring at her, but examining his coffee cup.

So the two of them had been in France together, had they? Dining together, staying at the same hotel. Was it at the château, she wondered, or in Paris? One way or the other, they seemed to be spending a lot of time together. And when Tony was so busy; and when he had to be so careful to be impartial and objective and all the other things ministers were meant to be.

And where did the woman fit into all this? When, in the middle of all these cosy evenings with Schenker, would Tony have had time to see *her*?

She put down her spoon and abandoned the last of her dessert. One way and another, this day had really been too much.

'Everything all right?' Schenker asked solicitously.

Susan looked up and realized she had been frowning.

'Delicious,' she said. 'Absolutely delicious.'


'Have we sent the flowers to Mrs Driscoll?'

'Yes, Mr Schenker.'

'What did we send?'

'A mixed bouquet of seasonal flowers.'

Schenker looked up from his desk. 'A mixed bouquet. But what was in it?'

The secretary flipped through her notebook, and Schenker knew immediately that she was stalling. He said briskly: 'Find out, would you? And next time, make sure there are plenty of roses. I think Mrs Driscoll would like roses.'

When the secretary had gone Schenker buzzed the intercom and a moment later his personal assistant Peter Cramm entered. Schenker always felt invigorated when Cramm arrived. Cramm, tall, fit and well turned-out, was the only person whose energy matched his own, the only person with enough imagination to get things done unprompted.

'Find out what charity work Susan Driscoll does, will you?' Schenker said immediately. 'She must be on some committee or another. It might be a cause we could support.'

Cramm, sitting in his customary seat at one side of Schenker's modernistic desk, did not reply but made a brief note on his pocket jotter.

'Now – Aldeb,' said Schenker. 'What's the update?'

'Still stuck on Senator Brisco.'

'Do we really need him?'

'He's on the Senate Appropriations Committee.'

'I know, I know, but haven't we got anyone else?'

'Our people are working on it.'

Like all large conglomerates, Morton-Kreiger employed a considerable number of lobbyists to look after its interests in Washington and other major capitals. When things were quiet the Morton-Kreiger board questioned the necessity for spending hundreds of thousands in this way, but when things got rough, as they had been with Aldeb, the board were only too happy to have made the investment.

'It's the re-test data that's the problem with Brisco,'

Cramm said. 'The environmentalists got hold of some of it, as you know, and they must have sent it to the senator, because he keeps quoting the figures at us. He sees himself as rather a science buff, I'm afraid. He's says even an idiot could see the data gaps and that he'd find it difficult to help until they can be explained.'

'What about the original tests? Hasn't he been shown a summary or something?'

'He says it's impossible to be sure they're unbiased.'

'Not unbiased?' Schenker echoed in an offended voice. 'What does he think he is, an expert? Does he have the slightest evidence for that sort of allegation?'

'He says TroChem is an industry-controlled laboratory and therefore incapable of delivering impartial data.'

'But everybody uses TroChem. Half the products on the US market have been tested at TroChem.' An exaggeration, of course – TroChem hadn't been going that long – but truthful enough for the purposes of the argument. Schenker tapped his fingers delicately on the desk. 'He must have been nobbled,' he declared. He didn't have to say who by.

The eco-mafia, as many people called them – and Schenker never discouraged the term – had loomed large in the lives of the agrochemical industry for some time. If the eco-mafia had their way, products would cost ten times as much and take ten times as long to bring to market, and this at a time when the number of new products getting through the system had already been squeezed to a trickle. These people also wanted to see products withdrawn on the most flimsy and far-fetched evidence, the sort of data that came from feeding rats virtually undiluted chemical for a month and getting a point-one per cent cancer rate.

'You know, I'd almost like the supply of products to dry up,' he remarked to Cramm, 'just to witness the anti-Green backlash.'

The anti-Green backlash was an old hope of Schenker's,

one he had harboured ever since the Environmental Protection Agency had first moved to ban Aldeb in the US – since, as he liked to put it, environmental fever had taken over the Western world and bludgeoned the media into submission.

Swivelling his chair, Schenker pushed himself smoothly to his feet and walked over to the window to stretch his spine. His back always gave him trouble first thing in the morning, the left-over of a water-skiing injury sustained when staying with the chief executive of Morton-Kreiger Incorporated in the Bahamas. Water-skiing, sports fishing, game shooting, snow skiing: Schenker had tried them all during his occasional and necessarily brief holidays. But the learning curves were too steep for his temperament and the available time.

Far below, the Thames flowed grey and sluggish. Even from this height he could see the whorls of polystyrene, plastic and aluminium cans swirling around the moored vessels. Soon the tide would turn and carry the debris back down-river in long ugly trails towards the East End, where doubtless it had originated. He bent over and touched his toes to ease the pressure on the lower vertebrae. 'That Senator Brisco should learn not to meddle,' he blew over his shoulder.

'Our people are working on one possibility that might swing him.'

'Yes?'

'It involves trading a few favours.'

That was always the way in American politics. 'And what are the chances?'

'Good, I'd say,' Cramm replied, and Schenker experienced the satisfaction he always felt when Cramm and the rest of the team had been beavering away behind the scenes. He didn't enquire further. It was quite enough to know that his people were working on it. The how and why did not concern him. Feeling brighter, he did some side bends, raising one arm in the air, putting the other hand on his hip and pushing over as far as he could go.

'A pity we never had conclusive data,' Schenker said more to himself than to Cramm, dredging up possibilities again. Although he, better than anyone, knew that Morton-Kreiger's scientific staff had been squeezed dry in the hunt for data favourable to Aldeb. 'Anyone else on that appropriations committee we should be attending to?' He breathed through a series of controlled pants.

Cramm shook his head. 'No one we haven't tried.'

'Keep at it,' Schenker said in the tone of a scoutmaster. 'This is still a number-one priority and I don't want anyone to forget it.'

Privately Schenker had already written Aldeb off in the US. That didn't mean that the battle wasn't to be fought to the bitter end, almost irrespective of cost. Not only was it a matter of principle to continue the fight, but it was essential to keep the environmentalists at bay and their resources stretched to the limit, if only to keep their attention from straying to other products.

Schenker had had plenty of time to get used to the idea of losing Aldeb in the US. The filing of the original EPA case, the unsuccessful appeal and the move for a rehearing had taken four years. Time enough to make contingency plans, salvage whatever could be salvaged, and divert remaining stocks of Aldeb elsewhere. Very sensibly, the poorer countries weren't so hysterical about overinflated cancer risks. They only cared about feeding their people. Schenker often reminded himself about the enormous contribution that agrochemicals made to the developing world. It made him feel his job was worthwhile.

After a few more side bends, a couple of toe touches and a number of deep breaths, Schenker returned briskly to his desk. 'Globally, we're still okay, are we?'

Cramm nodded. 'No change.'

'No more nasty surprises then.'

'I don't think so. Though that campaigning group Catch are trying to dredge something up.'

'Something?' There was reproof in his tone; he disliked inexactitude.

'They're advertising in farming magazines for people who've supposedly been affected by Aldeb.'

'Can they do that?'

Cramm shrugged. 'Nothing to stop them.'

'I'm surprised it's allowed. And how are these people meant to know they've been harmed by Aldeb?'

'Presumably they'll be self-diagnosed.'

Schenker raised an eyebrow. 'Self-deluded.'

'One interesting thing though,' Cramm offered with the tiny degree of dramatic emphasis he sometimes allowed himself. 'Catch advertised anonymously.'

'And that's allowed, too, is it?'

'Apparently.'

Schenker sighed in wonder at the magnanimity of English law. 'This secrecy, they're frightened of attention or what?'

'I think they've finally realized that farmers aren't great fans of radical lefties, and won't have anything to do with them if they announce themselves.'

'So what sort of a response have they had?'

'We don't know that.'

'And do we know what they're planning to do with this information once – if – they get it?'

'More media stories, presumably. Like the one on the potato farmers in Berkshire – they've been trying to push that as an Aldeb-caused-cancer story to the nationals.'

'And how are they getting on?'

'Nothing's appeared yet. But we're keeping an eye on it.'

Schenker pondered for a moment. It was all very well keeping a watch on the activities of these people, but that didn't stop them scoring heavily and without warning, as he knew to his cost.

'Where does Catch's money come from?'

'Membership. Fifteen thousand, fairly static.'

Schenker turned his palms up and gestured amazement. 'In admin terms, that must cost them almost as much as it brings in. Sure there's nothing else?'

'Unlikely. It's a shoestring operation. Just data-gathering and media pressurization. Nothing more ambitious.'

Schenker wasn't entirely convinced. 'Keep tabs on their financial situation, will you?' He pointed a long slow finger at Cramm, his favourite way of emphasizing a point. 'Lack of cash – that's the key to that lot.'

He sat back in the soft leather of his chair. It was time to move on.

'Silveron okay?' he asked Cramm, adding with heavy irony: 'No problems with the EPA on that, I trust?'

Cramm gave his small tight laugh. 'No.'

'And we're ready to go?'

'We're ready to go,' Cramm echoed.

Silveron, a new broad-spectrum pesticide, promised to be very profitable. Which was just as well because it had taken six years and sixty million dollars to develop, cash the division needed to pull back in a hurry. Silveron was Schenker's baby. He'd been in at the start of its development, had rooted for it all the way along the line, had overseen its progress.

'Any more feedback on UK performance?' Silveron was already on the UK market under a restricted licence, which allowed limited use for a period of two years, prior to the grant of a full licence.

'Just the normal sort of thing.'

'What does that mean?' snapped Schenker. Statements needed quantifying, tying down, putting in context.

'There's been a small amount of negative feedback, but

according to Marketing it's nothing – statistically insignificant.'

'They're sure?'

'They're sure.'

'Anything else?' Schenker asked.

A slight pause, then: 'Miss Kershaw called.'

Schenker felt a touch of alarm. 'Here? For me?'

'Oh no.' Cramm gave an astonished smile. 'Gracious, no. My home. Last night.'

'What did she want?'

'It was just a friendly call, to keep in touch.'

Schenker's fears were far from allayed. 'She didn't want anything?'

'No, nothing.'

'She didn't mention Driscoll?'

'Oh no. She wouldn't do that.' Cramm sounded very sure. 'No, I only mention it because I thought we might like to ask her to the opening of the Newcastle plant.'

Schenker was very still. Had Cramm gone mad? 'I don't think that would be a good idea,' he said coldly.

The very thought of Miss Kershaw made him uneasy – but then he felt uneasy about women at the best of times. He had always found them difficult and disturbingly unpredictable, and his brief marriage and unpleasant divorce ten years before had done everything to confirm his opinion. When he was forced to deal with them now, it was cautiously.

Angela Kershaw was the most difficult kind of female, pretty and vivacious, a combination which, in his limited experience, was likely to make her doubly unpredictable.

She'd first turned up at a cocktail party during a clean water conference in Birmingham some weeks before, an event partly sponsored by Morton-Kreiger. He gathered from Cramm that she was employed on a stand there, one of the army of pretty girls who made the rounds of motor

shows and exhibitions, demonstrating products and attracting business. No one seemed to know how she had come
to be invited to Morton-Kreiger's party but, whoever
brought her, it was Cramm who introduced her to Driscoll
and asked her to join them for dinner. To Schenker, she
seemed indistinguishable from dozens of other rather silly
young women, with her identikit smile, bright makeup and
inane conversation interspersed with gasps of girlish laughter, but to his amazement the evening was an enormous
success. The minister had been transfixed by her, almost
embarrassingly so.

Schenker had quickly forgotten about her until a month
later, when Cramm mentioned that she would be in Paris
during the European conference. Schenker's first reaction
had been alarm.

'What? Who invited her?'

'She's working there,' Cramm had replied.

'I don't think we need concern ourselves with her.'

'But it would be a pity, wouldn't it, not to repeat the
other evening? I mean, when she's going to be there
anyway, in Paris, and the minister has a free evening. I
know he'd enjoy seeing her again.'

There was something in the way Cramm said this that
made Schenker pause. He was not always terribly perceptive about these things, but his imagination weaved inexor-
ably towards an inescapable and disturbing conclusion.

'God – has she been seeing Driscoll?'

Cramm's impassive expression didn't falter. 'I really
couldn't say.'

This, doubtless, was the truth, although it left too much
unsaid. Schenker hesitated. He hated having to voice these
things openly, but it was necessary to be clear. 'Has Driscoll
said he'd like to see her?'

'Not in so many words, no, but . . .' His shrug was an
answer in itself.

Schenker felt resentment, distaste and a sense of opportunity in about equal measures, but opportunity, based as it was on Driscoll's burgeoning political career, won the day.

In the event Cramm's arrangements for the evening were discreet, though there were few arrangements that could be discreet enough for Schenker. They had gone to a château on the Marne near Epernay. To make up a tidy foursome, a second girl was found to accompany Schenker. Everyone arrived separately, the Kershaw girl registered as Mrs Smith, the dinner was held in a private room, the party remained sober, nobody attracted attention, and when it came to leaving the next morning, the cars arrived on time. Driscoll seemed delighted. Schenker was not so easily satisfied – he took up a couple of minor administrative details with Cramm later – but all in all the project could be judged to have achieved its objectives.

But invite Angela Kershaw to Newcastle for an official event? With the local press all over the place? Cramm was losing his sense of proportion.

Schenker said: 'No, Peter. Not Newcastle.'

'Oh,' said Cramm, lifting his voice slightly in unspoken dissatisfaction. 'A private dinner, then?'

'If you like.'

'A celebration in London perhaps? Shall I arrange it?'

Schenker shuffled the papers on his desk, suddenly impatient to be rid of these disconcerting trivialities and get on with the real business of the day. 'Do as you think fit,' he said curtly, waving Cramm away. 'But don't bother me with the details.'

# Chapter 7

—◆—

'You should be pleased, Mr Mackenzie. It's good news.' The doctor gave a professional smile, the sort designed to inspire, reassure and subtly reassert authority all at the same time.

Something dark and painful pulled at Nick's stomach, a lurking unvoiced anger. He did his best to suppress it: after all this man, a consultant physician named Plumb, meant well – all of them meant well – yet their habit of reducing everything to platitudes, of exuding this misplaced confidence, baffled and exasperated him.

'I wouldn't have called it good news,' Nick said evenly.

Plumb angled his head politely to one side.

'What you're saying is that you don't know what's wrong,' Nick said.

There was a pause. The juddering roar of accelerating traffic rose from the Marylebone Road below, reverberating through the room. The toxicologist sitting on Plumb's right, imported from a university especially for the meeting, studied his hands.

'We're saying that we believe there's nothing physically wrong with your wife,' Plumb explained gently.

'That you know of.'

'I'm sorry?'

Was it worth creating antagonism? Nick debated for a moment, then repeated quietly: 'Nothing wrong with her that you know of.'

'Mr Mackenzie' – Plumb gave a look of understanding

and compassion – 'we have very sophisticated tests nowadays. Your wife's been through all we can think of – and a few more. If there'd been anything seriously wrong, we would have found it, believe me.'

'But chemicals don't always show up in tests, do they?' Nick said.

The toxicologist blinked into life. 'It depends on the type of chemical, the dosage and how soon after the event you can run a test. And of course it helps to know what you're looking for. Then you know which tests to run.'

'And we've run all the obvious tests,' Plumb said in his plodding delivery. 'Several times. But with no trace of chemicals or chemical damage.'

Arguing technical points with this man was like playing tennis without a racquet: it was difficult to return even the most basic shot. Like all specialists, he was paid to have an opinion, and he wasn't about to admit that there might be the occasional yawning chasm in his knowledge, that, just possibly, he might simply be wrong. Nick rubbed a hand over his eyes. He felt dreadfully tired.

Aware that he was repeating himself for perhaps the twentieth time, he said wearily: 'My wife was overcome by fumes. She inhaled a large quantity of dangerous chemicals. You can't possibly say they had no effect.'

Plumb put on a serious but kindly face. 'Mr Mackenzie, your worries are very understandable, but this particular chemical that your wife inhaled, the wood preservative . . .'

'Reldane.'

'. . . Yes – Reldane – has no known harmful effects. Isn't that so, Blair?'

The toxicologist tore his eyes away from his hands. 'As wood preservers go, it's pretty benign really.'

Nick tried to remember what the people from Catch had told him over the phone. 'But that's not absolutely certain, is it?' he said. 'I understand that the research is fairly thin.'

Plumb frowned at that. 'But Reldane's been passed for

use by the safety people. It must have been. It wouldn't be allowed on the market otherwise, would it, Blair?' He flung a glance at the toxicologist.

'But I'm told that means very little,' Nick said before Blair had a chance to come in. 'The testing was done years ago. It could well be out of date.'

Plumb drew a deep breath. 'But there's no scientific basis for saying it's dangerous. No hard evidence to suggest it has any long-term effects. Quite the contrary. Isn't that correct, Blair?'

Given his cue, the toxicologist spouted facts. 'When ingested by mouth in any significant quantity, more than a millilitre, Reldane can cause nausea and dizziness, but it has no other known toxic effects. It's not carcinogenic or tetrogenic. And it doesn't affect the nervous system, not like the cholinesterase inhibitors.'

'What're they when they're at home?' Nick asked, beginning to lose patience.

'Substances that cause damage to the nervous system by inhibiting nerve transmitters. You find them in powerful pesticides. But not Reldane.'

'But when it's breathed in? That must be damaging, surely?'

'The Reldane was definitely inhaled, was it?'

'Yes. It was spilt on the ground, next to my wife's head. She was breathing it all the time she lay unconscious.'

'In that case, I have to say that it's even more unlikely that Reldane was to blame. You see, the effects of inhalation are invariably *less* severe than those of direct ingestion.'

If it was a trap, it had been neatly laid. Nick heard his voice rise: 'So you're saying it's harmless?'

Blair looked to Plumb for help.

'Not harmless exactly,' Plumb said. 'But not harm*ful* either. One has to accept that if Reldane had had any serious long-term effects in the population they would have come to light by now.'

Something in Nick died a little every time he heard a statement like that. Every answer was so plausible, every explanation so utterly reasonable, that gradually but relentlessly they wore you down and swamped your own instincts. He was weary of text-book solutions and standard assurances, weary of beating his head against the wall of scientific fact.

Plumb added: 'And the amount your wife inhaled was really quite small. After all, she was discovered in a reasonably short time, wasn't she?'

Nick didn't reply.

'Don't misunderstand me,' Plumb said. 'The chemical incident – contamination, if you prefer – might well have contributed to the trauma and the miscarriage. I'm not discounting that possibility, far from it.'

Nick looked away to the window, reaching for his breath. Even now he couldn't hear mention of the lost pregnancy without experiencing a mixture of conflicting emotions, all strong, all painful. He dimly recognized that there was a large dose of guilt in there somewhere, guilt at not having been there to prevent the accident, guilt at not being able to share or alleviate Alusha's anguish, misery that was all the worse for her attempts to hide it.

He forced himself back to Plumb's words. 'So you're saying it was trauma?'

Plumb settled back in the chair, a gleam of relief in his eyes now that that he was on the safer ground of his own expertise. 'I do indeed. The bump on the head, the inhalation, the miscarriage – I don't think they can be separated. One alone probably wouldn't have caused too much bother, but all three together – well, they'd be sufficient to cause significant trauma. And trauma – shock – whatever you want to call it, has profound physical effects.'

He paused for a moment to ensure that he had been understood. Nick understood all right; he was saying there was nothing wrong with Alusha. Overcome by the now

familiar sense of helplessness, he was silent, not trusting
himself to speak.

'There's no doubt your wife has endured a very *testing*
experience,' Plumb continued in a voice tinged with sympathy. 'But what has to be understood, Mr Mackenzie, is
that all this was a long time ago. Three months ago, to be
precise. After such a time there's absolutely no reason why
your wife shouldn't have recovered. At least, be well on the
way – '

'Then why in hell hasn't she recovered?' Nick said in
sudden exasperation.

'Ah. Now, the best person to talk to you about that is
my colleague, Dr Carter. He's *the* expert. He should be
here any moment – '

'But I want *you* to explain.'

'I assure you – Carter's the best person.'

Something shifted in Nick, a final thread broke in the
thin web of his control and his anger rose into his throat
like sickness. 'No. *You*.' His voice wavered and he fought
to control it. 'I want *you* to tell me.'

Plumb blinked at this unexpected show of emotion.
Finally he said awkwardly: 'Very well,' and, muttering
thanks to Blair, waited for him to leave.

'Please understand,' Plumb said when they were alone,
'there's no suggestion that your wife doesn't have physical
symptoms. Not for a moment. Her illness is very – real.'

'But you just said there was nothing wrong with her.'

'Well – ' Plumb glanced to the door as if for assistance
but it remained stubbornly closed. Looking back, he began
to feel his way slowly into his argument. 'Often, after some
physical trauma or disease, the brain remembers the symptoms of the disease and keeps producing them in the body,
even after the illness itself has gone. It's a well-known
syndrome. Pain is a common manifestation. Pain from
injury, pain from an accident. The brain gets so used to
receiving pain signals that it continues to manufacture them

long after the injury has healed.' He attempted a heartening smile which didn't quite come off. 'The good news is that this sort of syndrome usually responds well to treatment.'

Nick felt an icy calm, an absolute clarity. 'What you're saying is that it's all in her mind.'

Plumb gave a short bray of a laugh. 'Well – not in the way you mean, not in the sense that she's imagining it. Not at all, no, no. No, what happens is that the brain gets wrongly programmed and keeps sending out inappropriate signals – it's as simple as that.'

All Nick's instincts rebelled against this idea. This, surely, was nothing more than hot air wrapped up in elegant theory, intellectual verbiage invented to fill an inconvenient gap in the text books. But he resisted the impulse to say so. Instead, haunted by his responsibilities to Alusha and the need to consider every possibility, he tried to make sense of what Plumb was saying, to consider the idea rationally. Was it possible? Was there really no reason why Alusha shouldn't get well?

He thought back over the months, to the accident itself, to her fuddled brain, her streaming eyes and grey skin. There could be no doubting that. Nor the fact that her weight loss had started immediately, even before the mis-carriage. All the other things – the sweating, the diarrhoea, the memory problems, the jumpiness – they too had started straight away. Since then little had changed. If anything she'd got worse.

How could such awful symptoms come out of nothing? How could there be no real cause? These people kept forgetting one vital thing – that apart from the few days after the miscarriage Alusha had never given in to her illness, never stopped trying to get better, making the effort to walk even when she was exhausted which was nearly all the time, forcing herself to eat when it sickened her, putting on a bright smile when she must have longed to scream in despair.

No, he couldn't buy the idea that Alusha's brain was in some devious way blocking the way to a miraculous recovery. Quite apart from anything else, such a belief would be a betrayal.

Anyway, there was something about Plumb's little speech that made him wary; it had been too assertive, too facile, almost as if Plumb were convincing himself of his own argument.

And what was he really saying? What did the diagnosis actually boil down to?

Nick came full circle. 'So you *do* think it's in her mind.'

The other man's face reflected disappointment, but also lack of surprise. 'A lot of people have the same reaction,' he said. 'They think that any suggestion of, well, a *mental* component to a disease is some kind of a slur. But all illnesses have a mental component. Even a dose of flu. Really – all illness.'

If he hadn't been so close to despair, Nick would have laughed. He'd last had flu two years before, caught after crossing too many time zones. The only mental component he'd felt at the time was a desire to stop travelling in badly ventilated aircraft.

'Would you mind explaining that?' Nick asked with exaggerated courtesy. 'About the flu.'

'Well – people who have a positive attitude, their immune systems function better.'

'Ah, I get the idea. You mean people who are feeling good recover quicker?'

'Something like that.' Plumb nodded unsuspectingly.

'You mean people who are in good health, with no worries, no emotional problems and good strong bodies recover faster than other people?'

Seeing the way things were going, Plumb began to look cautious. He didn't reply.

'My wife was all those things, doctor. Strong in mind and body. So why isn't she better?'

Plumb drew a deep breath and began to wade through the morass of arguments again. Now, however, his tone was brisker, more uncompromising.

The sound of muffled female laughter floated in from the nursing station outside, then rose sharply as the door swung open and someone came in. Even before the new arrival had exchanged nods with Plumb, Nick knew this would be Carter. The man moved with the curious mixture of confidence and animal caution peculiar to specialists in private clinics, like a cat on a thick-pile carpet.

Nick shook the proffered hand but did not attempt to return the smile.

Plumb hurried into a rapid explanation of the conversation so far.

Seating himself elegantly in a chair, Carter nodded sagely, rubbing a finger across his upper lip in a practised gesture of concentration.

Carter turned to him. 'I'm sure we can help your wife, Mr Mackenzie.' His voice was beautifully modulated, like an actor's. For no apparent reason Nick took an instant dislike to him

'And what exactly is your angle, Dr Carter?'

'I'm a psychiatrist.' Carter watched for a reaction and, finding one, added smoothly: 'But from what you might call the new school. Not exclusively drug-based, you understand. We favour a multi-faceted approach. I deal with diseases with a mental component,' Carter continued. 'That is to say, *all* disease. Though sadly I don't have the opportunity to deal with half the cases I'd like to.' He gave a modest little shrug, as if he was in such demand that he had difficulty in allocating his time. 'Nowadays my sort of medicine gets called holistic. It approaches disease from the point of view of the whole person: mind, body and spirit. You really can't separate those three things, you see, though I have to admit modern medicine is slow to absorb the fact.'

'So what do you think caused my wife's illness?'

He went through the motions of considering the question. 'In a word – trauma.' The voice was low-pitched for reassurance. 'The fall, the knock on the head. The lost pregnancy. And I understand your wife suffered an assault some years ago. These events – all serious shocks – were bound to take their toll. It's been established that these things can have long-term repercussions – '

Nick was so incredulous it took him a moment to interrupt. 'You're saying that something that happened six years ago could be making her ill now?'

'Not directly, not perhaps in the way you think. I'm suggesting a cumulative effect. It's been shown that shock can have profound physiological effects for many years after the event.'

Nick felt the beginnings of a quiet but total despair. 'So . . . how exactly would you treat my wife?'

It was a moment before Carter replied. 'Our main approach would be cognitive therapy,' he said.

'Which is?'

'Basically, we'd concentrate on getting your wife up and about again. We'd draw up a programme of measured exercise involving a variety of activities.'

'What sort of activities?'

'Oh – things she enjoys. You know. Swimming. Walking. Getting out and about.' He sounded like a seedy salesman pushing two weeks at a holiday camp. 'And some physiotherapy, of course. As I'm sure you're aware, there's a danger that too much inactivity can lead to muscle wastage and fatigue, and then the patient gets caught in a downward spiral which is twice as difficult to break out of.'

A picture of Alusha pushed to exhaustion on a relentless exercise machine came into Nick's mind. He murmured: 'She doesn't like swimming.'

'Really? We'd take her to a lovely warm pool. It's really very pleasant.'

Now Nick saw Alusha out of her depth, foundering. Shaking himself free, he asked, 'And drugs. Would you use drugs?'

'Some. But the minimum possible.'

'Which? What kind?'

'Well – antidepressants mainly.'

'But my wife's not depressed.'

'No, of course not,' he agreed hastily. 'It's an unfortunate name, a misleading name. You see, alleviating depression is only one function of this type of drug. They have many other uses. Sometimes the hormones and neurotransmitters in the brain get out of balance and block the pathways . . .'

He elaborated at some length. The scientific terms came in a steady flow, the words at once impressive and chilling. Nick made the effort to listen with great care so that he should miss no detail.

Eventually he cut Carter short by standing up. 'I think I've got the picture.'

Plumb, who'd been fidgeting with his hands for some time, got thankfully to his feet. Carter, too, stood up, and stretched out his hand. They both looked relieved because Nick had finally understood.


Nick stared down at Alusha. She was asleep, her breathing shallow, her face thin and pale. She lay with one arm over the covers, her fingers clutching the edge of the sheet, as if for support. Her hair, which had lost its distinctive shine, looked tangled and unwashed. The nurse must have overlooked it; he would mention it when he saw them.

He longed for her to wake up so they could talk. He wanted to know what she thought of Carter's ideas, though he was pretty sure what her reaction would be; she would give a small snort of disbelief, a derisive smile and say the madmen were loose again. She called most medics madmen, often to their faces. He knew what she would say, but he needed to be sure.

He stared down at her as if the very act of examining her face might make her wake up. Her skin, taut, translucent and devoid of lines, was like a mask; her features, smooth and expressionless, were curiously inanimate as if she had slipped away somewhere.

After a time the strangeness of the mask-like face began to frighten him, and he went across to the window and looked out. Even four storeys up he could smell the stench of the traffic fumes. He allowed himself a brief moment of longing for Ashard.

He waited another ten minutes in case Alusha should wake, then went in search of the staff. Leona, a plump Jamaican staff nurse, was behind the desk. Seeing him, she grinned and called a cheerful hullo. He told her about Alusha's hair.

'I know. And I'm sorry. It doesn't look very good, does it? But she didn't want bothering,' Leona explained.

'But she's usually awake by now.'

'She wanted to go back to sleep.' Leona tutted in friendly remonstration: 'We're not meant to let her, of course, but you know . . .'

Nick was instantly alert. 'Not meant to? What do you mean?'

'She needs to get up and about a bit. Sleeping's no good, is it? Not if you have too much of it.'

'You've been told she mustn't sleep?'

Leona's normally open expression clouded slightly. She said solemnly: 'She's meant to keep active, Mr Mackenzie. Get the circulation going and that sort of thing. All patients are, unless there are medical reasons against it.'

What had the staff been told? Nick wondered. Had the

doctors already labelled Alusha a neurotic? Was Leona secretly planning to put Alusha on an exercise machine?

He pulled himself up short. He was getting paranoid. Leona was a perfectly nice straightforward girl who wouldn't force anyone to do anything. He managed a smile. 'Tell my wife I'll be in this afternoon, will you, Leona?'

He left by the stairs to avoid the public scrutiny of the lifts. As he approached the main lobby, he employed his usual technique for getting through busy places, putting his head down, keeping his eyes on the floor in front of him, and walking very fast. Half-way across the lobby, just as he was beginning to think he'd made it, a female voice called his name. Without breaking his stride he gave the briefest of glances over his shoulder to establish that he'd never seen her before in his life. Then, accelerating, he punched open the swing door and made it to the kerb in five seconds.

His car was nowhere in sight.

He heard panting at his elbow.

'I'm Daisy Field,' came the voice. 'We were going to meet.'

Nick stared obdurately ahead. There wasn't a single opening gambit in the entire world that he hadn't heard – it was astonishing what people would do to get his attention.

'Daisy Field, from Catch,' the girl persisted.

A memory stirred in his brain. Frowning, he looked down at her.

'The Campaign Against Toxic Chemicals,' she explained, reading the mystification in his face. 'We were due to meet at eleven, but they told me you were held up. Your manager suggested I come and wait here.'

Nick pressed his fingers against his forehead in a gesture of forgetfulness and apology. 'Sorry.'

'That's okay,' she said quickly. 'I mean really okay. You must be having an appalling time.'

Nick was silent. He had learned to cope with disbelief and puzzlement, but pity and understanding were altogether more difficult.

The car appeared at last, racing up to the kerb and swaying to a sudden halt. He was aware of wanting to be alone, yet not alone.

She must have sensed his uncertainty, because she offered: 'We could make it another time if that'd be easier.'

She was young, with an open face and a steady gaze. Making up his mind, he shook his head and gestured her into the car. She slid across the seat and settled in the far corner. As he climbed in after her he saw her inspect the car interior with open interest. 'How's it going with the doctors?' she asked. 'Are they saying there's nothing wrong?'

Nick hesitated, surprised that she should have guessed, but not sure that he was quite ready to discuss it. The car moved off; he looked ahead and gave a noncommittal shrug.

'It's their usual answer, I'm afraid,' she went on. 'Saying there's nothing wrong. That's what they told a forestry worker in Dumfries who'd inhaled 2,4,5-T. Not to mention a farmer's wife in Norfolk who miscarried after the next-door property had been sprayed with some cocktail or other – we never discovered what exactly.'

There was a pause; he was expected to respond. He shot her a quick glance, taking in those steady eyes, and an expression that was sympathetic but eager.

'Or are they saying it's all in her mind?' she asked in a sudden burst. 'That's another favourite, I'm afraid.'

She must have read the answer in his face, because she exclaimed: 'You mustn't believe it, you know. They only say that when they haven't a clue. And most of the time they haven't a clue, I'm afraid. That's what we're up against – a total failure to understand what chemicals can do to people.'

She was obviously very sincere and very idealistic. He dimly remembered feeling the same at that age, though his ire, directed as it was towards the Vietnam war and the arms race, appeared in retrospect altogether more aggressive and far less attractive. 'They're very . . . convincing,' he commented.

'Of course. That's their job, isn't it, to create confidence, to make you believe they have all the answers. It keeps the system going.'

He wondered how far to take this discussion. In his long experience of strangers it was best to be cautious until one was absolutely certain how far it was safe to go. It was amazing how little confidences got blown up into major items that ended up as so-called stories in the gutter press. On the other hand, this girl was a professional, she was offering help, and if he was going to take advantage of that he was going to have to trust her sooner or later.

He took another look at her. She was nice looking in a fresh unaffected sort of way. She was dressed carelessly, in a loose sweater and long flowing skirt with a diaphanous scarf of muted blues and purples tied round her shoulders. Her hair, which was copper-coloured and curly, almost bushy, was tied back to the nape of her neck with a loose bow, though several strands had escaped to form a soft frame for her face. Her skin was clear and slightly freckled, her eyes light-brown and very bright. She had a quick smile, a glowing energy and the sort of spontaneous sincerity that seems to leap out at you.

She was just the type to be an environmental campaigner, he decided: young – still in her twenties, he guessed – tenacious, unafraid and too sure by half.

'They say it's just trauma,' he said, and the admission was like a wrench. 'And when I try to argue they make me feel like I'm being difficult.'

'I can imagine,' she said, rolling her eyes expressively. 'Modern medicine's like an ancient religion. Full of mum-

bojumbo and powerful witchcraft, and anyone who dares
to question it gets labelled a heretic.' She had a chirpy voice
with a slight accent that he couldn't quite place – south or
maybe east London.

'Talking to them, I feel like I'm back in school,' Nick
said. 'They keep trying to explain the thing to me, first one
way then the other, and when I refuse to accept it I know
they're giving me another bad mark. One step nearer to
being chucked out of class.'

The driver wove the car expertly through the traffic
clogging Cavendish Square before grinding to a halt in the
inevitable jam behind Oxford Circus.

'But there are other doctors in the world,' Daisy said.

'Are there?' Nick gave a short sharp laugh, which
sounded caustic even to his own ears. He thought back
over the long weeks of tests and opinions and referrals.
'We seem to have tried most of medical London,' he said.
'I've even spoken to people in the US. They form a fairly
united front, believe me. None of them can say for sure
what's wrong.'

'What about the alternative doctors?' Daisy argued.
'They've been into environmental illness for years.'

'Oh, I've talked to them all right,' he replied.

'And?'

'And they said, sure they could help. But when it came
down to it, they couldn't offer much – vitamins, detoxifi-
cation, herbs, that sort of thing.'

'But holistic medicine's all about being gentle with the
body, letting it heal itself in its own time,' she said with a
conviction that bordered on the evangelical. 'You take the
load off the body and – '

'We've done all that,' Nick interrupted softly. 'Alusha's
used alternative medicine for years. She went on a total
health kick as soon as she could.'

'Oh.' Daisy withdrew, momentarily chastened before

flinging him an uncertain smile. 'Well, there's still the scientific data. That might produce something.'

'On the phone you said the scientific evidence was thin, that it didn't mean much.'

'I meant the original toxicology data. That's bound to be suspect, simply because it was done so long ago. Chemicals like Reldane, stuff that's been around for years, it all got waved through on a nod and a wink. Trials that would be a joke today. You know, they'd feed the stuff to a couple of mice for a week and, eureka, when they didn't immediately keel over and die, it was given the green stamp and put straight on the market.'

'That bad?'

'Yep. Well – not far off anyway.'

Was this as much of an exaggeration as it sounded? he wondered. Was she just saying this to help win him over? And if so, what else was she prepared to say to persuade him to her point of view? It occurred to him, not for the first time, that she was latching on to him purely for his publicity value to her campaign, and his heart sank, as it always did when people wanted something out of him.

'But there might well be something tucked away in the literature somewhere,' Daisy remarked with blithe confidence, 'something that shows Reldane has damaging effects.'

'But if anything like that had been published, surely the doctors would know about it?'

She sucked in her breath. 'Oh dear,' she said gently. 'You do have a lot to learn.'

Nick looked stiffly ahead, feeling rebuked and suddenly and inappropriately close to anger.

Turning abruptly, as if she had just appreciated her gaffe, Daisy added hastily: 'We have contacts with all the experts. Really – I'm sure we can find someone who can understand your wife's illness. We'll follow it through, I assure you. We'll back you all the way, for as long as it takes.'

He thought: Or until my publicity value runs out. Her support was a little too unconditional, her outlook too optimistic to be entirely believable. Aloud, he murmured a cursory: 'Thanks.'

'I think the press coverage went well, don't you?' she said breathlessly, rushing the conversation forward. 'Have you seen the cuttings?'

The truth was, he hadn't dared look at a single newspaper since he'd agreed in what he now realized to be a rash and ill-judged moment to go public on what had happened. Despair, the ache for crude revenge, the terrible piercing fear that Alusha would never recover, had overridden his natural caution, and, as he was doubtless about to discover, he had probably paid the price.

Daisy Field pulled a collection of newspaper cuttings out of a voluminous bag. 'The *Star* ran something on Friday. Did you see it? A full-page feature. It means we've made a clean sweep of the tabloids – every single one.' Her voice shifted into a minor key. 'Though I have to admit, the qualities weren't quite so good. Nothing in the *Guardian* or *Independent*. But the *Sunday Times* ran a good piece – the environment correspondent's a friend of mine. I thought *The Times* would run something too – they seemed so sure – but their medical correspondent probably killed it off. He's one of the psychosomatic school. You know, life events and all that – thinks everything stems from getting a nasty fright in the woodshed as a child.'

Suddenly she laughed, an earthy chuckle that came from the back of her throat, and he turned in surprise.

She was already on to the next cutting. 'And here – a front page, no less.'

Nick glanced at it and shuddered. The headline ran: *Pop Star Wife in Poison Horror*.

'God, I can do without this sort of stuff,' he said with feeling.

'Oh.' Her voice fell.

He was about to tell her exactly what was wrong with that sort of coverage, but stopped himself. It was he, after all, who, having given Catch permission to push the story, had failed to tell David or his own PR people about it, effectively ruining any chance of the story being handled properly.

Daisy was looking puzzled; she thought she'd done a good job.

He said: 'Not your fault. It's just – them.' He flicked a hand at the cuttings. 'If they didn't use photographs you'd have trouble recognizing yourself.'

'But they've got most of the facts right.'

Bracing himself, Nick glanced at the first few lines.

Ex-Amazon megastar Nick Mackenzie announced today that his Bahamian model wife is gravely ill after a poisoning accident. Alusha, 35, was found unconscious in a pool of poisonous chemicals on their hideaway West Highland estate in June, and has been lying in a coma at a London clinic ever since.

Close to tears, Nick, 46, stated yesterday . . .

Nick flung the paper down. Close to tears – Christ. He was only close to tears when he realized he'd never be able to get hold of the reporter who'd written that garbage and squeeze him by the throat until he screamed for mercy. It was extraordinary how they always got your age right but precious little else. Alusha was not and never had been Bahamian, nor a model, nor was she in a coma. He'd never even spoken to the reporter, let alone cried.

Daisy picked up the paper, read it, and said in a quiet ironic voice: 'Well – they spelt your name right.'

He gave a rueful grunt. She had a point: it was absurd to worry about the press. They simply weren't worth it.

'We're going the wrong way,' Daisy announced suddenly.

They were crossing Oxford Street, heading south towards David Weinberg's office. 'Where should we be going then?' Nick asked.

'To Gower Street. To see Dr Peasedale.'

Nick wondered if he should know who Peasedale was. Grasping the problem, Daisy explained: 'He's our toxicologist at University College. The one I told you about on the phone. Our tame pesticide expert.'

'Ah,' Nick said, though he remembered nothing about it. Leaning forward, he redirected the driver. 'A toxicologist?' he murmured. 'I met one of those this morning.' He told her what had been said in the hot airless room high in the clinic.

'Ah, well, they only know what they're given the opportunity to know,' Daisy declared, moving into her polemic mode. 'And that's only what other people have told them, isn't it? They believe in research, but they forget that the only research that's being done is what the chemical companies and the governments *choose* to have done.'

So clear-cut again; so sure. 'There must be other research programmes,' he argued half-heartedly.

'But why should there be? Who's going to fund them? Groups like ours don't have the money, and the big charities only support the projects the doctors advise them to support. And the doctors aren't interested in the idea of wide-ranging non-specific chemical damage. It upsets their neat little theories of disease. They want tidy little boxes – viral disease, bacterial disease, neurological disease, *any* disease as long as it can be seen under a microscope – and when their box theories won't fit, they throw up their hands and say the problem doesn't exist. What's failing, of course, is Western medicine itself – stuck in tight compartments, totally reliant on drugs and drug companies, spine-less, *visionless*.' In full flood, she had an extraordinary almost hypnotic fluency, so that her words flowed without break or hesitation. She gave an impression of both rehearsal and spontaneity, as well as vibrant indignation.

'And if things don't fit,' she went on, 'you throw them into a convenient catch-all, which in Western medicine is psychiatry, which has to have pulled off the greatest intellectual coup of the twentieth century, by passing itself off as scientifically based when in fact it's the only totally non-scientific speciality, based as it is on almost complete ignorance of the organ it's meant to know about.' She paused, as if to remind herself of what she had set out to say. 'No, they're simply not interested in difficult untreata-ble diseases. Untreatable diseases make them feel powerless, and powerlessness makes them resentful and uncoopera-tive. If they can't fire drugs at something, then they don't want to know about it. And I tell you' – she waved a finger, emphasizing her point like a seasoned politician – 'they certainly don't want to know about anything that suggests we're on the brink of widespread trouble, not to mention environmental disaster.'

But one disaster was more than enough for Nick; he couldn't take on responsibility for the rest of humanity as well. He let Daisy talk on for a while until, realizing she had lost her audience, she broke off quite amiably and lapsed into silence for the rest of the journey.

# Chapter 8

———————

PEASEDALE, A YOUNG bird-like man with thinning hair and spectacles, was summing up. 'Not much to offer you, I'm afraid,' he said. 'Consumed in large quantities Reldane would, of course, poison anybody. But in a small dose – I can't find any evidence to suggest it could cause such catastrophic symptoms.'

Daisy glanced across to Nick Mackenzie by the window. He was sprawled gracefully in his chair, one elbow on the sill, gazing intently out at the blank walls of the building opposite. Daisy, who for once had been keeping commendably silent, now burst out: 'But what about inhalation? Surely if you breathe something for an *hour* . . .'

Peasedale shook his head apologetically. He was perched on a high stool, his long limbs entwined in its legs like a double-jointed insect. 'If you breathe enough of almost anything over a long period, then you'll get adverse effects. That's true of even the commonest fumes – petrol, glue, spirit-based substances. And of course cigarettes. But you wouldn't get such dire symptoms after just an hour, not when the substance is mixed with plenty of air, as it was in this case. The only circumstance I can think of that might change that would be previous exposure to a chemical or chemicals that create extreme sensitivity, then – well, I suppose even something as modest as Reldane could provoke a strong reaction.'

There was a silence as they waited for Nick to respond. But he seemed to be completely absorbed by the view from the window, and it was left to Peasedale to prompt him.

'Has your wife been exposed to any strong chemicals in the past, Mr Mackenzie?'

'What?' He seemed to wake up only with an effort. 'No. Nothing unusual. Just the usual hotchpotch.'

'You mean . . .?'

He half turned. 'Oh, antibiotics, that sort of thing. But not recently – she won't take anything like that now – when she was younger.'

That was it then. Mixed with Daisy's disappointment was a creeping sense of guilt. All that chatter, all that confidence – she regretted it, not only because it now looked totally misplaced, but because normally she would have known better than to raise false hopes. Something had gone wrong; she had misplayed the scene in the car. It was partly that old demon of hers, optimism; partly her uncharacteristic nervousness at meeting Nick Mackenzie. She'd banged on like an inane schoolgirl.

'Can't you run some tests?' she asked Peasedale.

'What sort of thing? If you mean standard toxicology tests, they were done on Reldane's active ingredient years ago. I looked it up. There was some evidence that, given in massive doses, the active ingredient might eventually cause cancer in a tiny proportion of rats.'

Nick's voice drifted in from the window. 'They test these things on animals?'

There was a short silence. 'Certainly,' Peasedale said.

'That can't be necessary, surely?'

'There's no other way, not if you're going to be absolutely certain.'

Nick gave a visible shudder and resumed his study of the scene outside the window.

'The original tests,' said Daisy, picking up the argument again. 'If they show cancer, surely that's significant.'

But Peasedale wasn't going to have words put into his

mouth. 'Almost anything will cause cancer, given in sufficient quantity for a long enough period. But we're not talking cancer here, are we? We're talking about another sort of illness, a different set of symptoms. Now, if we were looking at something like 2,4,5-T, as found in Agent Orange, then we might have something. It causes all sorts of weird symptoms which don't show up in standard tests – immune dysfunction, enzyme and hormonal imbalance, that sort of thing.' He turned to Nick. 'You *are* sure it was Reldane and not something else?'

The sun had emerged from behind a cloud, driving golden shafts into the room and illuminating Nick Mackenzie's face in harsh brilliance.

Eventually he stirred. 'It was definitely Reldane,' he said in a soft voice.

'She's seen a toxicologist?'

A slight pause. 'A couple.'

'And the symptoms – these guys couldn't suggest anything?'

'Not really. They got excited about her memory loss, about mixing up her words – getting her sentences back to front, you know – and about her gut troubles. Then just as quickly they got unexcited again. Said they couldn't find anything.'

'Did they do a biopsy?'

'I'm not sure – '

'It involves taking a minute amount of tissue, usually with a needle.'

'Oh – that. Yes, they did it once – no, twice. I wouldn't let them do it again. Hurt her too much.'

'What about enzyme levels? Did they measure those?'

'I suppose so – yes. They said they'd looked at everything, anyway.'

Peasedale gave a wide shrug. 'In that case, I don't know what to suggest. And you say your wife hadn't been taking any prescription drugs recently?'

Nick shook his head. 'Neither of us ever took anything.' He added wryly: 'We went up to Scotland to escape all that, you see. Chemicals, pollution ... Funny, when you think about it.'

No one smiled.

'What about water? Could she have drunk contaminated water?' Peasedale suggested.

Nick didn't reply, so Daisy answered for him. 'Mr Mackenzie had a sample sent down from the house supply. We had it tested. Nothing wrong with it.'

'Tell him the rest,' Nick said to Daisy, looking at her for the first time in a long while. 'Tell him what you told me on the phone.'

Daisy drew a breath. 'They said it was some of the best water they'd ever tested.'

'You see,' Nick said with gentle irony. 'Clean air. Clean water. Perfect.' With a last look at the sky, he stood up. 'Thank you, Dr Peasedale. You've been most helpful. Very informative.' There was no sarcasm in his tone, only resignation, and Daisy had the feeling that it was only by this rather forced show of manners that he was managing to keep himself together.

She followed him towards the lift. His expression didn't invite conversation. When they came out into the street he strode towards the waiting car in the same cannon-shot way that he had emerged from the clinic. When she caught up with him he was holding the car door open and waiting for her to get in.

She murmured: 'But my office – it's out of your way.'

'Your – ' He frowned suddenly. 'Oh? I thought – lunch? You haven't time?' He asked it tentatively, with an awkward sideways look, as if he wasn't at all sure of getting a positive response.

'Of course – yes. If you want to. Of course.'

He gave a sudden fleeting smile, a look that flickered up to her eyes and away again, and she realized that for all his

apparent confidence and bodily grace he was essentially a
reserved man. It was hard to reconcile this with the image
of the seasoned stage performer who stood up in front of
thousands of people, but as they set off, she realized her
first instinct had been right. He hardly ever looked people
in the eye for very long, not when he could possibly avoid
it, and when he was forced to, he screwed up his eyes into
a tight frown, as if this could offer him some degree of
camouflage.

He said: 'I appreciate all you've done.'

Done? She caught the past tense with a twinge of alarm.
'I've done eff-all,' she said firmly. 'Yet.'

He was silent for a moment, then began haltingly: 'You
know . . . in the old days – in the Sixties anyway – we all
used to blame everything on the system. It was very . . .
well, convenient, I suppose.' He shot her a quick glance.
'But you wouldn't remember that. You're only – what?'

'Thirty-two.'

He squinted at her. 'Oh? You look younger.' He said it
as a statement of fact, not flattery.

He continued thoughtfully: 'Blaming the system used to
be a great let-out. It covered everything – the government,
the law, the welfare state – anything you liked. When
Alusha became ill I was desperate to find an *it* or a *someone*
to blame, just like in the old days. I longed to come face to
face with the person or *thing* that could let this happen. I
wanted to – well, create stink, show them – I don't know.
I just wanted *them* to suffer like Alusha was suffering.' He
gave a gesture of resignation. His hands were long and
slender. 'But really – what would be the use? Even if such a
person existed, or an organization or a *thing*, and even if
they were exposed or whatever, it wouldn't change much,
would it?'

'But it would!' she said emphatically, forgetting her
intention to show restraint. 'It *could*. It might prevent this
sort of thing happening again.'

His mouth turned down into a look that she was beginning to recognize, an expression that suggested she was being naive and idealistic.

'But it wouldn't get Alusha better, would it?' he pointed out, looking at her for the first time without frowning. She noticed the vivid blueness of his eyes, and how the skin at the edges was crinkled into islands of strong lines, as if under happier circumstances he smiled a lot.

'But it might,' she continued doggedly. 'Once they find out what happened – how this stuff actually caused the damage – then they might be able to find a treatment.'

'But they're never going to find out exactly how the stuff did what it did, are they?' he said patiently. 'Not if one's to believe Peasedale – which I do. So there's not much point in . . .' He paused, choosing his words. '. . . Well, going on with it. I'm sorry. I really feel my wife has to be my first priority. I have to concentrate on finding a doctor who can help her, a doctor who can find out what's wrong. I can't spend more time on this sort of thing.' He waved a hand apologetically. 'I don't mean your campaign's not *worth-while* – far from it. It's just . . . I really can't get involved.'

'You mean – ?'

'Your campaign – I wouldn't be able to do it justice.'

He was giving up, she realized. He was telling her that, despite everything – his apparent interest in Catch, his agreement to publicise the case – he didn't want to be involved any more. In which case the campaign had, within the space of just two weeks, won and lost the most valuable asset it had ever possessed. The odd thing was she didn't blame him at all, although this didn't stop her from feeling an unaccountable sense of loss, as if something really important had been taken from her.

'I understand,' she said, managing a small smile.

'I'll be pleased to help when this is all over, when my wife's better. Tell me over lunch, what I might be able to do.'

'Of course.'

The car drew up outside a sparkling neo-classical building behind Covent Garden. Nick got out and, holding the door open for her, led the way inside at his customary pace. As they sped through the main lobby, heading for an open lift, Daisy saw a wall sign and realized they were making for the David Weinberg office.

'I'll be about ten minutes,' Nick explained as the lift started upwards. 'Just a few calls to make. You don't mind?'

'Not at all.'

The doors opened to reveal a stage-lit reception area, all chrome and muted greys and arrays of large glossy photographs and golden discs. The place was surprisingly crowded. Two delivery men in overalls stood by a trolley loaded with cartons, apparently waiting for orders, various people were sitting on low sofas along two sides of the room, looking as if they'd been there for some time, while a party of four smartly dressed women was grouped around the reception desk.

Even as Nick launched himself across the room towards a door on the far side, Daisy could see that he wasn't going to make it. One of the well-dressed women was nudging her neighbours and, as Nick advanced, the four turned to face him. One was a young girl of about twenty, the other three were quite a bit older.

Seeing Nick, the older women's faces lit up like awed teenagers. Their ludicrous smiles, their round-eyed stares were both fascinating and rather embarrassing.

One of the older women stepped forward to intercept Nick. She was smiling hard, too hard, although, if you took away the smile, she was good-looking in a slightly overstated way. Her makeup, though well applied, was a little on the heavy side, and her fair hair, which was longish and layered like feathers, had that solid impenetrable look that comes from long hours with a hairdresser and a tall can of hairspray.

'Nick,' she sang, standing in his path. 'Hullo! How *are* you?'

Nick jerked to a halt like a cornered animal. Finding no escape, he produced a polite though unconvincing smile.

'It's been such a long time, I can't believe it,' the woman persisted, subtly but firmly blocking his way. She gave a nervous laugh, aware of the audience behind her.

Nick was grappling with his memory, and it showed.

'Twenty years,' she hurried on, the first hint of panic in her voice. 'It seems unbelievable!'

Nick blinked rapidly. 'Yes, of course . . .'

But it was obvious that he hadn't placed her and there was an awkward pause, the sort that seems to stretch out for ever. The woman's smile faltered, then, attempting to carry the thing off, she made a joke of it. 'Good God, I didn't think I'd changed that much! At least, most people tell me I haven't changed at all.' If she was hoping for some sort of affirmation, she was quickly disappointed.

She laughed again, a sharp discordant sound, then, before the situation deteriorated any further, announced: 'It's Suki Armitage. Well, that's what you'd remember me as. I'm not that any more, of course. My name's Driscoll. And now-adays people seem to call me Susan. The Suki got lost some-where along the line . . .' She went on for a bit, rather too fast, and after repeating herself a couple of times, trailed off.

A shot of recognition had flickered over Nick's face. 'Good Lord,' he murmured, and shifted his weight, on the point of flight again.

But Susan Driscoll wasn't about to give up. 'I was thinking about you only the other day,' she blundered on in her breathless Knightsbridge accent. 'I saw Annie and Roger Fenner. You remember them? And all those wonder-ful parties they used to give?'

The Fenners, as Daisy and everyone else in the world knew, were leading fashion designers. Susan Driscoll, it seemed, was rather practised at dropping names because she managed to squeeze in a few more as she rattled breathlessly through the brilliant people and parties of the good old days.

Daisy could tell that Nick had finally placed Susan Driscoll, though, from his expression, the realization did not seem to have thrilled him nearly as much as Susan Driscoll had hoped it would.

The one-sided conversation lurched on. Susan Driscoll's voice became shrill at the edges, and Daisy had the feeling she was less than pleased at not having been instantly remembered. Nick was looking increasingly hunted, and Daisy was not surprised when he flicked a glance at her, signalling his intention to escape.

'Well, it's good to see you again,' he muttered to Susan Driscoll.

'I'm so sorry to hear about your wife,' she said to his retreating back. 'I do hope she'll recover soon.' Nick gave a brief backward glance of acknowledgement.

'And we're so thrilled about the concert. I can't tell you what it means.'

Nick paused in the doorway. 'Concert?' He looked back at her in mystification. 'Concert?'

A pause, little short of electric. 'For Save the Children,' Susan Driscoll said bravely. 'I'm organizing it.'

He stared at her. 'What – ' He shook his head abruptly. 'There isn't going to be any concert.' For an instant he seemed to hover on the point of explanation then, thinking better of it, he turned and was gone.

There was a long moment while no one spoke and no one moved. Mrs Driscoll looked as if she'd got a very nasty taste in her mouth. Her lips were taut, her eyes narrow as a cat's. Humiliation then anger crossed over her face in quick succession, followed by something altogether more guarded.

Unobtrusively Daisy made for the door through which Nick had vanished. As she reached it, she heard a young voice saying: 'Oh, Mummy ... Perhaps there's a mistake ...'

Daisy looked back. Susan Driscoll was managing a brilliant recovery job. She was shrugging her daughter off, lifting her chin, putting on a smile. Only her eyes, in the instant before they swung round to face her friends, showed a last flash of bitter light.

Daisy escaped into a short corridor. There were several doors leading off it. The first stood open, revealing an empty office. The next was also open, and contained a young woman who seemed to know who Daisy was, and waved her to a seat.

After fifteen minutes Daisy's stomach started to rumble. After twenty she began to wonder if lunch might possibly have been forgotten.

She passed some of the time thinking about the rest of her week. She and Simon had been planning to go to a new film that evening but he'd cancelled. It was the novel again. The novel had become a fixture, like the lover in a *ménage à trois*, mysterious, vaguely threatening, but best left alone. Looking at the relationship coolly – and it contained precious little heat even in its warmer moments – it had not developed a great deal. They liked the same things all right: they went to environmental awareness parties and political conferences, they saw art films and exhibitions, they ate in wine bars and went to parties in Islington. But when it came down to it, the only thing that had really changed was that she was now the one feeling beleaguered, while Simon was increasingly relaxed and carefree. Well, who wouldn't look happier when he had someone to collect his laundry, and cook and wash up twice a week?

Now there was an unworthy thought. She was forgetting how Simon had come and fixed her kitchen door and cooked Sunday lunch two weeks running. She was forgetting the conversations, the evenings out and the occasional smiles. Perhaps that was all you could ever ask or expect.

She thought of Nick Mackenzie and tried to imagine Simon in his place, fighting for her as she lay in some hospital bed, searching the world for some way to cure her, but the picture wouldn't come alive and she abandoned it.

The time crept on. The secretary unwrapped a sandwich. Daisy began to wonder if Nick Mackenzie wasn't quite as unspoilt as he seemed and didn't perhaps make a habit of keeping people waiting.

At last, after what must have been half an hour, there was a murmur of voices, the door opened and Nick Mackenzie finally appeared. Behind him was a dark plump balding man – presumably David Weinberg – who, spotting Daisy, peered at her briefly as if to confirm she was of no great importance, before saying a hasty goodbye to Nick and disappearing into the corridor.

Nick flopped down on the seat beside her.

'Sorry, but I had to sort out that schemozzle,' he said companionably. 'For some reason my manager had decided not to tell that lady that the concert had been cancelled. He seemed to think I would change my mind.'

'And did you?'

'No.'

'I don't think the lady was too pleased.'

'I think you're right.'

Daisy couldn't resist asking: 'Did you remember her?'

He shot her a grin which quite transformed his face. 'To be honest, no, not to begin with. She looked completely different. I mean, like someone *else*. Then . . . yes, I realized who she was.' He looked away and shook his head, as if some memory had just come back to him.

'Come on,' he said abruptly. 'Let's go and eat.'

They got as far as the end of the corridor – Daisy was just allowing herself a vision of a nice restaurant some-where off the Covent Garden Piazza – when the secretary called Nick back to say his wife was on the phone. A look of surprise and pleasure leapt into his face as he turned to go. Calmly Daisy settled back against the wall and began a thorough inspection of the framed golden discs that decor-ated the corridor.

This time she didn't have to wait long; it was only a couple of minutes before he reappeared, emerging so quickly into the corridor that he was almost past her before she had realized.

Something had happened: his face was like thunder. She hesitated, uncertain whether to chase after him.

She caught up with him at the lift. As they both stepped inside, he flung her a fierce but impersonal look.

'Is there something the matter?' she asked. 'Can I do anything?'

He shook his head. 'No. No . . .' His voice was trembling with suppressed rage. 'No, no,' he repeated harshly. 'It's just that . . . I've got to go and move my wife.'

'Move her?'

'They made her swim. Made her swim when she hates it, absolutely hates it! And they've given her some drug, something that makes her feel terrible. They didn't even tell her what it was. Didn't even *tell* her! I can't believe it's possible. I can't – ' He broke off and screwed up his mouth, not trusting himself to say any more.

The lift was slowing down. Daisy tried to think of something useful to suggest. 'What about wheelchairs, ambulances and things? Can I – '

'No time for that. I'll carry her myself.' He said it as if it was the obvious thing to do, and Daisy thought: Lucky Alusha Mackenzie, having a husband like that.

The lift doors opened and he strode rapidly away, shoulders hunched, head down in that wary walk of his. As he stepped into the street, the sun caught him, illuminating his head with sudden light. It occurred to Daisy, not without an odd little pang, that she would probably never see him again.

After four visits to the Coach and Horses, Colin Hillyard had become quite a regular. It had got to the stage where the landlord, who went by the exotic name of Lionel Meredith-Peacock, greeted him warmly by name – Hillyard was using the name Meynell, a variation on Maynard, which was another favourite of his – and leant an elbow on the bar to exchange comments on the vagaries of the weather as if such things were quite unique to west Berkshire.

It was a Thursday. Hillyard made a point of arriving at more or less the same time every week and staying half an hour or so before leaving in a hurry, lending credence to the idea that he squeezed time out of his busy week to visit an ancient relative living nearby. He'd never elaborated on the elderly aunt or where she lived, nor had he said exactly what he did for a living; he spent too much time expressing quiet, almost languid interest in the local community and listening to the landlord's repertoire of well-worn anecdotes. Not that he ever pushed the local interest. Apart from establishing right at the outset that the Knowles family, who'd been featured in the local papers over an incident at the Berkshire Show, lived not far away and had been regular users of the pub, he hardly brought up a subject worth mentioning. In fact he'd once listened to the landlord holding forth on the merits of a cruise to Turkey over a package to the Canaries for all of twenty minutes before steering things gently back towards more parochial matters. He made such manoeuvres seem effortless, though he said so himself.

'People go for Turkey round here, do they?' he said to

Meredith-Peacock, looking ready to be impressed. And then he'd got chapter and verse on the holidays the locals took, and the likely price of them, and how even when farming was meant to be in deep trouble some of them were still off to Kenya and the 'Sea-shells' islands, as Meredith-Peacock liked to pronounce them.

Once it came up, Hillyard had pursued the farmers-in-trouble avenue, of course; it was too good to miss. But he went ever so gently, expressing just the right blend of vague commiseration and glaring ignorance befitting a true town-dweller. But though the opening was leading him nicely up to the subject of the Knowles family, which was precisely where he wanted to be, the conversation had had to be aborted. The landlord had gone to serve another customer and when he ambled back along the bar his mind had diverted, by some mysterious progression, onto the subject of rheumatism.

Now it was Thursday again and he was back feeling rather pleased with life, though no thanks to the weather, which was blustery with racing clouds and a sudden sneaky chill which on leaving the car had flipped at the vents of the tweedy sports jacket he had bought specially for the job from a countryman's outfitters in Hungerford.

It was three and the pub was quiet. There was only one customer at the bar, a ruddy-faced man in heavy boots, work trousers and waxed jacket. Hillyard sat at the next stool, exchanged ritual head-shakes about the gale-force wind with the landlord and ordered a pint of best. The farmer-figure – the landlord called him Bill – waited impatiently to regain the landlord's attention and resume the conversation that Hillyard had interrupted. He was complaining to the landlord about the sale of some farm, though why it should displease him Hillyard couldn't make out, since he seemed neither to know nor care about the owners of the property who, it appeared, had been forced to sell at a bad price.

This time Hillyard plunged straight in. No pussy-footing, as Beryl often said, not once you've laid the groundwork; no skulking in the woodwork. He came straight out and asked if it was the Knowleses who were selling. The farmer nipped gently at the bait, took the taste of it, and let himself be led forward, jerking only once at the line when something alerted him to Hillyard's curiosity, and he demanded: 'What's it to you, anyway?'

'I read about them in the paper, didn't I, Lionel? Sad business. Sort of stuck in my mind.'

'Well, it's not them that's selling,' said the farmer. 'Not Mrs Knowles, oh no. She'll stick it out. Family been there too long. As long as anyone can remember. Though she won't get much out of the place, not this year, oh no,' he added to the landlord. 'Hiring all the help in. Not cheap.'

The landlord pulled the conversation towards cancer statistics then, providentially, a new customer diverted his attention and Hillyard was able to lead Farmer Bill onwards, through backwaters of maize and wheat and into the mainstream of the Knowleses' future.

'Going to sue, of course.'

'Sue?'

The beady eyes shot Hillyard a confiding glance. 'Going to sue the chemical makers. Been advised not to, they've all tried to put her off, the lawyers and everyone, but she won't have it. Off her head if you ask me. Ain't going to bring her husband back, is it? Not in a month of Sundays.'

'No.' Hillyard shook his head solemnly. 'And the law – ' He sucked in his breath in a pitying hiss. 'Well, the only people who get rich are the lawyers, aren't they?'

'You're telling me,' gasped the farmer emphatically, and the idea triggered a blast of legal grievances that emerged blistering from the barrel of his memory. His protests finally spent, he murmured: 'That's what makes it crazy, see. She hasn't the money – well, not to spare. They'll bleed her dry.'

Hillyard made a commiserating face. 'No insurance money. Nothing like that?'

'Nope. Not that I've heard of, at any rate.'

And you would have heard, thought Hillyard. He said: 'You'd have thought she'd be able to get help. Some sort of legal aid.'

'Nothing handed out on a tray, is it? Not nowadays. Each man for himself.' He drained his beer and clunked the glass onto the bar with finality. He straightened up and patted his pockets. 'Right you are, Lionel,' he said, raising a farewell hand to the landlord.

He faced Hillyard for a moment. 'Not that people round here don't do what they can,' he said. 'The neighbours help out. They're in there right now.'

Hillyard maintained a look of polite interest. 'Right now?'

'Gone to the West Country for the week, Mrs Knowles and her son. First holiday in two years.'

Pure icing.

Hillyard almost danced his way to the car, checking his stride only with reluctance.

As he unlocked the car a silky-haired bundle pressed its nose to the glass and, as the door opened, hurled itself into his arms. 'Precious – were you waiting for your mum, were you? There, I wasn't so long, was I?'

The Pekinese snorted and snuffled and agitated its plume of tail like an uncontrolled metronome. Climbing in, Hillyard cradled it in his arms and sighed into its long coat: 'Did Beji miss me, did she? Of *course* she did, my little baby.' He gave the dog a rough squeeze and placed it on the sheepskin. 'Now be a good baby. Mummy's going to work.'

He didn't in fact get to work until eight that night. He parked in the spot he'd used before, by a gate on a quiet lane overlooking the Knowleses' farmhouse. It wasn't ideal – the house was too far away to see much with the naked

eye and he had to clamp the binoculars to the window arch
– but it gave as good a view as he was likely to get without
camping under a soggy hedge, which really wasn't his style
unless absolutely necessary. At six thirty a Land Rover
drew up in the farm yard and a figure got out and went
into one of the outbuildings, reappearing from time to time,
fetching and carrying between barns and outbuildings.

At seven Hillyard changed into what Beryl called his
Action Man kit – a dark track suit and trainers – and he
and Beji had their respective suppers. Beji's, being the best
marrow-bone chunks that money could buy, looked almost
the more appetizing. That wicked Beryl and her picnics;
always forgetting the cling-film so that the bread got
terminal dehydration, throwing in a couple of slabs of
processed cheese, a dab of pickle and, no doubt, a splash
of cigarette ash, and boasting she was doing him proud.
He'd give her a piece of his mind when he got back. Much
good it would do him.

At seven thirty he let Beji out to pee and almost missed
the Land Rover leaving.

He gave it another half an hour to be on the safe side,
and it was dark by the time he drove slowly along the
rutted drive towards the farmhouse. Lights had been left
shining on a couple of the outbuildings. One of the upstairs
windows of the house was also lit, but he guessed this was
merely a burglar deterrent.

He drew up just short of the house, turned the car round
and killed the lights. Beji growled.

'Quiet, you little bitch.'

The growl grew into the beginnings of a yap. Hillyard
clamped his hand over the back of the dog's neck and
squeezed hard. The growl changed into a whimper. '*That'll
teach you*,' he hissed.

Releasing his grip, he reached into the back for his bird-
watching bag and hitched it diagonally over his head and
shoulder. He opened the door and closed it almost noise-

lessly. With a bit of luck the farm dogs would be in a barn or locked in a back scullery. If they had the run of the house, things would be a bit more tricky. He could deal with one of the hounds, but not both, and he knew there were two, a collie and a Labrador-cross of some sort.

He approached the front door silently and listened for a few seconds before ringing the bell. An immediate frenetic barking came from the depths of the house. For a moment he thought he was in luck and the brutes were locked in a back room, but of course this was too much to hope for. The sound of wildly scrabbling claws on stone flags approached, and a dog threw its weight against the door with such force that it shook under his touch. Hillyard tutted and rolled his eyes in disgust. This door would have been easy – it had a single Yale lock – but on the principle that the dogs were unlikely to be permitted the run of the bedrooms, he would have to go to the infinitely greater trouble of an upstairs window instead.

Finding and extricating a ladder took twenty minutes. The only specimen he could locate was a long and ancient wooden relic with dubious treads. It was extremely heavy and it took all his strength to lift it against the side of the house without rasping the ends against the brickwork.

He rested for a while, listening hard, then climbed towards the window he'd selected, a wooden-framed casement job with what looked like a basic fastening.

Reaching the window, he flashed his torch through the glass and saw a bathroom with its door wide open. Well, he'd just have to risk that, because it was a dream of an entry: the catch was not fully engaged and, threading his bendy plastic through, he was able to slide it down without any trouble and pull the frame open noiselessly. There was all sorts of garbage on the sill – shampoos, toothpastes, old plastic mugs that would make one hell of a noise if they bounced around on the basin beneath. Painstakingly he moved them aside. In and over the basin. He took pride in the way he moved despite his build: smoothly, lightly, weight properly distributed, poised for sudden changes of plan. Beryl called him a bleedin' ballet dancer.

He had a good listen. His own panting was loud in his ears. He might be a bleedin' ballet dancer, but he wasn't as fit as he should be, a result of Beryl's daily expeditions to the cake shop. He'd have to get back to some sparring and weights.

Everything back in its place: window down, tall mug to the right, shorter one to the left and the clutter reassembled in between. Creep, creep across the lino floor and another listen, short truncheon, military-police issue, ready at his belt, just in case. He could hear the dogs prowling restlessly below and waited until the clack of their claws faded and ceased.

All the bedroom doors were closed. Quick recce inside each. Ma Knowles' bedroom had the light burning. Her bedside table looked promising but yielded nothing. Have to be downstairs then. Enough to give a girl the vapours.

He left the door to Ma Knowles' bedroom open and tying a thin cord round the handle led it diagonally across the landing and in through the bathroom door. Then he whistled from the top of the stairs and retreated behind the almost closed bathroom door. The dogs barked and stampeded around downstairs before coming tentatively up. From their furtive behaviour it was obvious this was forbidden territory. The collie trotted into the mum's bedroom, but the Lab-cross paused outside the door, its nose to the air. It had smelled a rat – or rather it had smelled him, which boiled down to the same thing.

He yanked on the cord, closing the bedroom door and trapping the collie inside, then, while the Lab-cross barked in bemusement at the closed door, he stepped smartly out from behind the bathroom door and gave it a sharp tap on the head. The animal was stunned but conscious, which was just how he wanted it, and he was able to take it by the collar and cajole and drag it downstairs to a sort of scullery and close the door.

There was a large kitchen, a living room, a dining room, cold and musty from lack of use, and a study-cum-office, which was quite the most untidy room Hillyard had ever seen, and that was saying something.

The cascades of paper emanated from an old roll-top desk, its every orifice stuffed with rolls of documents, its open flap piled high with correspondence, much of it unopened.

He settled down for a long night. The curtains were too flimsy to risk the overhead light, so he took a small battery-operated book-light from his bird-watcher's bag and clipped it to the top of the desk.

The bank statements were jammed into two pigeonholes. Ma Knowles had two accounts, the farm another two, and all four were overdrawn. Letters from the bank manager, which had been relegated to the floor, followed an unyielding tone, kindly but firm. The overdrafts had exceeded agreed limits and could under no circumstances remain unsecured.

The correspondence with the lawyers lay in a thick folder on the top of the desk. It took Hillyard an hour to photograph everything. As always he took pains – each page lined up, the exposure carefully monitored, the light adjusted – but was well rewarded because he got the lot: the letters from the lawyers, the evidence from the experts, the opinions of doctors and scientists, complete with names, addresses and dates.

There was even a letter or two from Miss Field, she of the Waldorf tea dance. Advising Mrs Knowles to give up, then in the very next letter, saying that she understood her reasons for wanting to carry on and could rely totally on Catch's support.

He was so absorbed in his work that when he sat back at the end of the job he hardly noticed that a full gale had blown up and was buffeting at the window.

Releasing the dogs took some ingenuity. The Lab-cross had recovered sufficiently to howl as he approached the kitchen. He found a tin of dog food and emptied it into the bowl. He opened the door a crack and after a token growl the animal buried its head in the bowl and was still gobbling as he ran up the stairs. He pushed open the door of the main bedroom and stepped neatly out of view as the collie shook itself out of its sleep and loped out, ready if it had but known it for its ration of short truncheon. He must have hit it a bit harder than the Lab because it nosedived onto the floor, out cold. But he didn't have time to worry about that because the Lab had finished guzzling and was on its way up, growling hard.

Bedroom door closed again, as he had found it, skirt round the poleaxed collie and across the landing into the bathroom again. A moment for a breather then out over the sill again, toiletries rearranged for a second time, down into the yard, ladder back into the outhouse.

It was ten thirty. Two miles clear of the farm he treated himself to a swig of brandy and a cuddle with Beji. Then he stepped on it, in a hurry to get home and bask in the old trout's praise.

# Chapter 9

———

'WHO IS THIS person?' Schenker held up the newspaper cutting between two forefingers.

'He was a rock star back in the early Seventies,' Cramm said. 'With a group called Amazon. Then he went solo. Very successful. Writes good stuff.'

'Good stuff?' Schenker asked doubtfully, narrowing his mouth.

'Sort of lyrical, a bit sad. Though some are a bit happier, I suppose. But good anyway. Intelligent sort of words, memorable tunes. Often got a message to them – conservation, save the world, you know the sort of thing.'

Schenker didn't know the sort of thing, not at all. It sounded like pseudo-Green nonsense to him.

'Well, he should stick to writing songs and stop spreading hysterical stuff he knows nothing about,' Schenker said firmly, flicking through the sheaf of cuttings. 'This preservative, it's definitely not one of ours?'

'No – Reldane, apparently.'

'Well, it doesn't make much difference whose it is, does it? This sort of thing does none of us any good. What I want to know is why the hell the federation didn't get quoted? They must have been contacted, surely.' The UK Agrochemical Federation was the trade organization of the pesticide manufacturers. One of its main functions was to counter the screechings of the Green lobby, though in Schenker's opinion it was largely ineffectual; it never moved without a committee decision and he, more than anyone, knew that committees nipped most effective action in the bud.

'They say they didn't have time to reply,' Cramm explained.

'How long do they need? A week? A year? Good God, this sort of thing can be answered in two minutes flat.' He shook his head irritably. 'Make sure the newspapers get a suitable complaint about unbalanced reporting. Make sure the federation gets *some* sort of statement in. We can't have this sort of thing splashed all over the papers and not put the record straight. Containment, Cramm. *Containment.*' He glanced anxiously at the time – he had to prepare for an important board meeting later in the morning – and reached across his desk for the next problem, which came in the form of a heavy document from the UK division. But Cramm hadn't quite finished.

'Catch was behind this,' he said, slipping the cuttings into a file.

'Mmm?' Schenker said vaguely, already absorbed by his reading. 'So?'

'They must have their claws into Nick Mackenzie. They'll try to milk him for funds.'

Tearing himself away, Schenker looked up. 'So?'

'This is a man with millions. He could – '

'Millions?' Schenker echoed with distaste. 'No wonder the country's in recession.' He waved a dismissive hand. He wasn't interested, not this morning, not when Research were manoeuvring for extra finance, which, if he wasn't very careful indeed, would be taken from his own marketing development budget. Research, under McNeill, had an independence from the executive which was intended to ensure that it retained a certain detachment and impartiality, but which only succeeded in splitting the power base and reducing effective decision making. McNeill was the thorn in Schenker's flesh, the one irritant that was impossible to shift.

'Deal with it,' he said vaguely.

Cramm seemed about to speak, but thought better of it.

Schenker returned to the notes which accompanied the fat document. The document, drawn up by Morton-Kreiger's UK Agrochemicals Division, dealt with the implications of a proposed new Food and Environment Protection Act. The changes brought by the last Act, in 1985, had been harsh but not, on the whole, unreasonable. But these new proposals went much further; in fact, they went so far as to be absurd. If enacted, it would become compulsory for certain foods to carry what amounted to a health warning. The mind boggled: what were these warnings going to say? 'These potatoes have been sprayed with X, Y and Z'? They might as well say: 'These potatoes will endanger your health.' Or 'These potatoes contain dangerous chemicals.' Lunatic.

According to the Green lobby, this labelling was needed to discourage growing methods that resulted in the build-up of pesticide residues. But it was these very growing methods that had been encouraged by the Ministry of Agriculture for decades, and which were still practised by vast numbers of growers. Were they seriously going to put all those growers out of business? More to the point, where was the scientific proof to back the contention that pesticides were dangerous? There was absolutely no firm evidence that residues were in the slightest bit harmful.

As usual, it was alarmism based on the scantiest of research. A typical Green stratagem.

But if the idea for food labelling was a nuisance, the other legislative proposals were deeply worrying, for the simple reason they had a much better chance of getting through. The amount of food sampling was to be increased – that is, more products lifted off the supermarket shelves, tested for residues and the growers held responsible – and the maximum permissible levels of pesticide residues were to be put in line with those of other countries. This, Schenker feared, would put a real squeeze on the UK market. Until now, the UK market had been much freer of petty restrictions than other countries in the developed world. There were something like thirty-eight pesticides still in use in the UK which had been banned or restricted elsewhere, and that included 2,4,5-T of Agent Orange fame, aldrin, dieldrin and lindane.

Of course the British market was only a fifth the size of the US market, but that wasn't the point. One compromise, a single concession, and before you knew it, customers would be paying through the nose for rotting, unattractive produce.

'How are we getting on with this?' he asked Cramm. The question wasn't intended to elicit information about the glossy presentation document sent to the parliamentary committee by the Federation, nor the slim fact-file sent to every member of parliament, nor the seminar and lavish lunch already held for scientific journalists, nor the generous grants and personal softeners handed out to leading scientists: all this (initiated and overseen by Schenker) was just basic groundwork. What Schenker wanted to know was how they were getting on where it really mattered: with the government and, in particular, the Minister of Agriculture, Fisheries and Food, a tough-minded wet called Cranbourne.

'Can't get near Cranbourne,' Cramm said. 'Keep getting frozen off by his staff.'

'Why?' Schenker asked simply. '*Why?*'

Cramm shrugged. 'The official line is that they've got all the facts they need. But the problem is still Cranbourne himself. He seems determined to stick to his guns.'

'What's wrong with the man?' Schenker exclaimed. 'He seems to have got a serious blind spot. Why else would he shut us out? He's meant to be a senior minister, for God's sake. He's meant to have an open mind.' Schenker chewed his upper lip, a habit of which he was unaware, but which

Cramm and the rest of his staff recognized as a sign of deep irritation.

Schenker's back was hurting. He got up from his chair and, stretching hard, went to the window. A thin drizzle was falling from a leaden sky, so that the grey of the river was indistinguishable from that of the sky. Schenker noticed the weather only in so far as it caused the traffic to clog up and slow his progress to meetings, or when, as now, it obscured his view of the City and the Stock Exchange, where even at this moment the market analysts would be reading indicators of Morton-Kreiger's soon-to-be-published half-year results.

'Still one of the PM's blue-eyed boys, Cranbourne, is he?' Schenker asked. 'Hasn't blotted his copy book?'

'No. Keeps his head down and his nose clean. Toes the line. Always has.'

'And no reshuffle before the next election?'

'Very unlikely. Though there are plenty of rumours of a snap election.'

'The spring. If they go early, they'll go in the spring. But assuming the worst scenario, Cranbourne could be sitting in that chair for another eighteen months. And he might just do it, you know. Push the Bill through.' Schenker turned to Cramm. 'No whispers about him? No rumblings of dissatisfaction?'

Cramm shook his head.

Schenker frowned. 'What – nothing?'

A look of understanding came over Cramm's quick face. 'I'll find out.'

Schenker sat down. 'You do just that. With a bit of luck, Driscoll will get Agriculture next time round and we'll be on to a better wicket. But in the meantime we've got to find a strategy for Cranbourne.'

'Containment,' offered Cramm, not without a faint smile.

The mention of Driscoll reminded Schenker of something. He buzzed his secretary. 'Contact Mrs Driscoll, would you, Elaine? See if she'd like a car on the morning of the opera. She might want to go to her hairdresser or something. And the flowers, Elaine, the ones for the next morning? Roses.'

He hadn't lost his certainty that Susan Driscoll would like roses. All real women liked roses. Real women dressed in feminine style, had tidy hair, pink lipstick and were a support to their husbands. Modern women, with their distorted values and almost masculine aggression, were unattractive, often alarmingly so. Fortunately career women were thin on the ground in the agrochemical industry.

Schenker surveyed his memo pad, and saw there was nothing more to discuss with Cramm. 'That's it then, is it?'

'Not quite.' Cramm rearranged the files on his lap. 'A small problem in Chicago. A report from one of our scientists.'

Schenker spread his fingers over the desk in two wide arcs.

'That's Research's problem, isn't it?' he said testily.

'Strictly speaking. But I thought you'd better see a copy of the report immediately, before it came to you through the normal channels. This scientist, Dublensky — if I've pronounced it right — he's gathered some data on the workers at the Aurora plant and — '

'Is that his job? To get data on the Aurora plant?' Schenker snapped.

'Well — no, I wouldn't have thought so.'

'What *is* his job then?'

'He's a toxicologist.'

'In charge of?'

'Er — ' Cramm glanced at some notes. 'Well, monitoring toxicology trials, I believe.'

'Then what the hell's he doing writing a report about the Aurora plant?' The Aurora Chemical Company of Aurora, Illinois, was a wholly-owned subsidiary of MKI —

Morton-Kreiger International of Chicago. It manufactured three of the company's best-selling US products, but as far as day-to-day management went, it was a separate entity.

'Aurora's got a chief executive, hasn't it?' Schenker said crisply. 'And a chief chemist?'

'Yes. Why this Dublensky got involved, I don't know. But he seems to have got hold of this data – '

'What data?'

'Medical reports on some of the workers on the Silveron production line.'

'Production line? It's hardly *in* production.'

Cramm looked at his notes. 'Two lines, all export.'

'I know, I know.' He had meant, hardly in production compared to the way it would be in the future. He waved Cramm on.

'Well, apparently a few of these people have been experiencing medical problems which, according to this Dublensky, should be treated as a serious cause for concern.'

'What's his game, huh? I mean, he isn't medically qualified, is he?'

Cramm shrugged. 'I wouldn't have thought so. I'll find out . . .'

'Of course he's not medically qualified,' Schenker leapt in. 'He's a scientist, isn't he? Come on, Cramm – what's the Aurora management saying about this? Have we got a report?'

Cramm shook his head. 'Nothing. Apparently, the company medical advisors are saying that the workers' complaints – and there're just three people involved, I believe – are nothing to do with Silveron at all. Just normal illnesses.'

'So in effect there's no problem at all!'

'MKI don't think so, certainly. But I understand they're authorizing a simple backup test on Silveron, just to be on the safe side. A repeat of one of the basic toxicology trials.

The results should be through prior to launch. That should put paid to ...' Cramm paused, choosing his words carefully, '. . . to any possible doubts.'

'So what the hell's this Dublensky moaning about, for God's sake?'

'He thinks the product launch should be delayed and a completely new set of trials undertaken.'

'Delayed!' Schenker protested. 'New trials! He must be joking. The trials would take years. The man's crazy. Listen – so long as MKI are happy, I don't want to hear another word about this.' He added reproachfully: 'Frankly I'm amazed it's got this far.'

Cramm gave it a moment, then said: 'I think it'd be wise to take a more cautious attitude.'

Sometimes Cramm spoke like that, quietly and insistently, and when he did so Schenker knew that he'd be foolish not to listen.

'Go on,' he said.

'The report came direct from this Dublensky. He bypassed the MKI management and somehow got it straight to us here in London. Not that he didn't try to get himself heard in Chicago. According to him he tried very hard. He says he sent a succession of memos and letters to the MKI board, but got palmed off, then threatened. He doesn't say how he was threatened. Dismissal perhaps.'

'So what's wrong with firing him?' Schenker asked. 'I would have thought it was an ideal solution for someone who's not prepared to follow proper procedures – for a scientist sounding off on matters that don't concern him.'

'My point is that this Dublensky must be a highly motivated man,' Cramm explained. 'He keeps at it when he's ignored. Then he jumps over his bosses' heads and risks his job. He might not appreciate being fired. He might run to the environmentalists.' Cramm added unnecessarily: 'Or the EPA.'

Schenker was silent for a moment. He needed to feel his

way around this one. People like this Dublensky were almost beyond his understanding. What made a man turn on the company that provided his livelihood? What made him want to cause trouble for everyone? A grievance, lack of promotion? Leftist leanings? Or simply a perverse and mean-spirited nature hidden under that all-embracing guise, idealism? He had a strong urge to send these visionary types to live in a communist state for a while, so they'd catch a heavy and incurable dose of realism.

At the same time he needed no reminding of what would happen to Silveron's launch if the Environmental Protection Agency got wind of this and filed suit.

'So what do you think we should do with him?'

Cramm answered straight away, and Schenker realized he'd had it all worked out from the beginning. 'Perhaps we should think about congratulating him. Then promoting him.'

Schenker considered this for a moment. It went against the grain to keep on a troublesome employee. At the same time Cramm's idea had certain advantages.

Yet the liturgy wasn't quite complete. Cramm should have said: congratulate him, promote him, then, most important of all, make him inactive. But then, being Cramm, this was undoubtedly what he had meant.

'Do it,' Schenker said and, seeing the time, hunched his shoulders over the desk and began reading to show that the session was over.


John Dublensky watched the first snowflakes of an unseasonally early winter swirl out of the darkness. A few stuck to the glass before melting into inconsequential droplets, defeated by the heating system of Morton-Kreiger International which was programmed to keep the staff in shirt sleeves right through till spring, when they were forced into sweaters by the air conditioning.

During Dublensky's college days at Columbia and his post-doc years at Syracuse, he'd looked forward to the snow; the eastern winters had a comforting enveloping quality that appealed to what he liked to think of as the mystical side of his nature, a side which Anne, his wife, constantly encouraged as an antidote to the absurdities of corporate life.

But the Chicago winters were different. Here the winds howled unchecked off the lake, the cold had a vicious edge, and the prairie landscape, open and urbanized, was bleak under its wrap of snow. He did not love the winters here. Come to that, he didn't much love Chicago, though he tried not to let that interfere with his enjoyment of life, which was considerable.

Shortly before five he began to tidy his desk. He did not usually leave on time, preferring to finish whatever he was doing at his own pace, but his son Tad's eighth birthday was coming up the next week and he wanted to get down to the sports store and look at a few things.

'What's this? Not staying late today?'

He recognized the strident voice of Don Reedy, his immediate superior.

Dublensky peered myopically at him. 'Hi.'

'Hi,' Reedy said, coming into the office. 'There must be a reason for this. Don't tell me – you're going on vacation!'

'That would be a little rash,' he smiled, searching his desk for his spare spectacles which he had seen only a moment ago. MKI operated a clean-desk policy, though no one would have believed it to look at Dublensky's desk.

'People have been known to benefit, you know. From vacations.'

Reedy perched on the edge of an adjacent desk watching Dublensky pack his briefcase. He was a large avuncular man, overweight by a good thirty pounds, with a benign smile which belied the very considerable committee skills that provided a welcome buffer between the senior management and the scientific staff. Reedy was tough but straight; Dublensky got on well with him.

Dublensky found his spectacles on the chair behind him. 'Well . . . I have to go now. Unless you . . .?'

His internal phone rang. In what was intended to be a practised move, Dublensky twisted the receiver up to his shoulder, but it slipped and he had to grab at it before it crashed to the desk. Anne, his wife, always said he was the clumsiest man she had ever met, a charge he gently refuted but which he had to admit had a grain of truth.

'Dublensky,' he said breathlessly.

'So glad to have caught you, Mr Dublensky,' the female voice said, and Dublensky felt a stab of surprise. Though he'd heard the clipped east-coast voice only a couple of times before, he recognized it immediately. It was Gertholm's secretary. Gertholm, president-in-chief of Morton-Kreiger International (US).

'Mr Gertholm was wondering if it would be convenient for you to see him in half an hour, at five thirty?'

It was convenient. It could hardly be otherwise. Ringing off, Dublensky sat slowly down at his desk, abandoning his briefcase to the floor. So. This was it. He shouldn't be surprised, of course. He'd stuck his neck out, and here was the guillotine, dropping fast. He supposed it was the report to London that had finally done it. The MKI management were not the kind of people to overlook a misdemeanour of that magnitude.

Well, there were worse things than being out of work, though the thought of Christmas without a pay cheque created an unpleasant sensation in the pit of his stomach.

'You okay?' Reedy asked.

'I've been summoned to Gertholm. It must be the axe. Has to be.'

'What? John, are you sure? No . . . *No!* You're mistaken. I would have known. Really. They would have told me.'

Dublensky wanted to believe him, but he wasn't sure

what to believe just now. 'I don't think I quite share your optimism,' he said unhappily. 'Why else would Gertholm want to see me?'

'Listen, John ... There could be other reasons, you know. Besides, why would he want to fire you?'

Dublensky looked at him in surprise. 'Hell, Don, we both know why. The Aurora business. Overstepping the mark. Exceeding my responsibilities.'

Reedy pulled up a chair and sat down. 'But that was a ... well, a brave report, John. A fine thing. I always said so. It can't be held against you.'

'It can't? Remember the Greek messenger?'

'I'm sorry?'

'Killed for bringing the news.'

Reedy leaned forward and patted his arm awkwardly. 'Listen, you're wrong. I'm quite sure you're wrong. Wait and see.'

Dublensky shook his head. Reedy was just trying to soften the blow. 'I'd like to be alone, Don, if you don't mind.'

Reedy shook his head firmly. 'I'll stay. Otherwise you're going to talk yourself into believing your own worst fears.'

Dublensky didn't want to argue – in most respects he was a mild man – but on this occasion he was going to have to insist. Dublensky got up and stood by the open door. 'Thanks, Don, but really . . .'

Reedy gave a long slow shake of his head and said, with a half laugh of disbelief: 'If that's what you want . . .'

Dublensky closed the door behind Reedy and sat down again. His first instinct was to call Anne – he always discussed everything with her – but he realized that she'd be on her way from work to collect Tad. Lifting his spectacles, he rubbed a hand viciously over his eyes. He suddenly felt very alone. He tried to imagine himself in conversation with Anne, tried to hear her arguments. What would she recommend? They'd long since decided that it was essential for him to expose the facts about the Aurora workers. How could he have acted otherwise? The situation was impossible to ignore. One of the workers on the Silveron production line had been paid off, permanently sick, two more were on indefinite sick leave. There was the medical evidence of Burt, the local physician who had originally contacted Dublensky with his suspicions, evidence which, though clinical and in a sense circumstantial, was impressive. And then there were the testimonials of the victims themselves, which made the most alarming reading of all.

Anne always used to say he wasn't tough or worldly enough for corporate life, and in some senses that may have been true, but Dublensky hadn't been so naive as to think his initial report would be well received. No one wanted bad news, far less a successful company like MKI. Up till now Dublensky had thought himself prepared for the consequences of his actions. Yet he'd never quite believed it would come to this. However you looked at it, however limited corporate vision was inclined to be, something was seriously wrong when a guy got fired for doing what was right.

He had less than twenty minutes before starting for Gertholm's eyrie in the main tower. He realized this might be the last time he sat at his desk, the last time he handled the projects which had become so familiar to him. He opened his briefcase and removed the work he had been planning to take home for the evening. For a while he stared at the empty case, miserable with indecision. Then, quickly, before he changed his mind, he stood up and lifted a thick pile of papers off one of the shelves. Here was the file that he had built up on the Aurora affair: the testimonials, the physician's notes, Dublensky's original report and copies of his memos and letters to the MKI management.

He fingered the papers thoughtfully. He should make a copy – he must make a copy – but it would be crazy to do it here. Quite apart from the time factor, such a thing might well be noticed, particularly if he'd just been fired. No, far better to take the documents out of the building and copy them in a late-night office supply store.

Alert to the sounds from the corridor, his heart kicking against his ribs, he placed the dossier in his briefcase and closed it. Then he sat down again.

Yet the decision-making wasn't over. The health of Aurora workers wasn't the only disturbing thing he'd come across; quite by chance he'd discovered another matter which also concerned Silveron. Until now he'd left this new difficulty on the back burner, progressing it slowly, almost reluctantly and, it had to be said, secretively. He had planned on doing a great deal more research on the matter, on assembling more facts, before putting his head on the block again; he was grimly aware that, if the state of the Aurora workers' health was unwelcome news for MKI, then this new information would be total anathema.

He opened a lower drawer and slid out a file. Though slimmer than the Aurora file, this bundle of papers weighed more heavily in his hands. For one thing the data was company property. Its removal from the MKI premises for the sort of purposes he had in mind would be a serious offence; the company could undoubtedly bring charges. And if he did manage to get the data out and copy it, what then? Hand it to the EPA? He tried to think through the consequences of such an action, but they were too enormous, too cataclysmic to settle easily in his mind.

The immediate decision was both impossible and disturbing. He postponed it by gazing out of the window. The snow was thicker now, swirling past the glass in whorls and eddies, the flakes illuminated by the hundreds of brilliantly lit windows of the Morton-Kreiger building.

Five minutes to go. Impatient at his own indecision, Dublensky moved with sudden speed, opening the briefcase, placing the second file on top of the Aurora dossier and shutting the lid with a snap.

It was done. He was committed. Curiously, he didn't feel as terrified as he'd thought he would. If anything, his heart had lifted, buoyed by the certainty that he had done the right thing.

He stood the briefcase at the side of his desk, ready to retrieve immediately after the interview. Then, like the Greek messenger, he went to receive his punishment.

The interview was brief – a bare five minutes. It passed for Dublensky in a haze of astonishment. MKI in all its might, embodied by the thin expressionless face of Gertholm, was pleased with him. His initiative and persistence were commendable. He was to be promoted. Chief chemist at the Allentown Chemical Works in Virginia and a raise of fifteen thousand dollars a year. With immediate effect. Removal expenses, hotel bills, relocation payment.

He was so astounded that the interview was almost over before the still small voice of caution made itself heard. What would happen to the Aurora dossier, he asked. Would it be acted upon?

This question was met with immediate reassurances. Although it would be impossible to postpone the launch, the company was going to commission an independent rerun of one of the basic toxicology trials. It was also going to keep a close check on health and safety procedures at the Aurora plant.

Dublensky returned to the south tower in a state of exaltation and stupefaction. He entered his office to find that Reedy had returned and was sitting in his chair. On hearing the door, the senior chemist swung sharply round and got hastily to his feet.

It was a moment before Dublensky, numb with disbelief, was capable of communicating his news.

'I knew it,' Reedy said with a congratulatory smile. 'I knew they'd never let someone of your calibre go.'

After a while Dublensky, settling into a pleasant state of shock, allowed Reedy to help him on with his jacket and walk him down the corridor. He was hardly aware of setting off on the drive home to Evanston. The road conditions were treacherous, the visibility poor, but he registered little until he passed the sports store and remembered his son's birthday. He turned back and bought Tad a Prince tennis racquet. Then, because this was a day for celebration, he added a set of Adidas tennis shoes, socks, shorts and shirt.

He arrived home jubilant. His exhilaration lasted twenty minutes, the time it took to tell Anne and Tad the full story, and for Tad to ask questions about Allentown, Virginia.

'They're buying your silence,' Anne said quietly.

Dublensky, taking some wine from the ice box, pulled an aggrieved face. 'Why d'you say that? I told you – they've followed up my report.'

'That's what they're telling you. But how do you know they'll progress it? You won't be around to find out, will you? You'll be tucked away in Virginia.'

Dublensky felt a flutter of resentment at the swiftness with which she had managed to put a dampener on things. At the same time he had great respect for his wife's judgement. Slowly, almost reluctantly, he considered the possibility. 'You're saying that all this is just a way of getting me to keep my mouth shut? But there's no reason to say that. They haven't asked me to drop the Aurora report. They haven't suggested a deal. I mean . . . you'd have to have an abysmal opinion of people to believe something like that.'

'Not of people. Of large corporations dedicated to profit.'

It was typical of Anne to be categorical. In fact, if Dublensky didn't love and respect her so much, he'd say she had a tendency to oversimplify things. 'You're seeing villains round every corner, sweetheart. I mean, they wouldn't go to all this trouble in the hope of keeping me quiet.'

'Wouldn't they? I'd have thought it was exactly the kind of thing they would do.'

Dublensky pulled the cork on the wine and poured two glasses. Already the celebration had gone a little flat. Now that the seeds of uncertainty were sown, doubts were beginning to creep in on him, each one weightier than the last. 'But I'll soon hear if nothing gets done,' he said in an attempt to reassure himself as much as Anne. 'I'll keep in touch with the sick production workers, with some of the other Aurora people. *And* with that doctor, Burt ... One way or another, I'll know what's going on.'

Anne took her glass but did not drink. 'Oh, I've no doubt they'll introduce some puny new safety measures at the Aurora plant and go ahead with trials of some description. But what does that prove? The trials will probably be meaningless.'

'Meaningless?' Now she had provoked him in so far as it was ever possible to provoke Dublensky. 'A trial is a trial. You can't alter results.'

Anne didn't reply but gave him a dry look. Dublensky was on the point of arguing until he remembered the slim file he'd put in his briefcase. The contents effectively challenged his own argument, and, throwing back a great gulp of wine, he sank despondently onto a kitchen chair.

Anne sat down next to him. 'How about keeping a copy of all the documentation?' she suggested earnestly. 'And using it if nothing gets done?'

'I was going to,' he admitted. 'I got the files ready – that was when I thought I was going to get fired.'

'Where are they? Have you got them with you?'

Dublensky had to think for a moment. In the confusion

of leaving the office and Reedy's kindness in seeing him off, he realized what had happened. 'They're still at the office. In my briefcase.'

Anne sat back with a harsh sigh. 'Well, that's the last we'll see of them then.'

Dublensky shot her a horrified look, dismayed at the implication. 'This isn't the Mob, you know. This isn't some kind of Mafia that makes things disappear overnight. Those documents will be there in the morning. Believe me. I'll bet my last dollar on it. They'll be there.' Even as he said it, the doubts flourished. Was it possible? Would someone actually remove the documents? If so, who? MKI's security people? No, they wouldn't know what to look for. Reedy then? No. Tough he might be, but a collaborator in dark matters of chicanery he was not.

'Listen,' Dublensky added. 'If those documents aren't there in the morning I'll make one hell of a stink, believe me! One hell of a stink.' Dublensky had never made a real stink in his life – he preferred to raise awkward matters on paper – but on this issue he was pretty certain he could raise enough steam to propel himself into action.

Anne was silent; but then her silences were far worse than anything she might say because she reserved them for her moments of greatest displeasure.

Dublensky drained his glass and poured himself another. A moderate drinker, he had the sudden urge to throw prudence aside and take the consequences. 'Listen, let's just wait until tomorrow, shall we?' he said plaintively. 'Let's just wait and see.'

He woke early the next morning with an unfamiliar headache and a dry mouth, and hurried out of the house before seven. The ploughs were barely out, the dawn little more than a glimmer, but the snow had stopped and the sky was hard and clear. Apart from a section of uncleared drift on Lincoln Avenue, he had a smooth run across town to the familiar copper roofs of the MKI building.

The security man in the main lobby glanced up and gave him a perfunctory nod. Dublensky felt a small burst of relief. In some of the wilder nightmares that had haunted him during the long night, the security men had refused him entry to the building. Now, amid the sounds of floor polishers and the chatter of the cleaners, his fears seemed absurd. They were promoting him, weren't they? They'd hardly give him the lock-out treatment reserved for abrupt departures.

Nevertheless his heart beat a little harder as he approached the security gate. He inserted his card. The green light flashed on, the gate opened, and he was through. When the elevator disgorged him at the sixth floor, his confidence had returned. Anne would be proved wrong; the documents would still be there.

The door of his office was open, an electrical cable snaking in from the passage. A cleaner was in the centre of the room, vacuuming in a desultory manner. Dublensky side-stepped the cleaning trolley and the cleaner and peered at the side of his desk. The briefcase stood there, just as he'd left it. He pulled it onto the desk and opened it. He allowed himself a small smile of relief and triumph.

Untouched.

He pulled the Aurora file to the top and opened it, just to be sure.

Complete. He'd known it. Anne had overreacted. There was nothing sinister going on at all. There never had been.

Nevertheless he would take the documents to the office supply store on his way home that evening, and get them copied, just in case.

After the uncertainties of the night, he felt a surge of euphoria which manifested itself in a spurt of manic energy, and he set about putting his papers into some sort of order, ready for the new incumbent, whoever that might be.

It wasn't long before he found out. Soon after eight

thirty there was a knock and Don Reedy entered with a young woman.

'Well, how's our new man in Virginia?' Reedy said with forced joviality. Dublensky thought he looked strained. 'John – meet Mary Cummins,' said Reedy. 'She'll be taking over from you here.'

'Where have you come from, Mary?' Dublensky asked.

'Pharmaceuticals.'

'Been there long?'

'A couple of years.'

She seemed rather young for the job, though Dublensky was far too polite to say so. 'Welcome,' he said amiably. 'I wish I'd had longer to get things straight for you.' He glanced apologetically at the disorder of his desk. 'If you can give me a couple of hours . . .'

'Sure,' Reedy answered for her. 'In the meantime it would help Mary if she could get on with some reading.'

'Of course, of course,' Dublensky said, surveying his cluttered shelves. 'Where would you like to start?'

They picked their way through product performance reports, field reports and projects in hand – mainly toxicology trials on development products.

'That should keep you busy,' Dublensky smiled.

'It'll make a good start,' Mary Cummins said earnestly.

Reedy looked over the selection. 'Oh, and do you have the Aurora file, John? I need to have a look at it. Then I'll pass it on to Mary. Now we're doing this rerun.'

Dublensky's smile faltered. 'Sure.' His eyes were held by Reedy's, and for an instant he felt like a rabbit caught in the lights of a car. He forced himself to look away, only to find he was staring down at his open briefcase. The Aurora file, complete with inscribed title, gazed up at him.

Dublensky felt his heart banging against his chest just as it used to when, in his teens, he'd attempted to challenge his father's awesome authority. He felt the same sort of paralysis, too, a progressive deadening of the will that always seemed to overcome him in moments of stress.

'Er . . . give me a moment, would you?' With an enormous effort, he lifted his head and made a show of looking over the shelves. 'I'll have to think . . .'

No one spoke. The pause extended and intensified. Reedy stood back, waiting stoically; Dublensky could almost sense his determination. What was behind this doggedness? Was it just a matter of professional competence? Or was Reedy forcing the matter? In which case . . . Dublensky shied from some of the more uncomfortable conclusions.

Moving back along the shelf, Dublensky stole a glance at Reedy. He was beginning to look irritated, though this could well have been in response to Dublensky's embarrassing display of inefficiency.

The next moment Reedy gave an unexpected laugh and said to Mary Cummins: 'I'm afraid John here is not the most organized of people.' Approaching, he clapped a friendly hand on Dublensky's shoulder and beamed at him. 'But he's done a fine job, and we shall miss him.'

Dublensky stared dumbly. Even before Reedy glanced down towards the desk, Dublensky knew what was going to happen, and his heart squeezed painfully.

'Here!' Reedy exclaimed. 'What's this?' He picked up the Aurora file. He gave a small indulgent shake of the head. 'Wasn't so far away after all.'

Dublensky could hardly breathe. Watching the file being removed was like seeing his own child kidnapped. The suddenness of it, the loss of all his painstaking work, overwhelmed him.

Yet – wasn't he overreacting? The file was coming to no harm, after all; it was just changing hands. But even as he tried to convince himself of this, he could hear Anne's weary sigh and harsh reproaches. She would say he'd been gullible and foolish. And he was depressingly aware that she might be right.

Reedy tucked the file under his arm and made for the door. Dublensky realized that, by some tacit arrangement, Mary was to remain in his office.

Reedy paused. 'Oh, and there are some documents which I can't seem to lay my hands on,' he said pleasantly. 'I thought you may have them, John. Perhaps you could look them out for me later this morning?'

He handed a sheet to Dublensky. On it was a list and there, among the ten or more items, were three documents belonging to the slim file still remaining in Dublensky's briefcase.

'Sure.' Dublensky tried to sound normal. 'Sure. By the end of the morning.'

It was two hours before Dublensky could persuade himself that it was safe to tuck the file in among some other documents and slip away. He remembered having seen a large automatic photocopier in the anonymous recesses of the west tower when he had visited the sales department some months before.

Perspiring, unable to prevent himself from glancing over his shoulder, he made his way across. Twice he had to ask for directions and then, having located the copier, he found himself explaining his visit to the clerk. A mumbled story about broken copiers and a meeting in the west tower seemed to suffice and, five minutes later, he had a duplicate in his hands.

Returning to his office, he waited until Mary Cummins went for a coffee then, rolling the duplicate into a scroll, slid it into the inner pocket of his overcoat.

Something, at least, had been salvaged. Anne couldn't accuse him of complete failure.

Now, only the doubts remained. Had Reedy been genuine? Had his request for the lost paperwork been the natural fruit of a tidy mind? Or had his apparent concern for Dublensky's welfare been fabricated from the outset?

Worse, had he been aware of what was in the briefcase? Had he been told to retrieve the missing documents?

It was possible. But if Dublensky accepted that, then the implications were almost too painful to think about.

# Chapter 10

NICK HAD FORGOTTEN how very long the nights were. He woke early, before six, and lay staring out through the uncurtained window, waiting for the dawn to light the giant beeches in the park and reveal, far beyond, the faint line of the hills of Cowal. But the darkness clung stubbornly to the house, dense and unmoving. Even at seven when, careful not to wake Alusha, he dressed noiselessly and slipped downstairs, no glimmering of light showed through the tall windows of the lower rooms.

Whenever he'd imagined Ashard in midwinter he'd pictured bare trees, grey landscape, snow, even a certain bleakness, but not darkness. In the old days he and Alusha had always left Scotland by early October when the dawns were still respectable early-morning occasions.

He gave up his plan for a pre-breakfast walk and wandered slowly from room to room, turning on lights, pausing in doorways. Everything was the same, yet disconcertingly unfamiliar. Not a thing was out of place, every cushion had been plumped, flowers had been placed on the tables, the polished surfaces of the furniture gleamed immaculately; and yet the effect was dark and cold and curiously lifeless.

Even his studio, which in his imagination was always as he had left it – cluttered with his favourite books and gadgets – was so tidy that it looked as if it had never seen a person, let alone a note of music. The sight rather depressed him.

Some non-essential bags still stood in the hall, waiting to be taken upstairs. Among them was a case belonging to the nurse who'd accompanied them from Boston. He hoped she wasn't planning on unpacking because she wouldn't be staying long. Nothing personal, but he never wanted to see another medical professional as long as he lived.

Sounds issued from the kitchen and he found Mrs Alton making coffee and laying out the breakfast things. She asked in a hushed reverential voice if Mrs Mackenzie would be wanting all her meals upstairs, and if so, would he be wanting to take them with her.

He got a fairly good picture of what Mrs Alton was thinking. Well, she'd have to think again.

'Of course not,' he said firmly. 'Only breakfast.'

'I see,' said Mrs Alton, nodding uncertainly. 'But if you'd like her to have something on a tray, in the library or wherever, you only have to say.'

'But she can tell you herself, Mrs Alton. Just like before.'

'Oh.' She blinked. 'Of course. It was just . . . I wanted to make everything as easy as possible . . .'

But he wasn't having any of this. 'Mrs Mackenzie's fine, Mrs Alton. Getting better all the time. And she's extremely happy to be back. So am I. We're really looking forward to Christmas.'

'Christmas,' she echoed, brightening a little. 'I've made the pudding. And a cake.'

'Good,' he said briskly. 'So – everything's fine then, isn't it, Mrs Alton?'

'Oh yes . . .' She was finally getting the idea. 'Yes, of course.'

Nick started to prepare Alusha's breakfast tray.

'Let me do that,' said Mrs Alton.

But he refused; he found an extraordinary satisfaction in choosing the food for Alusha, laying out the china, making the tray look attractive. He enjoyed the rhythm of the daily preparations and the challenge of finding new and exotic things to tempt Alusha's appetite. During the months in America it had made him feel useful.

He put out organic oranges ready for squeezing, some sesame thins, unhydrogenated vegetable margarine, organic marmalade and camomile tea, then added a slice of water-melon and half a papaya – also organic: everything was organic. He'd had it flown up specially from London.

When the food was set out, he opened the medicine box and started on the supplements, placing Alusha's morning dose of vitamins, minerals and amino acids in a small bowl on one side of the tray. Medicine box was actually a bit of a misnomer because it contained almost no medicines. Just before leaving Boston, he and Alusha had emptied every extraneous drug, antibiotic and allopathic medicine into the hotel waste bin. The cartons and bottles numbered an incredible fifty-eight, and that wasn't counting the stuff that'd been pumped into Alusha during her various spells in clinics and hospitals. Now, apart from vitamins and minerals, a few Chinese herbal medicines and some hom-eopathic drops, there were no drugs except for a few standard painkillers and sleeping tablets. And the mor-phine, of course. He kept that separately, with his own things. Originally the morphine had gone into the waste bin along with everything else, but a few hours later, when Alusha was asleep, he had retrieved it, despising himself for the deception, hating himself for admitting that there might be a need for it, yet doing it all the same. Doubter. Judas. Snake in the grass.

Dawn began to come at last, a grudging grey murk that seeped reluctantly through the kitchen windows. Chewing on some toast, he pulled on a jacket and, leaving Mrs Alton and the bright kitchen, escaped into the grounds.

The air tasted sweet and damp, heavy with the scent of decaying leaves fused with some indefinable tang – the peaty earth perhaps, or pine resin, or the faint salt breeze off the loch. Whatever, it was like nectar after the dry plasticky smell of aircraft and the stifling air of hermetically sealed service apartments.

Setting off at a cracking pace, he walked up through the park without pausing or looking back, delaying his first view of the landscape as a child postpones for a few agonizing minutes the opening of a present, in anticipation of pleasure, but also half afraid of disappointment.

Clear of the trees, he stopped at last and turned and looked out over the loch. A vast bed of thin mist lay enclosed in the long dark scoop of the hills, obscuring water, trees, everything in a dank grey blur. The murk of the sky was balanced by the gloom of the mist, grey and dark and chill. The very air seemed to be dripping silently with something like foreboding.

Yet in spite of this a sense of homecoming began to creep up on him. There was a comforting familiarity in the reach of the pasture, the pattern of the trees in the park and the sight of the house itself, squatting in its nest of gardens, its lights glowing brightly.

He walked a long way, up through the western woods to the glen, following the cascading river as far as the high moorlands, and returning through the northern woods to emerge at Meall Dhu. The mist was dispersing, and plumes of vapour rose from the loch like steam. Beyond on the hills opposite, bands of snow made white slashes against the dull brown of the winter grasslands.

He picked up the path which led down to the upper paddock. The paddock was empty now; Rona had gone months ago, sold to people near Oban who, after a month, had been forced to put her down. She had pined for Alusha, so they said, had refused to eat. There had been nothing they could do. He had not told Alusha.

He steeled himself to look at the stable. It looked innocent, as if nothing terrible had ever happened there.

As he turned to continue down the hill he paused, his attention caught by a slight movement, a flicker at the

periphery of his vision, somewhere across the paddock at
the edge of the trees. He stared for a long time, trying to
make out what it might have been, but there was nothing,
just the dark forest, the phalanx of silent trees and the
distant ticking of dripping leaves.

He was about to walk on when something made him
look back – an irregularity in the pattern of the trees, a
paler shape against the shadows – and then at last he saw
it: a man. Wearing countryman's tweeds so that he almost
blended into the background.

Was it Duncan? From this distance it was impossible to
tell. One of the foresters perhaps?

The figure was standing perfectly still, yet Nick felt sure
the man had seen him.

Maybe it was Duncan after all. Nick waved. For a long
while the man did not move, and Nick began to wonder if
the man hadn't seen him after all when, abruptly, the figure
raised his arm and waved back, a brief hesitant gesture that
was more like a salute. The next moment he turned into
the forest and was swallowed up by the trees.

Not Duncan – who then? At the thought of intruders,
all Nick's defensive reflexes returned with a vengeance, and
he was tempted to start off across the paddock in hot
pursuit. Almost immediately he thought better of it. This
was Ashard, for heaven's sake. The man was probably a
rambler who'd strayed off the path, or someone from the
next-door estate.

Nevertheless, he set off down the hill in a sombre mood.

Emerging from the vegetable garden, he saw Duncan
standing by the kitchen door. Beside him was Alusha. He
was both surprised and pleased to see her up so early. It
confirmed what he already knew: that coming home had
been the best decision they'd made in the whole miserable
time they'd been away.

Nick greeted Duncan then turned to Alusha.

'You're up early,' he said, kissing her lightly.

'I'm going for a walk!' she announced cheerfully. There was a hint of determination in her voice, like a child who won't be denied something she's set her heart on.

'What about breakfast?'

'I've had it. Thank you for making it for me.' Her eyes shone firmly, a smile danced resolutely on her lips. She looked transformed; Nick's heart twisted to see her so happy.

'Don't overdo it,' he said, thinking of the chill air.

At this public show of concern, she raised an eyebrow and ticked him off with her eyes. Then, with a small wave, she set off towards the rose garden. At first she walked briskly but soon the effort was too much for her, as Nick had known it would be, and she slowed to a gentler pace.

Duncan was watching her too, a deep frown on his face, and for a moment Nick saw Alusha as others must see her: far too thin, eyes unnaturally large, hair a shadow of its former glorious self. But then Duncan couldn't see what Nick saw, an Alusha vastly relieved at being home again.

The two men decided on a tour of the estate, and walked round the house towards the Range Rover.

'By the way, I saw someone up by Meall Dhu, lurking in the trees,' Nick remarked.

Duncan stopped in his tracks, looking mortified. 'A stranger?'

'I'm not sure.'

'Well, it couldn't be one of ours. Joe and Fergus are away by the loch, clearing brush. And the farmhands – well, they wouldn't be up in those parts.'

That's what Nick had thought. 'Oh well. Probably just a rambler.'

They climbed into the Range Rover. Nick added: 'Or a poacher.'

'But there's been no poaching!' Duncan exclaimed triumphantly. 'Not a dabble.'

'No?'

'Not since you left. Not a net, nor a peg, nor even a cigarette butt to be found. And not a fish disturbed, or I'm a Dutchman.'

'Well done.'

'Och, I'm not so certain it was my doing, to be perfectly honest. I rather think our friends decided to give up for some reason.'

Nick thought of the tall man and his partner by the pool. 'That was kind of them. They've reformed then, have they?'

'Not a bit of it!' Duncan shot him a guilty but not altogether serious glance. 'I rather think that those fancy managing agents next door are having their work cut out for them.' He gestured towards the Fincharn Estate.

'Oh dear,' Nick said straight-faced.

In mid afternoon, when Alusha was sleeping and the daylight was fading again, Nick ventured into the studio and tried to get the feel of the place again. He opened a few drawers, glanced at some abandoned songs and tapped out one of his old hits from years before. He remembered having thought it was rather good when he'd written it, but now it sounded flat and glib and rather pretentious.

His drawings looked all right though – the osprey series and some sketches he'd started making of the buzzards that inhabited the upper reaches of Ashard – and the sight of all his books cheered him further.

He wandered down the passage past the back stairs to the estate office, which had its main entrance off the courtyard to the east side of the house, a courtyard which housed Mr and Mrs Alton in a converted outhouse on the far side, and one of the forestry workers in a flat over the stables.

There was a pile of opened letters in the tray reserved for his mail. These would be letters that had come direct to Scotland and which Helen, who did the secretarial work in the estate office, thought he would like to see personally.

There was a letter from a writer friend who'd heard he and Alusha were coming back and wanted to know how they were. There was a note from an acquaintance in television asking about the possibility of making a TV programme about Nick's solo career. He apologized for not going through Nick's manager but, if Nick didn't mind him saying so, the man was totally impossible to deal with, since he never replied to letters or phone messages. Nick thought: That's David all right.

The next was a letter on Save the Children notepaper, written in a slanting female hand. He glanced at the signature. Susan Driscoll. Ever since his drinking years his memory for names and faces – sometimes even the words of his own songs – had been appalling. But he soon had it: it was Suki Armitage-that-was, organizer of charity concerts, and a touchy lady when she wasn't instantly remembered. She said she hadn't realized his wife was so ill. She was extremely sorry to hear about it, and of course quite understood why he couldn't do the concert. There was a PS. If at any time in the future things changed and he was ever interested in doing anything for her charity, she would of course be delighted to discuss it.

The next letter was also on headed notepaper. It was from the anti-chemical campaign, Catch. The signature was scrawled and it took him a moment to decipher it. Daisy, the eco-freak. He smiled, he wasn't sure why. He wondered if the realities of a heartless world had rubbed off on her yet.

The letter was short. She'd heard he might be returning. She hadn't stopped looking into Reldane, searching for evidence that it might have damaging effects, but she'd had no joy. However, she'd had some new thoughts. Could he send some more earth and water samples?

He put the letter on one side. She was a nice girl; he'd drop her a line. No, he'd call her. It would be easier to explain on the phone.

But something made him put it off; perhaps it was the thought of her persuasiveness and enthusiasm, which might prove altogether too powerful.

When after a week he still hadn't got round to calling, he finally scrawled her a note. *It's good of you to keep trying, but my wife and I really need to leave the past behind. That may seem selfish and irresponsible to you – and maybe it is – but it takes everything we have just to keep going. Hope you understand . . .*

He meant to finish there, but felt he owed her more of an explanation. *We've been making the rounds of the doctors and clinics for months now. The medics tried everything they could think of, and I know we should be grateful for that, but nothing helped. In fact, I don't think any of them really had the faintest clue of how to treat my wife. All they did was pump her full of drugs, which seemed to have terrible side-effects and to make her worse.*

He thought: I'm sounding bitter. I really mustn't.

*Though it's impossible to know how she would have been without the drugs, of course. The same, maybe even worse. Impossible to tell. Anyway, it doesn't seem to matter now, because . . .*

But he couldn't go on. How could he put the rest down on paper, and to a virtual stranger, when he couldn't even voice it to Alusha?

He crossed out the unfinished sentence, scribbled some best wishes and put it out for posting.

Concern over the cause of Alusha's illness seemed to be surprisingly widespread because two days later Nick got another letter on the same subject. This time the signature, which was small and childish, read A. Campbell. The address was Inveraray. Nick didn't know any A. Campbell, either male or female, but whoever it was, he or she thought Nick would be interested to know that some other people in the Argyll area had been suffering a mysterious illness, just like Mrs Mackenzie's.

For a moment Nick considered the wild possibility that
Alusha's illness might be contagious, but immediately dismissed it. If it had been catching, someone else would have
got it by now.

He skimmed on through the letter. Mr or Mrs Campbell
knew a young lad who'd been fit and well but was now
unable to leave the house. The boy slept all day, couldn't
eat, had lost weight, had an aversion to sunlight and
suffered badly from 'weeping attacks'.

Nick began to lose interest. This wasn't the same illness
at all. He felt a curious almost guilty relief; he was glad to
be spared the complications of other people's problems.

The letter ended with the description of another case
further down the loch at Lochgilphead. But again, the
symptoms didn't tally. Along with a number of vague-
sounding problems, this man apparently suffered vertigo,
skin rashes and panic attacks.

Nick had the picture: here were the local nutters and
hypochondriacs and depressives coming out of the woodwork, trying to win respectability and attention for their
illnesses, and finding a champion in the well-meaning but
deluded A. Campbell.

He scribbled a pencilled message across the letter, asking
Helen to thank A. Campbell for his interest, etc. Then,
chucking the letter thankfully into the out-tray, he forgot
about it.


The driving rain and gales came first, over Christmas
and the New Year, then, almost as a welcome relief, the
snow. Wet, slushy, damp stuff to begin with then, in late
January, crisp dry snow that fell and fell, forming a thick
blanket over the lower slopes of the hills and forests so
that the trees groaned and creaked with the weight. After
a few days a salty sou'westerly roared up the loch from
the Gulf Stream waters and shook the trees free, blowing

the snow into drifts and melting the surface into a heavy crust.

At Ashard House the days varied little. A few friends came to stay around Christmas, but after that, while no one was actually discouraged from coming, no one was openly invited either, and the trickle of company dried up. Nick was glad. Alusha wasn't up to it, and he wasn't sure he was either. People were very kind, but, being kind, they were also very wearing. Everyone was careful not to mention Alusha's appearance and to pretend she looked just fine, and questions about her health, if asked at all, were blatantly tactful. But they knew, and the worry and pity showed in their eyes, and it was like a ghastly game.

In the end it was easier to be alone, just him and Alusha, wrapped in the cocoon of the Glen Ashard winter. Being alone also gave Nick the opportunity to work again, or at least to attempt some sort of routine. Every morning at seven he crept out of bed and went down to the studio for a couple of hours' thought. In the old days thought itself, in enough quantity, had always resulted in a song or two but now, though he tinkered with a few ideas, nothing came. Even his great indulgence, the choral work that he'd been working on spasmodically for the past four years, didn't respond to this or any other approach. He gave it time – no point in forcing it – but even that didn't seem to do the trick. It was a situation he'd never encountered before and he began to feel a corrosive frustration. He was well aware that frustration itself could be highly counter-productive, and did his best to ignore it, but it ate slowly away at him, paralysing his will and deadening his mind.

He began to get headaches. His limbs began to ache, and he started to get irritable. He had no doubt it was psychosomatic. Too much stress – or how did the therapists put it? – the burden of suppressed emotion. Well, there was plenty of that. He lost some of his appetite, too, and his jeans started to get loose at the waist. He took to going to the studio late at night and, aided by forbidden cigarettes, tried working into the early hours, to see if that would hit the mental trigger. But though he went through the motions, tapping out one or two bars, he knew it was hopeless. After a few minutes, he'd start to read something light – the latest *Melody Maker*, or a Sunday colour magazine. Sometimes he'd try a sketch or, more usually, work on a detailed copy of an osprey illustration. Pencilling in the intricate featherwork of the wings was, he found, profoundly calming.

During these nights he also listened to the radio, to plays, discussion programmes, music – anything, in fact, to fill the long hours while Alusha slept. While she was awake, he could cope; there were the meals and the long ritualistic sessions in the kitchen with complex recipes and finicky ingredients, and the walks with Alusha – increasingly short – and in the evenings the videos and games of back-gammon.

But in the night there was nothing, just the grinding truth, and his inability to deal with it. He came to the studio to escape. Escape? From Alusha? It was true. He knew it, yet couldn't bring himself to face it, just as he couldn't bring himself to face the reason. It had got to the point where he almost avoided touching her. In bed, when she curved her back into his stomach and drew his arm round her, he was filled with such misery that he could hardly speak, far less sleep. He waited in despair and self-hatred until she slept, so that he could ease away from her and escape the sharp points of bone where the soft round-ness of her bottom had been, avoid the stick-like arms and the shrunken breasts where there had once been smooth firm flesh. In the day he could eliminate the picture of her wasting body from his mind and look her in the face and feel immense love and real bursting hope; he could, simply, believe. But the nights were impossible, because it was then that the evidence was at its most stark and inescapable.

In late February there was a change. She stopped sleeping at night. She began to mutter and turn, often for hours at a time. If he tried to touch her, she pushed him away and, still half-asleep, swore at him in French. At other times he woke and knew she was awake too. When he reached out to her he found her skin cold with sweat, her hands clenched. She'd murmur about dreams and feeling restless, but he knew it was the pain. She never mentioned it of course, but when she thought he was asleep, she'd flick on the light and wash down some pain killers.

He stopped his late night visits to the studio then, and a week or so later, his early morning ones as well. Curiously, he didn't mind; it was a relief to give up the farcical attempts to work. Now at least his course was clear, and his life revolved more than ever round Alusha's needs. When she woke in the night he'd ask if she wanted anything, and though she never did, she'd squeeze his hand and keep hold of it, and he liked to think he was helping to ease her pain.

To pass the long nights while he lay at her side he took to reading celebrity biographies, because they were straightforward and held his attention better than anything else. Often, though, he would just lie awake in the darkness, awed by Alusha's iron will and staggering perseverance. Where did this strength come from? How could she keep it up, day after day? How could she smile at him and chatter away and joke with him through the pain and sickness and despondency? Sometimes he caught her eyeing him thoughtfully, as if he were the one in need of inspection, and then the dogged uncompromising look disappeared from her eyes and was replaced by something altogether darker and angrier and softer.

She was amazing. He only wished he could be the same.

*

The thing came to him quite suddenly. It was on a day in early March or, more precisely, an early morning. He woke at five and there it was in his head: the choral work – theme, words, and orchestration, a whole bloody section, as if some ghostly superscribe had composed the entire thing, and, in case that wasn't enough for him, had obligingly written out the words and music in manuscript.

Checking that Alusha was asleep, he pulled on a robe and went straight down to the studio. He scribbled out some of the words, tried the melody on the piano, then the variation, and squirmed in anguish. Something was wrong; it didn't sound the same.

He tried again, but now something else wasn't right. The main theme had gone. Closing his eyes, maintaining his calm, he tried to recapture the sound that had been so vivid in his mind just ten minutes before. One phrase was crucial, he knew: a haunting minor cadence. If he could get that . . . He tried several ways, none of them right, and felt the mixture of elation and despair that always came at moments like this. Then, abruptly, the phrase came swooping back into his mind. At first it hovered there, amorphous and tantalizingly difficult to grasp, but slowly, patiently he began to pin it down until, quite suddenly, there it was: utterly complete, absolutely perfect. Well – as perfect as it was ever likely to be.

Once it was down on paper it began to look rather ordinary, and he could see plenty of imperfections – were the words a bit trite perhaps? Was the melody an unconscious rehash of an existing song?

Problems like these weren't new, of course. They came up all the time and, from long habit, he had learnt to ignore them, at least until the work was finished. The work . . . Having never written a choral work before, he wasn't too sure what to call it.

He scribbled down a few more words, fragments,

phrases, then started to work on the baritone and bass harmonies for the main theme.

At seven the ideas ran out and he realized he'd have to come back to it later in the day.

As he eased his way gently back into bed he sensed the stiff watchfulness of Alusha's body beside him, and knew she was awake. As the silence stretched out, he felt all his old helplessness slip over him, familiar as an old coat, heavy as lead.

'All right?' he whispered finally in the direction of the back of her head. She had been particularly bad in the last few days, stiff with pain, and withdrawn and irritable.

'Yes.' Her voice was low and rough. 'Yes . . . And you? Were you writing? Did you have some ideas?'

'Mmm. Maybe.'

'I know that maybe of yours,' she said in her increasingly halting speech. 'Good. I'm happy. It's been too long.' She paused and he knew she was sorting out her next batch of thoughts and assembling her words in the right order, something that she no longer found easy. 'You should write another album,' she said eventually. 'It would be good for you.'

This was so unlike her that he raised his head to peer at her in the darkness. Normally, she never commented on the pace or, more recently, the total absence of his work.

'You're right,' he said. 'I should.'

'I worry about you.' Another pause. 'About what will happen to you.'

If her earlier remark had surprised him, this gave him a ripple of alarm. Ever since the accident any conversation that touched on defeat, on the idea of Alusha not getting well, was never to be mentioned.

'Plans,' she said. 'You need plans.'

'What plans?' he said lightly. 'Since when have we ever made plans?'

'Always,' she said crossly. 'Always. And we need some

now. Listen – ' She paused, then gave a harsh little sigh of frustration because the words would not come out right. 'We've been doing things wrong, haven't we? Don't you think?'

He felt sick. 'What?' But he knew. He knew exactly what she meant.

'We never talk,' she said doggedly, 'about what will happen.'

He didn't reply. Although he'd thought about little else for the last few months, he couldn't begin to discuss it. He felt chilled, emotionally suspended.

The silence stretched out. Then she said: 'Thank you for the pain killer . . . for getting some more. It helps.' Her voice was low, laboured, and totally matter-of-fact.

'Does it?' This was the first time they had ever mentioned the fact that Alusha had found the morphine and was using it regularly.

'I tried without for a day or so . . . But no good. So I start again tonight. It makes me a little high, I think. And rather silly. Or more silly than usual.' She gave a snort of amusement that was almost a sigh. 'You'll just have to put up with that.'

Nick pulled her closer to him. 'I'll try.'

'You know . . .' She didn't finish.

After a minute, when she still hadn't replied, he prompted gently: 'Mmm?'

'You really must get on and finish that song or whatever it is,' she said.

He sensed that she'd been intending to say something quite different, but he didn't press her. 'I will,' he whispered. 'I promise.'

She pulled his arm further round her body, and tucked it under hers. Later she fell asleep again. Dressing quietly, he crept down to the studio to have another look at the song.

He played it several times but it didn't sound right. The

magic, such as it was, had gone. The grand chords, the mystical quality he was so sure he'd captured had degenerated into something tawdry and uninspired.

The dawn when it finally appeared was grey, dark and cold. He leant his elbows on the desk, thrust his head into his hands and wept.

# Chapter 11

A ROAD TO the edge of nowhere. Narrow and unmetalled, riddled with potholes, the track climbed tortuously through rough grassland and geometric blocks of forest towards empty hills. Then, just when Daisy felt certain nothing but wilderness could lie ahead, a patch of green appeared above, nestling in a crescent of forest, with a solitary dwelling at its edge.

The car bounced and weaved over the last few potholes, and Brayfield brought the car to a halt in front of a sagging picket fence. Daisy got out and, meeting the wind, pulled her jacket close around her. She wandered across the track and looked out over the broad landscape. The ground sloped gently away from her in a long sweep of newly planted forest and bracken towards a valley dotted with sheep and a meandering river marked by a snaking avenue of black trees.

She had never been anywhere like this before. She couldn't get over how quiet it was. No people, no noise. No real noise, that was. She didn't count the whistling of the wind, which sounded unreal, like the whooshing noises made by the special effects department in an old film. But beneath the wind, and almost as loud in its way, was a kind of mysterious silence, which was both weird and compelling.

After the sounds, the next thing she noticed was the space. Nothing but rolling hills, forest and water; miles and miles of emptiness. As she'd remarked to Brayfield on the drive up from Glasgow, it was hard to believe that this was the same country that contained London and Birmingham. It wasn't, Brayfield had reminded her sharply, not the same country at all. This was Scotland, quite a different country, and she'd best not forget it. Daisy had almost smiled until she saw he was deadly serious.

Presumably it was this very emptiness that brought the super-rich here. At five or six million for a nice little estate they probably thought the peace and quiet was cheap at the price. Nick Mackenzie's place was no more than fifteen miles from here; she knew – she'd looked it up on the map. She'd sent him a note to say she was coming and left a phone message with the David Weinberg office, but there had been no reply. Too concerned with his wife. Too reluctant to go over old ground. His original reply had, after all, been clear enough. But it would have been nice to have had a go at changing his mind.

She turned to find Brayfield waiting patiently by the gate. Brayfield, a heavy Highlander with a congenial manner and a terrifying smoker's cough, was her contact from the local branch of the Transport and General Workers' Union.

The house was small and single-storey, built of grey stone with small windows sheltering under deep eaves, a modern replica of a Highland croft. In the perverse way of small dwellings it had turned a blank side-wall to the view down the valley and chosen to face a stand of dense pines.

Brayfield led the way up a short path which ran through a patch of unkempt grass and dead plants. The curtains in the window to the left of the porch were drawn; as Daisy watched, one of them quivered and fell still. Brayfield knocked and the door swung open immediately. A stout grey-haired woman stood there, wearing a mauve sweater and grey tweed skirt with lace-up shoes. She had a square face with small eyes and a thin-pressed mouth. She looked about fifty but could have been less. Brayfield introduced her as Mrs Bell.

Mrs Bell gave Daisy's jeans, boots and bomber jacket a long dubious stare before standing back to let them in. The interior was dark and smelled of damp and fumes from some heating fuel. Mrs Bell led the way into a cluttered living room with a dralon three-piece suite adorned with sunflowers, a gold and orange rug over a threadbare brown carpet and fading pink rose-patterned wallpaper. In one corner was a television showing a football match with the sound turned down; in the other, a bed which was masked by the high back of the settee so that, from where they were standing, its occupant was almost hidden from view. Mrs Bell went up to the bed and bent over it, smoothing the bedcovers and talking in a low murmur. Finally she came back to them and said in a studiously low voice: 'Just five minutes now. He gets dreadful tired. And keep your voices down. He cannot manage with the noise.'

Daisy and Brayfield advanced. Brayfield had already told her a little about Mrs Bell's son, Adrian. His father, a forestry worker, had died suddenly eighteen months before, since when Adrian and his mother had been threatened with eviction. He had been ill for about nine months, and was now almost fourteen years old, though it would have been hard to judge his age from his looks. His face was narrow and angular, and the skin, which was stretched tightly across the bones, was extraordinarily white, with a scattering of livid pustular spots over the cheeks. His hands were long and thin and brittle-looking, and his frame, clothed in old-fashioned striped pyjamas, was sharp with bones.

He looked awful, and it suddenly occurred to Daisy that he might be dying. Yet his eyes were bright, and though he seemed to find the smallest movement a terrible effort, he managed a small wave.

Brayfield did most of the talking. 'Adrian was up in a field at the back here when it happened. This was in June last, wasn't it, Adrian? Up with the sheep, he was.'

Daisy asked softly: 'You were in charge of the sheep, were you, Adrian?'

Adrian hadn't heard. He was staring at Daisy with blank puzzlement, as if some exotic and unexpected creature had suddenly alighted by his bed. Becoming aware of their stares, he glanced away, looking embarrassed.

Brayfield took over again, calling over his shoulder: 'Just the three ewes, were there not, Mrs Bell?' A soft assent came from behind. 'Kept for their milk. Sent for cheese.' Looking back at Adrian, he continued: 'So there he was, young Adrian, up in back there, and he notices a strong smell drifting across the field. Coming from the forest. A plantation of young trees, were they not, Adrian? And then he sees the plane. A light plane. He remembers a red flash on the wing, going diagonal – a sort of stripe. Anyways, the plane passes right over. And after it comes the spray, and he's no hope of avoiding it. Very strong, it was. Made the lad ill directly, did it not, Adrian? Coughing and feeling dizzy, were you not?'

Adrian gave a faint nod. Daisy encouraged him with a smile, but he refused to meet her gaze.

'Right-thinking chap that Adrian was,' Brayfield went on, 'as soon as he stopped coughing, he went directly to find the estate manager. The man admitted to the spraying on *that* occasion – but it was the last time he ever did. And what did he say, Adrian?'

A pause then the voice came, soft as a whisper. 'Told me I shouldna' have been there. Said ... I should have kept clear. I . . .' He trailed off, as if he had lost the thread.

Brayfield nodded, urging him on. 'And then what happened?'

'I said about the sheep.'

'And he said to move them?'

Adrian blinked his agreement.

'What happened to the sheep?' Daisy asked.

'They took sick,' Brayfield said. 'Though it took some time. How long was it, Adrian, some months?'

Adrian took a breath that was almost a sigh. 'Aye. Two, three months.'

'They were taken for slaughter and examination.'

'And what did that show?' Daisy asked, trying to capture Adrian's attention.

Adrian stared fixedly at a point somewhere between the bedcovers and the window. He seemed to be shutting himself off from the conversation, as if the visit was already too much for him.

'There were no laboratories that could do the right tests,' Brayfield explained.

'Why not?'

'The veterinarians, they use the Ministry of Agriculture labs, but they're not equipped for pesticide tests.'

'Wouldn't you know it!' declared Daisy for Adrian's benefit. She caught him stealing a glance at her and, before he could look away, pulled a conspiratorial face at him. 'And what about you, Adrian? Did they do any tests on you?'

It was a moment before he responded, raising one of his thin fingers to point at his arm. 'Blood,' he whispered.

'And they tested it for pesticides?'

'We arranged it,' said Brayfield. 'In November.'

'And they found nothing?' Daisy guessed. 'Well, they wouldn't, I'm afraid, not so long after the event. You really have to be tested straight away. What about a tissue biopsy, Adrian, did they do that?' She explained: 'A bit of your arm. Or sometimes your bum, if you'll excuse the expression.'

A glimmer of a smile.

'Not even a sliver? Didn't sit you on a bacon slicer?'

He gave a small giggle and she risked reaching forward

to touch his hand. He still wouldn't look at her, but he didn't pull away either.

'They did all the standard tests,' Brayfield said. 'Or so they informed Mrs Bell.' He spoke over his shoulder: 'Is that not right, Mrs Bell?'

'And?' Daisy asked.

Brayfield shook his head.

'So they found nothing?' she said to Adrian.

The smile had gone, he was looking blank again.

'So what have they decided is wrong with you?' Daisy had never believed in beating about the bush with sick people or children.

Coming up behind Daisy, Adrian's mother said firmly: 'They canna' be sure. But they do know he'll mend in time.' She spoke in the uplifting tone people use to convince themselves, as much as others, of something they desperately want to be true.

'And treatment? What have they given you?'

Adrian's eyes travelled towards a table at the head of the bed. Daisy had already spotted the rows of prescription drugs, and had only been waiting for an excuse to examine them. Anti-depressants. Tranquillisers. Antibiotics. Not what Peasedale or any half-knowledgeable physician would have recommended, and that was putting it mildly. In fact they would have been horrified. But this wasn't the moment to say so.

Mrs Bell, looking defensive, her eyes on Daisy, had come to sit at the foot of the bed.

'And your symptoms, Adrian?' Daisy asked the boy. 'What did you notice first?'

He had to think about that. 'I felt just ... terrible. Dreadful sick.' He frowned, and there was that puzzlement again, as if he were attempting to dredge a memory that refused to deliver.

'His memory hasna' recovered,' confirmed Mrs Bell.

'Half the time he has no knowledge of what month it is, let alone the day. He was never like that before, *never*.' Her voice quivered with anger or bitterness, or both. 'Then there was the sickness. He couldna' eat, not for weeks. Lost a terrible amount of weight. We've got some back on him since, but not enough as you'd notice. Some foods don't suit him any more. He canna' take the things he used to love.'

Brayfield prompted: 'And you say he was dizzy, Mrs Bell?'

'Aye. Terrible unsteady on his legs. Kept fallin' over. An' weak. Could barely lift his arms above his head. Feeble as a bairn. Terrible, terrible.'

Daisy jotted the details in her notebook.

'An' sleep,' Mrs Bell went on, 'he slept all the hours God sent and a few more. I could never wake him. Sleep in the morning, sleep in the afternoon, an' all the night too.'

'Anything else, Mrs Bell?'

'Eh . . .' She considered. 'His talkin'. Words – he couldna' say his words.'

'In what way exactly?'

'Back about face. He'd say white an' mean black. Or chair instead of table. Dinner instead of tea.'

A memory stirred in Daisy's brain, a connection to something in the past, though she couldn't quite pin it down.

Mrs Bell leaned towards Adrian and brushed her fingers lightly over his hair. She didn't have to tell them he'd had enough. He looked drained, his skin grey beneath the bloom of ghastly spots. His eyelids were drooping, his mouth slack.

In the hall Mrs Bell asked in her stolid way if they could continue their talk later, when she'd given Adrian his dinner. Daisy and Brayfield used the time to climb the hill and inspect the site of Adrian's accident.

Brayfield indicated the forest at the top of the field. 'That is the place,' he said, raising his voice above the wind. 'It's not Commission land, I need hardly say.'

'Why wouldn't it be?'

'If it was, there would not be any problem in knowing what happened. The Forestry Commission are not perfect, but they are a sight more safety conscious than the private landowners. The Commission is unionized, and there's not one of our members who is not aware of who comes first in the firing line with these chemicals.'

Daisy hobbled over the grass tussocks in her slippery-soled ankle-boots. She had imagined she'd dressed for the country, but had obviously been mistaken. 'Who does the forest belong to then?'

'An insurance outfit. The Salmon Group. One of those firms that invested in forestry a few years back when there were the tax incentives.'

'But surely,' Daisy panted, trying unsuccessfully to keep her hair from blowing into her eyes, 'they could tell us. I mean, they must know what spray they used.'

'Them? Och, no.'

'What – they're refusing?'

'Not refusing. They are "anxious to assist us in our enquiries" – that is the way they put it at any rate. Which means they refer us to their forestry managers.'

'Who are – ?'

'Willis Bain.' He spoke the name with contempt. 'And *they* say it was fenitrothion.'

'But you don't think so?'

'No.' It was a long hoot of disbelief. 'Fenitrothion has never done that sort of harm.'

'So you think they're lying?'

'I think they are not telling the whole story.'

They had reached the edge of the plantation of firs – or were they pines? Some thirty feet tall, they were planted in ranks so dense that their upper branches were interwoven like a thatch, and their lower branches were shrivelled and brown from the permanent darkness around their feet.

'Lodgepole pine,' Brayfield said. 'See the crowns there, and the way the new growth is eaten back? That's the pine beauty moth. The larvae, they eat the young needles.'

'The trees don't recover?'

'Oh, they recover, so they tell me, but it takes years, and that is all lost income to the owners.'

'But I thought spraying caused more problems than it solved. I thought you killed the natural predators and the bugs got resistant.'

Brayfield snorted, and Daisy sensed the working man's scorn for all theory, Green or otherwise. 'One of our foresters took a look here. He says whatever they used on these trees, it worked fine.'

Daisy swung her bag down from her shoulder, and pulled out her sampling kit. 'Well, let's see what we've got.'

She cut a three-inch square block of grass and topsoil, placed it in a container, sealed the lid, then, climbing into the plantation, repeated the operation, taking soil from under the branches of the trees.

They set off down the hill again. The wind was blowing straight into their faces. Daisy, stiff with cold, a Kleenex clamped to her dripping nose, had to strain to hear what Brayfield was saying.

'Willis Bain are denying the conversation with Adrian took place. They are saying they never sprayed this part of the forest at the time Adrian got his dose. They say they sprayed it back in May.' Brayfield gave an exclamation of disgust. 'When I pressed them again over what they had sprayed it with when they *did* spray it, they would not confirm the fenitrothion. Said it was not company policy to give that sort of information.'

'How can they justify that?' She had to raise her voice to be heard over the wind.

Brayfield shrugged. 'Who can say?'

Daisy blew her nose, which had gone dead at the end. 'Who would have done the spraying itself? Do Willis Bain have a plane?'

'No, no. The work would have been contracted out.'

'Another contractor?' Daisy retorted. 'Blimey, doesn't anybody do anything themselves around here?'

'Willis Bain would not say which company they used for the job. They said it was irrelevant.'

'So the owners don't know anything,' she shouted, 'and the managing agents say there was no spraying, no pilot, no plane and no damage to Adrian?'

'We tried the local authorities and the local Health and Safety Executive to find out if and when they received the obligatory spray notifications, and they said what Willis Bain said, that this estate was done in May. Though they did at least give us the name of the flying company. We found them easily enough. They seemed right enough. They confirmed the May date. They even showed me their records.'

'What was the chemical?'

'They said that was for Willis Bain to tell me. Although they did go so far as to say the chemical was approved for aerial use.'

They paused by the fence at the side of the house. 'The only conclusion I can come to,' Brayfield said, 'is that the original spraying job did not cover this part of the forest, and that the moth suddenly spread and that someone panicked and called in another outfit in a hurry. Cowboys.'

Low clouds raced overhead, obscuring the hills, sending giant shadows chasing across the valley. Daisy's toes had lost all feeling, the cold seemed to have reached into her chest. 'Wouldn't there be some trace of them?' she managed through clenched teeth.

He shrugged. 'You would think so. We tried the local air traffic control people. Nothing. So long as agricultural pilots keep below the commercial air lanes, then they do not have to tell anyone except the military. And the military controllers, they have no record of a crop-spraying aircraft at the right time and place.'

They walked round to the gate. Brayfield held it open for her. 'A dead end, I fear.'

Well, that was nothing new, Daisy reflected. Investigations into chemical accidents were all about a succession of hurdles interspersed with dead ends.

As they entered the house Daisy noticed that another car had appeared in the lane, parked behind their own.

A man, presumably the car-owner, was sitting at the table in the kitchen. He was a big-boned fellow with a square face, a raw complexion and the broad bent nose and dog-eared features of a sporting man. His hair, which was an indistinct sandy-grey, was thin and clung to the mass of his considerable head. His eyes were small and quick-moving and creased up into a fierce expression, as if he regularly used it to frighten people.

He rose from his seat, an exercise that took his head within inches of the ceiling. He was both tall and broad, a giant of a man.

'My brother, Mr Campbell,' said Mrs Bell.

'Alistair Campbell,' the big man grunted. He didn't offer a hand, but dropped heavily back into his chair. 'So? What's to be done?' he demanded, elbows thrust onto the table. Before they had the chance to take off their coats or sit down he persisted: 'What are you proposin'?'

Daisy raised her eyebrows imperceptibly at Brayfield. She had met aggressive barn-storming types before.

As Daisy and Brayfield took chairs opposite each other on either side of Campbell, he threw yet more questions. Mrs Bell handed out cups of tea and retreated to the stove. Brayfield, who seemed unruffled by the verbal bludgeoning, calmly ran through a summary of the position, from the unhelpful response of the landowners to the evasiveness of Willis Bain.

Campbell swept all this aside with an impatient gesture. 'That's all very fine but where does it get the lad, eh? Where does it get him? Nowhere, that's where!' He spoke in a strong accent. 'He will be in need of care an' good food. That takes money.' He indicated his sister. 'Meg here canna' work, canna' leave him, so what's to be done, eh?'

Brayfield looked to Daisy for help.

'Well, there are two possible approaches, Mr Campbell,' Daisy said cautiously. 'First, we could use publicity, which is really all about shaming the opposition into coming to an arrangement – '

'But the money, what about the money?'

'I was just getting to that, Mr Campbell. The idea is that the opposition would eventually decide that some sort of ex-gratia payment is preferable to having their names spread all over the papers the whole time.'

Campbell swivelled on his chair and raised his shoulders at his sister. Neither of them seemed overly impressed by the idea.

Daisy pressed on. 'Another possibility is to go for a civil action in the courts, but I have to warn you that it could take years and an enormous amount of money, and even then – well, as things stand at present, it's simply Adrian's word against the managing agents'.'

Campbell gave her a truculent stare. 'So you're sayin' we should sit back and do nothin'!'

'I didn't quite say that,' Daisy explained patiently. 'What I'm saying is that the chances of getting full damages are not good. First, there's the problem of proving that the events happened as Adrian says they did, which means finding evidence that a chemical was sprayed on this particular section of forest on the day Adrian says the accident happened. Even if we managed to establish those events, in the absence of the aircraft operators and a precise identification of the chemical, we'd only have Willis Bain to go for, and the judge might decide that the company were only, say, fifty per cent liable, which means Adrian's award would get marked down by a half.' She took a sip of the dark tea.

'And then there's the matter of the permanence of Adrian's disability,' she went on. 'If Adrian recovers, well, the claim would by definition hardly be worth pursuing. Unfortunately there's only one way to find out if he's going to recover, and that's to wait and see. At least another six months, I would have thought. Just getting proceedings started can be a very expensive business, you see, so it's hardly worth going to the trouble before then. One would hope to get legal aid, of course, but that's very far from automatic in civil cases like this.' She took another sip of tea to see if the brew improved with familiarity, but it didn't.

'Then,' she continued, 'just when you might reasonably think you were getting somewhere, you'd face the hardest part of all – persuading the medical experts to agree that the chemical, whatever it was, was indeed responsible for Adrian's illness, and that his symptoms weren't the result of something else altogether, something unconnected with the accident.'

A spark of complicity passed between Campbell and his sister. It was the briefest of glances, little more than a flicker, but the warning lights came on in Daisy's brain.

'What have the doctors said so far?' she asked abruptly.

Campbell's brows shot together and he grunted, a deep growl of a sound, and Daisy was reminded of a large bear.

It was Mrs Bell who answered. 'When they first took him into the hospital – at the outset, it was, for two weeks – they said he would recover, that it was just a matter of time. Then, come September, when he was worse, they wanted him in Glasgow. He was there five weeks. He saw two, mebbe three of the specialists. At first they spoke of the chemical all the time, the likely nature of it. They seemed hopeful. They spoke about gettin' him better.

They were kind to Adrian, they couldna' do enough for him. Then . . .' She drew in her lips. 'Then it changed. Adrian was given to other doctors, ones I'd never seen before, ones they never told me about. But even then I didna' realize . . .' She gave a short sigh. 'I didna' see that things had changed . . . Not until Adrian became distressed, not until . . . At first he wouldna' talk to me. An' when I asked the staff, they wouldna' talk to me either. They tried to avoid me. It was as if – ' She broke off suddenly and, looking down at the table, picked harshly at the edge of the formica with her work-stained nails. 'Finally they took me into a room an' told me that, although the chemical might have caused a problem at the start, there was no reason it should now, that Adrian should be better. They said the illness he had now was in his mind. They had a name for it. They called it school phobia. They said it was to do with the death of his father. They said I was – ' She clamped her teeth onto her lower lip. 'They *said* I might not realize it directly, but that I was overprotectin' Adrian . . . that I was encouragin' ma own son to be ill.'

Daisy felt the customary stab of anger that this sort of injustice never failed to arouse in her. She said what she could, telling Mrs Bell that for every doctor who thought like that there was another who was prepared to take chemical damage seriously, but that the science of toxicity was in its infancy, that it was an umbrella science covering an enormous spread of specialities and requiring large teams of scientists which few governments were prepared to fund.

'They sent the education people around,' Campbell announced with a sharp exclamation of contempt. 'Tellin' Meg here to get Adrian back to school or else. I gave them *or else* all right, I can tell you.'

Daisy thought: I bet you did.

'An' the rest – I saw them off too,' Campbell scoffed with pride.

A small worm of alarm turned in Daisy's stomach. 'The rest?'

Mrs Bell answered: 'The social services.'

'Sheep,' Campbell declared. 'Followed the others like sheep.'

Mrs Bell said: 'They wanted me to agree to Adrian goin' back to hospital.'

'What did you tell them?'

Campbell answered for her again, pointing with a dramatic gesture towards the front room. 'That lad leaves here over ma dead body, that's what I told them.'

'Our doctor spoke for us,' Mrs Bell explained quietly. 'He's known Adrian from birth.'

'Over ma dead body,' Campbell echoed, slapping his palm on the table.

'And they accepted that, did they, Mrs Bell? Your doctor's opinion?'

'Aye, they seemed to. Although that hasna' prevented them from returnin' now an' again. To see how Adrian is managin' – that's how they explain it.'

'Pushin' their noses in where they're not wanted,' Campbell rumbled menacingly.

Daisy exchanged a glance with Mrs Bell, and saw in her face the knowledge that, but for the actions of the local doctor, things might have gone very differently.

Campbell, leaning forward, stabbed a finger at Daisy. 'Now this compensation business – what about these landowners, the folk makin' the money? Surely in God's name, they canna' escape fault!'

'They might be held liable for a small share of the blame,' Daisy began carefully. 'But even if everything was proved in our favour, they might well plead good faith and get away with it.'

Campbell gave a fierce jerk of his head. 'What about the makers? The chemical people?'

'We don't know who they are,' Daisy pointed out.

'And if we did?'

'If we did, it wouldn't make that much difference.'

'How can that be? They're makin' an' sellin' the stuff, are they not? Is that not negligent?'

'Oh that we could take them on, Mr Campbell. But negligence – or anything else for that matter – would be impossibly difficult to prove, and they'd throw everything they'd got into it – '

'Och, it's the money that talks, is it?'

'Well, yes – I'm rather afraid it is.'

There was a pause. Mrs Bell brought the teapot round again.

Campbell sat back, stretching his arms forward and splaying his broad hands palms-down on the table. His anger seemed to have given way to a genuine if dogged concern. 'So – his chances are na' very good?'

'At the moment, not brilliant,' Daisy admitted. 'Not unless we find more to go on.'

'An' this is what the lawyer people say, is it?'

'Yes.'

'The experts, eh?' He rolled the words round his mouth with contempt and Daisy thought that perhaps this wasn't the time to admit to her qualifications.

'I see, I see . . .' Campbell said musingly. 'So what must be done to start things movin' along the right road?'

'I suppose there are two – no, three – priorities,' she said. 'The first must be to get Adrian the best medical attention. We're not talking about instant cures, I'm afraid, but there's one specialist we usually recommend. I might be able to arrange for him to come up and see Adrian here.' As she said it she wondered how she could swing the expense of getting Peasedale's ally, Roper, to Scotland without Alan finding out. 'After that, well, we'd need to establish the name of the operators – the flying people – and the chemical they used.'

'Right,' Campbell said briskly. 'We canna' arrive before we begin, eh?'

'I'm sorry?'

'You arrange the doctor, fine. The rest, you can leave it to me.'

Daisy looked at him uncertainly. 'The rest?'

'You said – we canna' proceed until we have some facts, correct?'

'Facts would certainly help – '

'Aye, an' I'll be the man to find them.'

Daisy gave a nervous smile. 'And – er – how are you going to achieve that?'

Campbell stood up suddenly, pushing his chair back with a loud scraping noise. 'People not so very far from here know the answers to the question, do they not?'

'I expect they do,' Daisy agreed, thinking of the Willis Bain manager on the next-door estate and wondering what sort of information-extraction methods Campbell could possibly have in mind. It occurred to her that having Campbell on their side was going to be a liability of the most massive kind. 'But how exactly do you intend to persuade these people to tell you what you want to know, Mr Campbell?'

He didn't reply but gave her a long cautionary stare, as if she should have known better than to ask.

From the sidelines Mrs Bell gave an anxious: 'Alistair.'

'An' then?' he exclaimed, twisting round to shoot her an angry glance. 'They canna' be so hard to find, these people. The flyin' company, they might deny all knowledge. But the aeroplane Adrian saw in the forest there' – he jabbed a finger in the direction of the hill – 'that was real enough, was it not? An' there was a man flyin' it, was there not? They canna' have vanished into the mist. They canna' be so hard to find.' He added ominously: 'One way or another.'

'We did make the fullest possible enquiries,' Brayfield

ventured, sounding mildly defensive. 'Throughout Scotland.'

'An' then?' Campbell retorted. 'Scotland is not yet the centre of the planet, is it?'

Despite everything, Daisy found herself warming slightly to Mr Campbell. Whatever his shortcomings he couldn't be accused of being a lily-liver. Having met enough apathy in her time to run even the most inefficient nationalized industry, this threat of red-blooded action made something of a change. It was unfortunate that it was going in such an aggressive and potentially damaging direction.

Plucking his jacket from the back of the chair, Campbell thrust himself into it as if he were about to go and take on the world that very instant.

Taking a card from her voluminous carpetbag, Daisy got up and followed him down the passage. 'If you find anything out, you'll let me know?' she called.

He turned and, taking her card, read it slowly. 'Aye,' he said finally and, pushing the card deep into an inside pocket, opened the door.

Daisy followed him towards the gate. In flagrant violation of Alan's policy guidelines, she said: 'Don't think we won't give Adrian's case our support, Mr Campbell, because we will. I just didn't want you to think it was going to be easy.'

'Aye . . . Nothin's easy in this life.' He stood firm against the wind, a rock in a stormy sea.

Daisy asked: 'Is it far to Glen Ashard from here?'

Campbell turned his head and stared at her, the fierceness glittering in his eyes.

'Not so far,' he said.

Daisy would have asked more but a gust straight from the Arctic blasted up the lane and, with a quick farewell, she hurried back towards the shelter of the house.

But Campbell came after her. 'You know Mackenzie then?' he demanded, catching her at the door.

'A little.'

'You'll be seein' him while you're here?'

'I wish I was,' Daisy said truthfully.

Campbell followed her into the hall, standing so close over her that she had to twist her head to look up at him. 'That's a regret,' he said, 'a real regret.' He hesitated then seemed to make up his mind about something. 'It's the same sickness,' he said.

That took a moment to sink in. 'What is?'

'Mrs Mackenzie. Her sickness. The same as young Adrian's. There's no doubt in ma mind.'

'But she inhaled wood preservative.'

'Mebbe. But she could have inhaled a lot more without the realization of it, could she not?'

'Why do you think so?'

'Och, the look of her!' he exclaimed. 'The features of the sickness.'

Daisy was doubtful but curious. 'You've seen her? Alusha Mackenzie?'

He looked shifty. 'Not close up, like I am to you, but close enough. She canna' hardly walk. An' thin – she's no more than bones. Aye, it's the same thing all right. There's no doubt in ma mind.'

Daisy must have looked unconvinced because Campbell hurried on. 'Her skin – it has no colour, just like the boy's. An' she sleeps long hours.' He looked mildly embarrassed. 'At least, so I've heard. But most significant' – he paused to add weight to his words – 'she's also right next to Willis Bain forest.'

Suddenly Daisy realized what had struck a chord when Mrs Bell had described the way Adrian mixed up black for white and table for chair. She remembered Nick Mackenzie sitting in Peasedale's window, his elbow on the sill, his eyes screwed up against the brilliant light; she heard his voice describing his wife's symptoms, and the way she interchanged words of quite opposite meanings.

The same illness? The same chemical? It was possible. Of course it was possible. The geography alone was reason for suspicion.

With Campbell's words echoing in her mind, the idea took root and kept her occupied all the way back to London.

Dublensky had that wonderful feeling he always got when spring arrived – and the spring came one hell of a lot sooner in Virginia than it did in Chicago. Already the chestnuts were bristling with buds, the birds yelling their heads off. He felt like hollering right back at them, except that his neighbours – and there were a few fellow employees of the Allentown Chemical Company among them – might think he'd finally gone nuts. They already thought he was dangerously close to being certifiable because he cycled five miles to work each day and five miles back, an idea that seemed to sting his car-driving neighbours into nervous confusion.

The journey took twenty minutes on his ten-speed racer and, though the Allentown Chemical Company's works were not the prettiest of sights in the world and the air around it was not perhaps the sweetest, he always felt better for having been out of doors and taken the exercise.

This morning he arrived in his office, feeling like he could conquer the world. Before settling down to work – and maybe even to conquering the more mundane paperwork which seemed to cover every inch of his desk – he sat quietly for a moment, basking in the warmth of his good fortune. Anne had only last week landed a grant to run a marriage rehabilitation project, and would be setting up shop in a couple of months' time. Tad was doing really great in school: he'd made the seventh grade, the junior football team and won a math prize. A *math* prize, for heaven's sake. The boy was going to be a genius. Well, if not a genius, then a candidate for a top college. Perhaps even Yale. Why not? Dublensky had had to sweat his way through Columbia with precious little parental backup and even less money. Tad would have none of those disadvantages.

And Dublensky himself? Well, he was happy – yes, happy. The Allentown Chemical Company might not be the hub of the universe, and the chlorine-based water-purification products the company manufactured might not be of earth-shattering importance, but they were worth-while, they added something to the wellbeing of mankind, and he had independence, he ran his own department, he was well paid. What more could a man want?

He hummed as he started on the first stack of papers, and was quickly distracted by the latest issue of *Practical Scientist*. There was a four-paragraph item on Morton-Kreiger, he noticed, reporting on the loss of the company's final appeal against the EPA ban on Aldeb. The item closed with a mention of Silveron, and Morton-Kreiger's high hopes for it. Gertholm was briefly quoted as saying he was proud of the company's steady move towards safer cost-effective products.

Dublensky felt amazement and anxiety in equal and bewildering quantities. When he had last contacted Mary Cummins in Chicago just a couple of weeks ago, she had informed him that the results of the new trials on Silveron were due at any moment. Yet here was MKI's own president apparently unaware of what the results must surely contain. Otherwise, how could he be inflating the product like this? It was extraordinary how the company functioned sometimes, like an amorphous monster with several brains, none of them interconnected.

The office came to life around him. Still feeling aggrieved, he put the magazine on one side while he dealt with the day's incoming mail. There wasn't a great deal of it, for which he was extremely thankful, just two or three business letters and the usual collection of circulars, memos and journals. Plus, at the bottom, a typewritten envelope emblazoned 'Strictly Personal' with an Aurora, Illinois, postmark.

The letter was from Burt, the physician who'd been treating the sick workers from the Aurora plant. He was writing to say that one of the original workers had just had a diagnosis of lymph cancer and it was Burt's opinion that this was a direct result of the man's exposure to Silveron. The other two patients were still having severe health problems. Their personalities had changed, their reactions had slowed, their brains were affected in some way that was impossible to measure by any available tests. They also had a multitude of minor symptoms, ranging from eye problems, kidney and liver pain, digestive malfunction, myalgia, severe weight loss – you name it, he said, they seemed to have it.

Dublensky gave a moment's thought to the unfortunate victims. However remote he himself had been from events, he couldn't help feeling the weight of responsibility.

What was more, Burt went on, he was getting new patients from the plant, one who was suffering from similar symptoms, and another three with vaguer ailments that, though not so serious, were still giving him cause for concern. What the hell was going on? he wanted to know. Why weren't the new safety measures at the plant having any effect? And if they weren't effective, why hadn't they been reviewed? Or perhaps there *weren't* any new safety measures? he wrote, underlining the question twice. Perhaps the company had been pulling the wool over his eyes. What did Dublensky have to say about that?

Oh, he'd been given assurances, Burt continued. Dublensky's successor, Dr Mary Cummins, had given him a pledge only the previous week – but now he was damned certain he was being given the run around. Dr Cummins was saying that the product had passed its new toxicity trials with flying colours. How could this be? What did Dublensky know?

Dublensky thought: That's a very good question.

Burt finished by saying he was passing his case notes to the Environmental Protection Agency, and to the workers' union, and that if there wasn't a positive response from Morton-Kreiger soon in the form of confirmation of their toxicity results, he'd be forced to think of approaching the press too.

Dublensky sat back, stunned. Silveron passing its new trials with flying colours? It wasn't possible. He didn't believe it, either as a manager or a scientist. Silveron was trouble, he sensed it, he *knew* it.

He grabbed a piece of paper to draft a letter, a letter that in his mind's eye was going to be so hot that it wouldn't touch the envelope for smoke. Then, breaking off suddenly, he hesitated. Over the last year he'd scorched plenty of paper, he'd fired salvo after salvo of documents and letters in the direction of the MKI management, and look where it had got him. He could almost hear Anne's answer to that one: in Allentown, Virginia, a bought and silenced man.

He wrenched the phone off its cradle and, before he had time to change his mind, dialled head office in Chicago. He had intended to speak to Mary Cummins, but at the last minute found himself asking for Don Reedy.

'What the hell's this with the results on the Silveron trials, Don?' he heard himself bark the moment Don answered.

'The results, John? But they're not available yet.'

Dublensky made a supreme effort to keep his voice low and reasonable. 'According to my information, Mary Cummins already has the results.'

'I don't think that's possible, John. But why don't you ask her?'

'I'm asking you.'

A pause. Reedy's tone hardened. 'Listen, John, we'll let you have the results when they become available, as a courtesy. But I must stress that it's a courtesy. Silveron isn't your baby now, John. You know, it might be a good idea to remember that in future.'

Dublensky said with unusual firmness: 'So when are the results due, Don?'

'Shortly.'

'That's what you told me last time, Don. Everyone keeps telling me that. But when is shortly, Don? And what are the results going to say exactly?'

'Say? How can I know that? What a question, John.' Reedy's voice was heavy with impatience. 'They're trials, for heaven's sake. We can't know the results until they're complete, you know that.'

'But LKY must have given you an intimation.'

Another pause. 'It's TroChem. TroChem are doing the trials.'

'I'm talking about the new trials,' Dublensky explained. 'TroChem did the original trials, LKY Laboratories are doing the new trials.'

'I don't know where you got that idea from. It's Tro-Chem. This time and last time too.'

Dublensky felt himself go cold.

'Listen, I've got to rush, John. A meeting – '

'But Mary Cummins – she told me LKY was doing it!'

'I'm sure there's an explanation. We might have put the job out to tender. Yes, in fact, I'm sure we did. Maybe we considered LKY.'

*Might have put the job out to tender.* The vagueness was almost laughable. Reedy, more than anyone, knew exactly what job was going to tender.

'Why TroChem? *Why*, Don?'

'What the hell – I don't know. But what does it matter?'

'Why did we choose TroChem again, Don?'

Reedy sighed deeply. 'Because they're efficient, competitive and – oh, for God's sake, John.'

'And because they produce favourable results? I mean, don't they? Nice and favourable.'

Reedy's tone shifted again. 'You're letting your emotions rule your judgement, John,' he said coldly.

But Dublensky had the bit between his teeth. He had never realized he could sustain such a level of anger. 'Why TroChem, Don? Could it be because we can rely on them, huh? I mean, because we could be sure the results would be helped along a little, huh? Massaged – isn't that what they call it? Isn't that the right word, Don? Or hadn't you noticed the results came through so good – '

'John, I think you'd better stop – '

'The only reason I kept quiet about this, the only reason I tagged along' – he paused for an instant, aware that his voice had risen unpleasantly, like a fractious child's – 'was because I thought we were going to get some independent data at the end of it. I mean, some data that *meant* something. And all the time – hell . . .' His throat was tight, for a moment he couldn't speak. 'All the time . . . it meant nothing. I mean, if TroChem could make it come right once, they could make it come right again, couldn't they? Wouldn't you say? Christ, Don, don't tell me you hadn't thought about it. Don't tell me it hadn't occurred to you . . .'

He trailed off. There was a silence. Dublensky squeezed his temples in an agony of anger and self-reproach: he'd gone much farther than he'd intended to. Now Reedy would be able to guess the rest; what Dublensky knew about the original trial data – or what he thought he knew. Until half an hour ago he might have been prepared to concede that his suspicions were wildly out of court, that he might possibly be mistaken, but this news had crushed what remained of his fragile faith.

When Reedy finally replied his tone was placatory. 'Now listen, John, you're a fine person. You care, and that's a valuable commodity nowadays. But you *must* keep a sense of proportion. I don't know where you get these crazy ideas from, but there's no truth in them, none at all. You're building mountains out of molehills, and it isn't going to do you any good. I'm saying this because I like you, John, and I don't want to see you end up in trouble.'

'Trouble? Is that where I'm headed, Don?'

A sigh. 'Frankly, yes.'

'I see.' Dublensky screwed up his face into a fierce grimace. 'I see.' He was overcome by moral outrage; his voice wavered, heat pricked at his eyes. 'So what you're saying, Don, is that I'm going to be in trouble for uncovering the truth. Is that right?'

'The truth as *you* see it, John. As you see it. Though why you see it that way, I really don't know.'

Dublensky asked pointedly: 'And what about the plant, Don? What's happened there?'

'What do you mean?'

'The Aurora plant, Don. You keep telling me safety has been improved, you keep telling me about all these wonderful changes, but what's actually been done, Don? I mean *really* done?'

'Plenty. Plenty's been done.'

'Like?'

'Listen, I'm not on the safety executive at Aurora. I don't know the details. But when the people there tell me that the procedures have been tightened up, I believe them because I trust them. Trust, John. Maybe you've heard of it? I have to say I think you're running a bit low on that just now.'

'Yeah. I think you're right, Don,' he said with elaborate irony. 'I think you're right. Very low. The thing is, Don, what really takes my breath away is how you can let this just happen. How you can let it all pass you by and not stand up and *do* something. I mean – I simply don't know.' Without waiting for an answer, Dublensky put the phone down with a bang and thrust his head into his hands. Disbelief, anger and sadness roared through him in quick succession.

He looked up, his eyes turning instinctively towards the window and the light. The spring sunshine was illuminating the long roofs and tall chimneys of the works with brilliant radiance. Amazingly, it was the same wonderful day that it had been a few moments ago.

He thought of Tad and Anne and their settled lives; he thought of his own simple requirements for happiness. One wouldn't have thought it was too much to ask, a little simple happiness, but it seemed no sooner grasped than lost again.

When he got home, he would go to his desk and take out the file he kept there and study it again. He clung to the idea that this might help him towards the right decision, that somehow the figures would take on a new light. But he knew that this was too much to hope for. The figures would be just the same as before.

He would have to do something. But what? All the possibilities terrified him. He was no coward, but he was no hero either.

Anne would know what to do. Well, he hoped so.

Suddenly the end of the day seemed a long way away; all he could think about was getting home. Bracing himself to look his secretary in the eye while he told her an outright lie, he said he was feeling unwell, and, turning down the offer of a ride home, bicycled off into the sunshine.

At four that afternoon his secretary took an internal call from the office of the chief executive of the Allentown Chemical Company requiring Dublensky's presence, and had to inform them that he was away, unwell. That didn't stop the chief executive from calling Dublensky at home and asking him to come back in. The chief executive, a great one for doing things by the book, took pride in doing his firing humanely, face to face.

# Chapter 12

As always, there was something to be salvaged, the essence of the theme, some of the harmony, the best of the words. Nick worked all morning, smoking incessantly, phoning through to Mrs Alton for periodic cups of coffee. When he took a break, it was only to walk around the studio, to leaf through a book or read yesterday's paper. He didn't go out. There was a gale raging. For a time he stood at the window watching the trees pulling and straining under the force of the wind. The wind was not southwesterly, as was usual, but easterly, the one direction to which Ashard's park, even the glen itself, lay open, a wind that, if it continued for any length of time, was likely to bring down some of the more fragile and precious trees.

By early afternoon he was finally getting somewhere. He'd abandoned whole sections of the words and replaced them with new stuff which was much simpler, less impossibly pretentious. Now the theme, such as it was, seemed to fit.

At some point Alusha stole in, so ghostlike in her approach that he didn't hear her until she touched his shoulder. She announced that she was going for a walk.

'Very windy,' he said, scribbling down a word before he forgot it.

'But I like the wind,' she said in a curiously flat voice that was devoid of enthusiasm.

'It's easterly. Absolutely freezing.'

'I don't care.'

There was no answer to that. Perhaps a short walk round the rose garden would after all do some good. Walking was the one activity that, against all the odds, she had managed to keep up through the long winter months and which, even on her worst days when the effort of walking almost killed her, seemed to cheer her up.

He turned, intending to give her a brief kiss and return to his work, but there was something about the sight of her that made him pause. The skin of her thin face, already translucent, was tinged with grey, and her eyes, which were remote and unfocused, wore a dull absorbed expression, as if her mind was roaming over quite another planet.

After a moment her attention came back from wherever it had been and she put on a vague smile.

He stood up and put his arms around her. 'Love you,' he said. 'Love you,' she echoed. The smile was there, but he noticed she was smiling with her mouth, not her eyes.

'Crazy to go out,' he said. 'You'll get blown down the loch.' And he wasn't entirely joking; her balance was far from good.

'I'll be all right.' There was a stubborn note in her voice which he recognized only too well.

Releasing her, he said: 'I'll come with you.'

'No,' she said. 'No. I love the wind.' Her voice was at once sharp and unsteady. 'I love it. I want to go on my own.' Two livid spots of colour appeared high on her cheeks, and her eyes were suddenly bright and luminous, gleaming with a strange excitement. This change was so abrupt and so untypical of her that he stared into her face, puzzled and curious, but also alarmed. Her eyes glistened so brilliantly that for an instant he thought he had misread her mood and that she was for some reason close to tears. Then he suddenly knew what it was, and knowing, couldn't think why he hadn't guessed before. She was spaced out. Dosed up. High. The realization, like so many in the last few months, made him die a little inside.

He knew then that the pain must be very bad.

'I'll come with you,' he repeated quietly.

'No!' She was getting cross.

'But I want to.'

'No! I'm going on my own!'

Maybe it was the strange almost unrecognizable expression on her face, maybe it was simply that the winter had been far far too long, but something closed his emotions down tight as a drum. He knew he should argue, he knew he should prevent her from going out in this weather, but having finally broken through his creative block after so long he was loath to deflect his emotional energy from his work.

She knew she had won. She stood staring up at him for a moment, looking fierce and implacable and oddly emotional all at the same time. Then, pushing herself up on her toes, she gave him a last kiss, a peremptory brush on the cheek, and, turning quickly away, was gone.

He couldn't work after that, of course. Five minutes later he gave up trying and went out into the gale, intending to catch up with her. But though he walked quickly through the rose garden and round the edge of the lawns, there was no sign of her. Completing the circle, he made his way back through the kitchen garden, but she wasn't there either, and he went into the house again, wavering between the urge to search for her and the knowledge that she would bitterly resent any such intrusion on her space.

Leaving the studio door open, making a pretence of working, he kept an ear open for her return. Finally, just when he was getting prepared to risk her wrath by organizing some of the estate workers into a surreptitious search party, he heard the banging of a distant door and the murmur of female voices, and felt the tension drain out of him in a rush. He called, and echoing down the long passage came a distant response. By the time he got to the kitchen it was empty, but he saw Alusha's distinctive red scarf thrown across a chair. He thought of going to find her, but knowing she'd probably gone upstairs for her afternoon nap, he decided not to disturb her and, caught up by his work, he went back to the studio, anxious to make up for lost time.

It was two hours later and getting dark before he realized that the voices in the kitchen had been those of Helen and Mrs Alton, and that Alusha had never returned.


He stopped and, gasping for breath, shouted her name, but his call, like all of the calls before it, was sucked away and lost by the wind. He shouted again, straining to be heard over the thrumming and thrashing of the trees, but it was useless, like shouting under water. He shone the torch full circle, then upwards. The forest was alive with movement, the topmost branches contorting wildly, the pines creaking and groaning in loud complaint.

He pushed on fast, climbing steadily up the glen, his feet stumbling and jarring against the compacted earth and rock of the riverside path. He cast the torch-beam rhythmically from side to side, lighting the dead bracken and grasses and boulders on either side, and below, the fast rushing water. There was nothing to see. Just empty forest, and a ringing silence in his brain, and a deadness in his stomach.

He imagined her lying off the path somewhere, cold and barely conscious. Would he hear her if she was calling? Would he spot her? The answer was no, and no again. He'd probably missed her already, probably passed just inches away from her. Despair pulled at him out of the darkness.

With a conscious effort he tried to think logically and dispassionately, to imagine where she might have been making for, the route she would have taken. He realized that he wasn't absolutely certain where she went on her more adventurous afternoon outings. On their morning stroll, which they always took together, they rarely went further than the garden because that was usually enough to tire her out until lunch time. It had never occurred to him that she might go further in the afternoons, although in the past few weeks she had mentioned the glen several times in a nostalgic, thoughtful way, as if something had happened to remind her of it. He had assumed it was the drive they'd taken up the track to the moorlands one brilliant day in early March, but maybe he was entirely wrong, maybe she'd come this way on her own. Maybe.

And today – what had happened today? Had she meant to take a long walk? Or had she simply gone further than she intended, felt tired and stopped for a rest? Or suddenly felt too ill to drag herself home?

He pressed on, the uncertainty and fear clutching at his heart.

Above the low roar of the wind came the sound of thundering water. The fall below Macinley's Rock.

This was crazy – what was he doing here? She couldn't have made it this far, even at her most determined. It was a long climb, even for a fit person: he was panting hard and, despite the cold, the sweat was damp on his back.

He stopped, torn between the need to carry on and be certain of having covered all the ground, and the over-powering suspicion that he was wasting his time. He left the path, fought his way up the bank past rock and scrub and scrambled onto the main track. He forced himself to listen and heard nothing but the awful melancholy of the wind. Closing his ears, he turned quickly away, and realized that, for no reason that bore thinking about, he had decided to turn back.

The realization brought a new gust of despair. It was so very cold. Even if she was wearing a thick jacket, she'd be almost frozen by now. The thought was like something driven against his heart, almost unendurable, and to sup-press the agony, he began to shout her name again, forcing his voice over the rushing and roaring of the wind. His throat grew hoarse, his voice descended to a gasp. Momentarily defeated, he paused, shoulders hunched, and reached for his breath.

Down the track in the distance, through the trees, a light glimmered and flickered, and intensified steadily, growing into the long yellow beams of headlights. Behind it came another car, and another. Duncan's search party.

The first vehicle ground to a halt in front of him, and several people got out.

Duncan's voice said: 'We've a group searching the pastures, Mr Mackenzie. And another going east and south of the house. And a third starting up this way.' He stepped in front of the lights, masking Nick from the glare. 'What d'you think – shall we send a couple of men up the glen? Or just sweep down from here towards the house?'

Nick leant against a tree, his legs unaccountably weak. 'I don't think she could have got this far.'

'Right-ho.' There was forced optimism in his voice. 'We'll get set then. The police should be here soon enough.'

'The police? *Why?*'

'No avoiding it. The village . . .' Duncan indicated the men grouped around the cars. 'Everyone's here.'

Of course. No secrets in the village. Nevertheless the thought of the whole thing becoming public, of all the attention made Nick squirm inwardly. Once the police came thundering up the glen, the press wouldn't be far behind. Alusha would be furious.

Duncan drew closer and said in an undertone: 'The police were asking about kidnap. I said I didn't think it was likely. Was that right?'

Kidnap. Nick hadn't even considered it. *Christ.* He wasn't ready to make room for those sort of possibilities. 'You did right,' he said.

The cars were being backed round, ready to head down the hill again; their lights cut an arc through the trees.

Someone came out of darkness offering Nick a cup. A hot drink. Nick put it to his lips, scented coffee, and took a sip. It took him a moment to realize it was laced with whisky. He was gripped by an instantaneous and overwhelming urge to swallow it, along with the rest of the cup, a flask or two, and the contents of an entire distillery. Postponing the decision to swallow, he held the liquid in his mouth, moving it slowly over his tongue. It tasted fantastic. Memories flashed onto the screen of his mind, memories of liquid nights and technicolour days and wondrous oblivion.

He let the liquid fall to the back of his throat. Just one taste would do him good.

The next moment he gagged and spat the stuff onto the ground. It was several moments before he straightened up. A vast heat rushed over him, making the sweat run again.

A close thing. There'd been nothing that close since he'd left New York. What frightened him more than anything was how bloody marvellous it had tasted, and how deep his craving was, even after so many years.

He chucked the rest of the coffee onto the ground and realized he'd spattered someone's feet. He muttered an apology.

'No matter,' returned a voice. He wasn't sure why, but he felt the man had been watching him for some time.

People were moving about, sorting themselves into groups. There were twenty men, maybe more. Nick felt a sudden and savage impatience at the terrible slowness with which they moved. Finally, when Duncan had given a few last instructions, the groups began to start off.

Duncan called Nick towards the nearest car. Duncan plucked something off the back seat and waved it in the air. 'This should help!' It was the image-intensifier which Nick had given him for poacher-catching.

They drove slowly down the track, following the flickering pinpricks of torchlight that had fanned out through the forest.

The next hours were both vivid and dreamlike. Sometimes Nick felt alive and sick with fear, at other times he felt oddly apathetic and detached, as if someone had put the whole thing on film and slowed the projector. For the most part he simply felt ill, his mouth dry, his stomach light and jittery.

Halfway down the glen, they were met by a couple of police vehicles which disgorged men and dogs.

At the edge of the woods where the track looped towards the house, people grouped together again, smoking and whispering quietly, waiting for fresh instructions. Messages from the house brought reports from the other search parties: nothing had been found. The police took the opportunity to put questions to Nick. Gathering around him, their voices deferential but firm, they asked if Alusha always went for walks and how long she generally stayed out and if there was any reason why she should have gone for a longer walk than usual. It occurred to Nick that they were looking for a motive for her to have kept walking – a marital row, an unhappy marriage, a lover waiting at the end of the drive. It was all so ridiculous he didn't know whether to laugh or cry. He answered in monosyllables, if only to prevent himself from letting his rage show, and more than once they had to prompt him for a reply.

It was her illness that impressed them more than anything else. When it came to using police time, illness obviously ranked a long way above marital tiffs. He didn't tell them quite how ill she was. Apart from anything else, he didn't think it was any of their business.

It began to rain, a thin spiky inconsequential rain, then, all too quickly, a more determined rain that spattered against his face and trickled down his neck. He gulped some coffee – unlaced – smoked two cigarettes in quick succession and endured Duncan's well-meaning assurances.

Everything was dreamlike, then all of a sudden he awoke again. The urgency flooded back into him and he pushed

forward and began to argue with the police for an immediate return to the glen. The inspector, a soft-spoken man,
listened with attention but not, apparently, conviction.
There was no indication she had gone up the glen, was
there? the inspector argued. It wasn't very likely, was it,
not on such a stormy day. Wouldn't she have stayed closer
to home? Particularly since she was so unwell.

Forcing himself into a state of exaggerated calm, Nick
repeated stubbornly: 'We *must* search the glen!'

'The main paths have already been covered, have they
not, Mr Mackenzie? Would we not do better to – '

'The upper glen – no one's been there!'

'Why do you think she might have gone up there, Mr
Mackenzie?'

'*Because* – ' But he was beyond speech, beyond explanation, his mind a nightmare of half-realized fears and
confusions. Catching himself on the point of losing control,
he withdrew some way into the darkness and paced back
and forth, smoking hard. Just when he thought he'd got
himself into some sort of shape, the inspector announced
his plans for the search. It would be concentrated on the
area around the house and would slowly expand outwards.
The denser sections of forest and undergrowth would be
left until daylight.

The wind eased abruptly, and a heavier rain began to
fall, a drenching pervasive rain that drummed on the roofs
of the cars and kicked at the ground, so that people made
for the shelter of the trees.

Nick's vision of Alusha shifted agonizingly: he saw the
rain seeping into her clothes, saturating her already cold
skin, freezing her slowly to death.

He couldn't stand it any longer. Striding away, he
jumped into Duncan's car, rammed it into reverse, and,
twisting the wheel savagely, executed a tight turn.

As he jammed the accelerator down and shot off up the
glen he was aware of someone swinging into the back seat

and slamming the door shut behind him. He glanced over his shoulder.

'Duncan?'

'No. It's me, Alistair Campbell.'

Nick considered telling the man, whoever he was, to bugger off, then thought better of it. He might be useful.

The car bumped and leapt up the rough road. Nick didn't slow until he reached the point just below Macinley's Rock where his earlier search had ended. Then he parked and set off briskly up the main track, sweeping the under-growth with his torch-beam. As if by some previous agreement, the other man cut down to the path by the side of the river and walked in parallel, so that the dull glint of his light was visible through the trees.

Above Macinley's Rock, Nick saw the other man's light fall behind as it flickered slowly round the sides of the Great Pool. Eventually it came back onto the path and gradually drew level until they were once again in parallel. The wind had dwindled further and now the forest resounded to the steady drum and patter of the rain.

Half a mile later the other man's light rose to meet him as the lower path left the river and converged with the main track. The two men met without speaking and fell into step one behind the other.

To the right the forest thickened: they had reached a dense stand of pines. Nick paused. The stand continued for perhaps half a mile. Beyond it there was nothing but open moor and grazing sheep. It was just possible she had got this far – it had occurred to him that the morphine might have made her feel unusually energetic – but no further. Quite apart from the distance and the climb, she didn't like the darkness of the pine forest any more than she liked the bleakness of the open moor.

Desperate for a smoke, he stepped into the shelter of the trees and reached inside his jacket. His packet was empty. The other man, watchful as some shadowy manservant,

stepped forward and held out a packet which he illuminated with his torch. Nick stole a glance at him in the flare
of the match, but didn't recognize him.

Their cigarettes lit, the two men started back down the
track.

Campbell spoke. 'I could cross the river just by the pool
there an' follow down the other bank.'

'No.' The path was rough on the opposite side, the bank
very steep. It wasn't a possibility.

'She couldna' manage that, then?'

'No.'

'Not so good at the walkin'?'

'No.'

'Ma sister's lad's the same. Canna' hardly manage to
leave the house.'

What the hell was he talking about? Nick grunted
negatively and hurried on, swinging his torch-beam purposefully from side to side. The rain dropped over the beam
and cut across it like a curtain. He called Alusha's name,
and got the constant patter of the rain in return.

'It's the same malady, you know.'

Christ, Nick thought savagely, what a time for obtuse
social chat. He walked even faster, determined to shake the
other man off.

'It's a chemical,' the man persisted, matching his pace
effortlessly to Nick's. 'They were usin' it all over against
the beauty moth. The lad, he got a dose of it in June, just
before your wife. He's not been right since.'

Despite everything, a small memory triggered in Nick's
mind. A letter, something he'd received months ago – other
cases, the name Campbell.

There was something else though, something about the
man's voice, something familiar which he couldn't quite
place.

'Not the same thing,' Nick snapped with finality.

Now it was Campbell's turn to be silent. Eventually he murmured: 'If you say so.'

Suddenly Nick felt a jolt of recognition. The voice, the accent. Even the place. *God*. He swung his torch full onto Campbell. The face was square, with wet hair plastered down onto his forehead. The features were unfamiliar, but the build – oxlike and unusually tall – *yes*.

'You.'

Campbell raised a hand against the light.

'Christ! Christ!' Nick shook with rage. 'It *is* you!'

Campbell lowered his hand. 'I have to say that I canna' entirely deny the fact. But I've not touched a fish in this pool, not since June, an' that's the truth, Mr Mackenzie.'

'Get the hell out of my sight!' Nick turned on his heel and strode off, enraged by the intrusion, furious at the diversion. He went fast, swinging his torch rapidly, shouting Alusha's name until his voice descended into feeble infuriating croaks. It was some time before he glanced back over his shoulder. No sign of a light on the track. Then he saw it, down on the river path once more, a soft pinprick flattened and blurred by the rain.

He pressed on, suddenly aware of how long he'd been out of contact with Duncan and the main search party. Reaching the car, he jumped in and started up. Campbell could damned well walk back. Yet something made him switch off and get out again.

There was no sign of a light. He yelled Campbell's name.

There was only the rushing of the water and the drumming of the rain, then a voice came echoing back. From above, from beyond the invisible bulk of Macinley's Rock.

Nick bawled: 'Hurry.'

The voice came again, rising above the deathly splatter of the rain. A long call that sounded like: '*Here. O-v-e-r h-e-r-e.*'

Nick didn't move. He was gripped by an indescribable fear.

He waited, dreading the words, yet needing to hear them again.

They came once more, as he knew they would.

'O-v-e-r h-e-r-e.'

Finally he moved. Each step felt more unreal than the last; his body no longer belonged to him. He broke into an uneven stride, half run half walk, and made his way panting up the track until, abreast of Macinley's Rock, he began to climb down the slope towards the water. Hitting rock, he stumbled and fell, landing heavily on his hip and dropping the torch. Picking it up again, he remembered, by a great effort of will, to shine the beam in front of him. He blundered through undergrowth, past massive stones and across a mossy bank until, finally, he reached the edge of the pool.

'Here.' The harsh cry was unexpectedly close.

Nick shone the torch around, then down. The beam caught Campbell's huddled form, crouched at the pool edge. He was cradling a bundle which lay half in, half out of the water.

Campbell raised his head. His face was contorted into a terrible grimace. The bundle unfolded from his lap. First an arm, then a white face fell back over Campbell's knees.

Burning rage came over Nick like a hot sea, his brain exploded with pain.

'*Get off her, get off! You bastard! You bastard!*'

He was aware of screaming, aware of the other man moving away, aware, finally, of dropping to his knees and pulling Alusha onto his lap.

Then the heat left him as suddenly as it had come, cooled by the ice of Alusha's skin.

# Chapter 13

THE BEAUTY MOTH didn't live up to its name. Small, little more than an inch from wingtip to wingtip, a uniform and rather drab brown, it had no great claims to beauty although, when Daisy put her nose closer to the glass of the sample box, she saw that the upper wings were marked with an attractive and intricate tortoiseshell pattern.

She commented: 'It doesn't look big enough to eat a whole forest.'

The bugman shuffled his feet. 'Well, the moth itself *doesn't*, of course,' he said with a quick smile. 'It's the larva that's the gobbler.' He pointed to a striped caterpillar impaled on the next pin.

They walked back to the bugman's office, which was situated in a modernish wing of the Edwardian country house that was the headquarters of the forestry research station. The office windows, partially obscured by stacks of files and papers, looked out onto a dense shrubbery and, beyond, to the tall forest that surrounded the grounds.

Daisy asked: 'What would a forest manager do then, if he had a bad outbreak of pine beauty moth?'

The bugman settled in his chair. He was a bearded Welshman with the confident easy-going manner that comes from knowing his stuff and having the happy occasion to impart it. 'You'd have to spray the forest,' he said. 'There'd be no way round that. But we're developing virus applications that are absolutely specific to the moth and therefore very much safer – '

'Developing? They're not in use then?'

'Ah.' He gave a sight of regret. 'Still too expensive.'

'So a private contractor would still use an insecticide?'

'At the moment – yes.'

'And what would he use? Can you give me a list of the most likely chemicals?'

The bugman looked surprised. 'A list? Well, I could try. But really, there's only one in common use.'

'Only one?' Daisy echoed, adjusting rapidly to the likelihood of disappointment.

The bugman rasped a hand over his beard and puckered his lip, as if considering the possibility that he might have overlooked something. 'Aerial application, you said? No – there's really only one.'

Fenitrothion. He said the word slowly in case she wanted to copy it down. But there was no need. Fenitrothion was well known. It was an organophosphate that had been around for some time. If it had killed and maimed people on a regular basis the news would have seeped out by now. As it was, it didn't even rate a mention on Catch's 'dirty dozen' of the most dangerous chemicals. Although it was always possible that, despite everything, they had all been missing something.

'And there's really nothing else?'

'Not that I know of.'

There were questions she should ask, but her brain was thick with tiredness and it took a moment for her to grasp them.

'What follow-up studies have been done on fenitrothion?' she asked finally.

'Ah!' The bugman went to a shelf, selected two identical pamphlets and handed her one. The pamphlet was titled *Population, Biology and Control of the Pine Beauty Moth*. On the cover was a glossy photograph of the caterpillar, no longer the faded drab specimen of the show case but a smartly attired fellow in green, brown and white stripes, captured in the act of eating his way down a branch of pine needles.

The bugman leafed through his copy. 'There's a summary of all the major impact studies ... On birds mainly ...'

'What about the impact on people?' she asked.

'The operators, you mean? They have to take precautions, of course. Mixing the chemical, filling tanks and so on. They wear full gear – you know, space suits, masks.' The bugman found his place in the pamphlet and read: 'The effect on humans is ... insignificant. Well, that sounds fairly definite, doesn't it?'

'What about people caught in the spray drift, people on the ground?'

'Um ...' He referred again. 'Not discussed here. Probably not enough people to study. They're always careful to clear the area, you know, before they start spraying.' He replaced the pamphlet on the shelf. 'No, if you wanted to know more on that, you'd have to ask a toxicologist. Though I have to say I've never heard of anyone having any long-term health problems from fenitrothion.'

'A plane that was spraying the beauty moth – would it have to be specially equipped?'

'If it was using ultra-low-volume technique, yes.'

'What's that?'

'Ah.' He gleamed with quiet pride. 'It's what we've been pioneering. Much smaller chemical droplets, more efficiently distributed. Less chemical used, more effective, less damage to wildlife.'

'So the plane, what would it need for that?'

'Special atomisers. They fit them onto special arms under the wings.'

'And this ultra-low technique, is it in wide use? Would there be many aircraft fitted up for it?'

'Not yet,' he said with the disappointment of an ideas man finding himself pitted against the inertia of the real world.

'Otherwise . . . if a plane was using the old technique?'

'Then the regular spray booms, I suppose. But they give you nasty big droplets, and you miss the larvae who aren't right at the top of the canopy. A high miss rate.'

A high miss rate. Perhaps in Loch Fyne they had suffered a high miss rate during an early spraying, and had needed to dose the forest again in a hurry.

The Metro's heater choked a stream of luke-warm air, and Daisy had turned onto the Farnham bypass before her feet began to defrost. Even then she couldn't shake off a permanent sense of cold which seemed to have rooted itself low in her stomach. The drive back up the A3, far from being an opportunity to think, became a long exercise in staving off drowsiness and failing concentration. Maybe it was just lack of sleep; she had stayed up until one, sifting through the latest batch of case histories from EarthForce in Washington, going through the information from military air traffic control on the flights sanctioned in the Loch Fyne area. Then, when she'd finally got to bed, it had been to lie half-way between wakefulness and nightmare, her brain dogged by images of a featureless woman lying face down in water. Later, when she finally slept, it was to dream that Adrian, like Alusha Mackenzie, was dead.

She found a parking meter at the back of King's Cross, an unheard of stroke of fortune, and, dodging the ladies of the night who seemed to be out in force, she hurried through the litter-strewn streets to the office.

Jenny was perched at her desk, clad from spiky head to booted toe in black, long fringes of jet beads trailing from her jacket sleeves, like the wings of a recently alighted raven. Crouched over the telephone, she waved a batch of papers at Daisy and raised her eyebrows to indicate their importance.

A mug of coffee sat steaming at Jenny's elbow and, taking the papers in one hand, Daisy deftly removed the coffee with the other and headed for her office. Alan's door was partially open and she could hear his cool reasonable murmurings as he talked to someone on the phone. She padded quickly past and slipped into her office, closing her door silently behind her. Alan had been trying to catch her for a couple of days now but, having a fair idea of what he wanted to talk about, she was not too keen to be caught.

She sat down and, swigging at the coffee, glanced over the papers. They were copies of the legal correspondence on the Adrian Bell case which Mrs Bell had arranged for her solicitor to send over, though not without difficulty. Mrs Bell's solicitor had not taken kindly to the idea of Catch's involvement, and had responded to Daisy's phone calls with what could only be described as resistance.

Nonetheless, the correspondence was here, and there was quite a lot of it, including, she noted straight away, a letter from Willis Bain's lawyers.

The first part of the letter contained few surprises. Willis Bain absolutely denied any liability concerning the alleged accident. They also denied having treated the woodland next to the Bell home at any time during the previous June, or indeed in the weeks immediately adjacent to the alleged date in June. The block of forest in question had been sprayed only once during the year in question, in mid May, they said, when every possible safety procedure had been carried out: notifications posted to all neighbouring properties, including the Bells', and the police and local authority informed in accordance with legal requirements. Furthermore, the spraying method had conformed to Ministry of Agriculture and Civil Aviation Authority guidelines. The pesticide used was fully approved for aerial use.

Fully approved. Which meant that, unless Willis Bain were lying through their teeth, they had used fenitrothion.

Daisy went through the bundle once more before turning

to her messages. Peasedale, she saw, had called again. Like
Alan, he had been trying to get hold of her for the last two
days. The reminders to call him, penned in block letters on
yellow stickers, sat in silent rebuke on the body of the
phone.

'Fenitrothion,' she said immediately Peasedale answered.
'Could it possibly have been involved in the Bell and
Mackenzie cases?'

'Listen, it's appalling – Nick Mackenzie's wife.' Peasedale's usual tone of scientific detachment had escaped him
and he spoke almost plaintively, interspersing his words
with sudden sighs. 'Appalling. Was anything being done
for the poor woman? I mean was there any follow-up? Was
she under a competent toxicologist? I can't get it out of my
mind. I keep thinking about her. Do they know exactly
how she died? Was it the effects of some treatment she was
getting? I have this awful feeling that maybe I missed
something, that maybe I didn't look into it closely enough.'

Daisy told him what he wanted to hear. 'It wasn't you.
There wasn't anything you could have done.'

'Do they know exactly how she died?' Peasedale
repeated.

'I'm not sure,' she lied, remembering only too vividly
the minute details that Simon had relayed to her from the
*Sunday Times* news desk, and, by remembering, experienced some of the initial horror all over again.

'You haven't been in touch?' Peasedale asked.

'Hardly.'

Picking up the warning note in her voice, he retreated.
'No, I suppose it wouldn't be the right moment.'

'No. Now how about fenitrothion?'

'Fenitrothion?' he repeated blankly.

'Could it have done this sort of damage?'

There was a silence. She could almost see him sitting there
in his lab, perched on his stool like a stork on a chimney
pot. 'My first instinct is no. But let me have a think about

it, will you? A day or two? I'd really like to stick with this
one. I mean – I'd like to feel that I'd done my utmost. You
know.'

Daisy knew. It was all about making oneself feel better
about something one felt bad about.

'And Adrian Bell,' she said. 'It could well be the same
stuff. When can you and Roper get up there?'

'If you can fly us, I think we could make it this weekend.'

Return flights plus car hire plus meals. She wondered
what part of the expense budget could be expanded to
absorb it.

Ringing off, she managed to keep out of Alan's way for
another five minutes, but it couldn't last. She heard him
come off the phone, leave his office to chat to Jenny and
then, with the inevitability of a parent coming in search of
an unruly child, he was at her door and sidling in.

He sat at the side of her desk and gave her a sympathetic
but cautious smile. 'How are you doing?'

'Fine,' she said looking back at her work.

'Listen, the Mackenzie case – you have to look on it as
just one of those things.'

Alan took pride in being able to rationalize everything,
to take the cool dispassionate stance, to learn and grow, as
he liked to put it.

When she didn't respond, he tried: 'These things
happen.'

But Daisy wasn't in the mood for banalities. 'They do,
do they?'

'You mustn't take it personally.'

She sat back in her chair. 'Sure.' She heard the sarcasm
in her voice but was unable to suppress it. 'I could always
pretend I'd done a good job.'

'That's not fair. You couldn't have done any more than
you did, not when the Mackenzies had shut you out.'

'But I should have *realized*.'

'Realized what?'

'That it couldn't possibly have been Reldane.'

'But how could you?'

'Jeese, it was blindingly obvious, Alan. Or should have been, if I'd had a fraction of my brain in gear.'

'Okay, let's say you should have guessed,' said Alan, at his most conciliatory. 'But would the Mackenzies have listened? Even if you'd had some evidence to back you up? I doubt it. I get the impression Nick Mackenzie had made up his mind about what happened and wasn't about to change it, not for anybody. And even if you *had* persuaded him to listen, d'you think it would have made any difference? I mean, to what happened. I really don't think so.'

She was ready to accept that he might be right, but at the same time she wasn't ready to let the matter go that easily. She was still feeling too angry with herself. She needed time to come to terms with what had happened in her own time, at her own pace.

'It might have made a difference,' she said unrelentingly.

'Come on, Daisy. *If* someone had found out what it was that affected her, *assuming* it was a chemical – '

'What do you mean, *assuming*?'

'Okay, okay.' He held up a hand to signal his unconditional withdrawal. 'Okay, so it was a chemical, and if we'd known which one, *maybe* it would have changed things . . . But we never knew, did we? And we never will, either.'

Daisy picked up some papers and shuffled them noisily. 'Maybe we won't,' she said evasively. 'But then, maybe we will.' She could feel Alan staring at her, trying to work out what that statement might mean in terms of her own involvement.

'Well . . . It would be good to know, of course,' he said dubiously. 'But the cause and effect would be hard to prove. After the event, I mean.'

Perhaps it was the sleepless nights, but she was too tired to argue any more. She dropped the papers back onto the desk with a plop. 'Just so long as Adrian Bell doesn't go the same way.'

Alan looked suitably horrified at the thought. 'Of course not. We must do all we can.'

'Then you'll agree to Catch stumping up the cost for Peasedale and Roper to go and see him?'

Resentment sprang into Alan's eyes, as if he suspected her of having led the entire conversation up to this neat little trap. 'Can't Adrian come down to London?' he suggested weakly. She shook her head.

Alan was not graceful in defeat – he pulled a succession of unhappy faces – but he did at least recognize defeat when he saw it. 'Okay,' he grumbled. 'I'll swing it somehow. But just this once, Daisy.'

'Thanks, Alan.'

He grunted and made a hasty retreat. Daisy sat for a moment, staring at the wall, letting the last of her emotions subside. Then, turning with relief towards more positive thoughts, she lifted the phone and called Simon. He wasn't at home, but the *Sunday Times* seemed to think he was somewhere on the editorial floor. While she held, she allowed an indulgent vision to slide into her mind, a picture of herself in Simon's flat having a hot bath and a glass of wine while Simon got dinner and listened to her troubles.

He was sounding rushed when he finally answered. 'Pre-election hysteria,' he explained. 'The latest poll just put Labour five points ahead.'

She made her little plea – or maybe it was a cry for help.

'Dinner?' he echoed, and there was a sudden distance in his voice. She could almost see him calculating the time and effort it would take to shop and prepare the food and cook it. 'I won't finish till late, but I suppose I could pick something up from the Indian,' he suggested eventually, making no attempt to conceal the reluctance in his voice.

The thought of a featureless curry of unknown origin

did not enthrall Daisy, but tonight she'd have been happy with a can of beans so long as it was cooked by someone else. 'That sounds fine.'

'The fridge is rather bare,' he mentioned. 'I can pick up some milk, but we'll still need bread. And I think I'm out of fruit ...' He left the observation hanging in the air, awaiting suggestions. But her suggestions box, like the fridge, was bare, and when she failed to answer he rang off, sounding aggrieved.

Daisy reflected that Simon had many qualifications for the New Man – he related well to women, he made lists, pushed shopping trolleys, cooked adventurous Sunday lunches, consulted her religiously over film and theatre bookings – but this was one occasion when Daisy wished she could trade some of this refurbished masculinity for a burst of wild old-fashioned initiative, even – dare she say it – protectiveness.

It was late, but, unable to summon the energy to leave, she flicked half-heartedly through her mail. Alice Knowles had sent the latest news of her case, adding a note to say that despite the recent setbacks – she had been refused legal aid – she was still determined to go ahead with the legal action, come what may. Doubtless Alan would think Daisy had secretly been encouraging her, which she had not, but then there was nothing Daisy could say on the subject of the Knowles case that didn't bring scepticism into Alan's eyes.

The next note was from Peasedale's assistant, saying that the latest blood samples from the Lincolnshire farmer's wife suffering suspected Aldeb contamination still hadn't arrived. Daisy read the note with disbelief. This was the third time the arrangements had gone wrong, despite the most thorough preparations. When the farmer had replied to her advertisement in the farming magazine, Daisy had persuaded him to agree to a monthly monitoring programme for his wife's blood, whereby Peasedale would measure the samples for enzyme, hormone and liver-function levels. But with the samples continually getting held up, it was making a nonsense of the whole programme. The farmer's wife was called Ruth and she answered the phone in her habitually subdued manner, with a soft almost apologetic greeting.

'What happened to the blood sample, Ruth?'

There was a pause and she heard Ruth inhale a couple of times as if she couldn't quite bring herself to speak. 'I think you should talk to my husband,' she whispered finally.

'But why? What's happened, Ruth? Is there something wrong?'

Another pause, longer this time. 'Well . . . it's . . . I can't say.'

'Ruth –'

She gave a small sigh. 'He thinks it would be best not to go on.'

'Why, Ruth? Just tell me why.'

'They said it would . . .' Then she exclaimed, 'No – sorry! I can't – sorry!' and hung up.

Daisy slumped back in her chair. What had Ruth meant by 'they said'? Who was they – a doctor? An advisor? And what was it they'd said? What could have put Ruth and her husband off a straightforward medical investigation? Daisy couldn't begin to imagine – not just now anyway – and for the moment she gave up trying.

The advertisement stirred memories of another reply, and she called out to Jenny in the outer office: 'Jen, that funny man, Maynard, he hasn't been back, has he?'

Jenny appeared in the doorway. 'Not since the last time, when was it . . .' She pursed up her deep-purple mouth. 'Ooh, November, wasn't it?'

'No phone calls?'

'Nah – I'd 'ave told yer.' Jenny had a habit of lapsing into a Cockney accent: something to do with her new boyfriend. 'No, 'e seemed quite 'appy with all the bumph.'

'And he didn't ask any odd questions?'

'Nope, not a dicky bird.'

'Not especially nosy?'

Jenny squawked: 'You think he's a spy, don't you!' In her delight, her Cockney had momentarily disappeared.

'No, no. I just thought he was – odd.'

'Well, he didn't do anyfing exciting. I checked – remember? No secret mikes under me desk.'

'That's right.' Daisy clasped her fingers to her temples and shook her head. 'Just going nuts, Jen. Just getting paranoid.'

'Go home. Go on. You look half dead.'

She finally left the office at seven, glad to have the car for once, but not so glad at the realization that she'd forgotten to feed the meter. A parking ticket fluttered triumphantly from the wiper. Another sixteen quid up the spout, and little hope of getting it back on expenses.

Simon's bathroom was sparkling white with down-lights in the ceiling and a scorching hot towel rail and pukka tiles and a bath with a sloping back so you could fall asleep in it without getting a sudden snort of water up your nostrils. She poured the water so hot that it took her five minutes to get in but only two minutes to fall asleep. She woke when the flat door slammed and Simon called her name.

'I found some bread,' he called through. 'It's only granary, I'm afraid. Oh, and some mangy old bananas.'

'Sounds okay to me.'

'Didn't bother with curry though. Thought we could cook Sunday's chicken a bit early. You'll approve – it's organic – though what that means nowadays is anybody's guess.'

'Corn-fed, antibiotic-free?' she suggested.

'You'll be lucky.'

'Colonically irrigated perhaps?' She climbed out of the bath and reached for a towel.

He appeared at the door wearing a disparaging smile. 'Wrong,' he corrected her. 'Only free of continuously fed antibiotics. As the law stands at present there's nothing to stop the breeders feeding the birds the odd dose of antibiotics on a curative basis. And no guarantee that the birds are even free-range. It's a big con.'

'Why bother to buy it then?'

He regarded her carefully. 'You look washed out,' he remarked.

Maybe it was the sympathy, maybe it was a psychosomatic response, but she shivered violently. She wrapped the towel tighter round herself. 'I think I'm getting flu.'

She might as well have announced a case of yellow fever. Simon stepped smartly backwards, looking alarmed. 'God, I'm due to go to Madrid on Monday. The EEC conference.' Reading her expression, he rearranged his response and put on a solicitous face. 'Can I get you something?'

'Food'll do fine.'

He retreated to the kitchen. 'Then it can't be flu,' he called, not bothering to disguise the relief in his voice. 'You wouldn't be hungry if it was flu.'

'Just starvation then.'

She dressed and found Simon stuffing the bird with a mixture of crushed garlic, herbs and mushrooms. He had a bottle of Pernod out, not her favourite beverage, and she went in search of some white wine.

'Is the paper going to run anything more on Alusha Mackenzie?' she asked, pulling out a bottle.

'Not that one,' Simon cried in horror. He reached past her and grasped another bottle. 'This one. Nice and dry. The other one's an '85.' She wasn't sure which honoured guest he kept the special vintages for, but it didn't seem to be her.

'The Mackenzie story,' she prompted.

'Oh? Nothing, I don't think. Someone floated an idea for an in-depth piece on pesticides, but the editor killed it.'

Someone floated an idea, but not him. 'You didn't push for it?'

'Well – no.' He looked mildly defensive. Wiping his hands, he reached for his favourite corkscrew and began to work energetically on the cork.

'But why not? And why did the editor kill it?'

'You know why, Daisy. Not enough to go on. I mean . . .' He gave her his favourite let's-face-the-facts look. 'She killed herself, and while that's a tragedy it's not a story.' He pulled the cork with a plop.

'But you can't say she killed herself!'

'A river. A freezing night. A sick woman. It doesn't take a lot of working out.'

'That's making one helluva lot of judgements, for Christ's sake, one helluva lot of assumptions. God – how would you feel if you were sick and weak and you fell and died and the obituaries all marked you down as a suicide?'

'Fell? Daisy, you don't fall into rivers accidentally.'

She paced the kitchen. 'Sure you do. Sure you do. It happens all the time. People trip, they fall . . .'

'And if it's a poky little river, they climb out again.'

She threw out her hands. 'And what happens if people hit their heads and get knocked unconscious?'

Wiping the neck of the bottle with a professional polish, he poured a glass and thrust it into her hand as a doctor might force a palliative on a hysterical patient.

She took a long swig. 'You're totally pre-judging the issue,' she said. 'Branding someone who can't defend herself.'

'I'm not branding anyone with anything.'

'Oh yes you are! You're saying she killed herself and, whatever people say, suicide's still the ultimate crime – selfish and cowardly and messy.'

Simon poured some cooking wine over the chicken and

looked vaguely in the direction of the oven. 'There are worse things.'

'Like?'

He shrugged and, opening a cupboard, rummaged through a collection of herbs.

'Like?' she repeated harshly, feeling ugly and combative.

He selected a jar of marjoram and shook a dusting over the chicken. 'Like, well – being dishonest. Being a drug peddler. I don't know.'

She downed the rest of her wine and reached for a refill. 'There's no comparison. None at all. This woman's dead, and most of her death can be laid at the door of the stuff that poisoned her. You can't even begin to relate it to stealing or drugs.'

Simon gave the chicken a pat, as if the bird at least could be relied on to appreciate a sound argument. Then, waiting for Daisy to move aside, he bent over the oven and absorbed himself with the temperature control.

Daisy resumed her pacing, taking the length of the kitchen in five heartfelt strides.

Simon stood up from the oven, and said suddenly: 'She was doped.'

Daisy stopped dead. 'What do you mean doped?'

'They found drugs in her body.'

Daisy stood still, trying to make sense of it. And yet the sense was clear. He could only mean one sort of drug, otherwise he would have put it differently. But, needing to hear it in cold words, she asked all the same.

'Morphine or heroin or another derivative,' Simon said.

'Perhaps it was for pain. Perhaps it was prescribed.'

'Possibly,' he agreed. 'But apparently the levels were very high.'

'Then – ' She searched his face. 'What are you saying?'

He slid the chicken into the oven. 'It doesn't matter what I'm saying. Or anyone else for that matter. It's what the coroner says.'

'They don't have coroners in Scotland,' she replied mechanically.

'What do they have then?'

'Procurator fiscals.'

'God, what a title.'

'Will there be a hearing, an inquiry, do you know?'

He pulled a dead lettuce out of the fridge and looked at it accusingly. 'An inquest, you mean?'

'I don't think they have inquests. Just inquiries. Can you find out for me? If they're having one?'

'Mmm? Well . . .' He was losing interest. 'If I hear anything.'

By the time a powerful aroma of wine and garlic began to emerge from the oven she had lost her appetite.

'I think it's flu after all,' she said.

The wary expression came back into Simon's face.

Daisy took her cue. 'I think I'll skip the chicken if you don't mind.'

Simon put on a disappointed face, but didn't try to argue her out of it.

The flat was dark and cold when she got in. And a mess. She'd forgotten how behind she'd got with the chores. The ironing board stood in the middle of the room beside a well-filled ironing basket, the floor supported sprinklings of newspapers and magazines and a scattering of music cassettes. Her bed, only approximately made, was strewn with clothes and work papers.

On her way to the kitchen, her eye was caught by a note propped on the mantelpiece. She recognized the neat upright hand of Anthea, her flatmate. Anthea said she was sorry but she was giving two weeks' notice. She didn't quite think the flat was working out, nothing personal. She'd already moved her stuff out, she said, and would send the last two weeks' rent by post.

Despite the inconvenience, Daisy couldn't blame her. If

she'd been in Anthea's position, she'd probably have done the same.

In need of cheer, she made herself a hot lemon drink and slid a hot-water bottle into her bed before making a superficial attack on the clutter. She threw the newspapers into a pile behind a chair, hid the ironing board behind the bathroom door and thrust her tapes onto the shelf by the tape player. Something about the shelf made her pause. Though tidiness wasn't her strong point, she liked to keep her tapes in some kind of order, and now she had the sudden impression that something was out of place. She ran her fingers along the ranks of plastic, ticking them off in her memory until she realized that a number of work tapes had got into the wrong slot: recordings of interviews with chemical victims from which she transcribed notes in the evenings. She'd put them between Pink Floyd and Beethoven, where Bach should be. Or was it Brahms?

As she flopped into bed and clutched the blissful hot-water bottle she remembered the answering machine and, reaching out, pulled it across the floor towards her. It was off. Then she realized that it wasn't actually off but incorrectly set. The model was a fairly ancient one; to set it properly it wasn't enough simply to turn the machine on, you also had to flick the control switch away from 'answer set' and then back again before the tape whirred into the correct position. It was a sign of how brain-stormed she must have been that morning to have screwed up this simplest of tasks.

More out of habit than expectation she played back the message tape, expecting to hear a repeat of yesterday's messages.

But she was wrong. There were no old messages, just a brand new one in the form of her mother's voice announcing the date of her great-uncle Alf's seventieth birthday party, and asking if there was any chance of seeing her

before that, like for Sunday lunch. Daisy lay back, trying to
work this out. To have recorded that message, the machine
must have been properly set for at least some of the day. So
what had caused it to unset? It was some minutes before it
came to her. Anthea. Anthea must have unintentionally
switched it off at the wall as she was moving out, and
forgotten to reset it properly. That, or there had been a
power cut.

   She switched off the light and closed her eyes, ready to
let herself lose sleep over far more important things, like
what could have prompted the Lincolnshire farmer and his
wife to suddenly change their minds about the blood tests.


Hamish Macdonald didn't know what had hit him. One
moment he was minding his own business, throwing up
outside the back door of The Stag, peaceably wondering
why he'd wasted good money on those last four pints only
to review them so quickly, when in the next instant he was
lifted bodily from the ground. It was a curiously weightless
feeling, like flying, or being transported to heaven. Until he
hit the wall, that was. Then he knew that he wasn't flying
or going to heaven or suffering a malfunction of the brain.
The wall was too hard for that; through the considerable
haze and uncertainty, he was aware of the brickwork
meeting his head with a nasty tap.

   The sensation of flying ceased; his body slid a short way
down the wall then stopped with his feet still clear of the
ground, his weight supported by the grip of two vice-like
hands on his lapels. The hands, of course, had an owner,
as Macdonald feared they might, and now the owner's
voice was hissing in his ear.

   'Right, Macdonald, time for a wee chat.'

   Macdonald blinked and tried to make out his assailant's
identity, but the street lighting of Stirling, such as it was,
revealed nothing but the man's black outline. Was he a

thief? A man whom Macdonald had offended perhaps? That was always a real possibility. But whoever he was, whatever his business, Macdonald was only too happy to co-operate. Indeed, if only he could get his brain to respond he would tell the fellow so. But try as he might, much as his mouth moved, no words would come.

The other man was very close, his nose almost touching Macdonald's. 'Willis Bain, Macdonald. The sprayin' in the forest, the flyin'. Who did it?'

A memory stirred in Macdonald's mind. This conversation had happened before. This man had accosted him at his lodgings a few days ago and had asked him the same bloody stupid question. There was something about the man that Macdonald knew he should take into consideration, something really important, but for the life of him he couldn't remember what it was.

In the meantime, the thought of co-operating no longer seemed quite such a good idea. This harping on about spraying and dates and places, it reeked of trouble and the law and unpleasant consequences, and no one was going to nail Macdonald that easily, oh no.

The words came at last. 'Och, pish off,' said Macdonald.

He got another tap on the head for his trouble, a forceful push against the brickwork, and then Macdonald remembered what it was about this man he should have taken into account: the fellow was huge, huge and strong.

This called for different tactics. Although he felt no pain, Macdonald cried out, a loud moan intended both to frighten the other man and to vent his own fear.

It had no effect whatsoever. The other man pushed him harder against the wall, repeating the questions in an aggressive tone.

To give himself time, Macdonald moaned again. This, for some unknown reason, seemed to register and the other man relented slightly, letting Macdonald slide down the wall until his feet touched ground. The questions didn't stop, however. Time. Place. Aircraft. Company name. When. What. Which.

'A'right, a'right. Jus' let me go, will ye?'

The hands released him, and Macdonald felt a glimmering of hope that things might go his way after all. Leaving one arm propped against the welcome solidity of the wall, he resentfully shrugged his jacket back onto his shoulders.

'So?' demanded the voice.

'A'right, a'right.' Macdonald ran an unsteady hand over his lapels, both to smooth them down and to show the extent of his affront. Also to give himself time to calculate his chances of making a run for it. The odds were not good, he had to admit, even if by some miracle he could stand unsupported and sprint the five yards to The Stag's back door. No, he would have to rely on a bit of stealth: a smidgen of truth peppered with liberal doses of amnesia.

'When ye say this was?' he asked blearily.

'June last.'

'Tha's a long time. Cannae recall tha' long . . .'

'Try harder.'

The fella moved in again and Macdonald held up a protective arm. 'A'right, a'right. Ye're quick to take offence. So wha' was it agin?'

The explanation came, and Macdonald did his best to recall the circumstances. He remembered making various deliveries to airfields and isolated strips, he remembered seeing planes sitting around. But the names of the two or more flying companies? The names of chemicals? Even if his brain had been clear – and it was thicker than a Gorbals smog – he'd have had trouble knowing the where and when. All he'd ever done in his working life was to turn up more or less on time, pick up whatever he was meant to pick up, take it to the right place, collect his wages and mind his own business.

'I dunno, and tha's the honest truth.'

A massive hand shot out and grabbed his lapel again. 'A

wee aircraft,' growled the voice. 'Based out to the west somewhere. A field mebbe. Somewhere handy for the western lochs.'

Nothing stirred in Macdonald's brain.

'The aircraft,' the voice persisted. 'It mebbe had a red band on it. Diagonal.'

Ah, now . . . A bell rang in the back of Macdonald's memory, indistinctly at first, then with greater clarity. Gradually a picture formed; he saw the plane sitting on a piece of concrete, under an arclight, near a portable office. On a farm west of Stirling somewhere. Yes, he remembered all right. The question was, should he speak out? The whole thing reeked of consequences.

Better to be safe. He shook his head. 'Don't remember.'

The next moment it was all happening again, the flying sensation, the thud of his head hitting the wall, and a great deal harder this time, so that he cried with unprompted self-pity. The pain, which the alcohol for once failed to anaesthetize, finally persuaded him that enough was enough. This fella wasn't going to take no for an answer, and Macdonald wasn't about to suffer more insult and injury to prove otherwise.

He squealed: 'Mebbe there's somethin' . . . Mebbe.'

'Names, man, names.'

'Lemme think, lemme think . . .' The big man loosened his grip, but this did nothing to clarify Macdonald's memory, which was black as pitch. All Macdonald ever had to do was find the address on the delivery notes – the foreman at the depot near Stirling did all the paperwork, making sure the right chemical went to the right contractor – so how in heaven should he be expected to know the name of the flying company and the stuff they were using all of a sudden?

Seeing the big man looming above, he made an attempt to show willing.

'A field. By the wesht there. A wee plane. But A never

kent the name o' the plashe. Honesh to God, honesh to God . . .'

There was an answering growl and Macdonald cowered, fearing a reorganization of his face. Then, as if heaven-sent, something stirred in the back of Macdonald's mind, a memory so vague that he couldn't at first grasp it. But realizing it offered the only hope of salvation, he begged: 'Hang on, fella. Hang on . . .' and put his mind to concentrating hard, which was no easy task.

Finally it came, and in his haste to get it out before the big man got impatient he jabbered incoherently and it was a moment before he could make himself understood. 'A faerm . . . By a faerm . . . By a faerm name o'. . . name o' Auld . . . Auld-somethin' . . .'

There was a pause. The voice said angrily: 'The name, man!'

'Auldhome . . . Auldhame . . . Aye – *Auldhame*. Honesh to God, tha's all A ken . . . Honesh to God.'

Having said his piece, Macdonald's stomach threatened to go through its paces again and, to put off the evil moment, he slid further down the wall until he was almost bent double. When he next glanced up he was mightily relieved to see that the big man had gone. He celebrated by sinking the last distance to the ground and having a welcome lie down.

# Chapter 14

━━━━━

THE CALL CAME at midnight. Susan, surfacing slowly from a heavy sleep, knew there was no point in objecting to the lateness of the call, no point in mentioning that this was the first time they'd got to bed before one in the morning in the last two, maybe three, months. The call would be from party headquarters or a party colleague. Or maybe even the prime minister's office, in which case, even if it was five in the morning, you were incredibly relieved, not to mention pathetically grateful, to be hearing from them at all. It meant that you – or to be precise, Tony – was still up there where it mattered, in the PM's good books.

Through her sleep-drugged haze she suddenly remembered: this wasn't any old night. This was the night the PM was putting the new cabinet together.

She sat up groggily, eyes creased against the light, and tried to read Tony's face as he grunted a few monosyllabic yesses and noes into the phone.

Maddeningly, he wouldn't return her eye signals, and when he turned away to replace the phone, it was all she could do to get him to speak. She had to positively bully him before he finally told her: it was the PM's office. The PM had asked to see him at eleven the next morning.

It took her a moment to take this in, to realize the full implications of what he was saying. Then she knew without a doubt: he'd done it. She gave a great guffaw of delight and grabbed him in a fierce embrace. He didn't respond.

He seemed dazed, almost as if he wasn't expecting the call, which was ridiculous because everyone knew he was up for a top job. The PM's office hadn't told him what the job would be, of course – that little morsel would drop direct from the prime minister's lips – but the timing of the call was enough: the senior appointments were always announced first. It couldn't be anything less than full cabinet minister.

'Oh, honey!' She gave him another squeeze. He rubbed his eyes and blinked, as if trying to clear his brain. He didn't seem to have taken the news in at all.

'Are you all right?' she demanded. 'Are you ill or something?'

'What? No. No.' He didn't sound convinced.

'Tired then? Oh honey, you must be *so* tired.'

He gave a small shake of the head.

Susan eyed him fretfully. If he wasn't ill and he wasn't particularly tired, then what the hell *was* wrong? He should be grinning with delight and jumping up and down with excitement. Crying, even.

'Tony – it *has* to be a job! And a cabinet one. Got to be!'

'Yes.'

'Aren't you *pleased*?'

'Yes.' Then, with an effort, he smiled. 'Yes, of course I am.'

'D'you think it'll be Agriculture?'

He nodded absentmindedly.

'But isn't that what you wanted?'

'Yes.'

'*Well*, then.'

He squeezed her hand briefly and reached out to turn off the light. 'We'll see. In the morning.'

She was so baffled by this that it was a long time before she got back to sleep. And even as she finally began to nod off, she was suddenly wakened again by Tony getting out of bed and creeping noisily out of the room. If he slept at all during the night, he couldn't have slept for long because shortly after six, when she got up to go to the loo, she found the other side of the bed empty. She pulled on a dressing gown and, though she was feeling decidedly short of rest, tottered downstairs to see where he was and if she could do anything for him. She thought: Greater love hath no wife.

He was in the room they grandly called the study, but which was actually a ten-by-ten box squeezed out of a half-landing with a desk jammed under the window and a few bookshelves perched on the little available wall space.

The door was open and she could see his back hunched over the desk. She paused on the stairs, curious to see what he was up to. The answer was: not a lot. He was quite still, bent forward over the desk with his head cradled in his hands.

She started forward again, on the point of calling gently so as not to startle him, when he reached out a hand to pick up the phone. Something made her pull slowly back until she was hidden by the door frame. She told herself she'd done it so as not to interrupt him, but who was she kidding? His attitude, the stiffness of his body, told her this wasn't a routine call.

Whoever he was calling wasn't in a hurry to answer, but he was obviously prepared to wait it out. He sat motionless, the receiver pressed to his ear, his only sign of impatience a hand rubbed back and forth across his temple.

After what seemed a long time, he stiffened suddenly: he was in business. Susan craned forward.

'It's me,' he said. 'Tony . . . I know . . . I know . . . Yes . . . I'm sorry, but I wanted to be sure to get you.' His voice, already low, dropped to a whisper. As if aware of the dangers, he half turned his head, swinging round to glance over his shoulder. Susan pulled back out of view.

He was closing the door. It swung slowly towards the

frame, then stopped short, leaving a small gap. He didn't attempt to close it any more and after a second or two Susan crept forward and positioned herself by the jamb.

'It was the only time I could ring . . .' His voice sounded urgently. 'I know, I *know* . . . Look, I'm *sorry*, I really couldn't call before, I just couldn't. Listen, we have to meet . . . What do you mean? . . . But we *must* – we have to! We've got to discuss this thing! . . . What do you mean? What are you saying? *Christ* . . .' An anguished sigh. 'Listen, we *have* to talk. You can't drop this on me and then say you're not going to talk about it! Christ, it's got to be *discussed*. I mean, what are you planning to *do* about it, for God's sake? No . . . No . . . The only time I have is this morning, in an hour or so . . . No, the only time. Really . . . But I can't. No . . . *Please*. For God's sake, Angela.'

The small worm of jealousy turned in Susan's gut. So she had him crawling, this woman. Well, bully for her. She must be fantastic in bed; there wasn't much else that could reduce Tony to such creeping submission. From the sound of the call, it certainly wasn't her conversation, nor, presumably, her charm when woken at six in the morning.

Fine. In fact, it couldn't be finer. Why should she mind? In the time that Tony had been screwing this woman – at least eight months now – Susan had had plenty of time to get used to the idea. In the beginning she'd ignored it, then, when pretence had become impossible, Susan had entered what might be called her brave and noble phase, and forced herself to face the full facts in all their tacky unpleasantness. But all that had achieved was to make her miserable, tetchy and impossible to live with. Finally she'd learnt the trick: you rose above it. You became the perfect wife. You became sweet, charming and delightful, an absolute cast-iron asset. She had finally worked out that it was not only futile to worry, it was also unnecessary. A sexy number with black knickers and big boobs – or whatever amazing endowments she possessed – was never going to be a serious threat. Not to a marriage that had always muddled along reasonably well, not to a political wife who worked as hard at the job as Susan, not when Tony was on the up and up. It wasn't as if Tony had shown any outward signs of restlessness or dissatisfaction. On the contrary, he'd been sweet and affectionate, and, strange though it seemed, their relationship had if anything improved.

Tony's voice rose slightly, sounding peevish. '. . . But I can't *do* any other time. You don't understand. I'll be getting a new job later this morning. And then – well, it'll be hopeless . . . Angela, *please*.'

Despite herself, Susan got a curious satisfaction from hearing Tony grovel. She wasn't above feeling hurt and vindictive, and there was a part of her that thought: Serves you bloody right for being greedy.

At the same time his tone worried her. What was the urgency? Why was he sounding so desperate?

'. . . No, that would be difficult . . . No, it *has* to be your place . . . *No* . . . Seven thirty . . . No later. No . . . Bye.'

He had rung off. He was getting to his feet. She could hear the chair scraping across the carpet. Too late to vanish. Forward, then, in her mode of consummate actress. She tapped her nails on the door just as it swung open.

Tony gave a start, jerked his head up and stared at her in astonishment.

Susan smiled warmly. 'Darling, you're up early. Why didn't you sleep in for once?'

'Couldn't.'

'Darling, are you okay? You look dreadful.'

He gave a great sigh, lifting his shoulders then dropping them in a gesture of hopelessness. He reminded her of a bedraggled storm-tossed bird. The impression was accentuated by his hair, which was uncombed and stood up in feathery spikes around his head. She knew she should feel cross with him, but it was impossible, not when she was so worried.

'What *is* the matter, darling?' He wouldn't tell her, of course, but she had to ask.

'What? Oh, nothing.' He rubbed a hand mercilessly over his face.

When he met her eyes again, she gave him a come-off-it look.

'A problem,' he finally admitted. 'But nothing I can't deal with.' He put on his brave-boy expression, a look that normally worked wonders, as he well knew.

'I can't do anything then?' she asked.

'No.'

'Are you sure?'

He switched to his broad everything's-hunky-dory politician's grin.

'Sure.'

'Well, remember I'm always here if you need me.'

The words seemed to touch him. He looked grateful, almost movingly so, though whether it was because of the offer of help, or because she hadn't pressed him on the nature of the problem, she wasn't sure.

It would be easy to demolish him now. He looked about as confident as a five-year-old on his first day at school. Part of her longed to vent her anger and hurt, to tell him how pathetic his behaviour was, to make him see that he was just another plump menopausal male letting lust overrule his judgement; part of her even longed to point out how wonderful all this would look in five-inch headlines in the gutter press. But she held back. He wouldn't be able to take it. Like most successful men, his ego was paper-thin; he was apt to fall apart in the face of emotional crises.

But *was* this a real crisis? And if it was, what the hell was it about? She was burning to ask, yet loath to bring the whole beastly business out into the open.

She gave him a brief kiss on the cheek and was turning to go upstairs when without warning he caught her shoulder and pulled her back into a powerful hug, squeezing her so hard that her head was forced sideways, almost causing her to wince aloud. The awkward bearish embrace went on for what seemed a long time, and whenever she tried to pull away, he tightened his arms round her.

When he finally let go and she was able to twist her neck gingerly back into position, she looked sharply up at him in questioning astonishment. But, avoiding her eyes, Tony quickly dropped his head and turned to scrabble for a tissue from the box on the desk. He blew his nose with a loud roar. When he turned back, the brave little smile was in place again, though she noticed the moisture hadn't quite gone from the corners of his eyes.

Tony – sorry for himself? Tony – emotional? Never.

Now she knew it was serious.


She considered following him, like some private detective in a TV series, but it would really be far too difficult. Quite apart from the fact that she would have to get dressed in a hurry, something she'd never managed even in times of crisis, there would be the difficulty of finding transport. Tony would, presumably, drive himself in the Rover, so that if she tried to follow in the Golf, which was a most distinctive red colour, he would be bound to spot her in his mirror. A taxi would be more practical, but in this neighbourhood finding a taxi on the street was about as likely as getting the newspapers delivered before ten or finding the pavements litter-free. Even if one ordered a taxi on the phone, it was half an hour before the controller could find a cabbie prepared to penetrate the depths of SE5.

No: there was a better way, and she was rather pleased with herself for thinking of it.

Hearing Tony's splashings in the shower – not unlike the sounds of a large animal at a water hole – she slipped into the bedroom to look for the small wad of belongings –

wallet, cards and slim diary – that he always kept in his inside jacket pocket. Usually he left them over-night on his chest of drawers, but for some reason they were not there. She spent some time searching the jackets of his suits before deciding that he must have taken them downstairs.

His briefcase was sitting on the desk in his study. When she tried the clasps they flew open immediately. On top of the thick pile of papers was a black memo book that she had seen many times before, and which she knew he used for his work; but, though she looked carefully in every corner of the case, there was no diary.

She put the black memo book in the pocket of her dressing gown and, closing the case, went down to the kitchen and placed the memo book casually between a directory and a cookery book, as if it had got scooped up and put there accidentally.

Knowing Tony would be getting dressed by now, she prepared some breakfast. He'd already announced that he would be in a hurry this morning. He said he was meeting a journalist in Westminster. He was, she noted, an expert liar.

When he came into the kitchen, it was at the trot. He hung his jacket over the back of a chair, just as she'd hoped he would, and the moment he reached for the orange juice, which she'd carefully placed on the far side of the table, she flipped open his jacket, reached into the inner pocket and, grasping the contents, stuffed them into the pocket of her dressing gown.

Tony drained the glass and turned to say: 'I'll be back to drop the car off at about nine. Could you check with Central Office, to make sure they've arranged transport?'

'Of course.'

He gobbled his toast. 'Must be off.' He patted his trouser pockets. She realized with a lurch of disappointment that he would check his jacket the moment he put it on, and would quickly realize that his wallet and everything else were missing. Stupid of her: she hadn't thought this out properly.

He was glancing towards his jacket; he was going to put it on any minute.

'Darling, do have a vitamin,' she said.

'What?' He looked at her in surprise.

'A vitamin. You're very run down, you know. You don't want to start your new job with flu. There're some in the cupboard over there.'

He looked at his watch. 'Well ... okay. Where are they?' He was saying this without enthusiasm, waiting for her to fly past him, find the bottle and shake out a tablet. Tony was used to having things provided for him.

'In the cupboard over there, above the mixer.'

He gave her a questioning glance that revealed his disappointment at her lack of action, then started reluctantly across the kitchen.

As he peered into the cupboard, Susan pulled the bundle out of her pocket. Diary? It was in the middle, between the wallet and the credit card folder. She extricated it, fumbled, almost dropped it, and looked up anxiously. Tony, reading the label on a bottle, was turning round.

With the wallet and credit cards in one hand, and the diary in the other, she moved rapidly behind the chair and dropped both hands behind her back.

Tony was holding up a bottle.

'That's it,' she said.

'One?'

'I should think so. You'll need to wash it down though.'

He gave a small sigh of impatience as he went in search of a water container, eventually taking an upturned mug from the draining board and filling it from the tap.

Quickly, she opened the jacket again and slipped the wallet and credit card folder back into the inner pocket. She was aware of a childish excitement: if this hadn't been so serious, it would have been fun.

He was coming for the jacket now. He pulled it on, patted the lower pockets, then swung open the lapel. She stared as he checked the inner pocket, but the sight of the wallet seemed to satisfy him, and the next moment he was smoothing down his lapels and, with a quick kiss, was on his way.

She needed a couple of stiff coffees after that. As soon as the second cup was on the table in front of her, she set to work. She started with the diary. It didn't cover the previous year, of course, which meant it contained nothing of the Paris–Strasbourg trip, but if he was seeing his piece regularly then there had to be other entries, other trips that would give him away. The diary was pencil-thin, intended simply as an *aide mémoire* to his office diary, and contained only the most cryptic entries. Most had been made in his secretary's neat printed script. Appointments, meetings, dentist: there was nothing that didn't look entirely above board. And the social engagements – dinners, weddings, family gatherings – there was nothing that she couldn't verify there.

Perhaps he'd learnt to be secretive and write nothing down. Perhaps he'd guessed Susan might start getting suspicious. But if he was this careful now, perhaps he hadn't been so careful in the beginning. She wasn't sure where he kept his old diaries; she might have a look for them later. In the meantime, there was still the black memo book.

She went through it twice. Another disappointment. Plenty of names and phone numbers, but all government or party people or political journalists. The few female names were either researchers, identified as such in brackets after each name – Tony was meticulous about categorizing people – or well-known MPs or relatives or family. No mysterious initials beginning with A. No initials at all, in fact.

Damn.

She went back to the diary. There was one possibility she hadn't covered; that there was a link between the woman and that grey man Schenker from Morton-Kreiger. He'd been in Paris with Tony, and maybe in Strasbourg too, around the time of Tony's adulterous stay in the château. She found mention of his name quickly enough, first against a daytime meeting in January, then against a dinner, then on a trip to Covent Garden to which she'd also been invited. She flipped back to the dinner. It had taken place in late January. Apparently the two men had had dinner again in early February. And again two weeks later. And yet again just ten days after that. Rather frequent, these dinner meetings, even allowing for Schenker's smarmy little ways. Before she allowed herself a full measure of excitement, she went through the dates a second time, trying to match them to the occasions when her instincts had told her Tony was lying, but her memory wasn't good enough to be certain of the precise dates. Slapping the diary down on the table, she strode up to the study and, starting with the top right-hand drawer, went methodically through his desk. It took half an hour to find the old diaries, which were not in the desk at all, but on the topmost bookshelves in box files, sorted by year, along with all his correspondence, notes and political thoughts. Everything, she realized, for the writing of his memoirs, assuming he stayed in politics long enough and reached a high enough post for people to show interest.

She found the entry for the Strasbourg–Paris trip. There were EEC meetings, a conference. Schenker's name. Then not much else . . . Until, a week later – yes. *Yes!* The initial A. Ha, ha! she thought: Got you. She allowed herself a moment of satisfaction before continuing her search.

In the following weeks and months there were more A's until, in about October, they stopped abruptly. He must have realized he was taking risks, must have decided to get more careful.

But nowhere was there a phone number, or a clue to the woman's name.

Finding the date for the Strasbourg–Paris trip again, she went backwards through the previous months. In April she found an entry for a water conference in the Midlands, and under it for an evening engagement, Schenker's name again.

And in the top margin, a lone phone number. There was no name next to it, and perhaps for that reason she fastened on to it.

Back in the kitchen she thumbed through the memo-cum-address book, but there was no number resembling the mysterious entry in the diary margin. Looking through the current diary again, she went to the blank end-pages, which Tony had filled with densely packed jottings: notes, memos, names, frequently used phone numbers. And there it was at last: the very same number. And next to it, the name A. Kershaw.

She smiled to herself. This detective work was a piece of cake.

The phone book came up trumps, too. There was an A. Kershaw at the same number. The address was a flat in Wandsworth.

Yet, having got this far, Susan couldn't resist the final confirmation. It was getting on for nine: even allowing for Tony having arrived late and overstayed his allotted visiting time, he must have left the woman's place by now.

Before Susan had time for second thoughts or serious nerves, she picked up the phone and dialled the number.

It answered quickly, as if snatched· up from its cradle. A sulky female voice. 'Hullo?'

Susan realized she hadn't rehearsed this at all. 'Angela?'

'Yes?' The voice sounded grumpy, as if she hadn't had enough sleep.

'This is Naomi. How are you?'

'*Who?*'

'Naomi Attwood.'

'There's been some mistake ...' She was sounding irritated.

'Oh? Isn't that Angela Kershaw?'

'Yes it is. But I don't know any Naomi. You must have the wrong number.'

'Oh dear. I thought ... Aren't you Angela Kershaw from Tunbridge Wells?'

'No, I am most definitely not. Listen, you have the wrong number!'

Susan thought: Bad-tempered, too. 'Oh, sorry. I looked you up in the book. I thought ...'

But there was a click then the buzz of an empty line.

Susan put down the phone, glowing with self-congratulation. In her heyday as a model she'd posed for Bailey, Parks, O'Neill – all the best – she'd even done bit-parts in a couple of commercials, but until now she'd never quite appreciated the extent of her talent to impersonate.

She saw the time. Hastily she phoned Central Office to confirm Tony's car, and, breaking the habits of a lifetime, managed to shower, throw on some makeup and get dressed in twenty minutes flat, so that she was standing at the door to welcome Tony when he finally returned at nine twenty, delayed, he said, by heavy traffic. He looked preoccupied and grim. Two minutes later she was back at the door, the diary and memo book in hand, ready to pass them to him as he flew out of the house again. At the sight of them he looked startled, patted his pockets, and frowned at her.

'You left them by the phone,' she said.

'Good God. Thanks.' He peered into the street to make sure the official car was there, kissed her briefly, started down the steps and turned back. 'I'll call you the moment I get some news.' He grinned suddenly, a pathetic almost apologetic smile. 'Don't get too excited.'

'Ha! No less than the cabinet!'

He managed a laugh, but she could see that he was deep

in some torturous gloom. 'Oh, and Susan – the car. I
couldn't find a space for it. Would you?'

He indicated the Rover, which was parked on a yellow
line.

'Of course.'

She waved him goodbye. The perfect wife.


Drab utilitarian stuff. Hillyard wrinkled his nose slightly at
the Chairman Mao shirt and Castro fatigues, though that
didn't prevent him from flicking diligently through the
remainder of the hangers. There was only one frock that
could be described as stylish, and that was a drapy floral
number which would look rather fetching in a country
garden, taking tea under an apple tree.

Replacing the dress, he went quickly through the chest
of drawers. Cheap Marks and Spencer underwear. Nothing
remotely lacy or silly. Except for one nightdress, a present
from a rich boyfriend perhaps, although it was hard to
imagine Miss Field having friends who even began to verge
on the stylish. He ran his fingers over the fabric. Silk:
wonderful next to the skin.

There was a clutter of papers by the bed. Kneeling, he
went through them methodically, but there was nothing to
catch his attention, just periodicals and reports.

He glanced along the shelf of tapes above the tape
player. She'd tidied them, he noticed, even rearranged them
since his last visit. Put the classics at the far end and the
pop music, which accounted for most of the collection, at
the near end. While the case-history tapes, the ones he had
come to look at, had disappeared. He exhaled crossly and
it wasn't until he turned to look around the rest of the
room that he spotted the stack of tapes on the desk under
the window, perched on a pile of papers. He could almost
hear Beryl's gravelly voice saying: Who's a lucky boy, then?

The window, a bay, was tall and uncurtained, the sun

hitting the glass and spreading over the film of London grime like gold dust, so that even the most vigilant neighbour would have trouble seeing in. He sat at the desk and, slipping the tapes out of their boxes one by one, made a careful note of which tapes belonged in which boxes before exchanging them for the blanks in his pocket. Just as he was restacking the boxes on the pile of papers the phone rang with a loud shrill. Out of long habit he froze until, with the clicking of the answering machine, he could once more hear beyond the flat to the sounds on the communal stairs and the street below.

The answering machine spewed out its message, broadcasting it through the room. '*I'm not here just at the moment, but if you'd like to leave a message . . .*' The caller took up her invitation, announcing himself as Campbell from Loch Fyne.

Hillyard suddenly straightened and strode through to the bathroom. Springing onto the side of the bath, he opened a door set high in the wall and thrust his ear as close as possible to the cupboard inside. The hot water gurgled in the tank below, a pipe expanded with a tick-ticking sound, but even when these extraneous sounds ceased it was impossible to hear the whir of the tape in its hidey hole behind the thick bundles of old blankets and abandoned clothing that filled the available space. The caller rang off. There was a clunk from the answering machine in the main room, but from behind the high-set cupboard there was not the faintest sound.

He didn't disturb the machine – he'd already had it out once to change the tape and renew the batteries – but closed the door and stepped down, carefully wiping any trace of footmarks from the edge of the bath.

As he passed the bathroom wall-cabinet he took a quick look inside on the principle that you never knew what you might find, then, after a quick perusal of the street from the bay window, let himself out. He had obtained a full set of her keys, copied from the spare set she kept in the top right-hand drawer of her desk.

The car was parked in an adjacent street, guarded by Beji. He drove to the heath, to a popular parking place where old dears sat in their cars enjoying the sun and determined dog-walkers set off briskly, chins jutting, into the wind.

Hillyard collected a holdall from the boot, slid the driver's seat back as far as it would go and, settling himself comfortably with legs outstretched, began the time-consuming task of dubbing the tapes. He plugged the tape machine into the 12-volt lighter socket and, inserting the first pair of tapes, set the high-speed dubber in motion. He listened to the senseless jabbering for a moment before turning the volume down and making some cryptic notes in his personalized shorthand. These related to the message he'd heard in the flat. *Campbell, Loch Fyne. May have found (an)? airfield to west of Stirling.* There had been something else noteworthy in the message, but with the distractions of the bathroom expedition, it took him a while to recollect exactly what it was. He wrote: *No luck on the spray.* When the last tape had been copied he put the originals back in his pocket, repacked the holdall and returned it to the boot. As he headed back through Highgate, he hummed contentedly, thinking of the thick body of facts that would go into the next report. Some weeks it had been necessary to pad things out a bit. Then Beryl, exercising all her wicked ingenuity, had massaged the story forward, hinting at the promise of future disclosures without ever quite diverting from the facts, or, indeed, the lack of them. But this week no padding would be necessary, not so long as Beryl got moving on the transcriptions and had them finished in time.

He followed the same route back to Upper Holloway and parked within sight of the Field woman's flat. More from habit than the expectation of seeing anything, he watched the dust-coated windows of the first-floor flat for a couple of minutes before getting out and strolling gently towards the front steps. He was pulling the keys out of his pocket, preparing himself for a rapid entry, when he spotted a man at the far end of the street walking briskly down the hill towards him. At that distance Hillyard couldn't make out his face but he had a sudden and unpleasant suspicion that this was someone associated with the Field woman. A firm disciple of his own intuition, he accelerated into a more purposeful stride and, ignoring the house, kept walking.

Within a few yards Hillyard realized several things simultaneously: that he had been mistaken and didn't recognize the man at all, and that the approaching figure's resemblance, such as it was, had been to the Field woman's boyfriend, the *Sunday Times* journalist, Simon Calthrop, and it was this that had sounded the faint alarm in his mind.

If he'd had more time to think about it, he'd have known a visit from Calthrop wasn't likely. The boyfriend always liked the Field girl to go to him. But better safe than locked up, as Beryl liked to point out.

Passing the man, Hillyard carefully averted his eyes, and reaching the end of the street took a quick look back to make doubly sure that the man was not after all entering number fifty, before turning left and left again, to beat a circuitous path back to the car.

There he waited until there was a nice long lull in the business of the street. Letting himself back into the flat, he replaced the blank tapes with the originals, and stacked them carefully on the pile of papers, exactly where he'd found them.

He was in and out within two minutes. To a casual observer, a resident who'd just popped in for something.

There was a mammoth jam in Park Lane and it took him a good hour to get back to Battersea. He spent the time entertaining himself with Beji, dangling choccy drops above her nose.

# Chapter 15

NORMALLY SCHENKER NEVER ate alone in hotel suites – he resented the waste of executive time – but today he made an exception and ate breakfast in front of the TV so as to catch the first news of the British government appointments.

Cable news finally delivered at seven, but gave only the top four cabinet appointments. Schenker called Cramm's room immediately to find that his assistant, ever the great anticipator, had at that very moment plucked the information from the Reuters wire service.

Driscoll had got Agriculture.

Schenker beamed. He beamed at himself in the mirror as he adjusted his tie, and he smiled at Cramm as they descended to the Plaza's main lobby and went out to the waiting limo. There were still faint signs of pleasure on his face as they headed downtown to their appointment on Madison Avenue.

'The right man,' he remarked in a self-indulgent murmur.

'Absolutely,' echoed Cramm dutifully.

And the right man twice over, Schenker comforted himself. Not only was Driscoll a friend in the most beneficial sense of the word, but almost any change would have been a vast improvement on the last incumbent, Cranbourne, whose obstructive little ways had been a thorn in Schenker's flesh for a long time. Fortunately Cranbourne had overreached himself and made a slip just before the election. In better times the mistake – allowing the export of some unsafe meat – would hardly have rated more than a brief rebuke in the press, but Cranbourne had failed to realize that for a politician without friends, errors, however minor, were inclined to be fatal. Provided with the appropriate facts – and journalists existed to be fed facts – the media had developed the affair into a minor scandal. The timing hadn't helped the government's election chances of course, but that was a risk that had had to be taken.

'You always knew it would be Driscoll,' Cramm said with suitable admiration.

Schenker shrugged modestly. 'Not *knew*. Just weighed up the chances, and he always came out on top. Not too much of a high-flier, you see. Not too ambitious. Not foreign secretary or home secretary material. And he knows it. That's his strength. Steady, good grounding, solid ability, someone who can be relied on to spare the prime minister unpleasant surprises.'

'He's got a lot to deliver though, hasn't he?' said Cramm delicately. 'The manifesto, those environmental commitments . . . they were pretty heavy.'

'This government will never push Green issues at the expense of its economic programme,' said Schenker with confidence. 'The economy comes first and, whatever the British people may say, however Green they may think they are, the economy will always come first with them too.' Summing it up as he thought rather neatly, he added: 'Food before ideas. Always has been, always will be.'

The Food Bill, which everyone had got in such a panic about, had quickly got bogged down at committee stage, and the more extreme clauses gradually thinned down until, thanks to the snap election, the entire Bill had got killed off. The government had of course promised to reintroduce the legislation, which was only to be expected, but the details had been left acceptably indeterminate. With Driscoll safely in the chair, the insane warning-label idea for food was not likely to emerge again, and with a bit of luck – which, since Schenker left nothing to chance, meant a lot of hard work – the sampling and penalty proposals would lose most of their teeth.

As the limousine undulated down Fifth Avenue, Schenker allowed himself a rare moment of optimism.

Cramm cleared his throat and said: 'That problem at the Aurora works, the health scare – '

'I thought that was under control.'

'In so far as it was possible, yes. But there are ripples. EarthForce, the environmental group, are pressing the EPA to investigate the health reports, and a local congressman's got hold of the story and is hammering the press.'

'We don't need this now.' Schenker was thinking of the US launch of Silveron which, after interminable delays, was finally within sight. He was also thinking of the Stock Market, where Morton-Kreiger shares were still under pressure. 'Who's been talking?' he asked grimly. 'That scientist again?'

'MKI thinks it was this local doctor who's been treating the Silveron workers. Someone called Burt. They're looking into it.'

'I hope they're doing more than looking into it,' Schenker said with considerable irritation.

'Oh, sure. They've obtained some more medical opinions. No sign of chemicals in the blood, run-of-the-mill diseases: that sort of thing. And of course the results of the new toxicology trial are due fairly soon – '

'Soon? I thought they were due yesterday!'

'Technical problems at TroChem.'

'*Technical* problems?' He let his voice rise sarcastically. 'I thought these people were meant to be hyper-efficient. Why the hell can't they deliver?'

'They've given firm assurances that the results will be out within two weeks.'

'*Two weeks?* That'll be too late! Get through to

Research while we're in the meeting. Tell them *today*. It has to be today. Or I'll phone McNeill myself.' Perhaps he'd phone McNeill anyway. An opportunity to wave Research's inefficiencies in front of McNeill's nose was not to be missed.

Cramm looked doubtful.

Schenker turned on him. 'You're not trying to tell me there's some kind of problem?'

'No, no. I – ' He faltered uncharacteristically. 'I just thought you should be forewarned.'

Ominous remarks like that had the power to unsettle Schenker. 'About *what*?'

'The environmentalists. The press. Like I said.'

'Not the results?' He examined Cramm's face. 'Not the toxicology trials? God, if McNeill's been holding out on me . . .'

'No, no. Research say the results are going to be fine. As of last night, that is. Shall I check with them again?'

'You do that. *You do that*.' With the launch coming up, any sort of uncertainty frightened Schenker rigid. It took only the smallest scare to rattle the Stock Markets.

By the time they entered the gleaming portals of the advertising agency Schenker's mood was sombre.

Normally he made a point of avoiding advertising agencies, preferring to leave the control of their slick machinations to his executives, but on this occasion he'd been forced to make an exception. The marketing policy at Morton-Kreiger International (US) had been showing less than adequate results for some time and he'd pressed Gertholm into making some big changes in Chicago. The result was a new marketing team who, faced with the challenge of getting Silveron into the three top sellers within two years, had provisionally chosen this Madison Avenue agency for the Silveron account. They had chosen – but were they right? The team was too new, the decision too important for Schenker entirely to trust their judgement.

Advertising agencies, like public relations companies, rubbed Schenker up the wrong way. They always looked too affluent, too polished by half, and he could never quite forgive them for deriving their plump incomes from clients like him.

The agency people and the MKI marketing team were standing in stiff groups, coffee cups in hand, when he sped into the room. Conversation faltered, cups were abandoned as, without breaking his stride, Schenker shook a couple of hands and sat himself rapidly in the centre of the front row, staring pointedly ahead. The account director slipped into his welcoming spiel. The mixture of subservience and arrogance irritated Schenker beyond measure and, without removing his gaze from the screen ahead, he interrupted coldly: 'Let's go.'

There was a stir, a sense of having got off to a bad start, which was precisely what Schenker had intended, and the account executives lurched hastily into their opening routine.

Following normal practice, the presentation began with a summary of Silveron's market strategy, of which Schenker was well aware, but which the agency felt they had to regurgitate to show how brilliantly they understood the product. Finally they came to the proposed selling point: Silveron offered the broadest most cost-effective protection against pests yet.

It was to be a press campaign, the agency said, using saturation coverage in all the major target magazines, starting with a six-page pull-out section in the foremost growers' journals. This campaign would coincide with a free sampling operation, five Hawaiian holidays for the most successful wholesalers, and a $200,000 prize draw.

So far so obvious. Schenker waited to see how they intended to get the message across. The agricultural and forestry journals were bulging with ads, each indistinguishable from the next, each cluttered with facts, exhortations to purchase and glowing testimonials.

Finally they came to the bottom line: the treatment. The advertisement was to be a three-page spread, extended over successive right-hand pages. The first page was to be a tease, a page of solid green bled off at the edges, with just four words in small type in the lower right-hand corner: *Silveron covers almost everything*. Turning over, the reader was then hit by another almost totally green page with a list down the right-hand side, set in equally small type, a restrained, factual catalogue of Silveron's potential targets: *Spruce moth, Tussock moth, Boll weevil, Beauty moth* . . . The list was fifty bugs long. It looked good, Schenker had to admit. Finally, on the third page, came the hard sell: Silveron's cost-effectiveness, on a par with its main competitors; its persistence; the infrequency of application.

'Very good,' Schenker said. They were all watching him, trying to work out if this remark was as promising as it sounded. After a moment, he added: 'But will people really understand what a breakthrough Silveron is?'

The account executive made a show of looking mildly puzzled. 'A breakthrough?' he asked politely. 'We understood it was more of a development of existing products.'

'An *important* development,' Schenker corrected him. 'And we need to tell people that. Perhaps on that first page. Along with *Silveron covers almost everything*. Something to announce it's special. You know – It's new, it's special – something like that.'

There was a silence. They didn't like that, not at all. He'd forgotten how touchy these people got when it came to their words, as if they were Hemingway or Fitzgerald or somebody who could really write.

'Well . . .' the account executive said uncertainly. 'We could certainly examine the feasibility of that.'

'We also need to tell people it's safe,' Schenker continued. The agency people exchanged glances. No one seemed keen to take that one up. It was finally left to the copywriter to offer an opinion. 'Safety's a difficult one,' he said. 'There isn't enough to say.'

Schenker placed his hands in an attitude of prayer and pressed his fingers to his lips. 'Not enough? But Silveron has been cleared – or is about to be cleared – for sale in every country we've applied to market it. What do you mean – not enough?'

'We couldn't make the message sufficiently strong to make it worth saying. To use what you've just suggested would sound defensive. I mean, the consumer will know the product's been cleared by the EPA, otherwise we wouldn't be allowed to sell it in the first place.'

'Morton-Kreiger spends more on safety trials per product than any other major agrochemical company,' Schenker said calmly. 'We should make something of that.'

'That might be a useful selling point in corporate advertising, very useful,' the account executive said smoothly, 'but for a single product – well, it might be thought to imply that the product is in some way safer than its competitors – and that might cause problems.'

Schenker wasn't terribly fond of being told his own business. He said sternly: 'Might it?'

'Problems at our end I mean,' said the executive hastily. 'It would take time to get it past the advertising standards people. They'd want corroborative evidence.'

The copywriter chipped in: 'Even then it would only take one smidgen of bad publicity to make the whole campaign backfire.'

The account executive flinched visibly, as if he'd been stabbed in the back, which, in agency terms, he had. 'Of course that's not likely,' he said hurriedly.

'No one has ever been adversely affected by Silveron,' Schenker said.

Everyone nodded to show they had known this all along.

'Perhaps we could get the safety angle checked out by

our legal department?' the account executive said, trying to paper the cracks. 'And if there's anything we *can* say, we'll find a way of saying it. In an effective and meaningful way, of course.'

This was the usual advertising agency flannel. 'But it should have been a selling point from the beginning,' Schenker argued. 'The company has a fine safety record. We should use it.' He stood up. Those who'd been sitting quickly followed suit. There was a general air of expectancy. The agency were wondering if they'd got the account.

He made for the door. 'Oh, and the teaser,' he said. '*Silveron. It's the greatest yet. It covers almost everything.* That should do it, don't you think?' He flashed a quick smile to demonstrate that, given sufficient grounds for benevolence, he was capable of showing approval, and sped from the room with Cramm at his heels.

Back in the limo Schenker sat staring silently out of the smoked-glass windows. As they neared Wall Street and their next appointment, he said abruptly: 'Those rumours about the Aurora plant, Cramm. They could really hurt us.'

Cramm nodded.

'They have to be stopped.'


Dublensky sat at the kitchen table and drank his after-breakfast coffee. Under the new routine he allowed himself no more than ten minutes for this indulgence before getting into the den and starting work. But today he let the time spin out a bit, not only because it made a change, but because, for all his self-discipline, a minute here or there wasn't actually going to make any difference. Also there was the matter of the mail. He had checked the box but it still hadn't arrived, and he knew he wouldn't be able to settle down to anything else until it did.

He could never get used to being home at this time of

day, just as he couldn't accustom himself to the quiet of an empty house. It seemed strange that Anne and Tad should hurry out of the door each morning, leaving him to all this silence. Worse though was the bald unavoidable fact that he had nothing to keep him occupied. In the weeks since the Allentown Chemical Company had dispensed with his services he'd fixed the guttering, the kitchen faucet and Tad's bicycle, none of which had taken more than an hour or two even when he'd spun them out. The other household jobs, like painting the exterior and rehanging the damaged garage door, required money, thus relegating themselves to indefinite postponement.

When his ten-plus minutes were up he washed his cup, dried it carefully, put it away, and went out to the mail box. It was still empty. Returning to the den he started his fifth perusal of the latest issue of *Practical Scientist*. In the first few days of his unemployment he'd applied for nothing but the cream of jobs, but then, as the doubts began their relentless siege on his confidence, he'd started to glance over a few of the lesser jobs, positions he would not normally have considered. Even then it wasn't until he failed two interviews in succession that he began to write a second wave of applications.

The first turn-down hadn't surprised him too much – the job really wasn't his bag – but the second had been a definite surprise. In fact, it would be more accurate to describe it as one helluva jolt. He'd had every reason to think he was in with a good chance: the CV–job specification fit had been excellent, the interview had gone well, he'd established an immediate empathy with the chief executive, but when the answer finally came it had been a flat inexplicable no.

Anne took the news with narrowed lips, knowing eyes and a dark expression. For the first time in his marriage Dublensky avoided discussion with his wife, not only because he had a good idea of what she was going to say but because he wasn't sure he was ready to hear it. The hiatus left him isolated and dejected, yet oddly determined, and when he won an interview with a small corporation in Maryland, he made the decision not to tell Anne until he had the result. He wanted to surprise her. The salary was significantly lower than he'd been used to and he was most definitely overqualified, but it was a position which would allow him to sink into a peaceful kind of obscurity.

The mail man finally appeared, making his way fitfully up the street, and Dublensky ambled down the path to meet him.

There were two letters for him; the one from the Maryland corporation lay on top. He did not open it immediately, but took it into the den and laid it on the desk in front of him. Even then he did not open it immediately. The crisp white envelope seemed charged with all the might and inescapable power of the agrochemical industry. As he reached forward to run his finger under the flap his sense of doom deepened and he realized that, whether from a subconscious need to prepare himself or a sudden faith in his own instincts, he had already accepted the worst.

The realization did not stop his heart from taking a sharp turn as he pulled the single sheet from the envelope.

Position filled.

'They're nailing you,' Anne said as they lay in bed that night.

'Honey, how could they?' he argued despite himself. 'I mean, this last company, they're only a small outfit. They've no contacts with Morton-Kreiger.'

'Oh no? The references, what about the references? Don't tell me these corporations don't follow them up. Don Reedy may have said some okay things on paper – though they were no more than *okay*, were they? I mean, just *adequate* – but what does he actually say when they call him, huh? Don't tell me a quiet word doesn't get whispered in their ears. You know – Dublensky's a good man but *difficult*. Competent, sure, but slow. I mean, they wouldn't have to say much, would they? They wouldn't have to call you totally incompetent.'

'But why would they bother?' he asked, knowing the answer perfectly well but wanting to hear her say it.

'I'll tell you why,' she said. 'To squeeze you out. To make sure you don't get any kind of position again. To make people think you *are* incompetent. So that if you decide to spill the beans, they can say, well, he's just pissed off, isn't he? Got promoted beyond his abilities. Can't accept his own limitations. Disgruntled employee out for revenge. Who's the world going to believe then?' After a minute or two she added harshly: 'You should have sent that dossier to EarthForce straight away.'

'But Burt's already sent his medical notes to the EPA and EarthForce, for God's sake. And EarthForce are pressuring the EPA.'

'Burt's just a local physician. It's only his opinion. It's not the same.' She clicked her tongue and repeated: 'You should have sent your dossier.'

'But what would it add?'

'Everything. The workers' testimonials. The evidence about safety procedures.'

'But they can get the testimonials direct.'

'And the safety procedures? Since when will they be able to get that from another source?'

'It doesn't prove a lot . . .'

She sighed impatiently. '*God* – really, John! Of course it proves a lot. If Morton-Kreiger are forced to explain away this sickness, they may try to nail it on lax production-line procedures. While you – *you* – know damn well that the procedures were totally okay. Of *course* it proves some-thing.'

'I don't know.'

Anne gave a small grunt of derision and rolled away, turning her back on him, filling the space with one of her expressive silences.

Dublensky thought with a tremor of guilt of the other file, the one that Anne wasn't even aware of, that contained some of the Silveron toxicology results, and the fire which it would bring down on their heads if it were ever published. He had hoped never to have to use it; he hadn't been ready to face those sorts of consequences.

'I could still send them a dossier,' he offered.

'Oh, yeah? *Now?*' Anne retorted. 'And confirm what Morton-Kreiger are going to say about you? That you're just doing it because you're pissed off? That it's simply a case of sour grapes because you can't get another job? That would look great. I told you, I told you right at the beginning, you should have sent it straight away.'

'I thought I'd never get a job if I did.'

'Well, you're not getting a job anyway, so what's the difference? Jesus, John, what was it all for, if it wasn't to get this thing out into the open?'

Over the next days a wretchedness clung to Dublensky. Though Anne said no more, her words prowled reproachfully around his mind, nibbling at his conscience.

Even as he sat at the foot of Tad's bed in the evening, reading aloud from *Kidnapped*, he thought about what she had said. He managed the trick of reading one thing and thinking quite another until he came to some Scots dialect and had to pause and concentrate. His accent slipped from what may have been Irish to what sounded like Italian. Even if it had by some miracle bordered on Scots, he had no means of knowing. He glanced over his spectacles to find Tad hiding his laughter behind the bed covers.

'Okay,' Dublensky said with good humour. 'You try it.'

'No, Dad, you're great. Really. Go on, *please*.' A last giggle, then a straight face.

Dublensky found that he was staring unseeing at the page. He blinked himself back to reality. 'You enjoying this?' he asked doubtfully.

'Sure. It's good.'

'It is?' Dublensky realized he had taken in nothing of the last ten minutes' reading.

Grasping the situation, Tad explained: 'Davie Balfour and Alan Breck have escaped the redcoats and are making for Ben Alder and the Pass of – '

'Who's Ben Alder?'

'Not who – *what*. It's a mountain.'

'Oh. And it's important they reach it?'

'It's a place on their escape route.'

Dublensky frowned. 'I thought Alan Breck was the bad guy.'

Tad gave the sort of impatient sigh that children reserve for parents who are being particularly dumb. 'No, Dad. He's one of the good guys.'

'I thought he was involved in that shooting.'

'He was, sort of. But the guy who died was a traitor, siding with the English, so it didn't matter.'

'Didn't matter?'

'No,' Tad replied with exaggerated patience. 'The English are the bad guys, right? The ones who're down on the Scots. Alan Breck's with the Scots, fighting for freedom. Against the English,' he added just in case his father still hadn't got it. 'Anyway,' he said with a certain logic, 'you can tell Alan Breck's a good guy because he gets the good lines.'

'That makes him okay?'

'Definitely.'

'Isn't he a rascal, or whatever they used to call them?'

'Oh, sure. But he has to do what he has to do, right? And if that includes a few bad things – well, it's okay, isn't it, when he's got right on his side.'

Dublensky nodded slowly. 'I guess so.' And with that he lost whatever concentration he might have had, and put the book away.

The next day he sent a digest of the Aurora dossier to EarthForce. He did it cautiously – that is, anonymously and via his brother in New York, so it wouldn't have an Allentown postmark. He enclosed a covering note, briefly explaining the significance of the information, and would have left it totally unsigned except for a nagging reluctance to cut himself totally off from the prospective custodians of this, his precious and costly information. At the very least he wanted to be able to check that they'd received and understood it and, to do that, he needed a means of identifying himself. Feeling like a character out of a spy movie, he thought up a name and typed it at the bottom of the page. He chose the name Kalisz, after the city in Poland where his mother was born, then almost immediately thought better of it. It was pretty stupid to use a place name with which he had a connection, however tenuous. He briefly considered using an anagram of Tad and Anne's names, but rejected that for the same reason. Thinking of Tad, the answer suddenly came to him and he went upstairs to find the copy of *Kidnapped*.

An eighteenth-century rascal courtesy of Robert Louis Stevenson; you couldn't find a more remote connection than that. He reprinted the covering letter and signed it Alan Breck.

At the last moment, infused with a sudden gust of courage that had him shivering somewhere between exhilaration and fear, he added a postscript. *There is also something seriously wrong with the original toxicology data. Some of it was faked. I have the evidence.*

He hurried to the post before he could change his mind. Then he went and sat in the yard in the sunshine, and, closing his eyes very tight, let the light fall on his face.

# Chapter 16

———

'YOU'RE SURE THIS is it?' Daisy asked, surveying the wide expanse of rough grass.

Campbell leant an arm on the gate. 'Aye,' he grunted laconically. 'It's the place.'

The field seemed large enough and reasonably flat if you ignored the slight rise in the centre which hid the far right-hand boundary. But the ground was neither smooth nor firm. There was a quagmire fanning out from the gate, and, spreading into the distance, a progression of grassy tussocks interspersed with puddles. 'It's rather waterlogged,' she ventured.

'It's dry enough over there.' Campbell gestured towards the centre. 'You could land a jetliner.'

She shot him a glance but it was quite impossible to tell whether he was joking. 'You said there was an access road?'

He pointed towards the left, where a rough road was visible through a ragged boundary hedge. Some way up there was a wide opening in the hedge which led to what looked like a parking area just inside the field. Tucked in beside the hedge was a Portakabin, grey and weather-beaten, so that it blended perfectly with the landscape.

'Shall we get on then?' she said, aware that the morning was slipping away and that she would have to catch the four o'clock train if she was going to get back to London that evening. Officially – which meant for Alan's benefit – she wasn't here at all, but working flat out on a fund-raising campaign proposal due for presentation to Catch's executive committee the day after tomorrow. And she had been working on it, very hard, until Campbell's call had caused her to drop everything and jump on the night sleeper.

Campbell's unearthing of the airfield had sounded so very promising – an airfield would surely be thick with information on planes and flying companies – but now as she climbed into Campbell's battered Ford she reflected on what he had brought her hurrying all this way to see. A long-abandoned airstrip devoid of people and information. A possible interview with the field's owner who, since he wasn't expecting them, might well slam the door in their faces.

She had only herself to blame; too impulsive by half, too easily persuaded, too optimistic. Wasn't that what Alan was always telling her?

Campbell negotiated the car backwards onto the narrow lane, and they started off again. The inside of the car was like a fridge and, still frail from a heavy cold, she leant forward and twiddled with the heating controls.

'Too warm for you?' Campbell asked, rapidly winding his window down.

She stared at him.

'Not *cold*?'

'Well – a little.'

He grunted and, attacking the window again, closed it, though not, she noticed, right to the top.

'You work out of doors, do you?' she asked, blowing her nose.

'Aye.'

'Forestry?'

'Fisheries.'

'A fisherman?'

'No.'

She wondered if this terseness was habitual.

'What then?' she persevered.

'Work on a salmon farm. Top of the loch.'

'Ah. A large farm? Successful?'

'Does well enough. But the fish . . .' He shook his head briefly. 'They dinna' compare.'

'To – ?'

'Och, the wild fish.'

They came round a bend and saw an open gateway and a sign for Auldhame Farm. If the name Auldhame conjured up a picture of a quaint dwelling with whitewashed walls and dormer windows, the impression was soon dispelled by the austere greystone house that came into view as they turned in through the gate. The front yard was muddy and rutted with tractor tracks. In a decrepit outbuilding with a tattered metal roof a number of vehicles were rusting quietly. As the car came to a halt, a black mongrel raced from the outbuilding and, flinging itself to the limits of its chain, snarled and snapped at the empty air.

'Friendly place,' Daisy remarked. Picking her way through the mud, she followed Campbell to the grey-painted front door. Campbell rapped vigorously. The dog kept up its frenetic baying and from an open-sided barn on the far side of the yard, beyond a metal-bar fence, a morose-looking cow gave a mournful bellow. The front door remained unanswered.

'No one home,' Campbell remarked unnecessarily. 'We could try again in a wee while. The man'll likely be in for his dinner.'

They climbed into the car and started back along the narrow lane.

'Could take a look at that cabin,' Campbell suggested.

Daisy wished they could find something a little warmer to do. She could feel her throat swelling up and a small thread of pain worming its way through her sinus.

'You wouldn't close the window, would you?' she asked.

Reaching for the winder, Campbell gave a short grunt of amazement.

'I'm soft,' Daisy said. 'I admit everything.'

'Aye, you'd never last up here, that's for certain.'

They came to the access road and turned into it. Reaching the break in the hedge that they had seen from the lane, they drove into the field and onto a large concrete apron sprouting rectangles of weeds. Ahead lay the retreating ribbon of the airstrip, an avenue of smoother grass. On the edge of the apron and roughly three yards out from the hedge was the Portakabin. To one side, a clutter of bricks, wood, chipboard and assorted debris in various stages of decomposition lay in an untidy heap. A couple of oil drums sat under the hedge, a rusting storage tank stood on stilts close to the road and, at the far end of the cabin and partly hidden by it, there was a small wooden hut.

A blustery wind tore across the field, rippling the flattened grass like a fan. A cable rapped a dull tattoo against the side of the storage tank. Pulling up her scarf Daisy went round the Portakabin to investigate the small hut at the far end. Under a leaking roof was a filthy chemical toilet, its seat missing.

The Portakabin was grey and rectangular, about eighteen feet by eight, and raised on breeze blocks at each corner. There were windows in each side and a door reached by three rickety steps. High on the side facing the apron was a pale rectangle of brighter paint where a board or sign had once been. A telephone cable emerged from a hole near the top of one wall, led up to a post and looped off across country in the direction of the farmhouse.

Campbell was trying the door, rattling the handle noisily, apparently without success. Daisy, finding an empty oil drum, rolled it across to the side of the cabin and, righting it, perched herself precariously on the top and took a look through one of the windows. There was not a great deal to see. A bare metal table, a couple of fixed cupboards, a sink unit. There was something on the floor though, and she raised herself on tiptoe to see. Papers, a couple of sheets, lying under the desk close against the wall.

Climbing down, she went round to the steps again to find Campbell bent over the door lock. Ignoring her, he straightened and took a long look around him, taking in the field and the perimeter roads with a single sweep, then listening hard for good measure. The next moment his hand slid into his pocket to emerge with a metal bar flattened off at one end: which, as Daisy didn't need telling, was a jemmy. She was on the point of objecting but something held her back, and she realized that she was rather fascinated by this blatant display of criminal accomplishment and decidedly curious to see the outcome.

Campbell had the jemmy into the doorframe and was levering it forward when he stiffened suddenly and shot a look over his shoulder. The distant staccato of a tractor engine came floating across the field. The tractor must have been coming upwind because it was already quite close, spinning along the lane at a sharp lick, the cab and driver riding high above the hedge, heading in the direction of the farmhouse.

Their presence hadn't gone unnoticed. The white oval of the driver's face turned towards them several times. Then the tractor slowed and, turning abruptly into the access road, came thundering towards them. Campbell came down the cabin steps and stood at Daisy's side. She glanced down and noticed that the jemmy had vanished from his hand.

The tractor came hurtling onto the apron, narrowly missing Campbell's car, and ground to a halt beside them. The driver was a gaunt man with a cadaverous weather-beaten face and a sullen expression. He barked: 'Yer business?'

Daisy stepped forward and, raising her voice over the

rattle of the tractor's engine, answered politely: 'We were looking for the people who used to operate from here. The flying company.'

A long pause. 'No flyers here.'

'Are you the owner?'

Another extended pause. 'The farmer.'

'Well, perhaps you could help,' Daisy continued unabashed. 'We're trying to find this flying company. You wouldn't have an address for them, would you?'

An almost imperceptible shake of the head. 'No flyers here.'

'But there was – were – a short while back?'

No response at all. His mouth narrowed into a hard uneven line.

Daisy maintained a pleasant expression. 'We were told they flew regularly from here. Some time last summer.'

'Aye, an' they're away, so y've nothin' tae find oot, have ye?'

She was aware that Campbell was moving, that he was approaching her elbow. She saw the farmer's eyes lock on to him and fire up defensively.

'We just want to locate them,' Daisy said quickly, as much to forestall Campbell as anything else.

'An' why would that be?' the farmer demanded aggressively.

'To hire them,' she said off the top of her head. 'We've got some spraying work.'

He gave her a scathing look. Perhaps he was unconvinced by the idea of Daisy farming, and one couldn't really blame him. 'Recommended, were they?'

She shrugged. 'We heard about them.'

'From a faermer, was it?' He was beating her into a corner, and they both knew it.

Before she had time to think the idea through, she said: 'From Willis Bain.'

'Willis Bain, eh?' A gleam sparked into the sharp face. 'They knew the flyers, eh, but couldna' tell ye the name?'

Daisy thought: I fell straight into that one.

Campbell was agitating his feet, bracing himself for what she suspected would be some ill-chosen words.

Daisy threw in rapidly: 'The man I spoke to couldn't remember the name, only the place.'

The eyes narrowed, and he jerked his head in the direction of the road. Just in case they hadn't got the message, he snapped: 'Ye'll be off.'

Campbell was about to argue, but Daisy pulled at his sleeve and wheeled him firmly towards the car.

As they drove down the access road the tractor roared up behind them, its lights blazing, and hugged their bumper. 'Charming character,' Daisy remarked.

Campbell didn't reply. He was chewing his lip, though whether with fury or the effort of deep thought it was impossible to tell.

They turned into the lane and headed back towards the main road. Daisy watched the tractor stop at the junction. It was still there when she lost sight of it round the next bend. 'He knew all about it, didn't he?' she said disconsolately, blowing her nose. 'But he sure wasn't about to tell.'

'I'd say so, aye.'

'But, look, what about the local village?' she said, trying to salvage something. 'Wouldn't it be worth asking around?' She couldn't help thinking of the hostelries too, and the warmth a brandy would put into her stomach.

'I asked a time back,' Campbell said, rousing himself. 'Nothin'.'

'Not worth trying again?'

'Mebbe, but it'll be dark by six.'

The logic escaped her. 'Dark?' she echoed.

He shot her a conspiratorial look. 'The cabin there.'

Even then it took her a moment to understand. 'No,'

she said firmly as soon as she had got his drift. 'Absolutely not.'

'Be in and out in no time.'

'Absolutely not. What about our friend there? No. Really, Campbell, it's out of the question.'


Daisy held the torch while Campbell slid the jemmy between the door and the frame. After a moment he gave a grunt of exertion, there was the sound of grinding metal and the door swung open.

Daisy directed the torch-beam while Campbell went through the cupboards. She had to admit that they made a good team, working over each shelf systematically like a couple of seasoned villains. Their professionalism had extended to leaving the car by the main road in the pitch dark and tramping half a mile across sodden fields.

The cupboards themselves were disappointing. Crumpled chocolate wrappers – mainly Mars Bars – abandoned cigarette packets, paper clips and plenty of dust. Under the sink was an old telephone directory and the last few sheets of a jotter pad which Daisy pocketed in case there was an impression of the last message, like the fatal clues left by culprits in detective stories. The papers she had seen from the window, lying on the floor under the table, were blank.

They combed the crevices behind the fittings, in case they had missed something, but whoever had cleaned the place out had done a fairly good job.

There was a telephone socket, but no telephone and, of course, no telephone number.

They paused. Daisy didn't have to check with Campbell to know that he too had run out of ideas.

They left. Campbell pulled the door to and, using the jemmy, levered the doorlock back into its socket in the aluminium frame, so that to a casual observer the door would look more or less untouched. Close to, the deep dents and scratches around the lock wouldn't fool anyone, and certainly not the tenant farmer.

Daisy flicked the torch-beam across the air space under the cabin. Around the edge of the cabin a fringe of tall weeds reached almost to its base while in the centre a scattering of soft drink cans and unidentifiable metal sent back gleams of silver.

Campbell called her over to the rubbish dump, which he proceeded to pull apart, undaunted by even the heaviest items which he chucked to one side as if they were paper-light. The torch-beam revealed chipboard, formica, breeze blocks, bricks, lumps of concrete, earth and weeds.

They both spotted the red lettering at the same time, buried towards the back of the pile. The style and finish of the lettering was less than professional and the white background paint was peeling off the board in small blisters, but it was a sign all right. Perhaps if Campbell hadn't been lobbing breeze blocks noisily into the hedge, perhaps if she hadn't been humming with premature excitement, then they might have heard the engine noise a bit sooner.

As it was, the vehicle was already out of the lane and into the access road by the time they froze, mesmerized by the approaching lights like a couple of rabbits caught on a vegetable patch.

Daisy was the first to move. Instinctively she turned away from the lights to head down the side of the Portaka-bin towards the deep shadows at the end. She'd gone only a couple of steps when she looked back and realized that for some inexplicable reason Campbell hadn't moved, that he was bent over the rubbish again, digging at the board with his fingers. She felt a great thump of alarm.

Running back, she grabbed at his sleeve. 'Quick, for God's sake!'

But the big man continued to burrow at the board; he was immovable.

'*For God's sake!*' she cried.

She saw everything in a succession of frozen images, like a film being run through a projector frame by frame. She saw Campbell hunched over the dump, she saw the car beams back-lighting the hedge, throwing the tracery of branches into lacelike relief, and she saw herself rooted to the spot, like an idiot who couldn't decide which way to run. Yet she knew perfectly well which way to run; it was leaving Campbell that she couldn't bring herself to do, not until the immovable moron got the message. She yelled at him, and kept yelling.

The vehicle had almost reached the break in the hedge. At any second it would turn onto the apron and flood them with light. She felt a terrible rage as Campbell, moving with all the speed of a ponderous animal, finally pulled the board out of the dirt and began to move. Free at last, she sprinted off down the alley between the cabin and the hedge. Half way along she realized she wasn't going to make the end in time: the headlights were sweeping round, and fast. She took a dive onto the concrete. It was a trick she'd never had much reason to try before, and her chin ground into the concrete with an ugly grating sensation.

The lights flooded over her. She choked for air; something sharp and hard was digging into her ribs. But she kept still, reasonably confident that she'd got down in time, which was more than could be said for Campbell who at this very moment was probably giving the driver a floodlit view of his backside. The lights had swung round and faded. She raised her head and craned round.

No sign of Campbell; the alley was empty.

Under the belly of the Portakabin she could see the headlights shining out over the airstrip. The engine note slowed, and stopped. She twisted her head up again, but there was no doubt: Campbell had completely disappeared.

There was a pause, then the click of a car door opening. Heavy feet sounded on the concrete, walked a distance then stopped. The feet scrunched intermittently as their owner moved and stopped and moved again.

There was a long silence, then through the space underneath the cabin, she saw a torch-beam flash on and weave its way over the grass. The beam moved steadily around the edge of the cabin, coming towards the alleyway where she lay. Pushing herself up on her forearms she prepared to crawl under the cabin, but just then the torch-beam swung round and went back the other way, towards the steps.

After what seemed a long time the beam danced back towards the vehicle, the footsteps retreated, the car door slammed, the engine coughed into life and the car reversed into the road and drove away.

Daisy sank her head on to the concrete, took several deep breaths and picked herself off the sharp metal object that had been grinding into her ribs. She felt weak. One thing was absolutely sure: she wasn't cut out for a life of crime.

She rubbed her chin, which felt sore, and brushed ineffectually at the grit clinging to her hands and face. Footsteps approached and she looked up to find the dark outline of Campbell standing over her.

'Christ, Campbell, you gave me bloody heart failure!' she declared with feeling.

He didn't reply, but demanded: 'The torch.'

'Why the hell didn't you move! What the hell were you doing!' The torch wasn't in her hand, nor her pocket. She scrabbled about on the ground until she found it some distance ahead of where she'd come down. She fiddled with the switch, but it didn't work.

Campbell took it from her and gave it an almighty thump. It sprang into life. Nothing, apparently, failed to yield to his methods.

'Where the hell did you get to?'

'In the hedge there,' he replied. 'An' when he was past, I went round the road side.'

'Jesus . . . Jesus.' She was still shaking, barely capable of pointing the torch while Campbell led the way back to the rubbish dump. He picked the sign out of the hedge.

It had been quite a large sign, but now half of it was missing. The wrong half. It read: *lying Systems Ltd.*

'Terrific,' Daisy murmured.

She held the light while Campbell searched the rubbish heap for another ten minutes, but there was no more white board, no more red lettering. It was beginning to rain, a thin drizzle which threatened heavier things. She felt deathly cold.

'The village,' Daisy said wearily, thinking of the hot meal and warm brandy they'd had earlier and how she'd like to repeat it, thinking too of the long-departed afternoon train and the overnight sleeper that she really mustn't miss. 'Let's get back to the village.'

The village, two miles away, consisted of a string of low houses straddling a main road. Having tried the larger of the two hotels at midday, they now went to the smaller one, a dreary hostelry with frosted windows, dim yellow lighting, and the sickly-sweet stench of stale beer. The decor was a nicotine-stained sepia, the furnishings a uniform dark brown. Daisy spent ten minutes in the ladies sneezing, coughing and dabbing the blood from the graze on her chin before joining Campbell at the bar and ordering a brandy. She certainly felt she had deserved it. Campbell obviously felt in a deserving mood too, because he had ordered a double Scotch.

The barman was a vast man with a waistline that had defeated the local outfitters. His name was Jock and he tried very hard to help. 'A flyin' company, ye say?' He kept repeating it, as if this might be enough to jog his memory. 'Cannae say I recall a flyin' company. We had a construction company, right enough. Here a couple of months, they was.' He looked hopeful, as if the construction company might prove ān acceptable alternative.

The bar began to fill up. The customers had the sly laconic air of regulars. After exchanging monosyllabic greetings they stood silently at the bar waiting for Jock to pull their brew before slapping coins onto the counter and shuffling off to their tables. When Jock questioned them about the flying outfit they looked wary, then thoughtful, then shook their heads.

The atmosphere in the bar became heavy with smoke. Daisy felt her lungs turn raw.

A girl appeared behind the bar. She was about twenty, so far as it was possible to tell beneath the spiky hair and heavy eye makeup. The hair, which came low over her eyes, and the copious use of the kohl gave her the look of a black-eyed terrier.

Jock proudly: 'Ma daughter, Morag.'

Morag's mouth twitched grudgingly into what might have been a smile or a contemptuous pout.

'They're lookin' for an aero company,' Jock explained. 'Based on Auldhame Farm some time back.'

She slid Daisy a look of open suspicion. So much for the freemasonry of women.

Daisy tried to look friendly. 'They used to go spraying,' she said. 'Forests and that sort of thing. Over to the west. There must have been a mechanic. And a pilot. We thought they might have come in here from time to time.'

A sulky shrug and a hand pushed into the spiky mane.

'You've never heard anything about them then?'

Morag picked up a glass and polished it desultorily.

'I thought you'd know everything that went on around here.'

Morage flung her a look of mortal insult. 'I'm no tattler!'

'No, of course not,' Daisy said hastily. 'I just thought you'd have more idea. Than most people, I mean.' She flicked a glance in the direction of the male drinkers.

Morage rolled her eyes and said with feeling: 'Nothin' gets *their* noses oot of their beer, no' the roof fallin' in, no' nothin'.' She stalked up to the far end of the bar and slid a glass onto a shelf. Wandering back, she stopped some way away and looked sulky again, as if to show that she wasn't entirely won over, not by a long chalk. Then, taking her time, she sidled over again and, her back half-turned to Daisy, leant an elbow on the counter.

'There's a person might know,' she said in a bored voice, examining the far side of the room.

'Oh?'

'A friend a' mine. Doon Balintcith way.'

'Oh. This friend knew them then?'

Morag fixed Daisy with a wrathful soot-encrusted stare for daring to interrupt. 'Tha's no' what 'a said.'

Daisy looked suitably penitent, but Morag was not one to be hurried, not when every ounce of satisfaction could be squeezed from a waiting game, and it was another ten minutes and a third round of drinks before she deigned to drop a name and an approximate address.

Even then it was almost nine by the time Daisy managed to prise Campbell off his stool and escape into the cool of the night. After the stench and smoke of the bar, the air tasted sweet and fresh. There was a mist; auras of damp hung around the streetlamps.

Daisy led the way to the car. If they hurried to Balinteith and were sharpish with the interview there was still an outside chance of her catching the overnight sleeper.

Balinteith was ten minutes away along the Stirling road. The home of Morag's friend Jeannie Buchanan was easy enough to find. It lay at the end of a quiet cul-de-sac, a bungalow with pebbledash rendering and square windows adorned with arched frilly curtains in peek-a-boo style.

Jeannie Buchanan's father, a polite but monosyllabic man, informed them that his daughter was out for the evening and wouldn't be returning until after eleven.

Daisy hesitated, thinking of the train and all the work still to be done on the presentation charts. But she couldn't leave this now. Jeannie's father was reluctant to let them come back at eleven until Daisy explained that she was a lawyer and had come all the way from London just to interview Jeannie about the flying company operating out of Auldhame Farm.

As they left, Campbell scoffed under his breath: 'Lawyer!' There was a touch of admiration in his tone, and she realized he was congratulating her on being such an accomplished liar.

'True. Sorry.'

His step faltered, and he moved two paces away, as if she had a contagious disease. 'You didna' tell me that,' he said accusingly.

'And you didn't tell me you went in for breaking and entering.'

'That I do not!'

They got into the car. 'Just a hobby then?' she asked.

He seemed quite upset at the idea.

The Balinteith Hotel provided the sort of dinner that is known as substantial in the North, and solid elsewhere.

At first Campbell was uncommunicative, but by the end of the main course he was becoming almost garrulous, a result very possibly of his fifth double Scotch.

They discussed Peasedale and Roper's visit to Adrian and the progress of his new treatment, which mainly consisted of coming off the numerous tranquillizers, antibiotics and anti-depressants that he'd been on for months. It was too soon to know if there was any improvement. Daisy reached in her shoulder bag, a voluminous carpetbag that expanded to take documents, makeup and overnight things, and pulled out a footballing magazine. 'I thought Adrian might like it.'

'You'll not be passing through on Thursday then?' Thursday was two days away.

'No,' she said, surprised. 'Why?'

'For the inquiry.'

'What inquiry's that?'

'Why, into Mrs Mackenzie's death.'

She lowered her cup carefully into its saucer. 'But why an inquiry?'

'He requested it, so they say.'

'Nick Mackenzie?'

'Aye. Wasna' content with the findin's.'

'You mean there's been an inquiry already?'

'An investigation,' he corrected her. 'By the proc— proc – ' He pursed his lips and took another shot. 'Pro*cur*ator fiscal. An investigation, aye. Just that. No more.'

Daisy remembered that not only were there no such things as inquests in Scotland but that investigations into deaths were held informally and in private, and that their findings were not generally made public.

'I went before him, the proc'ator fiscal,' Campbell said. 'I went an' told him . . . About findin' her. About breathin' into her mouth. About trying to re-vive her. He asked if she felt cold . . .' His voice had got maudlin, his eyes glistened with sudden moisture. 'I told him . . . I said there was nothin' that could have been done.'

'And Nick Mackenzie asked for a public inquiry?'

'Aye.'

'He must be here then? In Scotland.'

'He wasna' just two days back. But by now – mebbe so.'

While Campbell ploughed through a large steamed pudding she thought about Nick Mackenzie being back at Glen Ashard, and wondered how she could manage to get away on Thursday, when that was the day of the presentation to the Catch executive committee. She also thought about Simon, and wondered why he hadn't told her about the inquiry when he must surely have known about it.

Jeannie Buchanan finally got home shortly before eleven thirty. She was a plump pale-faced girl with short cropped hair and large anxious eyes which grew even more circular at the sight of the waiting delegation. But if Jeannie was nervous, it didn't obstruct her memory.

'Aye, I worked there at the airfield,' she said immediately in a soft unobtrusive voice.

'And the name of the flying company, what was it?' Daisy asked.

'Acorn Flying Systems.'

Daisy felt a small chime of satisfaction. 'And where are they based now?'

'Och, nowhere,' came the mouselike voice. 'They . . . stopped.'

'Stopped?'

Jeannie glanced at her father, as if for corroboration. 'Closed down. I think they had some trouble with the bank. In fact . . .' She looked apologetic for mentioning it. 'They still owe me three weeks' wages.'

'When was this? That they ceased trading?'

'Och, it must be September last.'

So much for the easy run. 'What about the owners?' Daisy asked gently. 'The directors and so on – do you have any names?'

'There was a Mr Keen. He was the managing director. I only saw him twice – once when he took me on, and another time when he came out to the airfield and helped us out when we were busy. Then there was Davie, the mechanic. He came from Glasgow. And Reggie, he helped with the navigation system. And then of course there was Mr Duggan.'

'Mr Duggan?'

'The pilot.'

Daisy absorbed this for a moment. 'The director, Mr Keen, where did he come from, do you know?'

'The company had an address somewhere in Glasgow, but it wasn't his personal address, at least I don't think so. I tried writing to Mr Keen when the problem with the bank came up but the post office returned my letter. There was a phone number, a Glasgow number. I'd use it to phone Mr Keen when there were any problems. That was maybe two or three times a week. But when I last tried, the telephone people said the line had been disconnected.'

'Have you still got the number?'

Her face, which reflected her emotions like a mirror, immediately fell. 'I'm not sure I still have it. I'd have to look and see.'

'What about wages, paperwork, how was that arranged?'

'With the local branch of the bank. Or through the post from Glasgow.'

'What about other things – supplies – I don't know, whatever planes need?'

'The fuel, that arrived by tanker. It was arranged from Glasgow.'

'And the spray – the chemicals?'

'Sometimes Davie went off to the wholesalers. But most times it was delivered.'

'Who delivered it?'

'That would be Willis Bain,' she said without hesitation. 'Most of our work came from them. They're forest managers.'

'And the chemical used, what was it?'

She wet her lips and cast another glance at her father. 'Och, I'm not sure. There were two . . . They had such names. Long . . . I can't recall.'

'You don't remember a bit of a name?' There must have been a hint of reproach in her tone because Jeannie withdrew slightly. 'I only signed the receipts,' she said defensively. 'I didn't order the chemicals. That was done from Glasgow.'

'Of course,' Daisy said placatingly. 'Was there one that sounded like fenitrothion?'

'Mebbe . . . But . . .' Looking unhappy, she finished in a rush. 'I really couldn't say for sure.'

Daisy sat back. It had perhaps been too much to hope for. Fastening a smile over her disappointment, she asked: 'Duggan, the pilot – what was his full name?'

'Peter. Peter Duggan.'

'And where did he come from?'

'Och, he was from England.' She made it sound like Mars.

'Do you have his address?'

'Och no.' From the way she said it she wouldn't have wanted it even if he'd given it to her.

'You don't even remember the town?'

She was adamant: no.

'And Davie, the mechanic. Was he local?'

'No. He came from up Inverness way.'

'Have you an address?'

She shook her head. 'He said he was going to work abroad. The Middle East, I believe.'

'What was his second name?'

'Robertson.'

It might be possible to trace him, though God only knew how many Robertsons there were in and around Inverness. Daisy tried another tack. 'Acorn Flying Systems – what other work did it do?'

She shook her head. 'None that I know of. Just the spraying – we never did anything but the spraying. The trees, they had a bad disease, the beauty moth it was. We had plenty of work last summer, more than we could handle.'

'Do you remember any jobs up by Loch Fyne?'

She thought hard. 'There were a few. Around and about. But I'm not sure that I remember exactly . . .'

'Up by Inveraray way.'

She shrugged. 'I used to type the schedule and the job sheets and the notifications – but there were so many . . .'

'The notifications?'

'Notices to tell the police, the health and safety office, and the people on the adjoining land.'

'These were letters? Sent out by post?'

'Aye.' She dropped her eyes and started picking at the arm of her chair.

'And they were sent out for every job, Jeannie? To every neighbour?'

She didn't answer at first. When she finally spoke her voice was little more than a whisper. 'Aye.' She had a thread out of the fabric now, and was pulling at it.

Daisy wasn't sure what she'd touched on but it was something Jeannie wasn't inclined to talk about.

Jeannie's father stood up and made a remark about how late it was.

Daisy looked questioningly at Jeannie, hoping she'd elaborate, but she went on staring intently at the thread, weaving it back and forth between her fingers.

Campbell asked: 'This pilot fella, where did he board round here?'

Jeannie looked up; this was an easier one. 'Och, at Mrs Donald's,' she said as if everyone must know Mrs Donald. 'For a while, that is. Then he moved on to Mrs McKay's. Better breakfasts, he said.'

'These places, they're here in Balinteith?' Daisy asked.

'Aye,' she said.

Daisy tried some more questions about the flying schedules, but at the first mention of job sheets, Jeannie was fiddling at the chair arm again, and Daisy retreated.

As they got up to leave, Jeannie disappeared and returned a minute later with the address and defunct phone number of Acorn Flying Systems. 'There,' she said, handing it to Daisy with the formality of an offering.

It was quarter past midnight by the time Daisy drove Campbell's car out of Balinteith, heading west. Having seen the effect Campbell's last whisky had had on him and overcome by a strong desire to live, she had insisted on driving. The Ford was not the easiest car she'd ever tackled. The driver's seat was so low, battered into concavity by Campbell's bulk, that before she could see over the bonnet she had to prop herself up on top of her much-folded jacket and a smelly old fishing bag that Campbell dug out of the boot. The steering seemed only remotely connected to the front wheels, so there was a small but heart-stopping delay before the car responded to the turns.

'I was thinking,' Daisy said when she'd finally got the hang of it. 'That plane must have got serviced somewhere. At an airport, with proper mechanics. If we asked around we might find someone who knows this Keen person.'

There was no reply. She glanced across. Campbell had fallen asleep, his head back, his mouth open wide as if awaiting major tooth extraction. Daisy fiddled with the heating controls and was rewarded with a small but satisfying whisper of hot air.

The road wasn't bad by rural standards: not straight, but not too bendy either, and with almost no traffic she was able to keep up a good speed all the way to Loch Lomond. Here the road divided: south to Glasgow and the transport network, or west and north to Loch Fyne and Campbell's home. Glasgow was only half an hour away, while Loch Fyne was a good hour over the mountains. South was the obvious choice. If she stayed the night in Glasgow, she could take the early shuttle and still get to the office by morning. There'd still be difficulties, of course. Quite apart from having to justify the wild expenditure on hotels and planes – Catch personnel were meant to stay with friends and travel on cut-price rail tickets – she'd be landing Campbell with a long night-drive in an illegal state of inebriation.

If she took Campbell straight back to Loch Fyne now and stayed somewhere up there, on the other hand, she could interview the pilot's landladies in the morning. But then there'd be absolutely no chance of getting to the office in time to prepare the charts for Thursday. Given enough notice there was no reason why Alan couldn't have done the charts himself, of course. Maybe still could . . .

She had been stopped at the junction for some moments. Now a car was approaching from behind.

With a sigh of dread but also an indefinable clutch of excitement, she turned west onto the Loch Fyne road.

The low cloud that had darkened the sky all day had lifted. On the drive along the west bank of Loch Lomond first one star then another began to gleam through the layers of darkness. By the time she had urged the car up the long pass of Glen Croe to the summit at Rest And Be Thankful the mountains were etched black against a brilliant sky.

They reached Inveraray at one thirty. Campbell, who responded to her prodding with a massive groan, eventually directed her to a white-fronted hotel in the main street. It was ten minutes before the proprietor answered, looking far from pleased, and his displeasure was not mollified by the sight of Campbell, whom he seemed to know well.

Daisy took the key but did not go up to the room. Her brain was suddenly alive, almost feverish; she knew she wouldn't sleep.

She asked for a street-door key, and went out to the car with Campbell. He took some persuading to let her drop him off and keep the car.

'There's nothin' to see, not in the dark,' he grunted, adding superfluously: 'Be light by mornin'.'

'I'll come and pick you up first thing.'

'Is it Glen Ashard you wish to see?'

She gave a shrug, not quite sure of the answer herself.

'I can take you there, you know, right up behind the house. But best wait till day.'

'No. It's not that.' She couldn't explain.

'You could take away some earth, like you did for Adrian. See what it contains.'

'Yes, I know.' She pushed the gear in and moved off.

Campbell sighed, accepting defeat.

'I'll get the car back to you first thing,' Daisy repeated.

'Och no, no,' he declared. 'Keep it at the hotel here. I'll get a ride in, fine.'

His home was a mile or two out of town to the north, on a glen road that snaked up into the high lands. It was a squat cottage sitting on the ledge of a windswept hillside. She had no idea what Campbell's domestic arrangements were, but she rather assumed he lived alone.

As soon as she'd dropped him she headed back towards the town and, rejoining the main road, turned west. The houses thinned to a straggle then ceased altogether as the road ran close by the side of the loch. Though the stars shone as brilliantly as ever, the waters were very dark and it was impossible to see where the loch ended and the hills began.

Soon the road turned away from the water, deflected by high ground, and passed between fields and plantations of conifers. Occasionally there was the twinkle of a light in the distance and once a car came speeding past in the opposite direction, but for the most part the land was as dark as the night.

She briefly thought of turning back, but even as she considered it she knew she wouldn't. It couldn't be far away.

She passed one set of gates on a bend and reversed back to take a look at the sign, but it was some other house. After a mile or two the road left the loch again, passing through an arid landscape of newly felled forest, and she began to think she must have missed it. But then the road dipped into thickly wooded country again, tunnelling under a canopy of giant overhanging trees, and a wall appeared on the right, the sort of proprietorial wall reserved for parklands and large estates.

The gateposts when they finally appeared were prominent enough – fortified mediaeval-style towers, abutted by two gatekeepers' lodges. There was a conspicuous sign: *Ashard House. Strictly Private*, and tall wrought-iron gates which were firmly shut.

She drove slowly on, hoping for a glimpse of the house, but either the screen of trees was too thick or the place was set too far back, because no lights showed above the wall surrounding the estate.

She slowed down, feeling tired and slightly foolish, and looked for a place to turn. Eventually she came to a break in the wall where it curved in two arcs towards an entrance. She turned in and found herself on a rough track barred by a metal five-bar gate.

A point of light blinked through the undergrowth ahead. Switching off the headlights, she got out and went up to the gate, which was heavily padlocked. She stood for a while, undecided, tempted, drawn.

Feeling conspicuous despite the darkness, she climbed over and crept along the edge of the track.

After fifty yards or so the undergrowth became thinner, the trees more scattered until at last she was able to see the house. It was large with numerous tall uncurtained windows, several wings and a turret or two. She had no trouble in making out the size of the place, the number and shape of the windows: the two pinpricks she'd glimpsed from the road had been a mere sample of what was to come. Ashard House was a blaze of lights.

There was something sad in the sight of the bright house. When she crept away, it was in the certainty that she would stay for the inquiry.

# Chapter 17

'WAKE UP, SPORT.'

Nick, in depths black and heavy, senses obliterated by sleep, brain obliterated by chemicals legal but plentifully administered, heard the voice at the far end of an echoing tunnel.

'Nick, come on. Wakey-wakey.'

Someone was gripping Nick's shoulder, shaking it gently but relentlessly. Focusing on this sensation he used it to haul himself into the light.

It was Mel. Nick closed his eyes again and began to examine the messages his waking body was sending him. None of them was pleasant.

'It's three,' Mel announced. 'David's arrived. And the lawyer.'

Three. It took him a moment to realize it was afternoon. He felt a moment's resentment for not having been woken earlier, then remembered that it had been ten that morning before he had finally slept.

He muttered: 'I'll be down.' When Mel had gone he swung his feet to the floor and waited for his brain to catch up with his body. A nightmare still racketed round the edges of his mind and it was a moment before he was able to shake himself free of it. The half consciousness between sleep and waking was always the worst, worse even than jerking awake in the night, heart pounding, or lying with no hope of sleep, listening to the wailing of the wind.

He took a shower, dressed and went downstairs unshaven.

Mrs Alton was in the kitchen, looking flustered. She had risen to the challenge of preparing ready-to-heat food for all-night rehearsals, but she had not quite adjusted to finding Mel and Joe frying steak and chips at seven in the morning. 'Would you like something?' she asked tentatively.

'Coffee and toast, please, Mrs Alton.'

On his way across the hall he saw the envelope propped against a vase on the side table. It was marked urgent, in large letters. He scooped it up and carried it into the drawing room.

He found David and the lawyer either side of a roaring fire. David was sitting in a wing chair with Mrs Alton's full afternoon tea, complete with silver service, on a table in front of him. He had a scone half-way to his mouth but, on seeing Nick, put it down.

'How are you, Nick?' His expression was a blend of concern and faint alarm, and Nick realized that he was reading the full spectrum of bad news into his unshaven bleary-eyed appearance.

The lawyer rose from the seat opposite. He was a Glasgow solicitor called Bennett, a mousy little man with a mild manner and soft deferential voice which concealed a sharp mind.

'I was wondering if you'd given any more thought to what I suggested?' Bennett said as soon they were sitting down. 'It's rather late in the day but, given the circumstances, I'm sure we would find favourable consideration.'

Nick lit a cigarette and said nothing. He'd become adept at silences.

'The inquiry will be exactly what it says it is,' Bennett continued in patient tones. 'That is, a public enquiry. The press will not miss a moment, Mr Mackenzie, and if there's anything' – he paused to choose his words – 'if there's anything worth reporting – well, they will be bound to use it. It will all be very *exposed*. Very trying for you.' He paused then, getting no response, continued: 'I've been looking into precedents and it is perfectly possible that the Lord Advocate might consider withdrawing his recommendation for an inquiry, even at this late stage, since it was you yourself who pressed for it. I don't think he will take much convincing that, despite everything, it is not after all a matter of public interest and concern.' He looked across to David as if for support. 'Then the whole matter could be left to rest, Mr Mackenzie. In peace, one might say.'

They had been over all this before, Nick thought with bemusement. Perhaps Bennett hadn't listened properly when they'd first discussed it – when was it? A month ago? Two months? Last week? Time had become strangely elastic and shapeless, until whole images were wiped out or transposed. But he could see this particular scene all right: they had been in this room, the two of them, the fire burning brightly in the cavernous fireplace, Bennett sitting on the settee, Nick where David was now. Nick had explained it to him, carefully, at length. Bennett had argued, Nick had held his ground. In those weeks immediately after the accident he had felt a curious energy, he remembered, an extraordinary clarity of mind which had carried him forward, allowing him to tackle things in the most minute detail; he had even garnered an odd sort of pleasure in getting everything done in the correct and proper manner – in the way Alusha would have approved. Her presence had had form then; a bright living speaking thing. It was different now. Her face was fading. He could no longer see it clearly, could no longer hear her voice.

'It's not as if the inquiry would have gone ahead without ourselves specifically requesting it,' Bennett repeated, giving it one last shot. 'It's not as if the Lord Advocate had recommended it off his own bat, so to speak.' Casting an appraising look at Nick, he gathered himself to approach from another tack. 'What concerns me,' he began carefully, 'is the ambiguities that are bound to creep in, the ones I outlined to you.'

'Ambiguities?'

'Concerning the manner of your wife's illness. The differences of opinion. The uncertainties. Would you not agree that they might be best avoided? They could be very – disturbing for you.'

Nick roused himself to an argument for which he had little enthusiasm. 'But the evidence from the Boston man. There's no ambiguity there.'

Bennett dropped his head briefly over his clasped hands. 'I have to say as I've said before, Mr Mackenzie, that I believe it would be unwise to put too much reliance on Gravely's affidavit. Being an alternative practitioner, his opinion will not be viewed in the same light as an orthodox practitioner's. His views may well be – how shall I say? – put into question. And not being present in person, he won't be able to defend those views. It would be a different matter if we had some other opinion or opinions to back him up. Like those of a toxicologist, for example. Without what one might call hard evidence it is going to be almost impossible to establish our theory.' He broke off as Mrs Alton came into the room and put a tray of coffee and toast beside Nick. 'Of course there's always an adjournment,' he continued when the door had closed again. 'I am not sure whether the Lord Advocate would be persuaded to consider such a thing at this late stage, but I could but try. And given some extra time, then perhaps we could renew our enquiries among the toxicologists . . .'

He left the suggestion hanging hopefully in the air.

Nick drew on his cigarette and fiddled with the unfilled coffee cup at his side. 'No. No . . . I don't want a delay. No delay.'

There was a silence. Bennett clasped his hands more tightly and drew breath. 'The procurator fiscal's finding –

is it that which concerns you, Mr Mackenzie? Is it that which you feel must not be allowed to rest?'

Hardly trusting himself to speak, Nick said: 'Well, of course, of *course* it is! What d'you expect me to feel when it's *wrong*! Wrong and dangerous.'

'It's natural that you should be upset, anyone would be. It's always hard to accept something like that . . .'

'She didn't kill herself.' The quietness of his voice did not conceal its tension.

'No, no. I accept that, Mr Mackenzie . . .' Bennett used a kindly, humouring tone. '. . . But since the finding was not published, since the procurator fiscal's finding – erroneous though it may be – is to all intents and purpose a private matter, can the whole business not be put behind you?'

'No.'

'Mr Mackenzie, sometimes grief . . . the emotions . . . can colour our better judgement.'

'No.'

Nick was suddenly gripped by such a wave of despair and confusion that he had to get up and stand at the window until he regained the ability to speak. He longed for an enormous drink, a great big golden Scotch, just like the one he'd had yesterday at about this time and had followed with regular top-ups through the night. But he couldn't bring himself to go openly to the drinks trolley, not with David in the room. Already he could feel David's eagle eye on him, sizing up the situation, wondering whether he'd succumbed.

Bennett cleared his throat. 'Even allowing for your very admirable wish that nothing like this should be permitted to happen again, I am concerned that the inquiry will fail to deliver the appropriate sort of warning. I am concerned that the wrong message will come through, that you will be disappointed.'

David appeared briefly at Nick's elbow and pushed a

cup of coffee into his hand. Nick stared at it for a moment before nodding his thanks and draining the cup in one gulp. He stared out into the park, towards the wide spread of one of the larger cedars, its branches unbalanced by the loss of a lower limb in a winter gale. At some point he had meant to ask Duncan to prop up some of the more fragile branches, but could no longer remember if he'd ever got round to it. This memory, like so many of the recent and not so recent past, was lost in a haze that seemed to have invaded every part of his brain. The worrying thing was not that the fog existed, but that he had developed a strong need for it. Whenever it lifted he had to take steps to bring it back again; drink or Librium usually did the trick or, more effective still, both.

Bennett came back onto old ground. 'Peace of mind is worth a great deal, Mr Mackenzie.'

Peace of mind? Nick couldn't begin to imagine what that must feel like.

'We go ahead,' he said.

A reproving silence while Bennett regrouped. 'Just so long as you appreciate that I'll have very little control over what might come out in court.'

'What might come out?' There was a roaring in Nick's ears, like being under water. 'What do you mean – what might come out?'

Bennett held up both hands placatingly. 'I meant merely that we will have no control over the evidence that the procurator fiscal might introduce.'

'There's nothing to come out,' Nick retorted, refusing to be mollified. 'Except that my wife was half killed by a dangerous chemical, and that's exactly what I *do* want to come out!' Marching up to his chair, he dropped the cup and saucer onto the tray with a clatter. 'The only thing that can come out is the truth! What did you mean – what might come out? Christ.'

'The London psychiatrist, Carter . . .'

'Just one opinion!'

'But that will not stop them from introducing the evidence, will it, Mr Mackenzie! It will not stop those sorts of ideas from being discussed in public.'

'Well, it'll be your job to stop it, won't it!'

His anger was senseless, he knew it, senseless and destructive.

'I'll do my best, Mr Mackenzie, of that you may be sure.'

Sinking into his chair, Nick rubbed a hand over his eyes, and fighting for equilibrium said in a calmer voice: 'I accept the risks.'

Bennett reached for his briefcase and said regretfully: 'Very well.'

David, professional smoother of troubled waters, stepped in and asked Bennett how long he thought the inquiry would last.

Nick's gaze fell on the envelope that he'd carried in from the hall. He pulled it out from under the tray and, opening it, glanced down the handwritten letter. Daisy Field. There was no date and the envelope bore no post mark. He read the letter grudgingly.

An airfield, an aerial spraying programme. She asked if he'd considered the possibility that it wasn't Reldane at all, that Alusha had been affected by another substance altogether? There was a boy with similar symptoms, and a couple of other people who might be affected.

He rapidly lost interest. This sounded like the theory of that man Campbell, or a variant of it. The very thought of Campbell caused him to tighten his grip on the paper.

*With time and resources we hope to get firm evidence,* she wrote. Which meant she had no evidence at all. Just like the Reldane situation: all wishful thinking and wild promises and nothing to back it up.

She finished with an offer to give evidence at the inquiry if he thought that might help. She gave the telephone number of a hotel in Inveraray.

Bennett was getting up. 'Forgive me for mentioning it, Mr Mackenzie . . .' He gestured a slight apology. 'But tomorrow – a suit and tie might be a good idea.'

Ah, thought Nick, mustn't have the widowed husband looking degenerate.

Seeing the dangerous gleam in his eye, David interposed: 'They were rehearsing till six this morning. They've only just got up.'

'Of course,' Bennett said, with an indulgent smile to show that, as a man of the world, he understood the ways of artists.

Nick showed him to the door, grateful both for an end to the discussion and for the chance to slip upstairs and grab a nip of Scotch.

When he came down again he was revived and anaesthetized, and feeling a little more able to face the day, though this didn't stop him from needling David at the first opportunity.

David was standing in the hall waiting for him, wearing that mournful, mildly reproachful expression that Nick knew so well. It was the one he'd used in the old days when Nick had done things like falling downstairs and not getting up again.

'Well?' Nick demanded defensively.

David looked wide-eyed. 'I'm sorry?'

'Why're you looking at me like that? What's the problem?'

'There's no problem, Nick,' he replied, sounding hurt. 'There's never a problem.'


'I've managed to get another three bookings,' David explained, pouring himself another cup of tea. 'Chicago,

Detroit and Philadelphia. All cancellations from that Rotten Apple tour. Some tight logistics, I'm afraid, but otherwise good.'

'That's it then, is it?'

'Can't get any more bookings, not at this sort of notice. Lucky to get what we have.'

Nick got up and stood in front of the fire. 'How many's that then?'

'Seven. Start and finish at Madison Square. Well, not quite – actually Detroit will come last.'

Nick stared into the flames. 'It's going to work out, is it?'

What did he mean? David took a guess and replied: 'Sure. The Madison Square dates sold out straight away – I knew they would. We could have filled the Shea Stadium. Well – given more notice we could have. Next time, eh?'

'The material. It worries me.'

'In what way?'

'The new stuff.'

'What about it?'

'Not enough.'

'What – three songs? That's plenty, Nick, for this sort of gig at least. A major tour – well, that would be different. But with a low-scale comeback like this, most of the fans'll be coming for the old numbers anyway, you know that.'

Nick shook his head.

'It'll be okay, Nick, don't worry.'

But he was miles away, wearing the sort of look that rang alarm bells deep in David's memory.

'I'm booking the European tour, Nick. Is that all right?'

'What?'

'I should go ahead, should I?'

Nick pulled himself back from whatever had been detaining him. 'Sure.'

David thought: Give me signals, Nick. Let me know if you're going to make it. Let me know if you're in trouble.

He said: 'If you've any doubts, then you only have to tell me.'

Nick ambled back to his seat. 'No – fine. Go ahead.'

'What worries me is the timing, Nick. Will there be enough time to do the album? I worry that you're taking on too much.' He thought: I also worry that you won't be able to deal with it.

'It'll keep me out of trouble.' He grimaced at the platitude.

'So long as it's what you want, Nick. So long as it'll make you happy.'

'It's what I want.' He didn't sound too sure. In fact it seemed to David's sinking heart there was an edge of panic in his voice, an underlying appeal, like a child who can't admit to having made a mistake. Nick had always been stubborn. It was his greatest strength, and his greatest weakness. But desperate though David was to get an accurate grasp of the situation, this wasn't the time to press Nick, not on the day before the inquiry.

'I had an idea,' David said brightly. 'How about a one-off gig in London before you start the European tour. A sort of warm-up welcome-back we're-here date. It'd coincide with the announcement of the UK tour. Great publicity, particularly if it's a charity do – you know, hand-shaking with some royals and all in a good cause.'

'If you think so.'

'Well, I'll leave the idea with you, shall I? Then we'll bounce it off the others. Just thought I'd sound you out first, Nick. You're the boss.'

But he wasn't listening. He was staring at the fire, his hands moving relentlessly on the chair arms, a crossed leg swinging frenetically back and forth. David wasn't sur-prised when a few moments later he made a show of looking at his watch and, getting up, sidled towards the door in that hesitant way of his. 'Got to call someone.

Have some more tea, David. Make yourself at home.' He hovered at the door for an instant.

'Won't be long.' Then he was gone. He hadn't looked David in the eye.

David sank back in his chair, thinking: We've been here before, Nick. I recognize the signs.

Booze. Uppers. Downers. All three maybe. What difference did it make? The whole scene was like a rerun. Everyone knew their parts, everyone knew their lines. Everyone knew they had to pretend it wasn't happening. Everyone hoped it was going to be different but knew it was going to be just the same.

But the ending – that wouldn't be the same. This time there wasn't going to be anyone to catch Nick when he fell.


Mrs McKay's bed-and-breakfast establishment was at the far end of Balinteith, a dark two-storey villa of small proportions but grand design, set back from the road behind a damp garden of tall shrubs. Campbell chose to stay in the car, presumably to nurse his hangover, though Daisy hadn't enquired too closely about that.

A low gate with a broken latch and a short concrete path led to a porch and a glass-fronted door exhibiting a No Vacancies sign and the badges of two bed-and-breakfast associations. The bell sounded deep in the house and was met by a long silence. The glass door panels were draped with thick lace curtains, as were the windows on either side of the porch, and the whole place had a closed-up air to it, as if the owner had gone away. Daisy was hovering irresolutely on the path, searching the upper windows, when a large woman with a shock of white hair pulled back into an extravagant bun rolled in through the gate, a bulging shopping trolley in tow.

'Mrs McKay? Aye, that's me – for my sins. Only one

McKay round here.' She laughed as if it were a great joke and, scrabbling deep in her bag, came out empty-handed and threw up her hands in a theatrical gesture of despair. She reached under the frayed door mat and pulled out a key. 'I've no idea why I bother,' she exclaimed, her eyes dancing. 'The whole place knows where I keep it.'

Parking her trolley in the hall, she waved Daisy into the house with great sweeping movements, like a policeman directing traffic. The hall, dark with ancient furniture and elaborate wallpaper, smelled strongly of lavender polish.

'Now what can I do for you?' asked Mrs McKay, fighting her plump arms out of her voluminous plastic raincoat to reveal a tent-like floral dress that flowed over her bosom like water over a dam.

Daisy explained that she was trying to trace Peter Duggan, and invented an acquaintance who was anxious to find him.

'Come.' The great sweeping movements led Daisy to a parlour with four circular tables laid for breakfast, with overturned cups sitting neatly in their saucers, marmalade and honey jars and solid stainless-steel cruet sets.

'You'll be taking a cup of tea?' Mrs McKay sang gaily, waving Daisy to a table and disappearing into the adjoining kitchen. 'Peter Duggan – aye, he stayed here quite a wee while,' she called through the open door. 'A bit of a rascal if you ask me.' She gave a chortle. 'Not that I've the evidence for that statement, you understand.' She popped her head round the door and winked heavily. 'Just ma canny old instincts.'

'Did he leave a forwarding address?'

'No, no – not that one. Travel light, travel free, no questions asked. They're all the same.'

'Did he ever say where he came from?'

She pulled a thoughtful face and disappeared again, returning with a tray of tea things which she plonked noisily on the table. 'Now that you come to ask, I'm not sure he ever said.' She poured out the tea and sat down, exhaling noisily. 'That's strange, is it not?' she declared, affecting a look of cheerful puzzlement. 'I usually get the entire story, you understand – the *entire* story.' She giggled girlishly, raising a shoulder to her plump cheek.

'You must have some tales to tell, Mrs McKay.'

'Indeed. But I'm careful who I tell them to,' she said, her eyes darting up to Daisy's.

Daisy wasn't sure if this was an announcement or a warning. 'Did he say where he used to work?' she asked. 'The name of a company, an airline?'

Mrs McKay shook her head vigorously, so that her bun wobbled precariously on her head.

'Nothing like that?'

'I regret not.' She drained her cup and, under cover of her habitual smile, gave Daisy a long and careful look. 'This acquaintance of his,' she said drawing the words out like beads on a string, 'he just wants to get in touch, does he? Or might it be a she?' She wriggled her eyebrows suggestively.

'The friend simply wants to contact Peter,' Daisy confirmed. 'That's all.'

'Many would find that an unlikely story,' she crowed. 'Many would suspect that this friend might be a woman from his past, or mebbe someone in a wee dispute about money . . .'

'Nothing like that, really.'

'Many would not believe you,' she echoed, 'but then I've always gone where angels fear to tread.' She leaned across the table and tapped Daisy's hand. 'I always go by instinct. It's not let me down yet.'

Daisy ventured: 'So, Duggan – you might have some idea where . . .?'

But the ebullient hands were making flamboyant hushing gestures, the eyes closing, the face, absorbed with sudden concentration, tilting towards the ceiling. A moment of

silence then, with a sudden flash of the eyes she announced:
'He had family – ' Her hands described windmills in the
air. 'Somewhere in Surrey. Began with a D. Do-Doo-Da – '
  'Datchet?'
  'Dorking!' she cried triumphantly. 'A sister. In Dorking.
His only family, he said. I got the impression he was fond
of her. The sister was on her own. She'd married a free
spirit.' She lowered her voice waggishly. 'That is, a man
who felt free to go off and leave her with three children.
Peter played the uncle. He liked that. Fond of the kiddie-
winks, he was. Bought them presents.'
  'Her name – did he ever mention it?'
  'No, no ... He never told me that.' She tapped her
temple. 'Or else it's clean gone oot ma head, which is
entirely possible. But Dorking's not so large, is it? The way
Peter talked about it I got the impression it was just a wee
place. You could ask about, could you not?'
  'Well ...' Daisy didn't know much about Dorking,
except that it was one of the larger towns within commuter
distance of London.
  Her disappointment must have shown in her face
because Mrs McKay added brightly: 'Try the pubs. You'll
be sure to find him supporting a bar or two. I tell you, I
wheeled him to his bed more times than I care to mention.'
And she chuckled at the memory, the gleam of old desires
in her eyes.
  Daisy left her phone number, and as an afterthought
Campbell's too, in case Mrs McKay's memory should
undergo a sudden improvement.
  'Sorry I was not more help,' said Mrs McKay swaying
vigorously through the hall.
  'It's been a pleasure,' said Daisy.
  'You'll give him my warm regards?' she asked, opening
the door and leaning coquettishly against it.
  'Of course.'
  She called down the path. 'I wish you luck.'

Campbell was asleep when Daisy opened the car door. Stretching and unrolling his great frame from the seat, he shot her a bleary glance. 'Anythin'?' he asked.

'Not a lot,' Daisy replied. 'Just Dorking.'

'Eh?'

Daisy shook her head. 'Come on!' she cried, making gee-up-and-go gestures. 'The Stirling road.'

'Eh?'

'We're going to see Jeannie Buchanan at work. It's off the Stirling road.'

Campbell started the engine in silence though she could see all sorts of questions forming behind the lowering brows and narrow lips.

Leaving Balinteith, they drove eastwards through the flat farmlands of the Forth valley, between fields flecked with sheep and young lambs and the occasional white-blossoming tree. Everything was touched with the sharp yellow-green of early summer. To the north, in the far distance, the horizon was broken by soft grey hills that merged into a sky of milky radiance.

'The summer,' Daisy murmured.

Campbell peered through the windscreen as if noticing his surroundings for the first time. 'More colour in the Highlands.'

She smiled. 'Tell me, Campbell, what do Highlanders think of people like Nick Mackenzie, people who buy up the big estates?'

He waved a hand philosophically. 'We've been invaded by the English so many times once more is neither here nor there.'

'But there's resentment?'

'There's always resentment,' he grunted. 'We're still smartin' over the Clearances an' that was two hundred year' ago. The estates would not exist at all if the Scots had not been driven from the land.' He waved a hand. 'But Mr Mackenzie – och, he's all right.'

'No problems with people along the loch? No difficulties?'

Campbell shifted in his seat. 'No,' he said carefully. 'No. Why should you think that?'

'No reason,' she said.

It was one by the time they reached the village where Jeannie had said she worked. The Bonaccord Savings Bank was a modest stone building occupying a prominent position next to the grocery store. Campbell offered to come in with Daisy, but retreated, looking hurt, when she said: 'No, it would only frighten her.' Taking pity on him, she declared: 'You're too big, Campbell! You'd frighten anybody!'

The counter clerk looked disconcerted by the nature of her request, but, after ceremoniously locking his cash drawer, left his window to summon Jeannie. A minute later she appeared through a side door. Her child-like eyes rounded at the sight of Daisy.

'I hope you don't mind,' Daisy said. 'There was just one more thing.'

'More?' she whispered, glancing over her shoulder.

'Last night, there was something else, wasn't there?' Daisy suggested. 'Something you couldn't tell me?'

Jeannie's eyes grew, she seemed to undergo an inner struggle, then, with a sigh that was almost a moan, she began in a sudden and breathless rush: 'Aye, aye. It was the notifications – there was not always the time to amend them. It was not my fault, it was Mr Keen – always sending new instructions, pushing us, changing things, altering dates. There wasn't the time . . .' She paused, misgivings in her face, as if she realized she might already have said too much.

'Amend them – in what way?'

'When the spraying date was changed, when the weather was bad, to tell everyone who should have been told.'

'So you'd send out one set of notifications and then

when the date had to be cancelled you were meant to send out another lot with a new date on them?'

'Aye. But there was not the time. It was Mr Keen. Always changing everything. I did my best, I always tried to do my best . . .'

'Not your fault.'

But Jeannie was not to be reassured. 'It was wrong. I knew it was wrong, but what could I do?

'But were there mishaps, Jeannie – things that happened as a result?'

'Aye.' She closed her eyes for a moment. 'Sometimes I heard Mr Duggan joking about cattle and sheep and how he'd given them a dusting. That's what he used to call it, giving them a dusting. I knew what he meant. He meant he'd sprayed them. It didn't bother him. In fact, he used to laugh.' There was a glint of tears in her eyes.

'Not your fault,' Daisy repeated.

'I should have said something! I should have told someone!'

'How often did it happen – the notifications not getting amended?'

'Four times. Maybe five.'

'On jobs by Loch Fyne?'

The doors sounded and someone came into the bank. They both waited for the customer to approach the counter and begin to speak.

Daisy repeated her question in an undertone.

Jeannie looked imploringly at her, as if she would have given anything not to answer. Finally she whispered miserably: 'Aye. Up there, by Loch Fyne. Once . . .'

'Yes?'

'Once . . . I had no time at all.'

'No time to amend the notification, you mean?'

Her lower lip buckled, a tear plopped onto her blouse. Daisy fumbled in her bag and found a tissue.

'No time to send it,' Jeannie said, pressing the tissue to

her eyes. 'Nothing was ever sent, nothing at all . . .' Her voice was almost inaudible.

'And where exactly was it, this forest? Do you remember the name?'

She shook her head firmly.

'It wasn't the Fincharn Estate, was it?'

But try as she might Jeannie was past further remembrance. She thought it was on the north side of the loch, then the south and then maybe up towards Loch Awe.

'I didn't sleep last night for thinking of it,' Jeannie moaned, blowing her nose. 'I knew it would come out. I knew I should have told you.'

'Well, you've told me now.' Daisy squeezed her hand. 'Thanks.' She started for the door and turned back. 'By the way – did Duggan ever mention anything about Dorking?'

'Dorking?' Jeannie echoed. 'Dorking?' She touched her head, as if touching her memory. 'No,' she said. 'No.'

'Or a sister?'

'A *sister* . . . Oh, aye. Aye, he talked of her.'

'What did he say?'

'He talked about getting down to see her. He said he might take her on holiday. At least I think it was a holiday . . .'

'Did she have a name?'

'I never heard it.'

The clerk was pressing his face hard against the counter window in an attempt to get a look at them. 'You'll call me?' Daisy said. 'If there's anything else?'

She nodded effusively.

Daisy was almost through the door when Jeannie called: 'Wait – ' and hurried after her. 'His sister . . . I believe he said she had a wee shop. Clothes, I think it was. Aye, clothes. He said she went to London to purchase things for it. Perhaps it's there, the shop, in that place you said?'

Perhaps it was. But then again, perhaps it wasn't.

Jeannie held open the door and hovered, reluctant to let

her go. 'The notifications,' she said. 'I knew it was wrong at the time. But it was the job, you see – there were no other jobs to be found. I was frightened of losing it.'

'I know the feeling,' Daisy said, remembering a phone conversation she'd had with Alan that morning.

Heading west again, Daisy and Campbell took the first road south and spent the rest of the day in Glasgow attempting to trace the elusive Mr Keen. The address of Acorn Flying Systems turned out to be a converted stable at the back of an old house on the northern outskirts of the city. The windows were dirty but not so thickly covered that one couldn't peer through and see that the two interconnecting rooms were empty. There was a patch of hastily applied paint on the part of the door where a company name would have been positioned. The main house had also been converted into offices and was currently occupied by a firm of chartered surveyors who expressed an enthusiastic but resigned interest in tracing Mr Keen over the small matter of six months' rent.

Three aircraft supply and maintenance companies based in and around Glasgow Airport were also anxious to see Mr Keen again. As one manager put it, you could string Acorn's unpaid bills round the passenger terminal and still have enough to paper a house. Out of habit rather than expectation, Daisy called in on the Glasgow CID to discover that Keen's fame knew no bounds and that they too were interested in locating him, this time over a complaint of false accounting and embezzlement brought by an erstwhile co-director of Keen's in another defunct venture, a time-share company.

No one knew where Keen was now, but the police thought he'd moved to the Costa Blanca.

# Chapter 18

THE COURT OFFICIALS hadn't allowed enough room for the press. The four seats they had placed behind a single table were already occupied by the local boys, and a group of three journalists stood waiting for the ushers to bring more chairs. The officials hadn't made the same mistake with the public seating however and there was room enough for the eighty or so spectators.

Through the high-set windows the sky was very dark and the rain that had threatened since dawn was already beginning to spill down the glass. The photographers encamped outside would be getting wet, a thought that did not upset Daisy too much. Inside, the overhead lighting was poor and badly spaced, throwing deep shadows which added to the aura of gloom that seemed to pervade the room.

There was a raised top bench where the judge – by Scottish law, entitled sheriff – would sit, and to the right the oddly named procurator fiscal. Daisy had checked her Scottish law: the sheriff would decide the verdict, while the procurator fiscal, a full-time law officer who variously fulfilled the tasks of prosecutor, investigator and coroner, would lead the evidence. Interested parties could be represented by their own counsel. There was no jury. The clerk and a shorthand writer sat to one side of the bench while the witnesses, including Campbell, sat in the hall outside.

Everyone was waiting, and everyone knew what they were waiting for. It was only a minute before ten when a

sudden movement of heads marked Nick Mackenzie's
entrance. He strode quickly up the aisle, flanked by three
men, and took a seat in the front row. He was wearing a
well-cut charcoal suit with a white shirt. Only his hair was
a little on the wild side. Once seated, he kept his head
rigidly towards the front and Daisy could not see his face.
The plump dark man sitting on his left turned to whisper
in his ear, and she recognized David Weinberg. The man to
his right stood up and went to speak to the procurator
fiscal; this had to be his lawyer. As the lawyer returned to
his seat the usher handed him a note. Daisy knew it was a
note because she had written it. As she watched for the
lawyer's reaction some people in an intervening row stood
up and obscured her view. By the time they sat down again
the lawyer was back in his seat and she could no longer see
his face. But she noticed that Nick's head was bent forward,
as if he were reading the note. When his head came up
again, the lawyer inclined towards him and they had a
discussion. It was very short.

Then – nothing.

They didn't need her then. In a way she was relieved:
her evidence wouldn't have added a great deal, and unsupported guesswork never went down well in court.

The sheriff entered. They all stood. The proceedings
were under way.

First to give evidence were the police. It was the standard
stuff, delivered in the flat monotone affected by police
officers everywhere. The alarm being raised, the layout of
the estate, the search for the missing woman, the call to the
upper glen, the finding of the body beside the pool.

Nick's lawyer asked some ancilliary questions which
were clearly intended to establish that a well-planned
search had already been under way when the police arrived.

Next came the police surgeon, who had examined the
body on the night of the death. He estimated that death
had occurred some time during the day in question. It was

impossible to be more precise because of the temperature of the water in which the body had lain. Questioned by the procurator fiscal, he expanded on the methods used to estimate the time of death, and how they were complicated by temperature.

The pathologist was next into the witness box. Daisy braced herself. During her days as an articled clerk she had been to one or two inquests and she knew how clinical and merciless postmortem reports could sound. It had always seemed to her faintly demeaning that someone so newly dead could have the secrets of their bodies, complete in some cases with unmentionable diseases and unfortunate revelations, discussed in public.

The pathologist whipped through the usual preliminaries before stating that the immediate cause of death was drowning. Water had penetrated the lungs fully, indicating that the deceased was alive when she went into the water.

Prompted for his other findings he referred to his notes. 'I found bruising and abrasion on the left temple,' he said. 'The bruising covered an area of four centimetres by three. The skin was broken over most of the bruised area. I estimated that this injury occurred at the time of death or very shortly before. If it was before, then it can only have been a matter of minutes.'

'Could this injury in any way have contributed to death?' the procurator fiscal asked.

'Unlikely. It would not in itself have caused a loss of consciousness, although it could, I suppose, have caused confusion or loss of balance.'

'How in your opinion could this injury have been incurred then?' asked the procurator fiscal.

'It was obviously the result of a blow of some kind, but by what and in what circumstances I could not say.'

'Could it have resulted from Mrs Mackenzie being swept against a rock?'

'Possibly . . .' He sounded rather doubtful. 'If the water was very fast flowing.'

'Or a fall perhaps? Onto a rock or similar hard surface?'

'Yes.'

'Were there any other injuries?'

'No.'

The procurator fiscal indicated that he was satisfied on the point and the pathologist returned to his notes.

'Was the deceased otherwise in good health?' the procurator fiscal asked.

'She was considerably underweight for her height. Less than six stone on a height of five foot six inches. I would describe her as emaciated.'

'Was there any medical reason for this that you could find?'

'I could find no evidence of physiological disease, no. And certainly nothing that would account for the marked atrophy of the muscles. In my opinion the muscle atrophy could well have contributed to death.'

'In what way?'

'The deceased would have suffered much reduced muscle power compared to another woman of her age and build and would have had relative difficulty in swimming or extricating herself from the water. She was likely to have been weak.'

Nick moved then, bowing his head and rubbing a hand across his temple. The sheriff, a grey-faced man with a beaked nose and drooping eyes, peered at him over his half-moon spectacles, before returning to his scribblings.

'You suggest the deceased could have been weak,' said the procurator fiscal. 'But not so weak that she couldn't walk the' – he consulted the papers on the table beside him – 'almost two miles from the house?'

'Hard to say, but walking is not nearly so strenuous as swimming.'

'So it wouldn't have been impossible?'

The pathologist considered. 'Not impossible, no.'

The procurator fiscal waited for the signal from the sheriff that he had caught up on his notes before asking the pathologist to continue. Holding up his pad, the pathologist began to recite a long litany of test results. He spoke in a refined Scottish accent, his voice clear and well-developed like that of a trained actor, an impression borne out by his sense of timing; like a true performer, he left the scene-stealer till last. If the technical terms at the start of his speech had left people behind, morphine was a word they all understood. He had found morphine sulphate in the blood at a level of two hundred micrograms per litre.

'What sort of dose would that be? High? Low?' asked the procurator fiscal.

'For someone of the deceased's weight, high.'

A tiny ripple came from the audience, a collective movement that shivered through the hall.

'Is morphine sulphate a prescribed drug?'

'It is.'

'And what is it administered for?'

'The control of pain.'

'And this dose, it was commensurate with one administered for pain?'

'It *could* have been, but normally such a dose would only be given for really severe cases. As I've already said, I found no evidence of serious disease.'

'And it's normally given for cancer?'

'For that, and heart attack and injury. But as it's an addictive substance it's only given for pain that cannot be relieved in any other way. In cancer, only for terminal cases.'

'Can you say what effect such a dose would have had on the deceased?'

There was a sudden drumming on the high windows as

rain pelted against the glass. The sky was so black that the rivulets of water reflected the light back into the hall.

'I can't be certain,' said the pathologist, raising his resonant voice so it could be better heard above the rain, and it occurred to Daisy that he was enjoying his time in the spotlight. 'It would very much depend on the deceased's tolerance to the drug.'

'And what factors would influence a person's tolerance to morphine?'

'The individual's general health, the state of the liver and so on. But also usage – whether the individual was a habitual user.'

Another ripple, a collective intake of breath. Daisy winced inwardly: a disastrous choice of words, not something the reporters were likely to miss.

'I see. So you can't say precisely what effect this level would have had on the deceased?'

'All I can say is that even the most frequent user would have felt considerable effects from such a dose. What I can't estimate is the extent – the degree – of those effects.'

*User.* Again Daisy flinched, again she was aware of the effect that word would be having on the audience.

'And what are the effects of morphine?'

'Apart from reducing pain, it induces a feeling of well-being and euphoria.'

The procurator fiscal seemed to hover on the point of asking another question before saying: 'You found no other unnatural substances in the blood or tissue?

'I did not.'

'So what is the summary of your findings?'

'Death by drowning. I would add that low bodyweight and high blood-morphine level could have been contributory factors.'

The procurator fiscal nodded towards Nick's lawyer, who positively shot to his feet. First he went over the bruising on the head, clarifying that it occurred at or shortly before the drowning. Then he asked: 'Doctor, you say that morphine is used as a painkiller?'

'It is.'

'So it's widely prescribed by the medical profession?'

'I wouldn't say *widely*. I would say, not infrequently.'

'You mentioned cancer, but is it not also used for other diseases that cause intense pain?'

'Well it *can* be,' the pathologist replied grudgingly. 'But there are not many other diseases that cause such intense pain that they cannot be treated by other means like analgesics. As I have said, a medical practitioner would normally be reluctant to prescribe morphine for anything but the most severe cases, because of its habit-forming nature.'

'But whatever the disease, there's very little else that a doctor can prescribe for really intense and prolonged pain, is that correct?'

'For really intense and prolonged pain that did not respond to analgesics, no. Though, as I've already mentioned, the deceased did not appear to suffer . . .'

'That wasn't what I asked, doctor,' the lawyer cut in rapidly. 'I asked if morphine was appropriate for intense pain.'

The pathologist didn't like being interrupted and looked across to the procurator fiscal as if expecting him to intervene. Finding no support, he rearranged his mouth into a stern line of forbearance.

'You used the terms "habitual usage" and "frequent user" just now,' the lawyer was saying. 'Taking "habitual usage" first, what exactly did you mean by that?'

'Regular and extended usage.'

'And what did you mean by "frequent user"?'

'Someone who uses the substance frequently – often.'

'Regular – frequent – habitual. Aren't these all the same thing?'

'Well – yes.'

'So you might term a cancer victim an habitual user.'

A pause. 'I might.'

'Or an accident victim who suffers prolonged pain?'

A slight shrug. 'Possibly.'

'So the court would be correct to understand that the term "habitual" is interchangeable with "frequent" and "regular" and applies quite properly to someone who has been prescribed morphine as part of her medical treatment?'

The pause again, that oh-so subtle suggestion of doubt. 'Yes.'

'Thank you, doctor.'

As the pathologist left the box, Daisy glanced towards Nick, but he was motionless, shoulders back, head erect, and there was nothing to suggest the sort of face he might be showing to the front of the court.

The next to be called was a forensic scientist. Asked about the possible causes of the abrasion and bruising to the deceased's forehead, he ventured the opinion that the blow had come from a large flat surface such as a rock or large stone. He also confirmed that the water found in her lungs matched the water from the River Ashard.

As soon as he stepped down, the usher called Campbell, who, deserted by his usual assertiveness, walked awkwardly to the box and stumbled over the oath. Haltingly, his voice hardly raised above a whisper, he began to describe the search; how he had joined the main party sweeping down the glen, how he had joined Nick Mackenzie to go back and search the upper reaches.

The procurator fiscal interrupted him. 'Why did you decide to search the upper glen?'

'It was Mr Mackenzie. He wanted to go. I joined him.'

'There were just the two of you?'

'Aye.'

'And you left the main search party?'

'Aye.'

'Thank you. Please continue.'

He told how they had driven up the glen as far as the great rock then continued on foot, he by the narrow river path, Nick Mackenzie by the track, and how they had doubled back; how he had stopped by the pool a second time and shone his torch over the surface and seen a touch of white floating near the surface under the great rock, and waded in to investigate.

Campbell faltered, stopped and looked to the procurator fiscal for guidance.

'It was the body of Mrs Mackenzie?' the procurator fiscal prompted.

Campbell nodded.

'Please tell us what you did then.'

With a visible effort Campbell described in a tense hesitant voice how he pulled her to the edge of the pool and onto the bank and tried to revive her, laying her on her stomach and pressing hard on her back, then turning her and breathing into her mouth, and how his efforts had been of no use.

'And then?'

'I called Mr Mackenzie who came down from above. From the track there.'

'Go on.'

Campbell looked nervously about him. He wasn't sure what he was expected to say next.

'What did Mr Mackenzie do when he reached you?'

Campbell looked flustered and didn't reply.

'I'm merely asking what action Mr Mackenzie took when he got to you,' prompted the procurator fiscal gently.

'He . . . er, requested that I move to one side.'

'And then what happened?'

Campbell was silent.

'Did he try to revive her?'

Campbell blinked and ran a tongue over his lips. After

some thought he shook his head. Almost immediately he seemed to regret this because he stammered: 'No. That is, he . . . I'm no' certain.'

'Was it dark?' offered the procurator fiscal helpfully.

'That's it,' Campbell exclaimed, grabbing at the idea. 'I couldna' see.' He nodded at the sheriff to make sure that he too had got the point. 'It was dark,' he repeated, the relief evident in his face. 'I couldna' see.'

Daisy closed her eyes and willed Campbell to stop babbling. Not a moment too soon, the procurator fiscal told him to stand down.

Then they called Nick.

In the silence you could hear the wind bombarding the rain against the windows like pellets and the sound of the clerk's footsteps as he positioned himself by the witness box ready to administer the oath.

Nick paused to say something to his lawyer before getting up and crossing to the witness box. He faced the clerk while he took the oath, turning only when it was time to sit down. The women in front of Daisy craned their necks and darted their heads from side to side to get a better view, and it was a moment before Daisy could get a look at him. Skin pale, but not unnaturally so. Thinner perhaps; a little gaunt around that punished face. Eyes weary beneath the hooded lids, and touched with sadness.

The procurator fiscal began by asking him about events on the day the death had occurred – what time his wife had been missed, what form the search took, the return to the upper glen. For the most part he answered in monosyllables. Questions that required fuller answers he kept brutally short and occasionally the procurator fiscal had to prompt him to enlarge on what he had said.

'And when you came across Mr Campbell and your wife's body, what happened then?'

'Nothing,' he said in his quiet voice.

'You didn't try to revive her?'

'There was no point.'

'Why was that?'

Nick pressed his lips together. 'It was obvious my wife was dead.'

The procurator fiscal nodded, and went through some background about Alusha Mackenzie's daily routine and the walks she used to take. Then:

'Can you tell us about your wife's medical condition, Mr Mackenzie?'

'She had been very ill for some time.'

'What was the nature of her illness?'

Nick's glance flickered across the court in the direction of his lawyer. 'She'd accidentally inhaled a poisonous substance.'

'When was this?'

'Last June.'

'This substance – do you know what it was?'

'I believe it was a wood preserver called Reldane.'

'Could you tell us how you came to this conclusion?'

'My wife had been using Reldane on a stable door. She was found unconscious with the stuff – the Reldane – spilled on the concrete around her. She became extremely ill and never recovered.'

'Did you seek expert advice at that time?'

'If you could call it that.'

'You consulted a toxicologist?'

'More than one.'

'And what was their opinion?'

'Well, they couldn't say exactly how the damage was done, if that's what you mean.'

The procurator fiscal turned to the sheriff. 'Your honour, in view of the seriousness of the allegation concerning Reldane – a product which is freely available to the general public over the counter – and in view of the court's duty to investigate the matter as thoroughly as possible I will be calling an eminent toxicologist to give evidence about Reldane at a later stage.'

Nick's expression darkened. Hadn't he realized that this was inevitable? Daisy wondered. Hadn't he realized that his word would count for little against the experts'?

The procurator fiscal put his next question. 'Did the toxicologists you consulted venture any opinion on Reldane's role in your wife's illness?'

'Not really . . .' He shrugged it off. It was an unfortunate gesture, giving the impression that he wasn't interested in the question. Perhaps he realized his mistake because he added sharply: 'They all had different ideas.'

The procurator fiscal nodded solemnly. 'Did they not match the known effects of Reldane against your wife's symptoms?'

'They didn't seem to know a lot about Reldane.'

'So they could not be sure it was the Reldane?'

'Not certain, no.'

'You took your wife to America for assessment and treatment, I believe?'

'Yes.'

'And what was offered there?'

'Not a lot. They had no idea about treatment either.'

'But your wife was treated by a Dr Hubert Gravely of Boston?'

'Yes.'

'And he offered a firm opinion on the nature of your wife's illness?'

'Yes.'

The procurator fiscal reached behind him for some papers and announced that he was going to read the affadavit from Dr Gravely of Boston, Massachusetts. He read slowly, pausing occasionally to allow the sheriff to make his notes. The doctor's statement was impenetrable with jargon, but it seemed to boil down to the fact that he had attended Mrs Alusha Mackenzie at various times between November 15th and December 18th of the previous year in Boston, and that she was suffering from the effects of exposure to a highly toxic substance. The toxicity had affected, as far as one could gather, almost every organ in her body, including the heart, the liver, and the endocrinal and nervous systems.

'It appears, then, that your wife suffered a rapid and devastating decline in her health, Mr Mackenzie. Had she been well before the accident?'

'Yes.'

'Both mentally and physically?'

'Absolutely.'

'She was of normal weight?'

'Yes.'

'She had been expecting a baby at the time of the accident, is that correct?'

'Yes.'

'And what happened?'

'She lost it. Two weeks later.'

'What did the doctors say about that?'

Nick cast him a withering look. 'There wasn't a great deal they could say, was there?' It was the first time he had showed anything approaching emotion.

'And her weight loss, did that come soon after the accident too?'

'Yes.' He had pulled the mask back over his face.

'How did it come about? Did she lose the desire to eat?'

'No. She lost the ability to absorb her food.'

'So she ate as much as usual but still lost weight.'

'That's right.'

'What other symptoms did she have?'

'She was in pain nearly all the time.'

'I see. What sort of pain? Can you elaborate?'

'All her joints and – well, all over. And vicious headaches.'

'Did this pain disturb her a great deal?'

'It was unbearable.'

'And she was given drugs for it?'

'Yes. Morphine.' His voice had dropped until it was barely audible.

'And this was prescribed for her?'

He gave the briefest nod of his head.

'By whom?'

'The American doctor.'

'This doctor?' The procurator fiscal said, picking up the affidavit. 'Dr Gravely?'

He gave a slight shrug. 'Yes.'

'What dosage did she take?'

'It varied. I don't know.'

'Then she herself determined the dose?'

'Yes.'

'I see.' A pause. 'May I ask, Mr Mackenzie, was your wife depressed at all?'

He didn't reply for a moment. 'What sort of depression are you referring to? Endogenous or exogenous?' he demanded, and there was an edge to his voice.

'Well – I don't think we need to know . . .'

'It's an important distinction,' Nick said defensively, his voice rising. 'If you mean had my wife lost the will to fight her illness – absolutely not. Even at her worst she never gave up, never doubted that she'd get well. But the illness itself – sometimes she felt so bad that it got her down. Physically, I mean. But it was never so bad that – ' He broke off. He didn't need to finish; everyone knew what he had intended to say. But he said it anyway. 'That she would consider taking her own life.'

'On the day of her death, was she particularly depressed?'

'No.' There was a tremor in his voice, as if he were controlling himself with difficulty.

'She didn't make any remark, any comment that could have a bearing on later events?'

'No.'

'There was no note, no message of any kind?'

It was an instant before Nick managed to answer. 'No,' he said with emphasis. 'There was not.'

There was a short pause while the procurator fiscal consulted his notes.

'Your wife didn't have a family doctor here in Scotland?'

'No.'

'Why was that, may I ask?'

'She'd had enough of doctors. And before that she never needed one.'

'Thank you.' The procurator fiscal sat down. The worst was over; but then the damage had already been done.

Nick's lawyer did what he could, going over Alusha's health before the accident and the devastation of her illness, but there was no disguising the fact that, according to Nick's own evidence, the toxicologists had been unable to offer explanations about the cause of Alusha's illness, nor had they been able to support the allegations about Reldane.

Finally Nick was allowed to leave the box. He strode back to his seat, his face set, his expression guarded.

The court adjourned for lunch. The press were up and making for the door before the sheriff had left the court. As the spectators stood up, Daisy looked for Nick but there was no sign of him and she realized he had been ghosted away, perhaps into a side room. She spent the hour rebuilding Campbell's spirits in the nearest pub.

When the court reassembled, the procurator fiscal said to the sheriff: 'In view of the highly technical nature of the affidavit from Dr Gravely I think the court may benefit from some elucidation.' He nodded to the clerk who recalled the pathologist to the witness box.

The pathologist shook his head. 'I find it very difficult to interpret this statement, Mr Procurator Fiscal. Certainly it doesn't match with my findings.'

'In what way?'

'He mentions liver damage. I found no evidence of that whatsoever. He also mentions heart damage. Again I found no evidence of that. And as for hypothalamus malfunction – well, that's impossible to measure; there *is* no test for hypothalamus function. And he talks about T-cell damage of a type unknown to science.'

'So there would seem to be some discrepancy?'

'Yes, and I think I can offer an explanation. I took the liberty of looking up Dr Hubert Gravely in the United States medical register. I could not find him there.'

'You're saying he's not a registered medical practitioner?'

'Apparently not.'

There was a rustling in the room. The two women in front of Daisy exchanged glances at this unexpected turn of events. Nick had a hurried consultation with his lawyer. The two of them seemed to be in some disagreement because, though Nick was strongly arguing some point or another, the lawyer wasn't having any of it and kept shaking his head.

Then the procurator fiscal recalled Nick.

It was obvious that Nick's mood had shifted. The largely impassive expression of the morning had been replaced by one of guarded belligerence. He no longer sat erect, but hunched forward, one elbow on the chair-arm, knuckle against his chin, glaring at the procurator fiscal with what might easily be interpreted as suspicion. There was something else, too, a heaviness to his eyes, an unfocused look. It suddenly occurred to Daisy with slight shock that he had been drinking.

The procurator fiscal went back to the matter of Alusha Mackenzie's medical care in America. Nick left no one in any doubt as to his dislike for this line of questioning, grunting the briefest of replies, and executing some fairly obvious manoeuvres around direct answers. But it came out all the same.

Alusha Mackenzie had gone to Dr Gravely only after several stays in hospitals in London and New York, where, despite running every possible test, the doctors had been unable to offer an explanation for her illness.

'They could find no abnormalities whatsoever?' asked the procurator fiscal, clearly puzzled.

'Tests don't pick up everything,' Nick snapped. 'They're not perfect.'

'So in the absence of any diagnosis from the physicians, your wife went to Dr Gravely. He was an alternative practitioner, was he not?'

'Yes.'

'Forgive me, but I'm confused on two matters here,' said the procurator fiscal. 'First, what reason was offered by Mrs Mackenzie's physicians for the considerable pain she was in, the loss of weight and so on?'

Even from that distance Daisy could see Nick's jaw muscles working overtime.

'I have to ask, Mr Mackenzie.'

Still Nick didn't answer.

'Was it suggested that your wife was suffering from a nervous illness?'

Nick flinched slightly as the procurator fiscal touched the raw spot. 'She was damaged by a highly toxic substance,' he said bitterly, 'but it didn't fit the textbook, you see, so they were too frightened to give it a name! They couldn't find out exactly how the damage was done and couldn't see a neat list of symptoms, so that was that! They had to dredge their ideas bags and come up with something else – anything else.'

Wrong way to go, Nick. Looks bad. Too emotional, too defensive, too angry.

The procurator fiscal hesitated, as if genuinely regretting

the necessity to press the matter. 'So – what was it they finally suggested?'

'Ha!' It was several moments before he managed: 'They said it was depression. But it wasn't true. There's no way it was true.'

The procurator fiscal nodded slowly and for a moment Daisy thought he might let it go at that. But he was too professional to forget the other matter that had been confusing him. She had a good idea of what was coming, and she was right.

'One last question, Mr Mackenzie, you said that Dr Gravely prescribed the morphine for your wife, yet he was not a qualified practitioner. Could you – er – clarify this point?'

'I must have been mistaken,' Nick said impatiently, his face puckering warningly.

'It was another physician then?'

'Yes – what the hell does it matter anyway?'

The procurator fiscal looked a little taken aback at that and for a moment Daisy thought he would drop the point, but he pressed: 'You can't recall the name of this other physician?'

'No.'

'But it was prescribed by a doctor during your stay in the United States?'

Making little effort to hide his exasperation, Nick barked: 'Yes.'

After a last glance at Nick's face, the procurator fiscal allowed him to leave the box.

The next hour was taken up by evidence from the Mackenzies' staff corroborating the events of Alusha Mackenzie's last days. The housekeeper was adamant that Mrs Mackenzie had not been in low spirits; the estate manager, though fiercely loyal, was less certain. She had not looked well, he said. He could not say in what way, and in evading the question left the unfortunate impression that he had seen her looking depressed.

The toxicologist was last on. He didn't say anything unexpected, and he didn't say anything helpful either. Reldane was regarded as a relatively safe product, he stated. Of proven low toxicity, it had never been known to cause serious side effects among people regularly exposed to it.

As the court was adjourned until the next day, a shaft of weak sunlight the colour of amber splashed against the wall of the court, a sudden incongruous shaft of brightness.

Wherever Nick had been spirited to during the noon recess, he did not go there now. Instead, with his companions forming a tight circle round him like soldiers round their warrior king, he ran the gauntlet of the photographers and hurried from the building.

Back at the hotel Daisy called the office. She got straight through to Alan, and she had the strong feeling that he had been waiting for her call.

Having martyred himself on the field of the trustees' presentation all day, he was at his most scathing.

Going her own way, he accused, acting entirely at the expense of everyone else. No allowance for the load she was dumping on the rest of the team, no *consideration*. No pulling together. It was getting to the point, he added ominously, where Catch was becoming unworkable.

Ignoring the spirit of the last remark, Daisy made the appropriate noises: apology and entreaty, a little well-chosen flattery and some overt grovelling. Eventually Alan allowed himself to be placated, though grudgingly and with extremely bad grace so that she was left in no doubt that he was still highly displeased.

It was twenty minutes before she got to speak to Jenny, and even then she had to remind Alan she was calling long-distance before he would remove himself from the line.

'Tried the Civil Aviation Authority,' Jenny murmured,

keeping her voice down. 'They don't give pilots' addresses out to the public, but they do forward letters, so I wrote.'

'Good.'

'But they couldn't be sure the address they had for Peter Duggan was up-to-date. It was abroad somewhere – outside Europe, presumably, because they asked for extra postage. I turned on my persuasive powers' – she gave a self-mocking giggle – 'but they wouldn't say which country.'

'There must be other ways to find pilots,' Daisy said more in hope than certainty.

'I'll keep trying.'

'And the mechanic?'

'I've got someone trying all the Robertsons in the Inverness phone book. *Not* a simple task!'

Daisy spent the remainder of the afternoon with the local police, going over the flying notifications for the previous summer. The officer in charge was most co-operative. Acorn Flying Systems had sent out no less than twenty notifications for the Argyll area, but none of them was for any patch of forest adjacent to Ashard, and though they had posted their intention of spraying forest near to Adrian's, the work had been undertaken in July, well after he had been doused.

Dispirited, she took the last stuffy symptoms of her cold back to the hotel for an early bed with an aspirin and a cup of hot lemon. She slept until four, and then listened to the wind and thought of Nick Mackenzie at Glen Ashard.

The next morning it was raining again. The papers had been reasonably restrained. Only a couple of the tabloids had reported Alusha Mackenzie's 'heavy morphine usage', but had refrained from further comment, waiting, presumably, for the findings of the inquiry before running their main stories.

When the court resumed, just one witness was called, a psychiatrist named Carter, as smooth in appearance as he

was in speech. He had examined Mrs Mackenzie during
the previous October in London, he said, and had run
extensive tests.

'And what was your diagnosis?'

'Acute clinical depression.'

Daisy closed her eyes momentarily.

'And what was the treatment you recommended?'

'Antidepressants, graduated exercise, psychiatric therapy. But Mrs Mackenzie was removed from my care before
the treatment could begin.'

'Removed?'

'Her husband came and discharged her very suddenly.'

'And this was against your advice?'

'Very much so. I was extremely concerned for Mrs
Mackenzie's health.'

'In what way?'

Daisy bowed her head.

'I thought she might attempt to take her own life. I was
extremely concerned about it.'

Nick's lawyer did his best to shift the elegant Dr Carter
from his position, but he was not be ruffled and not to be
drawn. If exposure to chemicals could produce such symptoms, then he had never heard of a single case.

All that remained was for the procurator fiscal to
summarize the evidence. He was thorough and meticulous.
He recalled the pathologist's statement which allowed for
the possibility that the deceased's illness had contributed to
her death. But as to the cause of that illness, he believed the
evidence to be inconclusive. While Mrs Mackenzie may
well have inhaled Reldane, and it might have caused some
temporary symptoms, there was no evidence that it could
have caused the chronic debilitating illness of the following
ten months. The chemical Reldane had been in existence
for years; it was considered relatively safe. It seemed an
unlikely culprit. And then there was the evidence as to the
deceased's state of mind. Dr Carter had diagnosed clinical

depression, and had warned of the dangers of his patient's state of mind. And it must not be forgotten that she had experienced a traumatic year, with both an accident and a miscarriage. It was possible, therefore, that her illness and indeed her death were of nervous origin, and did not result from inhalation of the chemical Reldane.

Mr Mackenzie, on the other hand, was convinced that his wife had not been depressed, but if the court accepted that, then it left her considerable physical deterioration unexplained, and could well implicate some as yet unidentified factor.

As to the actual day of the death, he would only summarize the few facts, that no note had been found, that she had been seen to be looking unwell on the day of her death, that she had taken a high dose of morphine. The role which the drug may or may not have taken in the death was impossible to determine.

The sheriff announced that he would like the weekend to reflect, and would give his finding on Monday morning. The tension fell back uncertainly, people stirred discontentedly, as if they had been cheated.

Even before the sheriff had left the room, Nick was on his feet and striding down the aisle so rapidly that it was only by jumping quickly and awkwardly from her seat that Daisy made it to the door first and, passing quickly through, held it open for him. But before she had the chance to speak he had gone, speeding past with the barest flicker of a glance. An instant later his companions burst through the door in hot pursuit, one bumping into her with a muffled apology.

The party had almost reached the main entrance when it suddenly ground to an abrupt halt, the cohorts almost colliding with one another. It was Nick who had created the jam, she realized. He had stopped at the doors. He was turning to David Weinberg.

She hurried forward, aware that if she was going to

speak she must say the right thing and in the right words, aware that she would have only a few moments in which to say it.

He saw her, he frowned. Close up, he looked raw, defeated, heart-stopping. Suddenly anything she might have said seemed crass and inappropriate.

Finally she blurted: 'Can I talk to you?'

People were crowding round him. She could sense his panic, his need to escape. With an obvious effort he forced himself to look down at her.

She didn't know why at that moment of all moments she should look at anything but his face, why as she drew breath to ask him if she could come to see him that evening she should look past his shoulder and notice the head of the man passing behind him. But she did, and there was something about the retreating head, the greased-back hair and fat neck, that caught her by surprise. The words died on her lips, and in the second that she was distracted, in the very instant she was about to force her eyes away from the bull-like neck and back to Nick's face, something made Nick take fright because suddenly he was turning and before she realized what was happening he was pushing his way clear and his friends were rapidly closing ranks behind him.

Her heart bumped, she pushed after him, through the crowd, out of the doors and into the rain. Emerging, she realized there would be no second chance. The press were converging for their close-ups. As Nick made for his car they shouted questions, pushed shamelessly in front of him, held cameras in his face. Watching the mêlée, Daisy could only feel glad when he reached the shelter of the car and it tore away in a welter of spray.

She stood in the rain, filled with disbelief. She had let him go. She allowed herself a moment of sharp self-rebuke and something approaching misery, before peering through the sheeting rain, searching for the fat neck and slicked-back hair that had jerked at her memory. She began to half walk, half run along the street, examining the memory as she went. The image of the bull-necked head had been incongruous yet familiar.

It was only when she reached the main street and paused to look up and down its length that it came to her. Colin Maynard. The man from the Waldorf.

The implications confused her. Why should he be in Scotland? Interest in Alusha Mackenzie's case? Interest in Catch? If so, he must have done some serious homework to find out when and where the inquiry was being held.

The more she thought about it the more unlikely it seemed. She was seeing demons, she was having what Alan would call one of her windy phases.

The rain, which was gentle but relentless, dribbled down her face and flattened her hair coldly against her head. A few intrepid people were braving the shops, their heads hidden beneath lowered umbrellas. Two men appeared from a doorway and strode towards her. Both were short with fat bull-like necks, and by the time they had darted into the public bar of the nearby pub, their hair, too, had acquired a wet slicked-back look.

She turned back.

It was Campbell who called with the news on Monday.

Finding undetermined. The matter of Alusha Mackenzie's death was to be left open.

Daisy felt relief, as if Nick had been on trial and found innocent.

But of course it hadn't been Nick who had been on trial, it had been Alusha Mackenzie, the charge, mental instability.

# Chapter 19

———

DORKING, BACKBONE OF England, boasted several boutiques, small high-class establishments with two to three racks of tailored suits, floral dresses and glittery evening clothes.

Daisy drew a blank at the first two, but in the third the owner showed some interest at the mention of a pilot brother. She did not have one herself, but she had heard that Jane Ackroyd did, and directed Daisy to a boutique called The Dresser.

The shop was a few yards up an alley off the main street, the sort of place where the rents are only half the price. A door-operated bell sounded as Daisy entered and a well-groomed fortyish woman popped her head round a curtain at the far end of the shop.

'Are you Jane Ackroyd?' Daisy asked.

'Yes.' She was what some people might call faded, with pale washed-out eyes, soft blurred features, and a pair of deep vertical frown lines over the bridge of her nose.

'I believe you have a brother Peter Duggan,' Daisy said, diving in. 'I wanted to get in touch with him.'

A strange expression, half defensive, half curious, came over Jane Ackroyd's face. 'Oh yes? In connection with what?' she demanded.

So Duggan was her brother. Concealing a flutter of triumph, Daisy began the marginally adjusted story she'd prepared on the way down. 'I'm a solicitor making enquiries into the affairs of a company called Acorn Flying

REQUIEM                                365

Systems,' she explained, 'and in particular one of its
directors, a man named Keen. I believe your brother
worked for the company last year.'

Jane Ackroyd stared. 'You're a solicitor?' she asked
doubtfully.

'Yes.' When the disbelief in Jane Ackroyd's face failed
to recede she added: 'Though I'm what you might call off-
duty today.' She gestured apologetically towards her scuffy
clothes. 'I was on my way to the country. Going fishing.'

'Fishing?' She was incredulous.

That was the trouble with lies; they had to be repeated.

'Fishing,' she restated.

Jane Ackroyd gave the sort of nod she probably used to
humour difficult customers. 'Who are you acting for, Miss
– er?'

'Field. Daisy Field. I'm sorry, I'm not at liberty to reveal
the name of my client. I can only say that my client has a
direct interest in the matter.'

'Ah,' she said. 'It's money then, is it?'

Daisy shrugged regretfully as if ethics prevented her
commenting further, but allowed a small collusive smile to
slip onto her face which Jane Ackroyd could take any way
she wanted.

She got the message all right. 'Money,' she affirmed
knowingly. 'It had to be. They still owe Peter several weeks'
salary. It's outrageous when you consider he was doing all
the work and taking all the risks. Quite outrageous.' She
eyed Daisy one more time, as if making up her mind about
her. 'Wait here while I phone, will you?'

'Is he a long way away?' Daisy asked her retreating
back.

'Oh no,' Jane Ackroyd called over her shoulder, and
Daisy tried not to get too excited at this second unaccountable stroke of luck.

'Peter?' Jane Ackroyd's voice floated out from behind
the curtain before dropping to an inaudible murmur. Daisy

wandered closer to the curtain, touching the sleeves of the
dresses as she passed. Just as she began to catch the
occasional snatch of conversation, the street door opened,
the bell sounded with a loud buzz, and a customer came
into the shop. Jane Ackroyd peered round the curtain and
cut short the conversation with a 'Must go now.' She
emerged with a smile for the new arrival, then, returning
her attention to Daisy, politely but skilfully shepherded her
towards the door. 'My brother's on his way into town,' she
announced in a low voice. 'He'll meet you at The Saddler's
Arms in fifteen minutes.'

It was more than Daisy had dared hope for, and she
must have let it show in her face because the defensiveness
sprang back into Jane Ackroyd's eyes. She said sharply:
'This business – it's not going to involve Peter in any
unpleasantness, is it? I mean, no court cases or anything
like that?'

This was a promise that Daisy knew she couldn't make.
'A court case?' she murmured. 'There's no suggestion of
that at the moment.'

'You see . . .' Jane Ackroyd dropped her voice to a
whisper. 'Peter's been through a bit of a rough patch
recently. He . . . Well, he's not too . . .' Then with an
abrupt shake of her head, she abandoned her speech and
opened the door.

The lounge bar of The Saddler's Arms was empty except
for an ancient lady sipping a pint of stout which had left a
broad foam moustache on her upper lip, and a couple of
jovial salesmen arguing amicably over a sheaf of papers.
Daisy bought a Coke and sat at a table opposite the door.

After a few minutes Duggan came in. She knew it was
Duggan even before he caught her eye and raised his
eyebrows questioningly; he looked like something out of a
boys' comic, a parody of a flying man with his spotted
cravat, his cavalry twills and blazer, and his longish black

hair neatly parted and flattened against his head. The only thing lacking was a moustache.

'Miss Field?'

'Mr Duggan.'

He sat down, rubbing his hands energetically, and glanced in the direction of the bar. 'A drink?'

'No thanks.'

'God, not an abstainer, I hope,' he said with forced heartiness. 'Article in the paper today says all this health talk is claptrap. A little booze does wonders for the arteries.'

Close up, Duggan didn't look quite so dapper. His blazer had seen better days, his shirt collar was frayed, while his hair, which was heavy with grease or dirt or both, had discharged a sprinkling of dandruff over his shoulders. His face, which must have been quite good-looking once, appeared worn: his eyes were red-rimmed with pronounced pouches underneath, his skin was coarse and blotchy, and his teeth were heavily stained. It was no surprise when he lit a cigarette and drew on it with a deep gasp.

'Think I might have a little something,' he said, jerking his head towards the bar and ambling over. The barman seemed to know him well enough because he greeted him by name and, putting a glass unhesitatingly under the gin measure, gave him a double. Duggan returned to the table, cigarette jammed between his lips, eyes half-closed against the smoke. Sitting down, he dashed some tonic into his gin and took a quick swig. 'My sister said you were trying to find Keen.' He had a smoker's voice, deep and throaty.

Daisy ran through her prepared story, though she took care to shift the emphasis away from Keen to the broader canvas of Acorn Flying Systems.

'It was a limited company, Acorn, you know,' Duggan said. 'Can't get anything out of a limited company if it's got no assets. I know. I tried. Not a penny left in the kitty.

Stripped bare. It was that bastard Keen, of course. Cunning little shyster. Expensive cars, Italian clothes, that sort of thing. Bled the company dry. Left everyone else to carry the can. Should have known. Nasty common little upstart.' He took another gulp and sucked it through his teeth with a hissing sound. When he wasn't talking or drinking he was drawing on his cigarette, dragging the smoke deep into his lungs.

'How did you come to work for him?' Daisy asked.

'Had a job out in Oman which folded unexpectedly. Needed a job for the summer. Hadn't heard about Keen's reputation when I took it on, of course.'

'Had you done crop-spraying before?'

Duggan's lazy gaze fixed on her with new interest and he narrowed his eyes as if he'd got smoke in them. 'Yup. A bit.'

'It's quite tricky, isn't it? I mean, don't pilots kill themselves regularly?'

He liked that idea. His eyes came alive. 'It happens,' he said, tossing off the remark with a well-practised blend of nonchalance and bravado. 'But then just as many pilots get killed in road accidents, probably more.' The devil-may-care persona was obviously one he enjoyed and had doubt-less used to some effect over the years.

He drained his glass and, holding it at chest height, twiddled the stem slowly between thumb and forefinger. Daisy guessed she was meant to notice how empty it was. 'Can I buy you another?' she offered.

He attacked the next drink only marginally less slowly than the first, and she saw that his hand trembled slightly as he reached for the ashtray. It occurred to Daisy that this was not Duggan's first drink of the day. The bad patch Jane Ackroyd had alluded to began to take on a new dimension.

'You don't know where Keen disappeared to?' she asked.

He gave a dry laugh which turned into a phlegmy cough that rattled deep in his chest. 'Christ, no,' he said, recovering himself. 'Don't care either. It's no good knowing where the bastard is if I can't get any money out of him, is it? I just hope he's got his come-uppance. Wrapped his BMW round a lamppost or something.'

'He was difficult to work for, was he?'

'Christ – was he. Always buggering things up. Phoning new instructions through, trying to make me fly over my hours, wanting everything done pronto. It wasn't as if he provided any bloody backup. Just a mechanic, a field operator and an office girl who didn't know her arse from her elbow.' He stabbed his cigarette ineffectually into the ashtray so that it lay there smouldering. 'I must have been out of my tiny,' he snorted. 'Sweating my guts out to finance his flash lifestyle.'

'How long were you with the company in fact?'

'Oh – May till September. Something like that.'

'And the spraying – what sort of jobs were they exactly?'

'Forest stuff. Estates, that sort of thing. Everyone was in a tizz about this beetle moth or whatever it was. They all wanted everything done yesterday.'

'Willis Bain was one of your clients, I believe?'

He took a long slow drink, eyeing her over the rim of his glass, and she sensed a sudden caution in him. 'Yup,' he answered finally. 'Did quite a bit for them. But, um . . .' He hesitated, pulling out another cigarette and lighting it with an old-fashioned steel Zippo. 'Thought you were just interested in Keen? Tracing him and so on.'

'Wish it were that simple,' Daisy said. 'But I need a whole lot of background information. Evidence, facts.'

'You're actually trying to nail him, are you?' he said in sudden admiration. 'What for?'

She gave a shrug. 'Oh, financial irregularities. That sort of thing.'

'Bloody good. Bloody fantastic. Hope you get him!' He

drained his glass and grinned congenially, displaying teeth
which were so discoloured and unattractive that Daisy
couldn't help staring at them.

'Only thing I don't understand is what your client hopes
to gain.' He said it so casually that it was a moment before
Daisy realized the difficulties inherent in the question.

'I'm sorry?'

'Well, it can't be money.'

'No.' Daisy was thinking hard.

'Jail then?'

Daisy spread her hands to show that this might not be
so far from the truth.

'My God!' Duggan exclaimed with relish. 'Keen must
have upset your client very severely if they want to pin
something that serious on him.'

'You could say that.'

'So it might be jail?'

'It might be.'

Duggan gave a long lazy wink that was probably
intended to look conspiratorial but which merely appeared
lecherous. 'Well, you can count on me.'

Daisy thought: Now I wonder if that's true? For all his
affability Duggan didn't seem the steadfast type. Tricky
and difficult, she guessed; out for number one.

She offered him another drink. He accepted readily,
though not before going through the heavy drinker's time-
honoured ritual of insisting that he couldn't possibly drink
alone. She ordered a low-alcohol lager and a packet of
crisps to soak it up with.

'You don't look like a lawyer,' he said.

'What does a lawyer look like?'

'Older and uglier.' He winked again, and this time the
suggestiveness was deliberate though self-mocking.

She said: 'Well, you know how it is, one has to overcome
these handicaps.'

He laughed appreciatively, then, just as she was thinking

the interview was beginning to go smoothly, he added casually: 'You didn't say what firm you worked for.'

'Didn't I?' Was he trying to catch her out? Or was he just curious? She laughed it off. 'I'll give you my card.' She went through a pantomime of rooting through her bag. 'Well, I *would* give you a card, but I seem to have run out.'

He was waiting.

Aware that she was being forced into open lie, she heard herself give him the name of her old firm, the solicitors where she'd worked before joining Catch. 'Here – I'll give you the phone number.' She wrote down Catch's unlisted number on a scrap of paper. This lie she liked far less than the fishing story she'd told Jane Ackroyd, if only because there was a far greater chance of being found out. Duggan only had to look up her old firm and call their real number to discover she wasn't there any more. Or to call the Catch number before Daisy had a chance to brief Jenny.

But would he bother? It was all too easy to imagine that his mind was as languid as his body. Yet those sharp little questions hadn't come out of thin air.

She asked him about his dealings with Keen, routine stuff about paperwork, how the wages were paid, what money went through the Portakabin office.

'Never saw the cash,' Duggan declared, waving an expansive hand. 'In fact he kept us so tight that we had trouble getting enough petty cash for lav rolls. Not that we used the bloody place at all if we could possibly avoid it.'

Daisy smiled. 'You mean the hut?' The moment she'd said it, she could have kicked herself.

Duggan's glass paused half way to his mouth. 'You've been to the airfield then?' he asked.

'Yes.'

'Why? What for? Nothing to see.'

'I was just passing. On business.'

'Ah.' He nodded sagely, but she sensed him carefully weighing the information.

'Did you ever sign for things?' she asked. 'You know, fuel deliveries, that kind of thing?'

He shook his head. 'Nah. Though I bloody well checked the stuff once it arrived. Didn't trust Keen an inch.'

'In what way?'

'I wouldn't have put it past him to try and give me low-grade fuel.'

'Good God, really? Wouldn't that have been dangerous?'

'Probably.' Duggan chuckled to himself. He was back in the role of fearless daredevil pilot battling against unfavourable odds. All this boyish bravado, not to mention the heavy drinking, made Daisy wonder how Duggan was ever allowed in charge of an aircraft.

Keeping her tone light, she nudged the conversation forward. 'What about the chemicals – the stuff you used to spray the trees with – did you check that out too?'

'No. Didn't have to. Keen didn't have anything to do with the gunk, thank God. Davie, the mechanic, he was in charge of measuring and mixing and all that. The gunk was delivered direct from the customer most of the time anyway. They bought it direct from the manufacturers or whatever.'

'Of course.' Daisy nodded vigorously as if he had just reminded her of something she knew perfectly well.

'That way there was no chance of Keen short-changing them,' Duggan explained in case she'd missed the point.

'Quite. And the stuff you were using – er, remind me . . .?'

He shrugged. 'We used to call it "the usual". I'd say, is it the usual? And Davie'd say, it's the usual. And that would be that. But the name – it was feni – fenitri . . . Christ, never could say the bloody word.'

'Fenitrothion?'

'That's it.'

'Was that the only stuff?'

He brushed at a fall of ash on his lapel and managed to smear it deep into the fabric. 'Mmm – sorry?'

'What other chemicals did you use?'

'Other chemicals? No, that was it. Feni-whatsit.'

'But I thought . . . Hang on.' Daisy made a show of getting out her notebook and flicking through it. 'Something else was used for a couple of jobs near Loch Fyne, wasn't it?' She looked up expectantly.

He wasn't crazy about the question. He took a long sip at his gin, frowning at her over the glass. It was time for another refill, she noticed. She caught the barman's eye and pointed in the direction of Duggan's glass.

'Something else?' Duggan echoed coolly. 'I don't see what the hell that has to do with anything.' His voice had an edge to it, a note of truculence. 'I mean, how can your client be interested in the gunk we used on a particular job?'

'It's a matter of finding out if Keen did what he was contracted to do.'

'But like I said, it was a limited company. It doesn't matter if he delivered the goods, if he did what the client wanted – it's all bloody water under the bridge, isn't it? The only thing you can possibly get him for is fraud, and I don't see that what we sprayed on the treetops of Loch Fyne has got a blind thing to do with how Keen managed or mismanaged the bloody finances.'

Daisy held up a staying hand. 'It may seem that way, but the point is . . .'

The barman arrived with Duggan's refill and another low-alcohol lager. While she counted out the money coin by coin, she tried to think exactly what the point was. 'The point is,' she said finally, 'that if Keen was substituting cheap chemicals then it *was* fraud.'

But Duggan wasn't buying. 'Even if he'd pulled a fast one, it would have netted him a hundred quid at the most. Don't tell me they're going to nail him on a hundred quid!'

'They got Al Capone on a technicality.'

He sank slowly back in his chair, wrists draped over the arms, cigarette and drink in either hand. 'You're on the wrong track,' he announced with finality. 'Willis Bain delivered everything. It never came through Keen.'

'Oh.' Daisy looked disappointed. 'It'd still be useful to have the name of the other pesticide.'

'I never knew it.'

'But surely – you must have seen a name?'

'No. Does it matter?'

'I told you – every detail helps.'

He shook his head, his cat-eyes watching her through the curling spirals of smoke. 'Can't remember.'

Can't or won't, Daisy thought grimly. She took a sip of lager while she considered the way forward. He wouldn't take much more pressing, she sensed, or he'd clam up altogether. Letting the subject drop, on the other hand, would be to lose what might be her only opportunity.

There was a third option, she realized, something quite different. She let the idea grow and sharpen in her mind. She'd have to push hard to carry it off, and it wouldn't be very pretty – and that was putting it mildly – but it might just work.

She put her drink down. 'I need to know the name of that pesticide,' she said.

He picked some tobacco off his lip. 'I told you,' he said with an impatient sigh, 'I don't remember.'

'Or don't want to? Listen, Mr Duggan, I don't like to press you, but according to my information there were plenty of irregularities at Acorn Flying Systems, and they didn't just involve Keen.'

He was very still, the drink and cigarette for once forgotten in his fingers. 'What does that mean?'

'It means that rules and regulations were broken all the way down the line and Keen wasn't the only one responsible.'

His mouth twisted, his voice was hoarse. 'What the hell are you talking about?'

'About notifications not getting sent out. About livestock getting sprayed. About flying hours being exceeded. Shall I go on?' The excessive flying hours was a guess, but Duggan wasn't arguing.

He jerked forward in his chair, his face louring across the table. 'Who the hell *are* you? What the hell's this about?'

'Calm down, Mr Duggan. There's no need to get angry. I'm sure it won't be necessary to let this go any further, not if you can find a way to help me out.' As she said it, she wondered if this was the way practised blackmailers generally put their demands across. 'Just tell me the name of the pesticide, and we'll forget about the livestock.'

She thought: But not about the people. She couldn't make any promises on that. Which made her offer devious, even, if she were in the mood to be utterly scrupulous, dishonest. But remembering Alusha Mackenzie and Adrian Bell, she couldn't feel too heart-stricken about that.

Duggan was rallying from the initial shock. 'It's not bloody true, all you're saying,' he declared belligerently. 'Don't know where you got these outrageous bloody ideas from – '

'Reliable sources.'

Duggan's face contorted with something like fear. 'Christ, you b—' But the rest, which might have included the word bitch, was lost as he sat back in his chair and drained his drink at one go.

'It's a reasonable offer,' she said.

'Sounds like a bloody threat to me!'

'Take it or leave it.'

'But I don't bloody remember the name!'

'Try.'

His mouth was working hard and he looked as if he could cheerfully kill her, but he was thinking all right. 'I don't know – I don't know,' he said fretfully. 'It never had a name, just some stupid code number. ZX-something. ZX ... P. That was it. ZXP. No name. Well – it *did* have a name, but I only saw it once, about the second time we used the stuff. It was the day Keen actually deigned to come in. We couldn't believe it – never saw the bastard normally. Turned up out of the blue, treating us like bloody lackeys ... It was all his sodding fault that things went wrong, you know. He pushed us – '

'The pesticide,' she interrupted.

He glared at her. 'Yah, well ... There it was on the sheet. With the code number.'

'And a name.'

'Yeah, but only that once. The girl, she just put ZXP on the job sheets after that. And like I said Davie and I weren't into gunk names. We just got to call it "the old gunk" or "the new gunk". And that was it. I only saw the name that once, for God's sake.' He lit a cigarette from the butt of his old one.

Her silence finally drove him forward, fumbling resentfully through the remnants of his memory. 'I think it was some trade name or another. You know, one of those catchy made-up words. Something to do with forests. Leaves, needles, something like that . . .' He waited expectantly as if Daisy could in some miraculous way pull the name out of thin air. 'For Christ's sake,' he grumbled, 'it was last year – no one could remember that far back.' He glanced at her to see if this little appeal was going to earn him a reprieve, then lurched on: 'We had a lot of jobs that day. Too many. And Keen slapped on another. What could I say? If I'd caused trouble he'd simply have told me to get lost.' He ran a hand through his hair so that it stood out over his ears like feathers. 'White . . .' he murmured for no apparent reason. 'He was wearing white, Keen. Like a spivvy wop waiter. Top *and* bottom. White shoes too – I ask you! Standing there like some gift from God, ordering

everyone around. Changing the schedule. Putting the wind
up that stupid girl. Kept threatening us with financial
disaster if we didn't pull out the stops.' Catching her
expression he pulled himself back to the subject with bad
grace. 'Okay, okay.' He shook his head, fretting at the
problem. 'White . . . It was something like that. Pale,
anyway. No – glittery. Silver maybe. Yes . . .' He flapped a
hand. 'That was it. Silver.'

'Silver?'

'The name. The gunk. Silver-something.' He coughed, a
loose rattle deep in his chest. 'And that, I tell you, is all I
bloody remember.'

He thought she had finished with him, but he was
wrong. 'You did several jobs around Loch Fyne, didn't
you?' she asked.

He was very still, his eyes creased into a line of watchfulness. 'A few.'

She described the approximate area of Adrian Bell's
house.

He shrugged. 'Don't remember.'

'And the Fincharn Estate – you were up there, weren't
you?'

His face hardened. She could see him preparing a denial.
Then his expression lightened abruptly and he laughed.
'Barking up the wrong tree there, dear lady. Quite the
wrong tree. Had an equipment failure that day. The job
was aborted. Never did get to do it. Bad weather, no time.'
He sat back, blinking heavily, lips slack, ash spilling down
the front of his jacket. 'Quite the wrong tree,' he said, and
smiled.


Jenny flicked her eyes towards Alan's open door, indicating
that he was in or waiting to pounce, or both. Taking long
light strides Daisy sped past the door and into her office.
Plucking the Ministry of Agriculture's pesticides manual off

the shelf, she bent over the desk and started to thumb
through its 400 pages and 3000 odd products. She started
at the trade name index. Sickle, Sierra . . . Silvapron.

Then . . . something called Silveron ZXP.

ZXP. Silveron.

She checked it back to the main register. Insecticide for
professional use only, it said. Manufactured by Morton-
Kreiger (UK) Ltd. Registration number MAFF 05012.

The registration numbers were allocated historically, the
latest products being awarded the highest numbers. The
05000 numbers were the latest and suggested recent registration. She looked for the previous year's manual, searching her shelves and hunting through the most likely bumf
dump, which was located on the floor in the corner.
Nothing. In desperation she tiptoed to the door and mimed
to Jenny. Jenny, looking innocent, pulled her copy off the
shelf and sauntered over as if she were making for one of
the filing cabinets.

Daisy winked her thanks and took the manual to her
desk. It was as she thought: last year, no Silveron.

She went back to the current manual. Typically, the
ministry in their infinite wisdom omitted to state the type
of crops each product was actually approved for, and she
had to go to *The UK Pesticide Guide,* a publication of the
Crop Protection Council. Silveron wasn't listed. She
phoned the Council. Silveron had been approved too late
for the last edition. But they had the details to hand. It was
a broad-spectrum, contact organophosphorus insecticide.
It was approved for use against aphids, weevils, midge,
moth, thrips and numerous flies and beetles, for use on a
wide range of fruit and vegetables. Forestry use was considered such a low-risk activity that it was not listed.

They gave her the label precautions by reference numbers, which she looked up in the back of the guide. Silveron,
so the manufacturers advised, was not to be used by people
who were under medical advice not to work with organo-

phosphates (she'd yet to hear of anyone getting this advice until after the damage was done). Silveron was dangerous to bees and harmful to fish, livestock, game, wild birds and animals. It was harmful if swallowed, inhaled or put in contact with skin. Users were advised against breathing vapour or spray-mist. Protective clothing was to be worn.

This inventory, though chilling, was nothing out of the ordinary. In fact, if the consumer did but know it, it was typical for most chemicals in daily use on fruits and vegetables. What was almost as interesting were the omissions. No mention of special precautions or dangers, no directions to wear respirators when applying the stuff. In other words no one was treating Silveron like an especially dangerous chemical.

Neither was there any mention of approval for aerial application, she noticed. Which meant that Willis Bain had committed an offence in supplying the stuff to the flying company.

She felt a glimmer of hope. Getting warm, getting warm.

Forgetting the need to lie low, she gave a small whoop of triumph. Through the open door Jenny looked round and, catching the mood, laughed and raised a clenched fist in reply.

As Daisy hastily dialled Peasedale's number, she became aware of Alan striding swiftly into her office, a half-eaten sandwich clutched in his hand.

'Real progress, Alan,' she cried as Peasedale's number started ringing.

'I need to speak to you,' Alan said.

She gave him an unconcerned smile. 'Of course. In a while? I'm rather—' The number answered. 'Peasedale? It's me. Listen – I've got it. The pesticide in the Bell case.'

Alan thrust his face into her field of vision and mouthed an exaggerated 'now', repeating it several times, until his mouth moved like that of a newly landed fish.

Peasedale was making interested noises at the other end

of the line. 'Hold on,' she told him and, capping the phone, promised Alan: 'Soon. Really.'

'And when's *that* likely to be?' He was squeezing his sandwich so tightly that the honey was oozing through the bread in dark glutinous patches.

'But I've got the name of the pesticide.'

She might as well have been talking about the latest stationery order. 'Ten minutes,' Alan hissed.

Peasedale hadn't heard of Silveron ZXP, but he promised to ask around and see if anyone else had. She also called an industrial chemist at an independent laboratory who agreed to do an analysis for her. It wouldn't be free, of course, but he always managed to fiddle the hours to the minimum.

Finally, unable to find any more excuses, she made the excursion round the partition to Alan's office.

Alan had trouble in beginning his speech. He opened his mouth several times before sighing: 'For all the good our discussions do I sometimes wonder why we bother.'

'Alan, I'm listening,' she said, settling herself attentively in a chair. 'I always listen.'

'But you don't bloody take any notice of what we *agree*.' His voice cracked slightly.

'Whatever it is, I'm sorry,' Daisy said humbly.

'You can be sorry all you like, but it doesn't seem to make any bloody difference, does it? You disappear to Scotland, you abandon the presentation and leave me to face the trustees, then, just when I think maybe there's a chance of getting back to normal – you know, working as a team again, which is how it's meant to be in case you'd forgotten – you're off again and I'm up until midnight, preparing for the next meeting that I know damn well you won't turn up for.'

'What meeting? I had no meeting . . .'

'If you'd bothered to call in yesterday you might have found out about it. The EEC ban on Aldeb. The British

Euro MPs asked for a quick briefing, which seemed a pretty reasonable request. I mean, that is what we're meant to be here for, isn't it, briefing people who have the power, and that sort of thing? So I said yes. I couldn't very well refuse, could I? Even when I knew I wasn't going to get a single iota of backup.' He measured an iota between thumb and forefinger and held it up in front of his face. 'Not an iota!'

There wasn't a lot Daisy could say. 'Alan, I would have been there if I'd known, you know I would.'

Alan raised his glasses and rubbed his hand angrily across his eyes. 'It's not good enough,' he said.

'No, I suppose not.'

He pushed the glasses back onto his nose with such ferocity that the impact made him blink. 'I don't think it's going to pan out, Daisy. You might as well be working for a different organization. Sometimes I wonder if you're with us at all. I mean – well, it's just not going to work out, Daisy.'

An unpleasant little chill gripped Daisy's stomach. 'What are you saying, Alan?'

'I'm saying that it's hopeless, this doing your own thing. It's not fair to me, it's not fair to Catch.' He pursed his lips and looked unhappy. Eventually he managed to spit it out. 'I think you should think about resigning, Daisy. In fact' – he gave a small shudder – 'I *know* you should think about resigning.'

Daisy stared at him, totally taken aback.

'But I'm just getting somewhere, Alan. Everything's just beginning to happen. Identifying that pesticide is going to make all the difference to the Adrian Bell case.'

'That's it, Daisy. *You're* getting somewhere. Not Catch. Not the campaign. And as for the Bell case – Daisy, how often have we discussed our policy on individual cases? Just tell me, how often?'

'But, Alan – the case is going to expose all that's wrong with pesticide control – '

'Is it?' he said sharply. 'That's your opinion, Daisy. Not mine. Not the trustees'.' *Documenting* the Bell case is fine and useful and good anecdotal stuff and all that. But a detailed investigation – I mean, tracking down the pilot, going to inquests, all that stuff – is *not* part of our strategy.'

'But, Alan, we can't just leave it! Blimey, you might as well walk away from a road accident!'

'Daisy – ' He clapped his hands to his face in a gesture of despair. 'We've been through this before – how many times? It's just not possible to take on every injustice in the whole damned world and fight it personally. We don't have the resources.'

'Well, I do.'

'No you don't, Daisy. You don't!' He stabbed a finger at her. 'It's Catch's resources you're using.'

'Jesus, Alan!' But for once she made the effort to pull herself up short. This wasn't the time for a row, not when Alan was talking of her resigning and looking deadly serious when he said it.

A voice intruded, drifting over the partition from the outer office. Daisy recognized Simon's unmistakably authoritative tones. It was a moment before she remembered that he'd arrived to take her across town to an Arts for the Earth auction at Bonham's.

She said to Alan: 'Listen, I hear what you're saying, Alan. Really. But . . .'

'There's always a but, Daisy.'

'Yes,' she said momentarily defeated. 'I suppose there is.' She cast him a contrite look. 'I don't want to leave Catch, I really don't. Blimey, this is my life, Alan.'

'I think you're in the wrong organization, Daisy. I think it's as simple as that.'

Daisy took a moment to come up for air. 'Listen . . .' She waved in the general direction of the voices in the outer office. 'Can we talk about this later?'

Alan didn't reply but turned back to his desk with a

dark expression. He was still exhaling sharply as Daisy closed the door.

Simon was propped on Jenny's desk, chatting. He turned a smile on Daisy. 'Ready?'

'Can't make it. Sorry.' Another man, another apology.

He glanced at his watch, looking put out. 'Oh?'

'Something's come up,' she explained. 'To be precise – the pesticide in the Bell case.'

'Ah?' A spark of interest. 'What about it?'

'Got the name,' she announced, allowing some of her satisfaction to return.

'And – ?'

'It's something called Silveron ZXP. An organophosphate.'

He frowned slightly. 'Are you sure?' There was a touch of condescension in his tone.

'Yes, I'm sure,' she said, moving out of Jenny's hearing. 'Why?'

He went though the motions of considering her idea in more depth, but scepticism was still written large on his face. 'It just seems a little unlikely,' he said cautiously. 'Just when Silveron's about to get US approval, I mean.' The surprise must have shown in her face because he said, not without satisfaction: 'You didn't realize?'

'No,' she said, adjusting to the fact that Simon seemed to know all about Silveron. 'But then the EPA aren't perfect,' she said. 'They've had it wrong before.'

'They usually get it an awful lot righter than us, though, don't they?'

'You know a lot about Silveron,' she said accusingly.

'It's Morton-Kreiger's new baby. They seem to think it's got a great future.'

'Which means they think it's going to make them a lot of money,' she said waspishly. 'Anyway, since when did a company's opinion of its own product bear any relation to its safety?'

'I could ask around,' he said, putting on his magnanimous voice. 'Shall I? There *was* something, I know – a
problem on the production line . . .'

From Alan's office came the sound of a chair leg scraping
across lino. Unable to face a three-way discussion, Daisy
led Simon outside and up the steps to the street. A fierce
wind was blowing from King's Cross, spiralling litter along
the pavement. The front page of the *Sun* jammed against
Daisy's leg.

'A problem?' she prompted, kicking the newspaper aside.

'It was a scare. Some workers on the production line. A
temporary lapse in safety procedures, I think. But I'll dig
the cuttings out for you. Ask around. I've got to phone
some people in the US anyway.'

'They were sick, the workers – how sick? What sort of
symptoms?'

He shrugged as if he couldn't possibly be expected to
know. 'Must go.' He pecked her on the cheek. Turning
away, he hesitated and looked back. 'Oh, I'm seeing them
tomorrow – Morton-Kreiger. I'll ask them what sort of
safety margins it has, shall I?'

She laughed disbelievingly. 'They'll never tell you!'

'You'd be surprised. They're very PR conscious, very
anxious to show environmentally willing.'

She called after him: 'You won't let on, will you?'

'What? Who?'

'Morton-Kreiger. You won't tell them why you're
interested?'

Throwing her an offended look, he spread his hands as
if the idea was too insulting to be worthy of consideration
and hurried away.

She watched him go and wondered if it had been such a
good idea to encourage questions. Much as she was desperate for information, any probing, particularly on the part
of an environmental journalist, was likely to alert Morton-
Kreiger to the possibility of attack.

Back in her office, she closed the door to deter another Alan-led offensive, and sank into her chair, overcome by a sudden despondency. Never having been asked for her resignation before, it took some getting used to. Had Alan really meant it? Had she really gone too far or asked too much? It wasn't as if she'd asked Alan or Jenny to do anything she wouldn't have gladly done herself.

She said: 'Bugger it,' to no one in particular and sat up with a jerk. On her desk was an update on Jenny's investigations into Acorn's flying activities. Though she had managed to locate several Davie Robertsons in the Inverness region, none of them was or ever had been employed as an aeroplane mechanic, nor knew of a Davie Robertson who was. Further enquiries with the local Health and Safety Executive and the military air controllers had also drawn a blank, at least as far as flying in the Loch Fyne area was concerned.

The other messages did not interest Daisy and her attention returned to the pesticide manual still open in front of her at the Silveron entry. She stared at it for a long moment, then reached for a pile of worldwide environmental literature that she hardly ever had time to read in detail, and went through some of the latest issues. Silveron did not rate a mention on anyone's hit list: no warnings, no news of production-line sickness, no nothing. Abandoning the journals, she worked her way through the bulky contents of her in-tray. From somewhere near the top she pulled out the latest EarthForce bulletin, and there it was in the news section. Silveron ZXP. Sickness at the Aurora production plant in Aurora, Illinois; EarthForce making representations to the EPA; Morton-Kreiger tightening up their production-line safety procedures; a secondary toxicology study which, according to sources, was expected to show that Silveron came within statutory safety limits.

It was six p.m. and the cheap phone rate to the US didn't start until eight, but she dialled Washington anyway. Paul

Erlinger greeted her with a cry of delight, as if she were a long lost friend and charged into an effusive stream of questions, before cutting himself ruthlessly short and getting down to business.

'So what can I do for you?'

She told him she was interested in Silveron and what sort of damage it might be doing to people.

'You read our bulletin, did you?'

'I need more. The symptoms, the exposure, how those workers are doing. What *you* think.'

'Listen, er . . .' The line became muted as if he'd capped the phone. 'Listen, can I call you later, at home maybe?'

She gave him the number and they fixed a time.

She took a bus home, stopping at the Patels' to buy fish fingers, bananas and Greek yogurt. The flat was cold: she had left a window open. Her one pot plant had dropped most of its leaves, a victim of gross neglect. The mail consisted of three brown envelopes with windows. There were no messages on the answering machine.

She lit the gas fire and had a quick bath. The water hissed and spat in the tap, percussion to the hot tank's strings section, which sobbed and sighed and gurgled as it refilled.

Lying in the bath, she closed her eyes and the questions swooped in on her, one on top of another.

Silveron. Morton-Kreiger. Within statutory limits. Secondary trials. Was it that safe? How could it be that safe?

And the workers, how sick had they been? Did they have the muscle wasting, the problems in absorbing food?

She thought, too, of Scotland and Nick Mackenzie. Where was he now? she wondered. What was he doing? He wouldn't be in Scotland. He would have gone abroad, America, or a hot climate, the West Indies or Bahamas. Perhaps he was working again, perhaps he was beginning to pick up the pieces, but even as she nursed the thought forward, she remembered his heavy unfocused look during the inquiry, his uncharacteristic belligerence, and she wasn't so sure.

The call came through on the dot of nine. 'I'm sorry to have cut things short there,' Paul Erlinger said immediately. 'But I was with a journalist. Not known for his discretion – are they ever? Listen – is it safe to talk?'

'Safe? What do you mean?'

'I mean, is the line okay? Bug-free?'

The idea was so preposterous she almost laughed. 'I don't think Catch rates that sort of attention.'

'You'd be surprised. Might be worth getting it checked out.'

She couldn't see herself getting the idea past Alan. 'I'm at home anyway,' she reminded him.

He gave her the case histories of each of the Silveron workers, the numerous unexplained symptoms, the general malaise, the loss of weight, the single case of cancer which may or may not have been related to the Silveron exposure. Morton-Kreiger International were admitting absolutely nothing, but had tightened up their safety procedures at the plant 'as a precautionary measure'. He told her about the back-up toxicology trial and how the results, which had been carefully leaked by MKI, would show that there was no cause for alarm.

'And what do *you* think?'

A pause. He exhaled into the mouthpiece. 'I think there's a bad smell hanging around this one.'

'Why do you think so?'

'Just a feeling really. Hard to pin down, you know?'

'Nothing definite then?'

'Nothing *definite*.' There was something in his tone that suggested quite the opposite.

She felt a beat of excitement. 'Come on, Paul! I need this, I need it badly! I think I have two victims here, maybe more.'

'Look, Daisy, I wish I could tell you – but it's not that simple. You see, we took a decision to keep this under wraps, at least until we could be sure of protecting our sources.'

'So there *is* something!'

There was a silence interspersed with groans as if he were battling with his better judgement but quite enjoying the process. 'Okay, okay. I'll tell you this much – there could be hard evidence.'

'What sort of evidence? You mean, more victims? Or – *God!* – are Morton-Kreiger covering something?'

He laughed, but it was only to give himself time. 'Daisy, you're a one-woman interrogation machine.'

'Can I have this evidence?'

'Whoa, whoa. We ain't got it yet!'

'When? When will you get it?'

'Daisy, Daisy ...' He was objecting, but not that strongly. 'Ask me again after the thirtieth.'

Ten days away.

'You're not coming over for the PAN conference?' he asked. 'Maybe I'll have something by then.'

The Pesticide Action Network was a North American umbrella organization with which Catch attempted to keep close contact. Alan had considered sending himself to the conference in Boston but had decided against it, not on the grounds of expense, which did not anyway seem to pose such an insuperable problem where Alan's foreign trips were concerned, but because of pressure of work, a barb that had been aimed in Daisy's direction.

'Maybe I will,' she heard herself say.

'Hey, but I can't promise anything, Daisy. Don't come specially, will you? I mean, I might have absolutely *nothing.*'

'I was thinking of coming anyway,' she lied, trying to remember what she had in her savings account.

'You were?' He sounded pleased. 'In the meantime, Daisy, take my advice, don't leave anything lying around. You know what I mean?'

Involuntarily, she glanced around the room. Then, feeling faintly foolish at having caught herself taking the idea so seriously, she shook herself free and in her American-cop voice said: 'Listen – suspicion's my middle name.'

# Chapter 20

———

SUSAN WAITED FOR the hotel doorman to dart across the pavement and set the revolving doors in motion before sweeping through. She was ten minutes late, but since that was exactly how late she'd intended to be, she did not hurry. Nothing, anyway, could add to the considerable flutter of nervousness already dancing in her stomach, a nervousness that was tinged with an odd kind of excitement, like wearing a revealing dress for the first time.

The bar was dimly lit in the American style, so that it was impossible to see anything until your eyes had got used to the gloom. She stopped inside the door to get her bearings. Almost immediately the figure of Schenker appeared out of the shadows and taking her lightly by the elbow, guided her to a booth and took her coat. She ordered a glass of champagne. He ordered a mineral water with ice and lemon to add to the one already in front of him.

'Will you change your mind about lunch?' he asked her smoothly. 'The restaurant does a lovely *sole meunière*. Or there's smoked salmon in the bar here. Or club sandwiches.' He'd been polishing up on his culinary terms and social graces, she observed. The *sole meunière* was dished up far less obsequiously than before, and with the correct pronunciation.

'I can't, I'm afraid.' In fact she had no other lunch appointment, but Schenker was not her idea of a scintillating lunch companion, and she wanted to be away and free of him the moment the business was over. 'Another time perhaps.'

He asked her some dutiful questions about Camilla and how family life was surviving Tony's appointment. Susan kept her answers polite but short. She had no wish to discuss her domestic arrangements with Schenker, and if he had any brains, he'd realize that too.

He seemed to cotton on at last because he changed the subject, saying: 'And how's the fund-raising going? You've been doing great things for Save the Children.' He probably thought she was on the scrounge for more funds. This year alone she'd asked Morton-Kreiger for sponsorship for a major water project in India and to take fifty seats for a gala concert, and got both.

'You know how it is,' she said vaguely. 'The Third World's a bottomless pit.'

His small black eyes slid up to her face then away again several times. She could almost see him wondering why she'd asked for the meeting if it wasn't to beg for funds. He reminded her of a cautious reptile, waiting motionless to catch passing morsels.

They progressed unenthusiastically over the economic news, the state of the agrochemical industry and other equally thrilling topics until, unable to bear the sheer frustration any longer, Susan fixed him with her best gaze and said: 'Listen, something's come up. And I think you might be able to help.'

The raisin-eyes flicked away then back again, looking flattered, wary and curious all at the same time. 'Of course.' He reached for some nuts from the bowl on the table.

'You know a girl called Angela Kershaw, I believe.'

His hand hardly hesitated in its journey from the bowl to his mouth. He also made a pretty good job of hiding the glimmer of alarm that flashed into his eyes – a pretty good job but not a totally successful one, and Susan felt a tremor of satisfaction at the knowledge that she was on the right track.

He chewed on the nuts, a rapacious chomping. 'Umm . . . should I?'

'You and Tony had dinner with her in France.'

He made a show of trying to remember. 'Oh? Did we? Sorry – one meets so many people.'

Did he think she was going to be taken in by this sort of hot air? He must take her for a total idiot. Her temper rose and ripped away from her with alarming speed. 'Look,' she hissed, 'we can play games and pretend we don't know this woman, or we can get on and save ourselves a lot of trouble.'

He stared at her, taken aback, then, recovering, rubbed the salt fastidiously from his fingers. 'If you say so,' he said cautiously. 'Go on.'

'This woman. She's seeing Tony. I think she's causing him problems.'

'Ah. I see,' he said unevenly. 'I see.' He was thinking hard, playing for time. 'What sort of problems?'

'I'm not certain. But Tony's looking very worried.'

'And you say you don't know the – er, details?' he asked, picking his way over the words as if they were glass.

'No, but I thought you might.'

A glare of amazement. 'Me? Why?'

'You introduced them, didn't you?' she said.

'No,' he said indignantly. 'I did not. Absolutely not. I only met her the once. I don't know her at all!'

He sounded convincing. Doubt opened up in front of Susan like a crevasse. 'But you know her well enough to remember her name?' she asked accusingly.

He didn't argue on that point. 'I really have no contact with Miss – er, this lady. And I certainly don't know what the – er, details are. Really. No idea at all.'

'But you could find out,' she persisted.

The surprise again. 'I'm sorry?'

'Your company must be finding things out all the time. It can't be too difficult.'

'Difficult?'

'Finding things out. Using investigators, that sort of thing.'

He shook his head. 'Mrs Driscoll, I'm afraid the sort of investigations we undertake aren't anything like that. We commission reports on other companies, City personalities, financiers, that sort of thing. We don't investigate – well, *personal* matters.'

'No?' She raised an eyebrow.

'Besides, what could you hope to achieve? What would you expect to find out?'

'What she's up to, of course.'

'Dear Mrs Driscoll – '

Susan bridled at the dear. Little creep.

' – it would be most unwise to follow such a course on a matter like this. You see' – he dropped his voice and adopted a tone of patient explanation – 'it's not something one could pursue without actually compromising the minister further – without exposing him to the most terrible dangers. Investigators – people like that – one could never entirely trust them. There could be leaks. The press might get to hear of it.' He paused to emphasize the full horror of the idea. 'The risks would be enormous.'

'Risks?' she said briskly, finding her confidence again. 'But you don't seem to understand. He's already at risk. This woman's putting enormous pressure on him, pressure he can't take. She might already be planning to go to the press for all I know.'

Schenker's mask of impassivity slipped a little and he chewed his lip in mild agitation. 'So? What are you suggesting?'

'She's got to be dealt with.'

'Dealt with?'

'Dealt with,' Susan repeated with more conviction than

she felt. 'Given what she wants. Told to disappear. Paid off. Whatever it is she's after. And' – she fastened him with the full power of her considerable gaze – 'you're the best person to do it.'

He didn't reply, but she caught a hint of triumph in the staring black eyes. He liked the fact that she was having to grovel to him, she realized; he liked the fact that she'd had to come down to his level.

Schenker raised a beckoning finger and ordered another glass of champagne, and a Scotch and water for himself.

They didn't speak again until the drinks were in front of them and the waiter gone. Schenker took a long sip of his whisky. She noticed that his hair had been blow-dried to give the impression of thickness, the better to hide the receding hairline that reached almost to the bald patch at the back.

'Mrs Driscoll, even if I *could* find a means of helping,' he began in the sort of hushed condescending tone that pastors reserve for their flocks, 'I'm not sure it would be appropriate for me to get involved. In fact, entirely *in*appropriate. Behind your husband's back . . .' He sucked in his breath.

'But why?' she snapped.

'Why? Because quite apart from anything else, you might have misread the situation. Suppose there's no problem – '

'I haven't misread the situation. Believe me.'

He spread a hand, conceding the point reluctantly. 'But wouldn't it be better – more suitable, I mean – if a family friend, the family solicitor – '

'No. You're the only person who can do it. The only person I can trust.' It was flattery, of course, but it was also the truth. If anyone could deal with the matter effectively, it was Schenker. Not only did he have the power and the resources to do whatever should be done, but just as importantly he was a naturally secretive man, someone who could be relied on to keep things quiet.

He seemed affected by her unexpected declaration of trust. '*Dear* Mrs Driscoll, I wish I could help but ...' A condescending smile, a regretful shrug.

She thought viciously: Don't patronize *me,* you little worm! But with superhuman effort she suppressed the urge to say so. Was he being dense? Had he really not got the picture? Or was he just playing games? She decided to spell it out for him. She leant forward and rested a hand on his arm. He quivered slightly as if, given half a chance, he would have snatched his arm away, and it occurred to her that he didn't like contact with women. Perhaps he was the other way inclined. She lightened her touch.

'Tony could be finished by this,' she said. 'The strain could kill him. And if that doesn't, then the scandal most certainly will – and if this woman's as stupid as she sounds then there *will* be a scandal. Either way, he'll be finished,' she said, hammering the point home. '*Finished.*' She withdrew her hand and added in elaborate parody: 'And then, *dear* Mr Schenker, where would we be?'

His eyes dipped, his face closed down into an unreadable mask, he reached for his drink. Sipping it slowly, he looked at her over the rim of the glass, his eyes sly and pensive.

'Under the circumstances ...' He hesitated as if giving the matter further thought, though she had the feeling that he had already made up his mind. 'I will do what small amount I can to help ...' He looked up to catch her reaction, but she kept very still.

'... But I can only act in a *private* capacity, as one friend helping another.'

Was she the friend he was putting himself out for? Or was it Tony? The intimacy didn't bear thinking about.

'... But I can promise nothing. Nothing. I'm sure you can appreciate that.'

Susan picked up her bag and got to her feet. 'I'm sure you'll do your best, Mr Schenker. I'm sure you always do.'

And in the instant that followed, a brief look of understanding passed between them.

When she walked out into the foyer, Susan wobbled slightly on her heels, though they weren't especially high, and it was only when she was safely in a cab that she finally stopped shaking.

Dublensky tapped the corporation name into Anne's word processor, pressed the exit key and gave the print command. The daisywheel churned into life and disgorged the customized letter. A few weeks ago he would have sent nothing but a CV and a short covering note, but now he gave every application the fully personalized treatment.

By starting late and spinning things out a bit, this took him until noon, when he had an early lunch of cold cuts and salad, and set off on his daily bicycle journey to the gym for a work-out. He had been making full use of the sports club recently; his membership lapsed in a month's time and, due to economies on the home front, would not be renewed.

A fresh breeze was scudding over the lawns but once out of the shade the patches of sunlight were warm and sensuous on his back. It was the sort of day that would normally have made him outrageously glad to be alive, but in his present mood the coming of spring was dimmed by the reminder that time was passing and jobs were harder to find in the summer. He pedalled at a leisurely pace, saving his energies for the tyranny of the Nautilus equipment. At this time of day the street was quiet. A couple of pre-school kids were riding tricycles in their front yards, a housewife was hosing her car, a truck was making a delivery.

A car overtook Dublensky and, with a soft toot on the horn, drew in to the kerb. Dublensky recognized the green station-wagon of his neighbour, Joe Ankar, and cycled up to the driver's window.

'You got callers, John,' Ankar announced, gesturing back in the general direction of the house. 'A removal company. Arrived just a moment ago. Parked right outside.'

Dublensky automatically glanced over his shoulder. 'Removal company? I don't think so,' he smiled. 'I'm not going anywhere.'

'Well, they're there all right. Just a small truck, so maybe they're just delivering something. Anyways, they went right up the side of your house, like they were expected. Thought you must be in, otherwise I'd have checked it out.'

Dublensky couldn't think what goods Anne could have ordered, not when they were cutting back. 'Thanks, Joe.' Waving, he turned his bicycle for home. As he breasted the final rise he spotted the truck, parked out front just as Joe Ankar had described.

It was a well-worn vehicle, with *ABC Ready Removals* emblazoned on the side in paintwork that had seen better days, and underneath in smaller letters *Dor-to-Dor Express*, with a toll-free phone number.

There was no sign of the driver. Dublensky parked his bike against the garage and walked round to the back of the house expecting to find the driver leaving whatever he was delivering in the yard and maybe wedging a delivery note inside the screen door. But the yard was empty, the door closed. He walked across the width of the house at the back and looked up the other side. Nothing. Returning to the back door, he opened the screen and tried the door handle.

The door swung open. Dublensky felt a sharp chill. Had he left it open? He went over his departure in his mind, reliving his progress through the house. But there was no doubt about it: he had definitely locked the door.

He tried to calm himself, tried to think the thing through. The smartest move would be to go to a neighbour's and call the police, but he hesitated. Suppose he was mistaken? Suppose there was no prowler, suppose the delivery man was even now leaving the parcel or whatever it was at the next house?

Best not to be too hasty; he'd feel a fool calling the police if there was nothing wrong. Best to check things out first.

He hovered in the doorway. Fear held him back, but curiosity finally drove him forward and he stepped gingerly into the kitchen, listening hard. Nothing. Only the muffled sound of a dog barking somewhere up the street. He crept forward, aware of sharp excitement and a crazy disbelief at his own actions which seemed so daring as to belong to someone else altogether.

Measuring each step carefully, conscious of the appalling pounding of his heart, he reached the hallway door and peered through. The hallway was empty, silent.

Then it came: a slight sound, a rustling, like paper. Close by, within the house. *Someone.* Incensed, he felt a great leap of atavistic rage, quickly followed by the equally primitive response to get the hell out. The intruder could be armed. Knife or gun, what did it matter? You ended up dead all the same.

Yet for some inexplicable reason a paralysis gripped him and he held still. It seemed that the intruder was taking a break too because the rustling sounds ceased. Against all his better judgement, hardly believing he was capable of such lunacy, Dublensky inched forward into the hall, propelled by an appalling urge to see the intruder himself. The squeak of his soft shoes on the polished floor sounded unnaturally loud, like he was wearing suckers on his feet.

He crept towards the double doors to the lounge which were latched back against the wall and, squeezing himself hard against the wood, peered slowly round the frame.

It took him a moment to take it all in. The mess, the scattering of papers and books, the books standing up like islands in a sea of white. A dark-haired man dressed in overalls was crouching next to the wall units, searching the shelves. After a moment he sat back on his heels, a sheaf of papers balanced on his knee, and went through them methodically.

Mesmerized, Dublensky stood and watched. The papers on those shelves were Anne's – lecture notes and case studies. What could this man possibly want with them? And why had he made such a mess to get at them?

The intruder flicked through the last of the pile then, as casually as if he were throwing a ball to a child, chucked them to one side so that they fanned out over the floor. He went to the next batch of papers and it dawned on Dublensky that this was no ordinary prowler. What kind of burglar would bother to look through batch after batch of valueless papers, and so systematically?

He didn't pursue the realization further though he dimly perceived its significance. Instead he unbottled his anger, which was considerable, and stepped into the room.

Disconcertingly, the intruder, absorbed by his task, did not immediately see him. Dublensky drew breath to shout but the words died in his throat as he became aware of a flicker on the periphery of his vision, a movement that didn't belong. He jerked his head round. Too late, he remembered Joe's words. *You've got visitors . . . they went down the side . . .*

A second man was coming from the den. He too was dressed in overalls. He was a Hispanic, olive-skinned with a balding head and thick moustache. He saw Dublensky about the same instant that the crouching man did. Everyone froze, the Hispanic half-way through the door, the crouching man by the wall unit, and Dublensky in no-man's-land, three steps into the room with nowhere to go. They were frozen into a tableau, excepting that everyone's eyes were moving.

'Get out of my house!' Dublensky screamed, astonished at the aggression in his voice.

It seemed that the Hispanic didn't need a second

invitation. He moved quickly, accelerating from a standing start to a smooth and rapid walk in no seconds flat. Dublensky retreated slightly, suddenly alert to the risk of attack, but the Hispanic, though coming in the general direction of the door, kept wide, taking a loop out towards the wall as if to establish his non-aggressive intentions.

'Get out of my house!' Dublensky repeated, his attention caught by the crouching man, who had straightened up and was also beginning to move. He came forward at an almost leisurely pace, making no attempt to pretend he was heading for anything or anybody but Dublensky.

Dublensky felt a bolt of alarm, a fresh awareness of his vulnerability, and twisted his gaze back to the other man. Too late he saw that the Hispanic's loop had brought him close up behind him, that, far from continuing through the door, he was reaching out towards Dublensky. Dublensky's heart leapt against his chest, he heard himself cry out, and tried to duck away. The Hispanic's fist came punching forward, Dublensky countered with his forearm, only to find that the move had been a feint. With sickening helplessness he felt the Hispanic's free hand close in on his wrist, grip it brutally, and twist it up behind his back. The Hispanic kept twisting until Dublensky, yelping with pain, was forced to bend forward.

The least physical of men, Dublensky had time for a fleeting reflection on the stupidity of having instigated this encounter before everything was pushed from his mind by the arrival of a fist in his guts.

The top of his body jack-knifed forward and he sank slowly to his knees. His initial astonishment was eclipsed by ferocious and overwhelming panic as he choked for breath. His lungs were banded in steel, his stomach crushed in a vice, he thought he was going to die. So desperate was he for breath, so focused on the clawing of his lungs, that for an instant his brain failed to register the arrival of the next blow, which hit the back of his head with the force of

REQUIEM                    401

a power hammer. The impact seemed to drive his skull forward into his head, he was aware of a thunderous roaring, an astonishing weightlessness, then finally, with massive relief, the gathering balm of unconsciousness.

When his brain climbed slowly back to life, it was with a dragging reluctance. He lay motionless, his eyes and ears closed to everything but the needs of his lungs. He reached for breath, pulled at the air like a swimmer saved from drowning, yet when he finally managed to catch a long draught of air, it was only to cough it out again, along with his lunch. It was a while before he could be certain of breathing with any confidence, though it couldn't have been more than a few minutes. Then he lay still again, examining each of his senses in turn, muttering and whimpering with bewilderment and outrage, waiting for the worst of the pain and trauma to pass, half hoping he would slip back into unconsciousness again.

Somewhere outside, a bird sang. There was the hum of a car passing in the road. He opened his eyes and saw a scattering of papers, an overturned chair, an empty bookshelf and a vase of dried flowers balanced precariously on the edge of a table within an inch of falling.

No sounds came from inside the house. The intruders were long gone. He realized with a bitter sense of failure that he hadn't even managed to get the registration number of the delivery truck.

It was another fifteen minutes before he felt strong enough to lift his head, which ached with a nauseating intensity. He had trouble keeping his balance, and it was only by leaning hard on a chair that he managed to climb unsteadily to his feet.

His first instinct, as in any crisis, was to contact Anne. Her office told him she was in case conference, and he had to wait while she was called out. The sound of her voice, tinged with concern, sent him into helpless inarticulate weeping, and it was some time before he was able to explain haltingly what had happened. Anne, who in her determination not to fall into feminine stereotypes had spent a lifetime controlling her emotional responses, couldn't entirely suppress the quiver in her voice as she told him to sit tight.

While he waited for her, he sat in the lounge, staring at the sea of paper, shivering occasionally, murmuring and sighing to himself. When Anne arrived, he cried again and talked incoherently in a great stream of indignant rage. She gave him coffee and headache tablets, dried his tears and over his objections called the doctor and the police. The doctor wanted him straight down to the hospital for a skull X-ray, while the police, who seemed to think a bang on the head quite fortunate compared to some of the alternatives, were more interested in getting the suspects' descriptions and an idea of what was missing.

Anne led the police on a tour of the house. The upstairs was untouched, but the den, like the lounge, was a terrible mess, with overturned table and strewn papers. There were also broken lamps and damaged furniture, almost as if the Hispanic had had a more ambitious burglary in mind.

Even before Anne with her customary thoroughness started to check each item off in her mind Dublensky knew that nothing of monetary value had been taken. The fancy carriage clock Anne had given him one birthday was still on the windowsill. His four-hundred-dollar camera sat in full view on a shelf. Some cash in the top drawer of his desk was untouched.

Rapidly losing interest, the police took down the brief descriptions Dublensky was able to give them and, putting the incident down to a failed burglary attempt, said they'd come back when the inventory was complete.

Dublensky was relieved when they were gone. His out-pourings had drained him of speech, his head throbbed mercilessly. At the same time his mind had taken on a curious lucidity. Armed with more coffee and aspirin, and a pile of cookies which Anne insisted he eat for their energy value, he knelt on the den floor and began to sort through the scatterings of papers, books, journals and notes. The shock had worn off, to be replaced by a gathering anxiety, something akin to dread. He had a suspicion that, in one sense at least, the worst of the day was yet to come.

It took him almost an hour to sort the loose papers into rough batches and reorder the files, and another half hour before he was absolutely certain of what was missing. Then it was all he could do not to weep again.

His scientific notebooks going back to his student days were gone – all twelve of them – as well as a number of scientific papers, several diaries and his main correspondence file. A hurtful loss, but bearable.

More difficult to bear was the loss of the Aurora dossier, with its data on the sick workers and the safety procedures at the works. Although, when he really thought about it, it was not perhaps a complete disaster, since much of it duplicated Burt's work.

What was far, far worse than any of these was the loss of the slim unmarked file which he had hidden inside a folder of scientific papers at the back of a lower drawer of his desk. He kept on searching, but there was no doubt.

The secret file on the Silveron toxicology trials, with its ten irreplaceable photocopied pages, was gone.

# Chapter 21

———

THEY SAT BY the window, separated from the oppressive midday heat by a chill wall of air-conditioning. The restaurant was Ethiopian, the drinks American, and the food somewhere in between. Daisy ate spiced lamb and couscous, and an unashamedly American salad served with Roquefort dressing. Paul Erlinger was stabbing at some charcoal-grilled chick-pea rissoles with yoghurt sauce.

'Pity you couldn't make it to the conference,' he said between mouthfuls. 'There were some really useful people there, some great new initiatives. What was it, you couldn't get away in time?'

'Something like that.' Something like the fact that Catch was not funding this trip and that she'd got a bucket-shop ticket for a four-day trip sandwiched around a weekend.

'Any other time and I could have shown you a bit more of the town,' he said. 'Washington has great food – Mexican, Cuban, Creole – you name it.' He gave her a lop-sided grin. 'Food's my weakness.'

'I would never have guessed.' She grinned at him. He was far from good-looking, with his round face, snub nose and small mouth, and he was decidedly heavy round the jaw and over the belt, but his looks were redeemed by a beaming affectionate smile and a conspicuous sincerity.

'I could have shown you the Chesapeake,' he said warmly. 'Or the Appalachians. But like I told you, I've an appointment Sunday.'

'Another time,' Daisy said.

'I'll hold you to it.' His eyes sent unmistakable signals.

'That would be nice,' she said, trying to match his affability without offering open encouragement.

Guiding the conversation gently back onto the right track, she ventured: 'This source of yours – he never gave you his name?'

Paul lowered his voice theatrically. 'He calls himself Alan Breck.'

'But it's not his real name?'

'I doubt it. When he wrote us, he put it in quotes. I assume he's a Robert Louis Stevenson fan. It's a while since I read *Kidnapped* – like twenty years. I don't even remember if Alan Breck was a good guy.'

'And you've no idea who he really is?'

'Nope.' The waiter cleared the dishes and gave them dessert menus. Paul made a point of waiting for the waiter to go before continuing in the same confidential tones: 'But he has to be with Morton-Kreiger or TroChem – that was the laboratory Morton-Kreiger used to carry out the official toxicology trials on Silveron. It's just possible he could be with the Environmental Protection Agency, I suppose, but somehow I don't think so. We have our contacts there and – well, we'd have heard if they had something that hot on a big one like Silveron.'

'Why don't they have any suspicions? It seems incredible.'

'Not incredible – oh no. Not when the EPA have just had their funding cut, not when they only have the manufacturer's data to go on.'

'What will it take then, for the EPA to start an investigation?'

He spread his hands. 'Alan Breck's data, maybe.'

'That would be enough?'

'You bet. More than enough.' He picked up the menu. 'You want a dessert?'

She shook her head. With an obvious effort of will, he pushed the menu aside.

'He didn't send you the data itself?' she asked.

'No, I think he wanted to see if we'd treat the information seriously first.' He signalled the waiter for the tab.

'Why didn't he send it direct to the EPA?'

'Listen, the EPA's a government agency. They'd want names, dates, sworn affidavits – I mean, a heavy deal. And this guy may be in a real hot spot. Going public could lay him open to serious trouble. By sending the stuff through us he gets to lie low while we get to put ten times the political pressure on the EPA than he could ever achieve solo.' He paid the bill and they made their way to the door.

Outside, the heat closed around them like a blanket. The air was very still and a heavy bronze light hung over the street, as if there were a storm coming.

The EarthForce office was five blocks away, a broad red-brick converted warehouse on three storeys, between a used-furniture store and a Lebanese deli. The windows were heavily barred, the door faced with sheet metal.

'We take no chances,' Paul explained as he tapped a pass code into the security panel. 'A break-in would be seriously bad news.'

'You have a lot of break-ins round here?'

'Sure.'

'The drug problem?'

Paul led the way in and closed the door. 'Addicts? Oh, they're a problem, sure – but not so much for us. No cash here, you see, no valuables.'

'But you still get burgled?'

'You bet we do,' he said mysteriously. 'We've had a few kids try to hack their way through the windows – you know, just to show that no place in the neighbourhood is beyond their skills. But that's amateur stuff.' He paused, squeezing the suspense dry. 'No, we've had two professional break-ins in the last two years, and both times we've asked ourselves, now why would they bother?'

He led the way up the stairs, panting slightly, climbing crabwise so as not to lose a moment's conversation time. 'And we always came to the same unpleasant conclusion.'

'And what was that?'

'They came to get their secrets back,' he said with dramatic emphasis. 'Oh, they made it look like it was robbery – you know, spread everything around – but when we came to do an inventory, it was very particular kinds of documents that were missing. Since the first robbery we've made duplicates of all the important stuff and stored them in a secret hideaway.'

She followed him into the offices of EarthForce's Land Pollution Division. The layout was open-plan, the decor hi-tech rustic, with bare brick, tropical plants and six Meccano-style work stations.

Paul led the way to his work station and dragged over a second chair.

'So what exactly was taken?' she asked, sitting down.

'When I tell you that the Mafia controls the land-dumping industry in this country, you might be able to guess. All our hard-won evidence on illegal dumping – names, places, chemicals which got in the wrong barrels, chemicals which disappeared between destinations – you can imagine. Oh, and some major case files on river pollution – information which was going to nail some big companies. Companies who obviously had friends in all the right places. Pretty weird stuff, huh?'

It could only happen in America, she decided, the links with organized crime, the break-ins.

Paul, far from being disturbed by these incidents, seemed to relish them. 'We decided we were flattered by so much attention,' he announced. 'It meant we were on the right track.'

At last he seemed to remember what she had come for and, assuming a sudden seriousness, pushed himself to his feet and reached up to the shelves above the desk. The shelves had the usual lines of books, files and journals, but unlike the Catch shelves, everything was scrupulously organized so that journals were in sequence and files coded with coloured labels. 'I've got the case histories here.' He reached past the files and pulled down an unused pack of six A4-sized padded envelopes held together by a broad paper band and still in their cellophane wrapping. 'The ones I told you about on the phone – people who're all – or *were* until they got sick – workers on the Silveron production line in Aurora, Illinois. They were sent to us by Burt, the local physician. He's got no doubts about the cause of their troubles.'

'He can prove it?'

'That's the damnedest thing – nothing shows up in tests. Nothing significant, that is. The victims just feel and look like hell. One guy did develop a fatal case of cancer, like I said, but that happened so quickly that Burt thinks that the malignancy must have been brewing for some time, and was just accelerated by the chemical exposure.' He peered into the bundle of envelopes, levering their necks open with his fingers to view the contents. Finding the one he wanted, he pulled it out from between the rest.

'But these people, they lost weight?'

'Like they were starvation victims. And they got head-aches, and sick to their stomachs. Some can't eat. Some have bad pain.' He indicated the packet of unused envel-opes and grinned. 'My little hiding place. I don't leave this stuff in here at night of course. It goes in the safe.' He pulled a slim sheaf of papers out of the envelope. 'I thought of taking the stuff home every night, but it'd be no safer. I mean, I might get mugged.' He laughed at the thought.

Daisy couldn't help thinking that this obsession with secrecy and persecution was rather overplayed.

The bundle of papers was slim, perhaps ten sheets in all. Paul peeled off the first two and put them on one side. Gesturing her to draw her chair closer, he placed the rest in front of her. It was a report from the physician, Burt, containing a summary of his findings, backed up by the individual case histories of eight people, five male, three female, all workers at the Aurora Chemical Works, Aurora, Illinois. The symptoms were there: profound fatigue, severe weight loss, non-specific often agonizing pain, loss of memory and concentration, anxiety and depression. Not every patient had every symptom, but most had the fatigue and weight loss though, confusingly and perversely, one had actually put on weight. All had developed acute sensitivities to chemicals to the point where they had to stay away from even the mildest household products. All but two had also developed severe food allergies and were following restricted diets.

'We talked to Burt several times now,' Paul commented. 'He's pessimistic on the prognosis. He says the condition appears to be untreatable, and that these people don't seem to recover. In fact, four have steadily deteriorated. He thinks the chemical has long-term effects on the immune system, though he can't prove it. Nothing shows in the tests – at least not in the tests he has available to him.'

She read the cases through once again, slowly. When she'd finished, Paul took the report and, with a small flourish, handed her the two pages that he'd put on one side. It was the letter from Alan Breck.

The letter began with: *You don't need to know who I am*, and launched into a summary of what she had already read, listing the ailments of the Silveron workforce, and urging EarthForce to contact Burt the physician direct for detailed case histories. Morton-Kreiger had been given the facts not once but several times, the writer went on, but had continued to deny the problem. Only recently they had promised to tighten safety procedures on the production line, but the point was, there had never been anything wrong with the procedures in the first place. They had been checked at an early stage and found to be well structured and well implemented. Morton-Kreiger may have gone through with some cosmetic changes in the safety procedures in the last month, but that wouldn't achieve very much. The real point was, if Silveron could do this to chemical workers who were reasonably well protected, then what damage was it going to do the millions of people who'd handle the product once it got on sale?

But it was the postscript that put everything else in the shade. *There is also something seriously wrong with the original toxicology data. Some of it was faked. I have the evidence.* She looked up at Paul Erlinger.

'Dynamite, huh?' He took the letter back and fingered it reverentially.

Daisy tried to keep a sense of caution. 'How could it be faked?'

'Easy. Make up the results.'

'And Morton-Kreiger would do that?'

He made doubtful noises. 'Could be, but it was Tro-Chem who did the testing. They're a so-called independent, but since most of their shares are owned by the agrochemical industry, they're not what you or I would call independent.'

'But why would they want to fix the results?'

'Who knows? Found themselves in deep shit? Maybe they'd set their price too low and had to cut corners, maybe they wanted to please the client.'

'Faked . . .' Daisy's mind worked quickly through the implications. If it could be proved, there had to be a good chance of winning a UK ban. There might even be a chance of bringing Adrian Bell's case to court with Morton-Kreiger in the defendant's seat, if not in the UK, where courts were notoriously resistant to the idea of chemical illness, then here in the States. Then, with a great leap of imagination, she saw possibilities for press campaigns, for bringing fresh attention to the Mackenzie case.

'Your case histories,' Paul interrupted. 'It'd be interesting to compare.'

Daisy, pulling her thoughts back into shape, said hastily, 'Of course,' and dug into her bag for the slim folder that contained Adrian Bell and Alusha Mackenzie's stories, with those of the two less serious cases that had been reported by the union man, Brayfield.

Paul swung back in his chair, reading fast. 'Mackenzie . . . Isn't that Nick Mackenzie's wife? Didn't I hear something about this?'

Daisy was silent.

'Jeese, but I read about it,' Paul exclaimed almost immediately. 'She killed herself, didn't she? Just terrible. But I didn't hear anything about a chemical hit.'

'It wasn't suicide,' Daisy said defensively. 'It was an accident. And as for the spraying, the story just didn't come out at the time.'

He caught her tone. 'Oh,' he said carefully. 'Right. Right.' He watched her for a moment, gauging whether it was safe to continue. 'Has he brought charges, Nick Mackenzie? If anyone has the resources, he's sure the one to do it. I hope you've got him set up right.'

'Set up?' she asked stiffly.

'I mean, in with the right advice. Legal, specialist . . .'

'Yes.' She couldn't bring herself to tell him the truth; or maybe she couldn't bring herself to admit to it. 'But I don't think he'll go ahead. I think he's . . .'

'Not interested?'

'Not convinced,' she murmured. 'He thinks it was something else.'

'That's the way it goes.' Paul heaved himself forward in his chair and read the case history again, adding almost to himself: 'And I guess he's got troubles enough.'

'Troubles enough?' A faint squeeze in Daisy's chest.

'Well . . . you know.' Putting his hand up to his mouth, he spread his palm and made a fluttering gesture.

She chose not to understand.

'Drink troubles.'

'Old history,' she corrected him, feeling combative.

Paul pulled down his mouth, looking doubtful. After a moment's consideration, he rotated himself out of his revolving chair, went to another desk and scooped up a newspaper. Searching through it, he folded a page open and positioned it in front of Daisy.

He didn't have to point out the item. There was a large photograph. The pose of the three faces was fashionably disdainful, the juxtaposition carefully contrived, the lighting arranged to eradicate signs of age, but the face in the centre was unmistakably that of Nick Mackenzie. For some reason the reproduction had made his eyes unusually pale, almost white, so that they stood out in a disturbing way, like something out of a sci-fi film poster.

The headline was also large. *Amazon No-show Threat.* And the story: Lead singer Nick Mackenzie's health problems had caused the cancellation of a concert in Philadelphia. Disappointed fans had almost started a riot. The tour organizer was quoted as saying that Mr Mackenzie had been suffering from a recurrent chest infection which had necessitated heavy medication, but that he had now recovered and that the last two dates would most definitely go ahead. But the writer of the piece clearly thought otherwise. He reported that the lead singer's troubles had started in Chicago, where he seemed to be having trouble not only with his voice, but in remembering the words of his own songs. He'd made it into the second half, but only just. He'd looked unsteady on his feet and at one stage had almost tripped over.

'Maybe I was reading too much into it,' Paul suggested kindly. 'I mean, maybe it *was* just the flu.'

The rest of the piece was equally disastrous. There was the inevitable mention of tragic circumstances, the raking over of Alusha Mackenzie's death, then, most damning of all, a mention of Nick's former problems with alcohol. Clearly the reporter had few doubts as to the real cause of his so-called illness.

Daisy folded the paper with elaborate slowness. It hurt, and what surprised her was just how much it hurt. She felt a weight of responsibility. More than that, she felt angry at Nick Mackenzie for having shut her out. That's the real trouble, she thought: I believe that I could have saved him from this, if only he'd had faith in what I was doing.

But could she? People in trouble, people with habits they couldn't break, generally had a built-in resistance to being saved.

'So when are you seeing Alan Breck?'

She caught Paul by surprise, so that he didn't have time to prepare his lie and it came out on a false and guilty note. 'Eh . . . soon. I'm not too sure when.'

'You said the end of the month.'

'I did?'

'Paul, that's why I came.'

'Well – ' He fought it, looking unhappy, then, catching her expression, gestured defeat. 'Okay – it's Sunday. Look, I would have told you but – well, I promised not to tell anyone. And what am I doing now? I'm telling you! But, listen, I don't even know if he'll show. We fixed it weeks ago when he called to check I'd got his letter. I haven't heard from him since.' He threw open his hands. 'He may not show.'

'But I can come along?'

'Listen, I wish you could, I wish you could.'

'I'll be quiet as a mouse!'

He fell back in his chair, his hands clamped over the dome of his stomach, and stared at her for a long moment.

Then he gave a groan of half-hearted disapproval. He had
agreed.


He picked her up from her hotel in the Adams-Morgan
district shortly after breakfast, and they drove out over the
Potomac, heading, she thought, south-west. The sky was
hazy and bleached, the colour already leached out by the
sun. It was going to be another hot day. The car had no
air-conditioning and even as they passed the turn-off for
the Arlington Cemetery, rivulets of sweat dribbled down
Paul's cheeks and onto his neck.

They stayed on the main highway for over an hour until,
just short of a place called Culpeper, Paul slowed the car
and peered ahead, looking for landmarks. Sighting a turn-
off, he gave a grunt of recognition and a moment later they
pulled off the road and stopped in front of an Italian
wayside restaurant advertising Budweiser and home-baked
pizzas.

The interior was dark and chill and, at first glance,
empty. A waitress led them towards a booth. From the
ceiling Pavarotti was belting out a Neapolitan love song.

As they sat down Daisy was the first to spot the lone
figure seated in a far booth, a silhouette set against the
brilliant light of the window. Paul went over and held a
murmured conversation. After a time he beckoned her over.
Alan Breck had turned up.

He was in his mid- to late-thirties, with dark limp hair,
pale skin, anxious eyes magnified by metal-rimmed spectacles and nervous hands that flittered and settled constantly. Daisy sat opposite him, next to Paul. He viewed
the two of them with apprehension. Perhaps he'd hoped
they wouldn't come. Perhaps he'd almost not come himself.
Did he, too, have a persecution complex? Did he, like Paul,
believe that he'd stepped into some sort of spy thriller
where an all-powerful 'they' were watching his every move?

He did not volunteer his name. Paul launched straight into a speech of thanks and appreciation, sprinkled with reassurances. But though he radiated confidence and professionalism, this did nothing to impress their friend who, looking increasingly uneasy, tried to interrupt a couple of times until, in a final burst of desperation, he held up a staying hand.

'I don't know how to say this,' he said in a sharp off-beat voice. 'But – er' – he took a gulp of air, as if drawing courage from it – 'I think I may have wasted your time. I don't have, er, what I, er, suggested I might have . . .' He glanced up at their faces to see if they had understood. 'I do not have any data for you,' he said, drawing the words out ponderously. 'My, er, contact tells me that the information he had in mind, the data he *thought* was there – well, for one thing it wasn't exactly what he thought it was. I mean, it didn't add up to – what he thought it did. And then – '

He was interrupted by the waitress who deposited iced water and menus in front of them and, in an abrasive monotone, rattled off a long list of specials. Paul, momentarily silenced by the unexpected turn the conversation had taken, rallied sufficiently to order orange juice and eggs and hash browns with waffles and maple syrup.

Daisy ordered doughnuts. Their friend wanted only coffee.

'You never saw this data yourself then?' Paul asked.

Their friend shook his head. Despite the air-conditioning, he was sweating slightly. 'No. I just – heard about it.' He looked at the table, he looked at his hands; just occasionally he looked up at them in a series of darting uncertain glances. 'My contact – the one who told me about all this – well, now it seems . . . he built the whole thing up. You know, sort of misled me. I mean, he didn't *mean* to mislead me, but he kind of put the wrong interpretation on the figures. He thought they'd been fixed,

made to look good – like I told you in my letter. But now –
well – ' He took another gasp of air. 'He's pretty sure he
was mistaken.'

His words settled over the table like a blanket of lead.
For a moment Paul looked as though he was going to cry.

'This data, these figures – what were they exactly?' Daisy
asked.

He took a sip of water. 'Well, they, er . . .'

The waitress sped up in her soundless soft-soled shoes,
slid cups and cutlery noisily onto the table, and poured the
coffee.

'You were saying?' Daisy asked as soon as she had left.

He glanced past her, checking that the waitress was well
out of earshot but also, Daisy suspected, delaying the
moment. 'They were, er, some of the main toxicology test
results.'

'And how were they fixed?'

'But they weren't fixed,' he objected with an awkward
smile.

'Quite. But when your contact originally thought they
might have been fixed, how did he think it'd been done?'

He didn't want to go into that. He glanced at Paul as
though for help, then gave a nervous mirthless laugh. 'He
thought the results had been massaged . . . helped along a
bit. Improved.'

'Is that easy to do?'

He shifted his shoulders reluctantly. 'I don't know about
easy . . . But it's certainly possible.'

'Has it happened before?'

'Maybe. No one's sure. But once,' he embarked conver-
sationally, 'oh, years ago – there was a rumour. A product
was withdrawn.'

'Your contact – he's with Morton-Kreiger?'

He drew back again, considering whether he should
make this most basic of admissions. Finally he nodded

briefly but miserably, as if he was already angry with himself for having gone this far.

A door sounded. Some customers came into the restaurant, their voices raucous in the silence. Their friend stiffened and looked around him. Daisy knew then that it was only a matter of time before he made his escape. Outside, the sunlight had intensified, casting hard shadows.

'You were going to tell us something else,' she said, waiting for his eyes to drag back to hers. 'You said, for *one* thing the data wasn't what it appeared to be. What was the other thing?'

He made a show of searching his memory before saying with forced casualness: 'Oh, yeah ... I was going to say that, er ... my contact no longer has access even to the *summary* data. He found the file had been, er, removed from its usual place. It's never been returned. There's very little he can do to get it back. Officially he has no reason to call on it, you see.' He spread his hands. 'So ... That's it, I'm afraid.'

Why, Daisy wondered, has our friend gone to all the trouble of stringing these stories together? Why has he bothered to come and meet us when it would have been so much easier to leave a message saying he'd changed his mind or, even simpler, not to have shown up at all? Why, when he's scared sideways and every which way, has he risked showing his face?

The waitress brought the food and a fresh pour of coffee. The doughnuts were the size of cartoon car tyres and glistening with frosted sugar. Paul, faced by a large plate of eggs and hashed potatoes, dug straight in, though that didn't prevent him from cross-questioning their friend at length, going over each fact in plodding detail as if by sheer repetition he might coax more out of him. Daisy could have told him he was wasting his time. Their friend had already lied himself into a corner and, however uncomfortable he might feel about that, he wasn't going to back down now.

'Wouldn't your contact know if the figures had been massaged?' Paul began. 'I mean, wouldn't it have required collusion between a whole group of people?'

'But MKI didn't carry out the trials themselves,' he explained quickly. 'It was a company called TroChem.'

'Oh,' said Paul, feigning innocence. 'And who're TroChem?'

'They set up about eight years ago, offering specialist toxicology testing. They've earned a reputation for being hyper-efficient and cheap. They've been very successful.' Their friend's hesitation had disappeared, Daisy noticed. And it wasn't just that he was on safer ground; he spoke with the ease of someone who knew exactly what he was talking about. A laboratory technician then? No, he was brighter than that. A scientist.

'There weren't any checks carried out on the work? No independent assessments?'

He hesitated slightly then shook his head and frowned.

'So,' Paul continued, 'it'd be hard to tell that the figures had been massaged, would it? I mean, from the outside?'

He liked that question; it gave him another opportunity to pour cold water on the idea of any stray information just lying around. 'Absolutely impossible,' he said. 'You'd need complete access to all the lab results, all the data. You'd need to get full access to TroChem's records.'

'Or you'd need someone to talk,' Daisy suggested gently. 'Someone who'd seen the data and was sufficiently qualified to know what the figures meant.'

His eyes blinked up at her. He didn't say anything.

Paul picked up a waffle and, dribbling maple syrup over the top, used it to break the yolk on his fried egg. 'There's something I'm not clear about here,' he said. 'This contact of yours – he's a scientist, right?'

'I can't say . . . I really don't think I should say.'

'Of course,' Paul said hastily through a large mouthful. 'I just wanted to know if he – your contact – had the expertise to assess the data when he had it in front of him.'

Alan Breck's face was transparent; Daisy could see him fighting his way round his self-imposed obstacles. 'But I told you, he didn't have access to the full data,' he said. '*No one* could have made judgements about anything without having the data!'

'But he saw enough to suspect the possibility of – hell, let's be clear what we're talking about here – *fraud*?'

'I told you – he was mistaken. Really, he got it wrong!' His voice was taut and thin.

Paul nodded slowly. 'Right, right. Well . . .' He mopped up some egg and forked it rapidly into his mouth. 'Maybe we can still persuade the EPA to review Silveron.' He was thinking aloud. 'Approach them another way.'

'The Aurora testimonials,' their friend interjected with something like relief, and Daisy realized that he'd been trying to lead them to this point. 'If you're so concerned – that evidence should be enough, shouldn't it? You're in contact with Burt, aren't you? You only need some back-up – an expert or two – and then you can file for deregistration, can't you?' He looked back and forth between them, like a child seeking reassurance.

'We'll give it all we've got,' said Paul, licking syrup off his fingers.

'At the very least the EPA will have to postpone approval. I mean, won't they?' He sounded as though he needed to believe it very badly indeed.

'But if that fails?' she asked quietly. She felt Paul give her a questioning look. 'What happens if the Silveron launch doesn't get postponed? Suppose we have a repeat of the situation in Britain?'

Their friend didn't reply. His eyes were very large behind the lenses of his glasses.

'Britain?' he echoed.

'We've got two sick people, and another two possibles. And those are just the ones we know about.'

In a sudden movement he removed his glasses and rubbed the bridge of his nose. 'That's bad,' he said, and there was a gasp in his voice.

Paul tried to ease the moment along. 'It could be a lot worse.'

Daisy kept her eyes on their friend. 'Let me ask you one thing,' she said, 'do you believe Silveron is a safe product?'

He closed his eyes, then replaced his glasses very slowly and with elaborate care. 'Well, I can't judge – ' He caught her eye. 'No,' he said eventually, with a short baffled sound. 'I'd guess not.'

A noisy family arrived in an adjacent booth. 'More coffee anyone?' Paul asked brightly, looking for the waitress.

Their friend caught Daisy's eye. There were all sorts of messages in that gaze – fear, regret and something she couldn't quite read. A plea for understanding perhaps. As Paul turned back, he quickly looked down at his hands again.

She realized suddenly: it was Paul that was the problem. It was Paul that their friend didn't trust. Their friend had taken the trouble to come and deliver this message personally, not out of the goodness of his heart, but because it was vital for Paul to believe that he could be of no help in the matter, that he knew absolutely nothing, that, most important of all, there was nothing to know. The whole business had been an exercise in disinformation.

Why? Fear? Distrust of security at EarthForce? Or distrust of Paul himself? Did he know something about Paul that she didn't?

'Don't go away,' she said lightly, and went in search of the washroom. From her bag she took one of her visiting cards, emblazoned with the Catch logo, and, balancing it on the side of a basin, scribbled on the back: *If you ever*

*change your mind, please call me,* and added her home
number. Then, on an impulse: *Anything you say will be
safe with me.*

She went straight back in case he might try to leave
while she was gone. He was still there, though she noticed
that he had manoeuvred himself closer to the end of the
bench.

Paul was talking about the Aurora workers. She slid in
next to him, opposite their friend, and, leaning forward on
one elbow, slid the card under the table. She found his
knee. He looked startled, his eyes swivelling nervously
between hers and Paul's, then, as understanding dawned,
he moved his hand down to meet hers.

# Chapter 22

THE CLINIC WAS the last word in restrained elegance – or, as Hillyard liked to pronounce the word in his jocular moments, 'elly-*garnce*'. The place was new, built in muted brick with blue window frames, tinted glass, a ruthlessly landscaped strip of garden, and a large splash of flowers around the entrance. No expense spared. And one would hope not, at their prices.

He parked in a space marked 'Doctors only' and, whistling softly, marched into the foyer.

The accounts department was like a small bank, the customer service area separated from the clerk by a glass screen. Two Arabs in full garb were blocking the only window. They were bent over some papers as if they were having difficulty in understanding them. They were probably reading them upside down.

He inserted a shoulder politely between one of the Arabs and the window and said to the female clerk in his most attractive voice: 'Hullo there. I've come to settle Miss Kershaw's bill and I'm a bit pushed for time.' He gave her a collusive wink which she carefully ignored. 'You couldn't just hurry it along for me, could you?'

Turning away, giving no indication that she'd heard, the clerk tapped a code into her computer and looked idly at the screen.

Still smiling, Hillyard thought: Stone-faced bitch. The clerk swivelled in her chair and suspended her hand over a printer. The printer obediently spewed a document into her grasp which she ripped off and passed under the glass partition.

'Is this for me?' he asked with exaggerated surprise.

She gave a brief nod.

'Why, thank you,' he said, clasping his hand to his heart like some dreadful old ham on the steps of Elsinore, when what he really wanted to do was reach through the glass and grab the stupid woman by the throat and give her a good shake.

He went through the bill, item by item. Daily in-patient rate. Operating theatre hire. No mention of the actual operation, he noticed, no mention of that creepy word *termination*. Surgeon's fee, a healthy little three hundred and fifty quid. Now how many such jobs would that guy do in a morning? Six? Ten? It was all right for some; nice if you could get it.

He looked up to find the clerk watching him. He raised his eyebrows and gave her an exaggerated look of surprise, and she quickly looked away. He took the money from his wallet and counted it out. The notes were new and adhered to each other, and he took care to count them a second time. He didn't want to give old Stone-face the satisfaction of pointing out a mistake.

The Arabs, having asked a question and been rebuffed, had fallen back from the window to regroup. Hillyard thrust the bill with the money on top of it half-way under the partition. As the clerk reached for it, he dropped his hand back onto the money, pinning it to the counter. 'You'll tell them upstairs that it's paid, will you?'

'They usually call down.'

'But I'd like you to call up. Then Miss Kershaw will know she's free to leave, won't she?'

She pursed her lips. 'If you like,' she conceded.

He shone her a gracious smile. 'It would be so useful.' He kept his fingers firmly on the money. 'You'll phone immediately then, will you?'

She nodded, but he still didn't let go, not until she'd actually put it in words. Then he released the money with a gay flick of his fingers. When she had given him his change and stamped the receipt, he inclined his head. 'How very efficient you've been,' he said. 'It's been a real pleasure.'

He drove straight back to Battersea. Beji yapped excitedly round his feet as he let himself in, and panted up the stairs ahead of him, pausing hopefully by the flat door, asking for food. Ignoring the dog, he walked straight into the main office.

No Beryl. Cigarette butts in the ashtray, a half-drunk coffee, stone cold with lipstick marks on the rim, a newspaper folded at the racing selections. It was, he noticed, Ascot Gold Cup Day. She'd be locked in the betting shop for the rest of the day, the old bag. He bent over the typewriter to see how far she'd got with the transcription of the last tape. Not far, was the answer. But far enough to cause him a distinct spark of interest. He leafed back through the transcript, then, sliding the earphones over his head, he played the rest of the tape, making notes as he went along.

He looked through what he'd written to make certain he'd got the essential points, then dialled the number of the South Bank office. There was no answer.

After lunch in the flat he took a coffee down to the office. Miss Kershaw would have had plenty of time to get home by now. He dialled her number.

She answered.

'Ah, Miss Kershaw, how are we? All right, I trust. Was the clinic comfortable? It seemed a most pleasant place. As far as these places ever can be, I mean.'

'Leave me alone.'

Now that wasn't very pleasant. He adjusted his tone; friendly but firm. 'I was wondering how we were progressing towards Friday. Travellers' cheques, passports, that sort of thing.'

'Go to hell.'

'I only want to be of help,' he said, ignoring her little outburst and maintaining a cheerful and uplifting tone. 'Your flight's at eight, I believe. Why don't I order a car for five? That'll allow us plenty of time for the Friday-night jams.'

'Christ – ' She was suddenly tearful. 'Just leave me alone – '

'I understand,' Hillyard said, feeling magnanimous. 'Why don't I call you again tomorrow?'

'Listen, just piss off. I don't *ever* want to hear from you again. Not *ever* again, d'you understand?'

'Now, now. I only want to be of help. Make sure you get away for your little break. After all you *have* – ' He was going to say 'earned it', which, considering she was getting a very tidy sum for having got laid by a minister of the crown, wasn't far off the mark. But, checking himself, he said instead: 'You *do* deserve it. And then you'll be wanting me to give you your spending money, won't you? You'll be wanting to buy a nice swimsuit, and the odd frock – '

'Fuck off, you little pimp,' she screeched violently, and the line went dead.

Hillyard dropped the phone gently into its cradle. He said to Beji: 'Talk about the pot calling the kettle black.' The dog, who'd been hovering in the doorway, plucked up courage to come trotting across and sit at his feet.

'She'll be more herself by tomorrow,' Hillyard said to the dog. 'She'll be thinking about the rest of the money.'

Looking at the time, he tried the South Bank number again. This time it answered. He said immediately: 'Got something of interest for you.'

'Yes?'

'That Washington outfit, EarthForce, they're on to

something to do with Silveron. I quote their man, Paul something: "We might have some hard evidence." He meant, against Silveron. The Field girl's flown over. They've promised to give her the details.'

There was a silence from the other end of the line, then: 'That's it?'

'For the moment,' Hillyard said, somewhat piqued at the lack of reaction. 'I thought it sounded quite promising.'

'Well, keep me informed.' The interest, Hillyard noted, was not exactly overwhelming.

'I can't say when I'll have anything. The Field girl's due back in the morning. There'll be the usual delay.' Hillyard added peevishly: 'It's not easy having one hand tied behind one's back.'

There was a silence. This was an old argument and not, apparently, one Hillyard was going to be allowed to go into just at the moment. 'And the other matter, the one you dealt with today?' came the voice.

'All on schedule,' Hillyard replied. 'The main event was yesterday afternoon. She's decided to go to the Seychelles with a friend. I'll see her off myself.'

'No problems then?'

'No, all paid up.' Unable to let things lie, Hillyard returned to the old argument. 'You know, it's crazy to leave that office uncovered.'

'You know the policy. Too risky.'

'There'd be no risk, not with the new technology. I told you, no one'd ever know they were there.'

A pause. 'We'll see.'

'You talk about risk, but personal visits are ten times riskier.'

'I'll think about it.' He was sounding edgy. He didn't like being pushed.

'What about the boyfriend's place then?' Hillyard suggested. 'I could fix that up, no trouble – '

'No.'

'But she spends quite a bit of time there.'

'No.'

Hillyard gave a biting little sigh of annoyance. 'Right-ho, you're the boss. But don't blame me if I miss something.'

Hillyard replaced the receiver a little too hard so that it jumped out of its cradle and he had to replace it. The dog was still at his feet. He bent down and grabbed its head. 'No imagination, these people, eh, Beji?' he hissed into its ear. 'No imagination.'

The dog looked up at him, its eyes bulging beseechingly, and gave a little whimper. Hillyard pushed its head playfully from side to side, gripping the fluffy ears tighter as it tried to struggle free. 'None at all.'

Releasing the dog, he pushed it aside with his foot.


Daisy thought: Now how did I manage this?

She was standing in the main hall of the Greyhound depot at the Port Authority building, on her own, with a hundred and fifty-three dollars in her pocket, an empty folder of travellers' cheques, and a gaping ignorance of New York. Her homeward flight had left Washington two hours ago, making her return air ticket, which had been a cheap no-swap deal, worth nothing at all. Worse, she wouldn't have time to find a hotel, not if she was going to get to Madison Square Garden by seven thirty.

She looked for some bench space, no easy matter when the little available seating was taken up by sprawling family groups, back-packers, and sinister men with lizard eyes and large bellies. Taking her case to a corner, she laid it on the floor and sorted her way through underwear, a change of T-shirt and a toothbrush. A passing security guard paused to stare.

Pushing the bundle into her voluminous shoulder bag, she lugged her case towards a uniformed official. It took a

moment to establish that it was not a left-luggage office
that she wanted but a parcel check.

The depository was on the lower level, and cost two
dollars. Which left a hundred and fifty-one dollars for a
non-available ticket for a concert that may or may not
happen, and a hotel room she may or may not find.

Outside, the heat was oppressive, and a thin clammy
rain was falling, almost as warm and sticky as the air itself.
The traffic was heavy and the cabs all taken, and it wasn't
until Daisy leapt across the street at a run, yelling at the
top of her voice, that she managed to capture a cab
offloading a passenger.

The traffic was at a crawl and the ten or so blocks to
Madison Square Garden took ten minutes. The cab driver,
who spoke almost no English, did not understand her
questions about cheap but decent hotels, although she
noticed that his English improved dramatically when it
came to spelling out the fare.

The Garden was a massive circular building covering
two blocks. The entrances were choked with people. When
Daisy finally managed to get inside there was no misreading
the signs above the ticket windows. Sold Out. No Returns.

Back outside, the touts were asking upwards of a
hundred dollars and weren't about to haggle. One laughed
derisively when Daisy volunteered an English cheque.

Seven twenty-three. A passer-by directed her to a late-
opening bank in a nearby shopping plaza. At the bank she
discovered that money was easy to get, but only if you were
a paid-up card carrier. Gold card, dispenser card, charge
card: the automatic dispensing machine wasn't too fussy.
But if you were a non-plastic-carrying foreigner with scru-
ples about easy credit the place was a fortress. Sometimes,
Daisy reflected, pursuing one's principles was a pain.

It was after seven thirty. The rain was thin but penetrat-
ing. She ran back to the Garden along an uneven and
slippery sidewalk. A few latecomers were still rushing for

the entrances, but otherwise the street was empty. Even the touts had evaporated.

She walked round the curve of the building until she found the employees' entrance, a dark doorway hidden under an overhang. It was well-defended, a veritable Alamo, with rows of hefty security guards glaring out over metal barricades, looking for hostile forces.

She approached the nearest guard, who was staring at a point somewhere above her head. 'I've come to see someone in the show.'

His eyelids flickered. 'Passes only.' She noticed he spoke without moving his lips.

She nodded slowly. 'Suppose I said that I was expected, but I'd lost my pass – '

The guard swivelled his eyes in her direction. 'Look, lady, no one gets through without a pass, okay?' This time his lips gave the slightest quiver, as if he were exhaling sharply.

'I see,' she conceded. 'Could I at least leave a message?'

His mouth hardened.

'All I'm asking is to write it inside and come straight out.'

'*Lady* – it's no pass, no *pass*, okay?'

'Let's try it another way,' she said. 'Suppose I write the note out here and then hand it to you to leave inside the stage door.'

The guard blinked impassively. 'Lady, you can write an en*tire* book so long as you don't pass this point, okay?'

She eyed him, this fountain of assistance, then smiled to show that she had no trouble in moving her lips.

She retreated. A note – what would a note do? She felt a sudden gloom, a loss of energy. A note probably wouldn't even get through.

In the shelter of the overhang she extracted one of her cards and scribbled a few words on the back. *I'm here in New York. I have some news. I wondered if we could meet*

. . . The next moment she groaned aloud as the absurdity
of the exercise struck her, as she remembered that she had
no number to leave, no contact point. She leant her head
against the wall. What madness is this, Daisy? Not thinking
straight. Not thinking at all. Ever since the meeting with
Alan Breck she had been overcome by a driving compulsion
to act; and now it had lost her the last of her judgement.

Dropping the business card back into her bag, she
crossed the street to a phone and rooted around for a
number Paul Erlinger had given her. It was a friend of his;
someone environmental in Greenwich Village. The friend
had been out that morning when Paul had called, and now
as the line picked up Daisy heard the unmistakable click
and blip of an answering machine. Curious sounds came
singing down the line, a gentle twittering. At first she
thought it was a bad connection but then she realized it
was birdsong, a dawn chorus. After a few seconds, a voice
came winging over the symphony. 'Hi, this is Thomas H.
Raffety, working towards an integrated environment. I
can't take your call right now, but I'll get back to you as
soon as . . .'

Rain came shafting against Daisy's face. She twisted
away from it, and, out of the corner of her eye, saw a figure
emerge from the barricades around the employees'
entrance.

Tom H. Raffety's machine bleeped in her ear, awaiting
an answer. She gave her name absently, her attention fixed
on the briskly walking figure who was crossing the street
towards her. He was a young man in jeans, pale sneakers
and a bomber-jacket with the collar turned up against the
rain. As he drew closer she saw *Amazon* emblazoned across
the front.

Tom H. Raffety's tape was turning patiently, the bird
population silent. She muttered, 'Call you later,' and replacing the handset, hurried to intercept the striding figure.

'Excuse me – are you with the show?'

He cast her a sidelong glance but didn't break step.

'I'm a friend of Nick Mackenzie's. I'm in town unexpectedly.' She was almost running to keep up. 'You wouldn't
be able to get a note through for me, would you? I couldn't
get past the apes on the gate.'

His face grimaced, he rolled his eyes wearily heavenward. 'Come on, luv, I've 'eard it all before!'

She laughed: his accent was pure East End. And resusci-
tating the full ear-splitting beauty of her half-forgotten
south London accent, she gave her best performance yet;
she was the environmental campaigner over on a conference, she'd come to the show because Nick had invited her,
but she'd failed to let him know in time, hence the lack of
contact. After the long day and the succession of disap-
pointments, the little embellishments came easily.

His name was Les and he was a roadie and he wasn't
totally convinced. But he had at least come to a halt and
was standing in the rain, listening. The campaigner bit
seemed to hold him; he was impressed by the sight of her
card. He also took in the fact that she'd had meetings with
Nick, that they'd worked on an investigation together. She
could see from his face that he'd already worked out which
investigation that must have been.

He dithered for a while, his expression swinging between
caution and suspicion, then with a decisive grunt he jerked
his head towards the barricades and led the way back to
the Alamo. After a few minutes he came out with a pass
that got her as far as the stage door. As she passed through
the barricade Iron Lips, impassive to the end, made a point
of looking away.

Tearing a page out of her address book, Daisy scribbled:
*I'm here in New York. Wanted to see the show but you're
too popular. Have you a moment later? Or tomorrow?
Something's come up – extraordinary and important news.*

*Daisy Field (from the Campaign Against Toxic Chemicals).
PS Please leave a message at the stage door with a number
where I can reach you.*

'It'll be all right to pick up a message here?' she asked.
'I've no contact number, you see.'

Les shot her a doubtful glance, then, looking at his
watch, issued a sigh of inconvenience. 'Wait a mo,' he said
abruptly and before she could ask him where he was going
he'd disappeared into the backstage area.

At the barricades the guards lounged at their posts. Old
Iron Lips slid her a knowing look, as if he'd had her
number all along. Beyond the canopy, the rain fell steadily.
Above the hiss of wet tyres on the street, she thought she
could make out the twang of amplified music from inside
the hall.

Les was back in five minutes. He had an envelope in his
hand. It was unsealed and lying inside it was a ticket.

Daisy laughed with surprise and pleasure. 'How on
earth did you manage that? Thank you.'

He was half-way out of the door, resuming his interrupted errand. 'Don't fank me, luv,' he said. 'Fank the
boss.'


The sound didn't hang in the air, politely waiting to be
heard, it resonated through your body until your bones
vibrated and your ears drummed and your brain felt as if it
contained a billion megawatts of sound. And just in case
that wasn't enough to pulverize you into submission, there
were the special effects. Strobes, lasers, kaleidoscopes of
garish lights, and a stark fantastical set of girders and
reflective metal revolves.

It had been so long since Daisy had been to a live concert
that she found herself jerked sharply back in time, landing
somewhere between school and student days, surprised at
the vividness of her memories yet unable to relate to them.

The auditorium, a vast amphitheatre, was packed. There were ageing fans in Gucci shoes and designer jeans, jiggling around in their seats like fifteen-year-olds, having no trouble in recapturing the good old days. There were real kids too, who had ten years on Daisy, if not a great deal more, and for perhaps the first time in her life it occurred to her that, to some people at least, she was middle-aged.

From the stage, one number followed another. The band was in two sections: towards the rear a shadowy six-piece backing group, and to the front and bathed in ever-changing light, Amazon – or rather two-thirds of them. Nick Mackenzie had not yet appeared.

On first seeing this, she'd decided that it was part of the act, an old theatrical trick to build up the tension. Though it occurred to her that, in view of the press stories, the suspense might not be of the sort the producers had had in mind.

After a time it seemed to her that the audience was starting to get restive, although this might simply have resulted from the monotony of the music, the sort of tuneless rock that had fuelled a hundred forgettable bands. It was certainly not Nick Mackenzie's sort of music. This was all rhythm and amplification, while Nick's songs had striking melodies and words that you actually listened to, songs about issues, songs about the environment, songs that had been written before most people knew that Brazil had a rain forest. His biggest hits, though, had been love songs. Yet they too were different – sharp and funny, or, when they were sad, seriously sad, so that you didn't play them when you were feeling down.

The set finished. The band took their bow. The lights faded. A shiver of expectation passed through the crowd.

Was this it then? Or was this the big let-down? Had the others been covering for him? Would he fail to show?

There was a pause.

Then quite suddenly, without warning, he was there. No

special effects, no drumroll. He simply slipped out of the
shadows and stood there in the spotlight, centre stage.

The crowd roared its welcome. He gave a small gesture
of acknowledgement, a brief spread of the hands, and
launched straight into his first song.

The crowd fell silent. A charge seemed to fill the air,
partly expectation, partly, it seemed to Daisy, something a
little less comfortable, as if the crowd were daring him to
live up to their expectations, to match up to the collective
memories of a thousand middle-aged fans for whom, in
their imaginations at least, time had stood still. Or maybe
it was more sinister than that; maybe some had come in the
hope of getting altogether more dramatic kicks by witness-
ing a spectacular and highly public personal disaster.

Nick was dressed simply, in black jeans and open-necked
shirt. His hair looked different – longer, fluffier – and his
skin pale. Even from this distance she could glimpse the
brilliant blue of his eyes. He wore no jewellery, no gold
medallions or bracelets. In fact, there was nothing
extraneous about him at all.

The effect was powerful. There was something about
the way he stood, self-contained and uncompromising, that
made it impossible to drag your eyes away from him. And
she didn't try. For some reason she felt a proprietorial
thrill, as if she had in some way helped to get him there.

Amazon, finally complete, began with a rock ballad, a
hit from over twenty years before. The strobes flashed, the
lasers darted tongues of light, the crowd roared its
approval. Yet for all the heightened atmosphere, for all
Nick's presence, it dawned on Daisy that, while the other
two were squeezing every inch of attention from their
performance, Nick was withholding something from his,
something elemental.

The memory of the courtroom strong in her mind, she
watched his every movement, sensitive to the slightest
suggestion of hesitation, wary of any step that might

remotely resemble a lurch. But it wasn't the drink or, if it was, he was hiding it very well. He moved easily, almost lazily, and she remembered his extraordinary grace, the beautiful hands, the long stride.

More Amazon hits followed, a rock number, a rock ballad: standard stuff from the Seventies. Then a conscience song, one of his early ones, famous for its biting words and powerful message. But now, for some reason, the force, the intensity had gone. The singing of the song seemed to be posing an immense trial for him; she could sense the effort he was making to get through to the end. And then quite suddenly she understood: his heart simply wasn't in it. He was going through the motions all right, moving to the rhythms, creating the appropriate expressions, doing what was expected, but the effect was strained and contrived.

It seemed to her that the crowd's early excitement was also bleeding away. At the end of each successive song, the applause seemed to become less frenetic, more restrained. By the end of the set the air itself seemed cooler.

She noticed that, when Nick stepped back to take a bow, he was frowning slightly.

The applause died away. This was the moment for the opening chat with the audience, the ritual hi-there and how-wonderful-it-is-to-be-back, but the lights, instead of coming up, dimmed rapidly, leaving the stage in darkness. A single white spot grew at the front where Nick had been. It was empty. The silence drew out. The audience was very still, as if no one dared to imagine what might happen next.

Was this another stage effect? If so, it was in danger of being overplayed. The suspense was being pulled out to breaking point. Then, just as the silence became unbearable, he stepped slowly back into the cold white pool of light and up to the microphone, with a guitar in his hands. For a long moment he stared at a point a yard or two in front of his feet, then, coolly, almost absentmindedly,

started to play, very quietly, very slowly, and with rapt
concentration. After a few bars he began to sing, so softly
that his voice was barely audible above the instrument. A
verse later and the band came in, muted and unobtrusive.
He sang out a little then, but only enough to be heard. It
was almost as if the audience didn't exist for him, as if he
were singing for no one but himself. The effect was
extraordinarily intimate, and the crowd seemed to reach
forward to meet him, to try and join him in the intensity of
the experience.

A sea-change had come over him, Daisy realized, a shift
of mood and focus that had brought him back into his
performance. It was almost as if he had decided to reinhabit
his emotions. Now it was all there – force and feeling and
words and melody. And heart – yes, that as well.

. He came to the refrain and suddenly his voice soared
high above the music, and the sound was clear and strong,
and so full of pain that something squeezed tightly in
Daisy's chest.

. . . *Long nights, lying softly in the dark, waiting for you*
. . . *lost to me . . . in the long nights . . .*

As the song wound its way effortlessly through her
emotions, it occurred to Daisy, with the suddenness of the
obvious, that he wasn't singing for himself at all, he was
singing for his wife.

By the time he held the last mournful note, Daisy had to
dig out a hankie and give her nose a good blow. Music got
her like that sometimes.

The sound fell away. The crowd was still for an instant,
caught in a short collusive silence, then burst into loud and
ecstatic applause.

The lights came up. Nick seemed to become aware of
the crowd for the first time. He bowed and gave a brief
self-deprecating smile, the sort that comes with all sorts of
conditions and apologies attached.

Daisy felt an overwhelming sense of release, as if she

had personally delivered Nick from whatever fate had been lying in wait for him.

After that he was all right. Even in the fast rhythm numbers he managed to deliver all the dreams intact, while in the solo numbers he held everyone in an effortless grasp, and the crowd was his, and his alone.

It was after ten thirty when the last applause died away and the crowd surged out into the night.

The rain was still falling. Sheltering inside an exit Daisy searched her bag for the number of Tom H. Raffety and his performing aviary. Deep in the bag, next to her address book, was the envelope that had contained the concert ticket. She drew it out and took another look inside. Nothing. It was only then that she thought of turning it over and looking at the front.

It read: *Hotel Pierre, Suite 1605. Nick.*

# Chapter 23

BOURBON WAS SMOOTHER than Scotch, and sweeter. It slipped down more easily, like honey, though Nick suspected his liver didn't find it quite so attractive. Sometimes, as now, he mixed the liquor with dry ginger to persuade himself that it lasted longer that way. It was a reasonable deception so long as he ignored the proportionately larger swigs he took by way of compensation.

He took a big gulp now. If a drink had ever been essential, this was it. Well, perhaps the first had been really essential, but this one, his fourth or fifth since the show, was just as deeply deserved. He had abstained since two thirty, five hours before the concert, an exercise he often set himself on performance nights just to prove that he could do it. Though what exactly it proved, he wasn't sure. At the start of the show, just when he needed all the help he could get, he always felt lousy.

Now he sat back in the armchair, bare feet propped on the seat opposite, lit a fresh cigarette and stared out into the Manhattan night, just as he'd stared out into a million other nights across America, drink in one hand, cigarette in the other, waiting placidly for oblivion.

He reviewed his performance, although it took precious little analysis. It had been dishonest, second-rate. He'd faked it – faked the pleasure, faked the climaxes, like a woman deceiving a lover. And they'd applauded him. Which just went to show you could fool a lot of people a lot of the time. Though part of him couldn't believe they'd really been taken in.

Well, what did it matter? He knew all right. He knew that on the times he managed to carry it off – when he managed to carry it off at all – he did so by the skin of his teeth. Far from this uncertainty stimulating the adrenalin, far from providing a welcome edge to things, it filled him with a sickening panic.

There was a knock on the door. He didn't answer. The knock came again and David Weinberg's muffled voice called: 'Nick? Nick? How about dinner?'

Nick got slowly to his feet, walked through to the lobby, flicked open the door and returned to his chair.

David followed him across the room. 'So? How about joining us?'

'No, thanks.'

'Come for a short time. Just one course.'

Nick briefly considered the prospect of dinner with David. He knew exactly how it would be. Somewhere showy, like Sardi's, with a group of grey-faced backers, sponsors or recording company executives, providing sparkling conversation about percentages, contracts and promotional strategies.

'I'm fine,' he said.

David was silent for a moment, and Nick knew he was eyeing the glass in his hand and the bottle of bourbon on the side. 'Nick ... Take it easy, eh?' There was sadness in his voice, but also a note of censure. 'We've still got a long way to go.'

Nick almost laughed. 'Sure.' There was an album to record in the autumn, and the European tour at the end of the year. Twenty-four gigs in six weeks. A beautiful unimaginable nightmare, and there was no one he could blame but himself.

'Shall I call room service for you?' David asked.

Nick shook his head and, raising a hand, smiled

a goodbye. David, taking his cue, gave a small sigh and left.

Nick got up and made himself another drink, but without the dry ginger this time. When David took the trouble to look him out after the show, the pressure was really on. Usually David kept well clear of everyone else's troubles, but when he did make the decision to get involved then he did it wholesale, in full Jewish mama mode, complete with exhortations to eat and doctors armed with vitamin shots.

The problem had begun in Chicago, on the morning when Nick had failed to put the bourbon bottle away. It had started like any other day on tour, that is bleakly, with a homogeneous hotel room, a nagging hangover and no reason to get up. He'd read for a while, a fashionable and impenetrable novel, then turned on the TV to watch the news. A South American coup, an earthquake in Turkey, a mugging. The mugging was particularly vicious; a young female lawyer attacked and left for dead outside her New York City apartment. By New York standards it wasn't such a special story and probably would never have made the national news if the girl hadn't been the daughter of a senator, yet there was something about the story that affected him. Perhaps it was the girl's picture – she was very pretty – or because she was about to get married, or because she lived just a block away from his and Alusha's old apartment. Perhaps it wasn't anything to do with the mugging at all. But suddenly he found himself holding onto his pillow as if it were a life-belt and he were in danger of drowning, which in a sense he was. When the despair threatened to close over his head, he forced himself out of bed and into a cold shower and paced the room and tried to fight his way out of it until, with an almost laughable inevitability, he reached for a drink. There wasn't a thing he didn't know about himself at that moment, not a shaft of self-knowledge that didn't turn in him, but it made no difference. At that moment there was simply no other way to save his life. The binge lasted two days.

Since then he'd regained some sort of hold on things. Each day had become a precarious walk along a precipice, a contest to maintain his consciousness a notch or two below the critical level without actually falling over the edge. But there were still the dangerous days, the days when he lost his fear of heights.

Another knock came on the door. Mel or Joe, or a message from an acquaintance perhaps. He didn't move; there was no one he particularly wanted to see.

The knock came again, a gentle but insistent tap. Giving in with bad grace, he got up and, drink in hand, went to the door. A girl stood there, most definitely familiar, yet out of context, so that he couldn't immediately place her.

Reading his expression, the girl's smile faded a little. 'You didn't suggest a time,' she said, holding an envelope up in front of her face.

'Ahh.' Recognizing his own scrawl, the memory came stumbling back. 'Of course ... *Daisy* ...' He touched his head in apology.

'I thought I'd better come straight away,' she said. 'In case you were racing off somewhere.'

He stood back to let her in. 'Racing? No ... No ...' He gave a low chuckle. 'Where I was going, it wasn't fast.'

'This is the second time,' she said, walking through to the sitting room and surveying the lavish decor, 'that you've forgotten me, I mean.' She turned and gave him a jaunty grin. 'But I won't take it personally.' Then she laughed, and he realized that, for all her self-assurance, she was nervous.

'Have a drink,' he said.

'No thanks.'

He drained his glass. 'Well, I think I will.' He waved her towards a seat while he went to the drinks corner.

'I met your manager in the lobby,' she said. 'He got me through the security people and told me to come straight up. I hope that was all right.'

'Sure.' So that was it, he thought with a flash of annoyance: David exercising his good intentions, pushing female company his way. Next thing he'd be organizing social evenings.

Daisy sank into a deep chair, falling back with a small sigh, before straightening up and sitting rather stiffly on the edge of her seat.

He added some dry ginger to the bourbon and took another look at her. When had he last seen her? In London? Scotland? His memory of that time was poor but he seemed to remember her as pretty and fresh-looking, rather a one-off. She looked different now. Bedraggled, her hair hanging round her face in tight damp curls, and scruffy-looking, with her old denim jacket and worn, mud-splattered trousers.

'I was so sorry about your wife,' she said, her voice very clear. 'I wrote. I don't know if . . .'

There had been hundreds of letters, but he remembered seeing her name, remembered reading something, though he couldn't recall what she had said.

'Thanks. I got it.' He sat down opposite her.

'Thanks for the ticket,' she said.

He gestured that it was nothing. He didn't ask if she'd enjoyed the show; she'd probably tell him anyway. Most people did.

'I enjoyed the show,' she said.

'Aha.'

A slight pause. She was smiling at him. It was a generous smile, candid and full of goodwill. 'What about you?'

'Sorry?'

'Did *you* enjoy it? I mean, presumably you don't some-times.'

Well, there was a question. Lighting a cigarette he

pretended to consider for a moment, although there was only one possible answer. 'Not a lot,' he said baldly.

'I didn't think so.' Aware that he might take this the wrong way, she laughed to soften the impact.

He decided to take it the wrong way anyway. 'Why would you think that?'

'Well – you seemed – not quite there. At the beginning anyway.'

He experienced one of the rapid mood swings that characterized his bourbon evenings. 'You're right,' he said abruptly. 'I was lousy, and it showed.'

But she wasn't having any self-pity. 'Not lousy, and it was only at the beginning,' she said firmly. 'Up till "Long Nights". After that you were terrific. Particularly in the slow numbers.'

He almost argued, but got up to get another drink instead.

The bourbon bottle was beginning to look more empty than full. Normally he left the bottle on the side, to maintain some degree of control, but for convenience he brought it across and stood it on the table between them. 'Sure you won't have one?' he asked, speaking with care so as to get the words out right.

She gave a slow shake of her head. Apart from the smile, her expression was unreadable.

He gulped at his drink. He always gulped when he was with strangers; something to do with nerves. 'So how's your campaign going?' he asked to change the subject. He didn't terribly want to hear, in fact it was the last thing he wanted to talk about, but she would be expecting him to ask and he wanted to get it over with.

'Oh, one step forward, one step back,' she said lightly. 'Usual thing. You know.'

He wasn't sure he did know. He pushed himself to say: 'I thought people were coming round. More aware. What with all the scares.'

She considered for a moment. Her back was still ramrod straight as if she were sitting in a hard-back chair. It gave her the prim look of a school teacher. 'The public can only take so much,' she said. 'They're already frightened rigid by the greenhouse effect and the holes in the ozone layer. The idea of being poisoned on a daily basis is altogether too much for them.'

'Well, you can see why . . .' He lost his thread – or perhaps whatever it was hadn't been worth saying – and buried his nose in his drink.

There was a long pause; he was aware that he had run out of conversation.

'Perhaps I'll have a drink after all,' she said. 'Coke if you have it.'

'Sure.' He got up and went over to the side. He took a Coke out of the fridge and began to pour it. He misjudged the flow and some spilt down the side of the glass onto the tray. As he picked up the glass to dry it, it came into contact with a bottle and made a loud clink.

Well, that hadn't taken long. Things were happening fast tonight.

He was aware of her eyes on his back. He took a breath. Concentrate, Mackenzie, get it together.

He carried the drink carefully back to the table. He sat down and watched her sip at the Coke. There was another pause. He wished he could say something appropriate, but his brain was thick and treacherous.

She flicked a thoughtful glance at him, as if she were plucking up courage to launch into something difficult and wasn't sure what sort of a reaction she'd get. Of course. He realized then: she would hardly have gone to all this trouble if she hadn't wanted to ask him something. Everyone wanted something. He decided to get it over and done with.

'So what is it you want?' he asked.

That took her by surprise. She dropped her eyes and

gave a nervous grin, as if he'd caught her out in some trick. Her approach, whatever it might be, was not well planned.

'Well . . .' She took a deep breath. 'I could give you all the usual junk. You know – about wanting to get you involved in the campaign. The standard celebrity stuff, about needing your support on the publicity front and all that. Or . . .' She tipped her head to one side and gave him a sidelong grin, half embarrassed, half amused. 'Or I could come right out and tell you what I really want.'

He fiddled with his glass. 'Let me guess – a benefit concert.'

'A concert?' She was genuinely surprised. 'Well, I suppose – I mean, we wouldn't say no. Not if you were offering.'

She had such a gracious way of putting things. He stubbed out his cigarette and lit a fresh one. 'So what is it then? That you want.'

She hesitated. He noticed her eyes, which were hazel with very clear whites. For the first time since she arrived her expression was entirely solemn. 'Money,' she said.

He almost laughed. Most people when they wanted cash, which was often, usually approached the subject casually, as if money was so much garbage that just happened to have attached itself to him and which he was only too glad to be rid of. But Daisy Field said the word with the spiritual reverence of the dispossessed.

This, or something else about her, made him smile. He studied his glass for a moment. 'Daisy Field. There's a name.'

If she was disappointed in the sudden turn of the conversation, she hid it well. 'It wasn't my parents who had the sense of humour,' she said. 'It was my schoolmates. Deeply original, they were. You can guess the sort of thing – Potato . . . Corn . . . Turnip . . . There wasn't a field they didn't try on me. I gave as good as I got, of course, but it made no difference. We called a truce at Daisy. To tell the truth, I didn't mind too much.' She made a face. 'Anything was an improvement on the original.'

'Which was?'

She gave a cat-like smile and shook her head. 'Can't say it. Too shy.'

It occurred to him that she was far from shy, and that no one got anything out of Daisy Field that she didn't want to give.

'This money, what do you want it for?' He had to concentrate to get the words out right. That came from forgetting to eat, a mistake he made two or three times a day.

'A research programme.'

'What kind?' he asked.

'To investigate a pesticide called Silveron,' she said, launching earnestly into her subject. 'Or to be precise, an insecticide. It's been on limited sale in Britain for about a year, and it's due to be introduced here soon. We suspect it's unsafe. It's already caused serious problems.' She told him about some workers at a production plant in Aurora, Illinois, how they were seriously ill, how Morton-Kreiger, the manufacturers, were denying any link with Silveron. There was something about the way she talked, a breathless urgent quality, that made the story sound both convincing and a little unlikely. He remembered their car journey in London all those months ago, and how disturbingly simple she had made everything seem to him then.

'This programme,' he said. 'What would it give you at the en' of – ' He took another shot at it. 'At the end of the day?'

'Oh, evidence of toxicity, evidence of carcinogenicity,' she said, as if it was the most obvious thing in the world. 'Evidence that would get the chemical banned.'

'Can't the government people take care of that?'

'Oh, they won't do anything,' she declared derisively.

'Not just like that. Not until we push some proof right in front of them. These new products have a momentum all their own, you see – tests, approvals and launches – and once the bandwagon's under way, it just keeps rolling. You have to produce a bombshell to even begin to stop them.' She gave what looked like a shiver and pulled her arms closer to her body. 'At the moment it would only be our opinion against the manufacturer's, and the way things are, that ain't going to stop anything. Our word carries about as much weight as . . .' She blew out her lips. 'Well, the paper it's written on.'

'Recycled.' He thought that was quite good, particularly for this stage of the evening. Daisy's face lit up and she laughed, a light dancing laugh full of amusement, and he flattered himself that it wasn't just politeness. The evening began to look up; he was glad she had come.

'How d'you know they'll listen? The gov'ment people.' He heard the thickening of his speech, the slurring of his words.

'Oh, our work'll be done under the strictest scientific conditions. They'll have no choice.' Her jacket had fallen slightly open, and he saw a dark crescent of damp down the front of her T-shirt. Through his not inconsiderable haze, it dawned on him that she was sitting so stiffly because she was soaking wet, and that it must have been the air-conditioning that made her shiver. He pulled himself forward in his seat. 'You're wet,' he said.

'I *am* a bit. No, not a bit – ' That laugh again. 'A lot!'

'Give me your jacket,' he said. 'I'll put it to dry.' After a moment's hesitation, she took the jacket off. Somewhere in the process of getting to his feet, reaching for the jacket and turning towards the bathroom, he had to reach suddenly for the arm of the chair. He shot a quick look at her. Diplomat that she was, she was showing a sudden and absorbing interest in the carpet. But she'd noticed all right, and he minded about that. He always hated anyone to see him in this sort of condition. Anyone being outsiders, people who wouldn't make allowances, people who would judge him.

Moving off again, he still hadn't got it right and barked his shin hard against the table and swore, though not so quietly that she could avoid hearing. By the time he got to the bathroom, he was experiencing one of his periodic bouts of anger and self-contempt. He could imagine what she was thinking: another foul-mouthed performer with more money than manners.

He went into the bedroom and picked out his favourite Fair Isle cardigan, some five years old but still in shape. Giving the furniture a wide berth, he negotiated himself back to the sitting room and handed it to her.

'Thanks,' she said. She had to concertina the sleeves before her hands appeared at the ends.

'Shirt?' he asked, seeing just how wet her T-shirt was.

'This'll dry soon enough, thanks all the same.'

'Something to eat?'

'Oh . . .' She looked undecided. Then her eyes sparked with sudden pleasure. 'Something nice and junky? I've been living off ethnic food for three days.'

He dialled room service and passed her the phone.

She took the phone uncertainly, but was soon ordering king hamburgers and fries, with ice-cream to follow. 'What about you?' she asked. He gestured a why-not and she ordered the same again.

She was hungry. She ate like a stevedore at the end of an eight-hour shift, in great gulps, hardly pausing for breath. Her hair was drying now, springing out into a halo of curls round her head, and the freshness had come back into her face. She had a fine clear skin, he noticed, slightly freckled over the nose and almost devoid of lines.

She may have been nervous when she'd arrived, but she certainly wasn't now. She was perfectly happy to concentrate on her food and leave the conversation to him – which meant that as often as not she was eating in silence – and to throw him the occasional smile.

An uncomfortable thought came to him: Was she so relaxed because she thought he'd agreed to her request?

He tried to get the conversation going again, if only to iron out the possibility of misunderstanding. 'This money,' he said, picking his way through the enunciation. 'How much did you have in mind?'

She paused with the spoon half-way to her mouth, then returned it slowly to the dish. 'Brace yourself,' she said.

'Not suggesting I have another drink?' The wit. If it hadn't been such a joke, he might have laughed.

She grinned fleetingly, then fixed her eyes on him. They were large as lamps. 'It's a lot,' she admitted. 'We'd need at least two maybe three specialists and several assistants to get through all the work. And then there'll be the victims' blood to be monitored for maybe months at a time. That involves a lot of tests. I can't cost it fully until I get back to the UK and phone around and get estimates – '

'The UK?' he asked thickly. 'But . . .' There was a reason he'd asked the question but it took him a moment to remember what it was. 'The people are in Illinois – how're you goin' to test them if you're over there?'

'Oh, we can manage with the victims in Britain,' she said. 'There aren't so many, but there are enough.'

Two realizations began to filter through to Nick, both of which caused his heart to sink slightly. The first and the least surprising was that he was rapidly losing his nightly balancing act with the booze. Normally he put up no fight at all – the sooner it was all over the better – but tonight, just when he needed his brain, it was slipping away from him.

The second realization, which was slower in coming but just as inescapable, was that she was holding back, failing to tell him something, something that he wasn't going to like.

In a bid to salvage his brain, he pushed his glass across the table out of reach and braced himself to tackle the hamburger. It was spongy and dry.

'What's the rest of the story?' he asked, putting some briskness into his voice. 'Why's all this so important?'

She had picked up the shift in his tone because she started to speak quickly and urgently, in a level voice, very businesslike. 'There are three reasons,' she said, striking one finger with the index finger of the other hand. 'First, all the victims are little people, and the way things are at the moment they haven't a hope of getting compensation, not without scientific back-up from us.'

The meat was too much to swallow and, pushing it out from the middle of the roll, he ate the bread with a filling of onions and ketchup.

'The second thing is that as things stand there's absolutely nothing to stop Silveron getting full approval,' she continued, bending back a second finger. 'That means it'll be used on everything – cereals, vegetables, fruit. A disaster just waiting to happen. Oh, the effects may not be so immediate, but give it a year or two and they'll start to be reflected in the health statistics. By which time the whole bandwagon will be that much harder to stop. Once a product starts to make money, manufacturers and government agencies become that much more reluctant to admit that anything could be wrong with it. Not until millions of people have been exposed to what may be irreparable damage.'

He saw that this kind of speech, with its crisp well-used words and ready-hatched thoughts, came easily to her.

She began to elaborate but he held up a staying hand. 'Got it,' he said. Replacing the last of the bread on the plate, he asked: 'And the third thing?'

'Ahh.' Her eyes shone with suppressed excitement. 'We have good reason to believe that the manufacturers are hiding something. It's even possible that they have falsified their test results, which shows just how desperately unsafe the system can be. But the only way we can hope to prove that is to come up with our own results – '

'Got it,' he interrupted. 'Come up with your own results . . .' He focused on her with great care. 'And?'

'And?'

'Why me? Why should I help?'

She hesitated, her confidence suddenly plummeted. He was reminded of a child caught out in some minor subterfuge. 'We have evidence . . .' she began slowly, fixed those beautiful clear eyes on him again, 'to show that Silveron was used illegally on forests in the west of Scotland last year.' She took her time, anxious not to give him too much too soon. Then, with a deep breath, she added in a rush: 'And we have reason to believe it was sprayed on your wife. That it was the cause of her illness.'

He was silent.

Hastily, she reached down and pulled a file out of her bag and put it on the table. 'If you want to read the case histories of known Silveron victims, you'll find the symptoms are almost identical.'

He made no move towards the file, but stretched for the glass he'd carefully left out of reach across the table.

She began to tell him a long and involved story about an aerial spraying company which had been based to the west of Stirling, and a pilot who admitted to using Silveron in the Loch Fyne area, and how he had admitted to an abortive job on the Fincharn Estate. She went through every lead, explained every connection, described with considerable feeling the state of the sick boy on Loch Fyne – though he noticed that she was careful not to mention the boy's uncle, that loathsome Campbell – then jumped rapidly to her conclusions, explained them, interpreted them.

Facts, ideas, connections – they poured out of her like water, and like water they flowed over him and through him until his imagination foundered. Inventing a reason to get up, he went to find some dry ginger. The room swayed. That was a new one. Usually the room got progressively darker, like someone was turning down a dimmer switch.

He didn't realize she'd left her seat until she appeared beside him and touched his arm. 'Are you all right?'

'I'm all right,' he said.

'What about some water?' She reached for a Perrier.

'No.' He turned obstinately away and made his way across to the window and stared out into the night. A welter of sensations bumped and crashed around his head. Even if what she was saying were true, what the hell did it matter anyway? None of it was any use now. Investigations, diggings for truth, they didn't interest him, they were for energetic people like Daisy Field. But then, perhaps that was the point. Perhaps that was why he had let her come here, to let her take charge of it all, to let him work his way free.

He glanced back at her. She was watching him, her gaze steady, patient. Suddenly he warmed to her. Usually when he was the worse for wear people gave him infuriating looks of compassion, the sort they reserved for newly bereaved people and injured dogs.

Manoeuvring himself gently round the furniture, he walked past her and into the bedroom. He dug his cheque-book out of a drawer and sat on the bed for a while, letting the emotional dust settle.

He wandered back to the sitting room. 'How much was it then?' he asked.

She stared at him.

He shrugged extravagantly: 'How much?'

'Listen, I – ' She looked trapped. 'I – don't know.'

'Thought you wanted money?'

'But – are you sure?'

He tut-tutted and said with magisterial grandeur: 'Cheque-book's in my hand.' He held it up. 'Pen's in the other. An opportunity not to be missed. Might not come again.'

'Perhaps you should think about it.'

'This is all wrong,' he said, suddenly vastly amused. 'You're meant to be closing the deal. Meant to be standing over me with a gun.'

'Okay.' She ran her tongue along her lips and took the plunge. 'One million.'

She seemed to be reassured by his silence. She added hastily: 'It's possible we could do it for less, but that figure's a reasonable estimate, allowing for contingencies. Of course I'd keep you in touch, I'd provide full accounts – '

'Pounds or dollars?'

'Pounds.'

He took a breath. It was rather more than he'd expected. Even after all these years, he never got used to the noughts on the end of everything. The puritan in him was alarmed by the ease with which money came his way, while the child, the son of the local government official from Chertsey earning ten thousand a year, was terrified it would all slip away.

A million. Well, it wouldn't kill him.

He wrote a cheque.

Daisy kept sighing: 'I don't know what to say.'

'It's for two-fifty thou,' he said. 'More when you need it. Though don' try and cash it, not till I've had words with my accountant.' He sat back in the chair, holding the cheque up between his fingers. 'Two conditions.'

She nodded.

'One, don' ever link this publicly to me or my wife. No talk of this stuff causing her death. Understand? And no talk of me having anything to do with the money. Okay?'

She looked disappointed. 'Okay,' she said.

'If I hear anything, tha's it. No more money.'

She seemed a bit anxious at that, but nodded anyway.

'Two, I don' wanna know. I don' wanna see accounts, reports. Nothing. Just get on with it and do what you think's best.'

'But won't you want to know how we're getting on?'

'Nope.'

'But . . .' She bit back whatever she was going to say, then came in on another tack. 'Your songs – '

'My songs?' he echoed.

'I thought, with everything you've written . . .'

'Jus' songs,' he said stiffly. 'Not the same.' She'd managed to touch something raw in him.

She couldn't let it go. 'Perhaps I didn't explain . . . This research – it could blow the lid off a lot of things, it could be really important for the whole movement.'

'The movement? Listen' – he lurched sideways in his chair – 'I don't actually give a shit – ' This was sounding much worse than he'd intended. He started again. 'No, I . . . I mean . . . Course I give a . . . It's jus' . . .' He trailed off, suddenly uncertain of what precisely he was trying to say.

'Your decision, of course,' Daisy said, edging forward in her seat and pulling her bag towards her. 'But I just thought . . . Well, if you were in touch then at least you'd feel that' – she groped for the right words – 'that something *good* was coming out of the whole horrid business.'

Here was a fine example of instant half-baked wisdom. His blood pressure leapt and he gave an ugly chortle. 'Listen, if I need counselling I can get it from a shrink at two hun'red dollars a throw.'

She stared at him.

He heard the ugly words reverberating through the air and could have bitten his tongue out. He said awkwardly: 'Sorry . . . Sorry. I didn't mean to . . .'

She gave a quick bright smile. 'None of my business.' She picked up her bag.

'Look, I'm sorry . . . Please, don't go, don't go . . .'

She stood up.

'Please. Won't you, er . . .'

'I really must go. God, the time.'

Suddenly he couldn't bear the thought of being alone, couldn't bear her to leave with those ugly words still hanging in the air. He got clumsily to his feet. 'Please stay. I'd like you to stay.' Then before he realized what he was doing, he reached out and grasped her arm. He knew there was some reason he shouldn't, realized dimly that there was a risk of some misunderstanding, but by then it was too late: he'd asked her to stay, he'd grabbed at her, it was late and they were in his hotel room; a scenario not open to that many interpretations.

'I'd love to,' she said, sending out masses of signals to show that she wouldn't love to at all. 'But I really can't. My friends are waiting up for me.'

'Please – I didn't mean . . .' He took a deep breath. 'What I meant was, how about a film? Or a walk?'

She regarded him gravely for a moment, then dropped her head and smiled. She said: 'I thought no one walked in New York late at night.'

Sixteen storeys down, the rain had stopped. The streets were shining like mirrors and the air was heavy and damp so that the lights on the far side of Central Park were smudged and blurred.

They turned north along Fifth Avenue. Nick took several gulps of air and felt refreshed and slightly nauseous all at the same time. Daisy, looking small in his oversized cardigan, bounced along at his side.

They didn't talk much until they got to East 64th. His head was heavy; everything seemed remote and unfocused. But he recognized the block all right. 'We used to live up there,' he said. 'We – ' It was hard to shape the right words. 'Something bad happened.'

She was silent. A cab turned the corner, hit a pothole and sent a spout of water onto the sidewalk a few feet ahead of them. 'Someone attacked Alusha,' he said.

She was staring at him. 'How dreadful.'

'It was stupid, stupid . . .'

'What happened?'

'It was a kid – someone I'd tried to help. I let him do small jobs, deliveries – that kind of thing. But we never thought to check him out . . . He was a schizo. Unstable. Into drugs.'

'Oh.'

The lights went to *Walk* and they crossed the street. Nick's legs felt heavy; it was an effort to go on.

'Was she badly hurt?'

'Bad enough.'

Daisy was silent for a moment. 'And then you went to Scotland?'

'Yes.'

'A wonderful place.'

He gave a dismissive grunt.

'You'll go back?' she asked.

'Nope.'

'Never?'

'Never.'

He stumbled slightly and she reached for his arm, letting go when he was back on balance.

How must he seem to her? he wondered furiously. How must he look? Suddenly he felt ashamed and angry.

'It's touring . . .' he said, waving his arm by way of explanation. 'Gets to me . . . I don't mean to . . . I . . . After the show, you know . . .'

'I know all about it,' she said in a reminiscent tone. 'My father was a drunk.'

*Drunk*. What a word. He winced.

'Don't worry,' she said. 'I'm not going to try to talk you out of it. I'm not going to lecture you. I know better than that. My mum wasted thirty years trying to talk my father round.'

'I can stop.'

'Sure.'

'Any time.'

'Sure.'

He ground to a halt. He heard himself roar childishly: 'But I can!'

She stopped and turned to him and said simply: 'I know that.' She took his arm and they resumed walking. 'My father was a very charming drunk.' That word again. 'Hid it well from the outside world. Said he got early retirement because of his back, though if his back was bad, it was only because he spent so much time lying across the stairs.' She gave the ghost of a chuckle, which was more like a sigh.

He stopped. He felt crushed and dizzy.

'Are you all right?' she asked.

'I'm all right.' But he wasn't. He found a wall and leant against it. Closing his eyes was a mistake; his head spun faster and when he opened his eyes again he had to grip his temples to prevent lift-off. After a time he was aware of Daisy taking his arm and coaxing him into a cab and getting him back to the hotel.

It was midday when he awoke, in need of the bathroom. He was lying on the bed fully clothed except for his shoes. A bed-cover was spread over him and the curtains were closed. There was a glass of water beside him and he remembered that she had made him drink tons of it before she'd let him sleep.

When he finally got up and showered and took his hangover for a stumble through the suite he found a note on the sitting-room table.

*I took the cheque, but won't do anything with it until I've spoken to you. To say I'd be heartbroken if you changed your mind is an understatement* ... A line had been crossed out. He tried to make out what it was.

Something like: 'I'd shoot myself', followed by several exclamation marks. *But I'd understand*, she went on. *In the meantime, think again about staying in touch. We need you. Yours gratefully, Daisy.*

He dropped the note back on the table and forgot about it until later, when it was time to move out. Then he scooped it up and, crushing it into a small ball, threw it in the bin.

Three days later, sitting in a rented flat in London, he called his accountant and told him to expect the cheque. Then he called Catch and left a message with the girl there to say it was all right for Daisy to cash it.

When he put the phone down, he felt, against all expectations, as if the shadows were lifting.

# Chapter 24

———

SCHENKER HAD BEEN given a side table for the second time in a week. After three years in the wilderness of the Savoy Grill's centre tables, did this mean he had finally crossed the invisible divide and won the accolade of guaranteed occupancy? One could never be sure. Had Schenker's secretary told them he was going to be lunching with a cabinet minister? That might have decided the issue, of course, though Schenker preferred not to think so.

The minister, when he arrived, strode in at the politician's trot, energetic and fired with purpose, smiling broadly, greeting the head waiter like a valued colleague, acknowledging acquaintances with a regal nod as he motored across the floor.

It was five months since the election, and three months since Schenker had seen Driscoll, though not for lack of invitations. The minister had been too busy for Ascot, Wimbledon, Henley and Glyndebourne. Too busy or, it occurred to Schenker, too intent on quietly distancing himself from old affiliations.

The minister ordered mineral water, a wild mushroom and scallop salad followed by a plain grilled Dover sole. 'My waistline,' he laughed. But he said it with pride, patting his stomach to draw attention to a considerable weight-loss which had left him, if not quite slim, then certainly looking a great deal fitter. Power obviously suited him. He had the air of a man taking his responsibilities seriously but with huge enjoyment.

Schenker commented on how well he was looking.

'Thank you.'

'And how's Susan?'

'Oh, very well.' But it was said with a certain crisp-ness and Schenker got the impression that the conversation was not going to be allowed to drift into more personal realms.

The first course arrived and they talked their way through the economy, the latest food scare and an opinion poll on irradiated food. Schenker would have liked to leave the business of the day a little longer, but he sensed that Driscoll was going to make his escape as soon as decently possible.

'You'll have guessed why I wanted a chat,' Schenker began as soon as the waiter had cleared the plates. 'This extraordinary business about Silveron.'

Driscoll gave a rapid nod. 'My staff have been keeping me informed.'

His staff would have been alerted two weeks ago, Schenker guessed, when items had appeared in *The Times* and *Independent*. Neither story had been more than a couple of column-inches long, but that had been quite sufficient to put the wind up the Morton-Kreiger sharehold-ers. 'The point is,' he said, 'there's absolutely not a shred of evidence to back these claims. Not a shred. This is pure scaremongering of the worst kind. An alarmist campaign dreamed up by the American pressure groups.'

'We realize that,' Driscoll reassured him.

Schenker proceeded delicately. 'So the ministry will back us on this?'

'In what way do you mean?' He sounded guarded.

'Announce that the stories are absolutely groundless.'

'The ministry can't make those sort of statements, Ronald, you know that.' Driscoll's voice seemed to have altered, to have become plummier and more melodious than Schenker remembered, as if he'd been taking voice lessons.

Schenker tried another tack. 'But I can understand, can I, that your people privately condemn this campaign?'

'We always frown on pressure-group hysteria, you know that. Unless there's some basis in fact, of course.' He nodded to some new arrival across the room, his face breaking into a fleeting smile before resuming an appropriate seriousness. 'We certainly have no intention of responding to pressure, otherwise we'd spend all our time reacting, and not doing what the people elected us to do, which is to get on with implementing the government's election programme. No, I understand that my people are in contact with your people over this, and that we're all in contact with the Americans. I've no doubt the experts will sort it out. They usually do.'

Was he being deliberately unhelpful? Schenker couldn't decide.

'The thing is, Tony,' he said, 'this sort of thing can have repercussions out of all proportion – if matters are allowed to get out of hand, that is. If people panic.'

'Panic? *We're* certainly not going to be panicked into anything.' Driscoll spoke with vague condescension, as if he'd been a minister for years and knew the ropes backwards. 'Nothing's getting out of hand at *our* end.'

Schenker, bristling slightly, made the effort to smile. 'At your end, no, of course not. I didn't mean to suggest it was.' The next course arrived, and they waited while the waiter took the sole off the bone and arranged the fillets on Driscoll's plate. Schenker had ordered salmon, but was no longer hungry.

The waiter finally left. 'But there's still a small problem from our point of view, Tony,' Schenker said, forcing intimacy into his voice. 'I was hoping you might be able to put my mind at rest. Concerning a disturbing bit of news I heard, something to do with a possible delay in Silveron's full licence. And' – he gave an incredulous laugh – 'I even heard that the ACP might be reviewing the *existing* licence. It seemed so improbable I couldn't believe it.'

Driscoll took his time finishing his mouthful. 'You know very well that the ACP go their own way, Ronald. The *Advisory* Committee on Pesticides. And that's just what they are – advisory. They're the experts and I rely utterly on their judgement. They're my ears to the world of science.' He obviously liked the sound of the phrase because he paused to let it reverberate a little.

'But it's an extraordinary step to take on no evidence – '

'Well, not exactly *no* evidence, old boy,' Driscoll said reprovingly. Schenker noticed the *old boy*, a new addition to Driscoll's vocabulary. 'That's the point, isn't it?' Driscoll said. 'All these sick workers at your plant in Chicago – '

'*Three* people, Tony. Maybe only two. And even if it had – '

'I thought it was eight or more?' Driscoll cut in.

'Three,' Schenker persisted. 'And there's strong evidence to show that Silveron is completely innocent. We can show that at least four workers who *thought* their illnesses were chemical-related are suffering from diseases that have absolutely nothing to do with – '

'Of course, of course.' Driscoll waved a hand. 'I'm sure your people have done their homework. They ran a second batch of trials, didn't they, and the product looked fine? I know all that, Ronald. But the fact remains that some people are sick, and the thing has to be looked into. Don't forget the unions, Ronald. I've got them breathing down my neck all the time. They're never happy about these things until matters are properly investigated. And you won't need reminding, I'm sure, that they can do you far more damage than anyone else in the long run, with boycotts and that sort of thing. Far more damage.'

'I respect their anxiety. I do, sincerely,' Schenker said.

'But in this instance it is very seriously misplaced, Tony. Very seriously misplaced.' Driscoll had the blank look of someone who was rapidly losing interest.

Doggedly, Schenker pressed on. 'The Silveron licence, Tony. What I'd like to know is what possible reason the ACP have for taking another look at it?'

Driscoll gave a laugh, the sort people use to skirt around questions they have no intention of answering. 'Ronald, what can I say? As far as the ACP is concerned, my hands are tied. Utterly tied. It's a question of the due processes running their course, and being *seen* to run their course.'

Was this obduracy just a ploy? Schenker wondered. Was Driscoll taking a tough stand merely to make a future concession look doubly generous?

Driscoll pointed a knife at Schenker's plate. 'You haven't touched your salmon. I wonder if it's farmed. We export twelve thousand tons of salmon a year, you know. Amazing.'

Picking up a fork, Schenker began to pull half-heartedly at the fish.

'On second thoughts, probably wild,' Driscoll murmured reflectively. 'The Savoy, you know. Still caters for purists.'

Schenker put his fork down without eating. 'Tony, I don't need to tell you what this uncertainty means to us. A licence review would result in a serious loss of confidence. We've invested a hell of a lot in this product, Tony, one hell of a lot.'

'I know that.'

'Then where's the faith in our expertise? Where's the back-up? Where's the support? Delays and uncertainties will cost jobs, Tony. We'll have to lay people off – hundreds, maybe thousands.'

'I'd never let it get that far, Ronald, you know that.'

'But these things can happen overnight!'

Driscoll smiled benevolently and, folding his napkin into

a neat square, leaned confidentially across the table. 'Listen, this is what I'll do.' Ah, here comes the concession, Schenker thought; here comes the sweetener. 'I can't make firm promises,' Driscoll began like a true politician, 'but what I can do is to press the committee to consider the matter with all possible speed, and remind them of the inadvisability of proceeding any further without hard evidence.' He sat back looking pleased with himself. 'I think that should do the trick, don't you?' Reading Schenker's face, he spread his palms. 'More, sadly, I cannot do.'

Oh but you can, thought Schenker, his stomach twisting unpleasantly. In view of the favours you owe me, in view of the substantial donations Morton-Kreiger makes to party funds, you can. But Schenker wasn't going to beg, cap in hand, for a few additional crumbs of comfort that a grateful Driscoll might throw his way. That wasn't his style.

'That won't be enough,' he said firmly.

Driscoll looked surprised as well as cross at this lack of appreciation. 'What do you mean, not enough?'

'We need a firm statement, to reassure people.'

'Ronald, Ronald.' He gave a small pitying shake of the head and dabbed his mouth with the folded napkin. 'What do you expect me to do? Stand over the scientists and tell them how to run their committee?'

'I expect you to do whatever you have to do to save Morton-Kreiger from this totally undeserved and highly damaging attack – this victimization.'

Driscoll pulled himself upright, looking ruffled. He was just beginning to realize that Schenker might be calling in a number of long-standing favours. He didn't reply but buttoned his jacket, ready for a quick getaway.

Schenker spelt it out. 'I saved your bacon, Tony. Now I'm asking you to do the same for me.'

Driscoll looked at him uncomprehendingly and said tersely: 'I've said I'll do all I reasonably can. And I will.'

Then, casting an eye around him, itching for escape, he added dismissively: 'What do you mean anyway – saved my bacon?'

Schenker made a show of reticence, as if wild horses wouldn't drag such unnecessary details from his lips.

'Saved my bacon!' echoed the minister with a chortle. 'Really, Ronald, that's a little over the top, isn't it?'

He has no idea, Schenker realized, not even an inkling.

He'd probably erased the girl from his memory. Looking suitably reluctant at having to mention it, Schenker helped his memory along a bit.

'That unpleasant business.'

'Unpleasant business?' the minister retorted. 'It'd help if I knew what the hell you were talking about.' He was irritated, but also, Schenker sensed, curious.

Schenker pitched his voice just above a whisper. 'The business with Miss Kershaw.'

Surprise flashed across his face, and he gave a slight twitch as if he'd been attacked by an insect. Recovering, he raised an admonitory finger. 'Don't talk to me about Miss Kershaw. She was one of your least clever ideas, Schenker.'

'*My* idea?' He shook his head very slowly. 'I don't think that's quite accurate, Tony. Remember, I never even knew the girl until I met her with you.' Gesturing to show that the matter was hardly worth arguing about, he went on rapidly: 'But it was certainly my idea to settle her financially and make sure she kept out of your way.'

Driscoll was very still, his mouth sagging, the lower lip full and damp, revealing back teeth gleaming with fillings. When he finally managed to speak, his voice was thin and breathless. 'Settle her?'

Schenker flicked a warning glance as the waiter approached. They ordered coffee.

Driscoll's eyes were fixed blackly on his, waiting for an answer.

Schenker took his time. 'She had – er, ideas. We thought

that her ideas were the last thing you needed in your new job. We identified the problem and dealt with it. We also went to some lengths to ensure she would never trouble you again.'

Driscoll's mouth moved. He spluttered: 'You – ' But he never went on. He closed his eyes as if a lot of half-realized pieces were suddenly falling into place. Then he shot Schenker an agitated glance. '*We*, you said?'

'Sorry – I. Me.'

The coffee arrived. Schenker asked for the bill. Then he fixed his gaze on Driscoll. 'I valued our friendship highly enough to go out on a limb for you, to save you unpleasantness which might have been highly inconvenient to your career. This Silveron business means a lot to *my* career, Tony. I'm asking you to go out on a limb for me.'

Driscoll was recovering fast, the fight bouncing back into his face. He protested: 'I didn't ask you to interfere. In fact, it was a bloody liberty.'

'You would have preferred the business to' – Schenker rotated his fingers, as if plucking the right word out of the air – 'to, er, *progress*, would you?'

He got the meaning of that all right, and mashed his lips together. 'It wouldn't have got that far.'

'No?' Schenker was losing patience. 'Well, whichever way it had turned out, it would have cost you a great deal of worry, not to mention cash. I would have thought you were only too pleased to have that little lot taken off your hands.'

The bill arrived. Schenker signed it without reading it.

'It was rank interference,' Driscoll repeated bitterly.

Schenker could see what the trouble was. It wasn't that he had interfered – Driscoll could hardly be anything but grateful about that – it was injured pride, lost face, and the fact that the revelation had put Driscoll so completely in Schenker's debt.

'I acted as a friend,' Schenker said lightly. 'If I did wrong then I did it with the best intentions.'

That took the wind out of his sails, as Schenker had known it would. Driscoll, his eyes darting rapidly round the room, ran a smoothing hand down the front of his jacket and pulled his shoulders back, soldier fashion. 'I must go,' he said sharply, and got to his feet. Schenker rose and they nodded formally to each other.

'I'll be in touch,' Driscoll murmured, and marched off. This time he forgot to nod to his acquaintances.

Anne Dublensky gave a long shuddering sigh of exasperation. 'What do you mean, let's be positive?'

'I mean, let's be positive,' Dublensky replied with a short laugh.

'Sometimes you talk so much baloney, I think your head needs attention.' She stalked out into the yard, letting the screen bang behind her. Standing up wearily, knowing what was to come as surely as if they were reading a script, he followed her outside and found her raking the leaves with ferocious energy.

'What do you want, Anne?' he asked, genuinely puzzled. 'I mean, I have this job, don't I? We have a new start. It may not be much, but what am I meant to do – throw it all away?'

'I hate this place,' she hissed under her breath.

Automatically, he turned to look at the house. Okay, it wasn't perfect – truth be told, it was rather a dump – but it wasn't as if they were buying the place. They were just renting it while they waited for the house in Allentown to sell.

'When the agreement runs out we could try another place,' he suggested.

'*What?*' She looked at him as if he were a fool. 'I meant

*this* place.' She made an impatient all-encompassing sweep of her arm.

Ah, *this* place. This small town in New Jersey. It wasn't such a bad neighbourhood, at least Dublensky didn't think so. A little too satisfied with itself perhaps, not so friendly as other places they had been, a little too thick with country clubs that had mysteriously few Poles, Italians or Jews among their members, but not to be condemned for all that. There were always good unaffected people everywhere; you just had to go out and look for them. For some reason Anne hadn't shown much interest in meeting people. Nor, for that matter, in applying to join any projects, although in the past she had always complained bitterly when she had been denied the opportunity to work.

Each day seemed to be a burden to her, each conversation a source of profound irritation. Whatever he suggested by way of a diversion – an evening out, a weekend drive – she dismissed with now familiar contempt. And her displeasure, rarely far beneath the surface, was never more intense than when he tried to pacify her. Then, eyes glittering dangerously, she reacted with sharp-edged lunges of scorn.

'I never know what's wrong,' he said plaintively. 'You act like I've done something terrible but you never tell me what it is I'm supposed to have done. I mean, is it the job? Okay, so it's not great, I know it's not great – but I like it, I really do. I know you don't believe me, but it's true.'

'Oh, I believe you,' she said, picking up a sack and stuffing leaves in aggressively. 'Whatever else, you've always had the ability to adapt.'

Was there a touch of sarcasm in her tone? Even after all these years it was never possible to be sure with Anne. Observations, even compliments, were delivered conditionally, with overlays of meaning; she was incapable of seeing the simplest thing without sighting endless complications beyond. His job – as a toxicologist at a new contract

research company called Dalton Research International –
was an irony in itself, as the fast-growing Dalton had
aspirations to become another TroChem, and was even
now hungering after a contract with Morton-Kreiger. The
position was a step down in responsibility, status and
salary, but it was solid employment. Anne, despite her past
optimism, her remorseless encouragement, had shown only
a glancing interest in this success, her enthusiasm as
guarded as it was short-lived.

She stared at him, grasping the rake to her chest with
both hands. 'I've lost respect for you,' she declared suddenly. 'Yes,' she repeated more deliberately, 'I have lost
respect for you. I need to tell you that. You have a right to
know. That that's the way I feel about you now.'

'Anne . . .' He sighed. 'We've been over this so often.'

'Not often enough for me.'

'I can't take the world's burdens on my shoulders.
I've got you and Tad to look after. That's my first responsibility – '

'We can look after ourselves, thanks. In fact' – her face
hardened – 'I don't know if I wouldn't prefer it that way.'

Their arguments normally followed such well-worn
paths, such predictable channels of self-torture and mutual
frustration, that this new departure took him by surprise,
like a sudden blow.

The pain must have shown in his face because she
clutched a hand to her forehead with a groan of self-disgust
and said quickly: 'Forget that. I didn't mean it. I really
didn't mean it.' She turned back to her work, then paused
again and said grudgingly: 'You know I wouldn't mind so
much if you'd kept in contact with Burt, if you knew what
the hell was happening.'

She didn't always take this line. Sometimes she berated
him for not having stood up to the Allentown management
and sued for wrongful dismissal, other times she harped on
his stupidity in leaving the Aurora documents lying around,

waiting to be stolen. Most usually – and this was the nub of her displeasure – she'd rebuke him for hiding the existence of the second file from her, for not telling her about it until long after it was stolen, and worst of all, for having done nothing about it, for not being prepared to get up and tell the whole world what it contained. This was the real crime, the one that could never, it seemed, be forgiven.

'It's not in Burt's hands, I've told you,' Dublensky said sharply, still catching his breath from her unexpected salvo. 'It's EarthForce,' he said. 'EarthForce are the only people who can take the thing forward.'

'Well, they tried, didn't they? They had the publicity campaign, and where did that get them?'

'I don't know, how can I know?' He heard his voice rising; he felt a sudden heat at the back of his eyes.

'You could ask them, couldn't you? Why don't you call them?' she pleaded, her voice swooping low with entreaty. 'Why not? How long would it take – five minutes? Less? Speak to Paul Erlinger. Find out. Oh, this time *do* it, John. For me.'

His shoulders slumped, he gave a gesture of defeat. She'd made this request before and, though he'd genuinely intended to call, he'd never managed to get as far as the phone. At first he'd told himself it was a sensible move against the possibility of bad security at EarthForce, that he was merely protecting himself against a rerun of the burglary and other hostilities, but he knew this wasn't quite the whole story. He clung to the belief that Silveron would never get final EPA approval, that the product would come unstuck long before it got to the marketplace, that someone somewhere would denounce it; that, even on the slenderest of evidence, EarthForce would somehow persuade the EPA to demand a completely new set of toxicology trials.

In the meantime he had managed to salvage a large chunk of his life. His message of non-cooperation with

EarthForce had obviously been received loud and clear by
the powers that be, because it was soon after his meeting
with Paul Erlinger that he had landed this job. And now
Anne was berating him for having made the best of things,
for picking up the pieces of their lives.

'Okay, okay,' he said, hovering close to the edge of his
self-control, 'I'll call, I'll call. But I would like to know if
I'm going to be allowed some peace afterwards. Am I going
to be forgiven for whatever this crime is that I'm meant to
have committed?'

She sighed impatiently. 'There's no crime.'

'Well, you could have fooled me.'

She eyed him. 'If there's a crime it's that you don't seem
to care any more. That's what I find hard to take.'

'Don't care! How much am I meant to care? I mean, am
I meant to stand up and make these claims and get torn
apart in public and go onto welfare, all to achieve absolutely nothing, and then feel good with myself because I've
done it for some great principle?'

Shaking her head, she rolled her eyes skyward in an
expression of hopelessness, and, rake in hand, stalked off
across the grass. Even her back broadcast disappointment.

Two days later he got away from work earlier than
usual and, remembering that Anne had gone to collect Tad
from swimming practice, finally goaded himself into sitting
in front of the phone and calling Paul Erlinger.

In Washington the name of Alan Breck brought Erlinger
panting breathlessly to the phone. He betrayed his hopes
straight away. 'Your friend – are there developments?'

Dublensky felt a squeeze of shame. 'No.' As he said it,
the disappointment at the far end of the line was almost
palpable. 'No, I'm sorry. Nothing. No, I was hoping you
might be able to tell me about developments. How you're
progressing with the medical opinions and that sort of
thing.'

'Oh, well – you know. It's slow, like these things are

always slow.' His voice had lost its edge of excitement. 'At the moment I'd say it was one step forward, one back. Some of the Aurora workers – four in fact – have gone and gotten themselves rediagnosed with good old-fashioned ailments, non-chemical diseases that make it a lot easier to obtain welfare and insurance payouts. Can't blame them, but it's lowered our data base.'

'You think you still have a case?'

'Not such a great case that we couldn't do with a helluva lot more evidence.' The comment hung in the air, awaiting suggestions.

Dublensky was silent.

'We've been campaigning on Capitol Hill,' Erlinger continued, 'spreading the word. But you can imagine. They all say, where's the proof, let me know when you've got something to show me.'

'And the EPA?'

'Same. Took a second look at the test data, but can't act until there's something to go on.'

'So it's *not* looking good?'

'I wouldn't say that exactly. It's just the difference between catching someone with a smoking gun in his hand and having to patch a case together from circumstantial evidence. You can still get a conviction, but the jury may be out a long time.' There was a pause. 'Your friend – he hasn't regained access to that material?'

'No.'

'He wouldn't be prepared to swear to what he saw?'

Dublensky didn't speak. He was remembering how the robbery had occurred a short time after he had sent the Aurora dossier to EarthForce, how even if it was purely coincidental and there was no security leak at Erlinger's end, he couldn't risk exposure again. Unemployment, once sampled, was not a desirable option.

'No,' he said at last.

Erlinger absorbed this, then commented: 'There've been

more victims in Britain, you know. Daisy Field reports three new cases.'

'Three? Isn't that some sort of proof?'

'Not while the British authorities are pretending there's no problem and the cases don't get reported to Daisy until it's too late to run tests.'

'Can't she get publicity?'

'Not enough.'

Erlinger, sensing an opening, pressed home. 'There's only one way to cut the whole thing short, Alan.'

For a moment neither of them spoke.

'If you should ever see your way to getting us that information . . .' Erlinger let the idea hang in the air.

'I know,' Dublensky said tightly, battling with his thoughts. 'I know. I wish . . . I mean, I would if . . .' He pulled back, frightened of what he might hear himself say. He felt as if he was teetering on the rim of a volcano in a strong wind, his balance threatened by each gust of words. Finally he said: 'I'll see what I can do. Maybe there's something I can do.'

'You will?' Erlinger couldn't hide his excitement.

'Please, *please*. I'm not making promises. I'm not in any position – '

'No, no. Of course. I understand, I understand,' Erlinger said hastily. 'But any time you want to call, I'm here. Okay?'

Dublensky rang off, any relief he might have felt at having finally executed his chore more than outweighed by the realization of what he'd said. Why had he made even that vaguest of promises? But he already knew the answer: it was the thought of the people in Britain, the new cases. That reality couldn't be escaped, and the knowledge reduced him to a new state of wretchedness.

In the last minutes before Anne's return, he forced himself towards some sort of a decision.

He would call Erlinger again in two weeks' time and, if

there was no sign of a ban in Britain, he would commit a serious amount of time to rethinking his position. The decision, which he knew wasn't much of a decision at all, gave him a tangible sense of achievement.

The door sounded. Tad's call echoed through the house. Dublensky's heart lifted and, wrapping his mind in thoughts of family and home, he rose to greet him.

# Chapter 25

DAISY AWOKE TO a feeling of anxiety. She lay still, trying to make sense of this, placing herself in time and space. Early, very early, and dark; a homely back room in Mrs Biddows' bed-and-breakfast establishment in Elm Avenue, Chelmsford; the sound of a passing car in an adjacent road. She tried closing her eyes again, but the unease lingered on, cold as a draught. She remembered that she had an early meeting today. It was this, perhaps, which had made her wake. Or the thousand things on her mind. But unease? Fear? That was more difficult to tie down.

She got up and, going to the window, pulled the curtain aside. The row of semi-detached houses in the next road stood out sharply against the sulphurous rays of the street lighting, and the intervening gardens were dark as ink.

She went out onto the landing and listened, though she wasn't sure what for. Dressing, she went downstairs and left a note for Mrs Biddows to say she wouldn't be in for breakfast.

Usually the journey to the laboratory took three minutes, five on the rare occasions when she travelled as late as eight thirty, the height of the Chelmsford rush-hour. Now, in the pre-dawn, it took less than three.

She parked next to the chainlink perimeter fence that surrounded the laboratory and unfastened the padlock on the gates. She stepped through and stood for a moment, listening again. The estate consisted of a single loop road which gave access to twelve or more warehouses and light-

industrial workshops. Most of the companies employed
security firms – or so their warning notices proclaimed –
but she had never seen guards or cruising vans, not even
when she left at midnight, which was often.

Closing the gate behind her, she crossed the apron to the
main door of the building. Above the door, illuminated by
an exterior light, was the sign: *Octek Ltd.* The name had
come from an off-the-shelf name dealer, the sort that
registers and stocks company names for customers who
want to set something up in a hurry. The name didn't say
very much about anything, which was one of the reasons
she had chosen it.

She unlocked the single mortise lock. The door was in
need of two more heavy locks, top and bottom, but in all
the rush she hadn't got round to arranging it. She had,
however, ordered key-operated locks for all the windows
and heat-sensitive floodlights for the perimeter which were
due to be fitted in the next week or so. Ideally of course,
the place should be manned by a rota of security guards,
but people cost a great deal, as she had spent most of the
last two months finding out.

Opening the door, the alarm shrilled a warning until she
punched the code into the key pad. Turning on some more
lights, she locked the door behind her. Ahead was a
passage, with three offices and a washroom off it, and at
the end, the laboratory area, entered by two sets of double
doors.

Until three months ago the building had been occupied
by a health supplement supplier, churning out vitamin and
mineral capsules on a number of short assembly lines. The
benches and fittings had not met Peasedale and Floyd's
specifications however, and everything had been ripped out
and replaced by gleaming smooth-edged work surfaces
topped by shelving and interspersed with power points,
piped water, stainless-steel sink units and specialized

refrigerators. She knew the specification of almost every item, and she certainly knew its cost.

In the light from the passage the rows of polished metal fittings glinted darkly, and there was a tang of newness in the air. The place, though quiet, looked businesslike and productive. She knew she should feel some sort of triumph in having got so far in such a short time, but the elation, such as it was, was overshadowed by the worry which had become a permanent feature of her existence. The project had taken on a life of its own, monstrous and unpredictable, like an ungrateful child over whom one has lost control. The only thing that she could absolutely rely on, day after day, was that the money would continue to flood out.

She went along to her office, which lay to the left of the main entrance. She worked on some costings and estimates – figures which looked no better than they had the night before – until seven thirty when, hearing a car, she looked out and saw Peasedale's raincoated figure emerge from a taxi. He glided in on his long legs, soundless as a bird, and settled into the visitor's chair. He peered myopically at his watch. 'Mustn't miss the eight thirty.'

She spread her hands expectantly. 'Well – how did it go?' He had spent the previous evening at Floyd's house, hammering things out.

He considered his answer, canting his head to one side to reveal his long bony neck. 'We reviewed the protocols, and the time allocations . . .'

'And?'

'I think we've broken the back of it.'

A door slammed and Floyd entered, a small stocky figure radiating vitality and goodwill. He had recently joined them as chief scientist. Peasedale had suggested him for the job because, though Floyd wasn't the most highly qualified toxicologist around, Peasedale believed quite rightly that he was the only person likely to take the job. Most scientific staff were on fixed-term contracts and unable to change jobs at such short notice. Also, as Peasedale pointed out, most toxicologists didn't want their CVs sullied by involvement in renegade research projects. Such considerations didn't seem to bother Floyd. Irish-born, outgoing to the point of extroversion, he lived for work, horse racing and conversation, though not necessarily in that order.

'I'm not late, am I?' he said cheerfully.

'We hadn't really started,' Peasedale commented. 'I was just saying that we'd sorted the figures.'

There was a pause. The two of them exchanged glances and Daisy was reminded of a double act, except that no one was feeding the lines.

It was Peasedale who finally said: 'There's a problem.'

She'd rather thought there might be.

'The problem is that we can't finish in the time,' said Floyd. 'It's the enzyme assays. Oh, they're going fine,' he added, waving a confident hand in the direction of the laboratories, 'but we're only scratching the surface. We had a think about it and we decided that, to get a good picture, we should be covering another twenty or so of the major enzymes. But the way things are at the moment it'd mean another two months on the schedule.'

'Maybe more,' said Peasedale.

'We can't extend the schedule,' Daisy said firmly. 'And certainly not by two months.'

'No, no,' Floyd murmured supportively.

'Isn't there a way round it?' she asked.

Peasedale made a pained face. 'Another two technicians.'

'Ouch,' she said.

'Push us over budget, will it?'

'That sort of thing.' She pressed the tips of her forefingers hard against two points over the bridge of her nose. It was a trick based on acupuncture that was meant to relieve stress, but either it didn't work or she always tried it too late. 'These enzymes, we have to have them, do we?'

The two men, tall and short, bony and chubby, serious and sunny, like a couple of comedians paired up for their dissimilarities, nodded in unison.

She sighed: 'I'll see what I can work out. If you're absolutely certain.'

They were certain. Experts were always certain when they were asking for money.

'Otherwise we're okay?'

'With the usual provisos,' Peasedale said.

Floyd gave a short discordant laugh. 'Like getting that permit.'

Six weeks before, they had applied for a Home Office Project Licence but, despite continuous follow-up, nothing had come through.

'There couldn't have been anything wrong with the application?'

She'd asked this before, and now Peasedale gave the answer he always gave. 'Nothing that they could object to.'

'Except perhaps the research itself.' She tried not to voice that particular worry too often. She glanced at Peasedale and saw from his face that the idea had already taken hold in his mind.

Floyd, never a one for pessimism, said brightly: 'We could always move the whole shebang abroad.'

Daisy gave a mock groan. 'The problem is, you may well be right. Perhaps we should have been somewhere else all along.' She dragged her hands down her face. 'Like China.'

'You're forgetting,' Floyd said, 'if all else fails we'll have the cell-line results.'

'But they don't count. You said they don't count.'

'They'll count with the public well enough, I think.'

'But not with the committee. Anyway, it's academic. We don't have any results yet.'

A sly smile spread over Floyd's face. 'But we have things of interest.'

She glanced across to Peasedale for confirmation but found him with his watch pressed up to his glasses. 'My train,' he said anxiously.

Daisy picked up her car keys. 'Let's go then.'

In the car, Peasedale was tense and uncommunicative until they were safely over the first roundabout and clearly in good time for the train.

Daisy asked: 'I suppose it's useless asking what Floyd was on about?'

'What? Oh, the cell-line tests. Best that he shows you himself.' They continued in silence for a while, then Peasedale asked tentatively: 'The budget – you sounded worried.'

Something made her decide to confide in him. Perhaps she'd been grappling with the problem too long, perhaps she was tired of having no one to talk to. 'Quite honestly, I don't know if it's all right,' she said, accelerating past a noisy lorry. 'The money man – I haven't seen him in three months. He's abroad somewhere. I haven't even been able to talk to him. The money's been coming through all right, but . . . Well, you know how it is. Everything's gone way over estimate and . . .' There was no easy way of saying it. 'There's going to be a shortfall.'

'How much?'

'Twenty per cent. Maybe more.'

'So when do we run out?'

'I'm not sure. Some time around March maybe.' She couldn't admit even to herself that it might be as soon as Christmas.

They came to a stop at the end of a slow moving queue. She saw Peasedale's knuckles whiten at the thought of missing his train. 'Still plenty of time,' she said reassuringly.

'You can contact your – er, man?' he asked cautiously. He knew as well as anyone Daisy rarely answered questions about the source of money.

'Not directly.'

The line of cars was moving again. Ahead, the lights turned red.

'What, no means of contact *at all*?'

She gave a wry laugh. 'Oh, I leave messages regularly. With his accountant, with his – well, with all sorts of people – but I can't put it all in a message. I mean, it wouldn't sound too good to say thanks for all the money, but I need some more already. Not just like that.'

Ahead, the lights turned green. 'So what happens next?' Peasedale asked.

She considered for a moment. For the first few weeks she'd felt sure Nick would make some contact – a phone call, a message, something. But the silence had been as long as it had been absolute. 'I'm not sure,' she said baldly.

They reached the lights at last and got through on the amber. The station came into sight. Peasedale had five minutes to spare. He looked drained. He clasped his overnight bag to his chest, ready for the off.

'So what happens when the money's gone?' he asked.

Daisy turned into the forecourt and drew up in a taxi bay. 'Then we're out of business and it'll all have been for nothing.' She gave a brittle laugh.

Peasedale got out and popped his head back through the open door like an anxious bird. 'You think it could come to that?'

She raised her shoulders. 'Who knows? Don't miss your train.' He craned his head up in alarm and, slamming the door, flew into the entrance, the wings of his raincoat flapping out behind him.

She drove back slowly, thoughtfully, reviewing the decision to set up Octek as an independent operation. It had been a choice between that and waiting for laboratory space in a university, which could have taken as much as six months, and which required the co-operation of academics with both the time and the fearlessness to put their other research funds in jeopardy. The time couldn't be spared, not enough people could be found. So here they were, cobbling the thing together, throwing in people, equipment and commitment, and hoping it would be enough.

And if the money ran out? She couldn't bring herself to think about that now.

In A-Lab, the larger of the two laboratories, Floyd was sitting on a high stool talking to one of the technicians. 'Come on, sunshine,' she said. 'Cheer me up.'

Floyd got to his feet with a grin. 'I'm going to show you some pretty pictures.'

He led the way into the ante-room of B-Lab – commonly dubbed the robing room – where they put on green overalls and washed their hands before passing into the lab proper. Floyd navigated between the benches, exchanged greetings with the two young technicians, and stopped in front of a counter covered with rows of circular glass plates. Picking one up, he passed it to her. 'Salmonella. One of the control plates.' His voice hummed with anticipation.

The agar culture had been scored with bacteria, some of which had mutated and divided to form small colonies, visible as sporadic white dots on the clear jelly.

'And here is the result with ten micrograms of chemical per litre.' Like a magician, Floyd whipped away the plate and gave her another. On this plate the white dots, though still well spread, were clearly more numerous.

'And . . .' He produced a third plate. '. . . fifty micrograms.' Here the colonies had proliferated to such an extent that the dots formed a distinct white ribbon across the surface of the plate.

'What does it mean?'

'It means we have a dose-response effect – that is, the greater the dose of chemical, the greater the mutative response. Of course, it would be nice to know which individual chemical or compound is doing the damage . . .'

'But this is promising?'

'Oh yes. Looking good. Or perhaps I should say bad.'

'But not bad enough for the ACP,' she murmured. Neither the advisory committee, nor any of the government control agencies, accepted cell-line tests as evidence of a product's cancer-producing properties.

Daisy sat back. 'It's a start though, isn't it?'

'Oh, it's that all right.'

She felt heartened, though that didn't stop her feeling renewed anxiety at the delay over the Home Office permit. Without that, they were all set up with nowhere to go.

Coming out of the robing room, she went diagonally across the passage to what was known as Room 4. Here she was met by Vera, the animal welfare assistant. Room 4 smelled of hay or some other sweet-smelling substance. It was brightly lit and warm. The cages were well-spaced, and within each cage the mice and rats had plenty of room and clean bedding. Vera was already well into her morning chores, changing bedding and water, measuring out and recording feed. Later she would observe and log the appearance of each rodent.

It was all done by the book, the animals couldn't have been better looked after if they were pets. Daisy wished that none of this was necessary, but so long as the international safety requirements remained unchanged, there was no escaping the fact that it was. As Peasedale put it: rodents or people; safe chemicals or no chemicals at all. Until there were several billion fewer people in the world then managing without chemicals was never going to be a serious option. Cheap food and safe drugs, or a ramshackle vegetarian utopia: she'd left such stark choices behind, somewhere in her student days. Now she recognized that there had to be an in-between, a place that wasn't impossibly bad, and wasn't impossibly good either, where, though a tiny number of rats had to die to satisfy society's chemical requirements, it was always going to be far, far fewer than the number of cattle and pigs that died each day to make hamburgers. And under Vera's care these rodents, at least, would be given the best in analgesics and anaesthetics, and generally receive far better treatment than veal calves or intensively farmed poultry, which people with a so-called conscience ate every day.

No, there was no real answer, and there never would be.

Anyway, the whole thing was academic without the permit, because without it, they were not permitted to start testing anything on the animals.

When she got to the front office, the phone was ringing. It was Jenny. Jenny always phoned before nine thirty because Alan was rarely in by that time and she could make the call in peace. It wasn't that Alan minded the odd call now that Daisy had officially resigned, it was the extent of the message and information service Jenny was providing that he objected to.

Jenny relayed the messages, which didn't amount to much, followed by a progress report on the anti-Silveron campaign. The Aurora story had got coverage on both sides of the Atlantic, but, as with all such stories, the interest had rapidly fizzled out. In the US, EarthForce were continuing to lobby hard for an EPA review. In the UK, a few reliable MPs had promised to keep up what pressure they could during the long parliamentary recess but, apart from a single bland ministry statement, the government were living up to their reputation on environmental matters by taking the least possible action over the longest possible time.

'What about the rumour of a licence review?'

'Haven't heard anything more,' said Jenny. 'D'you want me to ask around?'

'Yes.'

'Who shall I ask?'

'Try Simon.'

'Simon?' Jenny sounded surprised at being given the job, but managed a tactful: 'Oh – right.'

The rest of the news was domestic. Alan was in a dither over the bill from the security firm who'd screened the office for bugs.

'But he okayed the estimate,' Daisy said.

'Well, he's saying it's extortionate, considering.'

Considering they had found nothing, she guessed. Alan believed in value for money. 'I was sure they'd find something,' Daisy murmured.

'Not a bleep,' said Jenny.

'So are Alan and I not speaking again?'

'Oh, you are, of course you are. But you know how he is.'

Daisy knew how he was, nobly agreeing the cost of her return flight from New York, bravely shouldering all the work while she was gone, and with no more than a muttered reminder every day for two weeks. Despite that, or maybe because of it, she missed having him and Jenny around. It was like leaving school; you couldn't wait to taste freedom, but, once gone, you became nostalgic. Since coming here, she'd got to know all about the loneliness of command.

She'd gone back to Catch a couple of times, but had found the sight of her old desk, cleared of her familiar clobber, disturbing. She couldn't help noticing, moreover, that the clobber of the new girl was a lot more orderly. A pin-board had appeared on the wall where her save-the-whale poster had been, an event chart with a neat array of coloured pins had been fixed over the desk, and the shelf of reference books had a whole new logic to it. Alan had found a soul-mate at last.

'Oh, and the security people,' Jenny giggled before ringing off. 'They even checked the loo.'

'I should hope so too.'

She tried Nick Mackenzie's accountant at exactly ten to eleven. On one memorable morning some weeks before, at exactly that time, she had managed to catch him at his desk and not in a meeting or being unavailable. Today, however, he was in a meeting, and she was forced to leave the standard message with his secretary, saying where she could be contacted for the rest of the day.

At noon she drove to the other side of Chelmsford to see a company about some equipment Floyd wanted. Whenever possible, she went to see people on their own patch because then there were fewer questions to answer about Octek. She had become rather expert at evasions and half-truths. At first she had quite enjoyed the subterfuge; now it was a strain. One became increasingly aware of how easy it was to get caught out.

She got back to Octek at one thirty to find a message from Jenny. It was marked very urgent.

'Thank God,' Jenny breathed down the line when she got through. 'It's your flat, I'm afraid.'

Daisy's first thought was that it had been burgled.

'A big leak from the floor above. The water tank burst in the Greek boys' flat and' – Jenny paused to break it gently – 'they think it poured through your ceiling.'

Daisy swore loudly. She could already see this absorbing great chunks of time that she simply didn't have.

'The Greek boys got a plumber in to fix their water tank, so the leak's stopped, but no one's managed to get into your place yet so . . . What can I do? Do you want me to go and see what's happening?'

Daisy thought through the alternatives. 'No – I'd better go.'

'Shall I meet you there? Would that help?'

'Thanks, but I'll see what it's like first.'

'Are you sure?'

'I'm sure.'

'Oh,' she said hurriedly, 'that Scotsman phoned.'

'Campbell?'

'He wouldn't say what it was about, but he said it was urgent.'

'I'll try and call him now.'

'And there's a letter from Mrs Knowles – Alice. I'll forward it to you.'

'What does it say?'

'Well . . .' There was a hesitant note in Jenny's voice.

Daisy prepared herself. 'Go on,' she said.

'Well    it's about that cancer doctor, the one who promised to be a witness.'

She could guess what was coming. 'He's backed out?'

'Yes.'

It wasn't worth feeling angry. You could never blame these people. When it came to dealing with its own non-conformists, there was no body so ruthless as the medical profession. The man had probably got ridiculed or warned off or threatened with the loss of his job, or all three.

'Any more good news? Tell me while I'm still sitting down.'

'That's it.'

She hoped Campbell's news wasn't going to make it three in a row. She tried to call him but he wasn't in, which at that time of day was no great surprise. More surprising was that Mrs Bell wasn't in and, though the phone was often left next to Adrian when he was alone in the cottage, there was no reply from him either.

She meant to start for London within half an hour but it was three o'clock before she'd made the last phone call and finished priming Mabel, the office typist-cum-fixer, to hold the fort. On her way to the London road she called in at Elm Avenue to pick up some washing things and write another note for Mrs Biddows, saying that she might not be back that night.

As she headed down the A12 she tried to work out when she'd last managed to get to the flat. It had been almost

three weeks ago, she realized, for a short weekend. Another
two weeks before that, she'd managed less than a day. A
neighbour in the flat below forwarded her mail to Catch,
and Jenny had popped in now and again to see that the
place was all right.

It would be strange to see it again – but not so strange
as seeing it with the ceiling spread all over the floor.

She'd forgotten what a pig the journey could be. She got
caught behind a pile-up on the M25, then a jam at
Edmonton, and didn't reach Holloway until after five.

Ominously, there was a section of ripped-up vinyl
flooring lying beside the front door of the house.

She took a deep breath before opening the flat door.

It was bad, but like all these things it could have been
worse. The water had poured through the ceilings of all
three rooms, but had brought down the plaster in only one,
though, with a certain inevitability, it was the main room,
containing her few valued possessions. It was as if a small
bomb had been detonated close to the ceiling, leaving a
long gaping hole. Lining paper hung down from the bulging
plasterboard in tattered rags, with shards of plaster still
attached.

She spent half an hour removing the larger chunks of
plaster from the floor, hanging rugs up to dry, mopping up
the remaining patches of damp, turning the mattress on its
side. But, like the aftermath of a flood, it was not a situation
that could be restored in a couple of hours.

On an impulse, in need of some sympathy perhaps, she
dialled Simon. He sounded rather huffy, and she had the
feeling she should be apologizing for something. 'Sorry not
to have called,' she said, trying to remember when she'd
last spoken to him. A week ago? No, eight days. 'I've been
unbelievably busy,' she said.

He gave a non-committal grunt, and the atmosphere
settled heavily, like the plaster-dust.

'I've had a slight disaster,' she said, and explained about

the ceiling not being in its proper place. She added, half
seriously: 'Don't suppose you'd like to come over and help
clear up?'

'Is it right down, the ceiling?'

'No, not completely.'

'What – a half? More, less?'

'A third.'

'Is the rest sagging?'

She looked up. 'Cracked in places. Sagging in others.'

'They'll only take the rest down, you know, when they
come to repair it. They'll never be able to patch it up as it
is. It's not worth clearing the place up. I wouldn't bother if
I were you.'

'But my things – '

'Send them to the cleaners.'

She closed her eyes and took a slow breath.

'While you're on,' she said, opening her eyes, 'you
couldn't do me a favour, could you?'

'I'll try.' The cautious tone.

'Have you got a mole at the Home Office?'

'A mole? What sort of a mole?'

A journalist's answer if there ever was one. 'The normal
sort,' she said. 'Someone who can find something out.'

A pause, a tinge of resentment. Was he still miffed
because she hadn't told him what she was doing up in
Chelmsford? Had he, the champion of discretion, taken
exception to being on the receiving end of his own brand
of secrecy?

'What department?' he asked.

She told him.

'I might know someone. Near enough anyway,' he
conceded.

'It's a favour for a friend,' she said. 'He wants to know
why there's a delay in issuing a project licence to a company
called Octek Ltd.' She spelt out the name and gave him the
date and reference number of the application. 'He thinks

there's a problem they're not telling him about. He thinks someone might be blocking things.'

His ears pricked up at that. 'Oh? Well, if I'm to have any hope of getting that sort of information, I'll need to know why anyone would want to block it.'

'My friend didn't say.'

Simon sighed fretfully. 'Really, I don't think there's anything I can do with so little information.'

'There could be a story in it.'

'How do you know?' he accused sharply.

A trap, a Simon-trap. 'All right,' she conceded. 'There *is* a bit more to it than I've told you, but I can't say what it is. I'm sorry.'

'This wouldn't be anything to do with your new job by any chance?'

What was one more lie? She raised her eyes towards the remains of the ceiling. 'No.'

'Well . . .' He made dubious noises. 'I don't suppose my contact'll be much use anyway.'

'But he's worth a go?'

'I don't know till I try.'

'The story – if anyone's going to get it, it'll be you, you know. You're the only one who could do it properly.'

That mollified him a bit. He always responded to a bit of flattery. It was one of his more endearing features.

'Okay,' he said grudgingly. 'I'll do what I can.'

'Thanks.' Someone walked across the floor above Daisy's head and disturbed a sprinkling of plaster dust which floated down around her. 'Simon, I couldn't come over, could I?' she asked suddenly. 'I'm a bit homeless, at least for tonight.'

'Look, I'd love to see you, but I can't.' He trotted out a story about having to meet a Euro-MP for dinner then drive straight down to Bristol. She noticed that he didn't offer her the use of his flat, although she still had a key.

'Can't you stay at Jenny's?' he asked, putting some concern into his voice.

'Oh, I expect so.'

'Well, then . . .'

There was a silence, the sort that says almost everything. Mainly goodbye.

She said it. 'Goodbye, Simon.'

It was a moment before he replied, but when he did she could tell that he'd read and absorbed the message in her voice. 'Goodbye, Daisy,' he said.

'I'll drop your keys in some time.'

He didn't put up much of a fight about it. 'Thanks.'

She put the phone down and poured herself another glass of wine and sat in silence for a long while. She remembered Campbell and dialled his number. She was relieved when there was no reply. Half the wine had disappeared before she found the energy to bundle her clothes into plastic sacks, pile up the soggy linen, and scoop the saturated sugar, flour and rice bags from the top of the kitchen units into the rubbish.

One of the few cupboards that was both dry and relatively free from dust was the one in the bathroom above the hot-water tank. Standing on the bath, unable to see into the recesses of the cupboard, she restacked the contents she could reach – the ones at the front mainly – and loaded in her clothes that were still dry and undamaged.

After that, there didn't seem much point in staying. She locked up the flat, lugged the plastic sacks of clothes and linen down to the car, and left a set of keys with the downstairs neighbours, along with a note, asking them to let the repair men in. It was already growing dark. She could go and grab a bath and a bed off Jenny, or she could fight her way across London to her mother's, or she could head straight back to Mrs Biddows'.

There was no debate really and, starting the faithful Metro, she headed north-east, back to Chelmsford.

\*

Removing the earpiece, Hillyard switched off the recorder and pulled out unhurriedly. He remained some distance behind until he reached an arterial road, where the traffic thickened and he was forced to close up. A few miles up the A10, he had an annoying few moments trapped behind some red lights, and thought he would have to rely on the pinger, but he managed to catch sight of her distinctive unmatched rear lights just in time to follow her onto the M25, heading east. After that it was easy. He kept two cars behind her all the way to the turn-off for the A12. Then it was a nice gentle run along the dual carriageway towards Chelmsford with the sound of the direction-finder pinging softly on the seat behind him.

He had just prepared himself for a drive into the depths of East Anglia when she left the Chelmsford bypass at the first roundabout and headed towards the town centre. They came to a straggling suburban high street lined with small shops and pubs. She indicated left, slowed and drew up in front of a Chinese take-away. He went past and, looking in his mirror, saw her get out of the car and enter the shop without looking to left or right.

He parked and waited. Beside him, Beji woke and pulled herself up to peer out of the window. She gave a tentative sniff, then another. He reached across and ruffled her head playfully.

The girl emerged from the take-away with her boxed dinner, got into the car again and drove straight off. Again, she didn't hesitate, didn't look about her. She hadn't used the journey to think too much then, hadn't linked the little water-tank disaster with anything more significant. Hadn't realized she'd been had. Not quite as smart as she thought she was. This idea offered him some consolation for the two months that she had managed to evade him.

As he followed, it occurred to him that she knew her way around this town. There was no hesitation in her driving, no pausing at junctions or craning to look at road signs. She was cutting skilfully across the suburbs with the confidence of someone who had used the route many times. After five minutes they came into a semi-industrial area where there was far less traffic. He dropped back a little and turned up the pinger. Suddenly, with hardly any warning and only the briefest flick of her indicator, she turned left into a slip road.

He slowed as he approached the turning, and took a quick look down it. The road looked more like an access road than a public thoroughfare. Making up his mind, he accelerated past, took another sideways glance, and realized he had made the right decision. It was a private road leading to some sort of industrial estate, and undoubtedly a no-through road. A little further on he turned around and made his way slowly back.

Just short of the entrance he drew into the kerb and twiddled with the dials on the direction-finder. The volume and direction of the pings were constant. He allowed himself a moment of satisfaction.

He gave it a full two minutes before turning into the estate and driving purposefully along, not too fast, not too slow. After a short distance the road forked. He continued along what seemed to be the most likely turning. Fifty yards on, he noticed a light flickering on in a building which lay ahead to the right. Simultaneously he spotted the Metro parked outside the perimeter fence. He drove steadily on, taking a careful look at the building as he passed. Lights were showing behind closed venetian blinds in a front room and in the entrance hall. Above the entrance was a sign: Octek Ltd. That, he remembered, was the name she'd mentioned on the phone, the company she'd asked her boyfriend to look into, though Hillyard would play back the recording later to make sure.

The road formed a loop, coming back on itself at the fork just before the main road. He drove out of the estate and turned right in the direction of the town centre. Plenty

of time now. Time for a beer and a sandwich, a walk for
Beji, and a call to Beryl. She would be pleased, she would
chortle lunacies down the phone at him, she would call him
a clever boy. And, he thought to himself, she would be
absolutely right.


Too much sweet, too little sour, and some dubious ball-
shaped protein that was, presumably, the promised prawns.
Nourishment of a sort. Daisy folded some rice into the
glutinous mixture and with her free hand leafed through
the pile of papers that had found their way onto her desk.

Turning over an invoice, she found a message in Mabel's
upright schoolmarmish script. A Mr Hotstart had telephoned. There was an office number and a home number.
Hotstart? She must mean Hopkirk. *Hopkirk*, she said
aloud, as if Mabel were in earshot. Hopkirk was Nick
Mackenzie's accountant.

A home number – he'd never left a home number before.
What did it mean? News? Bad news?

She dialled the number. It rang without reply. It was
nine thirty. Out to dinner perhaps. What time would he get
back – eleven? Twelve? Well, she would keep trying. There
was plenty of work to fill the time.

But her mind kept sliding back to what the accountant
might want, to what he might say. That the last instalment
couldn't be paid next month as she'd requested? Or, even
worse, that there would be no last instalment at all?

Finally, at ten forty-five, Hopkirk answered.

Mr Mackenzie was back, he said casually. If she wanted
to see him, he was free at ten on Saturday morning. Would
that be convenient? He gave her an address in West London
– Mr Mackenzie's new house, he said – and a telephone
number.

He rang off and she leaned weakly back in her chair.
Did she want to see him? *Did she!* God, she would have

trekked to Scotland, flown to America . . . What a question! The relief was warm and sweet. In her mind she was already going through her story with him, already explaining how the budget had managed to blossom, how the project needed this last injection of cash. He might be reluctant to listen, of course, he might be even more reluctant to provide the money, but he'd do it, she felt sure he would. At heart, he was all right. It was just a matter of *getting* to his heart, reaching him one more time. She checked herself, ashamed at such a manipulative thought. It was, she realized, a measure of her desperation.

Somewhere there was a sound. She listened but it didn't come again. She tried to place it. Muffled, from somewhere deep in the building, it had sounded like something falling or banging. A door perhaps.

She went down the passage and, unlocking the door to the labs, passed through and listened again. There was silence. She made her way down to the passage, into B-Lab's robing room and put her head round the door of the lab itself. It was quiet and dark. The windows were closed, the ventilation system whirring softly. Turning back, she looked into each of the store rooms in turn before coming to A-Lab. She switched on the lights and blinked for a moment. Then she saw a high narrow window which had been left open. Finding the pole, she inserted the hook into the ring on the frame and slammed the window shut.

She looked around to see if anything had been knocked over by the wind but nothing had been disturbed. It was very quiet. It didn't sound as though there was any wind at all. The sound must have come from somewhere else altogether, another building perhaps.

She left, double-checking each door before setting the alarm. Barring accidents, she should be asleep by eleven thirty.

She locked the gates, started the Metro, did her customary U-turn and accelerated towards the main road.

*If you want to see him.* What a question.

It was only when she drew up outside Mrs Biddows',
where the dial of the telephone was firmly locked against
improvident guests, that she remembered that she had
forgotten to call Campbell. Wearily she turned the
car around and headed back towards the lab. A half-
remembered phone box came into sight in a street radiating
from the first roundabout. She took the unfamiliar road
and, approaching the box, saw the green sign of a card-
operated phone. She stopped and, delving into her purse,
found three phone-cards, none of which had more than
two or three units on it.

If Campbell had a lot to say, she could always reverse
the charges, or even go back to the lab and call again from
there.

Campbell's number didn't answer. She left it ringing for
a long time in case he was sleeping heavily, but there was
still no reply. Then, despite the time, she tried Mrs Bell.

She answered straight away. 'Ahh,' she said flatly. 'I
thought it would be you. They're holdin' him for the night.
There's a hearin' in the morning.'

'What? *Who?*'

'Campbell. I thought you knew,' she said without surprise. 'There was trouble.'

'What sort of trouble?'

'With the therapist woman.'

'What therapist?'

'A psychotherapist, she called herself. Sent by the social
services. She came twice in a week, all the way from
Glasgow. Said she'd be comin' regularly. Campbell heard
what she was sayin' to Adrian. He didna' like what he
heard.'

'And?'

'There was an incident.'

'What sort of incident?'

'Well . . . They're sayin' it was assault.'

Daisy sighed aloud. Wonderful, Campbell, bloody wonderful.

The call meter started flashing a nil-units warning. Daisy said hastily: 'Listen, I'll be up. I'll try to get up as soon as I can – '

The line went dead.

Daisy leaned against the side of the box while she worked out what time she would get to Scotland if she grabbed a few hours' sleep and started at four.

Placing the car was half the art. Too far away and you could say goodbye to any hope of a quick bunk, too near and it was like hanging up a sign to say that you were in there, uninvited. There was another alternative, of course, and that was to look like you owned the place. Hillyard used a spike to spring the padlock, then swung open one of the gates and reversed the car close into the side of the building and, returning to the gate, latched it loosely shut behind him.

He marched purposefully up the side of the building until he was in the shadows, then went slowly about his business. He never hurried a recce, especially one like this. In fact, it was possible he might not go in tonight at all. It all depended on the alarm system, if there was one.

There was one. Shining a pencil beam through one of the windows, he sighted a magnetic contact attached to a window frame opposite. After that it was a question of cataloguing the type and location of each security device. It wasn't difficult. The windows around the rear of the building were numerous and large, revealing two laboratories full of equipment but not, as far as he could see, a great deal of security. There was no sign of heat sensors, nor of floor beams. The system appeared to be a fairly primitive

mix of magnetic contacts and vibration sensors, though it
never paid to make up one's mind about these things too
soon.

It took him half an hour to decide that his first assessment had been right, and the system was as basic as he had
first thought. It took him another twenty minutes to decide
on the best way in. The front of the building was out: too
well lit. On the open side where he had left the car there
was a side door, but it was solid and well bolted, and all
the windows were covered by vibration sensors. On the
other side however, reached by a narrow strip between
the building and the one next door, there was a frosted
metal-frame window which looked as though it belonged
to a washroom of some sort. As far as he could tell by
peering through the distortions of the glass, the opening
half of the frame, a conventional vertically hinged window,
had only a single magnetic contact. More to the point, the
other, fixed, window had a revolving draught-operated
vent cut into the glass.

From his tote-bag he selected some tools and, taking his
time, began to work on the vent. In the end he had to cut
around the fitting and lift the thing out wholesale. This was
not ideal – the refixing would require clips and putty and a
lot of fiddling about – but it was safer than trying to drill
out the fixings from the wrong side.

Padding the sharp edges of the cut glass circle with his
jacket, he reached through up to his shoulder until his fingers
touched the latch of the other window. It moved under his
fingers: it was not locked. He then checked the alarm fitting
to make certain that it was indeed magnetic.

From his bag he took a magnetic contact and, passing it
through the hole, stuck the magnet to its brothers on the
frame, ensuring that a circuit would be maintained when
he opened the window. Then, dropping his hand down to
the latch, he levered it upwards.

He pushed open the window. The alarm did not go off.

Climbing through, he came out of the washroom and into the passage and made his way softly towards the front entrance, looking for floor beams or heat sensors. Finding none, he looked into the rooms to right and left – offices, a stationery and equipment store – until he came to the office at the front of the building, the place where he had seen the light flicker on. This looked like the centre of operations: a large desk, a smaller one, two phones, filing cabinets.

He doubled back and went down to the other end of the corridor, to a pair of swing doors, just to check he hadn't missed anything. The doors were locked. He thought of trying to pick them, but it might not be possible and, since they undoubtedly led to the laboratories he had seen through the windows, it was unlikely to be worth the effort.

He returned to the front hall. Tracing the lightweight cable from the alarm touch pad inside the main doors, he found the alarm control box tucked inside a utility cupboard in a corner of the main office. It was a standard if outmoded model. He made a note of the model type, and the number of circuits.

Then he settled down to his main work of the night. Closing the venetian blinds, he draped his jacket over a desk lamp and risked turning on the light. Reading through the files, it took him half an hour to get the picture. Even then, he went back over some of the material a second time, just to be sure. Well, well. Cunning bitch.

He began to photograph everything systematically: correspondence, names of staff and advisors, scientific protocols, weekly progress reports, lists of so-called victims, accounts, bank statements. Everything was here. But just as he allowed himself a small chortle of triumph he realized there was after all something missing. The money: or rather, its source. This wasn't the sort of operation which the shoestring Catch budget could finance, not when the money was arriving in dirty great lumps, a quarter of a million at a time. Oh no, Miss Field had got herself a benefactor from somewhere, a nice little money machine. A rich lover perhaps; a sugar daddy.

In his mind he sifted through what he'd already read and photographed, but he knew the information wasn't there. By three, after a last search through the files, he had to admit defeat. But only temporarily. There were ways, and stuff the low-risk policy.

He hovered for a moment over the choice of items in the specially cushioned box in his tote-bag, and finally went for a small crystal handset transmitter. Better range than the wall-socket variety, and that was the main consideration when he wasn't sure how closely he'd be able to monitor it.

Opening up the telephone handset, he clamped the transmitter's tiny alligator clips to the connections, and stuck it to the inside of the plastic casing using double-sided tape. Neat as pie.

Closing the handset again, he tested the transmitter, then tidied up carefully, ready to leave.

He got as far as the door, then turned back as a memory struck him, something he'd seen in one of the files. It was a moment before he recalled the file's pedantic title: Home Office Project Licence Application. He didn't pretend to understand it all, much of it was in scientific-speak, but the relevant parts shone through all right, and a wonderful idea began to simmer and glow in his mind.

# Chapter 26

———

'YOU LOOK FINE, *fine*.' David's smile was the sort fathers use on adolescent children, fond but hesitant, in vague fear of rebuff. 'The rest's done you good.'

'It also drove me crazy,' said Nick mildly, and raised an eyebrow to show he almost meant it.

The waiter arrived with the drinks, a lager for David and a Badoit for Nick.

The restaurant was filling up. It was a nouveau-Italian place in Covent Garden, a cellar done out in neutral pastels with all the plumbing showing. Now and again someone looked Nick's way then just as quickly looked away again.

'She's late,' Nick remarked.

'The traffic. A state visit or something. Do you want to order?'

'No.'

David gave him that soft nervous smile again. He was unusually deferential, Nick noticed, almost as if Nick were some new client who might prove unpredictable.

'You've seen Mel and Joe?' David ventured.

'Yesterday.' Then, because it was what David wanted to hear, he added: 'I gave them a couple of songs to look at.'

David, terrified of overreacting, hid his pleasure behind a frozen smile. 'Stuff you might – er – put in the album?'

'Too early to say.'

David went into immediate retreat. 'Of course. Too early to say.'

'Might not be suitable, that's all.'

'Whatever you say, Nick. Whatever you say.'

Nick's irritation rose. All this eager agreement, all this backing away from the slightest risk of confrontation was getting on his nerves. David was sounding like a yes-man. Somehow, somewhere they'd lost touch with each other. Perhaps it had begun a long time ago and neither of them had noticed, perhaps it had happened during the brief American tour. Perhaps David wasn't even aware of it. Either way, it was a lonely thought.

David rolled his eyes towards the door. 'Here's our lady now.'

Nick glanced round. Some women enter restaurants, others make entrances. Susan Driscoll was not entering unobtrusively.

As she strode towards him and reached out to take his hand he tried to work out how she'd changed since he'd last seen her. It was her hair, he thought, though whether it was the colour or the style he had no idea. Grasping his hand, she kissed him warmly on the cheek as if they were old friends. He wondered if she was remembering their last meeting in David's office almost a year ago. From the breadth of her smile, he guessed not.

'Well!' she cried. 'How lovely it is to see you.' She leaned her chin on her hands to get a closer look at him. The movement caused her heavy golden hair to swing forward from her shoulder so that you couldn't help noticing it. He wondered if she practised the gesture. 'You look so well,' she said. 'Have you been away?'

'I've been drying out.'

Her smile didn't falter. 'Where did you go – Clouds? My friends tell me it's the best.'

'A place in Arizona.'

'Mmm. Sounds lovely. And do you do all that follow-up? AA meetings and all that. They say it's the most fantastic brotherhood. Better than a club.'

'I keep in touch.'

'Well,' she breathed, withdrawing gently from the subject. 'That's wonderful. You look wonderful.' And, giving a soft laugh, she reached out and brushed her fingers lightly against his arm in a gesture that was curiously intimate. His instinct was to pull up his drawbridge and retreat fast, yet there was something so direct in her manner, so well meaning, that he decided to reserve judgement, for the time being at least.

David launched the subject of the restored charity concert.

'It sold out in three days,' Susan said, throwing up her elegant hands in delight. 'Even at the extortionate prices we're charging. And the advertising's gone well. We should clear over a hundred thousand.' She turned her eyes to Nick's. He noticed their colour, a clear grey-green, and a distant memory came to him, of a morning when they had woken up together, long ago. But his recollection of his feelings at the time was strangely clouded, and no clear emotion came through. He knew that he hadn't loved her – though he had liked her well enough for a while – but there had been something disturbing in their relationship, something that had resulted in difficulties and unpleasantness, particularly towards the end, though he couldn't remember exactly what the problem had been. His memory, never brilliant, had faded dramatically during the drinking years.

'It's so inadequate to thank you, but I will anyway,' Susan said in her light dancing voice. 'It's such a nightmare this fund-raising,' she sighed. 'Such a hassle thinking of brilliant ideas only to find they've all been done before. But to get you *and* Amazon – well . . .' She gave an expressive little shrug.

'Glad to help,' he murmured.

She fixed him with those eyes again. 'I know it's probably a great bore for you.'

The first course arrived. 'It's just another concert.'

'Of course, but . . .' She paused, tucking her chin down and casting him a long upward look. 'Can I come straight out and ask you something?' She gave a sudden laugh that was self-deprecating and charming all at the same time. 'Then I can get it over and done with, and I won't have to spend the rest of the meal in misery, working out how on earth I'm going to find a way of asking you.'

It was bound to be something he didn't want to do, but at least she was asking. Some charity organizers just sprang things on you at the last minute, on the principle that once the event was under way it was almost impossible for you to make a scene. 'Ask away,' he said.

'It's our main donors – you wouldn't shake their hands at the party afterwards, would you? You know, say a couple of words to one or two of them. It wouldn't take long – fifteen minutes at the most, then you could slip away – through a back entrance or something. It's just so they can go away saying they met you. It makes such a difference.'

David tore himself away from his pasta. 'Can't be done in fifteen minutes. More like thirty. And Nick'll be very tired.'

'They're business people, are they?' Nick asked.

She wrinkled her nose. 'Corporate moguls, I'm afraid. *Seriously* boring. But what can you do? Some of them are very generous.'

'We know the sort,' David said drily, raising his eyebrows at Nick.

Nick smiled. 'They say they can't stand pop music. They say they only came because their kids made them, then admit they quite liked the show. They say it took them back to their youth.'

She laughed again, but her eyes remained on his, watching for his answer.

He made up his mind, though he knew he'd probably regret it. 'I'll come for half an hour,' he said.

David shot him a well-don't-blame-me look. Susan bowed her head and said simply: 'Thank you.' Her voice, soft and low, had a slight tremble to it, and she closed her eyes for an instant, as though saying a little prayer of thanks.

Before today, warmth was not a word he'd have associated with Susan Driscoll – brittle would have been nearer the mark – but he was rapidly opening his mind to the possibility that he had misjudged her.

Putting her salad aside, she began to talk about the old days which she seemed to remember with some fondness. But it didn't take her long to sense his lack of interest. 'So tell me,' she said, shifting onto safer ground, 'where are you based nowadays?'

'Kensington. I've just bought a house.'

'Oh? You've given up the country life then?'

'Kensington's quite leafy.'

She gave a soft laugh. 'But not many cows.'

'Not that I've noticed.'

'But then London has its compensations, doesn't it?' she ploughed on. 'Theatre and concerts and things. I adore London, but it might as well be Siberia for all I get to see of it nowadays.'

There was a small silence.

'Don't you get entertained a lot?' he managed.

'Oh, official entertaining, yes – dreary receptions, the occasional opera if one's lucky. But theatre, dinner parties with friends ...' She shook her head and a slight frown furrowed the smooth line of her forehead. 'I thought I was in for a quiet life but, well – ' She seemed to become aware of David who, having finished his pasta, was half listening to the conversation. She broke off with a brave little laugh. 'Let's just say things don't always work out the way you expect them to.'

What's this? Nick wondered. Are you trying to tell me that under all this brightness you're unhappy? Since

Alusha's death even the most casual of his friends had unburdened their troubles on him as if, having marked him as a fellow sufferer, they felt confident of a sympathetic response. Was the whole world suddenly unhappy, he wondered, or in his years with Alusha had he simply been too wrapped up in his own life to notice?

Aware that the conversation had faltered, he murmured: 'The Ministry of Agriculture, isn't it? Lots of farmers, I suppose.'

She rolled her eyes heavenward. 'Worse.' Her voice was heavy with ridicule. 'Factory openings. Beef federations. Milk marketing boards. Agrochemical giants.' Her mouth twitched with amusement, on the point, he guessed, of doing a sharp demolition job on the agrochemical industry, until the amusement drained out of her face, as if she had remembered something serious. He had a feeling he knew what that something was.

'Your wife— Did they ever find out . . . ?' she began cautiously. 'It was a chemical, wasn't it?'

David emerged from a mouthful of veal in cream sauce, looked nervously at Nick and took refuge in a hasty wave at the wine waiter.

'Well, no one's exactly sure,' Nick answered quietly.

'But . . . there was a suggestion, wasn't there?'

'It doesn't really matter now.'

'No . . .' she said uncertainly. 'I suppose not.'

No one spoke for a moment. The restaurant seemed very noisy.

'But you know, if you'd wanted any help . . . access to information . . .' She paused, her fingers lacing an intricate pattern under her chin, her eyes steady and clear. 'I'd have done all I could. Anything . . .' The word hung in the air.

'Thanks,' he answered simply. He caught David looking impressed at the calmness of his response.

Susan eased the conversation effortlessly away onto

food, recounting some disaster she'd had with an unknown fish in a foreign restaurant. She was good at smoothing things over, Nick noticed, something she'd probably learned in her years as a politician's wife. As he listened he realized she never mentioned her husband, either directly or indirectly. Was this intentional, he wondered, or a reflection of the discontent she'd already hinted at?

She told her tale entertainingly, with wide graceful gestures and frequent explosive laughter. His mood lifted. Against all the odds, he was enjoying himself, which just went to prove that you could never tell what might come out of even the most unpromising situation.

Yet was it really so unexpected? In the last year he'd been so careful to avoid new people and unfamiliar situations, so in dread of the effort they demanded, that he'd forgotten how refreshing a new face could be. Old friends, fond as they were, couldn't help humping the luggage of the past around with them. Susan represented the best of both worlds, he realized, an old friend with the virtues of the new.

There was something else about her too, an energy, an obvious and unquestioning appetite for life that in his present mood was rather beguiling. She was like a sun, sending out light and vitality in every direction. Her brilliance was a little remorseless perhaps, but with no dark shadows attached.

Catching his eye, she accused: 'You're laughing at me.'

'Not at all.'

'Well, I wouldn't be surprised,' she declared, looking rather pleased at the idea. He noticed her skin which was the colour of pale honey as if she'd been abroad a lot but had taken care to keep out of the sun.

David called for the bill.

'Already? And we've hardly talked about the concert!' Susan gasped in mock horror. 'Aren't there lots of things we should discuss?' she asked, striking a serious pose.

'Things you'll need on the day? Or anything you *don't* need? Mr Weinberg and I' – she indicated David with a slight movement of a long finger – 'we've covered security and transport. But what about home comforts – champagne, food, that sort of thing? I've looked backstage – it's a bit of a tip, but I can do something with the dressing rooms, jolly them up, you know.'

'It's really not necessary.'

'But it's no trouble. It's my living, after all.'

It was a cue. He took it. 'Oh?'

'I'm an interior designer.' She gave a jaunty little bow. 'Newly established but trying hard. All reasonable commissions considered' – she lowered her voice confidentially – 'which means I'll take on anything to get established.'

'You find the time?'

'Oh, I find it.' There was a note of determination in her voice. 'It'll be easier when I get a few big commissions, of course. Less rushing about. And I'll have our new place to practise on. We're moving closer to the Commons.'

She paused, then, with a spark of calculation she could only have intended him to see, her eyes brimming with amusement she asked: 'I don't suppose your new house needs doing up, does it?'

He played along. 'I hadn't noticed.'

'Let me show you some ideas,' she said instantly, her face alight. 'And if you hate them – well . . .' She raised her shoulders to suggest this was unlikely. 'If you like them – then we can take it from there.' She spread her hands like a showman.

Out of the corner of his eye Nick caught David giving him a stare which, if he'd chosen to look, was probably loaded with caution. Maybe in reaction to that, maybe because he'd taken a sudden liking to the idea of change, maybe because Susan had made him laugh, he heard himself agree.

She gave a small exclamation of pleasure. 'I'll need just

two things to get started,' she declared breathlessly. 'One's your address, of course.'

He put his hand out to David for a pen. 'And?'

'Some idea of the style you're looking for. Traditional, minimalist, neutral . . . you know.'

An image of Ashard flittered into his mind, the cavernous drawing room, muted and cool, the cosy library with its crackling fire and wood shelves, the bedroom overlooking the park, heavy with silks and soft brocades. 'I don't know,' he said.

She brushed the idea aside with a light twist of her wrist as if it had hardly been worth considering in the first place. 'Fine,' she said, 'absolutely *fine*. We can do it from another angle altogether. Just wander round the house, and you tell me what you *don't* like about the present decor. That'll tell me almost everything I need to know.' She broke off. 'How does that sound? Am I rushing things? Do you want to think it over?' She widened her eyes, giving him a look of apprehension that wasn't entirely convincing.

'No, that's fine.'

She grinned at him and, pulling a pocket diary out of her bag, opened it at a back page and pushed it towards him. He wrote down his address and phone number.

'Now tell me,' she said, 'when would you like me to come round?'

He shrugged.

She laughed, shaking her head as if he was a child whose little foibles were to be indulged as well as enjoyed. 'Well, what about tomorrow? Teatime? I love tea. I'll bring sticky buns.'

He didn't like sticky buns. He didn't like tea much either. He heard himself say: 'That'd be great.'


When he'd finished shaving, Schenker scrubbed a brisk flannel over his upper body, patted himself dry, applied

fresh deodorant and put on a clean shirt laundered by
Jeeves of Belgravia. He had a sudden doubt about the shirt.
Blue medium-width stripe on white – too City-ish? And the
style, with its deep collar – too Stock Exchange? Too
assertive? Maybe. But did it matter? The days when he
stood in fear and trembling of the group board were over.
Half of them had come up the hard way, like him, and
were unlikely to begrudge him a touch of style, while the
others, Establishment to the core, wore shirts with stripes
visible at fifty yards. Anyway, with what he had to tell
them today, they wouldn't be looking at his shirt.

Passing out of his private bathroom into his office, he
found his secretary standing expectantly by his desk.

'Hope it goes well,' she said.

'Thank you. It will.'

She slid soundlessly away and, sitting at his desk,
Schenker went over his notes for perhaps the tenth time.
The message would be best delivered briefly and low-key,
underplayed to the point of understatement. He would
merely say that, as of ten o'clock that morning, the Ministry
of Agriculture, Fisheries and Food had decided to grant
Silveron a licence for general use in the United Kingdom.

The board would show their delight. Then, after a decent
interval, they would express a wish for the situation in the
US to be resolved as satisfactorily, which would be their
way of asking how things were going over there. He would
assure them it was progressing, if slowly. He would remind
them that the number of new products being granted
licences in the US had dropped dramatically in recent years,
that product-development times had never been longer,
that, product for product, Morton-Kreiger was getting
more new lines onto the market than any of their
competitors.

No one would could argue with that. No one could say
he wasn't on top of the job.

Someone would ask about the Aurora scare, but he

would be able to reassure them on that too. All blown over, all illnesses accounted for, no new cases. Merely a storm blown up by the environmental activists.

Twenty minutes to go. In his anxiety to prepare himself properly, he had left too much time. He buzzed for Cramm.

Cramm was even quieter on his feet than Schenker's secretary, and it was a second before Schenker realized he had entered the room.

He waved him to a chair. 'I think I'll probably go to New York for the weekend,' he announced. 'Take tomorrow's Concorde. See friends on Long Island.' This wasn't quite true. The friends he was going to see – the senior vice president of a giant cola company and his wife – actually lived in Connecticut and weren't so much friends as new acquaintances. But Schenker, who'd been watching with growing interest some of the recent and highly dramatic cross-industry career moves of his contemporaries, wasn't about to tell anyone this, particularly Cramm.

'We'll meet in Chicago on Monday,' he said. 'So – is there anything before then?'

Unusually for him, Cramm didn't answer immediately.

Schenker gestured impatiently. 'Well?'

'It can wait,' Cramm said, but his eyes told a different story. They told Schenker it was something he wasn't going to like.

'I'll hear it now,' he said.

Cramm stared at him impassively. 'Perhaps we'd better speak outside.'

Schenker made a sound of irritation, already resenting the intrusion into his triumphal day. 'Is this really necessary?' But without waiting for an answer, he jumped to his feet and led the way through the adjoining conference room and out onto the terrace.

'Well?' he said tartly when Cramm had circled round to face him.

'Catch, they're setting up an operation – a whole lab – to run independent tests on Silveron.'

Schenker glared at him while he made up his mind how to react to this. 'So?' he said finally. 'They're going to spend a lot of money for nothing, aren't they? Might be a useful experience for them.'

'So you don't want us to do anything?'

'I don't know – keep an eye on it. Do what you think.' He waved a dismissive hand. 'Whatever. Is that all?' he added impatiently.

'It's the Kershaw woman. She's causing a bit of trouble.'

Schenker took a sharp breath of anger. He didn't want to hear about this, not now, not ever. 'What do you mean – *trouble*?'

'She wants more money.'

'What the hell *for*?'

'Distress and suffering.'

'*Distress and suffering*? She has to be joking.'

'Oh no, she's deadly serious.'

'But she's already been dealt with!' He glared into Cramm's impervious features. 'Hasn't she?'

'To the tune of fifteen thousand.'

'Jees-us,' Schenker hissed. He added: 'Remind me – where did that come from?'

'The Iraqi development budget.'

Schenker blinked. How Cramm managed these things he was never quite sure. 'So what's she after now, for God's sake?'

'Another ten.'

Schenker snorted with contempt. 'Offer her one thousand and if she's not interested tell her to go and jump.'

'What, call her bluff?'

'Why not?'

'She might spill it to the newspapers.'

'So? What's the bottom line? There's no link to us, is

there? She has no idea who contributed the funds, does she?'

'No. Oh no, none at all. But Driscoll?'

Schenker fixed Cramm with a telling gaze, and spread his hands in an expressive gesture of helplessness. Cramm read the message and for an instant looked slightly shocked.

Schenker glanced hastily at his watch and made for the door. Cramm got to it first and slid it open.

Schenker paused half-way through. 'No, we've done all we can for Driscoll. If the girl talks, he's on his own.'

Only eight minutes to go. On his way back to his bathroom to recomb his hair, Schenker buzzed through to his secretary to make sure she'd got the Concorde booking. His urge to renew his acquaintance with the cola magnate was growing by the moment.


Daisy followed Campbell out of the solicitor's office, and they stood for a moment looking down on Oban.

Campbell took a dark backward glance at the solid façade of the office, as if to check that he was really free of the law, albeit temporarily, then set off down the street at a brisk pace. Daisy ran to catch up as Campbell led the way down towards the harbour and into a solid hotel on the waterfront.

The lounge bar was gloomy but clean and uncrowded. Daisy ordered toast, marmalade and strong coffee.

'Well?' she asked when they were alone. 'Care to tell me about it?'

Campbell gave a solid grunt and for a while she thought he wasn't going to answer. Finally he declared: 'Wrong. *Wrong.*'

'Are you saying you didn't do it?'

He shot her an angry look.

'Assault's a serious charge,' she pointed out. 'You could

get a custodial sentence, you know. You were lucky to get bail.'

'I only tapped her.'

'Blimey, Campbell, a *woman*. Despite everything they're still meant to be *different*, you know. And a health professional! That makes her untouchable, Campbell, as close to sainthood as you can get without running for pope. *And* on official business . . .' She sighed: 'I won't go on.'

He was silent.

The waitress brought the coffee and toast.

She pushed him: 'Well?'

He looked angry again, then his expression relaxed into something more neutral and he gathered himself to speak. 'She struck him,' he said very slowly, to give it emphasis, 'she struck Adrian.'

Daisy settled slowly back in her chair and clasped her hands around her cup as if for warmth. 'From the beginning. Please.'

His mouth contorted with the exertion of memory. 'They said they were sendin' somebody – '

'They?'

'The social services. They said they were sendin' someone to look at Adrian,' he began hesitantly. 'They didna' say it was a – psycho*therapist*. No mention of that, och no.' He gave a caustic snort. 'We thought mebbe it was going to be some expert. Aye, we thought mebbe that they had found someone who could help. We were taken aback when this woman appeared. Och, not because she was a woman,' he added quickly, casting a defensive eye in Daisy's direction, 'but because of her manner. Very grand, she was, very cool. We were nothin' to her, she left us in no doubt o' that – hardly merited a civil word. She wouldna' answer questions, och no. Too high for that, she was. She requested we leave the room – she wanted to see Adrian alone, she said. There was no mention of bein' a psycho*therapist*, nothin' about what she'd come for. Not a shaft of politeness or consideration. Kept repeatin' she wanted to see Adrian alone.' For someone who normally kept things short, Campbell was doing well, stringing his sentences together with only the slightest pauses, though the effort had brought his brows low over his eyes. 'I should have had a notion, of course. I should have seen . . .' He gave a harsh sigh and, draining his coffee, looked towards the bar with transparent longing.

'Go on.'

He dragged his gaze back to her. 'Aye, well, we left her with Adrian for the time she wanted. Mebbe forty-five minutes – which was all too long for the lad, as you know. He can no' manage the talkin', not for that time. Och, lookin' back' – he took a great hissing suck of breath – 'like lambs, we were. Doin' her biddin'. Waitin' for her word from on high. Ha! When I think . . .' He gave a short bitter laugh. 'Well, finally she comes out, cool as you please, an' says she wants to talk to the two of us for a wee while. It was not a request, do you see, but an order. We agree right enough – we thought she would be tellin' us somethin'. But she says nothin' about Adrian, och no, she hadna' come to talk on a level with the likes of Meg an' me. She had *other* business, do you see? She begins pokin' her nose around. She asks about Meg an' her marriage an' the death of Jamie – Adrian's father. Then . . . then, if you please . . .' A pressure built up behind his face, his cheeks expanded and his voice, when it came, was tight and raw. 'She asks about Meg an' me. She wants to know how we get on, the two of us. If we spend time together. If we're close . . .' He blinked down at the table in dumb outrage, unable to meet Daisy's eyes. 'Brother an' sister! Brother an' sister. Och, I mebbe slow, but not that slow,' he cried, tapping the side of his head with a great squared-off finger. 'I could see the way her evil mind was workin'. I asked her straight out what kind of a doctor she was. We have the truth then. She's no doctor, she says, she's this psycho*therapist*. Ha! I could have murdered her – ' He clawed his hands. 'Her wicked mind had no place in that house, no place!' Calming himself, he narrowed his eyes and raised a finger. 'But I didna' let her see a sight of that. I didna' give her the satisfaction. No, I kept myself still, I said nothin' of my thoughts!'

'Then?'

'She was gone.'

'Just like that?'

'Eh?' He shifted heavily in his seat. 'Well . . . I told her there was no point in makin' another visit.' He pulled his shoulders back grandly. 'I told her Adrian was not in need of her kind of attention.'

'So she left?'

'Aye. But not for long. She was back just three days later, an' with no warnin'. I was away on the loch, I didna' hear until too late. An' this time, she brought another social worker. Och, but it was well planned, there's no doubt of that. The other woman, she was come to keep an eye on Meg, to make certain she stayed away while the dirty business was done. While the *person*' – he put a wealth of feeling into the word – 'had Adrian to herself. An' she had him to herself a long while – an hour, mebbe more – and when she left . . .' His shoulders rocked slightly, like a fighter's squaring up to an opponent. 'When she left, Adrian was broken, *broken*. Quiet an' wouldna' speak. An' that night – aye, he wept, wept like a babby. I saw him, but I couldna' get a thing out of him, he was that upset.'

During this last speech he had been getting increasingly restless and now, with what might have been a wave of apology, he lumbered to his feet and went to the bar. He came back with a large Scotch undiluted by water.

He took a quick gulp, his hand twitched, his eyes seemed to brighten. He went on: 'I had no doubts then. I told Meg that this *person* was to be locked out, that she was never again to enter the house. But Meg – she didna' see the sense of that. She said we would do best to make no complaint, not until we had good reason.' He pulled at his drink again and continued at what for him was breakneck speed. 'Good reason ... Aye, well there was only one way to find good reason. I took the loan of a portable telephone device – you know? – so that Meg could call an' tell me when they returned. An' they returned soon enough. A week, it was, to the day. I went straight to the parlour door and opened it – slow, slow – just a crack at first, an' listened. I couldna' hear Adrian – he wasna' speakin' – but I could hear *her* well enough. Aye, every word, every single evil word there was to hear. An' I heard other things too,' he said, his voice rough and low.

He paused and rubbed a hand mercilessly across his closed eyes so that it seemed he must do them damage. 'I didna' realize at first – what the sound could be. But then – aw – I knew,' he said.

Daisy waited.

'Strikin' him. She was strikin' him.'

The doubt must have shown in Daisy's face because he repeated emphatically: 'Strikin' him, aye. Slow, regular, like some – *machine*. You're not ill, Adrian, she says – *tak* – you know you're not ill – *tak* – ' With each sound he swung his open palm softly through the air, in a wide slapping motion. 'You're not ill, Adrian – *tak* – tell me you're not ill, go on, tell me – *tak*.'

Daisy stared at him, reading the signals in his face. Everything told her it was true; everything warned her it must be an exaggeration.

'It was not the entire time, och no, she had a rest now an' again, to give her time to put other notions in his head. It's attention you want, isn't it, she says, it's attention you want, isn't it, Adrian? – I heard each an' every word, each an' *every* one. You're tryin' to punish your father for havin' died, she says. You're angry with him, aren't you, Adrian?' He had raised his voice in a savage imitation of a woman's voice. 'You're angry that he's not here for you to tell him how angry you are. You're angry at your mammy for letting your uncle take his place.' He broke off and dropped his head for a moment. Daisy gave a sudden shudder.

'That's why you want to be ill, isn't it, Adrian?' he began again, coming up slowly. 'But you're *not* ill, Adrian, an' it's time you told me so. Now, tell me you're not ill, Adrian, tell me . . . Then . . .' His voice lowered, trembling with anger. 'Then I heard it again, the sound, the *sound*. *Tak, tak!* An' I went in an' I saw . . .' He sank the last of his Scotch in one gulp. He said flatly: 'I went in an' I saw what she was doin', an' I struck her right back. An' I tell you – there's not an ounce of regret in ma body.'

'You're not going to tell the judge that, I hope.'

He frowned and was silent.

'Where was she hitting Adrian?'

'The cheek. Here.' He put a hand to his face.

'Was he bruised? Were there marks?'

His mouth moved uncertainly. He looked at her with sudden suspicion. 'Red. The skin was red.'

Daisy sighed. 'Striking is a strong word.'

Campbell, putting a treacherous interpretation on this, became aggressive. 'An' what would you have me use?'

'Were they perhaps nearer to taps or light slaps?'

'Good God!' His eyes bulged with rage and she was reminded of how very frightening Campbell could be. 'Are you tellin' me this word or that would make it right?'

'Nothing would make it right. Don't misunderstand me. Even if she hadn't touched Adrian, it would still have been appalling.'

'Well then, taps, slaps – what's the difference?'

'With you, quite a bit, apparently. You said you just tapped the psychotherapist, but she ended up with a badly bruised eye. I'm just trying to get our vocabulary straight.'

Campbell hunched his shoulders and tried to look penitent. 'Well . . . Perhaps I put a mite more force behind it than I intended,' he admitted reluctantly. 'Will it count against me?'

But he asked it more out of hope than expectation. He knew very well that it would count against him. What worried Daisy was the other ways in which it might count against not only him but Adrian Bell and his mother as well.

'I think we should get straight back to Dermott's,' she said.

He did not look thrilled at the idea of seeing his solicitor again so soon. 'For what reason?'

'We might have to think about protecting Adrian.'

Expressions of alarm, perplexity and suspicion crossed Campbell's face in rapid succession. 'Protection? From what?' But before he had the chance to ask again, she had gone to the desk and paid the bill and was leading the way out into the street. It was how the social services might be taking all this that worried her, she explained as she set a rapid pace up the hill; how they could argue that Campbell's presence constituted a bad influence. At this, Campbell, with a certain predictability, ground to a halt and protested violently.

'I'm just telling you what they might be thinking,' Daisy argued quietly.

She painted the picture even more strongly then: how they might consider taking Adrian into care, how they could apply for a place of safety order on the grounds that Adrian's physical health was in danger from lack of essential medical treatment, or that his emotional health was in danger from unsuitable home influences, or both of these. Overriding Campbell's further explosions of rage, she told him how, unless Scottish law was dramatically different from English, the order could be granted in the absence of family representation, without anyone knowing anything about it – not until the police and social services arrived unannounced on the doorstep, and how Campbell and his sister would be powerless to prevent Adrian from being removed.

For a time Campbell fell into a furious inarticulate silence. 'They can be prevented?' he panted finally.

'I don't know. I'm not sure what the law allows here. In England a family can start ward of court proceedings. That way the social services can't do anything until the story's been heard by a judge. Even then there're risks – the judge might get talked into allowing some of the medical treatment – '

Campbell grabbed her arm, 'Hold it there! *Hold it there!*' he roared, sending a shower of spittle over her. 'You're sayin', you're sayin' . . .' It was a moment before he got a grip on his thoughts. 'You're sayin' we should apply to the court just so they can send that *person* back to torture Adrian?'

She grasped his hand and lifted it gently away from her sleeve. 'Whatever course we take involves risk. But anything's better than having Adrian removed altogether, surely.'

His rage made him speechless. 'But . . . Why should they want to take him?' he said at last in a broken voice.

'Because they want to get their way, that's why. You have to realize, Campbell, that these people are convinced they're right, and there's no stopping people who believe they've got right on their side.'

He couldn't take it in. 'I must talk to Meg. Must talk with Meg.'

A weariness came over Daisy, but also an acceptance. She could see that there was an inevitability to this, that Campbell would never dare move alone, that indeed he had no right to do so. But how long would these discussions take? It was Friday, midday. The legal weekend started early.

She offered: 'Do you want me to come back to Loch Fyne and go through it with Meg, then?'

He nodded doggedly.

She looked away across the water and took stock. Even if everything went smoothly, there wouldn't be a hope of getting anything before a judge before midday tomorrow. And tomorrow was the day of her meeting with Nick Mackenzie. A meeting, she hardly needed reminding, on which the financial future of Octek, if not the entire Silveron project, depended.

In the end she compromised with Campbell. While Campbell agreed to continue up the hill to see Dermott, to get the benefit of his advice on Scottish law regarding minors, Daisy promised to stop for an hour's discussion with Meg Bell before continuing on to London. She would return promptly on the Sunday, to help Campbell and his sister come to a firm decision.

To do the round journey by road would kill her; she would have to fly. But then when would she be able to get back to Octek? Monday night? Tuesday even? When she was away, the problems always seemed to pile up.

Waiting in Dermott's office it occurred to her that there was one further option, and borrowing a phone, she dialled Nick Mackenzie on the London number his accountant had given her. It rang for a long time then, just as she was about to give up, suddenly answered. For some reason, her heart did a leap against her ribs. Nerves.

A voice said: 'Hullo, can I help you?' It was a female voice with a northern accent, not young, probably quite old.

Mr Mackenzie was not at home, the voice said. This was the housekeeper speaking.

Daisy explained about the difficulty of keeping her appointment, and asked if there might be another time when he was free.

'He's going away,' said the voice. 'He leaves tomorrow evening. I'm not sure how long he'll be away.'

'Abroad?'

There was a pause, as if the housekeeper were uncertain whether to impart the information or not. 'Scotland,' she said eventually.

'He's coming to Glen Ashard?' she asked.

Yes, it was to Glen Ashard.

She left a message. She would be at the George Hotel in Inveraray, she said, and would come to Glen Ashard on Sunday at eleven, unless she heard to the contrary.

Dermott found a moment to see them, though in the way of lawyers who are not really very busy, he made it clear that it was not terribly convenient. There was no such thing as wardship in Scotland, he announced. And even if there was, such extreme measures were surely unnecessary. If anything needed to be done – and by his tone he clearly doubted it – then a reasoned dialogue with the social services would be the most sensible course. Everyone, after all, had the child's interests at heart. He spoke with complacency and a confidence that seemed to Daisy to spring more from inertia than good judgement.

In the car Daisy said: 'I think we should move Adrian. Take him to England.'

'You mean hide him away?'

'I mean . . .' She sighed. 'Yes, I suppose that *is* what I mean. But not too obviously. Not so we can't pretend that we were just taking him in search of medical treatment.'

Campbell shifted unhappily in his seat. 'Meg will never agree,' he sighed. 'She'll never be wantin' to leave Loch Fyne.'

This thought had also loomed large in Daisy's mind, and she fell silent for the rest of the journey.

It was three when they reached Loch Fyne. After a long chat with Adrian, who was up and sitting in a chair, looking a little fuller in the face but still very weak and with newly acquired liver problems, Daisy gave the idea of removing Adrian to England a first run past Mrs Bell. Later she went through it with her again in more detail.

But Mrs Bell was not to be moved, not for the moment at least.

After a supper of thick stew and dumplings Daisy left Campbell and Mrs Bell to talk it through in the kitchen and, lying on the sofa next to Adrian, fell asleep to the flickering of an old movie. She didn't wake till morning.

# Chapter 27

THE MASSIVE GATES were closed, the lodges at either side apparently deserted, the woodland beyond, impenetrable. High on one of the gateposts was a security camera and, lower down, an intercom with a bell and an integral camera lens. Daisy rang, and a light came on above the lens. She faced the camera and waited. A single low buzz, and the gates swung silently open. She got hastily into the Metro and drove through before they closed again.

The road wove gently through the woodland until, after a long bend, the Metro ground over a cattle grid, its suspension rattling alarmingly, and the shrubs gave way to a wide expanse of rough grassland dotted with large trees that rose like sentinels out of the mist.

It was only when the car had jangled over a second grid that the mass of Ashard House came into view. The place sprang straight out of a Walter Scott novel or an Errol Flynn film: heavily buttressed and turreted, windows not just leaded but mullioned as well, ivy growing dutifully up the walls towards a main tower which sported a tall undraped flagstaff.

In the porch was another security camera with a red winking light, its lens pointing to the spot a couple of feet in front of the door where callers stood to operate the old-fashioned metal bell-pull. But for all the hi-tech, security wasn't that rigid because the massive oak door was lying half-open.

She pulled the bell anyway, and heard an electronic ring

echoing through the house. No one came. She checked her
watch; she was dead on time. She gave it two more minutes
and another ring before stepping inside. The hall was large
and baronial, with a lot of dark wood and a wide staircase
towards the far end. Someone was moving house. Along
one wall a stack of cardboard and wooden packing cases
rose three-high.

Several doors led off the hall. She knocked and looked
in each in turn.

Beyond the staircase was a passage which led almost
immediately to a large and immaculate kitchen. This too
was empty, although she noticed that on the table a place
had been set for breakfast.

She retreated, feeling indecisive. A sound came drifting
down the passage from the far end, a sound so slight that
at first she thought it was the buzz of an insect. Then it
changed pitch, and she realized it was broadcast music of
some kind. She followed the trail to a closed door. She
knocked, and again, louder. There was no reply. She opened
the door.

The music surged up, amazingly loud, as if someone had
suddenly turned up the volume. The light from the three
tall windows was very bright, and it was a second before
she made out the figure sitting with his back to her, in
front of a control panel. His hands were moving over a
keyboard, and she realized he was playing along with the
music in some way. He stopped to scribble something,
and the music sped on, multi-stranded, but incomplete. He
put the pencil down, listened for a moment, then reached
out and flicked a switch. The music stopped with a squawk
and turned into a high-speed caterwauling as the tape
rewound.

'Hi,' she said.

Nick jerked round, looking startled, and stared at her
for a moment. 'It's not time already, is it? God!' Shaking
his head, he twisted back in his revolving seat and flicked

more switches until the noise stopped. 'You got my message then?' he said over his shoulder. 'Ten was okay, was it?'

'Yes,' she smiled. 'Fine.'

He hunched over the sheets he'd been scribbling on. 'Always the same,' he murmured. 'Have to stop just when it's going well . . .'

'If I'm interrupting . . .'

'No, no. Got to stop anyway.' He lifted the sheets of music and threw them onto a next-door table. Facing her at last, he shot her an oblique look that was both appraising and cautiously welcoming, before striding across to the window and looking up at the sky. 'Mist!' he exclaimed impatiently. 'No good while there's mist.'

'No good . . .?'

'Can't go till it's lifted.'

She gave an uncertain laugh. 'Go?'

He turned. 'Didn't I say?'

'Not unless the hotel clerk got amnesia.'

'Ah, I didn't say then.' He frowned at her, and it occurred to her that the omission had been intentional. Inviting her to follow he walked out into the passage. She caught up with him in the kitchen as he was coming out of a side room with a cool-box in either hand.

'Well, the important part's ready,' he said. 'Hope you like smoked salmon? And white wine? Otherwise it's mineral water – still or bubbly or in between. But look – would you like some coffee while we wait?' Running out of things to say, he looked down at her, his face pursed into an expression that was wary and watchful and amiable all at the same time.

'What's the occasion?' she asked.

His mouth twitched. 'Ah, well . . . I've got to go and see something. I thought you might like to come along.'

'Surprise time?'

He shrugged. 'If you like.' But he didn't mind the idea.

'Oh, I like,' she declared firmly. 'The surprises I've been getting recently have all been the nasty sort.'

A glint came into his eye, a tiny but unmistakable warning that he didn't want to hear about any of that, not yet anyway.

'You're moving?' she asked, gesturing towards the packing cases.

'Sort of.'

'A pity.' She meant, because the place was so beautiful. But she sensed it was the wrong thing to say.

'Oh well,' he remarked calmly. 'Things change, things move on.' He led the way across the hall and into a book-lined room with an open fire. 'Though I don't know about the house. I might keep it. Sell the rest – the farm, the estate.' He stood in the middle of the room and gave a small shrug. 'It seems to be the only place I can work. God only knows why.' Suddenly remembering his manners, he said abruptly: 'Sit down. I'll get some coffee.'

When he had gone she wandered over to the window, feeling unaccountably ill at ease, then turned and looked back across the room. To one side of her, in an alcove set into the book-shelves, were a number of photographs mounted in silver frames. She moved closer. Nick. Nick and Alusha. Alusha on her own, looking like her newspaper pictures but more so. An unusual face, arresting, beautiful.

The great house, the beautiful dead wife: shades of *Rebecca* – except that Nick had loved Alusha. And had not as yet taken a second wife.

Daisy reached out and lightly touched the frame.

'No time for coffee.' Nick dodged briefly around the door and beckoned.

She followed him through the hall and out onto the gravel. He pointed to a spot just above the trees.

The noise came first, the dull clacking of rotor blades, then a black dot appeared in the distance, coming in over the loch.

'I'll get the lunch,' said Nick, making for the door again. By the time he came back with the cool-boxes, the helicopter had clattered down onto an open expanse of lawn not far from the house, almost blasting the ivy off the walls.

Daisy felt an almost childish excitement. 'I've never been in one of these things before,' she shouted as they walked towards it.

He insisted she took the front seat, next to the pilot, while he sat in the middle of the three seats behind. They took off immediately. Daisy had barely slipped on the headset before the trees were passing under the glass window set into the floor, and the long expanse of the loch was opening out before them, a plate of blue steel glistening through the last smears of mist.

Soon they had left the water behind and were crossing the opposite shore, flying over hills reduced to mild corrugations, like crumpled paper, and forests condensed into strange geometric shapes.

Nick and the pilot were talking, their voices shrill in the headset, but she didn't listen until Nick's arm appeared over her shoulder, pointing towards two fingers of water ahead. 'Loch Riddon, Loch Striven. And beyond – you can hardly see it yet – the Firth of Clyde.'

Clyde. South. The city of Glasgow. But her disappointment was momentary. This was a day to let things happen, to sit back and enjoy.

They followed the right-hand shore for some minutes before cutting across to meet the Firth as it looped back towards the brown haze of the city. The helicopter slowed, and she realized they were coming in to land on the near shore.

The area was heavily industrialized. They came down on a derelict patch of concrete, surrounded by Victorian factories and warehouses, junk heaps and rusting corrugated-iron fencing, and tall blank walls.

As the rotors wound slowly down, a Mercedes appeared

out of nowhere, as if by magic, and bounced cautiously over the cratered concrete towards them.

Climbing out, Daisy laughed: 'That was wonderful! *Wonderful!* I didn't want it to end!'

Nick led the way to the car. 'It hasn't. Not yet.'

She got into the back of the car next to him and let the driver close the door for her. The heating was on, the seating soft.

'This could get too much, you know,' she remarked, only half joking.

He almost smiled, and she noticed that a couple of times after that he looked at her surreptitiously, as if to remind himself of what it was like to experience something thrilling for the first time.

After a few minutes the car slowed and turned in at a decrepit security gate manned by an elderly guard who peered at them myopically and waved them through.

They entered what appeared to be a shipyard, one that had seen better times, with rust-streaked cranes, vast sheds with patchwork iron roofs, and barren docks with long empty wharves.

The car picked its way carefully over the ruts, came to the end of a long shed and rounded a corner. The contrast could not have been more dramatic. In front of them was a flash of blinding, brilliant newness: a great, gleaming sea creature, immaculate and dazzlingly white, with shining metal trim and, high on the upper storey, sinister-wrap-around black-tinted windows.

The craft was out of the water, sitting at a backward tilt on a slipway. Maybe it was the low vantage point, maybe it was the sheer height of the hull, but the thing looked enormous, like a vast shark. It must have been close on two hundred feet long. It was sleek in an aggressively modern way, the front very sharp, the lines severe. Two enormously tall masts and a web of rigging rose from the deck, looking like later additions. Daisy supposed the yacht – or maybe it was a ship – carried sails, though from the ruthlessly aerodynamic lines it looked as if it ran on rocket fuel.

'Blimey,' she said. 'What an outrage!'

Nick shot her a quick glance and shifted in his seat. 'It's only a thought,' he said with a slight edge to his voice. 'I haven't decided anything yet.'

Getting a sudden idea of what this was about, Daisy murmured a diplomatic, 'Ah-ha,' and shut up.

A succession of ladders and platforms took them up the side of the vessel to the deck. A two-man reception committee stood waiting for them, like something out of a royal visit. One introduced himself as the agent, the other as the captain. The captain came complete with white uniform and brass buttons and scrambled egg on the shoulder.

The captain led the conducted tour. Not a stereo socket was missed from the inventory, not a built-in TV, heating control or en-suite bathroom. Each stateroom was close-carpeted in a different theme colour, every curtain and bedcover was ruthlessly co-ordinated. Even the loo-rolls matched. The kitchen had everything that baked, froze and chopped. The bridge was straight out of *Star Trek*, with wall-to-wall controls and raised swivel chairs, like the ones on sport-fishing boats. Desalination plants, air-condition-ing, ice-making machines: there was nothing this floating palace didn't possess, except, perhaps, the smallest sugges-tion of atmosphere or heart.

At one point they were asked to admire the Jacuzzi in the master suite, complete with gold taps and built-in stereo. Nick said nothing, but she saw his eyes roll slightly, though whether from disbelief or disapproval she wasn't sure.

When it came to the engine room, Daisy developed information fatigue and slowed down, intending to give it a miss, but Nick, turning back, widened his eyes in silent entreaty and beckoned her forward.

'I need moral support,' he whispered.

'Stay around here, and you'll be needing more than that!'

'Tell me what to say,' he asked in mock panic.

'Me? I don't know a cylinder from a carburettor.'

'Nor do I,' he said and gave a slight giggle.

'Pat the machinery – isn't that the thing? Give it a good stroke!'

He giggled again, a wonderfully infectious sound, before turning a serious face to the sales agent.

The ridiculousness of the vessel, the echo of that giggle, caused the bubble of suppressed laughter to rise in Daisy in ripples, and she had to look away until she had regained some sort of control. But for a time the laughter was never far from both of them, she could see it in the quiver of his mouth, and it wasn't until they returned to the sitting room – termed by the captain, the saloon – that she dared to look him in the eye.

Even then she thought it safer not to face him as they had coffee, and she sat next to him on the sofa while he talked with the captain and the agent. Yet in that moment of laughter in the engine room, something had overturned, had shifted inside her, and she found herself unable to keep from watching him, watching that wonderfully mobile mouth as it went through the motions of looking serious, of contemplating a question, of smiling suddenly, and noticing how these smiles were not always reflected in his eyes. Noticing, too, how beautiful his hands were, and how restless; seeing the way his hair curled on his neck and even, for a moment, seeming to catch the scent of him, woody and warm.

These were signs that even an idiot could read, these were warnings a mile high, and choosing to read them well, needing time to absorb the implications of this sudden bolt of feeling, she unlocked her gaze, leant over on the sofa arm, and paid studious attention to the captain.

Leaving the saloon, the sales agent smoothed his way

through some last well-practised selling points, and then
they made their way back down to the ground.

'Well?' Nick asked, as they walked towards the car.

'Well what?'

'What did you think of it?'

'Ah. Well . . . I think it's – um' – she made a show of
trying to find the right word – 'I think it's *unbelievable*.'

He cast her a sidelong glance, trying to gauge her
meaning. 'I thought I might take off for a year,' he
explained seriously. 'You know, get away. Sail somewhere
nice. Explore.'

'*Explore?* It won't exactly make it up the Amazon.'

'I wasn't thinking of – ' He made a face. 'You're very
hard on me,' he commented without rancour. 'You really
didn't like it?'

'I thought it was *dreadful*!' she laughed. '*Really*. I mean,
that's one seriously vulgar object, Nick.'

They got into the car. The driver sped round to his seat
and they started off.

'The owner went bankrupt in the middle of the refit,'
Nick said. 'And now if the yard don't manage to sell it, it
could bankrupt them too, put people out of work.'

'But the yard's already broke, isn't it?' she cried, waving
a hand. 'I mean, the docks are empty. You can't buy a
horror like that just to bail out a boatyard, Nick.'

'But it's something to take into account – '

'Not if they're going down the chute anyway.'

'And I thought you were the idealist, Daisy.'

He had spoken in a bantering tone, but there was a dart
of seriousness underneath. 'Ouch!' she said, with feeling.
'But what I do – that's different, that's – ' She creased her
face into a grimace. 'Okay, well, maybe it isn't *entirely*
different,' she conceded. 'But that doesn't change the fact
that the boat's a stinker, Nick. It's for flash-merchants,
the sort who drive gold Rollers and wear shades in the
dark – retired arms dealers and property developers and

men with shiny suits. The kind who buy their friends like they buy their clothes. You're not that loud, really you're not.'

It was out before she could stop it. 'I mean – '

But he was already saying solemnly: 'You don't think so?'

'I mean' – she felt the laughter simmering between them again – 'you're *better* than that.'

'Well, thank you.'

The irony came through in his voice, and seeing that she had made him smile again, she looked out of the window at the rows of gloomy houses in a state of sudden and quite unjustified happiness.


The pilot said he'd stay in the aircraft and have a sandwich there. It occurred to Nick that he was being diplomatic, that he thought the expedition had been organized for some romantic purpose. Realizing, Nick almost asked him to join them, but thought better of it. He and Daisy did, after all, have things to discuss, though they would be very far from what the pilot had in mind.

Taking the cool-boxes, Nick led the way across the springy turf towards a small rise. Carrying the rugs, Daisy strode along beside him, all energy and life, her chin set, her face tilted towards the sky, her eyes half closed as if to absorb the light.

Breasting the rise, a vast panorama opened out before them: to the left the hills of Islay, so close that they looked like a continuation of the land they were standing on; far to the right the long craggy outline of Mull, and, ahead, lying dark and low in a sparkling grey sea, the islands of Colonsay and Oronsay, conjoined in a single elongated reef. Beyond them, there was nothing but sea, the vast sprawl of the western ocean, stretching towards an invisible horizon.

'Where are we? Where are we?' Daisy gasped. Then in the next breath: 'No, no, don't tell me!'

He saw a perfect picnic place a short way below, an area of close-cropped grass within a circle of heather, and carried the cool-boxes down. He took the rugs from Daisy and shook them out. Opening a box, he offered her a drink.

She seemed dazed, only half listening. 'What?' she said, tearing herself away from the view. 'I'll have wine, thanks.'

He opened a bottle and poured her a glass.

She sat down on the rug with a long sigh. 'This place . . .' She exhaled, then shook her head, as if words could never adequately describe it. 'Is it an island?' she asked suddenly.

He nodded. 'A large one.'

'Don't tell me the name! Don't tell me anything about it! I don't want to know. I never want to know.' She stretched her arms lazily towards the sea as if to embrace it and gave a low almost sensual chuckle.

He recorked the wine bottle and poured himself a mineral water. He was aware that she had turned and was watching him.

'Not quite like when we last met,' he said, going carefully. 'How did I behave? I mean, was it bad, or just plain embarrassing?'

'You behaved immaculately,' she declared. 'You gave me all that money.'

He gave her a look to show that hadn't been what he meant.

'No, you were fine,' she said, with that quick open smile of hers. 'I mean – considering . . .'

'Not, I hope, *loud*?'

'Ha, ha.' She grinned. '*Not* loud.'

They looked out over the sea, which from this height seemed hard and flat, like steel. Eventually Daisy said: 'You know, you look at all this and you can't believe there's anything wrong with the world – you know what I mean?

Everything seems so strong here – so incorruptible. It seems unbelievable that we can screw it up so effectively.'

'I'll tell you what I see,' he said, loading his bread high with salmon. 'I see the sea.'

There was a pause while she thought about that. 'You think I'm bullshitting,' she said, her voice coming alive with the possibilities of a friendly argument.

'No.' He took a mouthful. The salmon was tender as butter. 'But I think you worry too much.'

She gave a short sigh. 'You're right, of course you're right.'

This sunny, reasonable, languid Daisy – was it an act? Even as Nick considered it, he thought it unlikely. She was too spontaneous, too transparent for that. She was like a guard dog whose ferocious exterior hides something quite different beneath.

She sipped her wine and, leaning back on one elbow, arched her neck until her head lay back against her shoulder. She had a long neck, he noticed, long and smooth.

'An island,' she murmured, her voice soft and low. 'Cut off from everything.' She half turned to him: 'Ever fancied an island? I mean, having one all to yourself.'

'I've got one,' he said. 'In the Seychelles.'

She propped herself up on one hand and stared at him. 'God, you've done it all!' she accused. Then, in further horror: 'It must be *awful* to have done it all!'

He thought about that for a moment. 'Not in my work, I haven't. I've still got a long way to go there.'

She accepted that. It satisfied her work ethic. But she didn't let him forget the island, not for a while anyway. She kept looking at him and sucking in her breath gently and shaking her head.

When they had finished eating they went for a walk, striking off parallel to the sea across the hilly moorland country. Daisy was well equipped in Doc Martens, he less so in trainers. They walked between dense patches of gorse and thistle, through knee-high heather, over wind-scrubbed slopes spotted with the occasional black-faced sheep. It was a while before they hit anything that resembled a path, and then Daisy was all for leaving it and making across rugged terrain towards a hill.

'You forget – I'm unfit,' he panted, hearing the wheezing of his lungs.

But she wasn't having excuses and urged him up the hill at a great rate. Twenty minutes later they reached the summit, he gasping, she triumphant. She would have led him down the following valley and up the next hill if he hadn't insisted on returning to check with the pilot.

The walk seemed to exhilarate her. As they retraced their steps she talked easily and rapidly, asking him about his childhood, his early life, listening with concentration, offering occasional comments. Her remarks were perceptive in an oblique off-beat way; they were also kind. The word echoed in his mind: *kind*, and he was aware of feeling a new trust in her. Even when she touched on dangerous territory – Alusha's illness, the inquest – he was able to answer with something like ease.

Back at the picnic site he left her sitting on the rug and went to find the pilot, who said it was all right to stay another half hour. When Nick returned, Daisy had dozed off. The way she lay – head tucked on one arm, mouth slightly open – and the suddenness with which she'd fallen asleep, reminded him of a child.

He sat close by, smoking steadily – too much, as always – watching a hawk hovering head-down over the heather, seeing the way the ocean glittered under the path of the sun.

When he next glanced down at Daisy she was awake, peering up at him through half-closed eyes. She smiled softly at him, and he smiled back.

She sat up and stretched. He said reminiscently: 'That

day, the day of the accident. There was a plane. I only remembered it when I was in Arizona. I had a dream one night, and it was there – in the dream. And when I woke up I could see it. A light plane. I don't remember anything special about it, no spraying gear, nothing like that, but then I only saw it for an instant. The plane was coming down Loch Fyne, heading straight for Ashard.'

'The plane that dumped its load on Adrian Bell, he saw it clearly,' she said. 'He said it had a red diagonal stripe on one wing.'

'I don't remember a stripe.'

'No,' she agreed quickly as if she hadn't expected him to.

She sat up on her haunches and pushed a hand through her hair. Her brightness had gone. 'One of the reasons I'm up this weekend is to try to find a way of stopping the local authority from taking Adrian into care.'

'Why would they want to take him into care?'

'To give him "essential" treatment – essential psychiatric treatment, that is.'

'Christ . . . Can they do that?'

'Oh yes.' She explained it to him. Her voice was flat and cool.

He remembered Alusha and the enforced swimming and the nameless drugs. 'Well . . . if I can help at all . . . Can I?'

'Ah.' She gave a nervous chuckle. 'You already have. I took some money out of the project – I didn't think you'd mind, it's not very much.' She looked up to him for approval. 'To pay their solicitor.'

He said he didn't mind.

Far below, the sea had softened under a mackerel sky. The breeze had strengthened. Turning to face it, she said in a neutral voice: 'They okayed Silveron for general use this week. MAFF – the Ministry of Agriculture, Fisheries and Food – they think the stuff's okay to be sprayed on food.'

She allowed herself a small snort of disgust. 'Morton-
Kreiger must have pulled some wires to get away with that
one. They probably nobbled that twit Driscoll.'

Driscoll. He thought immediately of Susan, saw her
walking through the rooms of the Kensington house,
redecorating them with a curl of her hands, and moved the
conversation onto different ground. 'What about the project – *our* project?' he asked. 'No results?'

'Not yet. And I'm afraid there won't be any, not for a
while.' She sat up on her heels, eyes round and bright, head
alert. The guard dog back on duty. 'Maybe months.'

Here was the bad news then, the news she'd been
preparing to tell him all day. He began to pack the bottles
back into the cool-boxes.

'It's been a combination of things,' she said, forcing
some of the lightness back into her voice. 'Unforeseen
expenses – we're running over budget, I'm afraid. But also
there's a problem with a licence. We've got to have this
licence to get started, and there's been a delay. I'd almost
believe it was intentional, except . . .' She trailed off, and
the worries of the world came across her forehead in a
sharp frown.

He stood up. 'So?' He knew what was coming, but he
thought he'd ask anyway.

She clambered to her feet. As she rose, he reached down
and picked up the rugs.

'The delay – it's going to cost a great deal. And we were
running tight on the budget anyway.' In her discomfort she
couldn't quite meet his eye. 'There were so many unforeseen problems, things we couldn't budget for. Everyone's
been great – the staff, trying so hard, working all hours,
getting everything set up . . . But without that piece of
paper it's useless – we can't even begin.'

A flurry of wind caught her hair and lifted it across her
face. She pushed it impatiently away. 'I've tried to find a
way round it – God, I even thought of moving the whole

thing abroad – but there'd be just as many problems.' Her
mouth tightened. 'So near and yet so far isn't in it.' She
gave a ragged laugh. 'You know I've never cared about
anything as much as I've cared about this. It's not just
Adrian, it's not just all the other people, it's the bloody
injustice of it all. It makes me totally wild!' She glared at
him, daring him to disagree. 'I know you think I'm totally
obsessed – well, I am, I admit I am – but why not – why
not? If this isn't worth doing, then what is?'

The old Daisy, fiery as ever. She must have caught the
look in his eye because she pulled back visibly. 'I wouldn't
ask if it wasn't important,' she said with sudden gravity. 'I
wouldn't even ask.'

He didn't reply immediately. Giving her the rugs to
carry, he picked up the cool-boxes and started up the rise,
using the time to go through the motions of conducting a
brief debate with himself, although he already had a strong
suspicion of what the outcome would be. His brain was
quite rightly shouting caution: any fool could have told him
it was crazy to let Daisy suck him deeper into what was
fast looking like a doomed situation, complete with financial and organizational catastrophes. His brain shouted,
but his mind wasn't listening. It was tuned to his instincts,
and they were saying: To hell with it. It was partly
stubbornness but it was also a fascination with Daisy's
uncomplicated view of justice, a need to believe that life
could be reduced to basic moral issues. He rather liked the
idea of an anarchic one-woman campaign against the
world. Daisy and Goliath.

Then of course there was the plane, the plane that
prowled around the edges of his memory. The plane
heading in over the loch.

He was nearing the top of the rise. He could hear Daisy's
footsteps coming up behind. He turned suddenly.

'How much?'

She stared at him. He noticed her eyes, which were

flecked with gold. 'Three hundred thousand. Well – ' she grimaced. 'That is – I *think*.'

He put down the cool-boxes and looked back at the sea for a long moment. 'All right.'

Searching his face for confirmation, she gave a low gasp and, dropping the rugs, threw her arms round his neck and pulled him into a large and very tight hug. Her body was small and warm against his. Slowly, not quite sure what he was feeling, he put his arms lightly round her, then just as gently withdrew them and pulled away.

Picking up the cool-boxes, he started off again. The Bell came into view over the ridge. Daisy caught up with him again.

'This licence,' he asked her, 'it'll come through all right, will it?'

'What?' Her face was radiant, her eyes shining. 'Oh yes,' she panted. 'We've checked. Should be quite soon.'

'What is it, this licence, anyway?'

'Oh, it's a permit really, it's – ' She seemed to hesitate. 'Well, we're not allowed to start work without it.'

'Why? What's it for?'

'It's – to ensure that things get done properly.' That suggestion of evasion again. 'To make sure one follows the rules.'

A thought came to him, a thought so appalling and so obvious that he knew it must be true. 'What rules?'

'For the tests.'

Grinding to a halt he looked down into her upturned face. 'What kind of tests?'

'Well . . . the mandatory tests. The ones that have to be done for all pesticides – '

He felt cold, the buffeting wind seemed to pass straight through him. 'Like?' he asked sharply.

She was pale, she knew what was coming. 'Like the LD50 test – '

'What's that?'

She tried to pass it off lightly. 'It's to see what dosage is needed to kill fifty per cent of the sample. Though you don't actually *kill* fifty per cent, you can work it out statistically without that – '

'Sample? You mean, animals?'

'Rats. Or mice. Usually rats.'

He stared at her, dumbfounded. '*Animals?*'

'Look, we wouldn't choose to use *any* animals, not in a thousand years, but we're forced to. That's the system.'

'The *system?*'

'Yes! Animal tests are the only kind they recognize – '

He still couldn't take it in. 'Jesus,' he kept saying. '*Jesus.*'

She began to rally. 'Look, every pesticide used on every vegetable has been tested that way. Every time you buy a carrot or a potato or an orange, anything that's not organic, you're condoning the system – '

His anger had been held back by his surprise, but now it surged up in his throat. 'Stuff the system! Christ – ' He could barely speak. 'All my money – *my* money – and you never even *told* me!'

'You said you didn't want to know! You said you didn't want to be involved!'

'Oh, come *on!*'

'Anyway, I thought you'd realize – '

'God!' Unable to handle his rage, he twisted away and strode towards the helicopter. The pilot was already at the controls, his headset on, making his checks.

She ran to catch up with him. 'What do you expect us to do? If there was another way, then we'd *do* it!'

Reaching the Bell, he threw the cool-boxes into the storage compartment and scoffed: 'Just tell me how I'm expected to get up and sing the songs I sing while you're in that lab murdering animals in *my* name. Christ!' – he beat a fist against the side of the helicopter – 'my stuff's all about *not* doing things like that!'

The pilot put his head out of the door and, making a

circling motion with his hand, questioned whether he should start up. Nick nodded abruptly. A moment later there was a whine, a cough and the rotor blades began to turn.

'What about Adrian and all those other people?' Daisy shouted above the gathering noise. 'What about your wife?'

'Don't you give me arguments like that!' he roared. 'Don't you bloody dare!'

She pulled back as if he had threatened her. Her lip wobbled, she mouthed air. 'But it's not as if . . . I mean, they're only *rats*! Just rats!'

He slammed the storage door shut and checked the clips. 'And where do dogs and cats come in the okay stakes,' he yelled. 'And monkeys?' His voice sounded ugly; he felt ugly. 'Before people, or after?'

He should have left it there, he felt confused enough as it was. But, pushing past her towards the open door, he couldn't resist a parting shot. 'Just imagine how the kids'd feel,' he cried, his voice rising harshly over the din, 'the kids who buy my music. *Betrayed.* They get ripped off the whole time as it is. Imagine how *they'd* feel.'

'You mean it wouldn't look good for you?'

'Yes – no – *Jesus* – ' But there was enough truth in what she'd said for him to feel rage at hearing it. 'I see!' he proclaimed savagely, 'I see!' having no idea what it was he was meant to be seeing.

Waving her fiercely into the back seat, he jumped in beside the pilot and gestured for them to leave.

She didn't put her headset on and later, when the pilot pointed out something of interest on the ground, she made no response.

# Chapter 28

THE MEDICAL SECRETARY went so far as to admit that
Dr Konrad was somewhere in the city of Reading, either in
the hospital or the nearby university. But his exact location,
whether he had received Daisy's message, whether he'd
have time to see her – these facts were not immediately
available.

After an hour Daisy took to hunting the corridors of the
hospital. Dr Konrad, oncologist lion, had the advantage of
perfect camouflage and good cover, but a passing house-
man eventually pointed her towards the right department
and she was rewarded with a sighting of a short hunched
figure loping head-down across a corridor. He was through
the doors of men's surgical and into a side room before she
could catch him, but a waiting game was one she knew
how to win and after fifteen minutes and a brief spurt
across the fifth-floor lobby she cornered him in a staff-only
lift.

'Dr Konrad?'

He looked defensive, then, seeing no possibility of
escape, gave a slight nod. He was a stocky man of about
fifty with blunt features, large hands and ruddy cheeks. He
looked more like a bricklayer than a cancer specialist.

She introduced herself. 'It's about the Knowles case,' she
said. 'May I ask why you changed your mind?'

'Changed my mind? I didn't change my mind,' he said
briskly. 'The evidence was quite simply inadequate. Regretfully, there was nothing more I could do.'

'But the affidavit – a year ago you were prepared to swear to it.'

'No, no,' he said with authority. 'Not swear to it – that's quite wrong. All I said was that I would do what I could to help. If Mrs Knowles and her solicitor thought I was saying something else then I'm afraid they were mistaken.'

This wasn't the impression Daisy had got from his letter to Mrs Knowles last December but she knew she wasn't going to get anywhere by saying so. 'I see,' she said. 'But tell me, do you still believe Aldeb was the causative agent?'

The lift slowed. His eyes flicked to the floor indicator and he was out through the opening doors.

'Aldeb,' she prompted, keeping pace with him as he strode off. 'You think it was responsible?'

'I thought it was the most *likely* cause,' he said cautiously. 'But that was just my opinion. Which isn't worth a great deal, I'm afraid, not without some hard statistics from the epidemiologists, some independent laboratory evidence.'

'The Americans have found enough laboratory evidence to ban Aldeb.'

'That was only with massive doses, wasn't it? Not conclusive.'

'Apparently not.' She tried again. 'Your opinion was worth a great deal, Dr Konrad.'

'Not on its own.'

'Well, the Knowleses' counsel certainly thought so.'

He slowed, his expression yielded into something almost apologetic. He stopped and said confidingly: 'Look here, without scientific evidence I'd have had nothing to back me up, Miss Field. The other side's lawyers would seize on me straight away, they'd demolish me. I've appeared in these cases before. I know what happens.'

'But without you – ' She shrugged. 'There's no case.'

'Look, I'm very sorry, I really am, but there's nothing I can do.'

She nodded reluctantly. 'Thanks anyway. Oh, one last thing, Dr Konrad . . .' She paused, trying to find a way of putting it. 'May I ask – is this your own decision?'

He halted, his head thrust forward. 'I beg your pardon?'

'I meant, did you decide this thing yourself or would it have been – well, something that was discussed?'

He didn't like the question any more than he'd liked it the first time round. 'It was a matter of judgement,' he said sternly. '*My* judgement, although I felt more than justified in sounding out my colleagues on the subject. As it happened, they all agreed with me.'

'I see.'

His eyebrows shot together, his eyes hardened. 'I'm not sure what you were suggesting there, Miss Field, but I take exception to it. I resent the implications – yes, I resent the implications very much indeed. Pressure, undue persuasion – that sort of thing could never happen here, and if it ever did then I'd fight it most vigorously! There *are* such things as ethics, you know, and we stand by them!' Giving a stiff little nod he pushed at the door and was gone.

Daisy sat in the car for a while, debating whether she should go and tell Alice straight away. Alice's place was only twenty miles to the west of the city, but it was twenty miles in the wrong direction and it was easy to persuade herself that she couldn't afford the time. Even as she argued the matter she was aware, with some feeling of shame, that there was more to it than that. She was already giving up on the Knowles case, she realized; she was already allotting it less time.

She drove out of Reading and headed east towards London. There was patchy fog on the M4 and a contraflow system just the other side of Windsor, but she calculated she could get to Catch before it closed at six to pick up her messages from Jenny, and still have time to drop in at the flat to see how the repairs were going before getting back to Chelmsford for a couple of hours' paperwork later in the evening.

Her conversations with Nick kept running and running in her mind, like a cassette player doomed to go on repeating the same tape. She heard every wrong note she had struck, every false comment, every idiotic statement. And hearing them, she was pricked again by uncertainty. Not just uncertainty over the money either – though there wasn't a moment when that particular dread didn't haunt her – it was the knowledge that he must be thinking badly of her, that he believed she had set out to deceive him over the animal testing. She minded about that. She wanted him to think well of her, she wanted him to enjoy her company, she wanted . . . Well, sometimes it was best not to think too deeply about what one wanted.

There had been moments – long moments – that day when they had been friends, when nice warm indecipherable messages had passed between them, when she had begun to think . . . But then whatever she had thought, it was too late now. It had been four days since the picnic, two days since she had left messages at the Kensington house and his accountant's. His mind was undoubtedly made up. He'd probably already instructed his accountant to cancel the last payment.

*I can't talk about it now.* She saw him striding rapidly from the helicopter and pausing at the door of Ashard House. *I can't talk about it now.*

It was just after six when she reached Catch to find Jenny and Alan gone, and Daisy's replacement, Candida, nose down at her desk, scribbling hard, beavering, presumably, on another flow chart. From the outer office Daisy gave her an encouraging wave and reached into the bottom of the pending tray where Jenny hid her messages away from prying eyes.

There had been five calls for Daisy, one from Peasedale, marked urgent, saying he'd be in his laboratory until six thirty that evening and could she come and see him on a very important matter; another from Dermott, the Oban solicitor. Dermott's call hadn't been marked urgent and he hadn't left any particular message, but Daisy snatched it up and reached for the phone straight away. It was three days ago, on Monday afternoon, that Mrs Bell had finally arrived at a cautious, irresolute decision regarding Adrian's future. She would speak to Dermott first, she had announced, to gather his opinion, and then, if he couldn't offer sufficient reassurances, she would consider Daisy's suggestion again more seriously.

'Ah, Miss Field,' declared Dermott when she got through to him. 'I had a meeting with the social services.'

'You did *what*?'

'I think we came to a good understanding. They appreciated Mrs Bell's concerns for Adrian's future, her worries about the psychotherapy. But they say that the doctors are unanimous in their judgement that the treatment put forward is, all things considered, the most appropriate. So I suggested a compromise.' His voice resounded with self-congratulation.

'*Why* did you go and see them? *Why?*'

There was a stiff pause. 'I was instructed by Mrs Bell to look into the matter, to take whatever measures I thought necessary to secure Adrian's future,' he said defensively, 'and I felt a conciliatory and reasoned approach would be the most beneficial, as indeed it has proved – '

'When did this meeting take place?'

'What? I don't see – ' He gave a soft tut. 'We met yesterday afternoon, at four.'

'*God* . . .' Automatically Daisy looked at her watch. 'God . . .' Her mind flew over the possibilities, but she could see only one outcome. 'Can you fend them off for a while? Can you keep them talking for a few days? *Please*, Mr Dermott. It's terribly important.'

'I cannot see the point – '

'It would give us time to get Adrian away to England.'

'*Really*, Miss Field, I think I'm best placed to judge the situation, and I cannot advise Mrs Bell to take such precipitate action. It's far better, surely, to keep the matter on a reasonable basis – '

'They've never accepted he was chemically damaged, Mr Dermott, never! Don't you see that this is the perfect excuse, just what they've been waiting for.'

'Excuse? Really, Miss Field. These are professionals – '

'But they won't be happy until they've got him in hospital, they won't be happy until they can try out their theories – '

'You make it sound like some *experiment*, Miss Field! You make it sound as if these people don't know what they're doing.'

'They're trying to say it's psychiatric, Mr Dermott. They're trying to say it's school phobia.'

'I think you're being a little overdramatic, Miss Field. From what I gather, the treatment that would be offered has been successful in the past. Adrian might be better off, you know. In hospital.'

'Did they promise not to take him into care?' she asked briskly.

'No such undertaking was necessary,' he protested, 'because no such suggestion was made.'

'Well, they wouldn't, would they?' Daisy snapped. 'The social services aren't known for sharing their plans with anyone, and certainly not parents. What about Mr Campbell?' she asked in increasing agony. 'Did they make a requirement that he stay away from Adrian?'

'The general advisability of such a move was discussed,' Dermott admitted cautiously.

'But not demanded?'

'No. As I'm trying to explain, Miss Field, it was a most amicable discussion.'

This was a bad sign. If they'd really been prepared to compromise, the banning of Campbell from the house would have been the very least of their requirements.

'Will you at least keep in touch with them, just in case?'

'If the situation merits it, certainly.'

Selecting a tone of exaggerated politeness, she said: 'Thank you for keeping me informed, Mr Dermott. I really appreciate it,' and rang off.

There was no reply from Mrs Bell's number. She tried Campbell, but he too was out. She thought of Adrian alone in the garish front room, propped up on the settee with his eyes fixed on the flickering soundless telly, and dialled again, just to be sure, but there was no answer.

A chair scraped behind her, in what had been her office. Candida was pinning up a wall chart. It was after six thirty. She called Peasedale and found he hadn't yet left. He wouldn't say what the matter was, but sounded relieved that she was coming over. Scooping up her messages she made for the door, only to be called back by Candida who sped out of her office, plucked a hard-back notebook off the top of a filing cabinet and presented it to Daisy. The cover was labelled *Phone Log: Daisy Field*. Inside were columns for recording the date, time, length and distance of calls. Daisy made admiring noises, and scribbled *Local call, 3 minutes. How are you, Alan? Hope the efficiency drive goes well*, and spread a large signature across three columns.

Peasedale was standing wedged against the window, his hair standing up at odd angles against the light.

He cleared a seat for her. He seemed curiously reluctant to start. 'I was summoned,' he said eventually, 'to the Lord God himself. Yesterday afternoon.' He plucked at his hair nervously. 'He said he'd heard that I was doing consultancy work for a private concern involved in speculative research. I told him I wasn't *working* for anybody, that I took no

salary, only expenses. But that didn't seem to bother him.
What concerned him, he said, was the effect on my
reputation.'

'He knew?' Daisy asked very quietly. 'But how did he
know?'

'He said my standing in the profession would be
affected,' continued Peasedale, not listening. 'Well, that
was the way he put it anyway. He said it wasn't just the
fact that I had taken the job on without departmental
permission – though that would have been a fair point – it
was the ethics of the thing. Ethics – God! I thought my one
bit of safe ground was the ethics!'

Daisy was still trying to absorb the fact that an academic, a head of a university medical department, tucked
away in an ivory tower far removed from government and
media contacts, had heard about Octek.

'How much did he know?'

'Oh, enough. What we were trying to do, the set-up,
that sort of thing . . . I told him more, of course, about why
we were doing it and so on, but he didn't seem too
interested. He said that however good our intentions it was
still a maverick project, and as such the results, if any, were
bound to be ignored by the scientific community. I must
say he got me there. I was a bit shocked. It had never
occurred to me that our findings would be done down just
because the project hadn't been hatched by the university –
just because there wasn't a big name at the top of the
letterhead.' He added: 'And I'm still not sure he's right
about that, you know.'

'But how did he find out?'

'What? Oh, I have no idea.'

'Did *you* tell anyone?'

He shook his head vehemently. 'Nobody. Only my wife,
and she wouldn't have told anyone. We don't mix in
university circles much anyway. No – however he heard, it
wasn't through *us*.' He pulled an emphatic face.

Who, then, had done the telling? Who had conveyed the information so very accurately to the spot where it would carry the most weight?

A further half hour with Peasedale didn't bring her any nearer to finding out, though it convinced her that, for all the head of department's apparent concern for Peasedale's career, the advice he had dispensed amounted to nothing less than a warning off.

Giving up any ideas of going back to Chelmsford that night, she joined the traffic snaking up York Way towards Tufnell Park. She drove automatically, her eyes locked onto the stream of tail lights and prepared herself to face the flat. A week ago the landlord had promised to send some men over to repair the ceiling absolutely instantaneously, so the chances of any work having been done weren't good.

But she was wrong. Once she managed to find a light that was still working, she saw that someone had been in and pulled down the remains of the ceiling and pinned up a layer of plasterboard. But if they'd gone to the trouble of throwing covers over the furniture, it certainly didn't show. Dust was everywhere, in a cloak far thicker than the original snowstorm. The stuff had penetrated every corner of every drawer and reached into the furthest depths of the highest kitchen cupboards. The shoulders of her clothes wore a white coating, like fine dandruff in a shampoo commercial.

She hunted around for a drink. There was some months-old cooking wine next to the stove, and in a cupboard above, an inch of vodka in a long-forgotten half-bottle hidden behind the Chinese spices. She took a sip, then, dispensing with formalities, knocked it back Russian-style.

Rummaging in a drawer she found a pad of paper, tacky with grit, and taking it to the table by the window, shifted some magazines, dusted off a chair and sat down. She compiled a number of lists: the first, of those who knew everything there was to know about Octek – barring of course the source of the funding. This numbered three: herself, Peasedale and Floyd. The second list, of those who knew some of the facts but not all of them: this contained the rest of the Octek employees, a total of five. Lastly, a list of outsiders, who knew bits and pieces, but not, significantly, the fact of Peasedale's involvement. This included Octek's accountant, Nick Mackenzie's accountant and sundry lawyers. After some thought, she added Simon's name, though again there was no reason for him to connect Peasedale to Octek. It was just possible he'd guessed, but it would have had to be one astonishingly accurate and assured guess. There was also Alan and Jenny, and, presumably, Candida.

None of it made sense. She knew all the Octek employees well. They were all committed; none of them would have talked. While the outsiders were either loyal or simply didn't have the information to know Peasedale was involved.

She tore the piece of paper off the pad and, crushing it, chucked it in the direction of the waste paper basket.

She tried Mrs Bell again. This time she was home. She listened quietly to what Daisy had to say, she seemed to appreciate the growing danger to Adrian, but she would promise nothing, not until she had spoken to Dermott about it in the morning. Then, on the point of ringing off, she added: 'But Dermott did well with the social services, did he not?'

With a sudden swoop of disappointment Daisy realized that she had understood nothing. 'But that's just the point, Meg,' she argued weakly. 'I don't think that the meeting achieved anything at all. I think it would only have spurred them into action . . .'

But it was no good. When it came to the law, Dermott's judgement was to be respected above all other.

Ringing off, Daisy was filled with an acute restlessness. She ranged up and down the room, kicked at the dust, lit the fire, went into the kitchen for coffee and, changing her mind, returned to her chair. A minute later she stomped back into the kitchen and, sweeping up the cooking wine, poured herself a glass. The stuff was dark, almost black, thick with sediment and horribly bitter. But two glasses later it had succeeded in dulling her brain. Not long after that, it brought a thumping tiredness, close to exhaustion. Curling up uncomfortably in the chair, she drifted into an uneasy sleep.

The phone woke her, slicing slowly into her mind from a great distance. She waited for the answering machine to pick up the call before remembering she had turned it off.

She scrabbled for the receiver and raised it slowly to her ear.

'Daisy? Daisy? Hullo – are you there?' It was Simon's voice.

'Hi.'

'You're there.'

'More or less.'

'You should answer.'

'What?'

'*Answer*. Say hullo or something. It helps, you know.'

'Yes.'

'Your friends the Octek people,' he said briskly, as if anxious to keep everything on a businesslike footing. 'I got the information,' he said. 'Or rather, I got all there is to get.'

'Thanks, thanks.' She straightened her legs and knocked over her empty glass.

'The answer, as far as they know, is that it's being processed in the normal way.'

Daisy sat forward in her chair, wishing the wine out of her head. 'You mean – ?'

'No story. Nothing abnormal at all. Frankly, Daisy, I felt a right berk, being so totally in the dark. He didn't believe I didn't know anything. Thought I was holding out.

Got shirty.' He added resentfully: 'And he's a useful guy too.'

'What did he think you should know, then?'

'What Octek was about, that sort of thing.'

'You didn't tell him?'

'Well, it would have been difficult, wouldn't it?' he said with heavy irony.

'Yes . . . Sorry.'

'Are you ill or something? You sound half asleep.'

'Uhm – just tired. So what exactly did he say?'

'Well – *nothing*,' he retorted, losing patience. 'That's the point. There was nothing to report. The thing's just going ahead in the normal way.'

Daisy lay back in her chair and closed her eyes again.

After a silence, Simon asked tentatively: 'You all right?'

Maybe the day had simply been too long, maybe her head was too thick with exhaustion and bad wine, maybe she had simply reached the point where she had to tell somebody, but she told him.

She told him about Adrian and her fears of a care order, she told him about the final setback in the Knowles case and, since the entire world seemed to know about Octek, she told him about that too. Why it had been launched, her involvement, the lab set-up, the testing programme.

'Jesus . . . That's a large undertaking, Daisy. You're doing it on your *own*?'

'Sort of.'

'But who – ? What – ? It must cost a fortune. Where's the money coming from?'

'Ah . . .' She gave a soft sigh. 'We had a backer . . . Though, as from this week, he may not be our backer any more.'

'Oh.' A sympathetic pause, and Simon said: 'Look – er . . . I'd, er . . . ask you over, but I've only two eggs . . . no bread. And I've got to go out again at nine thirty.'

'Thanks . . . It was sweet of you.'

'No, well . . . I'm always here, Daisy, you know that. This backer, tell me . . . What happened? Who is he?'

'Who is he?' she echoed dully, seeing Nick against the backdrop of the sea. 'No, I – I can't tell you . . .'

'Daisy, for God's sake, it's *me*.'

It was Simon, and in her exhaustion, in the skewing of her emotions, in her need, finally, to talk it through with someone, he took on rock-like form, a bastion of security.

Biggs, former detective sergeant, Metropolitan Police Notting Hill Division, in receipt of early retirement on health grounds, crouched in the Transit van and strained to hear. The reception wasn't too good at this distance, but he hadn't been able to park any closer.

He took a stab at the name the girl had mentioned, writing it methodically in his notebook, but though he had a strong feeling he'd heard it somewhere before, he wasn't sure he'd got it right. The tape might tell him when he played it back later. In the meantime he fiddled with the volume control, checked the recorder was running all right, and pressed the cans closer to his head.

The two of them were still talking about the guy, but not by name. It was all 'he' and 'him'. Biggs went on making notes, hoping the name would come up again, but the girl was getting tired of talking, you could hear it in her voice. She wanted to get off the phone and shift over to his place, she wanted a bit of the old how's-your-father. But her boyfriend wasn't sounding so keen, not since he'd heard the name of the character with all the gravy.

Suddenly the boyfriend said the name again. This time it came over loud and clear, and there was no mistaking it.

Biggs wrote it down in capitals. NICK MACKENZIE. No wonder the name had sounded familiar. Just like the rock star.

The girl ended the call and after a few minutes he saw her leave the house and walk past the van.

He took the tape from the recorder, pocketed it and put in a fresh one. He set the recorder to sound-activated operation and, picking up his mobile, dialled Hillyard's number. Hillyard answered straight away. From the sound of it he was out of doors somewhere. As if to confirm it, there was the sound of a car door slamming.

Biggs gave him a full report, leaving the choicest bit till last. The moment Hillyard heard the backer's name, he started crowing with pleasure, his voice rising in a series of outrageous sighs, like a tart catching sight of a rich Arab. If Hillyard hadn't been such a regular employer, if he hadn't been such a pro in his work, Biggs would have told him to stuff off long ago. In his Met days Biggs had duffed up lesser queens than Auntie Colin, and for no more than the way they twinkled their little toes.

A car door slammed again, there were voices, and Hillyard's sighs ceased as quickly as they'd begun. In one of his lightning shifts of tone he shut off with a blunt: 'See yer.'

'Shall I bring the tape over?'

A car engine fired. 'Not now,' he snapped as if Biggs had suddenly ceased to exist. 'We're off.' And with an abrupt click the connection was broken.


The room was hot and uncomfortably crowded. Nick looked round for Susan but she had gone. He was startled not only by the fact that she'd vanished, but the speed with which she'd done it. A moment ago she'd been at his elbow, protecting him like a seasoned diplomat, guiding selected guests towards him, cutting off more unwelcome advances, steering people firmly away when their allotted five minutes were up, while at the same time moving him slowly but steadily through the room in a curve that would have brought him to the door – and escape – within fifteen minutes.

Her dress was an unusually vivid blue, her hair swept up into an ingenious and very distinctive topknot, but even from his height, normally a good one for crowded rooms, he couldn't spot her. He looked briefly for David but he, too, seemed to have disappeared.

He tried to calm himself, but he'd forgotten how easily these things rattled him. He tried to move away but someone was pulling at his elbow. He turned, hoping for Susan, and found himself facing a vermilion-lipped woman. She waved a programme in his face. 'I *hate* to be a nuisance,' she crowed, 'but you *did* promise.'

No one had a pen. Someone called for one. A second arm descended, waving a programme, then a third. People pressed in from both sides. Several voices spoke at once. He felt the heat rise into his face and the sweat start on his back, and knew he was hovering close to some limit that didn't bear thinking about. He felt a snatch of bewilderment, a spurt of anger, and finally and more persistently, misery.

Signing, replying as best he could to the questions, he kept looking up for signs of rescue. He saw the distinctive topknot over the sea of heads long before he saw her face. She was shouldering her way through the circle of people like a small but determined tank, apologizing profusely as she came, but in a tone of such authority that no one dared challenge her. When she finally burst through and stood in front of him she rolled her eyes in an expression of apology and sympathy.

'God, what animals,' she breathed. 'Sorry, but I had to go and find the *one* person you have to meet.' Taking his arm, she extricated him firmly from the group and led him back the way they had come. She must have sensed his alarm because she said: 'After this, that's it, I promise. The end – *really*. I'll never bother you again.' Stopping abruptly, she smiled: 'Apart from our curtain and carpet sessions of course. There's no escaping that!'

She squeezed his hand, then, releasing it, led him to a less crowded corner where a man stood waiting.

'Can I introduce Ronald Schenker?'

They shook hands. Schenker's grip was cool, like his expression.

'Ronald's a great benefactor of ours,' Susan explained. 'In fact I don't know what we'd do without him.'

Schenker gave a smile, modest but tinged with complacency, as if he didn't really believe he had a great deal to be modest about. He stood in a small man's posture, upright and slightly defensive.

Schenker eyed Nick appraisingly. 'I found the concert very interesting,' he said carefully, 'and far more . . .' He paused to choose his words. '. . . *thought*-provoking than I'd imagined.'

Nick took it as a compliment. 'Thanks.'

A waiter appeared with a tray of food. Aware that he should eat, Nick spiked three pieces of chicken and balanced them on a paper serviette. When he glanced up, he caught Schenker staring at him.

Schenker said in his studied way: 'I noticed that a number of your songs had ecological themes. Harking back to some Golden Age we were meant to have enjoyed when we were cave men.'

'Well, not quite – '

'There never was a Golden Age, you know. Life was tough, life was harsh. It was dog eat dog. It's only civilization and technical advances that have taken the sting out of the daily grind. No one ever got anywhere by going backwards, and that's truer today than it ever was in the distant past. It'd be extremely dangerous to chuck everything away and start again. We'd be sabotaging our chances of survival. You can't stop progress, you know.'

'Some of us think progress has gone far enough.'

'Oh, it's very quaint to think of turning the clock back, running everything off water power, recycling junk, starting up crafts and cottage industries, but the average person wouldn't take kindly to having his electricity rationed, his rubbish charged by the metre, his food doubling in price. There'd be a revolution.'

'But you can be selective about progress – keep the good, regulate the bad.'

'Ah, regulations!' Schenker bared his teeth in something that approached a smile. 'The present government's fought three campaigns on the issue of the free market economy, and won handsomely every time. I think maybe the public aren't too keen on having their lives regulated.'

'But they're keen on a better quality of life.'

'Quality of life,' Schenker mused as if he wasn't quite certain what that involved. 'To most people I think that means having more of what they want at a lower price.'

'I think most people want to sleep easy in their beds in the knowledge that they're breathing clean air, eating clean food, drinking clean water . . . Creating a healthy world for their kids to grow up in.'

'You make us sound as if we're working against it, trying to prevent it.'

Susan saw the question in Nick's face. 'Ronald's one of the baddies,' she explained in a whisper designed to be heard. 'He makes chemicals. He's chief executive of Morton-Kreiger.'

'Just the Agrochemical Division,' Schenker elucidated.

Susan winked in Nick's direction. 'He's still in charge of billions! Ronald's a corporate star.'

But Schenker made no response to her flattery, he was too busy watching Nick's face.

'Time to go,' Nick said to Susan, sending messages to show he meant it.

One thing about Susan, she was quick. She picked up his signal straight away and, narrowing her eyes in reply, spirited a highly plausible excuse out of thin air and gave Schenker a charming goodbye.

Taking Nick's arm, she cut a swathe through the room and had him outside and into his car before the autograph-hunters looked up from their champagne. Telling the driver to wait, she perched beside him on the seat for a moment.

'You look exhausted,' she said. 'I wish . . .' She didn't finish but leant over and pressed her cheek to his.

She pulled back and regarded him fondly. 'Was it such an ordeal, the party?'

'No,' he lied.

'It meant a lot, that you came.' She gave a little smile and said cheerfully: 'See you tomorrow as usual?'

He remembered something he was meant to be doing the next afternoon, something financial with David.

'I've got a brilliant fabric for your bathroom,' she said. 'Hand-made for a rich Arab with more money than taste.'

'Should be just the job then.'

She laughed as if he'd said something really funny; she was good like that.

'I'll come over then, shall I?'

He nodded.

'I'll bring the buns,' she whispered and kissed him lightly on the lips.


Hillyard drove into the estate on the dot of two a.m. Drawing up outside the Octek building, he killed the engine, wound the window down another notch, and listened. Satisfied, he signalled to the shadowy outline of Len's face in the mirror. He watched a crack of light appear as the van doors opened, and saw the dark figure slip out. Len closed rapidly on the gates. A moment later the padlock was undone and the gates swung open. Hillyard drove through and backed the van up the side of the building into the shadows.

Hillyard checked his pockets to make sure he had everything and climbed out to meet the other three as they emerged from the back of the van, carrying their gear. The four of them went up the side of the building and rounded the corner just as Len smashed the floodlight over the main entrance and plunged the area into a darkness relieved only by the dim light that spilled out from the interior.

They assembled by the main doors. Again Hillyard listened, again there was silence. Len moved into the patch of light thrown out from the glass door-panels, and started on the locks. Soon there was a click, then another, and they were into the lobby, lit by a single fluorescent light.

The alarm buzzed its warning. In a certain time, probably less than a minute, it would go off. Len, moving with soft-footed agility, was in front of the control box, tools in hand, even before the last of them – the boy – was through the door and moving towards his station by the office window.

Hillyard shone a light onto the control box. Despite the surgical gloves, Len worked with extraordinary speed, running wires across three sets of connections, cutting two intervening wires without visible hesitation.

Nevertheless time was getting on. Getting into the box had taken a good ten seconds, while the wire work had taken another forty, maybe more. Still the warning buzzer sounded. If Hillyard hadn't had such confidence in Len, if there had been anyone else to touch him in the whole of south London, he might have said something. As it was he tightened his grip on the torch and kept silent.

Len paused, a third wire held loosely in the jaws of his palm-sized cutters, and checked the connections. Giving an imperceptible grunt, he severed the wire.

The buzzing stopped. The silence closed in, shockingly loud.

Hillyard exhaled.

Len peered at him through his spectacles and asked

hopefully: 'What about them?' He indicated the doors at
the end of the passage.

Locks were a serious disease with Len and it positively
hurt him to leave them untried. 'No, my old darling,'
Hillyard whispered firmly. 'From now on it's amateur
night.'

He went to the door of the front office. The boy was at
the blinds, staring out into the night. The remaining two
already had the pickaxes in their hands. At Hillyard's nod
they went down the corridor and began smashing through
the double doors at the end.

The doors gave up without much of a fight. Leaving Len
to tidy up his control box, Hillyard followed the others
through the remains of the doors and, overtaking, led the
way into the first room, immediately to the right of the
passageway. Lighting a path across the floor with his torch,
he lowered the venetian blinds at all four windows and
shone the torch around the room until he found a desk
lamp. Switching it on, he gestured to the others to begin.

They chose the most inviting equipment first: wooden
carousels of test tubes which smashed with the satisfying
crunch of crushed wine glasses; tiers of jar-lined shelves
which bent and crumbled, shooting cascades of glass across
the floor; complex electronic equipment with VDU units
which imploded on impact.

Leaving them to it, Hillyard explored the rest of the
place. Plain unmarked doors to the left of the passageway,
one locked, the next – a store room – open, the last locked
again. To the right, a small room with rows of white shoes
in plastic bags and overalls hanging on pegs that led into
another laboratory even larger than the first. He went into
this room and, closing the blinds, looked for a small lamp.
Finding none, he went back to the door and flicked on one
of the overhead lights.

Returning to the first laboratory, he saw that the lads
had finished with their pickaxes and were now creating a

pile of chairs, papers and miscellaneous rubbish in the centre of the floor.

When they had finished he led them back into the passageway and asked them to tackle the two locked doors on the left. The first door revealed stacks of stored equipment, the second a much larger room whose occupants were announced by the pungent smell that went before them. The room was lined with banks of cages containing an assortment of rodents. Mice and rats; white, grey, piebald, black. There seemed to be hundreds of them.

Leading the two men into the second laboratory to start work there, he returned alone to the cages. 'Now wouldn't Beji love *you*,' he said, dragging a gloved finger across the rungs of a cage of white mice. He tried lifting the cage, but it was fastened down in some way. Squatting, he examined the sides and base of the cage, and saw that it was clipped to the next cage. Once the clips were undone it was a simple matter to lift the cage and carry it out. He took it to the side door which he'd noticed on his first visit. The door was fastened with bolts, but also a bloody great mortise lock. Hillyard looked up the passage and saw Len still tinkering with the control box. Hillyard called to him. Len, perking up like a hunting dog, came hurrying along, pulling his skeleton keys out of his pocket.

It took him about five seconds to get the lock open, a speed which seemed to both please and disappoint him. The rest of the job took considerably longer. Hillyard carried the cages, a pair at a time, out of the building and round to the back area, which, though dark, was the only place that was sufficiently distant from the van. There, having opened each cage, he had to spend more precious seconds getting its inhabitants to leave. The first lot of rats fell out all right, but the mice clung stubbornly to their cages. He had to shake the cage quite violently to get them out. On the second to last trip, shaking out a cage of fat grey rats, one of them fell against his leg and clutched at

his trousers. Jumping clear with a cry of repulsion, he
landed on something soft which squelched and crunched
underfoot. Cursing, he ran back to the side door and
scraped his shoe repeatedly on the doorstep. Shivering with
disgust he took the last pair of cages to the door and threw
them out into the darkness unopened. He turned to go
back inside then stopped suddenly, and, retracing his steps
to one of the unopened cages, picked it up and threw it
into the back of the van.

The others had finished in the second lab and were
hovering tensely in the passageway, waiting for him to give
the go-ahead for the next stage. Hillyard noticed they had
already collected the jerrycans from the front lobby.

Hillyard looked at his watch. They'd been in the building
twenty minutes. It felt like a long time. The men's restlessness was infectious, the urge to cut and run almost over-
powering, but Hillyard suppressed it. He knew that this
job, above all, had to be done properly.

'Not so quick, not so quick,' he flung at them, leading
the way to the store rooms.

Only when the store rooms had received the pickaxe
treatment and all the filing cabinets in the front offices had
been emptied onto the floor did Hillyard finally give the go-
ahead for the jerrycans to be emptied over the piles of
furniture and papers. 'Not too much!' he barked at one
point. 'We don't want a towering bloody inferno!'

By the time he had supervised the fuelling, he was behind
schedule. He hurried into the office and, yanking the phone
out of its socket, smashed it hard on the corner of the desk.
Pulling off the casing, he removed the tiny transmitter that
he had put there on his first visit and put it in his pocket.
Passing the boy at the window, he went out into the lobby.
Pulling an aerosol can from his pocket, he paused at the
main doors. On the nod from the boy he stepped outside.
He shook the spray can until he could hear the metal ball
rattling inside its housing. He chose the long stretch of wall

under the windows of the main office for his first effort. Considering the poor light, it wasn't too bad. For his next site he chose the main doors themselves then, as a final offering, a stretch of wall on the side of the building, which, though poorly lit, was nice and large, like a blank page.

As he finished, he remembered that the side door was still open. Finding Len, he sent him to close it again.

When Len returned Hillyard gestured questioningly towards the control box.

'All set,' Len confirmed.

Now it was a matter of getting things in the right order. He sent the boy to the main door, Len to the burglar alarm, and the other two down the passage to wait outside the doors of the labs. When everyone was in position he gave the nod. The first lab went up immediately with a great whoosh and flash of light; the other one he couldn't see, but it must have gone up all right because the man in charge of lighting it came running out into the passage like a bat out of hell. As the two fire-lighters came through the smashed swing doors Len reset the burglar alarm and closed the box. Hillyard would have liked to wait and see the offices go up, but there wasn't time.

He ran out and round the corner and jumped into the van. The boy was already at the gates, swinging them open. Hillyard fired the engine, drove the van out onto the front apron and reversed it up to the main doors. Len was bending over the locks on the front door. The moment he straightened up and moved clear, the other two attacked the doors with their pickaxes, as if they were only just going in. The sound of the splintering wood was horrendously loud, but it was nothing compared to the alarm, which went off suddenly a few seconds later, its bells piercing the darkness. It seemed to Hillyard that the whole neighbourhood must be up and looking out of their windows.

The flames in the front office were filling the window.

The next moment there was a great whoomph! as the glass blew out. Hillyard pricked up his ears. Under the jangling of the alarm, he thought he could hear a siren in the distance.

He slid across the seat and yelled through the window: 'Come *o-n*!'

The rear doors of the van opened and first Len, then the other two, jumped in. The boy flung himself into the passenger seat as Hillyard accelerated through the gates. The boy panted audibly all the way to the Chelmsford bypass.

Hillyard was panting too. Reaching across, he brushed his hand against the boy's thigh.

# Chapter 29

———

A LOG SETTLED noisily in the grate, sending licks of gold up the oak panelling and into the dusty drops of the dark chandelier. The room was warm, the rug soft under Susan's back. Lazily, she rolled over and picked a crumpet off the dish by the hearth. The crumpet, sagging with melted butter, pliant as a sponge, was heavy with the scent of schooldays and other diet-free eras of long ago. She bit into it with a delicious sense of rediscovery. It had been a long time since she'd allowed herself anything so wicked.

Keeping her eyes off Nick – he mustn't feel she was crowding him – she looked casually towards the window. It was a filthy afternoon. Rain splattered against the glass, leaves streamed off the trees, and the sky was darkening rapidly. No sound penetrated the room – the double-glazing was too thick for that – and she was left with the curious but exhilarating sensation that everything that lay outside – London, people, family – was at a great remove, incapable of intruding on the afternoon.

She finally rewarded herself with a look at Nick. He was sitting on the floor with his back against the sofa, the wallpaper book open on his knees, his shoulders hunched, his face creased with concentration, like a student pondering some impossible maths problem. As always when she looked at him she felt a tiny proprietorial thrill, an involuntary spasm of excitement, the precise nature of which it wasn't necessary to examine. It was enough, she'd decided, to experience the surge of feeling, to ride the rush of elation which, after a week of these tea parties, seemed to be spilling over rather pleasantly into every part of her life.

She watched him, and smiled affectionately. He had a way of chewing on the side of his lip, of splaying his fingers over his cheek, of drawing sudden hissing breaths on his cigarette that suggested a bafflement, a mild helplessness that was really very attractive. This hint of vulnerability, and his habit of letting people get closer to him only by the smallest and most tantalizing degrees, made him rather a challenge.

She was making progress though, chipping softly away at his defences. She thought, not for the first time, of how satisfactorily things had changed. When they had been together all those years ago there had been passion – on her part at least – but also some beastly misunderstandings.

Nick flicked over a page and pulled at his chin. Unlike Tony, he was one of those men who had improved with age. Lean body, thick hair, intriguing face.

She had promised not to interrupt him while he studied the wallpaper samples – a rather professional-sounding assurance, she had thought – but what had been a reasonable pause had now stretched into an unwieldy silence, and silences were not something Susan felt comfortable with.

'I'm keeping quiet,' she said. 'I hope you've noticed.'

'It's no good,' he said, snapping the book shut and sliding it onto the floor. 'They're all beginning to look the same. You'll have to choose.'

'No problem,' she said happily. 'We could paper one wall and if you don't like it, we can take it down and start all over again.'

He nodded distractedly and she saw that she had lost him. This happened now and again: one moment he'd be there, listening attentively, sliding her the occasional glance in that oblique way of his, the next moment he'd slip away into a part of his mind that excluded her as completely as if he'd left the room.

'You were so brave at the party!' she said, pushing just the right balance of fondness and mockery into her voice.

His eyes flicked towards her but she could see he was only half listening.

'I still can't get over the way those women besieged you,' she went on lightly. 'People with money are the worst of all, I'm afraid. Think they've bought you along with the ticket.'

'Tell me about Schenker,' Nick asked suddenly.

She shrugged. 'Oh, he's just a mogul. You know . . . earnest. And dull.'

'Ruthless?'

'Ooh, that's a strong word!' she laughed. Sensing she had hit too flippant a note, she made a show of giving the question serious consideration. 'I don't know him *that* well,' she said, 'but ruthless – yes, I would think so. Why?'

But he didn't answer. Instead he asked: 'He knows your husband quite well, I suppose?'

Now where was this leading? Generally he never asked about Tony, not directly. 'Oh, they've met . . .' she said casually. 'You know – at functions, in the House. These companies always do quite a bit of lobbying. Oh, and he's taken us to the opera a couple of times. But then all the big companies do that – take us to things.'

Nick absorbed this slowly, staring intently at the fire.

The opportunity of deepening the conversation while at the same time airing the subject of Tony – something she'd been wanting to do for some time – was not to be missed. 'I hardly see Tony nowadays,' she murmured a little ruefully. 'He's in Luxembourg at the moment. Some trade talks, or whatever. But even if he'd been free to come to the party, he'd have persuaded himself he couldn't. In fact since he became a politician – well . . .' She gave a valiant little laugh and, though she didn't plan it, her breath caught rather attractively in her throat. 'We don't really communicate much . . . His work just eats him up. And he's so

incredibly hyped up all the time, rushing around like a
madman, that we don't have time to talk – about *anything*.
So I've rather given up, I'm afraid.' She looked down at the
rug and pulled delicately at the pile. 'I'm not complaining,
not exactly. Well, perhaps I *am*,' she added, shooting him a
fleeting smile. Looking suitably serene, she added: 'But I
think one has to try to make the best of things, don't you?
Even when they're – difficult. Make do. Muddle through.'

Nick lit a cigarette, propped an elbow on one knee and
looked into the fire. He was gathering himself to say
something in that cautious thoughtful way of his, but just
as he began to speak the phone rang. Usually he ignored it,
letting his housekeeper pick it up somewhere in the depths
of the house, but now he got up to answer it. 'My direct
line. Sorry . . .'

Direct line. She hadn't realized he had one. She certainly
didn't have the number for it, and she rather thought she
should. It was someone called David. David Weinberg,
presumably.

Nick was mumbling a perfunctory apology for having
missed some meeting or another. Susan reached for another
crumpet. It wouldn't do any harm when she was burning
up so much nervous energy.

'*What!*' Nick's voice was sharp and raw.

Susan abandoned the crumpet. Nick was sinking slowly
onto the sofa, reaching out a hand to steady himself.

'God!' he groaned, dropping abruptly into his seat and
clamping a hand to his face. 'I might have known! I should
have known!'

He listened for a few moments longer, muttering the
occasional 'God!' and 'Christ!', then, the conversation
apparently over, slumped wearily back in his seat, the
receiver forgotten in his hand until, looking down, he
swung it slowly back into its cradle.

Susan was on her feet. 'What's the matter?'

Almost immediately, the phone rang again. This time

Nick ignored it and after a few rings it stopped. He covered his head with his hands.

'*Nick* – what is it?'

He dropped his hands.

'Would you do something for me, Susan?'

'Of course.'

'Look and see if there's anyone hanging around the gate.'

'Of course.' She started across the room.

'Don't let them see you.' Nick's voice followed her.

A chill of excitement squirmed in her stomach; this was rather an adventure.

She approached the window at an angle, keeping away from the glass. The cloud had lifted a little, the rain abated, but now it was almost dusk and the streetlamps were burning a dull orange.

The house was fronted by a short garden of ornamental paving and thin strips of lawn, and screened from the road by a high wall.

'I can't see from here,' she called. 'Shall I try upstairs?'

'Would you?' His face was grim.

She went upstairs to the guest bedroom that lay immediately above the sitting room and peered cautiously from behind the edge of the curtain. Someone passed under the streetlamp on the opposite pavement, head down, small dog in train. A car was backing into a parking place. Otherwise nothing. She was rather disappointed. A man got out of the parked car and crossed the street diagonally, heading straight for the house. The next moment she heard a bell sound deep in the house.

She raced downstairs to hear Nick giving instructions that he was abroad and not available for comment.

'Didn't take them long!' he remarked bitterly.

'Nick, what *is* it?'

He lit a cigarette, shut his lighter with an angry snap and sucked the smoke in greedily. 'You're trapped as well,

I'm afraid – unless you want to get snapped, of course. They won't leave, you know, not until they get fed up. Or it's near closing time.'

She took a few steps closer to him. 'Who?'

'The papers! The tabloids!' He gestured towards the front of the house. 'They won't give up.' His tone was belligerent, indignant.

'Nick . . .' She made a calming voice. 'What's it all about?'

He gave a harsh chuckle. 'You might as well know. The whole of the rest of the bloody world'll know by the morning, so there's no reason why you shouldn't be the first.'

She went up to him and, kneeling at his side, tugged gently at his arm. After a moment's hesitation, he sat down beside her on the rug, resting his elbows on his knees.

'There's this research project I got involved with, a scientific project,' he began slowly. 'Well, the building – the laboratory they were using – it got burnt down in the night, totally destroyed.' He snorted mirthlessly. 'By animal rights campaigners, of all people. Angry at what the evil scientists were planning to do to the rats and mice. Protesting . . . Funny really . . .' He dropped his head onto his knees for a moment, then flicked a sideways glance at her. 'You see, I funded the place.'

Susan maintained her expression of concern. 'I see,' she said gently, not seeing very much at all. 'You, er – ' She grappled with her available ideas. 'It was a good cause, was it?'

He told her. He explained it fully, from the beginning, although afterwards she realized it wasn't quite the beginning, because he didn't disclose his real interest in the chemical called Silveron, not until a little later.

He told her about Catch and what they were trying to achieve with the Octek project, how the boy in Scotland had got sick, how several other forestry workers had been affected. How he had provided the funds on the condition that no one knew of his involvement.

A million pounds, a hidden laboratory: the extravagant whims of a rich man. The images were like breaths of excitement.

'I asked for total secrecy,' he murmured bitterly. 'I should have known.'

As if to emphasise the press interest, the phone rang. They waited for the unseen housekeeper to silence it. It rang again almost immediately and, with an exclamation of impatience, Nick jumped to his feet and took the receiver off the hook. He returned to the rug.

He went on, his voice thin and rough. He told her, haltingly, circuitously, why secrecy had been so important to him, and finally she understood. It was all about his wife. He thought this chemical had killed his wife.

He lit another cigarette, and she saw that his hands were trembling slightly.

'And now, just to put the lid on everything, they'll brand me a vivisectionist!' he cried painfully. 'Bloody great! Bloody terrific!'

She put a hand on his arm and squeezed it. 'They'll understand, once they know your reasons for doing it.'

He twisted his body away to look at her incredulously. 'Know my reasons?' he exclaimed. 'I'm not bloody telling them. Christ, no! It's bad enough them having this, without giving them . . .' He couldn't say it. 'No, I'm not going to tell them anything.'

She wanted to say: But they'll work it out for themselves. Perhaps he realized the inevitability of it, because all the energy went out of him and, turning back to the fire, he slumped his arms on his knees. His shoulder came up against hers. 'You mustn't tell them anything you don't want to,' she said reassuringly. She stroked a finger across the back of his hand, very lightly, as she had done for Camilla when she was small. 'Poor darling,' she murmured.

'Poor love.' It seemed to pacify him. She slipped her hand over his, and clasped it. He didn't pull away.

'What about a statement?' she suggested. 'To give your version.'

'I've done it,' he said exhaling smoke slowly downwards. 'I just told David what to say.'

'So there's nothing more to be done?'

'No.'

'Well, then.'

But he wasn't quite talked out yet, and it was another ten minutes or so before his despondency finally bordered on resignation.

She said again: 'Well, then.' He was very close. With her free hand she brushed the back of her fingers lightly across his cheek, once, and again.

'Poor love,' she breathed. A warmth hit her stomach, her heart fluttered nervously.

For a moment neither of them moved, then he flicked his cigarette into the fire. He closed his eyes, tightened his lips and, dropping his head, pressed his cheek against her fingers.

'Poor love.' She heard her voice from a distance, deep and uneven.

He twisted his head slowly towards hers, his eyes still closed; she turned her cheek to meet his. They stayed like that for a moment, their cheeks touching, then she reached up and put a hand on his neck and stroked it gently.

'Poor love.'

He moved first; she met his lips as they turned to find hers. He had moved first, and the triumph roared in her ears.


'Miss Field, would you mind?' The inspector leaned in through the open door and beckoned outwards. 'Something I'd like to discuss.'

Daisy pushed the remains of her cold hamburger back in its carton and climbed stiffly out of the police car. The inspector turned and led the way through the slanting rain into the Octek compound, past the last remaining fire engine, the flattened hoses, the piles of charred furniture. A group of workmen were hammering boards over the gaping holes that had been the doors and windows. On the outside walls the taunting graffiti stood out garishly, its lettering untarnished.

Inside, a fire officer was waiting for them. He introduced himself as a senior investigator and led the way into B-Lab, or what remained of it. Half the roof had gone, and most of the contents, blackened, pulverised or otherwise destroyed.

'Very methodical,' said the fire officer. 'Smashed everything first. All the glass, all the equipment, then stacked the combustibles in the centre here. Very methodical. Axes, from the look of it, like they used on the front doors. Then an inflammatory agent – undoubtedly petrol. You can see the way everything burnt outwards from here.' He indicated the concentric circles of water-soaked ash and debris.

'And the animal quarters . . .' interjected the inspector. 'Took every cage out – they were clipped down, you said?' – this to Daisy – 'Now *that* couldn't have been done in a hurry.'

The inspector's name was Brent. At the beginning of the long day, when she was still in a state of numbness and shock, she had misheard his name and called him Bent.

'They took their time,' commented the inspector enigmatically.

He was waiting for Daisy to draw some great conclusion. A gust of wind rattled through the remains of the roof.

'Did they?' she echoed dutifully.

With the air of someone grudgingly revealing a valuable card, Brent said: 'The alarm sounded at 0235 hours. We have a resident on the other side of the main road who can confirm that exactly. In the bathroom at the time, he was. Heard it go off and looked at his watch. Then a couple of minutes later, looked out of his window and saw the glow of the fire. Phoned the fire brigade straight away. Got here in six minutes.'

She still hadn't made the great connection. 'So? I'm sorry . . .'

'The fire was already well away when he looked out. Which means it was already burning when the alarm went off.' The inspector looked at her as if this explained everything. Catching her expression he continued heavily: 'Which suggests our friends got in well before it went off – must have done, to have got all this work done. Unless the alarm was faulty. But you said you had the security firm check it a month ago, so it doesn't seem very likely, does it?'

There was a pause. Rain dripped off a beam and spattered noisily onto a curl of charred roofing felt. 'I'm sorry, Inspector, I don't see . . .'

'Seems like they got in without setting off the alarm.'

She waited.

'Like they had access.'

He was watching her carefully. Ah, she was beginning to get the idea now. It was an insurance job. She herself had set it up for the money.

'There was very little insurance cover, Inspector. Certainly not enough to make it worthwhile.'

He absorbed this impassively, then ignored it. 'It makes the job very professional, Miss Field.'

Wherever this was meant to be leading, she really couldn't guess. 'But I thought animal rights groups *were* professional nowadays,' she said. 'You know, all geared up . . .'

'Not so professional that they'd reset the alarm as they

were leaving so as to make it look as though they hadn't
got past it in the first place.'

'I'm not sure of what you're getting at – '

The rain had formed a droplet on the end of his nose,
which vibrated as he spoke. 'I was hoping you might be
able to tell me, Miss Field.'

Guessing games. She shook her head firmly to show she
wasn't going to play. 'There's nothing I can tell you,
Inspector.'

Perhaps dusk had been coming on for some time and
she just hadn't noticed, but when she walked back along
the side of the building the firemen had rigged up a
floodlight on the forecourt to help the workmen fix the
last of the boards to the windows. The cast of the light
gave the graffiti on the front wall a new prominence, like
an advertisement for a coming attraction. *Animal Liberation! End Experiments!* Looking at it again, she noticed
the lettering which, like everything else, was rather professional.

Professional . . . Why shouldn't activists be professional?
Wasn't everyone nowadays? Charities, muggers, beggars
. . . masters of their various arts.

She noticed that the stringer from the local paper, a
spotty-faced young man in a Dick Tracy raincoat, had
returned and was loitering near the police car. By the way
he perked up at the sight of her, it wasn't hard to guess
who he was waiting for.

But Mabel, Octek's office factotum, reached Daisy first.
She brought a phone message from Jenny, who had managed to track Mabel down to her home nearby.

The message was succinct. It read: *Adrian Bell taken
into care at eight this morning under place of safety order.
Social services, police. Nothing anyone could do. Children's
panel hearing in a week.*

Daisy felt a lurch of bitter disappointment. Needing to

be alone, she walked rapidly through the gate and out of the compound.

'Miss Field, may I have another word?'

She walked on blindly.

'Miss Field?'

The raincoat bounced along at her side; she realized with sinking heart that, leech-like, it had attached itself to her and would have to be driven away. She hissed: 'I've nothing to add to what I said this morning, Mr – Bishop.'

'Brown, actually. Wayne Brown.' He took a couple of skips to get ahead of her as, turning, she went in the direction of her car. 'We've had a report come through, Miss Field,' he said, walking rapidly sideways. 'I was wondering if you'd care to comment. It's about Octek being involved in the unlicensed testing of chemicals – '

*Unlicensed?* God, where had this come from? 'No, no – I have nothing to say,' she insisted, digging into her pocket for her keys.

'The report says the financial backing came from Nick Mackenzie, the rock star. Is that right, Miss Field?'

She faltered, almost lost her balance, stopped. She stared at him. '*What?*'

'Nick Mackenzie,' he repeated with awful certainty. 'According to the report, he put up the money for this place. Could you confirm that, Miss Field?'

She managed to shake her head.

'Are you denying the story, then?'

'No . . . I mean – no comment. No comment!' Her head was light and bursting. She twisted round, momentarily disorientated, and looked for the car.

'Would you confirm that he was involved?'

'*No.*' She fastened on the car, and made for it, head low, blinking rapidly to clear the smarting from her eyes. Keys – where the *hell*? She scrabbled in her bag.

'It'll be all over the nationals tomorrow, Miss Field. All over. It'll look strange if you don't comment.' He ducked his head, trying to catch her eye. 'When did Mr Mackenzie become involved, Miss Field? Was it his idea? What were the animals involved? What exactly was being tested here, Miss Field?'

Her throat was dry, her head pounding. Keys, *keys*. Turning her frustration on her bag, she upended it on the car bonnet and shook it mercilessly.

Wayne darted forward ingratiatingly. 'Can I do anything?'

Extricating the keys, she jammed them into the lock and, losing her grip on her temper, told him tersely in words of four letters what he could do with himself. Looking aggrieved, he retreated. 'It'll all be out by tomorrow,' he echoed reproachfully. 'You'll be sorry you didn't give me your story.'

Shaking, still dangerously close to violence, she scooped up the contents of her bag and drove away. A hundred yards up the main road she swerved into the side and stopped, reaching for breath. She jammed her hands against her face and muttered furiously: '*God, God* ...' as the realization sank in: this was the end of everything – Octek, Adrian's freedom. Nick.

She groaned aloud as the full horror of Nick's position dawned on her. The papers – she could imagine the sort of line they would go for. *Rock star's secret lab attacked by animal libbers ... Singer's animal laboratory inferno ... Protest star silent on vivisection slur ...* As far as the animal-loving Brits were concerned, they might as well call him a child murderer and be done with it.

All he had asked was silence, a degree of protection, and she had let him down. For some reason she was certain it was she who had let him down. Somewhere, somehow she had let this happen. Somewhere, somehow she had trusted someone too much.

She blew her nose and angled the rear-view mirror downwards. She dragged at her eyes blindly, smearing the dampness away, and thought: *Who?* She realized it hadn't been so long ago that she'd asked that very question in relation to the leaking of Peasedale's involvement in Octek.

*Who?*

She reached Kensington just after eight. The rain had eased off. It took her a while to find the address, which was near Holland Park. It lay in a dark tree-lined street of ambassadorial residences with well-camouflaged house numbers. Nick's place was towards the end, a substantial house set behind a high wall. Above a screen of tall shrubs gothic gables rose sharp against the sky; no lights showed.

Beside the solid wooden gate there was a video-phone with a glowing buzzer. When she pressed it a light sprang on. She stared resolutely at the camera lens, her heart high in her chest.

The wind rattled the leaves of a nearby shrub, a branch creaked, a walker's heels clacked rhythmically along the other side of the street. The light went off with a slight click. She had the sensation of momentary disconnection, then, coming to, she reached up and pressed the buzzer again.

'Gone abroad.' A voice from behind, bored, knowing.

She twisted round. The man was close, but he had his back to the streetlight and she couldn't make out his face.

'At least that's what they're saying.' He shifted slightly then, stiffening, squinted at her. 'It – er – wouldn't be Miss Field, would it?'

'No comment.'

'No need to be like that,' he chuckled triumphantly. 'No need at all. I'm from the *Sun*. We've been good friends of yours in the past, Miss Field, very good friends, haven't we? *And* of Mr Mackenzie's – I think he'd agree about that, in fact I'm sure he would. Knows we can be relied on to give a fair quote. What about a quote, Miss Field? Can you tell me – '

'Get lost.' She stabbed at the buzzer, then, in a fit of desperation, left her finger on it.

'Miss Field – I'll take your words down verbatim. No aggro. You can say as much or as little as you like. No pressure. I'm good with the human angle. My speciality, you might say. They always give me the victims – '

A voice barked out of the video-phone. Hurriedly, guiltily Daisy jerked her finger off the buzzer as if it had stung her. It was a male voice, staccato, edged with fury. Nick.

For an instant Daisy stared vacantly at the camera before putting her mouth to the grille. 'Daisy. Daisy Field.' As she pulled back the reporter moved closer, coming in for Nick's response. Daisy slapped her hand over the grille as if that could prevent Nick's voice from emerging, and, parting her fingers, added hastily: 'Let me in – ' She almost said *Nick*, but stopped herself. 'There's a guy bothering me.'

A pause, a silence, she thought for a moment that he wouldn't let her in, then the door-release sounded. She pushed her way through into the garden and slammed the gate behind her.

No lights showed at any of the windows, nor at the door just visible at the end of a short path. She waited on the doorstep. A bolt shot back, a lock turned. The door opened and he stood there in a pool of yellow light, barefoot, hair tousled, an open shirt pushed haphazardly into the waistband of his jeans. He didn't speak but moved back a step and indicated with a small jerk of his head that she could come in. His expression was grim.

He pushed the door closed behind her, and stood there, feet apart, arms folded. She didn't have to ask if he'd heard what had happened, it was written all over his face.

'Well?' he demanded, and his tone was like ice.

'I . . . just wanted you to know that I have no idea how the press got hold of this . . . I wanted to say – I'm sorry, *really* sorry . . .'

'Is that it?' he asked caustically. 'If so, then – ' He moved to open the door again.

'No – I . . . Please. I wanted to explain.'

'Explain? You're joking!' He gave an ugly laugh. His gaze was unwaveringly hostile.

'But it's not the way it looks!' she pleaded. 'If you'd just let me explain.'

He hesitated, then, with the heavy air of someone overcoming his better judgement, moved away from the door and briskly refolded his arms. 'So?'

'It was . . .' She grasped at a half-formed idea, something that had taken root during the journey from Chelmsford, and developed it rapidly. 'I think the whole thing was planned. I think they knew all about Silveron, all about what we were doing, long before the raid. And the story about you – they leaked that specially, to get at you. To discredit you – '

'Well, they did a bloody good job, didn't they?' he interrupted bitterly. 'I'm for the slaughter tomorrow, and that's for sure.' He made another move for the door.

'No, no, you don't understand – ' She gabbled slightly in her rush to explain it to him, to get the idea straight in her mind. 'The animal rights people – we were meant to think it was them – but it wasn't! The police said it couldn't have been – too professional. The burglar alarm had been disconnected, and they said the animal people aren't up to that sort of stuff. Disconnected and reconnected, in fact – so it wouldn't go off until the fire started. That way they had time to wreck everything and get the fires going and get away before anyone knew . . .' Not certain that he'd absorbed the enormity of what she was saying, she explained: 'There were no animal rights people! They never existed. They were just a front, for someone else. Someone who wanted to stop what we were doing.'

Perhaps she was selling the idea too hard, perhaps he simply wasn't ready for it, but his face had become a mask of disbelief. 'These people are really dangerous,' she argued, hearing the desperation in her voice. 'They could have killed someone!'

'But they didn't, did they?' he exclaimed with a bark of sarcasm. 'Except *me*, of course.'

'Okay,' she said in sudden surrender. 'Okay.' She spread her hands wide. 'So it's my fault. Okay, so I fouled up. I take the blame. All right.' She fisted her hands. 'But, listen – if we give up now, then they'll have won. They'll have beaten us – '

'What are you saying?' His face was alight with incredulity. 'What are you suggesting? Are you saying we should go *on*?' He hit the heel of his hand against his forehead in an extravagant gesture of disbelief. 'Incredible! I don't believe it!' He let his voice rip. 'Christ – I've never known anyone with such – such total *tunnel* vision. God – you beat everything. *Everything* . . .' He took a stride closer. 'Tell me – what does it take for you to get the message? How can I get through to you?'

'I think you're getting through to me,' she said quietly.

'I am? Good! *Good!* Well, the message is – it's all over. Finished. *Finished.* I was crazy to agree to this thing in the first place! Crazy to think there was a hope in hell of keeping it quiet! Crazy to think that you – that you – ' He took a pace back, then swayed forward again, looming over her. 'I never want to hear about this again – got it?'

He was very close. She had a sudden memory of the island, and the touch of his cheek when she had reached her arms round his neck and hugged him.

She held up her hands in submission. 'Okay,' she said, trying to steady her voice. 'Okay.'

He hovered for a moment, not entirely convinced of victory, then let out a long breath and stood back.

Daisy cleared her throat. 'One thing. The boy – Adrian – he's been taken into care. No warning, the social services just arrived this morning and took him away. It'll take months to get him back. Lawyers, costs . . . The last of the cash – I thought perhaps you wouldn't mind?'

His hands unwound, his shoulders slumped. He was just beginning to focus on the idea when there was a sound from deeper inside the house, a loud clinking of china and a sharp exclamation, quickly followed by a crash, the sort that comes from a catastrophic breakage.

Nick started across the hall, calling: 'Are you all right?' Reaching an open door, he put his head through and said something Daisy couldn't hear. There was a reply, which she missed as well, but she could make out the speaker's gender all right. Female, a liquid voice, a rich laugh.

Daisy thought hastily: Well of course, there was bound to be somebody. There had to be. She did her best to sit hard on her emotions, but some of them bulged out untidily, like air in an unruly cushion.

Nick turned back. Sighting Daisy, his eyes hardened again. Clearly not in the mood to waste any more time, he raced for the door, his hand reaching out to pull it open.

'The boy,' she reminded him as he sped past.

'What?' He yanked open the door and glared at her. Finally he gave a short sharp nod. 'Okay.'

'Thanks,' she said. Stepping out, she turned back. 'And thanks for everything else, for your support.'

'Bye,' he said sharply, and shut the door.

In a state of emotional suspension, hardly aware of what she was doing, she set off in the general direction of Holloway. Nearing King's Cross, she changed her mind suddenly and made for Simon's flat. Yes, *you*, she thought with sudden viciousness. I want to talk to *you*!

But his car wasn't outside, there was no answer to her ring. She crossed the street and looked up at his windows. During his creative phases he had been known to ignore the doorbell, but tonight there were no seams of light showing through the blinds. Back in the Metro, she swore and hit her palm against the wheel. She thrust the key into

the ignition and twisted it brutally. The engine turned with
an agonized shudder and failed to start. With each attempt,
the turns became progressively more half-hearted until the
engine lapsed into silence, leaving only the tortuous whine
and click of the starter motor.

She sat back and laughed emptily. She was past any
other reaction.

Three lads from a nearby pub gave the car a push, but
the engine refused to show the slightest spark, and, thank-
ing her helpers, she abandoned the Metro in a meter bay
and took a taxi.

The stairway leading to her flat was spattered with dust
and debris that crunched noisily underfoot. Inside, the
builders had moved the furniture round again, but this
time, as if to make up for their previous lapse, had draped
almost everything with plastic dustsheets, so that only the
rugs had caught the splashes of plaster from the new ceiling.

Mess or no mess, it was still home. Within minutes, she
had set up the small table in front of her old red armchair
by the gas fire. While she waited for the water to heat in
the cistern, she sat down to call Mrs Bell. She dialled the
number then, jamming her finger on the rest, cut the line
before it had a chance to ring. Mrs Bell could wait. The
care order wouldn't be heard for a week, nothing could be
done for Adrian tonight.

There was time for six Jaffa cakes and two glasses of
wine before the water was hot. When at last she sank into
the bath, armed with a fresh glass, her mind felt dazzlingly,
dangerously lucid.

There was no doubt: Simon was the traitor. Oh, maybe
not in the way she had first thought. Conspiracy and
bribery weren't really his style: it was impossible to imagine
Simon lowering himself to dealing direct with the opposition. No, it was much more likely that he had trapped
himself into an error of judgement. He was egotistical
enough to believe he could weave his way effortlessly

through his web of contacts, sufficiently vain to think his judgement infallible. He had probably exchanged the information on Nick for something else, had probably used it to impress his editor, and come unstuck. Of course he'd never admit to it, not even to the slightest possibility. Even during the best of their relationship, Simon had not been able to admit to anything so prosaic as leaving a ring around the bath.

Illuminated by the wine, she saw everything with absolute clarity. Simon had been using her, manipulating her in that dry unemotional way of his. He had looked down on her from his intellectual pedestal, poured scorn on her ideas, then sold her short. Realizing this, she felt a wild irrational anger at all the food and creative support she had provided for him.

She slid down in the water and wet her hair. When she came up again, it was with a compulsive desire to tell him to his face. 'Ha!' she cackled aloud, and heard the drink singing in her voice.

After the traumas and confusions of the day, retaliation was a good clear-cut emotion, something nice and straightforward one could get one's teeth into, and wrapped in her old dressing gown in front of the fire, she dwelt lovingly and voraciously on the idea.

She was, she supposed, quite drunk – the bottle, she noted with some amazement, was empty: a whole bottle, for God's sake. But if the clarity of her mind was fading, it was compensated by an almost euphoric determination.

She lifted the phone.

Either Simon wasn't answering or he was still out, because his machine clicked on at the second ring. Drawing breath, she started on her little speech.

In case he'd been in Mongolia, she gave him the news of the fire and the daubed animal rights slogans. Then, her head singing with wine, her heart lurching with harsh excitement, she gave him her new version of events. The police had already established it wasn't animal rights campaigners, she declared, knew it had just been a front. Oh, they might not have the complete evidence to nail the real culprits, but they soon would. Then Morton-Kreiger would have to dig their way out of *that* one! As for the laboratory itself, well – no one was giving up, she said, and certainly not Nick Mackenzie. There were already plans for a new laboratory. She heard herself give a brief bray of triumph, a raucous discordant laugh. She had meant to stop there, but her voice took off, self-propelled, swollen with wine, and she heard herself saying there was more, much more – an immense scandal involving cooked data on Silveron. Picturing the disbelief in Simon's face, just *seeing* how he would be taking this, she said she had the hard evidence right *here*. And what was more she had someone in a key position who could verify it, back it up all the way. Then the lid would blow right off the whole rotten business. End of Morton-Kreiger. Pumph! But there'd be no story until the time was right – until *she* decided it was right – then she'd go public – though she would not, she implied rather subtly, bring the story to *him*.

She rang off with a brief sense of triumph. The feeling of release was soon overshadowed by a sense of futility. What had that proved? What had that done? Simon would merely think her stupid and drunk. And he would be right.

She woke once in the middle of the night, sprawled awkwardly across the chair, in a muck sweat from the fire which was still on at full blast. Switching it off, she lurched across the room, opened a window and burrowed under the plastic sheets onto the unmade bed. After a succession of nightmares peopled by men in white coats and arsonists working in full technicolour, she woke again at dawn, her mouth thick, her head clogged with EEC-approved wine additives. Getting up to fetch water, she passed the empty wine bottle, saw the phone.

In the cold light, she felt a sudden regret.

# Chapter 30

NICK FELT SOMETHING brush against his shoulder and woke with a lurch that sent his heart racing. In the instant before his memory came plunging back, he felt an upsurge of panic, a stab of something that almost overwhelmed him.

Then Susan spoke.

'Did I wake you? Oh, my love – I'm sorry.' She moved against his back and stroked his arm. He could feel the contours of her body, soft and bony, firm and warm.

He lay still for a moment, absorbing the sensation of female flesh against his, feeling a quaking relief at not, for once, waking alone.

He grappled for his watch in the semi-darkness and couldn't find it. 'What time is it?'

'I think we missed tea,' she laughed. The bed shook slightly as she put on the bedside light. 'Five thirty.' Her head came back against his shoulder. 'Were you dreaming, poor love? You were twitching and muttering so much, I didn't know whether to wake you. I didn't sleep. I always feel dreadful if I sleep in the afternoons – an absolute beast for the rest of the day.' Her hand came down his arm, following it round to his chest, weaving her fingers through his. 'Poor love – a nasty dream?'

He murmured, 'Not so good,' which was true, though he couldn't remember the details. Then, because he didn't want to set too depressing a tone, he said: 'I was being chased by a herd of reporters – or something like that.'

'Oh, those stories! I know you don't believe me – when I got here today I could almost *see* you thinking that I was only saying it to make you feel better – but they really *weren't* that bad, you know. Not bad at all! None of them said *anything* as remotely terrible as what you were worrying about last night.' She pushed herself up on one elbow. 'Honestly, they were *kind*, darling.' She put her cheek against his, and he caught the scent of her rather overpowering perfume. 'They *like* you, the press, they really do!'

He almost laughed. They may have been kind on one level – no one had openly called him an animal experimenter or an out-and-out hypocrite – but there wasn't a single newspaper which hadn't linked the story with Alusha's mysterious 'poisoning', and suggested, openly or not so openly, that he was involved in some sort of vendetta. And of course the tabloids had been unable to resist rehashing some of the more titillating evidence from the fatal accident inquiry. Yes, they may have been obliging on the surface, but they were still merciless about the past. He had been bracing himself for a frontal assault, only to find that they had stolen up on him from behind and taken him by surprise. Like old wounds, the memories had reopened painfully.

Susan tugged gently at his shoulder, and he rolled halfway onto his back. Leaning over him, she kissed him on the mouth, a fond lingering kiss. Then she smiled the broad contented smile she had been giving him ever since she'd arrived that afternoon. Whether it was the excitement of sneaking out through the garage at three that morning disguised with a scarf and old raincoat of the housekeeper's that appealed to her, or the rapid development of their relationship, he didn't want to guess. It wasn't that he exactly regretted starting this affair – although he wasn't entirely sure about that yet – but he rather wished it hadn't happened at this particular moment, when he was feeling besieged again; he wished he'd had more time to think it over.

But then it was the very fact that he was besieged that had made him turn to her. And perhaps it wasn't such a bad decision. He'd forgotten what a luxury it was to have someone to talk to, someone who wasn't otherwise involved in his life, someone who'd never known Alusha. He'd had the occasional relationship or near-relationship over the last few months – all brief, all highly unsatisfactory, all wanting what he wouldn't or couldn't give. Susan, by comparison, was undemanding. Well, so far. And though the arrangement, with its secrecy and lack of commitment, was far from ideal, it would do for now.

'What about a short break?' she suggested soothingly. 'Get away for a while. Somewhere you can relax.'

'I would, but I need to work.'

'But your European tour – surely you deserve some time off before all that?'

'No – you see, I *want* to work. There's something I have to finish.'

'Can't you work abroad?'

He sat up and stretched. 'Difficult.' He rubbed his face. 'I need a studio.'

'Oh.'

Her hands pushed up his back and started massaging his shoulders. The feel of hands on his skin . . . He closed his eyes.

'And where do you have to go to find a studio?'

He'd been thinking about that, but it was only now that he realized he had made up his mind. 'Scotland.'

'*Scotland*. Not to . . .? But I thought – ' She checked herself and gave a small exclamation, as if to tick herself off for straying into forbidden territory. She was good like that; she never delved too far. 'Well, if it'll make you happy . . .'

Happy? What he felt when he worked was too obsessive

for that, but it was a contentment of sorts, and, most important of all, a form of oblivion. Before going on the Arizona dry-out his mind had refused to wrap itself round anything even vaguely creative, but now it was showing definite signs of life. He'd spent a few evenings in a borrowed studio in London trying to push the choral piece forward, but though the familiar slow-burning excitement had begun to simmer away in his brain again, he knew there was only one place where he could really work.

Exhibiting her talents as a masseuse, Susan pushed her thumbs into the pressure points either side of his spine on a level with his shoulder blades. He winced at the perfect blend of pleasure and pain.

'Does all this work mean I won't get a decision out of you on the main guest suite?' she said in mock reproval. 'It was between the peach and the eau de nil, remember.'

He couldn't remember what eau de nil was when it was at home. 'You'd better decide,' he said. 'You're rather good at that.' Coughing, he reached for a cigarette. Smoking too much again.

'When will you go to Scotland?' she asked lightly.

He was suddenly able to make up his mind about that too. 'Tomorrow.'

Her hands paused. 'So soon? Oh. *Oh*.' She kissed his back. 'Wish I could come too,' she added in an undertone, and there was a hint of reproach in her voice that he'd not heard before. Then, in her cheerful tone: 'I'd planned – well, I'd thought I might be able to find out about that chemical for you. What did you say it was?'

'Silveron,' he murmured.

'*Silveron*,' she repeated slowly. 'You know – ask Tony's people to look into it.'

He twisted round and stared at her.

She shrugged slightly, pulling the sheet a little higher over her bosom, and asked charmingly: 'No?'

'I don't think that would be a good idea,' he said.

'Oh?' That hint of reproach again. 'But why not? That's what Tony's people are paid for, digging out information. They've nothing else to do, as far as I can gather.'

'Won't your husband . . .?'

'Oh, don't worry about him,' she said with a dismissive hand. 'He'll agree all right.' It occurred to Nick that the greatest single emotion she felt for her husband was scorn.

Perhaps she was aware that something unattractive was showing in her face, because she grinned suddenly and ran her fingers down his cheek.

But though her lips were smiling and her eyes unswervingly attentive, there was no humour in her expression.

From the past came memories of their earlier relationship. He remembered great outpourings of woe and abrupt emotional upheavals for which she had demanded his complete attention, sometimes for days on end. He couldn't remember what she had been so bothered about. Fitting in? Not being taken seriously? Something like that. And him not loving or understanding her – yes, plenty of that. The details were blurred, but he remembered the emotional exhaustion all right.

Looking at her now, the old and new Susan began to fuse, like one painting being scraped off another that had been painted underneath, until you couldn't be sure what you were seeing any more.

'So,' she said, 'I'll go ahead and ask, shall I?'

'I don't know.'

'But it won't be any trouble,' she insisted brightly. He couldn't help wondering if her eagerness didn't stem from a desire to show off her influence in high places.

He thought suddenly of Daisy – an image that never sprang to mind without a disturbing mixture of sensations – and remembered her conspiracy theories. With some surprise he found himself trotting it out. 'They won't have any information that hasn't been handed to them on a plate by the manufacturer. Might as well ask Morton-Kreiger.'

It was a moment before Susan spoke. 'Morton-Kreiger?'

There was someting in her voice that made him turn to look at her again. 'They make the stuff.'

'Oh.'

'Your friend Schenker.'

'My friend!' she retorted. 'Hardly.'

She moved behind him to resume her kneading and he could no longer see her face. 'My *friend*!' she repeated with a snort. 'Tedious little man!'

Her hands fanned out over the small of his back and found two points that no masseur of his acquaintance had ever found before. He gave a shiver.

'I should have used oil,' she said.

'Doing okay.'

Sighing, she lowered herself down beside him, and her touch lightened into a caress that travelled down his spine and over his backside. 'Next time I'll bring some,' she whispered, and there was something in her tone which told him he wasn't going to get to the studio that evening as he'd planned, not unless he made the effort to move straight away.

An hour later he was still there. But then, if working was one sort of oblivion, making love was another.

In the lazy time before they got up, he lay half listening to Susan's murmured recollections, his mind travelling lightly, soporifically, over thoughts of work and Ashard.

'You're not listening.' Susan tipped a finger at his chin.

He mumbled in mild apology.

'You're still thinking of those newspapers!' she accused. 'Why don't you put your side of the story?

'I gave them a statement yesterday.'

'No, not a statement – a story. The whole thing, from your point of view.'

'It wouldn't work.'

She stroked the hair clear of his forehead. 'Why not?'

'Telling your story only prolongs the agony,' he

explained. 'Then the tabloids would pick out the best quotes and use them out of context. They'd dredge things up, ask questions I couldn't answer.'

'But what could they ask that would be so bad?'

He almost laughed. 'Plenty.'

'You worry too much.'

'Oh no,' he said. 'They'd . . .' He hesitated, and wasn't sure why he hesitated.

'They'd bring up Alusha's death,' he heard himself say. 'And the evidence from the inquiry. They'd ask me about things I wouldn't want to talk about.'

Suddenly he had to move. Disentangling his arm, he sat up.

'You mean – her illness?'

'I mean, the psychiatrist's bloody report!' he retorted with sudden anger, and he realized that after all this time he had come to terms with nothing, nothing at all. And realizing this, his anger fed off itself. '*And* the morphine!' he added bitterly.

A pause, then she whispered: 'The morphine?'

He swung his legs to the floor and reached for his shorts. 'It was for the pain. She had terrible pain.'

'Well then . . .'

'They thought the pain was imaginary, like the rest. They thought she had a *habit*. I couldn't talk my way through all that again. Christ.'

'But *would* they ask – '

He stood up and tugged a cigarette from its packet. 'I'm not going to take that risk. They think I supplied her, you see.'

Susan gave a nervous laugh. 'What?'

'Oh, they didn't say so, not straight out, but that's what they *thought*.' Lighting the cigarette, he clamped it to his mouth and pulled on his jeans.

'But that's outrageous! They could never say anything like that.'

'No, well, maybe not – but I couldn't risk it.'

'But, Nick, they'd never *dare*.'

Changing his mind about dressing, he headed across the room towards the shower. He stopped in the doorway. 'You don't understand,' he said, suddenly inexplicably cross with her for failing to understand. 'I *did* supply her. I *did* get it for her.' He was already regretting this, already feeling that old sickness rise in his belly.

He went into the bathroom and closed the door and said aloud to the walls: 'I got it for her because she *needed* it.'


Alice scraped her chair back. 'Another cup?' She was already scooping up the teapot.

'Please.'

Daisy watched her go to the Aga, drop a fresh bag in the pot and stab at it absentmindedly with a spoon.

'I'm not surprised,' Alice announced. 'No . . . it's what I expected really.'

'I'm sorry, Alice, I really am.'

'These things happen.'

'We'll have to think again. Look elsewhere. Konrad's not the only specialist in the world. There'll be someone else. It's just a question of tracking him down.' Daisy heard the tired old reassurances, and wondered if she herself believed them any more. 'I heard about a new epidemiological study on agricultural workers in America . . .'

Alice twisted round and stood facing her, back against the stove, one hand gripping the rail.

'. . . I'm not sure who's doing the study,' Daisy went on, 'But they're looking into something very like Aldeb, something called – oh God, I can't even remember the name. Going nuts at last, Alice, but then it was only a matter of time – '

'Daisy – don't.'

There was a peremptory tone in Alice's voice that made them both pause and look at each other.

'I'm not going on,' Alice announced. 'I'm calling a halt.' In case Daisy still hadn't got it, she explained: 'I'm giving up the legal action.'

Daisy stared at her, not sure that she hadn't been expecting this.

'Why, Alice?'

'John's ill again. They've found two secondaries.'

'Oh, *Alice*.'

'I feel I'm letting you down.'

'Letting *me* down? You have to be kidding.'

'Well ... Whatever, I've no choice. What John needs now is care and support. And a bit of fun before it's too late. The promise of cash in five or six years or however long it takes isn't going to do him much good.'

'Oh, Alice, I'm so sorry. I'm so sorry.'

'He's only twenty-seven.'

'But what do they say? Surely ...'

'Oh, you know. The usual treatment, then wait and see.'

There was resignation in her voice. She'd seen too many courses of treatment fail on her husband to allow herself much hope.

'Alice, if there's anything I can do. Anything.'

'I feel I'm letting you down,' she repeated.

Daisy went across to her and put an arm round the wide curve of her shoulders. 'Alice, you've been a real trooper. I couldn't have asked for more.'

Alice gave a rueful grin. 'Wish I could have done more. Still makes me mad as hell.'

Daisy hugged her. Her old sweater smelled of animals and other unidentifiable farmyard odours, and her hair, wiry as horse bristles, tickled Daisy's cheek. 'You stay mad as hell, Alice. It's what gives you your get-up-and-go.'

Alice gave her a squeeze, then pulled back to scrabble for a handkerchief. She blew her nose with a loud hoot, then flicked the tails of her handkerchief across her eyes. 'Remember the agricultural show?' she said in a reminiscent tone. 'I promised myself then I'd never give up. Swore it.'

'But we gave them a fright. Don't forget that.'

'Did we?'

'You betcha. You'll be on a file somewhere, Alice. The one who nearly nailed 'em.'

She cheered up a little at that and, sluicing the hot water into the pot, took the tea back to the table.

Talking about her altercation with the law seemed to raise her spirits further. Her only regret, she declared, was that she hadn't been clapped in chains and taken to court, because then she could have aired the whole thing in public. But she wasn't to forget the impact of the hundreds of letters she'd written, Daisy reminded her, the dozens that had got published, and the numerous MPs who'd replied sympathetically. All that had raised public awareness.

'Wouldn't have given in,' Alice murmured from time to time, her eyes fixing on Daisy's in the failing light.

'I know you wouldn't,' Daisy said.

Shortly before six the gin came out. Alice produced it with a flourish which almost concealed the slight but unmistakable flash of guilt. 'Does me good,' she said. 'Always have a drop about this time.'

'I should hope so too,' Daisy said.

'You're a good girl, Daisy. I'll miss you.'

'Not half as much as I'll miss you, Alice.'

They blinked at each other.

'You'll have one . . .?' Alice tilted the gin bottle over a glass, her voice gently pleading, as if she already knew Daisy would take this as her cue to leave.

'Actually, I've had a bit of a time in the last few days,' Daisy said, allowing herself a measure of understatement. 'I've got to get back to see a few people.' Like the garage people, who had towed her car away that morning, like Jenny, whose VW Beetle she had borrowed, like the

Chelmsford police, the insurance agent, the Octek staff, and various other people who, weekend or not, would be wanting to speak to her urgently.

'You managing all right, Alice? I mean, for money, that sort of thing?'

'Hah!' she exclaimed, waving a vague hand, the gin already trembling in her voice. 'Another mortgage, another bank manager . . . I'll be all right.'


Before leaving, Daisy called Simon's number but there was still no reply. The *Sunday Times* features desk, never particularly well-informed on the whereabouts of its staff, was also unforthcoming until the unidentified voice on the end of the line broke off, capped the phone for a consultation, and returned to announce that Simon was expected back that evening from Prague.

'*Prague?* When did he leave?'

Another conference. 'Friday morning.'

The morning immediately after the fire. She drove away from Alice's in a state of bafflement and alarm. If Simon had left on Friday morning, then he would have had to pass on the information about Nick mighty quick. Impossibly quick. Like straight away, the very night he'd got her message.

But then if she was blaming Simon for revealing Octek's existence to people he shouldn't have, there was another problem. More than a problem – a great yawning gap. It was just after eight that morning, as she had faced her hangover in the bathroom mirror, that the realization had come to her; she had never told Simon where Octek was located. The set-up, the cell-line trials, the five-month testing programme, and of course Nick's identity – she'd given Simon all of that. But nowhere in the conversation had she given him the city, let alone the street, where it was all happening.

And if she hadn't told him, and he hadn't passed it on, then how had the fire raisers known where to go?

Unexpectedly, there was a parking place bang opposite the flat. She examined it for builders' skips, no-parking cones and upturned nails, courtesy of the local hooligans, but it seemed clear of hidden traps. Parking, she walked round the Beetle and flicked an unthinking glance up at the windows of the flat.

She stopped and looked again.

The lights were blazing.

The scene shook, her heart hammered.

As she watched, a shadow arced across the ceiling and the top of a man's head swelled briefly into the lower corner of the left-hand window.

She started across the road only to pause and retreat, struck by sudden doubts. Confrontation might not be such a good idea. Wait for him to come out then? Call the police?

She hovered uneasily in the road, looking up at the stagelit window.

Another movement. She scrambled back onto the pavement. A tall metal object appeared, glinting in the light, followed by the man's head, along with his shoulders and back. The man levered open the object – a stepladder – and climbed slowly towards the ceiling.

She leant against the car, weak and shaky, and it was some time before she managed to move in the direction of the house again.

The workman grinned down at her when she let herself in. 'You're working late,' she said.

'Didn't want ter 'ang about,' he said. 'Save me 'avin to come back Monday. Nearly done now.' He slapped some sort of filler into a hole in the wall where the falling ceiling had ripped a lump of plaster away.

'You gave me a shock,' she said. 'I thought you were . . .'

'What, doin' the place over? Nah,' he laughed, 'I was

lookin' after it for yer, wasn't I?' He smoothed off the filler and climbed down the ladder. 'Just leave it ter dry now. A week, I'd say, to be on the safe side. Oh, yer got some phone calls – seven, as I remember. Three left messages on the machine there. Oh, and a visitor. 'Bout free o'clock.'

Daisy pulled the plastic sheet off the red armchair. 'Who was it, did he say?'

'Nah.' He collected his tools into his bag. ''E just rings the bell. I put me 'ead out the windar and says there's no one 'ome, and 'e nods and goes off. Didn't 'ang about.'

'What did he look like?'

He climbed out of his overalls and dusted his hands thoughtfully. 'Blimey . . . now you're askin'. Brown 'air . . . Well-built. Nah . . .' He shook his head. 'Nah . . . didn't really get a good a look at 'im. Too busy tryin' to get me 'ead through yer windar without gettin' meself topped. You know you got a sashcord broke?'

'I have?'

He manoeuvred his ladder out through the door and came back for the dustsheets which he pulled off the furniture with great flourishes that sent billows of dust mushrooming lazily into the air.

'Only three messages?' she called after him.

'Yup. The other callers – four there were – they rang off when they 'eard the machine.'

'Thanks,' she said.

When he'd gone she played back the messages. A tense Peasedale pleaded for information, Inspector Brent requested in formal tones that she contact him as soon as convenient, and Jenny, in a no-nonsense message strong on emotional support, insisted that Daisy come over that evening for a meal with her and her boyfriend.

She was tempted by Jenny's offer. There wasn't much she could do in Chelmsford until Monday morning, although Inspector Brent probably thought differently, and there was even less to be done for Adrian until she could get up to Scotland, hopefully on Monday afternoon.

She called Jenny and said she'd be over as soon as she could. She thought of calling Peasedale, maybe even Brent, but couldn't face either. She felt like the pilot of an aircraft that had crash-landed in the jungle, miles from civilization, with a plane-load of demanding passengers.

There was a shout of laughter from the street, answered by a raucous exuberant yell. She felt a pang of loneliness, the sort you get when the rest of the world is having a good time and someone forgot to invite you. She scooped up some wine as an offering to Jenny and made for the door. Pausing, she went back to the answering machine and hovered over it uncertainly. No, she'd had quite enough messages for tonight. Leaving the machine off, she hurried out.

Remembering that Jenny was allergic to wine, she drove down the hill to Mr Patel's and picked up some cider. She added some bread and milk for her breakfast next morning.

She'd parked on a corner of the junction, pointing the wrong way. To save herself a trip round the block she backed cautiously out into the wider of the streets, peering through the tiny rear window of the Beetle, and was rewarded by the blasting horn and flashing headlights of a suicidal speed maniac screaming blindly out from behind the row of densely parked cars. Her adrenalin surged, her hands trembled on the wheel, she felt an abrupt exhaustion. Jenny's place suddenly seemed a long way away, the prospect of talking through the last couple of days altogether too much. Better to call it a day, better to get some sleep.

Wearily, she pointed the car up the hill again. Anticipating that the prime parking spot would be gone by now, she took the first space she came to, some way short of the flat on the near side. Getting into it involved a ten-point manoeuvre with a killing amount of wheel winding, but at the end of it the car was more or less parked.

Someone walked briskly past the car, going uphill. As she prepared to open the door, she glanced up and took in a jaunty gait, stocky build, and dark casual clothing. The lighting wasn't brilliant, he was largely in shadow, but something about the back of his head, or possibly his stride, made her pause, something that sparked the glimmer of a memory, and she canted her head to one side to observe him through the windows of the parked cars ahead. After a time the car windows offered more frame than glass, and she lost sight of him.

She opened the door and clambered heavily out. She noticed that the striding pedestrian had disappeared. For some reason, she wasn't sure what, this bothered her, and she took another look, balancing on tiptoe to get a view over the car roofs. Then she spotted him. He was climbing the steps to a house not far from hers. A neighbour, then, which accounted for the familiarity. A close neighbour at that, though from the oblique angle and in the darkness, it was hard to tell precisely how close.

Gathering the groceries, balancing them precariously on one arm, she closed and locked the car door, and made her way slowly up the hill.

She looked over to the prime parking place and saw that, far from being taken, it was still there. Automatically she glanced up at the flat windows.

Light.

She stopped, baffled. What lights had she left on?

But if she wasn't sure about the lights, she was absolutely certain about the curtains. She hadn't drawn them, either when she arrived or when she went out.

She stared at the familiar pattern of the Indian cotton, its peacock design thrown into colour-bleached reverse by the backlighting, the two curtains pulled around the bow of the windows and drawn together so tightly that there was no thread of light between them.

She had the feeling that this was happening at a remove, that she only had to pause for the scene to shift towards something more acceptable. But there was no escape from the curtains and the fact they were drawn.

Walking swiftly back to the car, she unlocked it and quickly restarted the engine. A car came ponderously over the brow of the hill. She knew the look; hunting for a space. 'Oh no you don't,' she breathed, winding viciously on the wheel to extricate the Beetle in fewer than ten moves.

She misjudged the final manoeuvre, clipped the bumper of the car in front with a loud scraping sound, and shot forward just in time to see the approaching car pause by the vacant parking space. She was accelerating, rehearsing reasons why the interloper should give up the space to her, when the car started towards her again, the driver's head bent forward over the wheel, peering at the house numbers. He was just lost.

She slowed down, made a conscious effort to unwind the tension in her hands, and parked quietly, without attracting attention. From here she had a good view of the front door and, when she shifted across to the passenger seat, the flat above. The lights were still on, the curtains drawn.

She settled down to wait, to catch him when he came out. She wanted to see his face.

Was it the man in the dark clothes, the pedestrian who'd passed her when she parked? There had been something about him, some echo of the past. She groped for the memory, but it wouldn't come.

Whoever he was, he was taking his time. How long had he been in there? Ten minutes? No, more like fifteen. She angled her head so she could keep the whole width of the bay window in view. What could he be doing in there? she wondered. What could be taking so long? Perhaps it wasn't the dark-clad man after all, perhaps it was a sneak thief who'd left even before she returned from Mr Patel's. Perhaps there was nobody in there any more.

Suddenly the light went out, the curtains absorbed the dull amber of the streetlights.

Her adrenalin rocketed. Fixing her eyes unwaveringly on the front of the house, she slid back into the driving seat. Her foot caught the edge of the milk carton, it fell. She swore and leant down to right it.

She glanced rapidly up at the window and her throat dried.

The curtains had been reopened.

She looked down at the front door.

It began to open. Whoever was opening it had not activated the time-lapse stair lights so that behind him the hall was in darkness, and she could make out only the barest shadow as he paused ghostlike in the open door, as if to watch and listen, before casually stepping out and pulling the door behind him.

Dark clothes, thick build: yes, the man from before. He ran quickly down the steps, head down.

Look up. I need you to look up.

He reached the bottom of the steps and, moving into an aureole of light, took a quick glance over his shoulder before setting off briskly in the direction he had come.

Got you.

Maynard.

The neck, the tight jaunty walk. *Maynard*. Plastered-down hair, thick lips, stocky build: crawling obsequious Maynard.

He was walking fast, his head and shoulders bobbing rapidly over the line of car roofs. She screwed around in her seat, watching the buoyant head retreating rapidly down the hill, and was fixed with a momentary indecision.

Should she leave it there? Be satisfied with the fact that she'd rumbled him? Or was she going to take it further? Make a complaint. All she had, she remembered, was an address in Hertfordshire, a phone number in Battersea. But suppose Maynard wasn't his real name, suppose the Battersea number wasn't there any more?

Undecided yet loath to lose him, she started the car and, straddling the street in a tight three-point turn, began to follow. Too fast, too fast. She slowed until she could see his head bouncing along at a comfortable distance ahead of her.

Turn off the headlights? No, too obvious. Best to crawl close by the parked cars, like the motorist she had seen earlier, so that if he looked back he would think she was lost.

Reaching a corner he turned suddenly, swivelling his body round abruptly until it was almost facing the way he had come. She resisted the urge to jam her foot on the brake and kept creeping forward, craning her head from side to side, so that, if his eyesight was that good, he would be able to see the dim outline of a face peering up at the house numbers.

When she glanced back he had vanished. She drove cautiously on towards the junction and stopped just beyond the last parked car, so that she could see along the pavement of the adjacent street.

No sign.

Now how had he managed that, for God's sake?

She looked down the hill towards Mr Patel's, then back the way she had come, then across to the other side of the side street again. Nothing.

*Hell.*

An engine started not far away. She wound down the window to get a direction on it, only for the sound to be drowned by a car lumbering up the hill towards her. The approaching car, a rumbling diesel, made ponderously slow progress and it was a long time before she could tune into the altogether quieter hum of the other car.

She had the sound now: it came from the side street where Maynard had disappeared.

It had to be him. Could it be him? But why, having started his engine, wasn't he moving?

A second later, the red glow of a rear light sprang on, then a second later the white reflection of a reversing light. The car moved back once, then curved out and accelerated away.

Daisy turned the corner and followed. It was a dark saloon, possibly a Rover. But was it Maynard?

Part of her accepted that this was crazy – even if it was Maynard he was probably the sort who'd know instantly if he was being followed – but the other part of her was damned if she was going to give up without a try.

The street led into another that ran parallel to Augustus Road. With hardly a hesitation to see if anything was coming, the dark car turned left, heading downhill through the web of dark residential streets. Reaching the arterial road at the bottom, it stopped in the face of a steady stream of traffic. Daisy saw an immediate problem: to close up or stay back? To invite attention or risk him seeing her in his mirror?

In the end she closed up, lowering the sun visor to hide her face. As she halted behind the Rover she saw with relief that the driver was not looking in his mirror: he was too intent on pushing the car impatiently forward, sticking its nose further and further out into the traffic, his head peering sideways as he waited for a suitable gap. Peering sideways and showing his profile to her.

Maynard. *Maynard*.

He spurted forward, then jammed on the brakes as someone hooted at him. As the brake lights flashed on and off, Daisy realized she was looking at his registration number. For God's sake. How many half-brained witnesses forgot to remember something as basic as a car number?

She got the number into her head just as the Rover finally sprang forward into the main road, accelerating fast. She rolled forward, knowing she must get out soon or lose him. The traffic was thick but tailing off, regulated by some unseen traffic lights. A small gap was coming up, followed, four cars later, by a larger one. She went for the earlier gap, pushing her foot hard down which, in the Beetle, provided little extra speed but some illusion of achievement. The approaching car braked uncomplainingly to let her in.

She was four, no five, cars back. Too far if there were traffic lights. One car peeled off to the left, then, in a straightish section, she risked overtaking another with nerve-racking slowness, hanging out in the centre of the road until she was almost squeezed against a traffic island.

Still two cars between them. The road curved to the right and she got a clear view of the Rover ahead. In the fluorescence of the shop lights it glinted dark red.

The road straightened then, enacting her worst fears, some traffic lights ahead of the Rover turned amber. As the line of cars slowed, she pulled out slightly to get a better view of the junction and waited with a sinking heart for the sight of the Rover speeding away. The lights were a solid red now, yet, though she waited, the car didn't appear. Maynard wouldn't be one to stop at anything short of red. Had he turned off then? She darted a glance to the left, but no car was turning off.

The cross-traffic had started, and she realized that he must have stopped at the amber after all.

Lucky, very lucky. More than she deserved.

Quickly, before the lights changed, before she forgot the registration number, she reached for her bag and scribbled it on a scrap of paper.

When the line started off again, she saw that the leading car was not after all the Rover, that Maynard had been caught behind another more cautious motorist. Now the Rover was jammed up against his bumper, as if this would encourage him to accelerate faster. She waited impatiently for an opportunity to overtake the car immediately in front of her and narrow the gap but they were into the twists of Turnpike Lane, heading north-east towards Tottenham, and it was impossible to pass.

The problem was eased by the car two ahead, which slowed and swooped into the kerb by a parade of shops, leaving just one car between her and Maynard. She couldn't decide whether she should leave it at this, whether the still considerable risk of getting separated at lights was preferable to being spotted. A few seconds later the problem became academic as the Rover suddenly indicated right and rocked to a halt in the centre of the next junction, waiting to turn.

As she drew up behind him she tweaked the sun visor for maximum shadow, and instantly regretted what must be an obvious gesture. But if Maynard had seen her tell-tale movement, if he had recognized her, he gave no sign.

The lights changed, Maynard lurched to the right across the junction, she followed. The road, not one she knew, was relatively clear of traffic, and Maynard accelerated away. She let him pull ahead a little, content just to keep him in sight. She was gripping the wheel so tightly that her nails were digging into her thumbs. Slow, take it easy. It's going well.

Even as she thought it, she drew a mental map and realised they had performed a loop and were now heading south. Perhaps Maynard wasn't sure of his way, perhaps he'd lost his sense of direction. In most people that would have been believable – this part of north London was enough to defeat most map readers – but for some reason she was certain Maynard knew exactly where he was going.

The thought made her pull back further.

'Still with me?'

The walkie-talkie gave a loud crackle, then Biggs' voice came through, gruff and terse. 'Affirmative.'

Hillyard gave a sharp sigh, intended for transmission. If Biggs' police jargon had once had novelty value, it had long since lost its power to amuse. Hillyard asked with heavy sarcasm: 'Does that mean yes?'

A silence. 'Affirmative.'

'Right. Close in. Make it snappy. I won't want to hang about.'

'Received and out.'

Hillyard braked hard and, keeping the radio to his ear, swivelled the wheel with the heel of his free hand and took the car round the corner into a dead-end street that led between banks of dismal council flats.

He continued to the end of the road, where there was a more recent though equally grim development, a series of concrete blocks with slit-like windows and peeling murals, partly raised on concrete stilts and connected by webs of poorly lit footways, halls and flights of high-walled steps.

Hillyard, who had been here before, bypassed the designated parking area and stopped the car under a raised block, between a massive concrete stilt and the blank wall of a service shaft. He parked unhurriedly, taking his time to slip the walkie-talkie into the inner pocket of his trainer jacket before getting out and locking up.

Resisting the urge to look over his shoulder, he sauntered past a sombre light and along the front of the building before disappearing into the shadows of a covered footway.

*

Daisy parked some way back. This was the sort of place you read about, where grannies locked themselves up at night and women didn't take their babies out for fear of thugs. The ten-storey blocks were ribbed with external galleries lit by row after row of dim bulbs, many not functioning. Several of the ground-level flats were deserted and boarded up, abandoned to the vandals. The wide concrete verges were speckled with litter.

She tucked her bag out of sight under the seat and got out and locked the door. Somewhere high up in one of the buildings, a thin shout echoed along a long empty space.

Ahead, in the dark area under one of the buildings, she saw the lights of Maynard's car go off. A moment later, he emerged from the shadows and strolled along the front of the building. He wasn't looking around him, he wasn't hurrying. He turned and disappeared into some sort of passageway. She waited for a minute to see if he would reappear, then wandered uncertainly forward. She wasn't about to follow him into the maze of walkways – she wasn't mad – but it might be worth taking a quick look at the car.

On the other hand she might just wait right here until he came out again.

You're frightened. *Yes, I know I'm frightened.*

Yet, as at so many times in the past, her old doggedness stirred, she was unable to let the idea go. Maybe it was the memory of Maynard at the Waldorf, his hamster cheeks full of cucumber sandwiches, maybe it was the idea of him poking around in her flat, but she set off along the pavement towards the towering end block, towards the shadows where the Rover was parked. Approaching, she kept an eye on the passageway in case Maynard should reappear, then ducked her head down to look in the rear window.

The back seats were in deep shadow: impossible to see anything. She moved to the front and put her eye closer to the glass.

The roaring snapping mouth reared up at her out of the darkness, aiming at her nose. She jumped back with a cry.

The mouth yapped frantically at the window, its teeth clacking against the glass.

'*Jesus!*'

She stood still, her heart racing.

The mouth subsided for an instant, revealing bulbous eyes, a flat squashed-back nose, a mane of, pale hair, then started its screaming again, yelping maniacally, crashing itself blindly at the window.

She retreated, her pulse still pumping in her ears, and headed back towards the Beetle.

Voices, loud and shrill, reverberated suddenly from the block to her right, and a group of youths spilled out from a doorway, jostling each other in aggressive horseplay. She kept her head down, aiming straight for the car. She sensed them catching sight of her, exchanging remarks. One of them called out something, though she didn't hear what it was. She caught it second time, though. It was the sort of graphic sexual invitation that yobs like to yell at women to make them feel threatened. She slowed a little and tipped her head up to show she wasn't going to be impressed. At the same time she was relieved to see someone coming along the pavement towards her, a man with a coat flapping round his knees: the sort of thin raincoat worn by clerks and insurance salesmen and other safe people.

She reached the Beetle just ahead of the man in the raincoat and thrust into her pocket for the keys. As she went round to the driver's side and bent to open the door, she was aware that the man in the raincoat was no longer on the pavement, that he had achieved some mysterious vanishing act. Then, by some instinct she couldn't name, she realized that he had moved around behind her, and realizing it, she instantly rationalized it: he was coming to ask her something, coming to ask if she was all right. She sensed his sudden approach as much as heard him, or maybe she glimpsed a brief flicker of movement, but either way she was turning when he hit her, which was probably why the weapon missed the back of her skull, where it could have been aimed, and caught her on the side of her head, above the ear and across the width of her cheekbone. *Thwack!* The weapon was both soft and enormously hard: she felt its soft edge, she felt its immense force. Even as it cannoned into her cheekbone, she thought: *He shouldn't be hitting me in the face. No one gets hit in the face.*

The blow threw her sideways and she felt herself sprawling untidily against the car. At some point two of her fingers got caught up somewhere and mangled, possibly in the door hinge, and at about the same time she must have sunk to the ground, where she was eventually found, but at that moment all she was aware of was a vast shock, a loud ringing in her ears, and a sensation that felt like drowning.

'Didn't tell you to brain her,' Hillyard sighed.

'You didn't tell me not to either,' said Biggs, with his usual mindless logic.

Hillyard straightened up and took a quick look around. 'Brought it on herself,' he commented waspishly. 'Trying to switch cars like that. Trying to be clever.'

'Didn't see it was her when she got on to you,' said Biggs. 'Just saw the car. That van's no good for gettin' a view, y'know. Can't see a bleedin' thing.' He gestured down at the girl. 'What shall we do with her?'

'A mugging victim, isn't she?'

They went through the contents of her shoulder bag, then the car itself, examining each item before either pocketing it or putting it back in the bag. Hillyard gave a grunt of satisfaction at finding one piece of paper, but otherwise he was not at all pleased. He had still not found what he had been looking for in that flat.

# Chapter 31

———

DUBLENSKY SAT OVER the newspaper and idly marked off the ball games that were showing on TV later in the day. Although it was ten he wasn't yet dressed and still wore a towelling robe over his shorts. His unclad feet were cold on the floor, his coffee in need of a refill, but indolence made him heavy, and he couldn't summon the energy to move.

The phone rang, a long sombre sound. Gathering his robe around him, Dublensky rose and shuffled over to the wall phone.

The voice wrenched Dublensky back to the past with a speed that left his mind stumbling. *Reedy?* But there was no mistaking the hearty tone, the sheer force of that voice. And then the name itself, announced with warmth and an extraordinary note of expectation, as if they were long-lost college friends due for a congenial reunion.

Dublensky managed: 'How are you, Don?'

'Never better! Never better! I'm in the Big Apple, John! Arrived yesterday. Attending a weekend meeting of the Institute. Dinners, lectures – you know, everyone applauds your speech then secretly tears it apart later.' He chuckled: 'You know the kind of thing.'

But Dublensky didn't know. He'd never belonged to the organization that he assumed Reedy was referring to, had never made a speech, nor torn anyone else's apart.

What did this show of brotherhood mean? When they had last spoken – it was back in March, shortly before he was fired from Allentown – it was to exchange bitter words over the Silveron affair. The memory of that conversation still had the power to shrink Dublensky's heart.

'What can I do for you, Don?' he asked tentatively.

'John . . .' Reedy lingered over his name, giving another chuckle. 'I thought we could meet. It's been a long time. How about dinner tonight? There's a conference event I'll be glad to skip. Can you make it? Say you can. It would be really great to see you.'

Dublensky fought for a reply.

'Would it be easier if I came down to you?' said Reedy, cutting into the silence. 'I could grab a hire car and get down by six thirty.'

This willingness to travel seemed to cast Reedy's invitation in a new light. Maybe the forced joviality hid a desire to make amends. Maybe he had come to apologize.

Not entirely free of suspicion, Dublensky found himself asking: 'Er, what is it you want to talk about exactly?'

'Why, nothing, John. I just wanted – ' Reedy paused suddenly, as if he had thought better of this approach, and murmured: 'John, you know how it is, there are things you can never talk about over the phone. I mean, like it'd be real nice to *see* you, John.'

'Is it Morton-Kreiger business?'

'What?' He sounded genuinely shocked. 'Oh no, John, no. This isn't business, this is entirely my idea!'

Dublensky knew then that he would agree. His curiosity was too great, his suspicions too sharp to leave it alone.

It was only after they had arranged to meet at a local inn and Dublensky was back at the table with a fresh cup of coffee, that it occurred to him that Reedy must have gone to a lot of trouble to track him down to this corner of New Jersey. In Allentown only two neighbours had known where he and Anne were moving to, and he certainly hadn't told anyone at the chemical works. Had Reedy traced him through his employers then? And if so, were Dalton now fully informed of Dublensky's background? Were they even now preparing to fire him? The thought filled him with new trepidation.

But then it was probably foolish to imagine that the mandarins of MKI were not aware of the fact that he worked for Dalton. Now and again it had even occurred to him that, incredible though it seemed, MKI might actually have fixed up this job in order to keep an eye on him.

Speculation, increasingly wild and torturous, filled Dublensky's mind until the evening when, telling an uninterested Anne he had a business meeting, he went to meet Reedy.

From the shadowy corner of the inn's bar area, Reedy rose with a smile that sent his chins creasing into the folds of his neck.

'John,' he sighed, taking Dublensky's hand and overlaying it with a fond pat. 'John.' He stood back and surveyed him like a parent eyeing a prodigal child. 'Hey, but it's good to see you.'

By the time they had finished their drinks and moved through to the dining area, Reedy had asked him about life in the town, about Tad and his schooling, about Anne. He did not enquire after Dublensky's work.

His tone was avuncular, though Dublensky thought he could detect a trace of briskness, as if he was anxious to keep the conversation moving at some predetermined pace.

Dublensky, needing to assert himself, if only modestly, made an abrupt interruption. 'What's happening at MKI?' he asked.

Reedy laughed at the question and tipped his fingers into space. 'Oh, you know. Unchanging. The monolith rolls on. Although – ' He shot Dublensky a slyly modest look. 'For some reason they have seen fit to kick me up a step. As of next month I become Executive Vice President, Research.'

'Congratulations.'

'Means getting my arse kicked more often.' He assumed

a long-suffering look that wasn't designed to convince anyone.

The food came and they paused to apply relish and sauces to their steaks. Reedy talked again, but more generally now, touching on everything from the national debt to bankruptcy among Iowa farmers. It was a screen of words, Dublensky realized, delivered both as a means of controlling the conversation and of giving himself time to prepare. But for what? There was something coming, of that Dublensky was certain. A formal non-aggression pact? An olive branch? A monetary deal?

He said with unaccustomed boldness: 'Was it about the Silveron affair you came, Don?'

Reedy put down his fork. 'The past is past, John,' he said, affecting surprise. 'That business – ' He waved a hand in the air. 'We all took the stance we thought was right at the time. Now, well . . .' He gave a slight shrug and said magnanimously: 'Let's say there were faults on both sides.' He returned to his plate, forking a lump of steak and lowering his head to push it into his mouth.

'Faults?'

'Mmm? Oh yeah, sure.' He chewed as he spoke, making little effort to close his mouth. 'Safety's the watchword at the Aurora plant now. My Lord, the safety! You can't move in that place for controls and regulations. We would never risk one worker, John, not one.' He pointed his fork for emphasis. 'But those early reports had us worried at one time, oh yes, I won't pretend they didn't.' He used the *we* as if he had long been operating at senior executive level. 'And of course we reacted appropriately. Now that the true facts have emerged we don't regret that. Some people might say that we'd overreacted, but no risk however tiny is worth taking, not where people are concerned.'

Dublensky was struggling to catch up. 'The true facts?' he echoed hesitantly.

Reedy gave him a polite, mildly puzzled stare. 'The

people who reported sick – what was really wrong with them.'

Dublensky looked blank and with a sudden exclamation Reedy slapped a hand to his forehead. 'You didn't know?' he asked incredulously. 'About the medical diagnoses?'

Dublensky remembered Burt telling him about the Aurora workers who had got themselves rediagnosed in order to claim welfare, but chose not to say so. Instead he stared across the table, awaiting a fresh interpretation of the facts.

Reedy, relishing his responsibilities, put down his fork and folded his serviette ceremoniously. 'Okay,' he said, holding up the fingers of both hands then folding down two, 'there were eight workers who reported sick in the early days. Except two weren't really sick – one had a nervous complaint from long before, the second was pregnant.' He knocked off two fingers. 'Of the six remaining, *two* had cancer – different forms – and the medics agree that chances are they both had the disease *before* they came into contact with Silveron. Which leaves four.' He spread the remaining fingers wide, thrusting his wrist forward for emphasis. 'Now these were the people we were really worried about – thanks in part to you, of course.' He gave a small bow of acknowledgement.

Dublensky's mind plunged back to the old Reedy, the man who had been indifferent to the Aurora workers, and wondered at how things could change.

'These four people were sick,' Reedy went on, curling his fingers into a fist, 'really sick. There was no doubt about that. But what we never realized – at least not for some time – was that they had not received the best diagnostic advice.' He dropped his voice confidentially. 'That physician Burt – well-meaning, of course – but he hadn't run half the tests he should have run. It seems he made up his mind in advance that it was a problem of toxic exposure and closed his mind to everything else.'

'But, but – ' Dublensky agitated a hand in his anxiety to get the words out. 'He ran all kinds of tests and they showed nothing.'

'Ah!' Reedy, smiling benignly, raised a correcting finger. 'All sorts of tests, but not the *right* ones. When we finally got these people to a top diagnostician, well! Two had identifiable ailments. One was a rare liver disease, I believe. Another an auto-immune problem. I don't know the details.' He gestured his ignorance. 'But I do know they would have gotten a lot more help if they'd come to MKI sooner.'

'To MKI?'

'Sure. We offered the diagnostician for free and were happy to do so.'

Dublensky wondered who this diagnostician was that he could find so much that Burt had missed.

'That still leaves two,' Dublensky ventured.

Reedy returned to his meal, spearing his fork into his french fries. 'Two,' he echoed contentedly. 'That's right. Well now, it's early days, but it seems that one of these people was a malingerer and the other had some sort of mental illness. The diagnostician couldn't be too specific on *that* – not his field, you understand – so he referred him to a psychiatrist. Sadly, this man refused to attend any sessions, diagnostic or otherwise.' He shook his head uncomprehendingly and spread a hand. 'What can you do when people don't want to be helped?'

All kinds of questions hovered on Dublensky's lips. Like why all these illnesses shouldn't have been brought on by the original exposure. Like why the first two victims – the ones with nervous illnesses and pregnancy – should be written off with a wave of the hand. And since when had pregnancy made a woman so ill she couldn't function?

But he did not put these questions. He said neutrally: 'I had no idea.'

Reedy, taking this as a positive response, beamed.

'Nothing to worry about, see. A scare.' He threw a last nugget of meat into his mouth and chewed it lazily. Catching sight of Dublensky's plate, he made a sound of dismay. 'You've not eaten!'

Obediently, Dublensky picked up his fork, only to prod at the food without interest.

Reedy finished his meal and, leaning forward, surveyed Dublensky with paternalistic satisfaction. 'You mustn't blame yourself, you know, John,' he said. 'You did what you thought was right. You followed your principles, and everyone respects you for that.'

Dublensky, stung by the condescension of the remark, was galvanized to ask: 'Is that what you came to tell me?'

Smiling, Reedy made a weaving motion with his hand. 'I came because I wanted to, John. It's been a long time and – well, I was grieved by what occurred. I wanted to check things out, make sure you were okay.'

Dublensky couldn't think of anything to say.

'You're happy at Dalton?' Reedy enquired.

Dublensky shrugged. 'Yeah.'

'Well, it's a company that's going places, that's for sure. They're up there with the high fliers, in line for some major contracts. And you'll get to fly right up there with them.' He drooped an eyelid into a half wink: one winner greeting another.

'It wasn't easy to find work,' Dublensky said flatly.

'But you're okay now,' he declared assertively. 'You're okay now!'

The waitress removed Dublensky's uneaten steak and took their orders for coffee and dessert.

As she left, Reedy leant across and said in a low sympathetic tone: 'Look here . . . There *is* something else, John. I've been debating whether to bring it up and I still don't know whether I should. But, hell – you're a good man, John. I'd hate to see you get the blame for something you didn't do. And as a friend – I hope a friend? – I couldn't let it pass without telling you. Otherwise I'd never forgive myself. You know?'

Dublensky thought: Here it is at last. 'You're making me nervous,' he said truthfully. 'What is it I'm supposed to have done?'

Reedy made a show of bracing himself, his face creased with regret. 'Please treat this in the greatest confidence,' he whispered, hunching over the table. 'But it seems . . .' He drew a breath. 'It seems that one of the environmental groups has gotten hold of some information, information that is *meant* to show inconsistencies in the Silveron trial data.'

Dublensky's heart bumped. His eyes fixed on Reedy's with ghastly fascination.

Reedy rocked back in his seat. 'Now we know this stuff is fake, we know it's been fabricated. Nothing but cheap disinformation. But the point is, this sort of subversive crap can be damaging – which of course is the intention.'

Dublensky pulled his features into the semblance of interest.

'Now none of this would affect you, John, except – ' He gave a great sigh of disbelief. 'Someone's trying to link your name to all this. Now don't ask me why. It seems incredible. But that's the way it is.'

Dublensky uttered a thin sound half-way to a question.

'They're saying you're the source, John. They're saying that you provided the information. More than that, they're saying you're about to go public on it – to get up and make a noise about all this.' He raised his shoulders and spread his hands in a further show of bafflement. 'Crazy.'

Dublensky hastily pulled his spectacles down his nose and pressed his fingertips into the corners of his eyes in the way he did when he needed time.

What made them imagine he would suddenly choose to talk now, after all these months? Then it came to him. It was his call to EarthForce the other day. It was his conversation with Paul Erlinger. Somehow MKI had got to hear about it, just as they had got to hear about his call to Erlinger back in March and instigated the burglary. They knew about it, and had interpreted that unhappy promise of his, that vague pledge to help, as a firm intention to act.

It had to be. What else could it be? *Jesus*. He knew he shouldn't have made that call.

Dublensky felt Reedy's eyes on him, gauging his reaction. Pushing his spectacles back up his nose, he said: 'The, cr . . . the information, it's fake, you say?'

'Oh yeah. The figures were obviously fabricated – '

'How do you know?'

Reedy drew his lips into a narrow line and regarded Dublensky with an air of forbearance beginning to wear thin. A forced note came into his voice. 'Now, John, really . . . We know. We just *know*.'

'But how?' Dublensky interjected quietly. '*How?*'

'How! For lots of reasons I'm not at liberty to divulge. For – ' He broke off and gave a harsh impatient sigh. 'Godammit, John, there's nothing *wrong* with Silveron!'

Dublensky realized then: Nothing has changed, nothing ever would. His anger stirred, a small spot of heat burned on his face. 'What exactly are these fake figures meant to show?' he asked.

'I don't know,' Reedy shrugged impatiently.

'Remember that conversation we had on the phone, Don? When I said I wasn't happy with the Silveron toxicology trials?'

Reedy was silent, his face a mask of disapproval.

'I wasn't happy because it looked like they'd been fixed up by TroChem. I told you about it, Don, but you wouldn't listen. I'd like to know why you wouldn't listen.'

'Come on, John,' Reedy exploded. 'You were irate, you were upset. No one would have taken you seriously under those circumstances!'

Dublensky considered this for a moment. 'Okay,' he

nodded gravely, 'okay. But suppose I asked you to take me seriously now?'

Reedy hesitated then laughed awkwardly. 'I'd listen, of course I'd listen. I'm listening now, aren't I?'

'Okay. I'm telling you now. The toxicology results were fixed up, Don.'

'Come *on*! Where's your proof, John? Give me some evidence.'

'It was stolen from me.'

'*What?*' He gave an unnatural laugh then examined Dublensky's face. 'You look at me like it was my fault or something. Oh, come *on*, John. You're trying to tell me these rumours are true? That you're going to go public on this thing and make one helluva fool of yourself? Jesus, what are you thinking of?' He reached over to tap Dublensky's elbow, as if to suggest that the whole thing could still be written off as a joke.

'You're not believing me again, Don.' Dublensky slid his coffee aside. His courage was developing a life all its own. 'Silveron's on the British market, Don. Did you know that? There are people there who've gotten sick after one-time exposure. Who've developed symptoms like the Aurora workers. Some of them are kids – '

'*John*. Unsubstantiated conjecture! Pressure-group propaganda!'

Dublensky's accumulated frustration rose into his throat like a wedge. 'These people are sick,' he repeated with difficulty, 'and you're telling me it's nothing to do with you?'

Reedy waved a hand. 'John, John – ' he wheedled. 'Come on – tell me you're going to give up this crazy idea!'

'I . . .'

'*John*. Not only are you totally *wrong* about all this, but you're failing to appreciate what you're taking on.'

The heat was suddenly very great. 'What am I taking on exactly, Don?'

Reedy gestured exasperation. 'For Christ's sake, John. MKI will eat you alive if you don't approach this reasonably.'

In that instant Dublensky felt himself lifted across some divide and deposited effortlessly on the other side.

'Eat me alive?'

'You know what I mean.'

'I don't think I do.'

'Be reasonable, John.'

'And how should I do that?'

'Well – talk the darned thing through, I guess. Sit round a table in a civilized way. Meet us in a spirit of co-operation – '

'Agree to a deal, you mean.'

'Aw, come on – '

'Agree to keep quiet.'

'We must be able to talk this through.'

'Am I set to lose my job? Is that it?'

'*John.* Come *on.*' He gave a false laugh.

The heat burned so hot in Dublensky that he could hardly keep still. He hovered on the edge of the precipice, the chasm clearly visible below, and, feeling no qualms at all, stepped out into the void. 'No deals,' he said.

Reedy sat back in his seat, his mouth puckered with cold displeasure. 'John ... What's all this about? What's it about? Just tell me.'

Framing his reply, Dublensky saw the irony of the situation. 'Until you came today I wasn't planning to do anything, Don. Not for sure anyway. But now ... I guess I don't feel too good about your attitude. In fact' – Dublensky exulted in his own boldness – 'it makes me sick.'

Reedy's eyes narrowed, his mouth slackened, he contemplated Dublensky with something like distaste. Crumpling his serviette and placing it deliberately on the table, he said: 'I feel sorry for you, John. I really do.'

Dublensky nodded blankly. 'You may be right.'

Reedy gave it one last shot. 'You won't see sense? You won't change your mind?'

Dublensky thought of Anne, he thought of Tad, and though he felt a sudden sharp fear for them, he knew that he wouldn't change his mind.


Daisy pushed the door shut behind her and stood, gathering her breath. From above, a muffled thump, the reverberation of a slamming door announced the presence of the Greeks, then the house fell quiet again, stifled by the Sunday morning hush.

She stood, matching the room against her memory of the previous evening. The furniture was still herded together in the same haphazard way, the books lay undisturbed on their shelves, the red chair sat by the fire.

There were no obvious signs of an intruder. But then Maynard would be too professional for that.

Out in the road, a horn tooted lightly and, going to the window, Daisy pushed up the lower sash and, supporting the weight of the frame on her shoulders, waved to the Beetle which was double-parked below. Jenny looked up at her, her face pressed close to the windscreen, and signalled a question: Are you sure you'll be all right? Daisy nodded: I'll be fine.

Jenny shook her head as if to say, I give up, then with a last glance to make sure Daisy hadn't changed her mind, drove away.

Daisy eased the broken sash down and, dropping her jacket over the red chair, went to check the answering machine, only to remember that she had left it off. She continued into the kitchen, still looking for signs of Maynard's presence. There were several mugs sitting unwashed on the draining board, an open jar of instant coffee, a coffee-soaked spoon sitting in the sugar bowl – the plasterer, most likely, making himself at home. Otherwise the

jars, shelves and racks were possessed of their usual disor-
ganised clutter.

She put a kettle on, prepared some coffee. A familiar
routine: a way of re-establishing her territory. Maynard
may not have left any visible trace, but like an alley cat he
seemed to have left a nasty aura behind him.

As the kettle heated, she drifted towards the bathroom
in search of a bottle of witch hazel which she remembered
having put in the back of the medicine cabinet somewhere.

Even after regular glances at Jenny's bedroom mirror
during the night, the sight of her face still held a lurid
fascination, and seeing it now in the surroundings of her
own place, it seemed even more macabre, as if a makeup
artist had run riot with the rouge and plasticine. The
swelling on her cheek had reduced her right eye to a little
more than a slit through which an iris swam darkly and
uncertainly in a brilliant sea of blood-red that had once
been the white. The skin of her cheek, distended by the
hugeness of the swelling, was red and taut and burning hot.
The bruising continued into her hair to a point somewhere
above her ear, which still rang loudly, like an alarm bell
going off after the event. But the ringing, though distract-
ing, was mild compared to the headache, a throbbing girdle
of pain which a double dose of Panadol had failed to shift.

She found the witch hazel and dabbed at the bruise.
What was really needed was ice, and she pottered back into
the kitchen to chip some chunks off the solidified lump that
was the ice tray.

The couple who'd picked her up off the ground and
propped her against the wheel of the Beetle the previous
night had pressed a handkerchief to her head, as if she were
bleeding. More welcomely, they had also fed her cheap
brandy, produced like magic from the inside pocket of the
husband's coat. Being long-standing residents of the estate,
they were not surprised when she turned down the offer of
an ambulance, and, in their relief at not having the bother

of explaining their side of the business to the Bill, took her
to their flat and put a call through to Jenny.

Wrapping an ice chunk in a tea towel, Daisy pressed it
to her face and, making coffee, went into the main room
and rooted around in her bag for the Panadol that Jenny
had put there. Breaking two out of the bubble pack, she
washed them down. Then, going to the desk, she opened
the centre drawer and pulled out a pile of notebooks going
back two years or so. These spiral-bound A5 pads were her
daily records: pages of names, phone numbers, information
and ideas jotted down as meetings occurred, as people
called or thoughts came to her. Most of her ideas she later
transferred to the relevant files or lists, and the phone
numbers to her pocket-sized loose-leaf folder which, despite
its striking similarity to a Filofax, she refused to call
anything but an address book.

It didn't take her long to find the phone number
Maynard had quoted in his original letter all those months
ago, the number of the friend in Battersea, the place where
he was staying for a while and could be contacted between
eleven and twelve.

Before she found reasons to put off the call she took the
pad to the phone and dialled the number. There was a
click, the usual pause, then a deathly whine. She tried again
but there was no mistake: the line was disconnected.

The Hertfordshire address would probably be just as
useless, though Jenny was going to dig the letter out of the
Catch files first thing in the morning and check it, just in
case.

Sitting down in the red chair she began to go through
her shoulder bag, compartment by compartment, an exercise she had carried out twice already at Jenny's. Her purse
had gone, along with its contents: cash, driving licence,
library ticket, Green party membership card. But her
address book was still there, also her cheque book, note
books, miscellaneous papers and documents. Also, her

keys. Didn't muggers usually take keys? If not for themselves, then for friends who might want to knock over your flat while you were in hospital?

But then it was possible that the mugger hadn't been interested in the keys because his friend, Maynard, had already had a good look around the flat. The scenario of the mugger and Maynard as a team had a disturbing ring of plausibility to it.

During the early morning, when her splitting head had woken her and she had lain on Jenny's sofabed, dazed with pain, she had attempted to construct another plot, to persuade herself that the mugging had been pure chance, that she had been the victim of nothing more than bad luck, but when she looked at it the other way round and considered how lucky that made Maynard, then her suspicions took on more life.

Besides, the man had been wearing a raincoat. What sort of mugger wore a raincoat?

But if any one thing was needed to convince her, it was the absence of the scrap of paper on which she'd scribbled Maynard's registration number. Looking again now, the scrap – roughly the size of a supermarket receipt – was definitely not there.

Late last night, while under the influence of brandy and Panadol, Daisy had tried to remember the registration. Now, sitting in her old red chair, her head buzzing with coffee, she had another go, jotting down possibilities and comparing them with her previous efforts. The first part of the sequence looked promising in so far as it came out the same each time – G412 – but the final three letters showed a depressingly variable pattern, and the more she worried at her memory the more uncertain it became. After a time, even the first part of the sequence began to lose conviction and, admitting defeat, she dropped the pad to her knee.

No phone number, an unlikely address, a lost car registration. Got me beaten, Maynard. Had me beaten all along. Ran rings round me, in fact. It must have made you laugh, to find someone this simple.

She thought back over the last few months, to the way everything that could possibly go wrong had gone wrong. Peasedale being warned off, the destruction of Octek, the publicising of Nick's identity. Looking at these events from her new vantage point – a half-closed eye, one might say – she now saw that bad luck had very little to do with it, that, on the contrary, there seemed to be an absolute inevitability to what had happened. Maynard – or his friends – seemed to have a flawless seam of information which allowed them to judge their tactics very finely indeed.

But how? What was this infallible source?

And what had brought Maynard here? What had he been hoping to find?

She went to the shelves. The tapes were undisturbed. The books were in their usual order, pressed back against the wall so that the spines of the differently sized volumes formed an irregular line. Yet when she looked more closely she saw that the dust on the shelves had been pulled into tramlines as the books had been slid out one by one. She ran a finger over the compressed page tops, and it seemed to her that some of them were missing their veneer of dust.

She went over to the desk and stared at the familiar stacks of papers, files and magazines that covered the top. Moving slowly round the side, she peered at the desk's ancient cracked leather surface. Finally she found what she was looking for: a shape made dark by being dust-free, a shape that was clear-edged and right-angled, marking the place where a pile of files had been standing before it was moved.

So he had been looking for papers. Yet what would he find that was on paper? She groped for the significance of this thought, fretted at the edges of it, but this too refused to come.

The phone rang. She reached quickly down and flipped on the answering machine.

It was Inspector Brent, sounding tetchy, wanting her to come in and see him the next morning, *if* it would convenient – a note of sarcasm here – and would she please confirm as soon as possible.

She decided to leave the machine on for the rest of the day. Even when Campbell called ten minutes later, she let his voice feed onto the tape. He sounded subdued, depressed, but though she felt a vague shame at not answering him, she couldn't get to grips with Adrian's case now. Time enough tomorrow when the lawyers were back at work, when she could think about returning to Scotland. When she had thought the Maynard business through.

Why had Maynard come looking for papers? She never put anything on paper.

Her brain finally made the connection. *That was it.* Peasedale, Nick ... Nothing had been in writing. Their connection with Octek had only ever been mentioned person to person. Or –

She was still for a long moment. Then, lowering the cold compress from her face, she went into the kitchen and found the collection of basic tools she had acquired during one of her self-sufficiency drives. Kneeling on the floor in front of the red chair, she unplugged the telephone cord from the wall, and took the cover off the socket. This revealed a simple array of wires and no space for concealment.

The phone itself then. But what was she looking for? How large were these things?

She removed all the visible screws and lifted the casing clear of its base. The inside of the casing was free of extraneous fixtures. She went over the guts of the apparatus wire by wire, connection by connection, but everything looked as though it had been soldered or welded; the two sealed cubes that had seemed vaguely promising had obviously been fixed on some production line.

She reassembled the body of the phone, dropped the handset back in place and rested her head against the side of the chair for a while.

The phone rang. She watched the answerphone whir into life and, watching it, thought: It's you!

Jenny's voice sang out, demanding to know if she was okay and insisting that she call back *immediately* otherwise she'd worry and have to come over again.

The moment she rang off, Daisy had the answerphone cable out of the wall and, a short while later, the front off the socket.

Nothing.

The answerphone itself, with its tape decks, windows, knobs and composite plastic casing, was more resistant to dissection, but finally yielded with the unfastening of four deceptively small screws in places designed to conceal them. The back, a single sheet of alloy, came away to reveal the interior, a dark conglomeration of electronic clutter. She examined it minutely under the table lamp. There were tape receptacles, circuit boards, sealed units, bunches of bound wires. And absolutely nothing that was loose or extraneous.

When at last the machine was together again, she took a rest, had a herb tea, and felt the effects of the Panadol lifting.

The handset was relatively easy: just two screws and a firm tug and it fell into two halves.

And there it was. An oblong, about two inches in length, half an inch square. Dull metallic black in colour, attached to the inside of the casing with some sort of sticky tape. Two wires coming from the ends, fastened to connections near the mouthpiece by tiny alligator clips.

She looked at it for a long time, but did not touch it.

Eventually she put the two halves of the handset back together and screwed them up.

She climbed into the red chair, her legs over one arm, her cheek against the back. The headache had returned, pumping more fiercely than ever, and new shafts of pain darted down the side of her skull and into her neck.

She realized that she'd been far, far too modest. She hadn't thought she was important enough for anyone to bother.

Well, Maynard had bothered all right, and Maynard had been well rewarded. Slowly, working through the drumming in her head, she catalogued the information. Conversations with Peasedale, the call to Simon, the explanation of Octek, the mention of Nick. He'd had it on a plate.

The next realization came to the surface with a great leap, like a submerged bubble.

*I've got hard evidence. I've got it right here!*

That was what Maynard had heard, that was what had brought him snooping around the flat. The evidence she'd embroidered for Simon, the proof about the Silveron data, the proof that did not exist.

She felt a flutter of satisfaction; she almost laughed. Serve him bloody right, serve his masters bloody right. Let them panic. With that thought, she wondered if the black bug in the phone might yet serve a purpose, though at the moment she couldn't quite see what.

When she woke the light had shifted round until it was shining in a golden rectangle on the wall above the bed. The answering machine had just clicked on. It was Jenny again. Daisy reached down and picked up the phone.

'Now *listen*, you; are you okay?'

'I'm okay.' She lay back, feeling drugged and heavy.

'You should have an X-ray, I'm sure you should have an X-ray.'

'No point. Can't put it in plaster, can they?'

Jenny made more clucking noises, threatened to come over, and was only placated with promises of doctors if things weren't better in the morning. On the point of ringing off, she said: 'Oh, there's a message from Alan. A call he took late on Friday. A Mrs Ackroyd. Came through on the unlisted line, asking for some company that Alan had never heard of. But also asking for you.'

'Ah.'

'She left a number. Dorking.'

Dorking? Duggan, the *Boy's Own* pilot Duggan. But Ackroyd . . .

But no, wait a minute – Duggan's *sister*.

'Keen to speak to you, so she said. Shall I deal with it?'

Daisy remembered the invisible black box under her hand and said: 'No . . . Don't worry. It's nothing important. Just give me the number.'

She had a wash and walked down the hill. She tried the Dorking number from the phonebox a few yards from Mr Patel's, but there was no reply. She went into the shop and bought some supper. Mr Patel, his expression twisted into a comic picture of concern at the sight of her face, popped a packet of marshmallows into her bag when she wasn't looking. On her way back she tried the number again, but there was still no one home. As she started up the hill again, she found herself looking over her shoulder. Was it possible? Would they bother with *that* as well? Surely not. And yet why not?

The thought powered her up the last of the hill and kept her occupied while she boiled up a steak-and-kidney pudding with frozen peas. Then she tackled the area around her bed, shifting furniture, clearing the dustsheets, making up the bed.

It was much later, in what felt like the depths of the night, that she heard the phone ringing from a long way off, as if from another room. The answering machine picked up, she heard a voice, a voice from another age, another world, a voice that had her stumbling awake and groping for the receiver.

'It's me,' she interrupted groggily.

'Daisy Field?' asked a soft male voice.

'Yes.'

'Umm. We met in Virginia. Back in July. Umm, Alan Breck. You remember? With Paul Erlinger?'

She pulled herself up on one elbow, struggling to clear her brain. 'Yes. Of course I remember.'

'I wanted to talk. Is this a convenient moment?'

'Yes, yes.' She sat up and fumbled for the light. There was a short silence and for an instant she thought she had lost him. 'Hullo?' she prompted.

'Look, I'm not sure you can help . . .'

'Please, I can help. I can help!'

He gave a short laugh, nervous, cautious. 'That day we met, you seemed . . . I got the feeling that you understood the, er . . . difficulties . . .' His voice hung in the air, awaiting reassurance.

'Oh yes,' she said hastily. 'I understood. I still do.' She saw the dark figure in the diner, the restless hands, the furtive eyes.

'It's . . . well . . . There have been particular problems with EarthForce. You know what I mean?'

She gathered her wits and plunged in, hoping she was on the right track. 'Security problems, you mean? Yes. Yes, I could see that.'

'You could? You could? But . . .' Another long pause. 'It's all right your end? It's – I mean, I'd be safe, would I?'

Even as she began to make firm reassurances, her mind took off in a great leap of fear and she stalled in mid sentence. The black box! Christ! What was she thinking of! Her heart raced, her mouth was suddenly dry.

'What is it?' he asked sharply.

She was silent, in a momentary panic, but even as she

fought her way free, it came to her that if she told him to
stop talking and the reason why, then she'd lose any trust
he might have, and that would be the end of that. She
heard herself stalling: 'Sorry – it's the middle of the night
here. I dropped the phone.'

A pause. 'It's a big step,' he said uncertainly, as if
debating the matter with himself.

'Of course it is,' she said, trying to urge him gently
forward without actually feeding facts to the invisible ear
under her hand. 'But I can guarantee you all the support
you need.'

He said suddenly: 'Look, if I went ahead I'd need some
sort of financial security for me and my family, at least
until the worst is over. Maybe other kinds of security as
well. Could you guarantee that?'

'I guarantee everything. Whatever you need!'

'And it's safe. You're sure?'

*God, forgive me this.* 'I'm sure.'

'And if I were to make a statement – go public – could
you arrange the right outlets – you know, newspapers?
TV?'

'Absolutely. I have contacts, good contacts.'

'But here in the US?'

She'd have to work on that, speak to Simon, but this
wasn't the time to show anything less than complete
confidence. 'Definitely. You just say the word. Just give me
the when and how.'

'The when?' He sounded alarmed. 'But *now*. I mean, I
don't think it's safe for me here any more, I don't think it's
safe for my family. And I thought you'd have the how. I
kind of assumed you'd know.' He was ready to be disappointed in her, she realized, ready to back off at any
moment.

'Give me a couple of days,' she said rapidly. 'I'll fix
everything. Money, security, media coverage.' Sensing he
still wasn't convinced, she insisted: 'You call back in two

days and if you're not happy with the way I've arranged things, we'll think again. Fair enough?'

'Okay.' There was still an edge of doubt in his voice. 'Okay. Tuesday.'

'Tuesday. Same time.'

When he rang off, she sat for a long time, waiting for her heartbeat to slow down.

Tuesday. Just two days. God.

And the black box: what would Maynard and his friends guess from all this? Had she already put Alan Breck in danger? Christ.

She slept less than four hours more, and started her day well before dawn.

# Chapter 32

———

SCHENKER, IN RARE good humour after a sporting weekend in the Scottish Highlands, hummed the melody from *Top Hat* as he unpacked in his apartment high above Bryanston Square.

On Friday he had been the subject of a feature in the *Financial Times* and he reflected happily on the thought that it would have been read by everyone of importance in the City.

A copy lay in his case and he glanced at it now. The photograph was excellent: it had caught the fire of intelligence in his eyes, made a virtue of his rather thin mouth, given him an aura of tension and energy. The interviewer had also been kind: effortless high-flyer; talented troubleshooter; tipped for greater things. And he had used Schenker's grittiest quotes: *I consider my learning curve hasn't reached its peak. The day you stop learning is the day you stop justifying your salary. Confidence comes from judgement, but growth comes from a certain degree of humility, from constant re-evaluation.*

Good stuff.

As he picked a suit for the morning, the telephone rang. Unhurriedly, he slid the trousers into the overnight press and laid the jacket over the integral hanger before strolling across to the bedside phone. It was, he noticed, almost one a.m.

'I need a word,' said Cramm.

'We'll have half an hour before the divisional meeting.'

'It can't wait.'

Schenker, who rarely slept more than five hours a night at the best of times, offered: 'Seven then. For breakfast.'

'But I'm here. In a box, down in the square. It'll take fifteen minutes at the most.'

As he waited, Schenker wondered if his purple silk dressing gown with quilted lapels wasn't a little too flamboyant for Cramm's eyes and, deciding that no risk, however small, was worth taking when it came to office gossip, he changed it for a black kimono.

Cramm appeared wearing holed jeans, an American-football jacket and a day's growth of beard.

'You look as though you've been sleeping rough,' said Schenker in a tone not totally devoid of criticism.

'I thought I'd better come straight over,' Cramm said in a tone that had Schenker bristling slightly as he waved him forward into the living room. Unexcitability had always been one of Cramm's greatest qualities, and it did not please Schenker to see that it seemed to have deserted him.

Offered a drink, Cramm took a Scotch and drank deeply.

'Well?' Schenker demanded.

'There was a fire – you may have read about it – at a research laboratory run by a company called Octek.'

'I hardly had time to read the papers. I was stalking at Lord Crowborough's. Why?'

'It was the laboratory I told you about, the one set up by the Catch woman.'

Schenker, pouring himself a ginger ale, lowered the bottle soundlessly to the bar top. 'You said it wasn't going to get off the ground.'

'There was a time when it looked like that. But in the end it couldn't be stopped.'

'You surprise me.' The sarcasm had been unintentional but he let it stand. If there were difficulties, then Cramm should have told him about them straight away.

Taking his drink, he sat on the sofa opposite Cramm and studied his assistant. In the past few months he had been leaving a lot to this young man. With a spark of unease it occurred to him that Cramm's eagerness to serve, his dogged pragmatism and his precocious grasp of office politics may not have been matched by a corresponding level of judgement.

'Tell me about the fire,' he said.

'It was an animal rights raid. Octek were using rodents. The activists broke in, liberated the animals and set fire to the place – '

Schenker interrupted with an upheld finger. 'These activists, why did they choose Octek?'

Cramm hesitated, uncertain as to the purpose of the interrogation.

'Why not choose a more obvious target?' Schenker persisted. 'One of our own places, for example?'

Cramm got the idea; they were playing detective. 'The place was unguarded,' he said. 'An easy target.'

'And how would they know that?'

An instant followed, a taut silence in which Cramm's gaze hardened. 'They must have been tipped off.'

Schenker felt his mood descend another notch. 'But it was definitely animal rights campaigners, was it?'

'Yes.' Cramm nodded emphatically, his eyes challenging Schenker to disagree, and in that moment Schenker's heart completed its descent. He was no longer in any doubt that Cramm had got carried away, that the situation, if unravelled, would prove ugly. Absorbing this, he felt a flash of anger, barbed with sudden fears and anxieties. Then just as rapidly, he pushed these feelings aside. Anger served no purpose, not until he could see his way clear.

He put his glass to his lips and sipped his drink. 'Go on.'

'They're going to try to pin it on us.'

'Who are?'

'Daisy Field and her group. They're threatening to go to the press.'

'On what evidence?'

'Apparently the police are saying the job was too professional for animal rights people.'

'That cuts both ways, surely. If it was too professional for one group, then why not for another?' Without waiting for a reply he pressed on: 'Is that all?'

Cramm shifted in his seat and studied his glass. 'No . . . There's something else apparently, some other evidence.'

'That could link us to the fire?'

'Yes.'

'And what is it?'

'We don't know.'

'We don't know,' repeated Schenker heavily. 'Well, what *could* it be?'

Cramm retorted defensively: 'I've no idea! There's nothing for them to know.'

Schenker regarded him carefully. This, he decided, was probably the truth. 'So what's the problem?'

Cramm looked surprised that he should miss the obvious. 'Well, the press could make it look very bad for us.'

'But how? No paper will print a story without some facts to back it up. What facts could they have?'

'I don't know, but the Field woman's boyfriend is a *Sunday Times* journalist.'

'So? He's a professional then, isn't he, with a tough editor. No stories without solid substantiation.'

'But she's got something, so she says.'

'Well, she's bound to say that, isn't she? It's called rattling the opposition. Come on, Cramm, if there are no facts, there are no facts!'

Cramm nodded uncertainly.

Schenker˙ said crisply: 'I suggest you draft a suitably

dismissive statement for the press, in case they try to run something.' He moved to the edge of the seat, ready to get up and show Cramm out, but the younger man obviously hadn't finished.

'They're planning to carry on,' he said doggedly, 'to start another lab and continue the work. They say none of this is going to put them off.'

'Did you imagine it would? These people have to martyr themselves,' Schenker scoffed with a wave of the hand. 'Let them! Silveron's okay. Nothing they can do is going to show otherwise. They're just going to waste a hell of a lot of money.' He slapped his knees and stood up. 'That's it?' he asked.

'No,' Cramm replied. 'They say they've got evidence that the Silveron trials were fixed. They say someone in a key position is prepared to talk. They're threatening to go public.'

Schenker had the sudden sensation of having been in this job too long, of seeing events come round for the second or third time, like the rerun of a tired old film. 'It's not that madman again, is it? That toxicologist in Chicago – the one with the name?'

Cramm nodded. 'Dublensky.'

He laughed derisively. 'He's just a nutcase!'

'But there's a chance, a risk – he might have documentation.'

'What do you mean, *documentation*?'

'He might have copied some data,' Cramm said eventually, picking his way cautiously through the words. 'Data that shows that some of the Silveron test results were lifted from another product.'

'Lifted?'

'Identical data, duplicate results.'

'And what's meant to be the significance of this – *data*? What's it meant to show?'

'That the Silveron trials were not carried out properly.'

Schenker let out a harsh guffaw that rang loudly in the quiet of the flat. 'You're not suggesting it's *genuine*?'

'Well . . .' Cramm spread his hands in a gesture of helplessness. 'It *looks* genuine, and that's the same thing.'

Schenker felt a shiver of anger. He slapped his palm down on the table. 'I want that document on my desk first thing this morning.'

'I'll try – '

'By ten. At the latest.'

Cramm looked unhappy but did not say it was impossible.

'So what's the bottom line here?' Schenker snapped. 'A press bonanza? A media massacre?'

'That's about it.'

Schenker got to his feet, fighting for air, and strode to the window. What a cock-up! Christ, and he had trusted Cramm to keep a finger on the pulse! With a swoop of resignation, he saw that he was going to have to take personal charge of this, that nothing would get sorted out unless he did.

'Okay,' he said, turning briskly. 'Let's go through it from the top.' He returned to his seat, leaning close over the coffee table, tapping the surface with a forefinger. 'I want a list of damage containment ideas by the morning. I want to know how this Dubinsky – '

'Dublensky.'

' – how this Dublensky can be effectively discredited the moment the first journalist gets on the line. I want to know how he can be neutralized.'

And, he thought to himself, I want to know how to guard my rear, to cover myself in the unpleasant eventuality that this thing blows up in my face. He thought of the cola magnate, and the discussions on Long Island, and wondered how close he was to being offered a new job.

'You might think of how to clip Miss Field's wings too,' he went on. 'Have another go at finding out where she gets all this money from – '

'You didn't hear then? I thought you'd have heard. It was all over the tabloids. It's Nick Mackenzie, the rock star. He was financing everything, the Field woman's salary, the laboratory.'

'How deep?'

'Must have been well over a million. Now he's going to finance Dublensky.'

'Finance him?'

'Bring him over, dish him up to the press.'

'Oh he is, is he! Jesus, who does he think he is? What the hell does he think he's playing at?'

'Saving the world?' sighed Cramm.

'Christ, these people!' Schenker exploded. 'Think they're a cut above the common herd! Think they've the God-given right to tell everyone how to behave!'

Cramm threw him a shrewd look. 'When it comes to behaviour, Mackenzie's got nothing to boast about.'

'Oh?'

'He's been seeing Mrs Driscoll. Every day.' He paused significantly. 'And some nights.'

Schenker stared unseeing at Cramm, then looked down at the table, gripped by a sudden pang, the nature of which he couldn't identify but which left him off-balance, almost breathless.

'Mrs Driscoll? Mrs *Driscoll*?' He glanced back at Cramm and, seeing that it was true, murmured: 'Well . . .' Then, aware of Cramm's gaze, added: 'What a very stupid woman she is.'

It was the same Rolls that had picked her up on the evening she had first met Schenker, Susan realized. Leather seats, walnut trim, glass partition screening the grey-uniformed driver and, best of all, something she hadn't noticed before, an old-fashioned voice tube with a brass spout.

'Does this thing actually work?' she cried delightedly, pulling the tube from its bracket and whisking off the cap.

Schenker glanced briefly across. 'Certainly.' But his look didn't encourage her to try it, and she replaced the tube with a shrug.

The car was heading up the Brompton Road towards Knightsbridge. 'Where are we going?' she asked brightly.

'I thought we'd drive round the park. Would you like to be dropped back at Harrods?'

'Round the park? How mysterious! I thought you were going to take me somewhere exciting. To the Dorchester at least.' She added teasingly: 'Rather clandestine, isn't it, a drive round the park? People will think we're meeting secretly.' She watched for Schenker's discomfiture, and was rewarded with the sight of his tongue flicking nervously over his lips. What a character he was! She was almost fond of him in a repugnant sort of way. So desperate to succeed, so childish in his anxiety to get things right, applying himself to London society with the same humourless intensity he applied to his business life.

He answered: 'I thought it would be better to talk here.' He was looking ahead, watching the traffic.

'Ooh dear,' she said, making a face. 'This sounds ominous.'

She kept her tone light. Whatever this was about, she wasn't going to be robbed of her mood, which was euphoric.

Schenker didn't respond immediately. It wasn't until they had passed under the Bowater building and were driving along the South Carriage Drive that he began to speak in a flat monotone. 'The Kershaw woman. She's been asking for money again. Additional expenses, was how she put it.'

Susan regarded the sky which until an instant ago had

looked unblemished, and, despite her intentions, felt her
euphoria deflating. She looked accusingly at Schenker but
his profile was unreadable. 'And so? Will you give it to
her?'

'We already have.'

She felt a flutter of relief. Of course he had. Schenker
knew which side his bread was buttered on.

'Unfortunately it's unlikely to finish there,' said
Schenker. 'She'll come back for more.'

What was Schenker trying to do to her? She shot him a
furious look. 'Oh?' she replied stiffly. 'And why do you
think that?'

He was examining the traffic with concentration. 'Well,
it's rather an attractive proposition, isn't it? A limitless
supply of cash.'

'She can't be that stupid, surely. I mean, she can't think
it'll go on for ever.'

'She's already making noises again,' he interrupted
smoothly.

A tremor of annoyance passed through Susan. Schenker
was playing games with her, trying to undermine her
happiness.

'But she can be stopped, can't she?' said Susan, unable
to suppress a hint of desperation in her voice. 'I mean, it's
ridiculous. The woman's behaving like a criminal.'

'And how would you suggest she be stopped?' He threw
her a questioning glance, and she caught a glint of something unfamiliar in his eye, a coolness, a spark of hostility.
It was another side of Schenker, one she had never seen
before.

'There must be a way,' she argued. 'I don't know . . . I
mean, can't she be threatened with legal action or something?' This, she well knew, was not a realistic proposition,
but then she could hardly be expected to provide serious
answers. Problem-solving was Schenker's province, and she
was surprised, not to say annoyed, that he should want to

consult her about it. He had seen to all the arrangements, had struck the deal, whatever it was, and now he would have to see the matter through.

Schenker said: 'Sadly, I really don't think there's much more I can do.'

Susan looked at him sharply. 'What do you mean?'

Schenker turned his head towards her, his black button eyes unblinking. 'Simply that I have done all I can and if this woman comes back ... Well ...' He lifted his shoulders slightly.

'What are you saying?' She almost prodded him on the arm, she was so irritated with him.

'That there'll be no more money.'

Susan stared at him, trying hard to interpret this. Did he simply mean he was going to get tough with the woman, keep her quiet in some other way? Or did he mean what she feared he meant, something so unpleasant she could hardly bring herself to think about it?

'But what happens if this woman gets difficult?' she asked, feeling her way forward. 'What happens if she threatens to go to the press?'

Schenker's eyes dropped slowly to the floor before coming back to her face to resume their steady gaze; his mouth curved down at the corners. She realized this was his way of showing regret.

'You'd let her ...?' she asked incredulously. 'You'd *let* her?'

'Hopefully it won't come to that.'

'*But you'd let her!*'

He turned a palm upward. 'I'd really have no choice.'

It was a moment before Susan could speak. 'But what about Tony?' she cried. 'What about everything he's done for you? God, you have an odd way of showing gratitude! After all he's *done* for you!'

'I'm not quite sure what you mean. We've enjoyed a pleasant working relationship, your husband and I, but I wouldn't have said we owed each other any favours. On the contrary, the minister has gone so far out of his way to avoid showing partiality since he's been in office that, if anything, I would say my company has suffered from our association, rather than the other way round.'

Was this what it was about, then? Sour grapes? Or was he after favours from Tony, in exchange for which he would find more money for the Kershaw woman? Was this an elaborate way of exerting pressure? Susan felt as if she had been plunged into a pit blindfold.

'But you're implicated in this business as well!' she protested. 'If the woman talks to the press, you'll get dragged into it too!'

'Oh? And how would that be?'

'Well, you introduced her to Tony for a start.'

'Hardly,' he murmured in a tone of mild distaste. 'They met at a party. I didn't even know the girl.'

'In France then. That weekend.'

'No, you're quite wrong. Your husband made all the arrangements.'

It came to her then: he was prepared to let Tony sink without trace.

But perhaps he wasn't quite so clever as he thought he was. He'd forgotten one rather important point. She rang triumphantly: 'Well, what about the money then? She'll say who gave it to her, won't she? She'll tell them it was you!'

With forbearance, in the tone of a teacher explaining basics to a child, he said: 'She has no idea where the money comes from. She certainly has no reason to think it comes from us. And even if she were to get the idea, she wouldn't be able to substantiate it.'

'Oh, come on! Who else could it come from?'

But even as Susan finished asking the question, she knew the answer. Tony. Of course. Tony.

She turned hastily to stare out of the window, trying to absorb the implications of this terrifying development. The car was approaching Speakers' Corner, passing the row of parked tourist coaches that lined Park Lane even in late October. In that moment Susan grasped what she should have understood from the beginning, that Schenker had thought this out very carefully, that he had left nothing to chance, that if there was a scandal then one person at least was going to emerge unscathed.

'You'd *let* this happen?' she repeated weakly, feeling herself close to tears.

'Really, we did what we could.' It seemed to her that he was suppressing a sigh. 'Under the circumstances . . .' He waved a hand as if it wasn't worth explaining all over again.

Lifting her chin, she asked bravely: 'So why are you telling me all this? What d'you want?'

'Want?'

'From me.'

'From you? Why, nothing. Nothing at all.' He seemed surprised and mildly offended. 'No, no. The only thing I wanted was to warn you about the wo— about the situation. To tell you I could do no more.' But his tone was a little too emphatic, his surprise a little too polished to be entirely convincing, and she knew she wouldn't feel any confidence on this point until the drive was over. But if he was planning to say anything he wasn't in a hurry, and they sat in silence as the car swept into the north carriageway.

Finally Schenker said: 'Things are very tough at the moment.'

Was this her cue? Maybe. But she wasn't in the mood to make things easy for him.

Schenker, seeing he wasn't going to get any help, went on: 'Your friend Mr Mackenzie's causing me a few headaches.'

Before she could prevent herself, she had jerked her head round to stare at Schenker. Of all the lines he might have taken, of all the approaches, this was the last she had expected. For an awful moment it occurred to her that he might know about her and Nick, but in the next instant she rejected the thought. No one, and especially not Schenker, could possibly know about that. Much as she'd wanted to shout it from the rooftops, much as it had killed her to suppress her exhilaration, she hadn't told a soul, not even her best girlfriend. But then, unless you wanted the entire world to know, you never told your best girlfriend.

No, it couldn't be that. What could he mean? Then it came to her. 'The laboratory, his project . . .?'

Schenker twisted in his seat to face her. 'He has this obsession with one of our products. I don't know why. He seems to think it harmed his wife. Though at the beginning the villain was meant to be something completely different – a wood preserver named Reldane. But when that proved harmless, he lighted on Silveron. Frankly, we're mystified as to why he should go to these extraordinary lengths to try and prove that there's something wrong with what is basically one of our best products, a substance that's been tested to within an inch of its life.' He leaned closer and, resting his arm along the seat back, extended a finger as if to touch her shoulder. 'Oh, don't misunderstand me. I'm sorry he was the victim of those animal rights people. But at the same time I can't pretend I'm actually crying about it.'

Here was the confident approachable Schenker again. It was as if the unpleasantness of the last few minutes had been an unfortunate interlude which, now it was out of the way, could be ignored. She realized how little she understood this man, and how much he alarmed her.

'Well, he's finished with all that now,' she said. She added quickly: 'So I understand anyway.'

'Finished? Really?' His tone was polite but unbelieving. 'I'm reliably informed that he's already setting up a second laboratory, that he has every intention of continuing with this obsession. More unfortunate for him, I also understand that he and these Catch people have fallen victim to some forged laboratory data and are planning to make allegations to the press that they cannot possibly substantiate. We would have to sue, of course. It would be an ugly business, do him a lot of harm. As well as causing us a great deal of trouble.'

She had got the idea. Somewhere in here was the bargain, the price of Tony's safety. She heard herself say: 'Perhaps I can help . . . Speak to him . . .'

He considered: 'Well . . .' he said doubtfully. 'I hardly think an appeal to reason is going to have much effect, even coming from you.'

Even from her? Did he know after all? The thought bewildered her. And what did he want if he didn't want her to speak to Nick? A small worm of dread curled in her stomach.

The car was heading south through the park towards the Serpentine. The driver half turned his head. Schenker, catching the movement, picked up the voice tube and told him to carry on. So there had been a plan to stop, a plan which was no longer necessary. Schenker obviously expected to finish his business before they reached Harrods.

Unable to bear the uncertainty any longer, she asked: 'What do you suggest then?'

He put on a show of faint surprise, shrugging slightly. 'Suggest? Why, nothing.' He waved a hand into space. 'No, I'm just surprised that Mackenzie should want his life subjected to scrutiny, and by a press which holds nothing sacred. It's a rare man who has nothing to hide.'

Susan was very still. A chill crept up from her stomach.

Schenker interleaved his fingers and pushed out his lips, his movements drawn out, almost languid. The dark eyes travelled slowly across to Susan and stared at her with a look that, while pretending to be quizzical, was deeply knowing. 'And Mr Mackenzie has a great deal to hide, so I believe.' Any last doubts she might have had as to his meaning were dispelled by the glint of personal contempt that he couldn't quite conceal.

She looked quickly out of the window before her face crumpled.

He knew. The realization was only marginally less shocking than the knowledge that this was no idle disclosure, that at the end of the day this dreadful little man wouldn't hesitate to make use of it, to betray her in the same way that he was preparing to betray Tony.

Chemical-campaigning pop star and agriculture chief's wife. The papers would have a field day. Tony's career would never survive it. She leaned her head against the glass.

They were in the traffic queue at Alexandra Gate before she felt steady again.

'I could talk to him,' she offered, gaining strength as she said it. 'Persuade him that publicity wouldn't be a good idea.'

'Mmm?' Schenker seemed almost bored. 'And d'you think he'd listen?'

'Yes,' she said defensively. Then she remembered Nick and his principles and felt a sudden doubt. If it came to a choice between her and his beloved project, how would he decide? Publicity about their affair wouldn't frighten him at all, she realized bitterly. He wouldn't care, he would tell her to go to hell, just like he'd told her to go to hell all those years ago. Nothing would frighten him. Nothing except . . .

The answer came to her then. Part of her was shocked and repulsed by the idea, but another part of her reached out for it avidly. There was a sort of justice in it, an awful sort of satisfaction.

A last instant of uncertainty, then she said: 'There's something he wouldn't be happy about, something he'd hate the world to know.'

She could feel Schenker watching her. 'Oh?' he said casually. 'And what's that?'

Susan told him and for the first time during that dreadful drive she felt a glimmering of hope.

Hillyard whistled as he bounded up the stairs two at a time. In this sort of quiet he reckoned it was less obvious to make a bit of noise than to creep around surreptitiously. As he came up the final flight he switched the tote bag he was carrying to his left hand and prepared to let himself into the flat, spinning the door keys round his finger as if he owned the place. On the landing he paused for a moment, listening hard, before resuming his whistling, more softly this time.

There were footsteps on the stairs, coming down; males gabbling in some foreign language. He was sliding the key into the lock when they turned onto the landing. He took his time before looking round, his lips still pursed into a whistle, and smiled briefly and impersonally at the two swarthy men approaching. They fell silent, eyeing him liberally as they passed. Well, they might not know what to make of him, but he had their mark all right. A pair of queens, and no mistake.

He let himself into the flat without looking back. By this time he knew his way around the place so well that he could see at a glance what had changed. The furniture was different – she had moved two chairs round – a dust sheet lay in a tangle on the floor, and a new pile of papers had appeared on the desk. And then there was the ceiling. The fresh plaster was dry in the centre but still damp at the edges where it met the cornice, and a right mess down one of the walls where the water from the tank had got behind the wallpaper and bubbled it away.

He went straight to the phone and, careful to weight the rest so it would ring if someone called, unfastened the handset with a screwdriver and eased the halves apart. He looked at the microtransmitter for a moment, remembering the sounds on the tape recording, the clunks as she had unscrewed the fastenings, the creaking of plastic as she had removed the casing, and then the long silence. She must have seen it: she couldn't have missed it. And if she hadn't been looking for this, what else could she have been looking for?

She had seen it, but she had left it in place. She hadn't told anybody, she hadn't called the police. Clever girl. Well, almost.

The transmitter was fixed with double-sided tape, and now he pulled it free, and unclipping the tiny alligator clips slid it into his pocket.

He put the halves back together and refastened the screws. Then, going to the main telephone socket on the skirting board, he removed the socket plate and replaced it with a new one from his bag, his work interrupted only by a squawk from his walkie-talkie, which gave him a moment's fright. He checked with Biggs down in the van, but there was nothing brewing; just interference.

He had a quick look through the new pile of papers on the desk. Insurance claim forms, magazines.

Then the final task. He took some time mulling over the exact location for his little present. He went through her hanging cupboard and bathroom drawers, but lingered longest over the underwear in the top drawer of the chest in the main room. All in all, it would be the most fitting place. He fingered a pair of panties and dangled them in the air, both repelled and fascinated by the thought of catching her bodily scents. Then he ran his hand up inside the chest to make sure there would be no gaps once the drawer was closed again.

He pushed the drawer closed except for an opening of about three inches, then went back to the tote-bag. Shuddering with physical excitement, unable to suppress a crow of anticipation, he pulled on a glove and slipped his hand carefully into the holdall. After a moment's scrabbling, he had his prey. A big beauty who went into the drawer good as gold.

Hillyard was all finished and out of the place in eight minutes flat.

# Chapter 33

NICK BUZZED FOR Mrs Alton and looked at the house phone accusingly when it failed to respond. He peered at his watch. Nine. Could it be that late? He looked up and realized it had probably been dark for some time. Rolling his chair clear of the console, he leaned back and stretched, pushing his arms high over his head and giving a long shuddering sigh. Eight, no, nine hours he'd been here.

He had completed – what? He leaned forward to count the pages – ten pages of manuscript; maybe five minutes' finished music. It had come with breathtaking speed. The orchestration was still a bit rough, of course, definitely in need of refinement, but it had begun to develop the sort of texture he was after and he didn't think he'd be too ashamed to hear it performed in its present form. Since Sunday he had finished one complete section, or, to be more accurate, a movement, though that was rather a grand title for something that was just eight minutes long. It was a lyrical section entitled *In a Summer Garden*. Next would come *Dawnlight*. The movement he had been working on today, an allegro section which would come before both of these, had not yet found a name. Something that suggested life or joy, he thought. The whole thing was going to be called simply *Thanksgiving*.

The structure of the piece, with its elegiac choral tone, was loosely that of a requiem, but he wasn't going to call it that, not only because it would sound presumptuous and people would think he was trying to put himself up there with Mozart and Fauré, but because he didn't want to be constrained by the conventions of the form. Also, and even more to the point, the requiem mass was about death in its direst sense, quite the opposite of what he was trying to achieve in this celebration of life.

Perhaps *Thanksgiving* was too bland; perhaps *Last Song* would be better. While he considered this he got up and went down the passageway to the kitchen, suddenly ravenous.

Mrs Alton, who knew him only too well, had left a large notice on the table, directing him to the various dishes in the fridge and larder, with instructions for microwaving.

The sounds of the night, inaudible in the heavily clad studio, now wafted softly against the dark window. Irrationally, he felt conspicuous in the light, as if someone were out there watching him from the rising land beyond the window, and he went to lower the blind. He paused to take a look into the darkness. He could just make out a tall beech, caught against the glimmer of the sky. It moved gently, the last of its thin leaves causing the stars to wink uncertainly. From somewhere a long way off came the faint whistle of a night creature.

That morning he had walked to the western woods. The smell of autumn was strong, the air sharp and damp. He had felt a great surge of feeling, something close to exultation. It was partly the work, of course, the humming of the music in his brain, but something else too: a sense of liberation, a growing feeling that he was breaking free of the old patterns of despair and hopelessness.

Eating in solitary splendour he listened to the silence, feeling the emptiness of the house around him, and decided that, in spite of everything, he might learn to love the place again. When he wasn't here he might offer it to other people, make it into a retreat for composers and musicians, set up a special trust named after Alusha.

The ideas kept him occupied to the end of the meal.

Soon his mind was darting back to his music and, restless, he scooped up some fruit and started for the studio again.

At the kitchen door a faint sound caught him and he stopped to look back over his shoulder, thinking the fruit must have overbalanced in the bowl. But the room was quiet, the fruit undisturbed. He tried to pin the sound down – the microwave cooling? The contents of the dishwater settling? – but the sound had been too indistinct.

He thought of security. Had Mrs Alton locked all the doors when she left? Were the sensors on?

He hovered indecisively before depositing the fruit back on the kitchen table and beginning a round of the house.

The passage beyond the studio was dark, the estate office darker still. The outside door which led from the office into the courtyard on the east side of the house was securely locked and bolted. Retracing his steps, he checked the front door then, skirting the packing cases which still lined the walls, went to the door of the drawing room. Switching on a light, he glanced towards the french windows at the far end, then continued into the boot room, which had been a gun room in another life. Here another external door gave out on to the western side of the house, close to the rose garden. He didn't bother with a light, but felt his way past the coats in the half darkness, watching his own outline approaching in the dark reflections of the glass-panelled door. As he tested the locks he looked out into the night, but the sky seemed darker on this side and he couldn't make out the shapes of the trees.

Back in the kitchen he picked up the fruit before remembering the last and most frequently used door. Biting off a piece of apple he went through the small hall at the rear of the kitchen into the scullery, which served as a back lobby. It was a large room and dark, its shadows pierced by the green eyes of three giant freezers. From the boiler room next door came the low hum of the heating plant.

Next to the door was a narrow window. As he reached

for the door handle he peered through it and saw that the starlight had faded and the outline of the beech had become less distinct: a deeper blackness against an uncertain sky.

Then the darkness shifted.

He thrust his eye closer to the glass.

Something had moved, but what?

Suddenly his eye was brought down to the splash of light falling from the bottom of the kitchen window. A foot had come into view. A booted foot, heavy, large. It was placing itself cautiously on the flagstone. After a moment, the other foot appeared, feeling its way forward. The figure above was in darkness apart from the side of the leg, the shadow of a hand.

Not Duncan: Duncan would come straight in. Not one of the estate workers: they'd ring at the courtyard door. No: this person was too furtive, this person was hoping not to be heard.

Pulse racing, Nick abandoned his apple, threw the banana on the floor, and reached for the door to throw the lock. The next instant he wavered and pulled back. No, let the bastard come in, let him get the appropriate welcome.

Reaching down to the door again, but stealthily, he tested the key to make sure the lock wasn't set, then, trembling and hot for battle, he went on a feverish hunt for a weapon – a stick, a metal bar, anything that would carry some weight.

Panting fretfully, cursing under his breath, he worked his way rapidly round the room, feeling for implements, long, sharp, heavy – he would have taken anything – and found nothing but cans, sacks of potatoes, catering-sized coffee tins.

A knock. Soft, like a tap.

He froze. It came again, a little louder.

He tiptoed along the front of the freezers until he was in the shadows to the far side of the door, the best position from which to spring an attack. An elbow locked around the throat should do it. If not that, an arm-lock up the back. His hand-to-hand technique wasn't too hot, but he mentally rehearsed the grip and twist needed to immobilize his enemy.

The knocking came again, a louder more confident rap that was designed to be heard. It figured: he'd want to be sure the house was empty, he'd want to know he wasn't going to be disturbed.

A scrunching of feet as the man shifted his weight, then a thunderous rap that had the door bouncing on its hinges. Through the window the outside light sprang on; the man's rapid movements must have triggered the vibration sensor.

Nick felt a moment of doubt. Could it be friend rather than foe? Should he take a look? But no – what friend crept up to one's door so as to avoid activating the security lights?

In the ensuing silence, the sound of the handle turning had his stomach barrelling up into his ribs. He retreated slightly, to get a better run at it.

The handle ground on. The sound ceased. It was a moment before he realized that the door was already swinging open, coming rapidly towards him. Then it stopped. In the light from the kitchen, the man was clearly outlined as he stepped into the room. Large, heavy.

The man paused, as if to listen, then pulled the door closed behind him.

Perhaps Nick made a sound, perhaps the other man suddenly sensed his presence, but the next instant he was spinning round with an audible gasp.

Nick, himself startled, went in a split second too late. He knew it was too late because as he went for the man's arm to try for the arm-lock he saw the arm curling upwards to block his strike.

Having missed his move, he went for anything he could get, scrabbling to get a grip on his opponent's shoulder, flailing for the wrist of the blocking arm. At the same time he tried to hook a foot round the intruder's ankle and knock him off balance. The man was shouting something, but whatever it was Nick didn't hear and pressed on. The advantage of surprise was gone, and the other man was recovering fast. He kicked Nick's foot away as easily as if it were some mild obstruction, and, neatly reversing the position, hooked his leg behind Nick's.

Nick might have been able to cope with that if it hadn't been for the hand that came from somewhere under the cover of the blocking arm and splayed itself against the underside of his chin, snapping his head backwards with a nasty jerk. Abandoning all thoughts of attack, Nick tried to twist away, at the same time pulling the iron-clawed fingers away from his chin. But as his weight was driven back, he came up against the man's leg and, feeling his balance going, pushed out a hand in the direction of the man's head to grab what he could.

The man was trying to speak again, but Nick was too busy finding hair and part of an ear to listen. Getting a firm grip, he twisted hard. He heard the other man yelp with pain, but any triumph he might have felt was short-lived when the pressure on his chin failed to lessen; if anything it intensified. He made a last effort to twist away, but somehow the intruder had got a vice-like grip on his shoulder. God, he was strong. It was like tussling with a machine.

Finally Nick felt his weight begin to topple. Determined not to go down alone, he held on grimly to the patch of scalp. The other man came down all right; his weight – what felt like a good eighteen stone – landed right on top of Nick. But even as the man was on his way down, he must have been planning his next move because he quickly straddled Nick's body and, letting go of his chin, pinned his shoulders effortlessly to the floor with one arm, while conjuring up a spare hand from somewhere to bolt itself round Nick's throat. One didn't have to be a martial arts enthusiast to realize he had done this sort of thing before.

One feel of those steely fingers closing round his neck and Nick felt a punch of real fear.

'I'm not here to harm you!' came a deep voice. 'Just let go ma head, for God's sake.'

For an instant the hand around Nick's throat increased its pressure, to show what it could do if it really tried. Not needing a second hint, Nick loosened his grip on the man's scalp and immediately felt the hand withdraw from his neck.

For an instant neither of them moved, their panting loud in the gloom.

'Aye, but you gave me a shock!' came a deep voice.

'Who the hell – ! Get the fuck off me!'

'Sure. Sure.' His tone was surprisingly contrite. He moved hastily, rolling clear and clambering to his feet. 'I didna' mean to go fightin' you. It was just the shock. By God, but you were like a devil there.' He gave a low gasp. 'You nearly had me . . . And no mistake.'

Nick, recovering fast, scrambled to his feet. 'Who the hell – !'

In the gloom he saw the man leaning against the wall, gathering his breath. 'It's Campbell,' the voice said. 'Alistair Campbell.' He held up a defensive hand. 'Now don't go mad, Mr Mackenzie. You'd best listen to me, or you may regret it. I came specially to warn you, do you see?'

'Jesus,' Nick howled angrily, still feeling the fingers at his throat, 'I could get you arrested for this. Trespass, for Christ's sake . . . You've no right to go creeping about, scaring the shit out of people. What the hell's wrong with ringing the door bell like everyone else?'

'What, at the gate there? You mightna' have let me in.'

'Up here then, for Christ's sake!'

'I didna' want to meet with the police.'

Nick, suddenly exhausted, propped himself against a freezer. 'The police?'

'That's what I came to tell you, Mr Mackenzie. They're on their way. At this very moment.'

'What the hell are you talking about?' He felt like a drink. No – not a drink. Coffee. Striding shakily past Campbell, he tottered into the kitchen and made for the percolator.

'They're comin' right now, Mr Mackenzie,' said Campbell, hurrying along behind. 'I have it on good authority' – a tone of confidentiality came into his voice – 'a friend at the local police. I thought you might need to know.'

Nick wasn't in the mood for this obtuse conversation. He was still smarting from the speed of Campbell's victory. 'Look, I don't know what the hell you're on about,' he retorted, pouring his coffee.

'It's a squad from Glasgow.' Campbell drew in his lips. 'From the drug squad.'

Nick guffawed. 'The drug squad? Don't make me laugh. I've never touched the stuff. No, laddie,' he wagged an irate finger, 'you've got things wrong! If anyone's going to get into trouble tonight, it's going to be you!'

Campbell shuffled, his face creased into an expression of almost childish alarm. 'Mr Mackenzie, you have to believe me. This is no joke.'

There was an earnestness about the man that caused Nick's anger to subside a little – his anger, but not his incredulity. 'No joke, eh? Well then, they're in for a big disappointment, aren't they?'

'They've a warrant, Mr Mackenzie.'

Nick paused, the coffee half-way to his mouth. There was a certainty in Campbell's tone that was beginning to unnerve him. For the first time he considered the possibility that there might be some truth in what he was saying.

While he was trying to make sense of the idea, there was a loud buzz from the far side of the room.

The two men exchanged glances.

Nick slowly put down his cup. 'The gate,' he said.

Campbell bounced forward on the balls of his feet, poised for action. 'Shall I hold them off? Keep them busy?'

Nick didn't dare imagine what Campbell had in mind. 'But I tell you, there's nothing here!' he said harshly, striding across to the videophone and looking at the screen. Two cars, two men standing in the foreground, both in plain clothes. He felt a sudden unreasoned panic, as if he had something to feel guilty about.

On the screen one of the men reached forward, his hand growing disproportionately large in the distortions of the fish-eye lens. The buzzer sounded again.

Nick lifted the handset. He saw the two men cock their heads as they heard the click.

Suddenly the scene lurched in front of him, the heat drained from his face.

'What is it?' Campbell's hoarse whisper sounded at his elbow.

Nick fell back, staring dumbly at the wall as he tried to fight himself clear of the thought that was ricocheting round his brain. '*God . . .*'

'Here.' Campbell took the handset from Nick's faltering grasp and barked a peremptory. 'Hullo?'

It took Nick a few seconds to gather his wits, about as long as it took Campbell to have a grudging conversation with the men at the gate and, capping the receiver, to turn questioningly to Nick. 'They've a warrant all right. Shall I . . .?'

Nick gave a dazed nod, already retreating. By the time Campbell had pressed the entry button, he was beginning to run, sprinting into the hall and up the stairs. In the bedroom, he pulled open the wardrobes, now largely empty, and progressed rapidly through the drawers, scrabbling through the contents and slamming them shut again.

At Alusha's bedside cabinet he pulled himself up short, thinking: Slow, slow. Don't miss anything. Crazy to hurry now.

Her clothes had gone months ago, donated to charity, but smaller belongings remained, things he hadn't got round to clearing away. He dropped to his knees and went through the main compartment, a wide cupboard with two shelves. Books, Walkman, tapes, magazines. As he moved to the drawer above, he was aware that Campbell had entered the room and was hovering at the window.

Jewellery, Panadol, face cream, hairbrush, hairbands, pencils, tissues, cotton wool . . .

Campbell made a warning sound, but Nick had already heard the scrunch of car wheels on the drive.

His hand closed over a small jar half hidden by the bag of cotton wool balls. Rapidly he unscrewed the top and put his nose to the white powder. Sticking a finger in, he took a lick, resealed the jar and jammed it in his pocket. There might be more somewhere. *Where, Alusha?*

A car door slammed. He caught Campbell's eye as he sped past him into Alusha's bathroom and started on the double stack of drawers either side of the dressing table. Eye makeup, skin makeup, lotions, creams.

The front door bell sounded deep in the hall.

'I'll keep them busy, shall I?' called Campbell from the bedroom.

'No!' He shot a drawer home and wrenched out the next. Belts, scarves, trinkets, haircombs. The travelling drawer next: sun lotion, fly repellents, stomach remedies.

The door bell sounded again.

Straightening up, he lunged for the corner cupboard. Nothing. *Where, Alusha?* Feeling the sweat on his ribs, he brushed past Campbell and hurried into the dressing room that he had shared with Alusha.

The door bell rang again, but this time someone was leaving his finger on it.

Her cupboards were empty, the shoe racks bare. He began to lose hope.

'Let me search!' hissed Campbell, grabbing his arm. 'Just tell me where – '

'I don't know! I don't know!' he replied fretfully. '*Somewhere . . .*'

The police were hammering at the door now, their shouts floating up through the window.

'I don't know!' Nick cried as much in anguish as exasperation.

'They'll break the door.'

Nick slouched, his energy gone, and realized he had resigned himself to giving up the search. He made for the stairs, turning sharply at the top so that Campbell almost bowled into him.

'Get rid of this,' he said, thrusting the jar into Campbell's hand. 'And I mean, get *rid* of it.'

Campbell gave a fierce nod and slipped soundlessly away, heading, it seemed, for the back stairs whose location he seemed to know as well as he knew the rest of the house.

Nick's story about having been in the soundproofed studio unable to hear the doorbell and the staff having inexplicably disappeared did not impress the police, and certainly not the detective inspector, a fiftyish man, short and overweight with heavy jowls and a broken nose, nor his second-in-command, a young detective sergeant who, with his black leathers and razor-cut hair, looked like something out of *Mad Max*. The rest of the men immediately fanned out and, though he couldn't be sure, he had the feeling some of them made straight for the lavatories to see if they could find evidence of recently flushed drugs.

He thought suddenly of Campbell. Would he – ? Dear God, let him have had more sense. Anywhere but the lavatories.

There were seven or eight officers altogether, sullen men with hard staring eyes, all Glaswegians as far as he could make out, their accents as impenetrable as their expressions.

They were thorough, or at least he assumed they were, because they were there a long time. After calling his solicitor, a privilege grudgingly permitted half an hour after he'd requested it, he sat in the library, looking into the fire, trying very hard not to think of the snooping hands going through Alusha's things, occasionally glancing up to find the sergeant's eyes boring into him. Despite himself, aware that he shouldn't be rattled by such transparent bullying, he felt unnerved.

What had triggered this little visit? It was no accident, that was for sure; they wouldn't have gone to all this trouble without a tip-off. His first thought was that the dealer had talked. Going by the unlikely name of Ned Sunshine, he was supplier of drugs to the aristocracy and other branches of show business, and had been recommended by Joe. But why now? Why after so long? And why single out Nick?

After a time the inspector came back into the library and began a plodding question-and-answer session. Was Nick in possession of illegal substances? Had he ever purchased illegal substances? Had drugs ever been used on the premises?

Nick kept his voice level, showing what he hoped was the right degree of indignation without actually losing his temper, although as the inspector's questions grew more asinine and repetitive his control became patchy.

A knock on the door brought a welcome if astonishing interruption. It was all Nick could do not to stare as Campbell appeared, preceded by a hazardously balanced tray of mugs, and came cautiously across the room, eyes fastened on the drinks as if his life depended on it. He managed the transition onto the persian rug all right and, after a moment's alarm, successfully negotiated a protruding table, then, his breath rasping audibly, his mouth puckered with concentration, he lowered the tray to the inspector's elbow. His old tweed jacket, visibly frayed, a large and mysterious stain on the hip, added a certain distinction to the idea of Campbell as a butler, and Nick watched in fascination as he straightened, set his sights firmly on the mugs again, and advanced across the hearth.

As he lowered the tray, he looked directly at Nick and dropped a heavy wink. Nick, needing more reassurance, raised a questioning eyebrow. Campbell gave an imperceptible nod. 'All gone,' he whispered.

The mug contained coffee, not bad coffee at that. As Campbell paused at the door, Nick called: 'Thank you, Campbell.'

Tucking the tray under his arm, he gave a slight bow. 'Not at all, sir.'

After that Nick allowed himself some optimism, which, as he should have known, was bound to be fatal. Five minutes later a young officer came jauntily into the room and, with an unmistakable flourish, handed the inspector a small screw-top jar.

'A bag in the bottom of a wardrobe, sir.'

The inspector unscrewed it and sniffed. He held out the open jar and said: 'And how do you explain this, Mr Mackenzie?'

# Chapter 34

——

NUMBER NINETEEN LINDEN Gardens, the home of Jane Ackroyd, sat at the end of a road of identical bow-fronted houses with pebbledash rendering and steep gables, distinguished from each other by the colourful paintwork of the mock-Tudor beams on the gable ends and the various sugary hues of the pebbledash.

Daisy walked up the path an hour late. There had been a morning meeting with Mrs Bell's new lawyer in Glasgow which had overrun, a long call to Jenny in London to check on progress on the arrangements for the arrival of Alan Breck, and, as a final hurdle, a delay on the Glasgow shuttle. But then it was an achievement to have reached Dorking at all.

In Chelmsford the previous morning, Inspector Brent had kept her for over an hour, asking questions about insurance cover, business associates, and – his favourite expression – those who might wish her *harm*. He floated concepts that would have been quaint if they weren't so unlikely – a spurned boyfriend? A disgruntled former employee? The possibility that there might have been an entirely different sort of villain didn't seem to occur to him, and she hadn't bothered to put him on the right track. At each mention of *harm* his gaze invariably travelled to her swollen and multi-coloured eye until, unable to contain his curiosity any longer, he asked in his deathless style if it was possible that the circumstances surrounding her injury might have a pertinent bearing on the damage to the laboratory.

The insurance assessor kept her another half hour. Then it was back into Jenny's car – borrowed again at six that morning – and a hasty drive to the Glasgow shuttle via Hertfordshire. She found the address given by Maynard in a parade of shops on the outskirts of St Albans. It was a print and duplicating shop which rented out accommodation addresses by the week. They did not keep a record of past transactions and, even if they had, would not have been prepared to reveal them.

From Glasgow she had taken a hire car to Loch Fyne and spent a challenging hour persuading Mrs Bell to dispense with Dermott and use a Glasgow lawyer named Munro, an expert on family law. A hurriedly arranged meeting with Munro followed, then, aided by some legal muscle from Munro, the three of them gained permission to go and see Adrian in hospital. They found him grey-faced, subdued, unresponsive to everything but the sight of Daisy's black eye, which produced a stare of amazement. He hadn't been able to say what drugs they were giving him, only that they made him sick. The physiotherapy was hurting him, he said, and he felt very weak.

Later in that long day, perched in her Glasgow hotel room Daisy tried a few press contacts to see if she could drum up some local interest in Adrian's case. But she had underestimated the opposition: Munro called to tell her that Strathclyde Council had been granted an injunction banning all publicity. Such was the power vested in the authorities: the power to remove a child and the power to prevent the world from hearing about it.

Suddenly Monday was almost over, and Alan Breck's call was only twenty-four hours away. Jenny, working alone and under pressure in the Catch office, had found a firm to cover security, had looked into flights and accommodation. But the media deal hung insecurely in the air. Simon wasn't back, an opposition newspaper was showing only limited interest. No guaranteed coverage; no money. Daisy didn't need telling that Alan Breck wouldn't come for that.

The door of number nineteen was painted Cambridge-blue to match the gables. Bypassing the heavy Victorian-style brass knocker, Daisy pressed an electric bell set into a ceramic plate under a reproduction carriage lamp. At once a dog barked, a woman's voice shouted 'Quiet!' and the door was pulled open by Jane Ackroyd in a dark blue suit with white-edged lapels and rows of chunky jewellery.

'Oh, it's you!' she declared more in relief than irritation, holding on to the collar of a snapping Jack Russell. 'I was beginning to think you weren't coming.' She peered closer as Daisy came into the hall. 'Good God! What *have* you done to your face?'

'A car hit me. Well, a car door.'

'Oh,' she murmured, already losing interest. She closed the door and released the Jack Russell which immediately jumped against Daisy's leg and bared its teeth.

'Listen,' Jane Ackroyd said, dropping her voice conspiratorially, 'I think you should know – I only told Peter a couple of hours ago. That you were coming. And he's still a bit – well, *unhappy*.'

'I thought it was his idea. I thought it was urgent. You said it was urgent.'

'Oh, he's keen, oh yes! Absolutely! It's just – well, he wasn't too happy to hear it was *you* that I'd phoned.'

Daisy didn't attempt to hide her annoyance. 'Perhaps I should go then?'

'Oh no! Please don't go.' She gripped Daisy's wrist, her jewellery jangling in agitation. 'He's talking about going to South America. Apparently they're desperate for pilots – and not too worried about the state of one's licence.' She released Daisy's wrist and took to twisting her rings. 'He'll get work, I've no doubt he will, but all those mountains.

The bandits. No spare parts. No, I couldn't stand it, I really couldn't.' She glanced over her shoulder. 'He went back to the medical board to ask for a review, you know,' she said, whispering again, 'but they wouldn't reconsider. It was that Scotland job, he's sure of it. Never been the same since. When I saw your name in the paper and I realized you were with – what is it?' She gestured forgetfulness. 'The Campaign For . . .?'

'Against Toxic Chemicals.'

'Then I guessed you might know what to do. It's a scandal.' Her colourless eyes showed a pale outrage. 'He was only doing his job. An absolute scandal.'

Through a closed door came the sound of a muffled cough and the energetic shaking of a newspaper. 'You'd better come in . . .' She led the way into a living room, small but grandly decorated, with a pale carpet and matching curtains, a chintz drop-arm sofa with extravagant gilded cords, silk-shaded standard lamps, and a fake open fire.

Duggan was sitting in a high-winged chair to the right of the fire, a newspaper on his knee and a cigarette dangling loosely from the fingers of one hand. Taking his time, he folded the paper, balanced the cigarette on the rim of an ashtray and lumbered to his feet. He was still dapper in a boy-flyer sort of way, but it seemed to Daisy that his blazer, resplendent with brass buttons, hung loosely on him, and that his cheeks had lost some of their fullness. His hair still sported its razor-line side parting, but his eyes were watery and his skin had a dry spongy quality to it.

He shook hands, but his gaze harboured old grievances and as soon as his sister had left the room he couldn't resist taking a stab at her. 'Someone hit you back, did they?'

'Someone who couldn't take the truth when he heard it,' she smiled.

He sat down again, looking defensive.

Daisy asked after his health.

'Bloody awful.' By the way of illustration he gave a terrifying cough, the sort that anti-smoking campaigners would be glad to have broadcast to every schoolkid in the country. 'But not so awful that they had the right to take my licence away.' She noticed his hands were trembling.

'What grounds did they give?'

'No grounds. Don't have to give grounds. Like bloody insurance companies.'

'And you think your health was affected by chemicals?'

Resting his elbows on the chair-arms, he brought his cigarette in front of his mouth and regarded her through the spiral of smoke. 'You lied to me,' he said. 'You said you were with some solicitors' firm or other.'

'Did I?'

'You know bloody well you did.'

'Perhaps I thought you'd be less than forthcoming if I said I was with Catch.'

'Too right.' He took another drag, sucking so hard that she could almost feel the smoke biting into his lungs. 'Could have your licence revoked as well, perhaps?' The thought appealed to him and he creased up his eyes with malicious amusement.

'Maybe.'

It didn't satisfy him. 'Bloody cheek, you know. Bloody cheek. And those threats – ' He stabbed a finger at her, eyeing her down the length of it, like someone sighting along a rifle. 'I don't take kindly to threats, you know. Not on. Not on.' His voice shook slightly.

'You had important information. I needed to get it.'

'Bloody cheek.' But the venom had gone out of his voice.

He got up and poured himself a liberal glass of Scotch. 'So what can you do for me?' he demanded truculently.

'Hard to say. What sort of thing did you have in mind?'

'Why, compensation. It was that damned gunk I worked

with, I'm sure of it. Felt off-colour ever since. That blighter
Keen. Took no precautions, you know. Hired fools like
Davie. Couldn't read a label to save his life.'

'When you say off-colour, what do you mean exactly?'

'Well . . .' He waved an impatient hand. 'You know,
*low*. Can't bloody concentrate. Hands all over the place.
Head feels woozy, that sort of thing.'

Putting down his drink, he reached for a packet of
cigarettes and lit one, steadying one trembling hand against
the other as he operated the lighter. Daisy could see that
there might be difficulties in persuading a court that this
trembling was purely the result of chemical exposure.

'Any particular chemical you had in mind?' she asked.

He gave a series of short coughs which he dampened
greedily with a drink. 'Pretty obvious,' he declared sullenly.
'That stuff you were so curious about – '

'Silveron.'

He wagged his cigarette in confirmation.

'Did you come into direct contact with it then?'

'When the wind was in the wrong direction.' He glared
morosely into space from under drooping eyelids. Then his
eyes dipped back towards hers and his voice rolled on
reminiscently: 'Gunk slopped all over the place when we
were filling the tanks, too. Couldn't help it, not with that
prehistoric equipment.'

'And the spray, did it ever land on anyone else accidentally? I mean, that you know of?'

His mouth hardened. 'What sort of question's that?'

'It'd help to know.'

'I'd bet it would!' he said in a voice suddenly vicious
with injustice. 'Trying to trap me, eh?'

Daisy, her patience already frail, stood up and said
briskly: 'Obviously I can't be of help.'

'So what d'you want me to say?' he bellowed as she
made for the door. 'We've all made mistakes, for God's

sake. You show me a spray pilot and I'll show you someone who's made a cock-up!'

She paused at the door and looked back at him. He threw out an expansive arm, slopping his drink in the process. 'What the hell difference does it make anyway?'

'Everything,' she said.

'Christ Almighty!' he spluttered. 'I'm meant to incriminate myself, am I?'

'No.' She came back into the room. 'Just tell it all to a newspaper.'

'*Just!*' His eyes darted imploringly around the room, as if seeking the sympathy of an invisible audience. 'And that's not incriminating myself?'

She sat down again. 'You could stay anonymous.'

'Ha. That's what *you* say. The licensing department of the CAA would bloody know. I tell you, they'd soon bloody work it out.' He snorted vaguely until, with a sideways glance, he said coolly: 'And what'd be in it for me?'

'We'd find the right lawyers and experts to help you fight your case. If that's what you decided to do.'

He gave a non-committal grunt and eyed her leerily over his glass. Finally, after a last thoughtful glance, he chucked his cigarette onto the fake coals. 'I did my best, you know. Never knowingly hurt a fly. Never.' He looked up at her mournfully.

'But there were cock-ups?'

He tensed and looked into his drink. For a moment she thought he wouldn't answer. Then he drew in a slow breath, hissing it through his teeth. 'The bloody guidance system ... sometimes didn't work. Or the flow line – that jammed once. Not my fault. It was the no-good ground staff. Bloody incompetent. Keen's fault. Wouldn't pay a decent rate.' He reached slowly for a cigarette, spinning out the movement so that he could avoid looking into Daisy's eyes. 'One day . . .' He hesitated and said with sudden anger: 'Shit, I don't know – '

'This is off the record,' she murmured.

He risked a look at her and nodded unhappily. Perhaps he knew that what he was about to say wasn't going to sound too good. Perhaps the memories had been bothering him for some time. He lit his cigarette and started to play with his lighter, swivelling it on the arm on his chair.

'The time with the flow line. Bloody thing seized up. Then suddenly got going at the wrong moment.' He held the cigarette in his fingers like a peashooter, drawing short puffs from it. 'Doing a patch near a big house. Loch Fyne, it was. Thought I saw someone. Couldn't be sure though. There was a horse. Saw that all right. And a hut, a stable. Thought I saw something else. Behind the horse. But then I had to turn away fast. Impossible to go back and see. Fairly sure they must have got a pretty good whiff though.' He gave a joyless chuckle. 'Surprised not to hear anything about it, if you really want to know. Thought all hell would break loose.'

'And the other time?'

Baring his teeth, he sucked in his breath. 'Think it was a boy.' His fingers tightened on the lighter so that it stopped turning. 'Not absolutely certain . . . Only saw him for a flash. Standing in this field at the end of the run, he was. So close couldn't have missed him if I'd tried. Flew right over him.' He grasped the lighter and squeezed it hard. 'Turned back and took a look, but hard to see. Hidden behind the animals or something . . .' He blinked rapidly. 'Flew straight back to the strip, sent a telex to Keen telling him to stuff it. Told him that if I wasn't given proper recce time I'd be off. Same bloody answer. He'd see to it. He was always seeing to things that never bloody happened.' He glanced at her, gauging her reaction. 'Felt bad about it,' he said in a rough voice. 'Just a kid. Often wondered if he was okay. But it was too late by then, wasn't it? No good telling everyone. What good would that have done?'

Daisy spent a moment examining her hands. She said: 'Can you remember what you had in the tanks that day?'

'Yup. It was that stuff of yours,' he offered gladly. 'Silver-whatsit.'

He peered at her through the wreaths of smoke, his lids drooping knowingly. 'Did I say the right thing?'


Jenny was waiting in the Catch office with good and bad news. The good news was that Simon was due back from Prague at any moment and that she'd managed to arrange a meeting in the editorial office of the *Sunday Times* for seven that evening. The bad news was that she'd got a price from a security firm for guarding Alan Breck and it wasn't going to be cheap.

As bad news went, it could have been a lot worse. There was still something left in the Octek kitty.

Then Jenny showed her the day's newspapers, and Daisy saw it was going to be worse after all. The story took up a quarter page in the tabloids, a more restrained side paragraph in the qualities. Charged. Bailed. In possession of drugs at his Highland castle. All the tabloids called it a castle, which suggested they had got the story from a wire service. In the absence of other facts, they had rehashed the usual history: Alusha, the financing of the laboratory, the fire.

She wondered: Can it be true? Then in the next instant: What the hell difference did it make anyway? They should leave him alone. He doesn't deserve this.

It was nine before the Alan Breck deal was struck. Simon delayed the final agreement, worried by the apparent lack of documentation, throwing up what seemed to Daisy to be unnecessary obstacles. The offer wasn't as good as she'd

hoped – travel expenses and a ten-thousand-pound fee –
but with foreign rights the money could double. Would it
be enough? Would Alan Breck be hoping for more? And
what about all his other expenses? She had the feeling he
would be expecting her to find them, along with the cost of
the security people.

The flat was cold when she got in. As she bent down to
light the fire something made her pause. She listened for a
second or two. A sound, a gentle scraping, like a leaf on
the window, except it hadn't come from the window. The
kitchen then? She went in. The kitchen window returned
her reflection dustily, like a sheet of black metal. Outside it
was very dark and, though she put an eye to the glass, she
couldn't make out anything in the small patch of paved
garden below. Above, the yellow oblongs of lighted windows hung in the blackness.

Whatever the sound was, it had gone, or else it was lost
in the ringing that was still buzzing like a run-down alarm
clock in her ear. She switched on the kettle then heard the
sound again.

It was more distinct this time, coming in clearly over the
chiming in her ear, not so much a scraping as a scratching,
emanating, so it seemed, from the main room. She crept
soundlessly towards the door, but as she stepped into the
room it stopped. She waited, cocking her good ear from side
to side. For perhaps half a minute there was nothing but the
murmurs of the street, the faint beat of reggae music from
the flat below and the humming of the heating kettle. Then
it sounded again, but so soft, so vague, so lost in the insistent
caterwauling of her singing ear that she was no longer sure
that it was inside the room. She crept into the centre of the
room and stood still, preparing to wait it out.

When the scraping came again it was so sharp that it
seemed to be very close by, and she started slightly. A
grinding noise, as if someone were running his nails over a
rough surface. She'd got the direction now – close by the

kitchen door and lowish – but by the time she had inched forward the kettle was rumbling to the boil and if there was any other sound she missed it.

When the kettle had clicked off and grumbled into silence there was still nothing, and after another couple of minutes she gave up and went and made herself a coffee.

She unpacked her bag, hung up some clothes.

In the flat below the reggae music stopped and a door slammed.

She went to the chest to throw a jersey into the bottom drawer. As she leaned forward she caught a whiff of an acrid almost fetid smell.

She pulled open the top drawer to drop in some clean clothes and the smell rose up in a wave. At the same time her eyes were drawn to a series of yellow stains and black dots scattered over her underwear.

'What the hell – ?'

She reached into the drawer. As her hand closed over her one and only pair of silk panties, the clothes at the back of the drawer gave a distinct twitch. She stared, immobilized. She looked into the shadows at the back of the drawer and was met by a single shining dot. Yellow, glistening. An eye.

She jerked back, and in the same instant her clothes burst into movement; there was a violent scuttling and scrabbling, and a missile thundered wildly round the drawer. She gave a shriek that sounded unnaturally loud in her ears. The missile, brown and trailing a low tail, leaped at the side of the drawer, propelled itself over the edge, landed on the ground and, its claws skittering furiously on the floorboards, shot past the red chair, across the hearth and disappeared under the bed.

She stared mutely at the bed then back at the ruins of her underwear. Suddenly and without warning, something folded inside her, the tears leapt hotly against the back of her eyes.

'Shit,' she murmured. '*Shit.*'

It was a moment before she realized the door bell was buzzing.

The route to the window – her normal vantage point for the inspection of callers – would take her too near the bed and other dark places. She backed towards the door and pressed the entry. Opening the flat door she heard the street door open and close, she heard footfalls in the hall.

Then, inexplicably, the footsteps ceased. A second later the stair lights clicked off. Darkness and silence.

Something rose up in her, something close to panic. She roared: 'Who is it?'

There was the heavy sound of someone stumbling, and a muffled oath.

'Who is it?' she yelled, her throat raw.

'Daisy? Where are the lights, for God's sake?'

That voice. That *voice*.

She reached out onto the landing for the push button and the lights came on. She went to the stairs and peered over the banister.

'God!' she cried.

Nick, climbing the stairs, began to speak but, looking up, the words died on his lips. 'Jesus . . .' He came to an abrupt halt. 'What the – ?' His expression was so astonished that she slapped a hand over her black eye to cover it.

Coming up the last few stairs, he said: 'Daisy . . . What *have* you been up to?'

He laid a hand against her bruised cheek and murmured a sympathetic: 'Ouch, ouch!'

The lights clicked off and for a moment Daisy thought she'd landed in heaven.


She found him a rolling pin, part of a set of kitchen implements she'd bought off a stall in Camden Lock.

Clearing the furniture away from the bed he advanced slowly.

'Careful. It's enormous,' she warned.

'Not nearly as big as I am,' he said.

'I'm not so sure.'

He looked back over his shoulder. 'Whose side are you on?'

'The winner's.'

'I'd better not let him get away then.'

He slid the bed slowly away from the wall, one end at a time, then crept round behind it. He poked the rolling pin into the assortment of luggage, scrolled paper and plastic-wrapped bundles that made up the subterranean clutter under the bed, then moved with sudden speed as the creature scuttled between a suitcase and a roll of paper. He took a swipe at it, missed by a tail, and chased it to the other side of the room, tripping and almost sprawling over the rug as he scrabbled round the end of the bed in hot pursuit.

The creature was fast, but he finally cornered it by the bathroom and dealt it a blow. Finishing it off quickly, he wrapped the carcass in newspaper and took the parcel down to the dustbins. While he was away Daisy hastily sponged her face and daubed some makeup over her bruise.

She came out of the bathroom to meet him. He was still catching his breath. They stared at each other for a moment.

'I'm not too practised at rat-catching,' he said.

'Oh, you'll do,' she said. 'Believe me.'

'Thanks.' He smiled but distractedly.

'Please – sit down.' She straightening the red chair and brushed a hand over it. 'Coffee?' she said brightly.

He stopped just in front of her and said: 'How *did* you get that face?'

'Ah! That's another story.'

He raised his eyebrows slightly and she could almost see

him thinking: If this was a boyfriend, he must be something else.

'I'll make the coffee,' she said and turned quickly towards the kitchen.

His voice drifted in from the living room. 'What happened to the ceiling?'

Tapping the coffee gently into a mug, she went and stood in the doorway. 'I was wondering about that too.'

He was looking mystified, trying unsuccessfully to fit this into the boyfriend scenario.

'I think they did it on purpose, when they came to install the bug – ' Her hand flew over her mouth. 'Hell,' she breathed and, going back into the kitchen, found a screwdriver. Putting a finger to her lips, throwing him a significant look, she stabbed a finger towards the instrument. Kneeling, she unscrewed the handset and pulled it apart. Her heart skidding, she peered inside, held it up to the light, ran two fingers along the casing and sank slowly back on her haunches. 'It's gone,' she gasped.

He slid forward onto his knees beside her and peered at the handset. 'What's gone?'

'The bug. The microphone. The thing they were listening with.' Her voice was flying high, sawing all over the place.

'What are you saying?'

'They were bugging this place. Listening to everything.'

He hesitated as if he needed to understand it correctly. 'Listening?'

'Yes! It was a bug all right, otherwise they wouldn't have gone to all the trouble of removing it, would they?'

He nodded uncertainly.

'They must have realized I'd found it, you see,' she argued. 'They must have been frightened that I'd use it as evidence.'

'You're shivering,' he said. 'Are you okay?'

'I'm okay.' But she wasn't, not quite yet, and he seemed

to realize it, because he got up and went into the kitchen and came back with the coffee.

He sat hunched forward in the chair above her, watching over her as she drank. 'All right?'

'I'm glad you're here.'

He smiled, and the tiredness seemed to go out of his eyes for a moment.

'Tell me about it,' he said, sitting back in the chair. 'The rat, the ceiling, the bug.'

'Not overlooking the eye,' she said.

'Not overlooking the eye,' he said gravely.

She sat on a cushion at his feet, her profile outlined against the fire, her bruised cheek turned away from him. Her hair was untied and swelled out in a cloud from her neck. It was the sort of curly pre-Raphaelite style much favoured by models, but which in Daisy's case was almost certainly achieved without a hairdresser. She had a fine profile, with a straight nose and arched brows, and he noticed the outline of her lips.

When she began to speak her voice was hesitant and low-pitched.

The Greeks' water tank was the first real clue, she said, the first thing that should have made her stop and think. But she had too much on her plate, too many things to organize; it simply never occurred to her that it might have been intentional. Why should it? But looking back she could see that they must have been desperate to locate the laboratory, and that the tank was the only sure way of getting her back to the flat. If anyone had tried to tell her people would go to those sort of lengths, she wouldn't have believed them. But now . . .

She gave him a quick sideways glance. He smiled briefly by way of encouragement. She looked back to the fire.

She told him about the succession of things that had
started to go wrong, small things, not-so-small things, and
her feeling that she was constantly being outmanoeuvred,
that however hard she tried, someone was always there
ahead of her. The problems with the licence, Peasedale
being warned off by his boss, Adrian getting made a ward
of court, the disintegration of Alice Knowles' case ...
Always something. Looking back she couldn't be sure what
was inevitable, what might have been prevented. All of
those things perhaps, or none of them; it was impossible to
know.

The fire, though, that was something else. She arched
her head back and gave a laugh of disbelief. He noticed the
long smoothness of her neck, and remembered having
noticed it once before. Animal rights! she scoffed. You had
to hand it to them. The slogans, the freeing of the rats and
mice – well planned. And they did a brilliant job at
destruction, nothing left intact. And the burglar alarm:
disconnecting the thing, then setting it to go off when they
left and it was too late to save anything.

She was silent for a moment, then shifted on her cushion.
For an instant her leg came against his, but she moved it
quickly away.

Then there was you, she said, her voice calm now. Only
three people knew about your involvement, she said. You
yourself – she ticked him off with a solemn gesture in his
direction – and me – she pressed a splayed hand against her
chest – and your accountant. Until the night of the fire, that
was. Then – yes, she had to admit there had been someone
else – Simon Calthrop of the *Sunday Times*. But he
wouldn't have told, she added; she was certain of that. And
even if by some wild chance he'd gone against everything
he believed in and told someone, it certainly wouldn't have
been another newspaper, not in a thousand years. No, no,
the point wasn't that she'd *told* Simon; the point was that
she'd made the call from *here*, from this phone. She looked

back to him to make sure he'd grasped the significance of what she was saying.

Then she gave an exclamation of disgust, directed at herself. She should have guessed then. Why she hadn't, she couldn't imagine. So stupid, so stupid. She said it over and over again, screwing her eyes down and shaking her head.

'But why should you have guessed?' he said.

She began again: Friday night, the night after the fire, the night she had come to see him in Kensington ... She faltered uneasily, as if this was a part of the story she'd rather not relive.

'Sorry I got mad,' he volunteered.

She spun round. 'No, no. I don't blame you!' she said. 'Really. Really.'

Then, looking back to the fire, she continued, speaking in a pedantic un-Daisyish fashion, all bare bones and no emotion, running briskly through facts like so many on a file: how after she'd left him in Kensington she'd gone home and drunk too much and left the wild overblown message on Simon's machine, how next evening she'd spotted Maynard leaving her flat and followed him into the dead-end trap of the north London estate. She skimmed over the attack itself with a cartoon-strip 'Then, pow! That was it!' and was on to the discovery of the bug in the phone before he could pull her back to the mugging.

'It must have been one hell of a clout!'

'Don't remember much. Just that he wore this unlikely raincoat. More like a flasher.'

He leaned forward and turned her face towards him, tracing the bruise across her cheek and into her hair, feeling the lump above her ear.

'God,' he said.

'Don't be too sympathetic.' She laughed feebly. 'Might feel sorry for myself.' She spoke lightly, but not so lightly that there wasn't a trace of emotion in her voice.

'Can you hear all right?'

'What did you say?'

'Ha, ha. He could have killed you, you know.' He dropped his hand. 'And the rat?'

'A charming little thought of Maynard's, I'd guess. Probably one of the ones from our own lab!'

He thought suddenly: And I killed it. And with no compunction at all. Daisy had obviously appreciated the irony of the situation already, because she turned and gave him an oddly flustered look.

'Is that it?' he asked.

'Not quite.' She twisted around until she was facing him and, laying an elbow over the chair-arm, told him all about the man known as Alan Breck and how she needed to get him over to Britain.

'Can I help?' he said.

She looked questioningly at him.

'I mean, money?'

'Amazing.' She was laughing with disbelief.

'Well, it's about the only thing I'm good for, isn't it? Money.'

'Not true!' Impulsively, she knelt forward and, reaching an arm round his neck, pulled his cheek against hers. He felt the softness of her, felt her warmth. But after a reciprocal squeeze he disengaged himself. He was in too uncertain a state of mind to be embracing someone like Daisy; he might cling to her, a piece of buoyancy in the wreckage.

Sitting back on her heels, she regarded him gravely. 'Why did you come? Was it . . .?'

'Something happened.'

She said quickly: 'I read about it.'

He murmured: 'And that was only the half of it.' He thought of Susan and felt a lurch of bitterness, but he didn't want to talk about that, and certainly not to Daisy. 'My manager's having hysterics,' he said instead. 'Our European tour starts in two weeks and with this drugs thing the insurance people are threatening to withdraw cover, which means if anything goes wrong I could get wiped out financially.' He snorted with an amusement he didn't feel, then added: 'I won't put up a defence, you see. They'd want to know where I got the stuff. They'd want to rake over old ground.'

She didn't say anything.

He said: 'No, why I came was . . . I talked to Campbell.'

'You did what!'

'He dropped in on me. Unexpectedly. He told me about Adrian.' And all about you, he almost added.

'Adrian,' she echoed.

'I realized . . . Well, anyway – I've come to offer my help. *Again*. If you want it.'

'Even after everything?'

'*Especially* after everything.' He thought: Oh, you have no idea!

'You won't regret it.'

'I don't expect you'll let me.'

She grinned, her bruise like a carbuncle on the side of her face.

'Your Mr Breck, you said he's calling? Shall I wait?'

'Would you? *Would* you?'

He went down to his driver and sent him for a pizza, which they ate sitting on the floor in front of the fire.

They talked. He stretched out in the big red chair with the creaky arm. After a while he felt drowsy; he hadn't slept the previous night. Without meaning to, he dozed.

'Sorry,' he said, waking suddenly.

She couldn't resist it. 'Like old times.'

'Ha, ha.' He smiled.

When he woke next it was midnight and the phone was ringing.

# Chapter 35

A BRILLIANT SUNDAY morning. Daisy stood waiting by the window. It had stormed and blown for three solid days, the media had talked about a repeat of the 'eighty-seven hurricane, but by now the air was still, the last few leaves hung exhausted in the plane trees and a strong yellow light was touching the chimneys of Augustus Road.

Seven twenty. She made her calculations again, working backwards from the time Simon would need to leave for Heathrow to the latest he could reasonably get up. It was possible he'd got up early to work on the novel of course, but as she knew from many a gruff encounter it was safer to interrupt his work than his sleep.

Finally, worried that she might have miscalculated and missed him altogether, she dialled his number fifteen minutes early. The telephone was answered at the first ring: she could almost see him snatching it up.

'Yup?' His brisk tone.

'I checked with the airport,' she said. 'The flight may be early.'

She could imagine him pursing his lips, putting on a look of forbearance. 'I'll be there in good time,' he grunted.

'Terminal 3. Jenny'll be waiting from nine thirty – '

'Yes, yes.' He was openly impatient now. Stress was not kind to Simon.

She asked: 'The US agreement, it got signed?'

'There were problems, they wanted one of their own

people to take over the story. In the end we agreed to split it.'

Of course you did, she thought, because this story will make your name and the US deal will make your newspaper some money. 'Well done,' she said.

But he wasn't to be deflected from his bad temper. 'This secrecy's ludicrous, Daisy. I *cannot* go away without leaving a number. The office have *got* to be able to get in touch with me.'

'I told you – it's not possible, not at the moment anyway.'

A sigh of exasperation. '*Really*. You've been seeing too many films, Daisy. Life isn't like this.'

'Maybe not, but I promised.'

'*Jesus* . . . Anyone would think I was going to broadcast it from the rooftops!'

But Simon had lost the power to intimidate her. 'Jenny'll tell you at the airport,' she said mildly. 'Like we discussed.'

Another sigh, some more huffing and puffing, but he rang off without further argument.

She drove down to Hammersmith by a circuitous route, stopping several times just past tight bends, taking detours through drowsy streets. By the time she was onto the Great West Road she was sure she was quite alone.

At eight thirty only a few dedicated Sunday travellers had ventured onto the roads and the M4 seemed unnaturally wide and empty, like a runway. Soon she was turning off and running along the road skirting Heathrow's northern perimeter, with fifteen minutes to spare. She decided to use the time on a last check, a final look for fellow travellers. She circled a roundabout, turned into a cul-de-sac, parked for a few minutes outside a garage. She watched, but the scene, like the morning, was fresh, clear and innocent.

After that it would have been tempting to take a few shortcuts, but she stuck to her plan and, avoiding the

Airport Inn and its car park, left the car at the next hotel
along and walked back, taking a couple of rearward glances
as she went. These precautions, which would have seemed
ludicrous a couple of weeks ago, were now a bare and
reasonable minimum, and never mind the scorn that Simon
would pour on them if he knew.

The hire car, a grey-green Escort, sat on the far side of
the Airport Inn car park, in the tight space she had found
for it at eight the previous night.

It was a moment before she got it started, a moment
that brought the time up to nine exactly. She drove round
to the front of the hotel and peered under the canopy.

Campbell must have been watching for her, because he
came straight out and, throwing his bag into the back, sank
wordlessly into the seat beside her. He was wearing his
usual tweeds, she noticed, though as a gesture to town life
he had forgone the headgear he had been sporting when
she met him off the flight – a countryman's narrow-
brimmed hat of great age and uncertain shape. What
Campbell thought of her costume he wasn't saying. She
had deliberated long and hard over the choice of clothes
that would achieve both transformation and anonymity,
finally borrowing from Jenny some loose charcoal-grey
trousers, a black cossack jacket and a deep-brimmed grey
hat, turned back at the front in Paddington Bear style. She
had tied her hair up inside the hat and added tinted glasses:
a student traveller, an artist, a would-be actress on her way
to New York.

At Terminal 3 she stopped in one of the drop-off lanes
and instructed Campbell on the various manoeuvres that
would be needed to elude traffic wardens: moving the car a
few yards along the lane, hovering at the far end, in the last
resort making a circuit of the traffic system.

Leaving Campbell, she went to the arrivals hall and,
having established the flight was on time, took up station
in an ill-lit corner furnished with two lines of bucket seats

and a wide pillar. There was a dense crowd at the barriers around the customs exit. Shortly after nine thirty she saw Jenny arrive with the two security men, who looked like everyone's idea of bodyguards, large, with jackets that sat uneasily on their shoulders and heads that swivelled continuously. Led by Jenny, the three of them took up a position at the corner of the barriers, where Jenny's hand-held sign was visible to the emerging passengers. At ten, when the 'landed' sign lit up next to the American Airlines New York flight, Simon was nowhere in sight, and when he still hadn't arrived by ten fifteen it occurred to Daisy that he was putting them through this uncertainty on purpose.

It was ten twenty when Jenny and the two security men finally pushed their way free of the crowd and closed around a family negotiating their trolley out of customs: Alan Breck, instantly recognizable behind his owlish spectacles, and next to him his wife, a dark-haired, intense-looking woman, and their son, ungainly and sullen in a football jacket and cap.

As Jenny shook their hands Simon appeared as if by magic with a photographer at his elbow, and, in his effortlessly dominating way, took charge of the party and guided them towards the exit.

*Now*, Daisy. Use your eyes, stay back, don't hurry, don't lose them, stay back.

She started forward, then halted at the edge of the flowing crowd which was dense with relatives and high-stacked trolleys, sometimes three abreast. Through the heads she saw Simon lead his group down the concourse towards the side exit.

She manoeuvred into the crowd, scanning faces, heads, clothes, people who might be making for the side exit, people who might be hanging back. There was nobody. As the party disappeared out into the light, she doubled back and made as rapidly as possible for the only other exit, inexplicably located at the far end of the building. Getting

out at last, she made her way to the corner and looked
down the side of the building to see that the group had
wandered in her direction and were close enough for her to
see that Simon and Jenny were in urgent and visibly
acrimonious discussion. Alan Breck and his family were
looking on apprehensively, the security men were hovering,
the photographer was diplomatically observing airport life.

Daisy inwardly raged, and had to restrain herself from
striding down and taking Simon by the neck. What *was* he
up to? What did he think he was playing at? She deflected
her frustration into rooting for Jenny. Come on, she
shouted silently, don't let him talk you down, girl. Stand
firm, tell him where he gets off, ease the moment over.
Come on, Jen. *Come on.*

At last Jenny turned her back on Simon and went over
to the Brecks. Daisy was so intent on their reactions that
she almost forgot her watching job, and twisted hastily
round to scrutinize the steady trickle of people continuing
to ooze from the building. A bus drew up with a screech of
brakes, a child screamed inconsolably; no one looked her
way.

The security firm's car, an excessively showy limousine
with darkened windows, had drawn into the kerb beside
Jenny. The bodyguards loaded the baggage for the short
journey to Terminal 1. Simon, having struck his journalist-
of-the-world stance, all weariness and tested patience, now
roused himself to talk to the photographer and gesture in
the direction of the other teminal. A moment later, he set
off on foot with the photographer in train. There wasn't
room for everyone in the car, but it wasn't that which had
annoyed him, she guessed. No, it was Scotland. He
wouldn't have taken kindly to having such an out-of-the-
way destination sprung on him, particularly when he knew
it had been planned by Daisy. Well, he would survive. The
fresh air would do him good.

Daisy lowered her head and, skipping across the traffic

lane, walked hurriedly to where the Escort was waiting. As she climbed in Campbell gunned the engine like some getaway driver.

'Easy, easy,' she murmured.

They watched as the limousine drew out ahead and, threading itself into the flow of traffic from the other lanes, turned into the one-way system and disappeared around the side of the multi-storey car park. Daisy mentally logged the traffic that followed: a transit bus, a beat-up pink jalopy, a black cab, a Volvo estate, two more cabs. None of which, from what she could see, had started its journey from that side exit, or even hovered near by.

'Anything?'

Campbell shook his head and they started off, resighting the limousine as it set itself at the Terminal 1 ramp and snaked its black body up to the departure level. Coming over the lip of the ramp, they saw the limousine at the far end of the car lane, a security man stationed on either side as a porter unloaded the baggage.

In the adjoining lanes there was no Volvo, no beat-up jalopy, nothing that might be hovering at a careful distance, only travellers wheeling their trolleys over the crossings and the usual procession of buses and cabs.

Campbell leaned forward and rested his arms over the wheel. 'What about the red car there?'

It wouldn't be red; whatever colour, it wouldn't be red. But she followed his gaze anyway to see a business-suited man get out and pull on a thick camel coat.

'No,' she said.

Jenny and the Brecks were negotiating the passenger crossing, the porter ahead, the security men back and front; the limousine was pulling away. Reaching the terminal building, Jenny led the way towards domestic departures.

In the drop-off lanes taxis squealed to a halt, cars came and went, people humped bags onto trolleys and kissed each other and hurried away; only two cars showed no signs of activity, but neither had been following the limousine when it came up the ramp.

'I'll watch them to the gate,' said Daisy with a baffled sigh.

She went into the building by a central door. This terminal was a little less crowded, and she took care to walk briskly across to the far side of the concourse and place herself between a roundel of postcards of the Royal Family and a Sock Shop before looking round. She spotted Jenny immediately, standing at one of the British Midland check-in islands, in conversation with the ground staff. Her flock was gathered moodily around her. Alan Breck looked a little more relaxed, though that wasn't saying a great deal, but his wife still wore the thunderous expression she'd acquired during the altercation outside Terminal 3, and Daisy knew whose feathers were going to have to be smoothed once they arrived at Glen Ashard.

After five minutes the walking party arrived, and Simon, characteristically impervious to atmosphere, chose to stand and talk to Alan Breck in a close shoulder-hunched way that conspicuously excluded the wife. Even at that distance Daisy could pick up her resentment which flashed like so much dark electricity across the hall. More of Simon's winning ways and the party would be in danger of falling apart.

Watching Mrs Breck's grim face, Daisy almost missed the raincoat. It was on the near side of the same island, standing by a closed check-in point. The wearer, a shortish man with cropped gunmetal hair, was turned towards her but his head was bent over an information leaflet, so that only a wide forehead and the tip of a flat fleshy nose were visible.

Nonetheless there was a familiarity, an echo, to him – or was it just the raincoat? In her present state of nervousness she had no trust in her jittery memory. She saw again the striding jaunty walk of the man approaching her on the housing estate, the raincoat flapping around his knees. Was he short like this? Was his nose squashy and flat?

Jenny was shepherding everyone towards the domestic departure area. Typically, Simon, engrossed in his conversation with Alan Breck and apparently in no mood to hurry, was slow to move. Mrs Breck began to follow Jenny then, realizing her husband wasn't with her, hung back to let him catch up, while the son, looking mutinous, arced off in the direction of a newsstand. As the party fragmented, the security guards showed their first signs of agitation, fanning out on either side, as if to round up a dissipated flock.

The man in the raincoat glanced up from his timetable. He looked in the direction of the straggling group and his stare did not waver. From this angle the blunt face looked unfamiliar.

He put the timetable on the counter and, leaving it there, sidled round the island and spoke to the check-in clerk. Head on, he was suddenly promising again; there was a squareness to his face, a set to the jaw, that could have belonged to the murky figure of the council estate.

The raincoat man was gesturing, pointing towards the departure area. The clerk leaned forward to follow his gaze, then nodded and jerked a hand in the same direction. He asked her another question and seemed satisfied with the answer he received because, with a brief nod of thanks, he set off towards the departure area.

Daisy moved clear of the postcards and watched him crossing the concourse. That stride – cocky, jaunty. It looked right. Even from side on, she could see the roll in his walk, the swagger in his shoulders. His image slipped effortlessly into its night-time guise.

Making her way along the fronts of the boutiques, her eyes on the striding figure ahead, she felt the unaccustomed sensation of sweat against her shirt.

The departure hall was L-shaped. The short arm led to

the domestic departure gates by way of a waiting and information area. Reaching the corner, Daisy saw the raincoat man come to an abrupt halt half-way across the area and stare up at the information board. Reaching into an inside breast pocket he pulled something out and began to write on it.

Another man stopped beside him to look up at the board. The raincoat man, without any sort of acknowledgement, held out a scrap of paper to the second man, which he took and read. The second man – fiftyish, balding, draped in a shapeless waterproof jacket – said a few words then went off towards the departure gate.

She was still watching the balding man when the raincoat man turned and walked straight towards her.

She stood still, transfixed by the suddenness of his movement, unable to unfasten her gaze from his face so that, when his glance flickered onto hers, their eyes met. In a reflex that seemed to come far too late, she managed to drag her eyes to a point a few feet above his head, to the information board which she read with apparent concentration.

He was coming quickly, his step showy, purposeful. The rain-coat flapped around his knees. *Muggers don't wear raincoats.* He gave her another brief glance as he passed. He did not appear to recognize her. But now it seemed to her that she recognized him very well indeed.

She kept on staring at the board for what seemed a long time but which was only a half a minute or so, then turned very slowly and fumbled in her bag as if searching for something. Keeping her head down, she looked out over the top of her dark glasses. He was not in sight. Sweeping the concourse more openly, she began to walk unhurriedly towards the nearest exit, then, remembering the speed with which the raincoat man had been travelling, more urgently.

Move, she thought; take it slow. Mustn't lose him; mustn't rush it. *Hurry. Slow.* He might be waiting outside, watching for her to burst out and give herself away. *Careful.* Think this through. Take your time.

Unable to decide on the most sensible course, she swerved towards another door, wrenching the hat off her head and pulling the elastic bands out of her hair as she went. She was still pushing the hat into her bag and agitating her hair into some sort of frizzy disorder when she came through the doors. The scene was cluttered: in the first lane were coaches and buses and cabs; in the next cars; and close by on the pavement, a large group of package-tourists blocking her vision. She couldn't see the raincoat man. She couldn't even see Campbell.

She ran across to the pedestrian island, then, conscious of the risk of exposure, held back and shifted sideways instead. Take your time, take your time. She had got Campbell now – he'd been hidden by a black cab. He was standing beside the Escort talking to a traffic warden. She kept moving, following the edge of the pavement, dodging past a hotel bus, peering into blind spots. A knot of people stood at the taxi rank. Beyond them were two isolated figures searching vacantly for transport. Neither was raincoated.

With a growing sense of futility, she crossed to the island and looked along the line of cars, then across to the car park.

She walked disconsolately back towards Campbell who was easing himself gently away from the warden and into the car, bowing slightly, fingers tipping a salute against the brim of his absent hat. The warden, a small woman with violently bleached hair, was looking charmed and had just placed her pen firmly back in its holder. Immediately ahead of the Escort a second warden had found a less amenable citizen in the form of a black-cab driver, who was arguing vehemently over some transgression. His passenger stuck his head out of the window, trying to intervene.

The head was square-shaped with a gunmetal crop. The

wrist, appearing suddenly over the sill, was wearing a raincoat. He turned slightly and she saw his face. It was the raincoat man.

She dropped into the seat beside Campbell while he was still completing his conquest of the warden through the open window. 'I'm supposed to be meetin' ma granny,' he hissed at Daisy out of the side of his mouth.

Ahead, the argument ceased, the driver slammed his door and the black cab roared off.

'Tell her Granny's been delayed.'

They followed, staying on the cab's bumper until they were safely into the airport tunnel, falling back when they came onto the motorway proper. Campbell, in a state of grim concentration, did not speak. Daisy too was silent as she plodded morosely through a sudden burst of doubts. That walk, that stride, had they really been so familiar? And the face, she'd never really got a good view of it that night. Even the interest the man had seemed to show in Jenny and her group could have been innocent. And while she had been watching him, had there been someone else? Someone she'd never seen, someone who'd seen her?

While Campbell stared stoically ahead, she changed her clothes, swapping the cossack top for an old donkey jacket and the loose trousers for some jeans, and tied her hair back with a band.

They were forced to close up on the cab at Chiswick because of the lights, and, except for the run over the Hammersmith fly-over, had to stay close all the way to the junction with the Earl's Court Road, where the cab peeled off to the right and headed south.

The Earl's Court Road was jammed. They inched forward, one car between them and the cab. Daisy checked the batteries on the pair of walkie-talkies that she had hired from the security company and, sliding one into her shoulder bag, laid the other on the seat where Campbell would be able to reach it.

In the next lane was a black cab with an illuminated for-hire light and no one hurrying to bag it.

'Feeling brave?'

Campbell raised his eyebrows uncertainly.

'Remember,' she said as she prepared to open the door, 'stay with him until I tell you.'

She did not look back as she wove between the cars to the free cab and climbed in. Only when she was in the darkness of the interior did she peer forward, but if the raincoat man was looking back he wasn't doing it just then. Neither was the driver, whose face was just visible in the wing mirror.

'You want to follow that cab?' Daisy's driver repeated phlegmatically. 'Well, I'll tell you straight off, it ain't so easy as it looks in the films.'

The traffic was moving now, filtering slowly down to two lanes in the narrow section by the tube station. Campbell was three cars ahead and two behind the raincoat man. Approaching the junction with the Old Brompton Road the lights turned red and Daisy watched in sudden tension as the raincoat man's cab sped over the junction into the beginning of Redcliffe Gardens. The car behind also scooted across on the red and then, to the sound of indignant hoots and a near collision, the Escort.

'See what I mean?' the cabby called as they ground to a halt.

Daisy thrust the walkie-talkie to her ear and when after a few seconds Campbell hadn't come through she called him up. Finally there was an answering crackle, and Campbell's voice informed her he was at the next lights, with the cab just ahead, looking as though it was going straight on. She described the next junction and how, once over it, he would come to the river and curve round to the left and that he should call her if the cab showed any signs of turning off. Whatever happened, he was to stay as close as possible.

When the traffic moved off again, the cabby put his foot down, skilfully cut up a couple of cars and gained three places. They beat the next two sets of lights, so that they caught up with the Escort on the Embankment just as Campbell's voice winged over the radio to tell her that their quarry was indicating right to turn over the river.

On Battersea Bridge they overtook Campbell and came up behind the cab. Daisy checked the registration number and, once her tension had subsided a little, she radioed to Campbell to drop back.

Over the bridge they survived two more lights before plunging into the web of back streets that was Battersea. There was no order to the streets, just one-way systems with sudden twists and roads squeezed in beside tall railway arches, and row after row of squat two-up two-downs. Daisy relayed the route and street names to the invisible Escort until Campbell, with panic in his voice, declared himself confused, and after a short pause, lost.

Ahead, the other cab turned into successively smaller streets. 'Hold back,' Daisy commanded the driver sharply.

'I'll lose 'im!' he declared in an injured tone.

'We're too close!'

The driver shook his head and slowed down. Ahead, the cab turned a corner. When, after what seemed a long time, they also turned, it was to find themselves in a road of terraced houses, and to see the other cab fast approaching the far end of the road where it formed a T-junction with a street of shops.

'Too far back now,' Daisy urged. 'Get a bit closer.'

With an admonishing sigh the cabby pushed his foot down. The taxi was starting to accelerate nicely when the vehicle ahead swerved unexpectedly into the left and stopped, just short of the junction.

'Drive past, don't slow down,' Daisy said sharply. She drew back from the window and did not look out until they were past the stopped taxi and turning left into the shopping street. Then, glancing quickly back, she saw that the raincoat man had been very quick off the mark; he was already across the pavement and stepping into a doorway set into the side wall of the corner building.

Daisy stopped the cab a safe distance along the main road and radioed fresh directions to Campbell. Then, paying the cabby off, she walked slowly back and examined the front of the corner building, which at street level contained a cycling shop. On the floor above were some sort of offices. The two windows were labelled Reynard Associates in the sort of gold-block lettering much favoured by solicitors and accountants. This firm, however, gave no hint as to its function.

She walked on, crossing the side street – its name was Peregrine Road – and continuing along the main street until she was well out of sight of the bicycle shop.

The Escort appeared soon after, approaching cautiously from the north. Campbell's head swivelled from side to side as he looked for shop numbers and street names. Spotting her, he broke into a brief grimace, and pulled in.

They parked the car in a street on the other side of the main road and walked back to a baker's shop which stood on the corner diagonally opposite the bicycle shop. Daisy, looking obliquely through the double thickness of the baker's side and front windows, watched Campbell continue alone, crossing into Peregrine Road and ambling down the long side wall of the bicycle shop.

He paused at the door in the wall, gazed intently at whatever information it had to offer, then, glancing up as if to admire the architecture or perhaps to check for windows, he continued on his way down Peregrine Road. He reappeared five minutes later from a parallel road, having cut across the back somewhere, and, keeping largely out of sight of the bicycle shop, rejoined her, looking for all his tweeds like a thoroughly urban animal. It would be all too easy to think the two of them were getting to be rather good at all this.

'It's a firm called Re*y*nard Ass*o*ciates,' Campbell announced, drawing the words out in a long string. 'Investigation an' security.'

'But what now?' she murmured. 'We can't very well walk in and ask them to own up, can we?'

Campbell threw her an odd look, both shrewd and innocent.

'No, Campbell,' she warned, getting his meaning. 'Are you nuts? Far too dodgy.'

He looked away. 'If you say so.'

'I do. All I need is to *see* Maynard. That's all. Just to make sure.'

Before starting the watch, she went in search of a phone box to call Scotland. As she dialled, a slight heat came into her face, a butterfly of anticipation, and it was with disappointment that she heard the housekeeper answer and say that Nick was out on the estate. The helicopter bringing the party from Glasgow was not expected for another hour. Daisy left a message saying she would try again later, but that she and Campbell might not make it up to Ashard until the morning.

She found some take-away tea and sandwiches and, making her way back to the baker's shop, thought of Nick. Thinking of Nick had taken up quite a lot of her time in the last few days. Since he'd left the flat on Tuesday night, they'd spoken, what? – eight or nine times, and met once, for a quick meal. She had gained his support and goodwill, but had she gathered a bit more along the way? Was there something to be read into his willingness to talk when the business was done, his near-confidences, his subtle teasing?

It was two hours later, as Campbell was preparing to go in search of pizzas, that the raincoat man suddenly emerged

from the side door and, striding a short way down Peregrine Road, stopped by a car and got in. When the car
drew out from the line of parked vehicles, it was pointing
the other way and there was no chance of seeing the
registration number as it drove off.

After that she and Campbell split up. While Campbell
stayed by the baker's window and called in on the walkie-
talkie every half hour, Daisy took the Escort and, circling
the backstreets, came up Peregrine Road and parked in the
slot vacated by the raincoat man, just fifty feet from
the doorway. When she leaned across the passenger seat,
she had a good view of the side wall and the rear of the
property: three storeys of grimy brickwork with a two-
storey extension pushing back into the yard to create the
long outside wall.

The stillness of the morning had given way to a sharp
breeze and the clear sky to a succession of bold black-
rimmed clouds. Daisy pictured Alan Breck and his wife in
the warmth of Ashard, perhaps in the room Nick called the
library, with a roaring fire and a hot meal, and wondered if
Simon would have tried to begin the first session yet. It
would be nice to think he wouldn't rush things, but that
might be hoping for too much.

Would he let Nick sit in on the sessions? She tried to
imagine the two of them in conversation, tried to guess
what they'd make of each other. Journalists were not
among Nick's favourite people, not even when they were
on his side, while Simon would, she guessed, try to be
amenable. Like many people who publicly distrusted
excesses of money and power, Simon was at the same time
fatally attracted to them.

The day slowly wore on. A couple of dogs met, bristled
and briefly scrapped. The traffic increased to a steady
trickle, a few residents of Peregrine Road dawdled out,
returning with Sunday newspapers under their arms.

Regretting the tea, Daisy at one point went in hasty search of a loo, finally inveigling a newsagent into letting her use his.

Towards four the thin winter sun began to settle over the roof of the bakery, there was a brief flare of rich buttery light, a moment of glory for the houses of Peregrine Road, then twilight came quickly and the streetlamps began their uncertain flickerings. Taking pity on Campbell at his wind-swept station, Daisy offered to swap places. While they were talking, there was a sudden movement at the door in the wall. A dog appeared.

The animal was fluffy and low-built, a Pekinese maybe. She wasn't too good on makes. It seemed to be unaccompanied. It raised its nose to the air then snuffled along the base of the wall, the model of a well-trained pet.

But we know better, don't we? Daisy thought with a stab of savage excitement. We know what a vicious little agitator you are! In dark cars, under tower blocks, in well-laid traps. She saw again the white shape as it hurled itself against the glass, the bared teeth, the goggle eyes.

The walkie-talkie crackled and she realized she was still pressing the transmit button. She released it to hear Camp-bell repeatedly calling her name. She was about to answer when the dog acquired an owner in the shape of a hunched female figure with high heels and thin legs beneath an over-short coat that did not quite cover her knee-length skirt. She was pulling the door shut with one hand, locking it with the other. A cigarette hung from her lips. Her hair was blonde or grey – it showed white-rimmed against the shop lights in the main street – and was styled into a tall starched beehive rolled into a sausage at the back, like well-moulded candy floss. But if the beehive was enjoying a fashion revival and could have belonged to a young woman, the legs could not. They were thin and slightly bandy and, in the way of older women who lose weight, her feet looked a little too large for her body.

The woman dropped the keys into a handbag and stood watching the dog, puffing on the clamped cigarette while she buttoned her coat more closely.

Campbell's voice was becoming increasingly agitated.

'I'm okay,' Daisy whispered. 'There's a woman – ' She broke off as the woman strolled towards her.

Daisy shifted rapidly across to the driving seat and prepared to engross herself in something on the opposite side of the road. The woman halted alongside the Escort, one foot resting coquettishly out to one side like a model's in a fashion still, one elbow tucked tightly into her waist as she alternately pulled on the cigarette and let her hand swing wearily away to the side. Her face was long and angular and adorned with heavy makeup; in the fading light, her arched eyebrows and mascaraed eyes were like black ink strokes, and her thin mouth, painted with some deep colour, made a dark gash across her face.

She stared along the length of Peregrine Road for a minute or two then turned and strutted slowly back, stopping once to call the dog.

Daisy eased herself back into the passenger seat and watched as the woman paused by the door in the wall, called the dog to her and snapped a lead onto its collar. Then, walking as briskly as her heels would allow, she disappeared around the corner into the main street, jerking the loitering dog after her.

Daisy gave a report to Campbell. A few minutes later he came over and got into the car beside her. 'She locked up as she left, did she?' he asked.

Daisy didn't answer. She knew where this was leading. But since she knew it, she had to ask herself why she had allowed this watching exercise to go on for so long, and why indeed the two of them were here at all if she didn't intend to let Campbell progress the thing to, what was for him at least, its natural conclusion.

Campbell tried again. 'No lights at the front. None at

the back either, eh?' He had taken several looks at the rear windows, but now he craned forward to stare again. 'No one home at all.'

'Campbell, this isn't like breaking into Portakabins. No talking our way out if things go wrong. No hedges to dive into.'

'Och, I wouldna' be so sure of that.' His confidence had driven him to an unnatural heartiness.

The place seemed crowded suddenly: a couple came round the corner and walked briskly past; a hunched man shuffled slowly over the junction; a lone cat trotted by. The long wall, black with shadows, its upper features lost against the dark mass of the buildings, was beginning to pick up dull reflections from the shop lights, and the door itself, far from getting lost in the gloom, seemed remarkably prominent.

'I don't like it,' she said.

'Have I led you wrong in the past?'

'Our criminal partnership hasn't lasted that long, thank God.'

'But what could happen, eh? No one home. All closed up for the night. And a Sunday at that.'

'Why am I so bloody scared then? My hands are shaking.' She held them up accusingly.

He laid a rough hand on hers and patted it briefly. 'You'll be all right once we're in.'

'I'll be better once we're out.'

'I could go on my own,' he suggested.

She looked up at the dark walls of the building, towards the invisible windows and the offices beyond.

'No . . .' she said. 'You might miss something.'

'Don't go sayin' I didna' offer.'

'I'll tell the judge,' she sighed.

\*

'A helicopter? Go on.' Hillyard removed his gaze from an intriguing smooth-skinned creature on the far side of the restaurant and, addressing his dessert once more, dragged curls of ice-cream off the top with a spoon.

'Couldn't find out where it was going,' said Biggs defensively. 'Tried a touch of financial persuasion, but no go. Too few in the know, and they weren't talking.'

'So what's Phillips doing now?'

'Asking around some more.'

'Well, that's not very bright, is it?' Hillyard said, larding his voice with exasperation. 'Glasgow Airport's a small place. Don't you think it's just possible people might notice someone asking the same bloody stupid questions time and again?' He clicked his tongue and gave a harsh sigh. 'Pull him off, for God's sake. Get him on the next plane.'

'But – don't we need to know? Where they was going?'

Hillyard slid him a pitying look over his spoon. 'We do indeed, Biggs. But luckily for you and Phillips it doesn't take a master brain to work it out.'

Biggs looked reproachful.

Hillyard glanced up to see his lunch companion, whose seat Biggs was temporarily occupying, emerging from the gents. An old partner in crime – crime, it had to be said, of a youthful and entirely different nature – he made a face when he saw that Biggs was still in his chair. Hillyard signalled to him to stay away a while longer, and watched him stalk sulkily off towards the bar.

'And the Field girl?' Hillyard asked Biggs.

'I told you, she wasn't with them.'

'But she was at the airport?'

'She saw them off.'

'Then what did she do?'

'Drove back to London. Well, I suppose.'

'You didn't follow her?'

'I tried.'

'Doesn't make sense.' Abandoning the delicate scrapings, Hillyard scooped up the last of the ice-cream in a single mound and jammed it into his mouth. He had a sudden certainty that Biggs was lying. 'She was on to you, was she?'

Biggs' eyes gave him away immediately, a sharp dart of resentment. It was a wonder he'd ever made inspector. Not for the first time Hillyard regretted the boom in business that had forced him to take on staff in the shape of incompetents like this.

'On to me?' bleated Biggs. 'I told you – I lost her, that's all. Blimey, what do you expect on me tod? Bloody miracles?'

'When did she suss you?'

'Oh, for Christ's sake – '

He gave a squawk as Hillyard's hand closed over his wrist, an exclamation of outrage which subsided into a slow hiss as Hillyard's grip tightened. He looked wildly across to the neighbouring tables to see if people were watching, which one or two of them were, then brought his affronted gaze back to Hillyard. Hillyard could see what Biggs was thinking, that in the Met no one would have dared treat him in this way without dire consequences to their health. Hillyard almost said aloud: But it's me you work for now.

Hillyard dug his nails into the other man's flesh and whispered: '*Don't bugger about with me, you little sod.*'

'The airport,' he admitted furtively.

'And then?'

Biggs wrenched his arm free but made no reply.

'I'll be grabbing more than your wrist next time.' Hillyard smiled sweetly.

Biggs stared morosely at the glass of wine in front of him then, seeming to focus on it for the first time, knocked it back in one. 'She tried to follow me.'

'Tried?'

'She lost me.'

'Where?'

'Battersea Bridge.'

'You're sure?'

'*Sure* I'm sure,' he said, his voice rising with fresh indignation. 'I got the driver to hook round the houses. No way she could have stayed the course without me clocking her.'

'What was she in?'

'An Escort. Greenish.'

'Got the number?'

'Oh, no chance,' he replied with overblown sarcasm. 'I twiddled my thumbs all the way from Heathrow, didn't I? Never even *looked*. Why would I ever think of something that obvious? Christ Almighty . . .'

But Hillyard wasn't listening any more. One section of his mind was rehearsing the call he would be giving Cramm in a few minutes' time, hatching the phrases he would use to break the bad news of the American scientist's arrival while managing to convey the impression that there was still plenty of useful work to be done on the ground. Reynard Associates' turnover – not to mention Hillyard's lifestyle – wouldn't look so rosy if there was a withdrawal of Cramm's very considerable custom.

The other section of his mind was working on how he was going to tell his lunch companion that the meal was over, and that he was about to leave with this plodder Biggs on rather more urgent business.

# Chapter 36

DUBLENSKY WALKED DOWN the broad staircase and paused to get his bearings.

Whatever he'd imagined about his arrival in Britain, it had involved nothing like this. The strange mansion in the northern wilds somewhere; the shadowy servants who slid in and out without a word; and the owner, a singer – a rock singer, for heaven's sake. Dublensky remembered his songs from college days. They had been all the rage. For all he knew, they still were. The whole thing was very strange.

The girl Jenny had tried hard to make them feel at home, but with that ring through her nose and her weird makeup and crazy clothes, her appearance only added to his feeling that he had landed in the middle of a TV drama, an Agatha Christie perhaps. In his present mood, maybe even a Munsters.

He hadn't asked Anne what she thought of the day so far; he could read it in her face. While Tad, disgusted at not being in London, had decided to sulk in his room.

He entered the room to the left of the front entrance.

Simon Calthrop the journalist was there, also Nick Mackenzie. There was no sign of the photographer; perhaps, having got his pictures, he'd left.

'Ah!' Calthrop jumped to his feet. 'All ready, Mr Dublensky?'

Dublensky wasn't certain he was ready for this and perhaps it showed on his face because Mackenzie said: 'Maybe you'd prefer to rest, Mr Dublensky?'

Calthrop threw Mackenzie a sharp look before saying to Dublensky: 'I really don't think we have the time for that. I need to get back to London by Tuesday at the latest. We've a great deal to get through.'

Unseen by Calthrop, Mackenzie raised his eyebrows kindly at Dublensky, as if to say: I'd make up your own mind if I were you.

Dublensky asked: 'Miss Field, has she arrived yet?' knowing that he wouldn't be reassured until she did.

Calthrop shrugged as if it wasn't a matter of great interest, but Mackenzie looked worried, which only served to add to Dublensky's feeling that something wasn't quite right.

'I'd really like to see Miss Field,' Dublensky echoed dully.

'Is it the contract?' Calthrop demanded, moving in front of Dublensky. 'Are you worried about something in the contract?'

'Not exactly. I . . .'

Calthrop motioned him towards a chair, holding the gesture until Dublensky had sat down. 'Well, what is it then, Mr Dublensky?' He dropped into the seat opposite and fastened Dublensky with a firm gaze.

'I just . . . I guess I would have liked to talk things through with Miss Field.'

'Well, that doesn't seem possible just at the moment, does it? So I suggest we get on, and then when she turns up you can talk about anything that's still worrying you.'

'It's what'll happen when we leave here,' Dublensky said, putting a shape to his anxieties. 'No one's told me what's going to happen.'

From the fireplace Mackenzie said: 'You'll be looked after, Mr Dublensky. I guarantee it.'

His voice was reassuring, his manner amiable, yet how far could a rock singer be trusted? 'Perhaps a rest might be

a good idea,' he muttered indecisively. 'I'm really very
tired.'

Calthrop pressed his lips together. 'I think it might be
best to start now, Mr Dublensky.'

'Well, I . . .'

'Simon.' Nick Mackenzie beckoned to Calthrop, and the
two of them went into a huddle by the door. Dublensky
couldn't hear what was being said, but he knew they were
arguing. Finally Nick Mackenzie came back and crouched
on the edge of the opposite chair. 'How about a walk
before it gets dark, Mr Dublensky? I rather wanted to show
you something.'

They took warm coats from a cloakroom and went out
of the house by a side door which gave on to a hedged
garden with neatly delineated rectangular beds. It was cold,
but not unpleasantly so. Patches of white cloud skated
across a low winter sun. Mackenzie began again: 'You
mustn't let them persuade you into doing anything you
don't want to do, you know.'

'No, but . . . Well, I've burnt my boats. There's no
turning back, that's for sure.'

'But take it at your own pace. Don't let them pressure
you.'

They turned out of the garden and joined a path that led
upward between shrubs.

Mackenzie slowed a little. 'You were worried about the
future . . . Well, I just wanted to say that there's a job
waiting for you if you want it.'

Dublensky looked across at him in surprise. 'There is?'

'It's a trust, a research charity. It's going to be set up in
the next month or so. They'll be needing people.'

'But . . .' He floundered for a moment. 'Will they want
to employ me?'

He gave a small smile. 'Oh yes.'

'What kind of research are we talking about?'

'Research into the effects of chemicals, how to help people recover from them. That sort of thing.'

Dublensky paused. 'Well . . .'

'No interference. No strings.'

'Sounds . . .' He was going to say unbelievable. 'Unusual.'

'It might mean being based over here.'

Dublensky, who a minute ago would have considered any suggestion of moving abroad with dismay, now found himself turning the idea over in his mind. 'This trust, could I present research proposals?'

'Sure. Anything you liked.'

They continued until, breasting a rise, they reached a paddock surrounded by a wooden rail with a stable on one side.

'We could look at Silveron, for example?'

'Oh yes.'

They stopped and leant on the paddock rail. 'This trust,' Dublensky said, 'it's yours, right? You yourself would be setting it up?'

Mackenzie gave a slight shrug which was an admission, but not so much of an admission that it invited further comment.

'Well . . .' said Dublensky. 'It sounds . . . interesting.'

They stood in silence as if all had been agreed between them, which in a sense it had.

The wind seemed to bite suddenly, and Dublensky felt the cold. 'You were going to show me something?' he prompted gently.

Mackenzie was staring up the slope of the paddock, towards the forest. 'What?' He came out of his thoughts with difficulty. 'Was I?' He blinked at Dublensky in mild surprise. 'Of course.' Turning, he raised a hand to the panorama below. 'I was going to show you the view.'

\*

Now and again during that long evening Dublensky's words would dwindle and his eyes travel from face to face as if to be sure that he had people's attention. Strange that he should be in doubt: it seemed to Nick that the room was held in a breathless hush of concentration, broken only by the settling of the logs on the fire and the clinking of Anne Dublensky's coffee cup. But then Nick realized: it was not attention that Dublensky craved, but belief.

Simon Calthrop, hunched over a glass of best claret, armed with two tape recorders and a large note book was taking Dublensky painstakingly through the procedures used in toxicology trials: the day-to-day recordings, the tests and examinations.

Nick found he was able to listen to the statistics of rodent extermination with a new and undreamed of detachment. It wasn't just the ease with which he'd clobbered the rat in Daisy's flat, it was the realization that, when all was said and done, people like Dublensky hadn't been able to find a better way.

He also recognized that moral dilemmas belonged to a world of hard practicalities and uncomfortable truths, a world in which he felt poorly qualified to make sweeping judgements. Alusha had died because the safeguards had failed; perhaps that was all he needed to know.

Calthrop was leading Dublensky firmly onwards. 'So when did you begin to suspect irregularities?'

'Oh, not straight away. I mean, not until the Silveron toxicology results had been in for quite a while, like over a year.' Dublensky was crouched forward on the sofa, arms resting on knees, hands pulling nervously at each other. 'Then one day I was looking through the full set of data. Not many people bother with that, believe me. It runs to five or six heavy volumes: computer printouts, daily observation sheets, test results – and here you're talking about maybe five, six specialities: immunology, oncology, dermatology, histology, pathology. I mean, these things can go on for ever. Anyway, my particular interest is haematology. That's because I'm a chemist and I don't know a darned thing about it.' He smiled wrily. Beside him on the sofa, Anne Dublensky shifted in her seat and frowned at him.

'Blood,' continued Dublensky, drawing back into himself. 'I always look at the blood tests, because it's there that you often get the first hint of trouble. Anyway, there I was flicking the pages and I stop at this one page – a computer analysis of standard haemoglobin tests with statistical significance calculations – and I see that the figures have thrown up this strange pattern, a succession of three identical numbers. Like on a roulette wheel you'll occasionally get a number repeating itself. Mathematicians will tell you these things can happen quite easily and that it's well within the normal range of probabilities, but it still seems sort of strange when it appears. So I see this row of identical numbers and I think, hey, what a crazy set of figures, then I notice another oddity, a really low figure in the first column. It could be a testing error, of course, or a statistical error. Then, again, it might be a genuinely low result, just like it seems. Nothing really unusual about any of that. In fact if you didn't get the occasional crazy figure, then things really *would* look strange, like too good to be true, you know.' He jerked his head from person to person, searching out reactions, then paused modestly to recount his moment of glory. 'Except that I suddenly get this feeling I've seen these figures before,' he explained. 'Now this isn't possible – I mean, that's what I tell myself. It's just a trick of my mind. But the more I think about, the more uneasy I get. And you have to remember that by this time the production line at Aurora is pumping out Silveron for export and I've already had the first letter from Dr Burt. So I don't need all that much encouragement to think unhappy thoughts.'

Calthrop, keen as ever to get his chronology right, interjected with a request for dates. While Dublensky leafed through some old diaries he had brought, Nick helped Jenny to stack the supper plates onto a tray. As he bent over the table he became aware that Anne Dublensky was staring at him.

'Where's Daisy Field?' she asked tensely.

'Something important must have come up,' he said.

'Important?' Her tone demanded to know what on earth could have been more important than this.

Returning to his chair Nick too wondered what could be so vital that it could keep Daisy away from this meeting which she had fought so hard to stage.

'I thought and thought, but it didn't get me too far,' Dublensky was saying. 'So I got methodical. I went through all the test data I'd read in the last three years or so. Quite a job. Even then, I missed it first time round because the 8,3,5-Q file was never on my official reading list, so to speak. Picked it up by chance and zoomed through it, you know.'

'What product was that?' asked Calthrop.

'8,3,5-Q? It was an insecticide that never got beyond development stage. It was in initial development at the same time as our big seller Bulwark — was quite similar to it chemically in fact — but once it was realized that Bulwark was the more effective product, 8,3,5-Q was put on what turned out to be permanent hold, and the data buried, forgotten. But not' — he made a sound of fresh surprise — 'by TroChem.'

'TroChem had carried out trials on 8,3,5-Q?'

'They had.'

'So when you looked through the 8,3,5-Q data you found what?'

'I found that many of the haematology results between Silveron and 8,3,5-Q were identical.'

'When you say identical . . .?'

'I mean identical. Ten sheets of results that were the same in every respect. Coincidence wasn't in it. I mean the chances were so remote as to be mathematically incalculable. No – TroChem had simply lifted the data and reused it.' With this, a dreaminess crept over him as if he were reliving the moment of discovery. It was a moment before he responded to the next question. 'Why would TroChem do it?' he echoed. But he'd obviously thought about it a great deal because his reply flowed easily: 'Commercial pressure. Lack of staff. Human nature. The temptation to take short cuts. A desire to please the client. A belief that no harm would come of it.' He spread his hands. 'Any of those. All of them. Who knows.'

'But how could they expect to get away with it?' Nick chipped in.

'Oh, easy. It goes like this. They sincerely believe the product's okay – I mean, it's been developed by Morton-Kreiger, hasn't it? All the expertise, all those expensive labs – they think the trials are just a question of waving things through, of rubber-stamping something that's bound to be okay. They've no reason to think the data will ever be queried. So they cheat things – or maybe only one man cheats things, an overworked head of department, a guy who's under pressure to hurry things along, who's got problems with his budget. He just slips in some ready-made data that no one's ever seen – or he *thinks* no one's ever seen, stuff from a defunct product. No problem. End of story.'

'Were no genuine tests done at all then?'

'Oh, I've no doubt TroChem got the trials under way; it was just the analyses they didn't get round to doing.'

There was a silence. Dublensky rubbed his eyes, Calthrop shuffled thoughtfully through his notes, Anne Dublensky watched, looking worried.

'Can we move on to your dealings with Morton-Kreiger then?' murmured Calthrop. 'How you reported your worries to them and what sort of a reaction you got?'

Just then Mrs Alton buzzed through to say Mr Weinberg

was on the line and needed to speak to Nick 'very urgently'. Nick took it in the hall.

'Where the hell are you?'

'I'm here, David.'

'You're meant to be bloody rehearsing.'

In all their years together Nick couldn't remember David swearing at him, however mildly.

'A couple of days won't make much difference.'

'The tour starts in one *week*, Nick! Not only can't it wait, it's beyond a bloody joke. I never thought I'd get this sort of prima donna shit from you, Nick. Never! Joe, Mel – I've never expected anything but grief from them, but *you* . . . Christ, the entire band managed to turn up at the studio at ten sharp this morning, just like yesterday and the day before, and what do they find? What are you trying to do to us, Nick? Just tell me? Mmm? *Mmm?*' Words temporarily failed him.

'I'll be there, David.'

'But *when*? Listen, I've been on the phone the whole bloody day getting these lawyers to pull out the stops and get these charges dropped. The rest of the time I've been telling the underwriters it's all a terrible mistake and you've never touched drugs in your life and the newspaper stories are crap and begging them on my hands and knees not to pull out the rug from under the tour, and all to no bloody avail because their hearts are made of concrete, and I find I'm wasting my breath anyway because I'm getting shot in the back by my own team. You're killing me, Nick, killing me. Tell me, just tell me, *why* are you trying to stymie the whole goddam thing? Huh? Is it that you don't want to do this damn tour?' He sounded close to tears.

'David, I'll be down tomorrow.'

There was a silence. 'You promise?'

'I promise.'

'First thing?'

'Well . . . No. Can't do first thing. Later, David, later.'

A weary pause. 'Nick, you're the one person who can kill me, you know that?'

'Tomorrow, David, I'll be down tomorrow.'

'Suppose there's an alarm?'

But Campbell, having pocketed a torch, was already hoisting himself up the low wall at the back of the property and hooking his heel over the lip. After a great deal of heavy breathing he heaved his bulk onto the top and for an instant lay there, face down, limbs hanging loose, like a lion resting on the branch of a tree.

Someone came round the corner: a leather-jacketed youth in a hurry, hands thrust in pockets, head down. Daisy glanced up to warn Campbell, but he was already gone. She passed the youth at a stroll, face low. Rounding the corner she went a few yards along the main street, looked in the window of an electricity showroom then sauntered back. Reaching the door in the wall, she gave a sharp tap. Someone came out of a house in Peregrine Road. Moving quickly away from the door, she went to the car and pretended to let herself in. Two minutes later she returned to the door and tapped again.

There were two bells by the door, she noticed, a large brass-mounted one next to the engraved plate of Reynard Associates, and above it a small plastic type marked by a blank label stuck into a cheap metal surround. Campbell hadn't mentioned a second bell. A second bell meant a flat, a flat with occupants who came back at all times of the day and night. She began to feel jittery again.

There was a sound, a scraping scrabbling noise to her left; quite close. A movement took her eye up to the top of the low wall, and she watched Campbell's dark bulk appear over the top and drop untidily to the pavement.

'Couldna' make it up the back. Nowhere to get a grip,' he panted as he dusted himself off.

'Well, we tried.'

The sweat shone on Campbell's temples, he blew out noisily through his lips. 'We're no' finished yet.'

'But how?'

He jerked his head towards the door in the wall.

'Jesus, Campbell.'

He was already sliding the jemmy out of the warren of pockets and compartments that lined his jacket.

'Isn't there another way?'

'Eh?' he answered distractedly, already moving towards the door.

'What about keys – can't we use those skeleton things?'

He threw her a protesting look. 'I dinna' carry stuff like that!'

Now you tell me, she thought as she took up station to one side of the door, trying to shield Campbell from casual observers in the main street, a fairly ludicrous exercise when she was half his size.

'Isn't it going to show, the damage?' Daisy called nervously. 'The Bill always check doors.'

In reply, there was a grinding sound, a vicious groaning of timber and an almighty report, so loud it was like a pistol shot. A pedestrian on the far side of the main road paused and looked across. When he didn't move on, Daisy uttered a loud yelp of laughter. Behind, Campbell gave a startled exclamation and grabbed her am. 'What is it?' She laughed again and jerked her head towards the pedestrian who, convinced he was hearing nothing more than a couple of people returning from an alcoholic afternoon, gave one last look and moved on.

Inside, Campbell found a light switch and Daisy held the door while Campbell wedged it closed with rolled pages torn from a stack of telephone directories sitting on the floor. The door was severely damaged, the wood badly splintered around the lock and jamb so that, even when it was closed, a large chink of light showed through from the

street outside. No bobby in his right mind would miss
something that obvious, but she tried to close her mind to
that as Campbell led the way through the narrow hall to a
flight of stairs which wheeled round a blind turn to a first-
floor landing.

Daisy's back crawled, she felt a deep foreboding: what
Campbell would probably dismiss as first-time nerves, and
he would be right.

Campbell found the next switch and the landing was
flooded with light from an array of spots splaying out from
a central ceiling rose. There was new carpet, bright paintwork, a prosperous look. The area contained five doors
and no windows. Campbell took the left-hand doors, Daisy
the right. The first door on the right was marked 'Private'
and opened onto a continuation of the stairs. Here the stair
carpet was very far from new, the paintwork visibly worn,
and a musty aroma of ancient damp and old cooking fat
wafted down the stairs, mixed with an odd animal odour,
like wet fur.

She moved on. Next was a toilet, the door labelled with
a cheap stick-on sign. Last was an unmarked door, also
open, that led into the rear extension that she had seen
from the street.

From the sound of rattling door handles, it appeared
that Campbell was having less success with the two doors
at the front of the house. One was a frosted glass-panelled
door with 'Reynard Associates, Investigation & Security' in
concentric arched gold lettering and on the rail underneath,
a stick-on sign: 'Please Enter'; the second had ribbed glass,
and was marked 'Private'.

Daisy called: 'This one's open.'

Abandoning his rattling, Campbell swept past her into
the back extension. She followed and in the light from the
hall saw what appeared to be some kind of conference
room with easy chairs, a low table, a coffee-making
machine and a tall metal cabinet in one corner. An odour

of newness mingled with the strong smell of stale cigarettes. There was a large spill of some dark liquid on the carpet near the door.

Campbell switched on the light, cutting off her objections with a gruff: 'Might be keys.'

'Keys?'

'The office there.' He indicated the door he had left, and started to search the filing cabinet.

Daisy went to the window to watch for signs of approaching danger in Peregrine Road but, feeling conspicuous, pulled back.

Campbell, tiring of his search for keys, went back across the hall to the office door.

'Try not to make so much noise,' she called as Campbell grew more ferocious with the door handle.

He made a sound, a non-committal grunt before punching a hole in the glass with his elbow. Daisy sucked her breath as the sound reverberated into the night.

She warned: 'No lights, Campbell' as he reached through and slipped the latch.

There were blinds at the windows, venetian blinds with knotted cords and jammed pulleys which she closed before allowing Campbell to switch on his torch. Then, with Campbell angling the light, his body masking any stray beams that might find their way through the blinds, they went to work.

The offices consisted of two rooms separated by a chipboard and frosted-glass screen. The first room contained two cluttered desks, a photocopier and a wall of filing cabinets, the second, reached through a connecting door stamped 'C. Hillyard, Director' or by means of the locked ribbed-glass door from the hall, had one much larger desk clean of papers, two easy chairs, an exercise bike and four gleaming filing cabinets.

It was a mistake to start at the filing cabinets, but she didn't realize that straight away. In its time, Reynard

Associates seemed to have dealt with large numbers of clients. Each drawer contained dozens of files, and while the file tabs bore numbers which suggested some sort of system, the files themselves appeared random, and she began to realize that, approached this way, the job could not be done in a single night.

One of the cabinets in the inner office refused to open, and leaving Campbell to pick the lock – which in Campbell's repertoire meant to break it – she went back into the outer office and, by the light from the hall, searched the tops of the desks. The larger desk was the more obviously occupied, with in- and out-trays, two telephones, piles of papers and files, a couple of unemptied ashtrays and a stack of tape cassettes. She picked up a cassette and, holding it up to the light, read the label. There was a date – it was five days back – and the word 'Jackie'. The rest of the cassettes – there were twenty or more – seemed to relate to Jackie as well, with the exception of two labelled 'Charlie'. On the windowsill beside the desk there was a cassette player with headphones. Dropping one of the Jackie tapes into the slot, she sampled the buttons until, hitting the right one, the machine gave a click and began to play.

The voice when it sprang into life was both strange and familiar. She recognized the inflections and flat south London vowels and other oddities of her own voice, even recalled the precise conversation – she'd been speaking to Jenny early one morning – yet at the same time the voice sounded disconnected and alien, grotesquely so. Partly it was the recording, which was distorted, partly it was the sheer surprise of hearing her unguarded words relayed back to her in this unlikely place.

Slowly, calmly, she sorted through the stack of cassettes. The most recent was dated yesterday. She jammed it into her pocket, along with three others picked at random.

Campbell reappeared and she beckoned him across to shine his torch over the desk while she searched the papers.

A file also marked 'Jackie' was on top of the largest pile of documents. She might have thought this was a lucky find if she hadn't spotted the next file, which was also entitled Jackie, and the one beneath that. Examination of the bottom file – no surprises on the title – gave her the picture. The transcriptions in the files were rough, the typing erratic and littered with errors, but they faithfully recorded every telephone conversation she'd had over the last few months, in many cases word for word.

Then her gaze lit on a report which read: 'Conversation with painter?? Workman?? Tells her she got some calls, also that she had a male visitor who left no name. Painter couldn't give a description. *Who's a lucky boy, then?* NFI.'

So obvious, thought Daisy. So obvious, and I missed it. Why should they restrict their listening to phone calls? Why not bug the entire flat and record every conversation with visiting house painters, repairmen, friends, and lovers? Catch every private moment, and, if they were lucky, a few intimate ones as well to relieve the boredom and give them a few laughs. Well, they would have been disappointed on that score. No lovers in her bed for a long while, nor anywhere else in the flat for that matter. Only that long conversation with Nick by the chair. She thought abruptly: Did they get that too?

She glanced at the report again. NFI. No further investigation? No further interest?

'We should have brought a camera,' she muttered, eyeing the photocopier and wondering how long it would take to copy a complete file.

'What for?' Campbell declared as he went through some of the papers she had cast aside. 'Just take the stuff. It's not as if they will na' be knowin' we were here, nor what we came for.'

With Campbell life had a certain simplicity. She tucked three Jackie files into her capacious carpetbag and went through the remaining papers on the desk. They yielded little: surveillance reports on errant husbands, security reports on business premises, bills, invoices, VAT forms.

Campbell disappeared into the inner office. Outside, a lorry thundered past and slowed with a long piercing squeal of brakes. She held still, listening, and realized that for the last few minutes at least, she had forgotten to be frightened. As if to punish her, one of the phones began to ring.

After half a minute the ringing stopped. She returned to the desk top. Her hand settled on the invoices again and she held them up to the light one by one. Each one had the name and address of the creditor typed into the appropriate box with an invoice number above and a reference number below. In the main section came the itemization – hours of surveillance, office expenses – and the amount owing plus VAT. In some cases there were no details, just the statement 'paid on account' or 'paid in advance against expenses'. Roughly half the invoices were made out to individuals, the other half to companies, and the majority were for between £100 and £500. Only two were for significantly more, one, for the amount of £5,575, made out to Workham Overseas Holdings Ltd, covering 'security for the month of October', the other for £2,310, made out to PKL Electronics, covering 'employee security'. Workham Overseas Holdings Ltd had an address in the Cayman Islands, and a postal address care of a bank in London.

She made a note of the two reference numbers on the invoices and, after briefly checking the drawers of both desks and the stacks of papers on the windowsills, returned to the filing cabinets. But the gloomy light from the hall defeated her and she had to summon Campbell, torch in hand, before she could make progress through the files. The reference numbers seemed to bear some relation to logic and sequence and, working her way along the wall of cabinets, she found the drawer with the numbers most closely related to that on the PKL Electronics invoice, and then, an instant later, the PKL file itself, more or less in the

right place. From what she could see PKL was everything it
purported to be, an electronics company, indulging in a
little surreptitious spying on its employees. There was no
mention of Jackie, nothing relating to agrochemicals.

The locating of the Workham file took a little longer. In
the place where the file would most logically be found –
two cabinets away in the top drawer – there was a gap, a
large one, as if several very bulky files had been removed.

Outside in the street a siren screamed and Daisy stiffened, senses reaching out beyond the room.

'Try next door,' suggested Campbell, his voice cracking
with something that might have been tension.

In the inner office, in the top drawer of the filing cabinet
Campbell had forced open, they found a mound of papers,
none of which referred to Jackie or Workham Overseas
Holdings, while in the lower drawer there was a batch of
eavesdropping equipment: recorders, batteries, and foam-
lined boxes containing small black oblongs like the one she
had found in her phone. As Daisy squatted to search the
lower drawers there was a resounding *crack!* She twisted
round to see Campbell at the desk, manoeuvring his way
into the drawers with the jemmy.

'For God's sake!' she cried weakly.

A moment later she forgave him as he called her over to
inspect the contents of the top right-hand drawer. The
Workham file – or rather the first of three – was sitting on
the top.

Surveillance reports, digests of the Jackie transcriptions,
a study of developments at Catch and Octek, even – she
drew Campbell's attention to it – a report on the fire.

She muttered excitedly: 'Bloody hell.'

'Aye, well, take it an' let's be off then!'

She pushed the file into her now bulging bag. 'There's
more,' she said, shining the torch on the files underneath.

'You've enough,' Campbell whispered, his voice alive
with sudden anxiety.

The second file contained detailed expense sheets covering the rental of cars and vans, the salaries of two 'operatives', sometimes three, along with equipment hire, phone calls and numerous incidentals.

The third file was a bit of a mystery. Though it had the same reference number and must presumably relate to Workham Overseas Holdings, it concerned someone called Angela Kershaw who lived in Wandsworth, and contained a number of surveillance reports, some hospital bills, a few scribblings and not much else. One of the scribblings said: *Paid in full. Subject has agreed not to see M again.* Then underneath: *Cramm – But will Driscoll stay away from her?*

'Campbell . . . look at this.'

But Campbell wasn't looking. 'Hurry,' he said in agitation. Daisy snapped the files shut and threw them back in the drawer. Then something made her draw the last one out again.

'Come on!' urged Campbell.

But she was taking another look at the note. '*Driscoll* . . . You realize who that – '

Campbell made an abrupt hushing sound. His fear transmitted itself across the darkness, and she felt a creep of alarm. The street had gone quiet, the traffic had fallen into one of those inexplicable lulls that occur from time to time. Inside the house there was a deep stillness. It was broken by a faint sound, a muted ticking. Expanding metal. 'The heating,' she whispered.

She sensed him relax. Sitting the torch on the desk she stacked all three Workham files and tried to force them into her over-stretched shoulder bag, but there wasn't room. Even the surveillance file on its own was a squeeze, and reluctantly she put the other two back on the desk. Even then she couldn't bring herself to leave them and, ripping the contents of the Kershaw file from its covers, tearing five specimen sheets from the expenses file, she rolled them up and pushed them into her belt. This, she immediately realized, was not ideal either and, removing them again, she thrust the bundle at Campbell who, after some complaint, jammed it into an inside compartment of his jacket.

'That's it,' she said.

Campbell didn't reply. He seemed to be listening again. Abruptly he moved towards the outer office, waving at her to turn off the torch. Following, she came into the hall as he reached for the switch and killed the lights.

In the darkness all she could hear was the soft rasp of Campbell's breathing and the vibration of the traffic humming against the windows.

A creak, a flow of sounds billowed into the stairwell: someone had opened the street door.

Suddenly the lights in the lower hall sprang on and spilled round the turn in the stairs, and Daisy's hand gave a slight involuntary spasm. Campbell touched her arm and jerked his head towards the blind spot between the toilet and the door that led to the floor above, where they would be hidden from anyone coming up from below. Having installed her there, he advanced slowly towards the head of the stairs, setting his feet down with such caution that in other circumstances he would have looked comical, like an actor in a farce.

A floorboard creaked beneath his foot. She could almost feel him wince. He paused and tried again, but as he shifted his weight the wood creaked again.

No sound came from below, no shout, no footfall.

Reaching the top of the stairs Campbell put his eye to the corner and peered cautiously down the first flight, ready to spring out at anyone who came up. The silence ticked on. Numerous thoughts jostled in Daisy's mind: the absurdity of the situation, the weight of the files dragging at her shoulder, the desire for something – anything – to happen, the urge to make some appalling noise, to shout or maybe even laugh.

Just as it seemed the silence would go on for ever the lights went off below, plunging them into darkness again. A moment later there was a scraping of mauled wood against a frame, and an uneasy silence rippled up the stairs.

It was perhaps two minutes before Campbell reached back and touched her arm and whispered: 'Stay here.' In the darkness she sensed rather than saw him move. A couple of treads creaked as he made his way down the stairs. With each sound Daisy's foreboding returned.

There was no way of knowing how far he had got when the loud thud rumbled up the stairwell. It was a deep and solid sound, like the thwack of a bat hitting a ball, like –

She saw again the open door of the Beetle and the raincoat man's arm raised above his head.

A shuffling, a grunt, the sound of a scuffle. The dull thwack again. A crash, then silence.

She opened her mouth to call Campbell's name but the word died on her lips. Someone was already speaking. The murmur of a voice, not Campbell's.

After a moment the lower light sprang on again.

She felt a moment of overwhelming helplessness, then the options spread themselves out before her: the conference room with its sheer drop to the yard below, the office with its windows that might or might not open, the toilet with its tiny window and no way out at all.

From below, the voice rose, the words indistinct. The sound seemed to be coming up the stairs towards her.

Catlike, her instinct cried out for height and, reaching for the knob beside her, she pulled open the door that led upstairs, and, stepping silently around it, closed it softly behind her. Feeling her way up the narrow stairs in the darkness, she stepped on every second tread, using the edges where the wood was least likely to give her away.

Her back prickled with the heat of pursuit, she felt the terror of every small girl's nightmare – the man panting at her heels, the weights pulling at her limbs – and it was with difficulty that she suppressed the urge to hurry.

Rounding the dogleg in the stairs she heard feet pounding up to the floor below. Under cover of the noise, unable any longer to control the need to run, she made it to the top floor in three swift strides, two steps at a time. She stopped to listen, her heart hammering in her chest.

The pounding feet were not following. Not yet anyway. She felt her way softly round the edge of a small hallway to an open door. Lights from the main street cast a fan of rectangles over the ceiling of a kitchen. In the next room, which was charged with the odours of ancient meals, tobacco and animals, the street reflections outlined chairs and the glint of glass-fronted pictures. To the back was a room in pitch darkness. Here the scent was of stale sweat and aftershave.

She felt her way across the room to a sliver of night light showing through curtains and peered out. Below was the black bulk of the rear extension. Was it a flat roof? For all the times she had looked up at it from the car, she couldn't remember. And what sort of a drop was it? A few feet? Six at the most.

Slipping the bag off her shoulders, she opened the curtains a short way, hearing the clink of the rings sliding along the rail, and tried the window. It wouldn't budge. She felt along the top of the lower sash for a catch, and finding one, slid it open. Still the frame wouldn't shift. 'Come on!' She heard the desperation in her voice, felt the cold dampness on her forehead. The upper sash was a little more forthcoming and, after she had swung her weight on it, finally permitted itself to be lowered a grudging twelve inches or so. From somewhere in the house came the sound of a banging door, rapidly answered by the thudding of her heart. She thought: Dear God, I'm no good at this. Not without Campbell.

She pulled at the window again, to see if she could open it further, but it was solid, and she realized there were security stops on the frame.

A strange sound rose from below: a faint scratching. Hurrying now, she zipped up the bag, heaved it onto the lip of the open window then, giving it a firm shove, watched it bump past the sill before disappearing into the darkness and landing almost immediately on the roof below with what seemed to be a grossly amplified thud.

A dog barked, a sharp furious yapping. The sound was coming from inside the house. A voice yelled for it to shut up. The barking continued. Claws scratched frantically against wood. After a moment a door was opened and she knew instantly which one it was – the door to the stairs. A male voice came floating up the stairwell: 'Fuck off, Beji.'

She heard the skittering of the animal's paws as it scrabbled up the stairs. She made for the door, intending to slam it shut, but even before she stumbled over the bed she realized she had left it too late. The dog was fast; it was already racing across the hallway. Her brain, acting on its own initiative, was making a few simultaneous calculations: if she lunged for the door and pushed hard she might catch the animal against the jamb, while if she held back, the dog would get in and try for a chunk of her leg. Either way someone was going to get hurt. The question was, who would make the least noise?

She held back. The dog shot in, braked hard and spun round to get a run at her. She kicked out a defensive foot but the animal had seen plenty of those and was past it in a flash and under the cover of semi-darkness was coming in to her leg from the other side. Daisy tried to grab at the mass of fur, but it was surprisingly hard to grip. The animal snarled and wriggled and howled, its snapping teeth grabbing at her legs. Any last self-control she might have felt vanished in the heat of her panic and, letting the teeth get to grips with her jeans, she caught the animal by the scruff of the neck and yanked it screaming into the air and clamped a hand round its throat. She wasn't sure how much pressure was needed to kill, but she soon found out how much was needed to cut off the noise. When the animal stopped screaming, she eased the pressure, and cocked an ear towards the door, straining to pick up sounds over the dazed gasps of the dog.

The silence reached out, unsettlingly quiet.

She dropped the snuffling rasping dog onto the bed and looked longingly towards the window. There might still be time. But even as she assessed the precarious climb onto the sill and the impossibly narrow squeeze through the high opening, she heard the creak of a tread on the stairs.

She was very still.

And again, faint but unmistakable.

I don't think I can deal with this, she thought; I want to scream.

A light came on in the hall beyond the open door.

She moved deeper into the room. The window was out of the question now. Under the bed? She felt an anticipatory lurch of something like claustrophobia. In the wardrobe? It stood to one side of the door, a narrow old-fashioned free-standing wardrobe in dark wood. Too small. To the other side of the window then, in the corner, a door to what could be a walk-in cupboard?

There had to be a better way.

Bluff it out? Stand her ground?

The dog began to whimper. In the light from the hall she could see it clearly – two globular eyes in a squashed face, a mass of pale fur – and then it came to her with sudden certainty: this was *his* room.

For a moment she was the child again, fear panting at her heels, limbs dragging in water, unable to move.

Another sound. Much closer, almost at the door. She moved at last, stealing deeper into the room, towards the far corner and the narrow recessed door. It pulled open soundlessly. She met hanging clothes, a floor covered with shoes and soft unidentifiable bundles. Easing her feet through to the boards beneath, she stepped into the dark sweat- and musk-scented world of Maynard's shirts.

The long journey and the time change were finally taking their toll on Dublensky, and his memory was giving trouble. It wasn't the contents of the memos he'd sent to the MKI management that were failing to come to mind – he remembered them quite clearly – nor even the responses he'd got back – they'd been few enough – but the order and timing of these events, which Calthrop was determined that he should recall. But with each new effort of memory Dublensky's mind was only becoming more confused.

Mackenzie suggested a break. Calthrop didn't look too happy about that, but then matters were brought to a natural halt by a buzz on the internal phone which had Nick Mackenzie leaving the room like a rocket. The girl Jenny followed immediately, then a few minutes later Mackenzie put his head round the door and summoned Simon Calthrop as well, leaving the Dublenskys alone.

Anne said: 'There's something bad going on, I know there is. And they're not telling us.'

'Why d'you say that? I thought it was going well. I mean, they've done everything they said they would.'

'I meant something else.'

'Like what?'

'How do I know?' she said impatiently. 'That's what they're not telling us.'

They sat in silence for a while, aware of the murmur of urgent voices wafting through the partly open door.

Dublensky got to his feet. 'I'll go and make sure Tad's okay. Should he be in bed?'

Anne shrugged. 'He's half-way through a video.'

Dublensky decided to go anyway. Reaching the door he pulled it open to see Mackenzie, Calthrop and the girl in the centre of the hall. Calthrop was saying in a fast low-pitched voice: 'I can't possibly get involved with this! Christ, you shouldn't even be telling me. It's *crazy* to tell me. If the paper gets a whiff of this, they'll have hysterics. *God.*'

Dublensky would have moved then if he hadn't heard Mackenzie say: 'But what about *Daisy*?'

Calthrop held up both hands and said with a chilly little laugh: 'I'm sorry – I'm really not listening to this. I've gone totally deaf.'

'She could be in trouble!'

'Daisy's a resilient girl. She'll be all right.'

Calthrop began to retreat, but Mackenzie grabbed him by the shoulder. 'What do you mean, *all right*? Suppose she's been beaten up like Campbell? Suppose she's lying somewhere, hurt?'

'Listen, Mackenzie, perhaps I'm not making myself clear,' interrupted Calthrop smoothly, shaking his shoulder free. 'I won't – I *can't* – have anything to do with this.'

Even from where Dublensky stood he could see the set of Mackenzie's jaw, the anger in his face. 'I see,' he hissed. 'So Campbell's beaten up and Daisy's missing and you're not prepared to help?'

'Now wait a minute,' Calthrop argued virtuously. 'Don't let's forget what they were doing to get into this mess, shall we? A *burglary*, for God's sake. What do you expect me to do, find a tame policeman to help out?'

'You must have contacts!'

'Nobody could have contacts that good,' Calthrop scoffed. 'They were committing a criminal offence, and my paper can have *nothing* to do with it. *Nothing*. And' – he raised an admonitory finger – 'nothing to do with the perpetrators, either. Daisy's finally gone over the edge this time. Killed her chances. If this comes out she'll be finished, believe me!'

'They were only looking for evidence,' Jenny chipped in defensively.

'What evidence?' Calthrop jeered. 'We could never use that sort of evidence, it's useless!'

Mackenzie hunched down into his shoulders. 'What do you mean?'

'I mean we can't use stuff which has been stolen in a bloody burglary. God, we'd be bombarded with writs and injunctions, not to mention arrest!'

There was silence. Mackenzie glowered at the floor, then, sensing Dublensky's presence, swung round to stare at him. Dublensky tried to pretend he'd just that minute come into the hall.

'Fine,' Mackenzie said to no one in particular. 'Fine.'

And with that he strode over to Dublensky. 'I've got to leave,' he said in a rough undertone. 'You won't go away, will you?'

'What's happening?' Dublensky asked in agitation.

'Nothing that need bother you.'

Dublensky protested: 'But I think I should know.'

'Just don't go away, that's all!'

And he disappeared up the stairs at a run. The next morning the housekeeper told Dublensky that Mr Mackenzie had been driven south the previous night. She thought he had gone to London.

# Chapter 37

THE SILENCE CLOSED in around Daisy, steady and tantalizing, and at that moment she might have been able to convince herself she was alone in the building if it hadn't been for the sickly scent of Maynard's clothing, the blend of hair gel and unidentifiable body scents that were like a presence in the darkness.

She had eased the hanging clothes away from her face and was standing propped against the wall, her ear close to the door, waiting and listening, though for what she wasn't sure. More silence? Some sign that it was safe to get out? Even perhaps a sound in the room outside.

The pipes ticked gently, and a muffled sound, something like the banging of a car door, drifted up from Peregrine Road.

How long had she been here? Ten minutes? No, longer, much longer – more like twenty. It had taken a good five minutes for her heart to regain its rhythm after she'd stepped into the cupboard and discovered that not only were there no means of pulling the door closed after her, but it was threatening to swing open again. Gripping the edge of the door with her fingers she had run a hand over the inner surface and eventually located a clothes hook which had given her sufficient leverage to pull the door gently into the jamb. Then, just when she thought the worst was over, the spring-loaded ball closure had given a slight click as it went home. The sound, no louder than a breaking matchstick, had seemed to reverberate across the silence, gathering volume in her brain. Her throat dried, her heart squeezed against her chest.

There had been no sound from the other side of the door.

It was another five minutes before she convinced herself that it was silence that she was hearing in the room beyond, that the rustlings of her own movements, the sound of her own breathing were not masking some other breathing or the creep of footfalls on the carpet or the soft snorts of the lurking dog.

There had been no one moment when she had realized the dog had gone, no one moment when the snuffles had stopped; rather the sounds had faded imperceptibly, probably early on, when she was still listening for something much closer, like a touch on the door, a sudden pull on the handle.

Once the snuffles had faded there had been no other sound. Whoever had come up the stairs had come and gone silently.

Now the silence was long and seemingly uninhabited. She would have to move sooner or later, and this was as good a time as any. She slid her hand to the edge of the door and began to exert pressure on it by degrees. It resisted her first efforts and, realizing she'd have to push a little harder, she felt for the hook so that she could restrain the door from flying open once it sprang past the catch.

Finding the hook, she was on the point of giving the door a solid push when a sound came, catching her by surprise.

Loud, close, just beyond the door. Her hand jerked away from the hook.

Loud, close. The bitter complaint of wood sliding against wood, the squeal of ancient pulleys: the window.

But if the loudness was startling, so was the realization that someone had stolen into the room without a sound, had crossed to the window without the creak of a floorboard. Had even – the thought unnerved her – been there all the time.

Her knee gave way, she jerked it taut. She realized she was holding her breath and exhaled rapidly. She shifted her weight and put her head closer to the door. Had he realized why the window was open? If so, why was he closing it? Then it occurred to her that the frame was complaining so much not because the window was being closed but because the upper sash was being opened further; either that, or somehow he'd managed to prise open the solid lower sash.

There was only one reason he would be opening the window further: to search the roof below. He must think she'd got out that way. Or maybe he was checking to see if she was trapped there, unable to get down.

Whatever, he would see the bag. The realization came to her with sickening certainty, and she grimaced in silent frustration. Stupid. *Stupid.*

She pressed her ear back to the door. Faint scrabbling sounds, a soft rasping like clothes dragging over the window-sill.

That was it then, she thought, adjusting to the full weight of her disappointment: he'll have seen it by now. She pictured him leaning out of the window, torch in hand, casting the light over the roof until the bulky shape of the bag caught in the beam. In a few minutes he would climb out and retrieve it. Then he would discover the bulging files and, knowing she would never have left them behind intentionally, he would realize that she couldn't have got very far after all.

She listened for the sound of feet on the sill, for knocks and scrapes as he climbed down onto the roof. She prepared to open the door and run while he was out on the roof, but though she waited, nerves beating at her throat, the pause stretched on and on until, finally, it was broken by an abrupt and unexpected sound: the screaming pulleys again, louder than ever. The window being closed. And not just one sash either: there was the thud of a second sliding home, and the click of a clasp.

What did it mean? He couldn't possibly have had time to get out onto the roof and retrieve the bag and climb back in. Maybe he'd decided to leave it till morning. Maybe he didn't have a torch. Maybe – it seemed too much to hope for – he hadn't spotted the bag at all.

But hope comes cheap and she allowed herself a large ration. She almost persuaded herself that he'd given up on her, that he thought she'd escaped. From there it was a short step to an even more promising thought: that he didn't realize she was there or had ever been there, that he believed Campbell had come on his own. The open window could after all have been Campbell's doing, while the dog, catching Campbell's scent, could have become hysterical and run itself into the door.

Arguments that didn't bear much examination; but they kept her going while she waited breathlessly in the darkness. The silence was worse this time because she knew he moved soundlessly, and, while he might well have left the room, he could just as easily be inches away, his hand reaching slowly for the door, or, worse, just standing there, waiting.

The silence stretched out. The sounds in Peregrine Road, now stifled by the closed window, were barely audible: a dog barking, the occasional car, a jet rumbling over on its descent to Heathrow. After a time she persuaded herself that the room was empty again. When ten minutes' silence had passed she murmured inwardly, *This is ridiculous*, and reached for the door again, one hand to the hook, the other to the door edge. She pushed gently but the door didn't shift. She tried harder. It was very stiff. She ran over her memories of the door: the soft click when she had pulled it shut, the operation of the simple spring-ball arrangement, the knob on the outside which had been of the fixed non-turning variety, the impossibility of a latch or anything heart-stopping like that.

She pushed again, really hard this time. And again.

And then for an instant her heart really did stop, because as she put her whole weight against the door, she realized it would never open. It had been locked from the outside.


'Are you sure?'

'Sure I'm sure. Over the bicycle shop. An' look, the hire car's still there. Three down, behind the white one.'

Nick looked at the Escort, then surveyed the building. It was on the opposite corner, on a junction with a small street called Peregrine Road, whose name, set on a plate on the side wall, was just visible in the streetlights. A single white light glowed dimly in the window of the shop. The windows above were in darkness.

'The door, it's at the side there.'

Campbell's voice tightened oddly, and Nick took a quick look at him. He sat stiffly in the passenger seat, his head pressed back against the rest, his lower lip pushed out fiercely, like a bulldog's. In the thin light it was hard to tell if he was in pain or just exhausted.

'You all right?'

'Huh? I'm a'right,' he replied testily. It was the answer he'd given at the hospital when Nick had picked him up from the casualty department an hour before. His only visible signs of injury, then as now, were a puffy left eye and a long cut over the lid which had been fixed with Elastoplast, giving him the look of a boxer after a choppy fight. The nurse had mentioned something about concussion, but Campbell had brushed the idea aside.

Nick turned off the engine and peered forward to take another look at the building. Was Daisy still there? He tried to imagine her somewhere behind the dark windows.

Was she lying unconscious? But no, why would they have
attacked her? There wouldn't have been any need to subdue
her, not like with Campbell. Trapped then? But why would
they have kept her there, why would they bother?

He sighed fretfully: 'We should have gone straight to the
police. There's nothing we can do here!'

'Ha!' Campbell brayed his contempt. 'An' what would
*they* be doin' that we canna'?'

'Having the law on their side,' Nick replied.

'Aye, an' they'd just listen like lambs, would they?
They'd just come along an' do as we asked, would they?'

Nick, remembering that he was up on drugs charges and
Campbell on bail for assault, reluctantly felt himself giving
way, though it went against his better judgement.

'But why would she still be here?' he argued.

'Huh? Well, she didna' come out, did she?'

'How do you *know*? You were in the gutter unconscious.'

'But she'd have made a call if she'd have got out, would
she not? She'd have taken the car. She'd have called
Ashard.'

There was no denying that and, momentarily silenced,
another idea came to Nick: that she'd had an accident,
tried to climb out and fallen from a window. The idea,
dramatic and unlikely though it was, began to fix itself in
his mind.

'Perhaps we should ask at the hospitals.'

'Eh?' Campbell dismissed it with a blow of his lips. 'But
they'd have brought her to the emergency there' – he
gestured over his shoulder in the general direction of the
hospital they had just left – 'I would've seen her.' He moved
his bulk towards the door, impatient for action.

But Nick had a good idea of the action Campbell had in
mind, and he didn't want any of that, not if it could
possibly be avoided. 'Wait,' he insisted firmly. 'Let's decide
what we're going to do – to say.'

'Say?' Campbell sucked in his breath disapprovingly. 'Best to go straight in' – he thrust an arrowlike hand in the direction of the building – 'take a look around, see if she's there, an' talk later.'

'That's a sure way to get into trouble!' Nick snapped. 'They might call the police.'

Campbell threw him an incredulous look. 'What? They'd no more call the police than I would!'

'We don't know that,' Nick argued, zipping up his jacket with finality. 'But whatever happens violence isn't going to help.' He was aware of sounding sanctimonious, but he didn't know how else to dampen Campbell's insatiable appetite for action.

'Stay here,' Nick instructed, and before Campbell could argue he got out and strode across Peregrine Road to the entrance in the wall. It was barely six and still pitch black; there weren't many people around yet, just the occasional car in the main road. The door was in a bad way, splintered and bent around the remains of the lock. It had been patched up with pieces of plywood, nailed roughly into place. A square of white card had been pinned to the door. Peering at it closely, he read: *Reynard Associates are temporarily closed for staff holidays.*

Nick pressed the bell, waited, then pressed the second bell. After four tries he left his finger on both bells.

No one came.

He returned to the car with a sense of anticlimax.

'Should a' gone straight in,' mumbled Campbell, a note of censure in his voice. 'Now they'll know we're here.'

Nick clenched the wheel. 'I want to find her, Campbell, just as much as you do.'

His remark seemed to trigger something in Campbell for, without a word, he got out of the car. Nick shouted, but there was no stopping him.

Nick watched half in agitation, half in fascination as Campbell strode up to the door and beat on it with both hands. Ignoring the stares of a passer-by, he then kicked viciously at a point half way up the door where the lock should have been. When that failed he ran the full weight of his shoulder against it, and looked surprised when the door withstood his advances. He was rallying himself for another go when a man on the corner of the main road started shouting and gesticulating at him. Then Nick saw that the gestures weren't aimed *at* Campbell, but *towards* Campbell, as if directing someone towards the scene. Suddenly appreciating his danger, Campbell abandoned the door and, looking over his shoulder, half walked, half ran back to the car. Nick, falling into the required role of getaway driver, had the engine running and the car moving even as Campbell climbed in. Braking to turn out into the main road, he saw a uniformed policeman pounding up to the passer-by, who was pointing towards the car.

Nick shot out into the road and accelerated away, his ears singing, his heart pumping, feeling the policeman's eyes burning into the illuminated car registration. The car lights – he should never have turned them on! What a stupid mistake! Then, when the worst of his panic had subsided and he'd got things into some sort of proportion, he realized that it wasn't the lights that had been the mistake, but allowing Campbell to talk him into such a crazy idea in the first place.

He wasn't capable of speech for some time and it was Campbell who broke the silence as they crossed the river.

'A regret,' he said with feeling. 'A real regret. I was almost there!'

Nick pressed his lips together and parked in silence just the other side of the King's Road. Using the car phone he called Jenny at Glen Ashard, but there was no news. They walked back to a café-brasserie that was just opening up, ready to catch the yuppie breakfast trade.

Nerves partially restored by strong coffee, Nick made Campbell go through the whole evening again in more detail, from the time he and Daisy had got inside the place until the moment he woke in the street with the ambulance-men leaning over him. Campbell, speaking haltingly, got as far as the tape recordings and the invoices and the Work-ham Overseas Holdings files when his ruddy cheeks turned ashen and he clutched a hand to his injured head.

After that he wasn't much good for anything. Nick offered to deposit him at a doctor but with some predicta-bility Campbell wasn't having any of that and lay back in his seat, pale and uncommunicative, as they drove through the first knots of rush-hour traffic to Scotland Yard.

'What was she doing there exactly?'

The inspector's manner was deceptively benign, making it only too easy to overlook the directness of the question.

Nick replied carefully: 'She went there for information.'

'What kind of information?'

How much to tell? 'Information about the illegal bug-ging of her telephone – and other things.'

The inspector smiled blandly and raised an eyebrow to show that he was prepared to be moderately impressed. Having become something of a judge of policemen over the last months, Nick put him down as shrewd rather than bright, a man who had carved out a niche that exactly suited his talents. Greying and pouchy, he seemed poured into his seat. The benevolence, the unhurried speech, the appar-ent sloth were, Nick suspected, part of a well-practised approach, designed to lull, lure and, quite probably, to drive people to confession through sheer frustration. It was almost an hour since Nick had announced himself at the desk downstairs, and forty minutes since he had been ushered in to see this man Morgan. Yet far from responding to the urgency, it seemed to Nick in his present mood that Morgan was taking pleasure in slowing things down.

Morgan asked: 'And what makes you so sure she's still in there?'

'I told you – the car. And she would have called if she'd managed to get out. It's the first thing she would have done.'

'So why would she be having trouble in getting out? Why would anyone want to prevent her?'

At Campbell's insistence, Nick hadn't mentioned the fact that Campbell had been there, hadn't suggested that Daisy was anything but alone. 'These people had been spying on her,' Nick offered. 'They knew she was on to them, they knew she was going to expose them. They would have had good reason to shut her up.'

'But she hadn't called us in?' Morgan murmured. 'She hadn't thought it serious enough for that?'

Watching the inspector, Nick was suddenly reminded of the roomful of doctors he'd faced during Alusha's illness and how they had worn the same look of condescension and quiet disbelief. Goaded by tiredness and old anger, Nick added testily: 'You don't seem to believe me.'

'If I didn't believe you, Mr Mackenzie, I wouldn't have sent a car to go and look, would I?'

'But can they get in? Can they search the place?'

'Not without a warrant.'

'And will you get a warrant?'

'Not without some evidence.' He gave a humouring smile. 'Which is the purpose of these questions, Mr Mackenzie.' He took a long languid breath. 'Now this company, Reynard Associates – you say they're private investigators?'

'I told you . . . Look, can't we do this later?'

'But why not now, Mr Mackenzie? Is there some difficulty?' The ingenuous smile.

'Because – ' Nick could almost hear Campbell's voice, telling him that this was just what he had warned him about, all talk and no action. 'Because there's no time!'

The inspector dropped his eyes slowly to the desk and examined his pen. When he looked up there was an obdurate look beneath the benevolent gaze. 'We'll hurry as best we can, Mr Mackenzie. In the meantime, Reynard Associates – would you mind?' Nick saw that there was to be no escape, not for the time being at least, though that didn't stop him from burying his head in his hands. Then, drawing a deep breath, he started to go through it again.

It was nine fifteen by the time Nick called an exasperated halt. The patrol men sent to ring on the side door in Peregrine Road had drawn a blank, and the inspector was showing no signs of trying for a warrant. Leaving Morgan to dig up what he could on Reynard Associates, Nick got down to the car to find Campbell half asleep in the passenger seat. He was grey-faced and groggy, but that didn't stop him remarking: 'What did I tell you, hey?' with a glint of satisfaction.

Nick called Jenny at Ashard again, but there was still no news.

Intending to drop Campbell off into the care of his housekeeper in Kensington, Nick headed west. His route took him close by David's place in Knightsbridge and, realizing David might still be at home, he diverted into Montpelier Square.

David emerged from the door of his immaculate town house and stared at Nick disbelievingly before his face lit up like a child's for whom a long-heralded promise has unexpectedly come true. 'Nick! You made it! You made it!' He must have been shaving because he was still in his dressing gown and there were smudges of foam on his ears.

Nick remembered his promise of the previous afternoon. 'David, I'll try to get into the studio later, I promise.'

David's expression underwent a painful transformation

from open joy to the sort of dull hurt shown on the faces of ill-treated dogs in advertisements for animal charities.

'David, a favour. Could you trace a company for me? It's called Workham Overseas Holdings.'

With a sigh David turned away and padded off across the hall and down the stairs. Nick followed him into the basement kitchen, a mock-German-farmhouse affair with a dazzling ceiling of recessed spotlights, walls of dark oak fittings and a central island that sported hanging copper pans which gleamed from lack of use.

'It's based in the Cayman Islands,' Nick prompted.

David flicked on a coffee percolator, filled it with water and, opening a cupboard, pulled out two cups and deposited them noisily on the work surface. His movements were slow and heavy, as if he was suddenly very tired. 'Can't be done,' he said laconically.

'Why not?'

'Half the reason people put their companies in the Cayman Islands is so that people like us can't trace them.'

'But haven't I got a company in the Caymans?'

'Exactly.'

'But there must be a way surely.'

'You asked me, and I'm telling you there's no way. Zilch.' He made a chopping movement with his hand. This was David at his steeliest, the David encountered by record companies trying to negotiate contracts.

Nick persevered: 'Have we no contacts?'

David turned slowly to face him, his emotions hidden behind layers of hard-won impassivity. 'Contacts are only as good as the favours they owe you.'

'But you could ask, David?'

'Asking'll get me nowhere,' he drawled. 'Secrecy's sewn into the system tighter than the coins in my grandmother's hem when she escaped the Russian revolution.'

'But *asking* . . .?'

A slight pause which Nick took as a hopeful sign.

'When can I tell the others you'll be coming to rehearsal?' David replied, apparently changing the subject but not, as they both knew, changing it at all.

'David, as soon as I can. This afternoon. Maybe sooner. Look, I wouldn't ask if it wasn't important.'

David filled the cups and, taking them across the kitchen, plonked them saucerless on a rustic wooden table that matched the dark oak units. 'Everything's important with you, Nick, everything except what you're meant to be doing at the time.'

Smarting under the unprecedented rebuke, Nick sank onto a stool.

'Someone's gone missing,' he tried to explain. 'Daisy Field, the campaigner from Catch. You remember . . .?' He began to tell him about the weekend's events but a veil of indifference had dropped over David's eyes and Nick recognized the look he usually reserved for the stream of hard-luck stories that regularly came his way each working day.

'Not your problem, surely,' David murmured at last.

'But it *is*. She was— She's— I have to find her, David!'

'I see,' he said, and his eyes carried a wealth of meaning.

'It's not like that,' Nick replied sternly. 'It's not like that at all. It's just – I feel sort of responsible. I feel . . .'

He trailed off, aware that David was watching him with open puzzlement. He repeated: 'I can't leave it, David.'

David reassumed his world-weary mantle.

'Okay,' he conceded with a slow sigh, 'okay. I'll do what I can, but I promise nothing, you understand, *nothing*. I'll have to ask a lot of favours, serious favours I have no right to ask. It could take time.'

'How long?'

'Well there's the time difference for a start, five hours, and favours never come quick. Several days, at the least. But even then I can't promise a *thing*, Nick, not a *thing*.'

'I thought . . .' What had he thought? That it would be a question of lifting a phone and getting a quick answer.

'Having got that out of the way,' said David heavily, 'can we now discuss a few small items like this tour we're meant to be starting next week? I won't begin to tell you what I'm going through with the insurance people – '

'I was fixed up, by the way.'

David's eyelids drooped lower. He didn't speak.

'The drugs. Someone set me up.'

David kept all expression out of his face. 'Who'd want to do that, Nick?'

Nick downed his coffee and got ready to leave. 'People who wanted to warn me off.'

This was too much, even for David, and a sort of regretful wariness came across his eyes. 'But, Nick – do you mean they *planted* the drugs?'

Nick stood up. 'I mean someone tipped them off.'

'Who?'

A vision of Susan slipped into Nick's mind, and, as always when he thought of her now, it was against the backdrop of that South Kensington flat all those years ago. Whether from an improvement in his memory or some trick by which his brain had patched in conversations from other times, he seemed to hear the very words she had used in the argument that had finally broken their relationship, words that were uniformly violent, bitter, and ugly. It occurred to him, as it had occurred to him soon after the drugs raid, that she had hated him then, and probably still did.

But this wasn't the moment to deal with that. There would never be a right moment. Thoughts of vengeance and recrimination had never formed an important part of his repertoire. It was quite enough that he was rid of her.

Yet as he went out to the car and half turned to wave to David it suddenly struck him that Susan, far from being someone to avoid, was probably the very person he should

go and see. Much as he loathed to admit it, much as it
infuriated him to think of facing her again, Susan might
just be able to wave a magic wand: Susan with her
knowledge of Schenker, her many dealings with him, Susan
who liked to show off her contacts, Susan the perfect
messenger. Even – it wasn't totally impossible – Susan with
a sense of shame at what she had done.

Campbell raised his eyebrows expectantly as Nick got
into his car.

Nick fought an increasingly miserable battle with himself before starting the car and driving round the square.

'Well? Anythin'?' Campbell demanded eventually.

'What? No, nothing.'

'So?'

'We're going to see Mrs Driscoll. Well, I think so.' And
saying it he realized he still hadn't made up his mind.

'And who is she?'

'The wife of the agriculture minister.'

Coming into Eaton Square, Campbell gave a sudden
peremptory exclamation, half-way between a grunt and a
shout, and seemed to clutch his stomach. Imagining sickness or worse, Nick swerved in to the kerb. 'What is it?'

Campbell made an odd sound, and it was an instant
before Nick realized it wasn't a bark of impending nausea
but of gruff excitement. He was brandishing a half-rolled
bundle of papers which he had extricated from the inner
reaches of his jacket.

'Daisy, she had no room for them, she gave them to me.
That name, that name – it's in here!'

Nick shuffled through, reading quickly. 'I don't see . . .'

'Look – *Driscoll*!'

Nick stared at the papers for a long time, reading
and rereading them until their meaning was both clear and
confused in turns. Workham Overseas Holdings. The
Cayman Islands. Expenses. Operatives. Vehicles. And then
hospital bills. The name Angela Kershaw. And: *Cramm* –

*But will Driscoll stay away from her?* Who was the her? The Kershaw woman? And Driscoll, could it really be the same ... Yet if all these papers came from a Workham Overseas Holdings file, if Workham was in fact Morton-Kreiger, then why on earth not? Reading the cryptic message again, he tried to imagine a situation where a man in a prominent position couldn't be relied on to keep away from a woman, and ended up with a sexual scenario. The hospital bills sent him further along the same path. He tried to push his mind in other directions – hate, guilt, debt – but nothing else rang with anything approaching conviction.

He threaded the car back into the traffic, aware of two simultaneous and equally disturbing thoughts: that this might be something extremely valuable, and that he hadn't the first idea what to do with it.

He remembered that Susan had moved to a place somewhere off Vincent Square but had to call his house-keeper on the car phone for the exact address. He found the house at one end of a narrow and uninspiring street of variable architecture. The place was a dark-bricked Georgian town house with newly painted window frames, a royal-blue front door that shone like glass and baggy-knicker curtains in the upstairs rooms. Waiting outside was a black car with a uniformed driver.

Nick hesitated a moment, struck by nervousness and an odd beating excitement that, in an ancient reflex, had him momentarily longing for a drink. Leaving the car keys with Campbell, he went up to the house and rang the bell. The door opened instantly as if someone had been waiting behind it, and a soberly suited man in horn-rimmed glasses stepped forward. The man had clearly been expecting someone else because an expression of surprise darted across his face. Deciding that Nick was harmless, exercising a politician's versatility, he recovered quickly with a brisk enquiring look.

'Good morning,' he said, angling his head as if to catch some airborne clue as to Nick's identity.

'I've come to see Susan.'

'Of course, of course.' The professional smile, broad but bleak, flashed across his face. He looked like his photographs but smaller and plumper, and, despite his vigorous manner, less intimidating.

'One of her interior people, are you?' Driscoll said. He allowed himself a moment to enjoy his turn of phrase before deciding that his time was too valuable to be spent hanging around on the doorstep. Retreating into the hall he shouted Susan's name up the stairs while shrugging on his coat. Picking up a battered ministerial dispatch box, he advanced on the door again.

'With you in a moment.' He ground to a halt on the threshold, faced by the impropriety of leaving Nick in front of an open door, and yelled over his shoulder: 'Susan, your guest's waiting. Mr – ?' He turned questioningly.

'Mackenzie.'

Driscoll repeated it up the stairs without visible recognition, then, assuming the benevolent but preoccupied look of someone with good works to do but not enough time to do them in, he scuttled across the pavement to his waiting car.

When Nick looked into the house again it was to see Susan standing on the stairs. She was wearing a Japanese wrap, long and flowing, in a blue which intensified the colour of her eyes. Her skin was pale and luminous and apparently bare of makeup, her hair a shining gold. Her loveliness shocked him, it seemed so inappropriate; and for a moment he was bowled back in time and remembering all kinds of things he would rather forget, like the warmth and suppleness of her body, and the long afternoons in Kensington, memories now inextricably mixed with anger and remorse.

She gave an abrupt laugh. 'Well, talk of the devil!'

'Were you?' he asked.

'What?' She took his hand and drew him inside the house and closed the door.

'Talking of me.'

'Not exactly,' she said, kissing him chastely on the cheek. 'But I was *thinking* of you, which was a hundred times better.' Still holding his hand, she stood back and examined him carefully, like a fond and long-lost friend. He looked for signs of embarrassment or shame in her face, but apart from the peculiar concentration of her gaze there was nothing to give her away, and she wore her confidence brilliantly, like a piece of jewellery. She thought she was safe, he realized. She thought she had got away with it.

'Now why would you be thinking of me?'

She caught the edge of sarcasm in his voice and for the first time a glint of doubt darkened her eyes. But it didn't trouble her for long; with a small chuckle, she started across the hall, gesturing for him to follow. When he didn't move, she looked back and asked in mock reproach: 'What, no coffee?'

'I won't stay,' he said tautly, knowing he mustn't antagonize her, yet unable to prevent the disapproval from showing in his voice.

She caught the message all right because her eyes lost some of their sparkle and she said a small 'Oh.' Then some sort of realization came to her and, clapping a hand theatrically to her forehead, she came back and gripped his arm. 'Of course, forgive me . . . The papers, that beastly story. I was so glad to see you that I almost – ' She made a face of suitable mortification, her eyes already inviting forgiveness. 'Listen, I tried to call you several times. I left messages, but they told me you were in Scotland.' She gave a soft groan and pressed a hand against his cheek. 'Poor, poor Nick – the *last* thing you needed. But they can't charge you with anything, surely – can they? I mean, *drugs*. It just isn't *you*, anyone could have told them that.'

The anger rose suddenly, without warning, and then he couldn't stop himself. 'They knew what they were looking for.'

She looked surprised then puzzled. He had to admire her: it was really a very good act. 'Knew?' she asked.

'Someone tipped them off.'

'Oh?' Her forehead crinkled gently into a frown.

'Told them about' – he couldn't say Alusha's name – 'the morphine in the house.'

She searched his face, and read there the meaning he had intended her to see. Her mouth twitched, her eyes narrowed and then came understanding, disbelief and hurt.

'You think . . .' She gave a soft gasp. 'You think *I* . . .'

She looked so appalled, so genuinely hurt, that his certainties uprooted themselves and swam around, dissolving the moment his mind touched on them. He couldn't think of anything to say.

'Well!' She was sawing away at her mouth, biting back tears. 'Well!' Her eyes brimmed suddenly, and she drew away.

'I think you'd better go,' she choked, hiding the contortions of her face with a splayed hand.

There was nothing he would have liked better than to go, to be free of the swooping and churning of his emotions, but there was still the business of Daisy. He said: 'That wasn't why I came.'

'It wasn't? I see!' she retorted in a sudden fury. 'That was just a little aside then, was it? My God, you're making me wonder what's coming next!'

He plunged in, desperate to get the whole thing over and done with. 'Daisy Field's gone missing,' he said quickly. 'We think your friend Schenker might be able to find her.'

She stared at him for a moment. '*What?*' She made an exaggerated gesture of disbelief, stabbing the fingertips of both hands against her chest. 'You want me to – ?' She rolled her eyes expressively. 'You came to ask me *that*?'

'We think she might be in danger.'

'But' – through the tears came an incredulous laugh – 'God, you've got a nerve! Schenker's nothing to do with *me*. Why should you think he's anything to do with me! If you need to ask him, why don't you go and do it yourself!'

'I thought the request would come better from you.'

She shook her head slowly. 'I can't help you. And now I think you really must go.' Her voice rose suddenly.

'He'd listen to you.'

'Oh yes! And what would I tell him!'

'That we have evidence to show Morton-Kreiger have been involved in dirty tricks, that we know who was responsible. That we know about Workham Overseas Holdings.'

Waving this aside, she stood up suddenly. 'You'll have to find another messenger boy.'

'You don't understand –'

'Oh, it's not that I don't understand,' she cut in sharply. 'That's not the problem. The problem is that you've just accused me of the most incredible breach of trust, and now you expect me to do you some sort of favour. My God.' She laughed outright, a bark of disbelief.

She's acting again, he thought suddenly, and in the tilt of her head and the twist of her mouth he caught the profile illuminated by the sunlit South Kensington window all those years ago, saw again the fierce expression, the white rage, the mouth distorted with the stream of bitterness; and seeing them, his intuition and anger took fresh shape.

He said abruptly: 'You could give him the name Angela Kershaw as well!'

There was a moment of startled silence. Susan was absolutely motionless, her eyes round and enlarged as she stared up at him.

'Schenker's been paying some of her bills.'

Her mouth opened slightly and she was so still that she

seemed to have stopped breathing. Then her eyes narrowed, she blinked rapidly. 'I'm sorry . . .?'

He might have hesitated then if it hadn't been for her tightly fisted hands and the chalkiness of her skin, which betrayed her shock.

He said: 'There's a file on her.'

'A file?'

'We've seen it.'

But he didn't have to elaborate. This was quite enough for Susan. Her mouth set into a grimace of despair. She sank back onto a chair. 'Oh God, oh God.' She looked as though she'd been punched in the stomach. In that moment he realized – if there had ever been any doubt – where her loyalties really lay, where they had always lain.

She recovered a little. 'How did you come to see it?' she asked. Then, in horror, as if it had only just occurred to her: 'Who else has seen it?'

'All sorts of facts about Schenker are going to come out,' he said, 'facts that Schenker won't want the world to hear.'

'Facts? You mean, evidence, documents?'

'Yes.'

'And there's evidence' – she braced herself to say it – 'about Angela Kershaw . . .'

'Yes.'

She gripped her forehead as if to contain her agony. 'But this evidence – it's not out yet?'

'No.'

A glimmer of hope dashed across her face. 'So we've got time!'

We? The assumption was so brazen he let it pass. 'Possibly.'

'So? *So?*' She was taut with impatience.

So? What came next? He thought of the thin sheaf of papers in the car, of what they would represent to Susan if she knew about them, and what she would give for them;

and the next move loomed up in front of him, obvious and horribly enticing. Yet he balked at the thought. However one viewed it, however many excuses one larded over it, it would be blackmail, ugly and repugnant. Even looking at her now, even knowing without a doubt that, finding herself in his position, she wouldn't hesitate to use whatever weapons were to hand, just as she hadn't hesitated to bargain away his most precious and painful secret, he couldn't bring himself to do it. He didn't like the idea of sinking to her level. He had enough of a bad taste in his mouth already.

'Can't we do something?' Susan pressed, beginning to recover her fighting power. 'Get hold of this file?'

He hesitated, playing for time. 'It's possible.'

'Can you get hold of it? *Can* you? I'd do anything,' she said, '*anything*.' Then, realizing this might have revealed too much, she pulled back a little, adding: 'It's not fair, you see. Whatever Tony is, whatever he's done, he doesn't deserve this.' She consolidated her selfless image with an appealing, pathetic smile. 'This thing's been hanging over his head for ages, it's been making him ill. That dreadful woman . . . It was nothing, *nothing*. But she's made his life an absolute misery ever since. *No one* deserves that sort of thing.'

He was silent.

'If there's any way of getting the evidence back, any way . . .' She was going more carefully now, concealing her determination. She must love Driscoll a lot, Nick decided; or she must love being his wife, which probably added up to the same thing.

He heard himself say: 'There might be a way,' and realized that she had presented him with an easy way out, and that he was about to take it.

'There might?' She brightened visibly. 'So what do we have to do? Is it a question of money?' She had no trouble using the word.

'Not money.'

'Something else then?' She was bargaining eagerly, and he saw that the doing of deals, the trading of favours, were the only currencies she really understood, that for her everything had a price, that everything – and that included people – only had value in so far as they contributed to her own wellbeing. Where had he come in her grand reckoning, he wondered? Well, it didn't matter. He had little doubt where he stood now.

She was waiting.

'Daisy has the file.'

'Ah!' She let out a long breath of comprehension. 'So if we find Daisy, we find . . .' She smiled collusively, and he shrank from the new and ugly intimacy in her eyes.

'That's about it,' he said.

'So you want me to approach Schenker?'

'Yes.'

'I see, I see.' Her mind was working overtime, the effort visible in her face. 'He'll know how to find her? Are you sure?'

'I'm sure.'

'Doesn't it . . .? Why shouldn't . . .?' Thinking better of whatever she was going to ask, she gave him a searching almost suspicious look. 'You *have* been busy,' she commented, and it wasn't entirely a compliment. 'So how much should I say?'

'Say that we believe that his associates know where Daisy is and that we want her back. And that they'd better make sure she turns up quick. Mention those company names.' He went through them with her.

'I see, I see.' She was painfully anxious to get it right. 'But what about Schenker, aren't we going to promise him something too?'

He didn't understand immediately.

She explained with slight impatience, as if it should have been obvious: 'The facts you were talking about, the ones he's not going to like – can't we get hold of those files as well?'

The machinations of her mind were quite amazing, they quite took his breath away. 'No,' he said vehemently. 'That's different, totally different. Schenker's not going to get off the hook. There are things that have got to come out, things that Daisy's worked on for months. Things that' – he didn't know how to express it to her – '*matter*.'

'Right,' she said at last, having come to some sort of decision. 'I see.' She got to her feet and pulled the lapels of her robe together and drew herself up, as if she was about to step out on a stage and play a great role. 'I'll phone now.'

'Don't say anything about getting any files back,' he reminded her. 'They might think we're willing to do a deal and we're not.'

'Right.' Preoccupied, already rehearsing what she was going to say, she turned away and went down the hall and disappeared into a back room, closing the door behind her.

Nick went to the front door and looked out. He could just make out Campbell in the front of the car, his head slumped to one side, asleep.

Susan was gone about five minutes. He spent the time circling the hall, thinking of Daisy, imagining where she was now, remembering all the work she had put into the Silveron case and what an uphill struggle it had been for her. Looking back, he felt a sort of dazed admiration for her. Her perseverance seemed to run like a constant thread through the upheaval and horrors of the last year or so, a point of light in an otherwise murky sky.

He had treated her badly, and he minded about that.

A click of a door and Susan reappeared, coming swiftly up the hall. Her expression was withdrawn, unreadable. 'I gave them the message,' she said.

'Them?'

'Schenker's man – his assistant.'

'And?'

'I imagine they'll look into it.'

'Imagine?'

'Oh, he bleated about not knowing anything about your friend,' she explained quickly, 'but he understood all right.' She came closer, and her face was hard with new questions. 'Tell me' – and she paused to fix her eyes firmly on his – 'how is it that you know all about the Kershaw woman when your Daisy friend still has the file?'

He started for the door. 'Listen – it doesn't matter.'

'What do you mean it doesn't matter?' She caught his sleeve and jerked him round again, her lips tight with suppressed fury. 'You'd better be telling the bloody truth!' she hissed. She looked older now, older and not at all lovely.

'Don't worry, Susan, you'll get what you want.'

Her fist twitched as if she would punch him with anger.

'I'd better,' she said bitterly. 'I'd better or . . .'

Something overturned inside him. 'Or? Or what, Susan?' he said brutally. 'Or you'll tell your friends even more things about me? Well, I've news for you. There's nothing more to tell. My real secrets I keep for my friends.'

Her mouth opened to speak but nothing came out. Instead she shut the fury neatly away and reached out a hand towards him, as if to take back what she had said. Perhaps she thought he might change his mind and she wouldn't get the Kershaw papers back after all.

But she needn't have worried. She could have them. He didn't care any more. He was already opening the door, making for the fresh air. He didn't look back.


Hillyard turned up the volume and angled the cassette player to carry the sound further into the room. The music blared out. It was a Forties-style big band number with plenty of brass and a noisy vocalist, one of three tapes he'd

given Beryl for Christmas because they took her back to
her youth.

Moving softly back to the door he picked up the broom
that he had brought from the kitchen and went to the
window. With the arrival of the music, the beating had
started again on the wardrobe door, an irritating thud-
thud, rising after a moment to more aggressive thumps as
she took some hard object to the wood – a shoe, he
imagined. She'd better not be using one of his new shoes or
he'd thwack it right back at her. Or better still, give her a
taste of what Beji had suffered, a twist to the throat and
some hair out of her scalp.

Thankfully the music spared him the sound of her voice,
or maybe she'd simply run out of volume. Throughout the
evening no sooner had she shut up than she'd started again,
disturbing his work and his rest, bash bash, yell yell.
Finally, partly to teach her a lesson, partly to give Beji some
satisfaction, he'd opened the flat door and let the dog race
upstairs to bark herself silly at the vibrating door.

Now, in the early morning, he slipped the catch on the
window and raised the lower sash. Feeding the broom out,
brush-end first, he found he could just reach the bag.
Hooking the broom under one of the straps was more
difficult. The bag was much heavier than he'd thought and
kept sliding off. Clicking his tongue at this tiresome development, he went in search of the small stepladder from the
office and manoeuvred it out of the window and onto
the roof. The roof was pitched, making the firm positioning
of the base tricky, and he had to run a rope from an upper
rung over the sill and across the bed to the door handle.
This extra work did not please him at all, not after the
many aggravations of the long evening, during which he
had had to patch up the street door, barricade it from the
inside, and then feed endless files into the shredder. What
with one thing and another, he hadn't got to his makeshift
bed on the back-office sofa until two, and then it was to

have his fitful sleep interrupted shortly after six by someone who had first rung, then hung, on the bell, and finally tried to break the door down. From the vibrations that had resounded through the building he had no doubt it was the girl's muscle man again.

There had been more callers at a quarter to eight. Stationing himself at the blinds in the front he had seen the marked police car pull out into the main street.

It had occurred to him then, with some force, that he didn't have a lot of time.

Now with the benefit of full daylight he clambered onto the ladder and climbed cautiously down to the roof. Hitching the bag over his shoulder, he remounted the steps and made his precarious way back into the room.

He went through the contents immediately, there on the bed. As far as he could tell, nothing was missing – or was it? Retrieving the ladder, he took everything downstairs and double-checked each file as he put it through the jaws of the shredding machine, sheet by sheet. Nothing seemed to be missing from any of the files – the girl would hardly have had time to remove individual pages – but were all the files themselves there? Had the cow stuck any in her pockets?

He made himself a coffee and, sitting at Beryl's desk, made a mental list of the files he had shredded last night, along with the files he had found in the bag, and matched them against his memory. He went next door into his own office and went through the smashed drawers of his desk again.

It was then that he saw something that he had missed during the night, lying on the floor in the desk well: the edge of a file. Pulling it out he saw it was a Workham file. It was empty. He certainly hadn't shredded the contents. He muttered: 'Cow, bloody cow,' and, returning to the main office, he went through the cabinets and the clutter on the desktops. The papers weren't there. At one point his

mobile phone rang, which he chose not to answer. A
minute later the desk telephone rang. Turning up the
volume on the answering machine, he tilted the blinds open
and gazed across the street to the opposite roof. He
watched a couple of seagulls shrieking and raging over a
scrap of booty while he half listened to Cramm's voice
asking him to call 'very urgently indeed'. With a sigh he
lifted the receiver just before Cramm rang off.

'The Catch woman, have you got her?' demanded
Cramm. The voice had a nervy ring to it, a note of panic.

Hillyard replied harshly: 'She was here but she's gone.'

'*There?* What do you mean she was there? What
*happened*?'

'She was hiding upstairs. I didn't realize.'

'Christ – how long was she there?'

'All night.'

'Jesus – and she's gone?'

'I said. She's gone.'

'Christ, but what the hell did she take with her? What
did she find out?'

'Nothing. She took nothing.'

'That's not what I bloody heard! They're on to us, you
fucking idiot! They've got some of your bloody files!'

'Not possible. Guesswork. No proof.'

There was a new stream of invective which Hillyard cut
off by putting the phone down. He muttered: 'Stuff you,
Cramm.' As for the girl, she wasn't going anywhere, not
until he'd finished with her, and he hadn't finished with her
yet, oh no.

In the hall Beji was whining softly, agitating to be let
out.

'Shut up.' He aimed a quick kick which, despite the
animal's wild evasions, managed to meet its rump. As usual
the screams were out of all proportion to the pain. 'Anyone
would think I'd killed you, you bitch.' Shutting the creature
on the other side of the flat door, he mounted the stairs on

light feet and crossed the landing to the bedroom. On the cassette player a female vocalist was trudging her way through some dirge about true love. Rapidly, he stopped the tape and, flipping it over, restarted it on the other side to ensure a reliable half-hour's musical accompaniment. As the music started again, so did the knocking, but much fainter now, as if she'd lost enthusiasm.

Taking his time, Hillyard closed the window, fastened the latch and drew the curtains, tugging the edges meticulously across each other to obliterate the daylight.

Then, treading carefully around the one creaking floorboard, he approached the cupboard door and slowly and soundlessly turned the key in the lock.

# Chapter 38

'THE PLANE WAS late, then?' Schenker's secretary asked, rising fluidly to her feet and following him to the door of his office.

'A little.' In fact it had been on time but Schenker had spent half an hour in the first-class lounge at Terminal 4 talking to his American lawyer at home in Greenwich, Connecticut, hearing the words he had banked on hearing, the words which had finally put him out of the nervous agony he had endured ever since leaving New York.

Everything had gone through, the lawyer reported: the final terms were agreed, the contract was signed. Some ground had had to be given away on profit sharing, termination pay and perks, but no more than Schenker had reckoned for, and this morning, as his car had eased its way through the jams from the airport, he had allowed himself a measure of euphoria, ready to carry him through the considerable challenges of the day, which would mainly consist of ensuring that it was his last at Morton-Kreiger.

'Orange juice? Coffee?'

'Coffee.'

His secretary retreated and he entered his office alone. It looked strange to him, as if he'd been away a long time. The river, grey and sluggish, had a decayed air about it, and the city in its wash of rare sunshine wore the unreality of a picture postcard. He realized that in his mind he had already left the place behind.

His secretary reappeared with the coffee. 'The chairman asked you to call him straight away, before anyone else.'

Schenker pressed the internal number.

'What's this additional agenda item?' said Sir Harry without preamble.

'I thought it was self-explanatory, Chairman.'

'It sounds like a no-confidence motion in McNeill to me.'

'That would be accurate, yes.'

'Ah.' A thoughtful silence, then: 'You'd better spare me five minutes then.'

Rising from behind the desk, Sir Harry gestured Schenker not to the chairs by the floor-length windows which, as a devotee of the informal avuncular approach, he usually chose for his confidential chats, but across the desk to the chair in front of him.

'This sounds serious,' he said.

'It is,' Schenker confirmed briskly. 'Bad news from Chicago. We've been seriously let down by Research.'

'Explain, if you will.'

'It's very simple. McNeill's people have been holding out on me – on *us*. The toxicology trials on Silveron could, apparently, be unreliable after all.'

He sat up at that. 'On what evidence?'

'A former MKI toxicologist and – '

'But I thought there was no substance in that rumour.'

'So did I!' said Schenker with a bitterness that was perfectly genuine. 'Research consistently denied the possibility, as you know, but now it seems that his little man might have been right all along. Apparently TroChem took *shortcuts*. Duplicated a bit of data here and there. Adjusted a few results. What can you *do*, for Christ's sake?' He got to his feet and started pacing the room. 'McNeill's never allowed anyone *near* Research. Never allowed anyone to question the controls . . .' He paused to ensure that the chairman absorbed the full implications of the last remark.

'And the controls were at fault?' said the chairman.

'You bet your life they were!' He came up behind his chair and gripped the back. 'McNeill finally admitted it yesterday at MKI. We were fed a pup by TroChem, data which was – *is* – highly dubious. If anyone had taken the care to lay down proper protocols, to install proper control mechanisms, none of this could have happened! Any confidence one might have had in Research has been totally destroyed!' He slapped his hands down on the chair to add resonance.

'Oh dear,' said the chairman, who liked to see things running smoothly. 'That bad?'

'Most certainly.'

'But what are you saying – that Silveron is back to square one, that the trials are invalid?'

'Yup.'

'My God.' The chairman was not much given to expletives, but he repeated this several times. 'There must be a way to salvage the situation, surely?'

'Possibly, but I really don't feel able to take it on. This thing has made my position untenable. All my work has been totally undermined. I've put everything behind Silveron – *everything* – both publicly and privately, and now I find myself stabbed in the back. How can I continue to support the product?' He made a wide gesture. 'How can I defend it in public?'

'But will that be necessary? To defend it publicly?'

He thought: Of course it will be, you stupid old fool. But perhaps this wasn't the time to tell Sir Harry of the press storm that was about to blow up under Morton-Kreiger's feet. Instead he said: 'Yes, I very much suspect it will be.'

'But surely it will be possible to reassure, to tell the world that we're looking into it and doing everything in our power . . .'

Schenker came round the front of his chair, tweaking

the knees of his trousers, sat down again. 'In all conscience I couldn't do that.'

'You couldn't?' He seemed surprised.

'No.'

'But . . .' Sir Harry's shaggy brows shot down, he seemed to swell at the enormity of what he was hearing. 'You feel that makes your position untenable?'

'Yes.'

There was only one direction in which this conversation could possibly lead – and indeed only one direction in which Schenker had been leading it – and Sir Harry, who in matters of this kind was sharp as a razor, was not slow in recognizing it. 'You intend to resign?'

'I can't see any alternative,' Schenker said with as much regret as he could muster.

Sir Harry leaned slowly back in his chair and, making a cage of his hands, puckered his mouth into a tight oval and regarded Schenker over the arch of his fingers. 'You can't be persuaded?'

'No.'

'I see.' He gave a brief smile of regret, but it was a mere token. 'You would not consider a – er – bridging period. Getting us through the crisis. With your expertise – ' Seeing the expression on Schenker's face, he broke off and said sombrely: 'I see.' He drew a deep and troubled breath as a new thought occurred to him. 'There could be – er – difficulties,' he murmured.

Schenker was well aware of the difficulties he had in mind, but it would not be appropriate to say so. 'Oh?'

Sir Harry assumed his favourite role, that of the senior diplomat feeling his way slowly over treacherous ground. 'The difficulties would surround – er – the timing. There must be no doubts about Silveron, no perceived link with your departure, no *rumours* – not until the matter has been properly investigated.'

'Of course not. I see that.'

'You do?'

'Absolutely.'

'There would have to be assurances . . .' He hesitated delicately.

'Of course!' Schenker looked marginally offended at the implication that he would have objected to any such suggestion.

'Good. Good.' Sir Harry gave a small self-satisfied smile, as if he had brought about this most satisfactory understanding singlehanded. 'These assurances would have to be a condition of – any arrangement.'

'Yes.'

'A sad day for Morton-Kreiger, a sad day indeed.'

Sad enough for the board to decide that his departure could be judged to have occurred by mutual consent? He didn't ask, although the answers would be worth an extra two hundred and fifty thousand on his golden handshake. He didn't ask because the extra money hardly rated beside the importance of being free to take up the cola job at short notice.

He had an hour before the board meeting, an hour to prepare for what would be a much tougher version of his interview with Sir Harry, complete with merciless attacks from McNeill. His preparations certainly did not involve Cramm, who was waiting for him in his office, looking grim and, unless he was mistaken, doom-laden.

'Later,' he announced sharply before Cramm could speak.

'It can't wait.'

He glared: 'You'd be surprised,' and sat down, glancing rapidly over the lists and messages that had been arranged neatly over his desk.

'The Kershaw business,' Cramm rushed in. 'It's about to get out.'

Schenker sighed impatiently: 'I'm sorry, but really, that has nothing to do with us any more, does it?'

There was a pause and Cramm said painfully: 'There are other things that might have got out as well.'

'Like?'

'Our connection to a security firm in south London, people who undertook some investigations for us – '

'Not my problem, Cramm.' He fixed Cramm with a hard stare. 'Though if you intend to stay on here, I suggest you make it yours.'

Cramm looked like a man being stoned, with missiles flying at him from all directions and no idea which part of himself to protect next. 'Won't there be dangers?'

'For us? You've always told me not, Cramm. You've always said there would be no difficulties for us.'

Cramm's throat moved soundlessly.

'If you're worried about it, Cramm, I suggest you make certain the story gets told in the right way.'

Cramm craned his head uncertainly. 'I don't understand.'

Schenker raised an eyebrow.

'You mean – leak it?'

Schenker shrugged gently as if to deny anything quite so extreme. 'I would just point out that once a story's got fixed in the public mind in a particular way, then it's almost impossible to change it again later, isn't it? Better for people to think it was Driscoll who dealt with the whole unsavoury matter himself – the payments and so on. Better for Driscoll, that is. Looks more gentlemanly.'

Cramm seemed confused.

'Better for you, too,' added Schenker with an emphasis which was not lost on Cramm.

Recovering, Cramm managed: 'I'll draw up some ideas and come back to you.'

'No time for that.' Schenker's mind was already on the board meeting, his eyes scanning the papers in front of him.

'You don't want to check – '

'You'll handle it very well, I'm sure,' he replied crisply.

Cramm finally moved uncertainly towards the door. 'Containment,' he said, making a painful stab at humour.

Schenker looked up for the last time. 'Very good, Cramm.'


The daylight vanished quite suddenly. Daisy had watched it creep under the door barely half an hour ago, a lozenge of grey which had slowly rimmed the heel of her shoe with a curve of light. Putting her hand to the base of the door, she had watched the smudge of grey harden into a sliver of brightness against her fingers.

When the music suddenly blared out it had sent a tattoo of adrenalin knocking against her ribs, and half in reflex, half in fear, she'd picked up a heavy shoe and started beating on the door again. When she gave up, which was quite soon, she had looked down and seen dark beams flowing across the splinter of light, as someone moved back and forth across the window. After a time the flickerings stopped. When they returned a minute or so later, it was only to cease again almost immediately, and this time the dart of light stayed unbroken for a long time, leaving nothing but the tinny bray of the music and the taunting swoops of the singers' voices, pounding through a heavy refrain.

Adjusting to the possibility of another wait, Daisy settled back on her makeshift cushion, a coat she had taken from its hanger and folded twice to soften the impact of the floor, and leant back into the corner, which she had also padded with clothing. Not too uncomfortable if one ignored the lack of leg space. At the beginning, the possibility of claustrophobia hadn't entered her mind, but during the long night, flutterings of something like panic had struck her, and now she was aware of it loitering not far away, like a giant mugger in the shadows. Strangely, it wasn't the lack of space that seemed threatening, nor even the darkness, but the air, which sometimes seemed so viscous that it was an effort to breathe.

During the earlier part of the night she'd had other distractions, first the cold which had necessitated pulling one of Maynard's jackets over her, later the demands of her bladder, a mild annoyance which rapidly grew into a major crisis. Nothing, she decided, was worth doing damage to herself and when her kidneys began to ache she reached out a hand to examine the selection of receptacles on offer. Tempting though it was to leave Maynard with a lasting memento of her stay in the form of a fluid-filled Chelsea boot, she finally chose a plastic bag which she found bundled up in a corner. Thankfully it proved to be watertight. In films, she reflected bleakly, the leading characters never encountered problems like this.

After that, at what seemed like midnight but which was probably much earlier, she exercised herself by throwing her weight against the door, partly in the genuine hope of breaking out, partly to remind Maynard, if he was still there, that she wasn't about to give up, and partly to break the sound of the silence, which seemed to stretch out endlessly. But lack of space prevented her from gaining momentum and the door didn't budge. Pressing her back against the rear wall and punching her heel against the lock was more promising, but the door, seemingly made of steel, continued to stand firm. After a short rest she began a new assault which was interrupted by the yapping and screeching of the dog on the other side. She thought briefly: I should have silenced you more permanently. Then she realized the dog was a message from Maynard, telling her that he was still out there, that it would be futile for her to try to escape.

She retreated and thought again. Perhaps in the morning . . . Perhaps he would simply open the door and let her walk out of the house. Why not? Why not? If she said it often enough, it acquired a sort of credibility. After all, what else would he do? Well, that certainly didn't bear thinking about.

After a time the dog stopped yapping and she thought she heard it pad away. Raiding the hanging clothes to fold into cushions, she settled down on the floor. If this was to be a waiting game, then she'd learn to play it her way, and rest while she could.

She thought of Campbell again, and wondered where he might be. Lying unconscious downstairs? Trussed up perhaps? Or dumped miles away, unable to remember what had happened, incapable, for some other reason, of getting help?

And everyone at Ashard, what would they be thinking? She pictured Nick in the book-lined room wondering where on earth she'd got to. Feeling let down perhaps, thinking she was tricky and unreliable, regretting his change of mind. She allowed herself a few moments' pure fantasy, a scene in which all this was long over and everything they had fought for had been vindicated, and she was standing at the door of the studio, waiting for him to finish whatever he was doing. This time when he turned it was to smile. Then . . .

Best not to let the reel wind on.

The picture of the others at Ashard was even more confused. Was Simon managing to coax the story out of Alan Breck? Was he doing it sympathetically or was he steaming ahead in his usual oblivious way? Only one thing seemed fairly sure, Simon wouldn't notice her absence except to remark on the inconvenience and added difficulties it was causing him. And Alan Breck? He would be closest to the truth, she suspected. He would be seeing disaster at every turn.

At some point she must have dozed because her mind filled with dogs that pulled at her legs and grasping hands that reached out of the darkness to drag her down. She woke with a start, and stared with blind relief into the darkness. She didn't mean to sleep again, but it stole up on her and she found herself dreaming quite another sort of dream in which the Nick fantasy came alive. This time, after turning to smile at her, he got up and reached an arm round her shoulders and pulled her against him, just like he had at the flat, but this time he kissed her, and, needing no encouragement, she kissed him right back. Then, in the maddening way of dreams, the scene shifted and the two of them were standing close to the burning laboratory, which somehow seemed to be located close to Ashard, though it wasn't the equipment that was burning, but her carpetbag with all the hard-won evidence against Morton-Kreiger.

She had woken, disturbed at the reality of it, not quite persuaded it wasn't true, wishing the dream had stayed firmly on Nick. Then she had looked down to watch the lick of dawn light creep onto the shoe.

The music must have been going for half an hour when it stopped in mid-song. Pulling herself hastily up, putting an ear to the door, she heard a mechanical click and the music started again. She hammered on the wood, though not so hard that she couldn't hear what was going on outside. '*I see the moonlight, baby, and I dream of you . . .*' The music was louder than before. She sighed with frustration, and the wardrobe was suddenly uncomfortably hot, and the mugger in the shadows moved several inches closer. Finally she sat down again and did some breathing exercises, and it was then that she looked down and realized that the splinter of light had gone. She ran her fingers along the crack and leant her face lower to the floor, but there wasn't the smallest whisper of light. She stared at the place where the light should have been, and a chill crept into her stomach. The curtains had been drawn. Or – a ridiculous overblown thought – something had been pressed against the outside of the door, something designed to seal the cracks and prevent the air from getting in.

She fought down the nudge of panic. She thought: Get a

grip! Ten deep breaths, slow and steady; count to five, hold five, exhale five.

She stopped abruptly on an in-breath. Beyond the door one song had finished, another, a slow mournful number, was starting. And in the slight pause in between – what? Nothing she could be sure of, nothing she could pin down, yet –

What? A faint rustling?

Her senses reached out into the darkness, she forgot to breathe, resuming abruptly with a gasp. Slowly she got to her feet and, resting her hand against the door, put her ear to the edge. The dog? No: too quiet, no snuffling. Something else, something huge and furtive.

The female voice sang: '. . . *nothin' ain't the same without you . . .*'

Daisy flattened her hand against the door and applied a minute amount of pressure. The door seemed to give a little. She felt very hot suddenly, and when she reached up to find the hook, her hand was trembling.

The slow song ended, there was a short pause, and the band crashed into a swing number screeching with brass. The sound seemed to pulsate through the darkness, smothering everything in its path. Gripping the hook, she increased the pressure on the door. Finally she gave it a distinct push.

A slight resistance, then it gave suddenly and opened with a plop.

Reflexively, she yanked on the hook to prevent the door swinging out too far and in her anxiety pulled the door back against the jamb so that it almost closed again.

She waited for the thumping of her heart to subside. She felt the heat inside her shirt, the looseness in her stomach.

Part of her was crying: *Stop!* Suppose he hasn't gone. Suppose it's a trick. Something elaborate and unpleasant, something –

She forced herself on. No good wasting time over questions without answers; no good hanging about.

Gripping the edge of the door, she pushed it slowly open. She saw a faint thread of light reflected vertically down a wall, revealing the edge of the drawn curtains. Another faint dusting of light showed against the ceiling.

She stepped over the threshold. The curtains must have been very thick or lined with a particularly dense material because almost no light permeated the room. It was impossible to make out the position or shape of the furniture. Keeping a hand on the open door, she took another tentative step forward, senses reaching out into the darkness. She strained to hear something – anything – over the shrilling trumpets; she strained to see, but the blaring music seemed to intensify the darkness.

The scent came suddenly, a distinct smell like the one in the cupboard but sharper. It wafted towards her as if blown from some invisible source, and she had the impression that it was coming from close by. She half turned. She sensed him before she saw him; his closeness was like an unbearable heat. Then he seemed to loom above her, huge, suffocatingly close, a giant black shape against the greater darkness of the room. The fear shot into her throat. Instinctively she tried to step back, but he was very quick. Somehow his arm came up from behind and, before she could dodge aside, it looped around her neck with a force that pushed her head back with a snap. Reflexively, her hands flew up and tried to pull his arm away, but he was massively strong. Even as she clawed ineffectually at his arm, he was forcing her forwards, over and down. She struggled to keep her footing, to try to get some leverage from the floor, at the same time twisting violently to free herself from the stranglehold. But his power was remorseless, like a massive weight pressing down on her. He caught her unimpeded arm and twisted her wrist round and backwards. She felt the screaming deep-seated fear that comes from complete helplessness, and opened her mouth to cry out. No sound came. She lost the last of her balance, her foot skidded away, her leg twisted over, the bed came up and pressed into her face.

His weight continued to bear down on her, crushing into her back, while he slipped a hand round the front of her throat. She thought: He's going to kill me. Somewhere in the far distance the music had paused, and she heard ragged gasps which she dimly recognized as her own.

Another number started, a duet with a sickly violin accompaniment. The pain was excruciating as he twisted her wrist inwards over her back. Something breezed against her ear. It was only when he spoke that she realized it was his breath.

'Where are the other files, you little cow?' His voice was high and uneven. The odour of his breath hit her, pungent and stale. 'Where?' he repeated in a hiss, giving her throat a squeeze.

Her head throbbed, the blood pounded in her ears, she felt herself choking. Perhaps he realized he was half killing her because he suddenly eased the pressure.

'Where?'

'Gone,' she gasped.

'Gone where?'

'Gone.' A realization nagged at her; she couldn't think it through.

'Gone where?' He gave a savage twist to her wrist.

'Away.' Most of her mind was registering pain, but another part was working overtime, trying to read the message her brain was attempting to deliver.

Suddenly he jerked at her throat, and his hand was tight as a noose. She couldn't breathe. The fear rose up and burst like an explosion in her head. She fought for air, her lungs heaved, a loud drumming filled her ears.

He let go suddenly, and she sucked in a long shuddering breath. The blood came back into her veins with a roar.

'*Where?*'

He didn't know. It came to her suddenly: he didn't know where the other papers were, which meant he didn't have Campbell, had never searched him.

'Campbell. With Campbell,' she managed.

He couldn't have heard her properly, or perhaps he wanted to hear it a second time because he wrenched her wrist backwards and snapped: '*Who?*'

Through clenched teeth she told him again and he gave her a great shove of rage. 'In that case,' he said in a vicious tone, 'we're going to have to get them *back*, aren't we?'


'He'll have contacted the police,' she said.

'I don't think so, somehow.'

The tones were harder, none of the solicitousness remained, but it was unmistakably Maynard's voice, complete with sing-song and that strange indefinable accent, and she saw again the table at the Waldorf and the fat neck beneath the pasty cheeks and the stomach pushing against the shirt and his lips folding daintily over the scones and the pale eyes following the spinning dancers.

She coughed; her gullet was raw. 'I know he'll have gone to the police,' she rasped.

He didn't reply. She tried again. 'He'll have handed the evidence in by now.'

'No time.'

'He won't agree to hand the files back – '

He snapped: 'Shut up,' and his voice sawed higher.

He had stopped the music but left the room in darkness. She was sitting on the bed, facing the dim outline of the curtained window, following his movements around the room by the sound and scent of him. He was behind her now, somewhere on the other side of the bed.

'*Shut up,*' he repeated savagely for no apparent reason,

and she felt a fresh flutter of fear. His hand came from across the bed and grasped the back of her neck loosely, almost caressingly. Her flesh crept, she longed to recoil. She spoke, as much from the need to break the spell of fear as to argue with him.

'Keeping me here won't do any good,' she said. 'It'll make things far worse, worse than anything – '

He shook her slightly. '*Shut*' – his grip tightened on her neck and he shook her again, more violently – '*up*.'

She kept very still then, looking blankly ahead. His hand stayed on her neck and she sensed that he was considering his next move. The following moments were very long; there was only the closeness of him and his sickly scent and the deadness in her stomach and the ache in her throat.

'Don't turn round,' he announced at last.

When she didn't answer he gave her neck a shake.

She agreed quickly: 'No.'

His hand fell away.

*Snap!* A light came on, a low lamp on the other side of the bed which threw her shadow large against the curtains. An instant later the outline of Maynard soared massively up behind her shadow, filling the whole wall.

'Strip.'

'What?'

'You heard.'

'But . . . *why?*'

He exhaled impatiently. His voice came in a vicious singsong. 'You could be *lying*, couldn't you? *Hiding* things!'

'I'd have given them to you.'

'I don't think I'm going to believe that. Why should I?' His voice rose sharply. She decided quite suddenly that he was unhinged. 'Don't turn round,' he added quickly. 'Clothes on the bed. Nothing on the floor. *Now*.'

Several thoughts converged on Daisy's mind: how he

would react if she refused, what he would do when he
discovered the tapes in her pockets, whether she had time
to hide them.

Although he wasn't touching her, she gave a large
involuntary shudder as if to slough him off. She realized
she had decided what she must do and, feeling faintly sick
at the thought of going through with it, she got to her feet
and began to undress. As she unzipped her jacket and
pulled it off she reached into one of the pockets and,
grasping a tape, hid it in one hand as she passed the jacket
backwards onto the bed with the other.

She heard him begin to rummage through the jacket.
She slipped the remaining tape down the front of her jeans.

'Bitch!' he yelled suddenly, and she heard him rattle one
of the cassettes. Then: 'What else have you got, *bitch*?'

She went on undressing. As she unzipped her jeans she
pushed the tape down the front of her pants. When she was
down to her underwear she stopped and waited, watching
his shadow on the wall as it swayed and billowed against
the light, thinking of the times Maynard must have been in
her flat, realizing he must have searched through her clothes
before.

'Bitch!' he echoed. He stopped moving. 'Where's the
rest? *Where's the rest?*'

'There isn't any more.'

His shadow shot upwards, growing huge. She ducked
but he was too quick and, grasping her hair, he pulled her
down. Gasping, she threw her hands back to stop herself
sprawling flat on the bed, but she still fell far enough for
him to see down the front of her body.

He uttered a bark of rage; the sound reminded her of
the dog. He gave her a small punch of fury and reaching
down grabbed the tape from the front of her pants.

'What do you think I am – *stupid*?' The exaggerated
singsong had an oddly mesmeric quality to it. '*Mmm?
Stupid?*'

She sat up again, moving slowly so as not to attract his attention, then remained very still. She realized she was behaving like a victim. She made herself speak. 'You were right about Campbell. He won't have gone to the police – '

'*Shut up!*'

She could hear his breathing; it was coming in shallow angry pants.

She said: 'He's got form, he wouldn't dare – '

'Shut up.' She felt a movement of air on her back. *Don't show your fear, don't let him see.* The telephone was dropped onto the bed beside her. The hand came back onto her neck. His voice had a malevolent slow-beating rhythm to it now.

'All right,' he said, 'call your friend, but no silly business!'

'He's – I don't know where he is.'

'Then you'll have to *find* him, won't you?' On the *find*, he jabbed a finger in her back.

'The number – it's in my bag.'

He gave an exaggerated sigh of annoyance. '*Wait.*'

His shadow expanded and shifted; he left the room. While he was gone she stared at the phone, unguarded beside her. Tempting, but not enough time, nothing to be gained, too frightened: more to the point, no number.

He returned quickly, throwing her carpetbag onto the bed. His hand came onto her neck again.

Moving with care, willing her hands not to tremble, she found her address book in the outside pocket of her bag. She began to tap out the Ashard number and got one digit wrong. She cut the call. The fingers squeezed, biting into the sides of her neck. 'Come on, *darling*,' he hissed. 'Get it right.'

She waited grimly until he eased the pressure, then wriggled her neck free. 'Keep off me,' she protested. 'Or no call.'

'Or no call,' he mimicked in a piping voice. 'Ha! You

break in, you half murder Beji, then you start bitching. Jesus . . .' He came at her suddenly, put two hands round her throat and dug his fingers briefly and savagely into her windpipe. '*Make the call.*'

She choked, bent double and coughed herself dry. When she could breathe again she pulled herself up and started again.

She did better this time. The number connected and began to ring. Jenny answered with a squeal: 'Where *are* you?'

'Never mind. Where's Campbell?' She heard her own voice, gruff and raw and strange in her ears.

'He was beaten up. He was – '

'Is he all right?'

'I think so.'

'Where is he now?'

'With Nick. He's with Nick.'

'What, in Scotland?'

'No, London. Are you all right? You sound – '

'London?' She hesitated. It was a mistake; a thumb pressed hard into her flesh.

'Daisy? Daisy?' Jenny was sounding worried.

'Where are they?' she managed.

'I'm not sure. Look, is everything all right?'

'You *must* know where they are!'

'Daisy – there's something wrong. What is it?'

'I've got to find Campbell.'

She could almost hear the thoughts rumbling through Jenny's brain. There was a heavy pause then, catching on, Jenny said briskly: 'You could try Nick's house, but you might have more luck with his car phone. Have you got the number?'

Daisy reached into her bag for something to write with. Out of the corner of her eye she caught the blurred outline of Maynard's head against the light, and, more clearly, his left hand resting loosely on his bent knee. His hands were blunt, she noticed, blunt and very white.

She took down the number and rang off before Jenny could ask any more questions. She dialled the car phone. The line produced a strange screech, and she had to try again. Maynard made sounds of irritation, sharp sucking noises. His hand was clammy on her skin.

Her fingers were stiff; she dialled with concentration. The line connected, the number rang. It went on ringing. And on, and on.

'No answer,' she whispered.

'Try something else then!' The thumb bit deep into the sensitive spot at the side of her spine.

She still had the phone to her ear. As she moved to cut the line and dial Nick's house, the ringing tone stopped suddenly. Perhaps, being a car phone, it had disconnected automatically. Her finger was moving to cut it off again when a voice grunted: 'Yus?'

It was a moment before she realized. 'Campbell? Campbell!' She gave a shrill cry of relief. 'Oh, for God's sake.'

'Daisy? Is that you? Where are you?'

But she wasn't allowed to answer that, and the warm moist fingers closed on the back of her neck as a reminder.


The day had not kept its promise. The sky, which had been darkening as Nick gunned the car away from Victoria, became positively black as they crossed Chelsea Bridge and ran down the side of Battersea Park. Rain came suddenly, falling in long perpendicular lines like pencils, drumming loudly on the roof and bouncing off the bonnet in a dense ridge of spray that obscured the Mercedes insignia on the front and much of the road besides.

'The *western* entrance?' Nick asked Campbell.

'That's what she said.'

They reached the south-western corner. Here the black iron gates were closed. Was there another entrance on this side? He couldn't remember. Or had she meant them to wait here? He turned right, along the western side of the park, heading for the Albert Bridge. The spray from the other vehicles had him slowing to peer at the line of parked cars and railings marking the edge of the park. Finally he saw an entrance, black gates again but open this time.

They drove in. There was a circular turning area, various roads spoking off, all of which sported barriers against traffic, and, to the right, a large parking area. Nick stopped on the circle beside a sign warning against stopping at any time, and looked through the trees towards the river. A woman ran head down along a path, dragging a small stiff-legged dog in her wake. A bent figure stood beneath a tree, huddled under an umbrella.

They went on into the car park.

'A blue Vauxhall?' Nick asked Campbell.

'That's what she said.'

'What the hell does a Vauxhall look like?'

A slight shrug. 'The name'll be written on it someplace, will it not? We can look as we pass.'

'What, in this?'

Nick heard the edge in his voice, and knew he was sounding unreasonable.

They rounded the circle and headed into the car park, a long thin rectangle of hard-packed gravel interspersed with deep potholes and landscaped with trees. The blades flipped fluidly over the windscreen at double time, the rain continued its pounding. There were a cluster of cars at the near end. Further down there was just a scattering of vehicles: a Range Rover with steamed-up windows, a Fiat disgorging dogs, a saloon of indeterminate make, undoubtedly blue – also, on closer examination, undoubtedly a Honda and unoccupied. The fourth car was a metallic-grey Volvo, the fifth an ancient black Mini.

Suddenly the wind came with a vengeance, picking up the rain and slamming it against the car, so that the wipers were momentarily overwhelmed. A car appeared out of the blur, parked at the far end of the parking area. They both craned forward. The car was canary yellow: the shape unmistakably that of an old Renault.

Nick sank back in his seat. 'Too early anyway, isn't it? How long? Ten minutes?' He knew perfectly well how long there was to go. Campbell looked at his watch and grunted in confirmation.

'Definitely the western entrance?'

'That's what she said!' He could hear the tension in Campbell's voice. He remembered Campbell's voice as it had sounded on the phone in the CID office high above Victoria Street, when Campbell had called up from the front desk and interrupted Nick's second meeting with Inspector Morgan. There had been a bark of concealed excitement in his tone, and Nick had turned away in case Morgan should hear it or see the mixture of relief and alarm on his own face.

Nick drove back towards the top of the parking area and pulled in at a place where they could see the western entrance.

The rain eased, the drumming melted into a mild tattoo. Only the wind kept up its racketing, spiralling the rain upwards through the stands of black trees, buffeting at the doors of the car.

Campbell broke the silence. 'Suppose these people try some trick or other?'

'What do you mean?'

'Suppose Daisy's no' there?'

'Then – ' The thought, which had been lurking with others at the back of Nick's mind, pulled at him. 'We leave it to Morgan.'

For once Campbell did not argue.

Pulling his jacket tight around his neck, Nick got out

and walked up to the circle and looked out through the
gates, then wandered a short way along a path towards
the river. The mist had thinned and the trees stood out in
ranks, like a waiting army. The thin suspension cables of
the Albert Bridge were like long strands of cooked sugar
falling towards the white haze of the river.

He returned to the car. Time was up. Absurd fears flew
through his mind. That this was just a game for some sick
mind, that the car phone would ring and he would hear
someone laughing down the line and telling him to go
jump; that Campbell had got it totally wrong and they
shouldn't be here at all but in Hyde Park.

Campbell made a sound. Following his pointed finger,
Nick saw the car coming in through the gate. It stopped on
the edge of the circle. The bodywork was dark; it could
have been blue.

It started off again, rounding the circle and heading into
the parking area. It was definitely blue. He felt a lurch of
excitement. He tried to make out how many people were
in it, but it was hidden by the line of cars as it passed down
the far side and when it emerged at the end he couldn't see
properly through the streaming side windows.

The blue car continued towards the less inhabited end
of the parking area and, executing a sudden U-turn,
stopped on the near side, quite a long way down, facing
the way it had come.

In his eagerness to turn and follow, Nick stepped a little
too hard on the throttle and the wheels spun. He eased off
but not enough to prevent the car executing a flamboyant
turn. He was aware of another vehicle, a large saloon of
dark but indeterminate colour, emerging from between the
lines of parked cars and braking in plenty of time to let him
pass. He accelerated away.

Passing the blue car on the far side, he made another
much slower turn to come up behind it. He stopped five
yards short.

It was a Vauxhall Cavalier. Its exhaust was spewing vapour. Its back window was rain-soaked but demisted. There was only one head visible above the outline of the headrests.

Nick put out a hand to Campbell for the documents.

'But she's no' there!'

Nick gestured again for the documents.

Campbell glared at him. *'But she's no' there!'* he shouted as if Nick were deaf.

Nick glanced away to the right and saw that the dark saloon was trundling slowly down the far side of the parking area. There were at least three people in it. He said to Campbell: 'The documents! Don't bloody argue!'

With a rasp of exasperation, Campbell pushed the roll of papers into Nick's hand and reached for the door. 'I tell you,' he said threateningly, indicating the car ahead, 'this fella's no' going any place till *we* say so!'

Paying no attention, Nick got out and looked back at the dark saloon, which was turning itself round and parking twenty yards behind. Jamming the papers inside his jacket out of the rain he walked towards the Vauxhall with Campbell at his heels. As he came up to the driver's door, the window opened. Nick bent down and saw a dark-jowled man with hooded eyes and a weary expression.

'Maynard?' Nick asked.

Ignoring the question, the man drawled: 'The delivery, is it?'

'Are you Maynard?' Nick pressed.

'Look, I'm just the messenger boy, right? Like I take the delivery and radio through that I've got it. Right?'

Nick, aware of Campbell hovering at his elbow, said: 'What guarantees do we have?'

The man shrugged. 'Look, I've just been told to radio through, haven't I?'

Campbell had lowered his head and was glowering into the car. 'I know you!'

'Shut up!' Nick hissed out of the corner of his mouth.

'The one at the airport,' Campbell growled in Nick's ear. 'The one we followed.'

Nick motioned him silent with a sharp movement of his hand, and handed the roll of papers through the window. The man in the car spoke into his walkie-talkie, listened for a moment, then signed off. Throwing the radio on the seat, he reached forward to engage the gear lever. At about the same time he also opened his mouth to speak but before he could say anything Campbell, seeing treachery in the movement, roared, 'An' where d'you think you're goin'?' and, elbowing Nick aside, pushed a hand through the window.

But the other man's reflexes were quicker; he had the gear engaged and his foot down before Campbell could get at the keys. The car jumped forward, Campbell was nearly pulled off his feet. For a few surreal moments he managed to stay with the accelerating car, his legs wheeling and kicking into the air like a racing cyclist's, before his feet got mixed up and he nosedived towards the gravel. He saved himself with an astonishingly effective roll, all roundness and no arms like a barrel, and was already struggling to his feet as he came out of it.

Nick loped forward, eyes on the disappearing car, choking with disbelief and fury. He was about to bawl at Campbell, to give him a small but furious taste of his mind, when the blare of a horn had him twisting round and jumping instinctively to one side as a car tore past, shooting out a heavy wedge of spray. It was the dark saloon.

Nick ran back to the Mercedes and, jumping in, roared after the others, rocking briefly to a stop to let Campbell scramble in beside him.

'Who're that?' gasped Campbell, barely articulate.

Foot hard down, Nick blasted towards the exit without replying. Slowing to negotiate the bend at the entrance he shot out into the circle in time to see the tail of the dark car disappear through the gates, turning left. He accelerated across the circle and slewed out into the Albert Bridge Road as a car nosed its way across the junction from the opposite direction, turning south. Missing it by a couple of feet, feeling a brief surge of fear, Nick ignored the agitated bleats of the car's horn and, straightening up, accelerated once again.

The rain and spray mingled into curtains of moisture which closed in and lifted like drifting fogs. The dark saloon, lost one moment, reappeared the next. He saw that it was jammed up behind the Vauxhall's bumper, flashing its lights. At the corner of the park, the two cars swerved in beside the closed gates.

'Who is it?' demanded Campbell.

'Morgan,' Nick said, adding firmly to crush any argument: 'My idea. I asked him along.'

By the time they pulled in behind the dark saloon, Morgan and his men had the driver out of the Vauxhall and into a tight box of tall backs. As Nick ran up the man was showing his driver's licence and protesting rapidly: 'Just delivering a message, lads! That's all! Just doing a favour for a friend. Listen, the name's Biggs, ex-Notting Hill CID.' Turning to Morgan he added with forced camaraderie: 'Don't I know you?'

'The message,' Nick interjected, shouldering his way past the coppers and pushing his face close to Biggs. 'What was the message?'

'The message?' Biggs had a ghastly smile on his face.

'What you were meant to tell me!'

Biggs looked at the waiting policemen imploringly. 'I was just pickin' up and deliverin'. I didn't know what it was about. I was just told to – '

'The *message*.'

'Yeah, well. It was "Albert Bridge", wasn't it? That's all I know. Just doing a favour . . .'

Nick didn't hear the rest. He was already running back to the car.

Susan threw the swatches of fabric onto the sofa and paced over to the window. Restlessly she turned away and went down to the kitchen to make another cup of coffee, then changed her mind and poured herself a drink. Only midday, but what the hell.

It was the waiting that was killing her. Would Nick ring as soon as he'd retrieved this beastly file or whatever it was? On the whole she thought not; he was too puffed up with wounded pride, too self-obsessed, too self-righteous. Should she try Cramm's man then? God only knew what sort of a reception she'd get from him. Or Schenker himself? No, she hated the thought of grovelling, and however mildly she couched her request, it would be self-abasement of an odious kind.

Taking her drink, she went up to the bedroom and combed her hair and repencilled her eyebrows. The sound of a closing door echoed up from the hall. The front door? It couldn't be. The daily had gone for the day. Camilla was away at college. She strode out and hung over the stairwell. 'Who's there?'

'It's me.' Tony's voice, flat and sombre.

Balancing her drink, she hurried down the stairs. 'Good God, what are *you* doing home?'

He was very still, his face set, his eyes black and staring.

'*Well?*' she demanded, suddenly irritated at him for taking her by surprise.

'I have to talk to you.'

There was something about his tone and the oddness of his expression that infuriated her. 'What *is* it?'

He dropped his gaze, ran a hand up his cheek and over his forehead, and turned towards the drawing room. He walked untidily, as if he had just got out of bed.

She followed at his heels. '*Well?*'

He reached for a drink, lifting the gin bottle then letting it fall again. 'I'm afraid – it's bad news,' he said with difficulty. 'I've made rather a foolish mistake.' He made the effort to look at her, but his gaze slid away again. 'A stupid error of judgement.'

Susan clutched at his arm. 'What? *What?*'

He looked back at the bottle and began to unscrew it slowly. Stopping again, he said suddenly: 'There was a girl. It was nothing, absolutely nothing, believe me. She was just ... Well anyway, it all got out of hand, I'm afraid.' Abandoning the bottle, his hand dropped wearily to his side and he said in an abject tone: 'I'm sorry, Susan.'

'What do you mean? What's happening?' In her agitation she yanked on his lapel, pulling the shoulder of his jacket awry.

'I'll have to resign.'

'*Resign?*' She heard the shriek in her voice. 'But why, *why?*'

Grasping the gin bottle again, he poured himself a large one. 'No choice. Money changed hands. She was a tart. They know all about it.' He took a large swig.

Before Susan could think, she had exclaimed: 'But it wasn't you! It wasn't *you* who gave her the money!'

Tony's head jerked back, he almost spilled his drink. He stared at her in astonishment.

'You mustn't resign!' she rushed on. 'Why should you! Lots of people have women, half the cabinet are bloody divorced, for God's sake – why should *you* have to resign?'

He couldn't take it in. 'You *knew?*'

'Of course I knew! Of *course* I knew! Just as I know that you *don't need to resign!*' She spaced the words out so that he would understand. 'It's all under control, you see. It's not going to come out after all. By the end of the day we'll have all the evidence back – all of it!' She saw the amazement in Tony's face. In her anxiety to convince him she gave an odd laugh, almost a shriek. 'Trust me, trust me! All of it – *back here*! Every single bit. Then no one can touch you! No one!'

She went on – she couldn't stop – while he stared at her half in shock, half in something like wonder. Finally, keeping his eyes on her face, he put his drink down. 'Susan. *Susan!*' He touched her hand. She fell quiet, gripped by a fear she couldn't name. 'Susan . . . it was the *press* who called.'

She felt a stab of terrible cold, for a moment she couldn't speak. '*Why? How?* They couldn't! They *couldn't!* Was it that woman? But it's just her word against yours! It's just – '

'They've got the whole story.'

'How *can* they? How *can* they?' Susan heard her voice rising and knew her face was ugly. 'She's just making things up, she's got no proof!'

'They've got details of hotels.' His tone dropped to one of near despair. 'And of three separate payments. And . . .' His face creased into a mask of anguish. 'A hospital visit.'

'No! No!' She pulled her hand free with a jerk and in her rage almost punched him. 'No! They can't! They *can't!* It's all in the file! All in the file!' She gave a cry and stumbled away, making for the hall.

He caught her at the telephone. 'Susan – don't!'

'I'll call that bastard Schenker! How *dare* he? *Bastard, bastard!*'

'Susan – don't. It's all over.' He grasped the receiver and for a moment they both pulled at it before she released her grip and burst into tears. 'It's not fair!' she cried. 'It's not fair!'

He put the receiver firmly back in its cradle and put an arm round her shoulders.

But her rage was vast and inconsolable and, punching him on the chest, she struggled free and screamed at him.

She was still hurling invective as she ran up the stairs and raced into the bedroom and fell raging onto the bed.

The towers of the Albert Bridge rose like ornate candles out of a damp mist. The rain had eased a little, more of a steady drizzle than a downpour, and the wind had died right away, although as they came onto the bridge it produced a last fleeting gasp that pattered the rain against the side of the car.

The traffic was heavy and when Nick slowed down he got an impatient horn from behind. There were a couple of pedestrians and a jogger braving the pavement on this side of the bridge. All of them were men. The tooting car overtook, sounding its horn again as it passed.

They went on steadily, they crested the rise of the bridge. Campbell made a sound and pointed to the far end of the bridge on the opposite side, to an old-fashioned red telephone box just visible beyond the neat hexagonal band box which housed the cable anchor. A figure stood huddled against the box. Jeans, jacket, slight build, hair flat against the head. A boy. Or maybe not a boy. With shoulders hunched high and head dropped low as if to ward off the rain, it was hard to tell. Then the figure moved, folding its arms together as if in disgust and there was something in the movement that was so completely Daisy that Nick jabbed the accelerator, pulled out into the fast lane and roared towards her.

She saw him coming. She straightened up, she bent to peer at the car, she moved forward and, reaching the kerb, began to gesticulate or wave or both. Nick stopped in the middle of the road, indicating right, and met a fresh volley of abuse from the vehicles behind. Seeing a tight gap in the oncoming traffic he stepped on the throttle and bolted across, causing one driver to stand on his brakes and flash his lights in rage.

He shot onto the pavement ahead of Daisy and had to brake suddenly as she ran towards him, swerving round the bumper. He jumped out and they nearly cannoned into each other. She was already talking: she must have been talking even as he opened the door. If he hadn't been so alarmed by the look of her he would have laughed. Her skin was very pale, her eyes dark with shadows, her hair plastered onto her head by the rain.

He grasped her tightly by the shoulders. 'God – are you all right?'

But she was gabbling insistently: 'You didn't give him the files, did you? You didn't, did you? *Did* you?'

'Slow down! Slow down! It's all right.' She was shivering under his hands.

'You didn't, did you?' Her voice was wobbling dangerously.

He spread his lips into a grin. 'Not quite everything.'

'Not everything?'

'I gave them what we didn't need,' he said truthfully. 'And kept the rest.'

'Kept the rest, kept the rest.' She was taut as a wire, humming with a furious electricity. 'Maynard – he took it all back, everything. I couldn't stop him. I couldn't – ' She broke off. Her eyes had a dark and empty look.

'Morgan'll be after him by now.'

'Morgan?'

'From Scotland Yard.'

She seemed to take that in. 'Alan Breck – is he all right? Is he – '

'He's all right.'

'Must get to him. Must get to Scotland. Must – ' She tugged at his sleeve in agitation and looked around as if some airborne transportation might at any moment manifest itself.

'Daisy, it's all right. Slow down.'

She froze. She had caught sight of Campbell getting out

by the passenger door. For an instant she stared at him
blankly, then she hissed: 'Campbell!' and from her tone
one might have thought she was cross with him.

She looked back at Nick and then at Campbell and her
expression folded inwards. She dropped her head against
Nick's chest and gave a great shudder and said: 'Oh, I'm so
tired.'

Hillyard's hands were wet on the wheel. Furiously he
rubbed them one at a time on the side of the seat. Turning
a corner into the Wandsworth Bridge Road, he almost
clipped a parked car. Christ, he thought, I'm falling apart.
Get it together, get it together. The cow won't talk, not
when her big friend has form, not when she herself could
get debarred or whatever they did to lawyers caught
breaking and entering.

No, she wouldn't talk. But hearing himself repeat this,
he realized he was far from persuaded. *Christ*. He must
think this through, must get his story fixed up. He'd say
that if the cow got trapped in the flat then it must have
been accidental. He'd say that on discovering the burglary
he'd taken a quick look around, repaired the door – the
hammering would have covered any sounds from upstairs
– and gone to Beryl's to sleep. He would flatly deny the
rest. Beryl would back him up. She'd provide an alibi for
the evening. Biggs and his lunch companion would cover
for the earlier part of the day.

Would it be enough? Yes, yes, of course it would be
enough. The girl could never prove otherwise, not without
incriminating herself. The thought calmed him, and he
indulged in a different scenario, one in which he was above
all suspicion, and the police, on the strength of his evidence,
were forced to charge the Field bitch with burglary.

Approaching Battersea, he tried Biggs on the walkie-
talkie but either he was out of range or he was already

back inside the office because there was no answer. Parking, he looked for Biggs' car but couldn't see it. He approached the door in the wall and saw that the door which he'd wedged tightly shut was now slightly open. He prodded it with his finger. It swung open further. He listened. Somewhere upstairs, Beji began yapping, but without enthusiasm.

Hillyard stepped inside. He heard a voice drifting down from the office. He recognized the inimitable sound of Beryl gabbing on the phone. He felt a mingling of relief and anger. He did not need Beryl in her shrewish mode, carping at him for screwing up, telling him exactly where he'd gone wrong, going hysterical about the carnage to her beloved files. At the same time the sound of the old trout's voice was oddly reassuring.

As he began to trudge upwards, Beji appeared on the turn of the stairs, growling softly. 'You can shut your face for a start!' he hissed. The dog bared its teeth. Continuing past, he aimed a blow in the dog's direction, a blow which, as his hand travelled through the air, took on all the considerable force of his pent-up fury and caught the animal a clout that sent it sprawling against the wall.

He was seven steps up and almost onto the landing when two unpleasant sensations hit him one after the other. The first was a sudden, sharp pain in his lower calf which, as Beji's teeth cut deeper into his flesh, grew to such excruciating proportions that it was a moment before he could find the breath to scream. The second sensation was of a dark shape coming up the stairs behind him, a shape that wasn't Biggs. As he twisted round to beat Beji away from his leg the shape was no more than a blur, a snatched impression of a tall figure stepping round the bend of the stairs, but by the time he had torn the dog's teeth quite literally out of his calf he had recognized the confident step and heavy expressionless gaze of a CID man. Seeing the second one coming up behind, Hillyard realized they must have been waiting for him. He fell back against the wall sobbing and spitting, and it wasn't entirely because of the pain in his leg.

# Chapter 39

——•——

IT WAS A day of brilliant light and deep winter shadows. Snow lay on the hills and across the floor of the pass and on the north-facing slopes where the January sun couldn't reach. The landscape seemed to reflect itself upwards into the whiteness of the sky, but as the road dropped down towards the loch the colours came back into the earth, rich and golden, and the sky turned a pale crystalline blue.

The potholed road to nowhere wound its way upwards through the conifers towards the low roof of the Bells' cottage. As Daisy turned the last corner Campbell's figure came into view, waiting motionless by the gate. It was just as they had planned: no one else at all.

In the back of the car, Meg Bell said prosaically: 'Well, here we are then.' But the calmness of her voice could not entirely conceal her emotion. Daisy glanced in the mirror. Adrian was staring ahead, holding the dazed, gravely incredulous expression he had worn since they had picked him up from the hospital.

She drew up at the gate. Campbell opened Adrian's door and helped him out and when Daisy looked again Adrian was enveloped in Campbell's awkward hunched embrace.

Daisy looked away over the broad landscape. There was no wind, and in the stillness it seemed to her that there were strange imperceptible sounds echoing softly from the hills, sounds that had always been there but which she had never heard before. She looked away towards the west, to where the head of the loch lay unseen around the bend of the hills, and thought of the parkland and the empty house beyond. In her mind the house was cold and barren. He would sell it eventually, she thought; he would sell it and move on to another life.

She turned. Campbell, one arm around Adrian, was helping him up the path and into the cottage.

The four of them ate in the front room, sitting around a table in front of the small open fire. Daisy had syphoned off some cash from the legal fund to install four dimple radiators and put something aside for the fuel bills, and now the cottage was warm and dry and free of fumes.

Adrian seemed to wake to his freedom by slow degrees until, fired with something approaching energy, he gave a sudden smile. Daisy's pleasure was tempered by the lingering frustrations of the seven-week legal battle, and the knowledge that, though Adrian was out of hospital and clear of the place of safety order, he was not completely free, since the local authority had obtained a supervision order. Adrian would not be able to travel or start new medical treatment without the social services' permission, nor could his case be publicized in any way. Daisy reflected that, when doing battle with the authorities, there was no such thing as a good clean win. The best that could be hoped for – at least until Adrian reached sixteen and had more hope of establishing his right to refuse medical treatment – was a truce, albeit an uneasy one.

On the plus side, the whole process could have taken a great deal longer. Six months, or even more, was not uncommon in child-care cases. And Adrian, though he had been virtually comatose on the heavy drugs given him in the early weeks and had lost a great deal of the weight he had fought so hard to gain, seemed at the same time to have acquired a fresh determination, a new resilience to his disabilities, exhibited by his insistence on leaving the hospital on foot under his own power.

No amount of will-power could sustain his energy for

long though, and at the end of the meal he lay on the settee, looking drained. But he was not so tired that he didn't want to inspect the book of press cuttings that Daisy had brought with her.

'The show that runs and runs,' Daisy remarked, not without a certain satisfaction. The *Sunday Times* had made Silveron a lead story for three consecutive weeks, then, after a break for Christmas, had picked it up again for another two. They ran Dublensky's story for the first two weeks and the anonymous pilot's the next, with appropriate responses or evasions from Morton-Kreiger, politicians and pressure groups. The rest of the press had been forced to cover the story – giving due credit to the *Sunday Times* – because numerous questions had been asked in the Commons and the new Minister of Agriculture had been forced to make a statement. Coming on top of Driscoll's sudden resignation for 'family reasons', with attendant rumours of unsuitable women, blackmail and late-night parties – rumours subsequently confirmed by Angela Kershaw who had sold her story to the *News of the World* for £45,000 – the ministry had been pushed firmly out of its complacency and into the political spotlight, and there was talk of a major rethink, of imposing more stringent regulations on all pesticides, of having data independently analysed. There was even renewed talk of splitting Food from Agriculture, and creating two separate ministries with non-conflicting aims.

But the item that thrilled Adrian more than anything was the *Sunday Times*' New Year lead feature. The cutting had been smuggled into hospital to him, he had already read it twice, but now, looking proud and embarrassed in turns, he could not get enough of it, and who could blame him, since he himself was the star of the piece. Well, the unacknowledged star. To work its way around the injunction on publicity, the newspaper had been forced to use pseudonyms, to move the Bell home to 'somewhere in western Scotland', to alter all other facts that could in any way identify Adrian. But for all that, the story was very much Adrian's, some of it told in his own words, courtesy of a tape recorder and a list of questions that Daisy had taken into the hospital when posing as an assistant to the Bells' solicitor.

But if Adrian was intoxicated by his stardom, Daisy got most satisfaction from the two items that had appeared in last Sunday's paper. First, the bald front-page news that Silveron's UK licence had been suspended, and that in the States the EPA had announced an urgent and thorough investigation into Silveron and all other chemicals tested by TroChem.

The second item, another massive four-page leading article, was the exposure of the dirty tricks and surveillance campaign mounted against Catch and its sometime employee Daisy Field by Reynard Associates at the behest of the mysterious Workham Overseas Holdings. There were facsimiles of the expense sheets detailing the operatives and vehicles used to keep tabs on 'Jackie' (no suggestion of how this and other material had been acquired, Daisy noted), an invoice made out to Workham Overseas Holdings showing the accommodation address in the Cayman Islands, a photograph of the bug like the one found in the phone socket at Daisy's flat, a calendar of the long series of unexplainable and violent events culminating in the Octek fire, and a detailed re-examination of the facts surrounding the fire itself.

The newspaper also noted the arrest of the managing director of Reynard Associates, one Colin Hillyard, on certain charges which, being *sub judice*, were closed to further comment.

Then, just when it seemed that no more revelations were likely to be squeezed out of the story, came the punch, the point where the newspaper, at possible risk of an injunction and almost certainly amid the violent screams of its lawyers, had taken the plunge and stated that Cayman Islands sources had linked Workham Overseas Holdings to an offshore subsidiary wholly owned by Morton-Kreiger. These sources, as Daisy knew, had first consisted of friends and contacts of Nick's manager David Weinberg, but the information had subsequently been corroborated by the newspaper's own investigations, the nature of which Simon wouldn't reveal to her.

Significantly, Morton-Kreiger had neither confirmed nor denied the allegations. The company seemed to be in much-denied turmoil. Their chief executive (agrochemicals) had left in early December to join one of the big cola companies, their head of research had taken early and abrupt retirement just before Christmas and then, with the breaking of the Silveron story, their share price had taken a very nasty bump on the stock market. Although just days ago Daisy had noticed that, with the announcement of better-than-expected profits and with high contingency reserves, their share price had recovered to within a few points of its previous level.

Adrian had fallen asleep. Leaving him, they went into the kitchen, Mrs Bell to prepare tea, Campbell to thirst after a celebratory drink of a stronger nature, which he satisfied by spiriting a flask out of his jacket. For someone who in less than two weeks faced an assault hearing, he was extraordinarily sanguine. But then Daisy suspected he was making the not uncommon mistake of believing too heartily in his own defence – a defence first suggested by Daisy and subsequently endorsed by his lawyers. The plea was to be guilty – no escaping that – but with lashings of mitigation: emotional strain, an over-developed protective instinct – which was one way of putting it – and a misreading of modern psychological techniques which had resulted in Campbell's not unreasonable belief that Adrian, far from being helped by the psychologist, was actually being attacked by her. The lawyers reckoned that, with luck and a good performance from Campbell – patent regret and no aggression, he would get a hefty fine or maybe three months suspended.

'Well then! Very fine! Very fine!' Campbell beamed across the table in a surge of bonhomie. He insisted on pouring a large measure of whisky for Daisy, and his sister as well, although she never took more than a sip. 'Everyone home, everyone well and good,' pronounced Campbell with magisterial pomp, an emotional wobble in his voice. Everyone home. Everyone well and good. Contemplating this, Daisy thought of Adrian and a future in which his hopes of recovery had improved little, at least in the short term, but which promised a much better chance of compensation, although the fight would undoubtedly be long and bitter, a grind through the courts which might well take five, six, even ten years. She thought, too, of Dublensky and his family setting up home near the new trust headquarters in Oxford, a Dublensky who, delivered of his moral burden, blossomed with pride and zealous energy, who, far from retiring from the fray, had offered to visit Washington to testify publicly before a congressional committee on the Silveron affair.

But there was someone Campbell had forgotten. Nick was not back yet. His European tour had closed in Amsterdam just the previous night. He had last telephoned a few days ago, wanting to hear the news, agreeing proposals for the trust, confirming that he'd seen the latest *Sunday Times*. He had been surviving the tour reasonably well, he said, had even, to his surprise, enjoyed parts of it. As always during his irregular calls she had, to her slight shame, listened for traces of drink in his voice, for small signs of despair, but he had sounded happy, and if anything caught her attention, it was perhaps a hint of preoccupation in his tone. He had apologized for not phoning more often, but he'd been very tied up. At which Daisy's imagination had bounded off in new and unwelcome directions.

He had been vague about when he was coming home, murmuring about studio time and a recording that he must finish. He hadn't even said which home he would be coming to.

But Campbell knew. 'Ashard,' he declared. 'It's been readied.'

She looked away through the window then back at Campbell. 'You're sure?'

Campbell waved a hand, as if to indicate that his sources were impeccable. 'Aye, expected this mornin'.'

She thought of phoning but changed her mind. Ten minutes later as she was on her way out, Campbell called: 'And tell Mr Mackenzie I'll be after my jacket directly. Tell him it was never in the wood store, though I must have searched a dozen times.'

The gates were open, the housekeeper let her into the house. The hall was warm, there were displays of flowers. But it was not until her knock on the studio door went unanswered and she pushed it quietly open that the dream from the long night in Hillyard's flat came back to her. Nick sitting at the console, music pouring from the amplifiers, the strong white light at the windows: the scene was a mingling of old and imaginary images, so that she wasn't sure if this hadn't already happened and she wasn't in some extraordinary way reliving it.

But then, with a certain inevitability, the reality diverged. Though she waited several moments he didn't realize she was there, he didn't look round, and after standing uncertainly for a while she went and sat on the arm of a chair.

The music was rich and orchestral, with an overlay of voices, sometimes in chorus. Most of it was taped and he seemed to be adding strands of sound on the keyboard as he went along. After a pause which was no more than a beat, he came in with a solo written for a voice much higher than his own. First he hummed the melody, then he sang in a strained falsetto. The words were from a poem, she thought, or maybe a lament. Despite the odd pitch of his voice and the patchwork of different sounds, the effect was unusual and rather lovely. She tried to imagine how it must feel to create something like this, and felt a thrill of excitement for him.

He stopped suddenly, flicked the tape off, and made a small grunt of dissatisfaction.

Standing up, she said: 'Sounds beautiful.'

He swung round, not at all startled, and a slow grin spread over his face. '*Daisy*.' He got up and came over and kissed her firmly on both cheeks. He looked wonderful.

Holding her lightly by the shoulders, he pulled back and stared at her. 'Daisy,' he murmured again. He appeared pleased, though whether with her or with life in general, it was hard to tell. 'What, no black eye?'

'Not today.'

He dropped his hands from her shoulders. 'No one left to fight, huh?'

'Oh, I wouldn't say *that*. But I was thinking of giving up hand-to-hand combat.'

'Getting soft?'

'Just thought I might try a quiet life. You know – for a change.'

He made a disbelieving face and grinned again. 'Adrian's free anyway. That's great. Well done.'

'Adrian's out,' she agreed. 'But then Campbell might well be in, and the place he'll be going to has a lot more bars on the windows.' She explained how Campbell was finding the idea of public repentance difficult.

'Can't you coach him?'

'A gorilla with stage training would be more receptive.'

'Oh well,' he laughed, refusing to take the threat too seriously. 'I'll keep him company. Two old lags doing our time.'

'I thought they were dropping the charges. I thought they understood why you had the stuff – '

'Bad joke. Sorry,' he said rapidly, grimacing an apology. 'They *do* – they *have* dropped the charges. But what about you? There was a time when I thought we'd all be inside together. The Three Musketeers up shit creek.' The idea entertained him.

'Oh, Morgan knows I did it,' she said blithely. 'I mean, he knows that I know who broke Hillyard's door down, and I know he knows. And I know he knows that I was in there when I shouldn't have been. But we don't talk about any of that. I just say I knocked on Hillyard's door and got invited inside and we ended up making a deal over the documents. No unlawful imprisonment, no kidnap, nothing nasty. That way I don't get to perjure myself and Campbell keeps out of further trouble, all at the same time. Well, that's the theory anyway. Hillyard's busy pushing his side of the story.'

'Which is?'

'That I sent some thugs to break into his place, and he found me there next morning.'

'Are the police buying that?'

'They're doing their best to overlook it. They're rather keener on getting Hillyard for breaking and entering my flat, for illegal surveillance and assault and a few other things.'

'And will they get him? I mean, on all of that?'

'Enough. Though' – she bared her teeth – 'I'm not sure anything could be enough.'

'Nightmares?' he asked, and she saw his own nightmares reflected in his eyes.

'A few.'

He reached for her hand and squeezed it.

She put on a look that said it was all right really, which at that moment it most certainly was.

'Come on,' he said suddenly, 'let's go out before it gets dark. I haven't seen around the place yet.'

Pausing at the door he jerked his head in the direction of the console. 'You really liked it?'

'Oh yes.'

'Well, it's finished,' he declared, making a broad arc with his hand as if to encompass an enormous volume of music. 'At least *nearly*. I worked on it almost every day while I was away.'

She couldn't help asking: 'You had the time?'

'Sure. In the afternoons before the show . . .'

'You said you were tied up.'

His expression changed from puzzlement to wry amusement. 'Now what else would have tied me up, Daisy?'

'Will you be performing it soon?' she said rather too quickly.

He was still laughing at her, trying to catch her eye as they went into the hall. 'I'll get a rough on tape first. Then . . . well, we'll see.' He added more thoughtfully: 'Once maybe. With a full orchestra and choir. Yes, just the once. Who knows.'

'Why not more often?'

He led the way into a small room that was entirely given over to coats and boots. 'I don't know . . . Hearing something once, sometimes that's enough.' He held up a quilted jacket for size before helping her on with it.

She sensed he wasn't ready to explain further, and she didn't press him. 'Oh, Campbell wants his jacket back,' she said.

'What?'

'He says he's looked for it in the wood store a dozen times.'

He frowned as he searched his memory. 'A jacket?' Then he gave a short laugh. 'Oh *that*. He wants it back, does he? Ha! He'll be bloody lucky.' But going to a hook behind the hall door he rooted through a pile of coats and, with a grunt of satisfaction, emerged with a well-worn tweed jacket. He held it at arm's length. 'This,' he said scornfully, jerking it up and down until it danced, 'was used to wrap me up one night. Campbell bloody *tucked me up* with it!' For a moment he was lost in the past somewhere, but then he turned and looked at her, and there was nothing of the past in his smile. 'Come on,' he said.

He threw the jacket on a bench and they went out of the side door and into a formal garden. The air was fresh, the hills were so finely drawn that they seemed to be etched into the sky. They stood looking out over the water for a minute before taking a well-trodden path that led across the park towards the trees.

'I won't be staying here,' he said.

'Where will you go?'

'There's a place in Oxfordshire I thought I might go and look at.'

'Nice?'

'Could be.'

'A farm? Land?'

'Just a bit of land.'

'Quiet?'

'Quiet enough. But much more convenient, much closer to everything.'

Closer to the trust headquarters, to London, to *me*, she thought.

'Will you come and look at it with me?' he asked, almost shyly.

'Yes! Of course I will!'

'I want to be sure it's not too *loud*, you see.'

Daisy clasped her chest as if she had been stabbed. 'Whoever *said* that word!'

They started off again. She asked: 'The tour – how did it go? Was it all right?' But he wasn't going to miss that opportunity either.

'Rather tied me up,' he said.

'You're victimizing me!' she complained.

He said more seriously: 'No, it went well. In the most important way anyway.'

'The most important way?'

'It made money.'

'Ah.'

'Well, I have to keep you and your projects in the manner to which they've become accustomed, don't I?'

'In that case,' she declared, 'I hope it made pots and *pots*!'

And then the dream converged. He gave a hoot of laughter and, pulling her into the curve of his arm, squeezed her close against him.